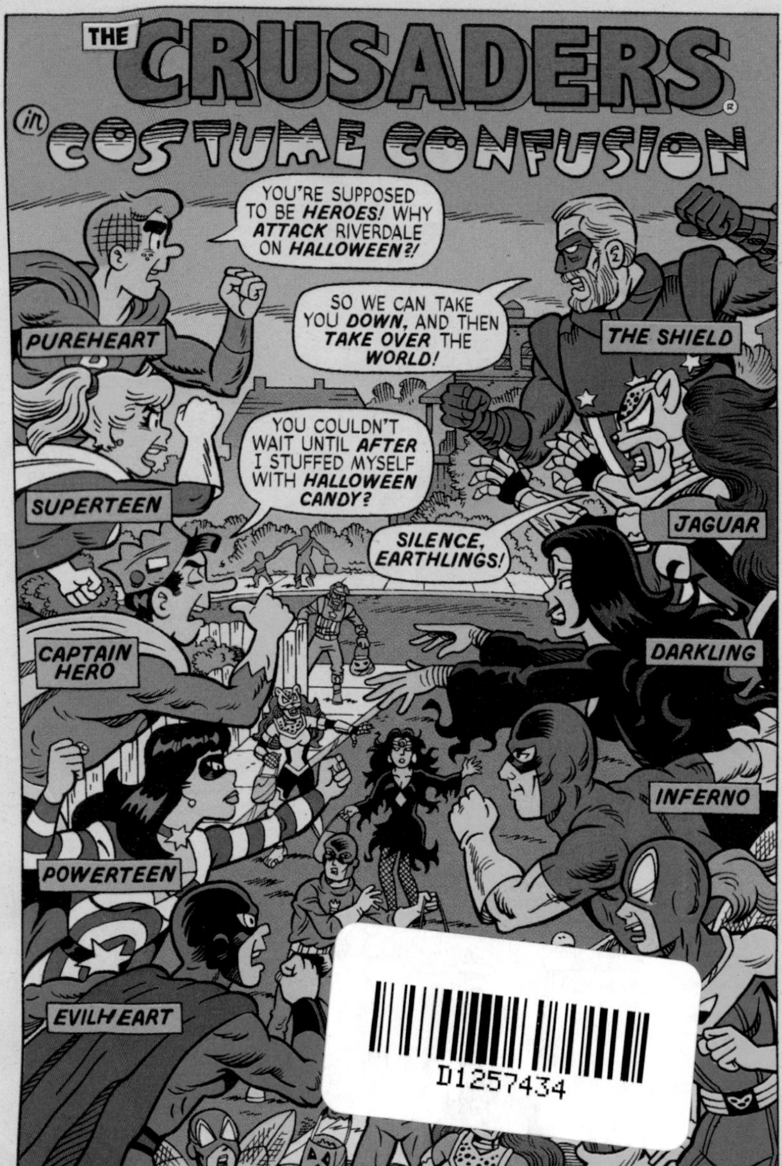
THE CRUSADERS
in COSTUME CONFUSION
YOU'RE SUPPOSED TO BE HEROES! WHY ATTACK RIVERDALE ON HALLOWEEN?!
SO WE CAN TAKE YOU DOWN, AND THEN TAKE OVER THE WORLD!
YOU COULDN'T WAIT UNTIL AFTER I STUFFED MYSELF WITH HALLOWEEN CANDY?
SILENCE, EARTHLINGS!
PUREHEART
THE SHIELD
SUPERTEEN
JAGUAR
CAPTAIN HERO
DARKLING
INFERNO
POWERTEEN
EVILHEART

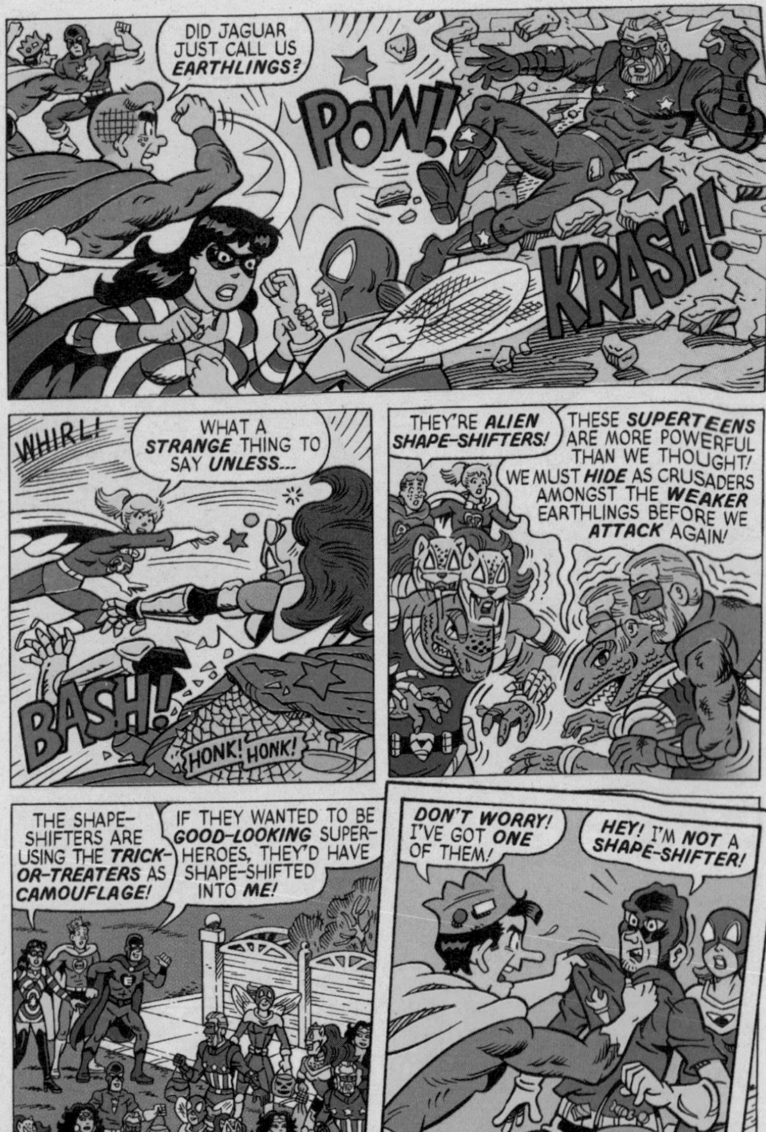
DID JAGUAR JUST CALL US EARTHLINGS?
POW!
KRASH!
WHIRL!
WHAT A STRANGE THING TO SAY UNLESS...
BASH!
HONK! HONK!
THEY'RE ALIEN SHAPE-SHIFTERS!
THESE SUPERTEENS ARE MORE POWERFUL THAN WE THOUGHT! WE MUST HIDE AS CRUSADERS AMONGST THE WEAKER EARTHLINGS BEFORE WE ATTACK AGAIN!
THE SHAPE-SHIFTERS ARE USING THE TRICK-OR-TREATERS AS CAMOUFLAGE!
IF THEY WANTED TO BE GOOD-LOOKING SUPER-HEROES, THEY'D HAVE SHAPE-SHIFTED INTO ME!
DON'T WORRY! I'VE GOT ONE OF THEM!
HEY! I'M NOT A SHAPE-SHIFTER!
2

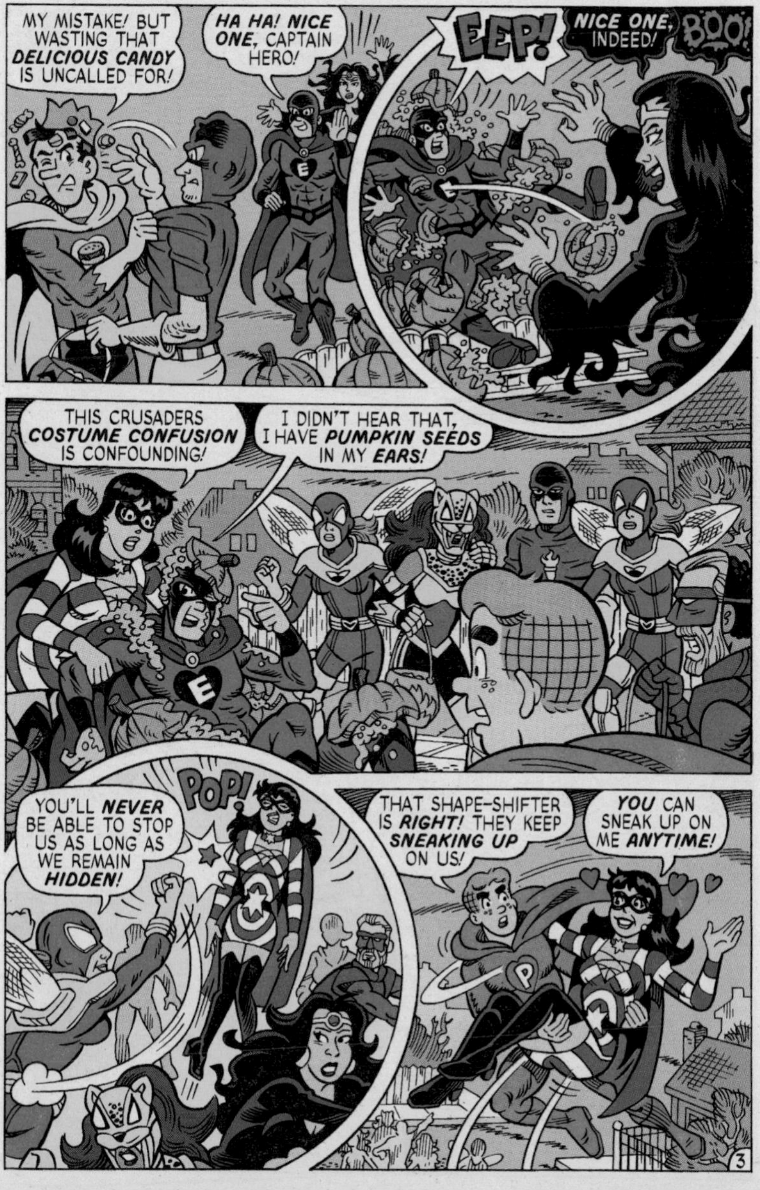

MY MISTAKE! BUT WASTING THAT DELICIOUS CANDY IS UNCALLED FOR!
HA HA! NICE ONE, CAPTAIN HERO!
EEP!
NICE ONE, INDEED!
BOO!
THIS CRUSADERS COSTUME CONFUSION IS CONFOUNDING!
I DIDN'T HEAR THAT, I HAVE PUMPKIN SEEDS IN MY EARS!
POP!
YOU'LL NEVER BE ABLE TO STOP US AS LONG AS WE REMAIN HIDDEN!
THAT SHAPE-SHIFTER IS RIGHT! THEY KEEP SNEAKING UP ON US!
YOU CAN SNEAK UP ON ME ANYTIME!

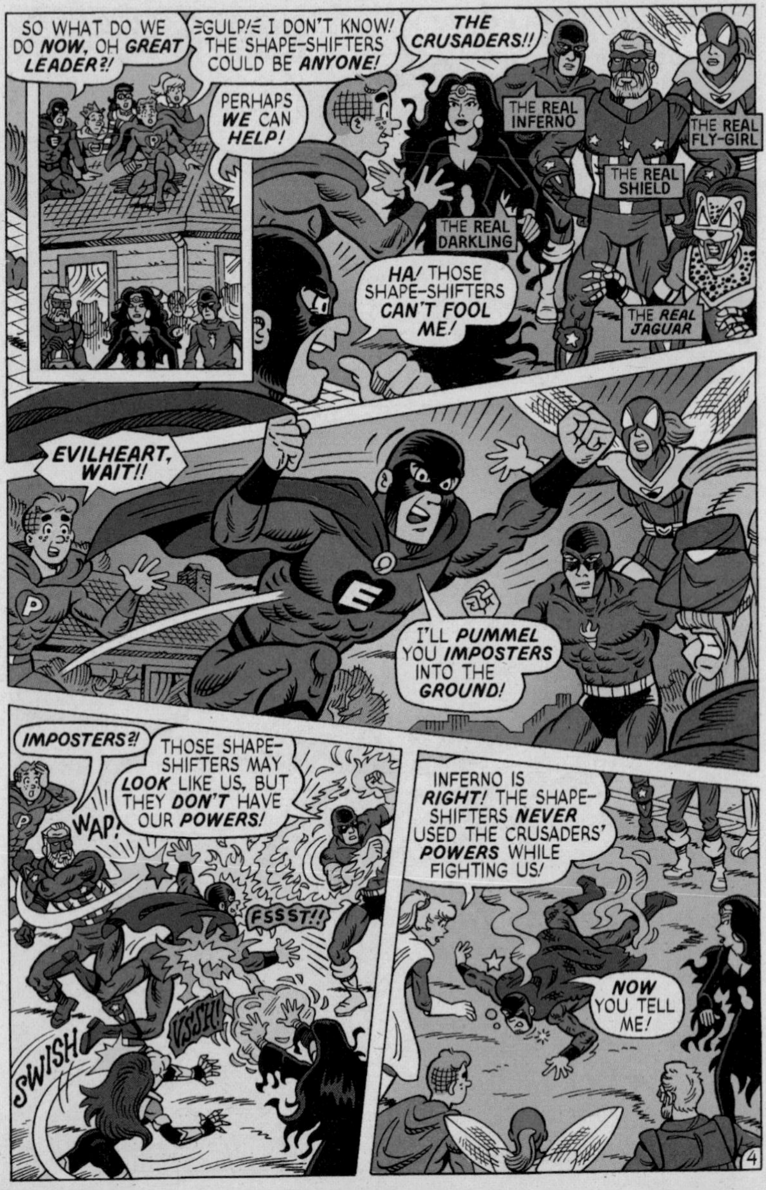

SO WHAT DO WE DO NOW, OH GREAT LEADER?!
=GULP!= I DON'T KNOW! THE SHAPE-SHIFTERS COULD BE ANYONE!
THE CRUSADERS!!
PERHAPS WE CAN HELP!
THE REAL INFERNO
THE REAL FLY-GIRL
THE REAL SHIELD
THE REAL DARKLING
HA! THOSE SHAPE-SHIFTERS CAN'T FOOL ME!
THE REAL JAGUAR
EVILHEART, WAIT!!
I'LL PUMMEL YOU IMPOSTERS INTO THE GROUND!
IMPOSTERS?!
THOSE SHAPE-SHIFTERS MAY LOOK LIKE US, BUT THEY DON'T HAVE OUR POWERS!
WAP!
FSSST!!
VSSH!
SWISH
INFERNO IS RIGHT! THE SHAPE-SHIFTERS NEVER USED THE CRUSADERS' POWERS WHILE FIGHTING US!
NOW YOU TELL ME!
4

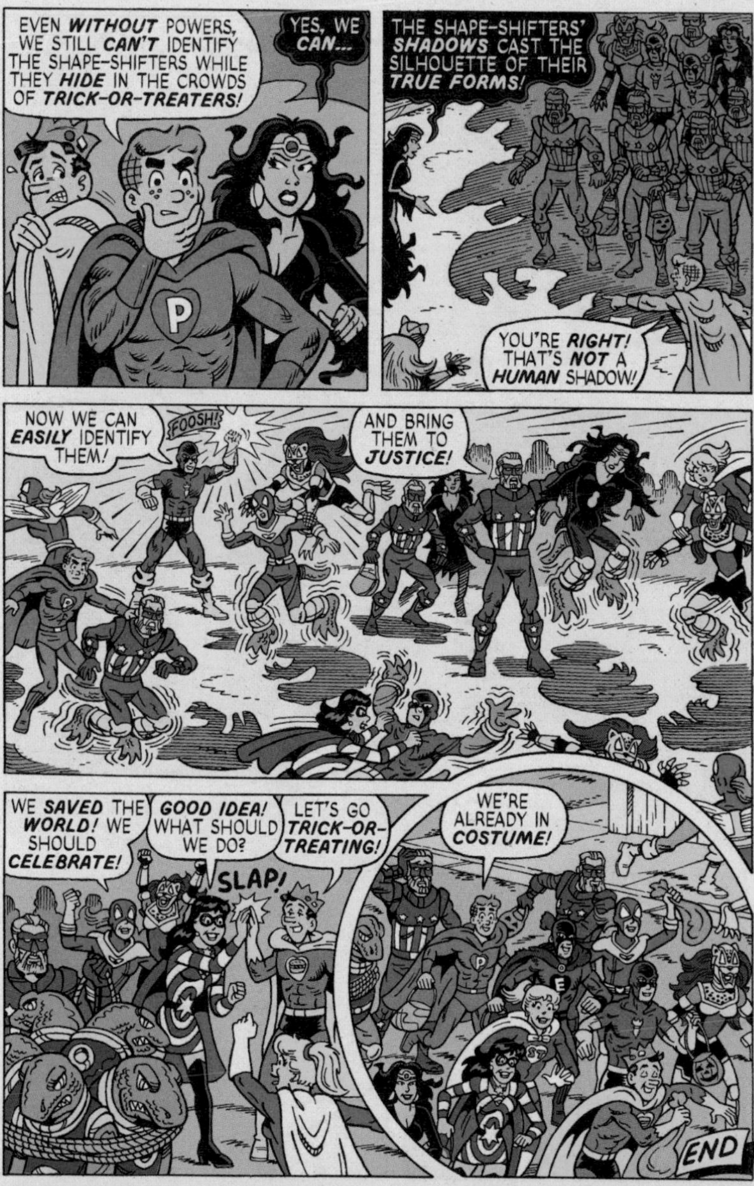
EVEN WITHOUT POWERS, WE STILL CAN'T IDENTIFY THE SHAPE-SHIFTERS WHILE THEY HIDE IN THE CROWDS OF TRICK-OR-TREATERS!
YES, WE CAN...
THE SHAPE-SHIFTERS' SHADOWS CAST THE SILHOUETTE OF THEIR TRUE FORMS!
YOU'RE RIGHT! THAT'S NOT A HUMAN SHADOW!
NOW WE CAN EASILY IDENTIFY THEM!
FOOSH!
AND BRING THEM TO JUSTICE!
WE SAVED THE WORLD! WE SHOULD CELEBRATE!
GOOD IDEA! WHAT SHOULD WE DO?
LET'S GO TRICK-OR-TREATING!
SLAP!
WE'RE ALREADY IN COSTUME!
END

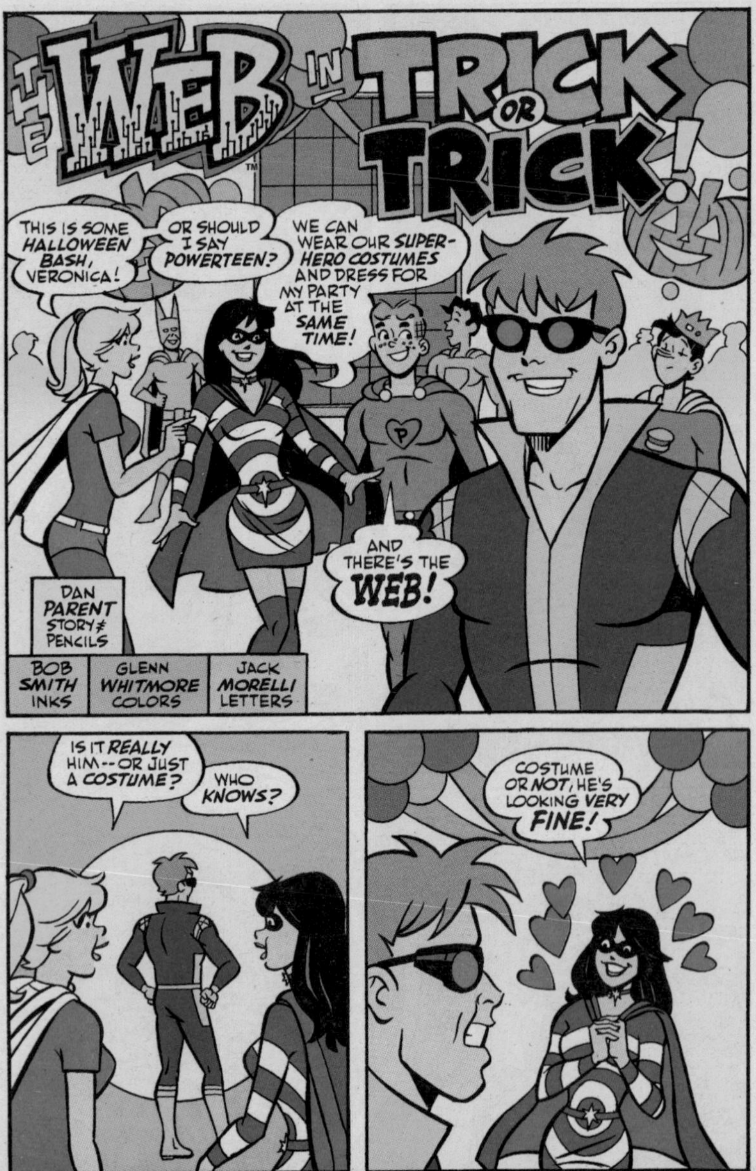
THE WEB™ IN TRICK OR TRICK!
THIS IS SOME HALLOWEEN BASH, VERONICA!
OR SHOULD I SAY POWERTEEN?
WE CAN WEAR OUR SUPER-HERO COSTUMES AND DRESS FOR MY PARTY AT THE SAME TIME!
AND THERE'S THE WEB!
DAN PARENT STORY & PENCILS
BOB SMITH INKS
GLENN WHITMORE COLORS
JACK MORELLI LETTERS
IS IT REALLY HIM--OR JUST A COSTUME?
WHO KNOWS?
COSTUME OR NOT, HE'S LOOKING VERY FINE!

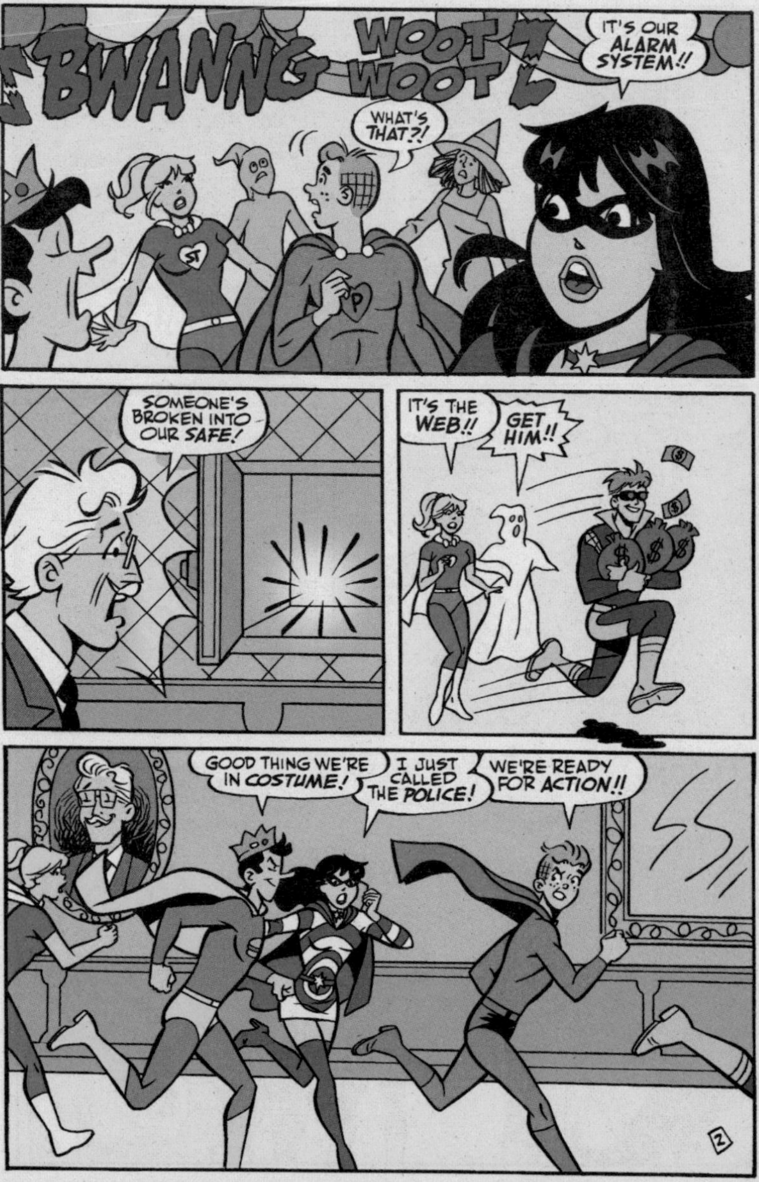
BWANNG
WOOT WOOT
IT'S OUR ALARM SYSTEM!!
WHAT'S THAT?!
SOMEONE'S BROKEN INTO OUR SAFE!
IT'S THE WEB!!
GET HIM!!
GOOD THING WE'RE IN COSTUME!
I JUST CALLED THE POLICE!
WE'RE READY FOR ACTION!!
2

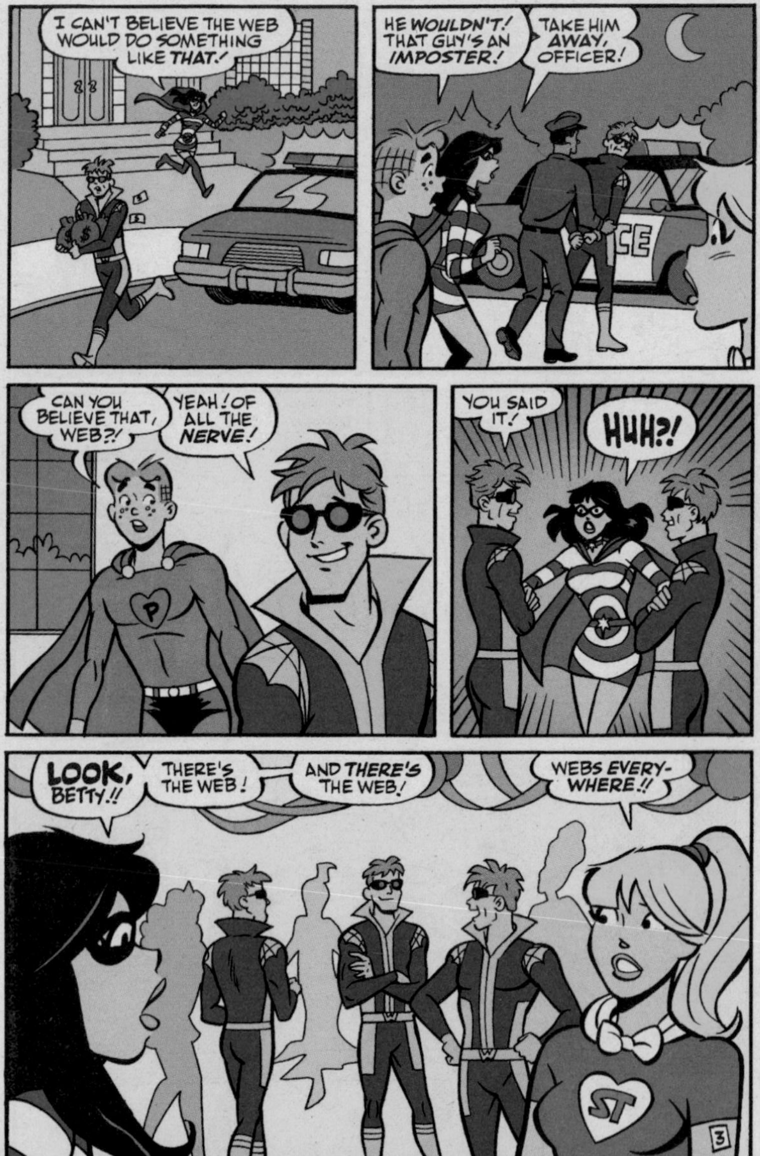

I CAN'T BELIEVE THE WEB WOULD DO SOMETHING LIKE THAT!
HE WOULDN'T! THAT GUY'S AN IMPOSTER!
TAKE HIM AWAY, OFFICER!
CAN YOU BELIEVE THAT, WEB?!
YEAH! OF ALL THE NERVE!
YOU SAID IT!
HUH?!
LOOK, BETTY!!
THERE'S THE WEB!
AND THERE'S THE WEB!
WEBS EVERY-WHERE!!
3

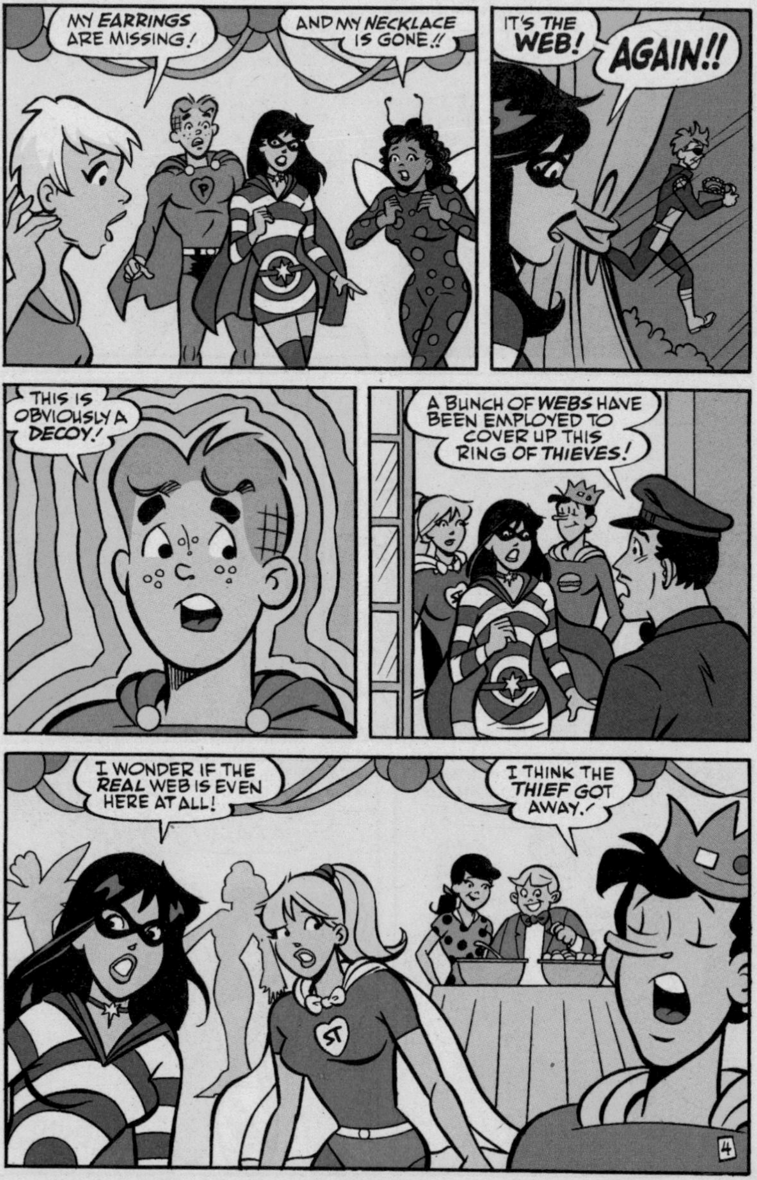
MY EARRINGS ARE MISSING!
AND MY NECKLACE IS GONE!!
IT'S THE WEB!
AGAIN!!
THIS IS OBVIOUSLY A DECOY!
A BUNCH OF WEBS HAVE BEEN EMPLOYED TO COVER UP THIS RING OF THIEVES!
I WONDER IF THE REAL WEB IS EVEN HERE AT ALL!
I THINK THE THIEF GOT AWAY.!
4

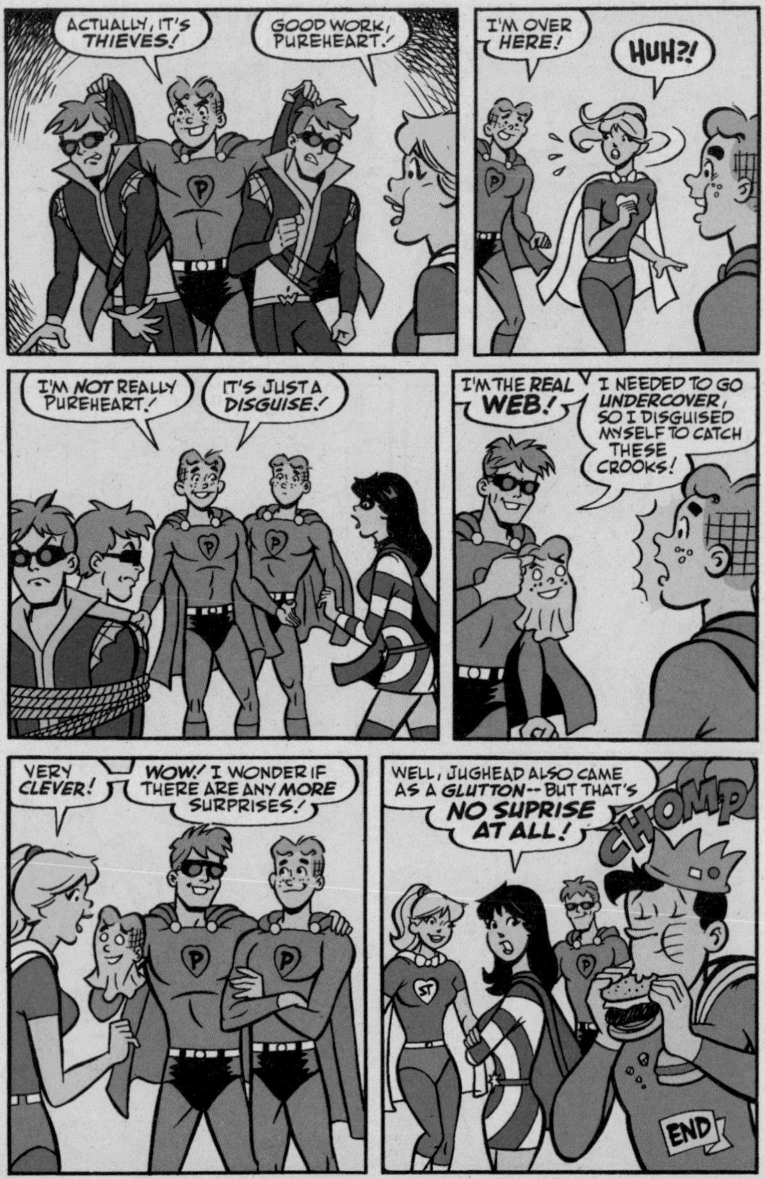
ACTUALLY, IT'S THIEVES!
GOOD WORK, PUREHEART.!
I'M OVER HERE!
HUH?!
I'M NOT REALLY PUREHEART.!
IT'S JUST A DISGUISE.!
I'M THE REAL WEB!
I NEEDED TO GO UNDERCOVER, SO I DISGUISED MYSELF TO CATCH THESE CROOKS!
VERY CLEVER!
WOW! I WONDER IF THERE ARE ANY MORE SURPRISES.!
WELL, JUGHEAD ALSO CAME AS A GLUTTON-- BUT THAT'S NO SUPRISE AT ALL!
CHOMP
END

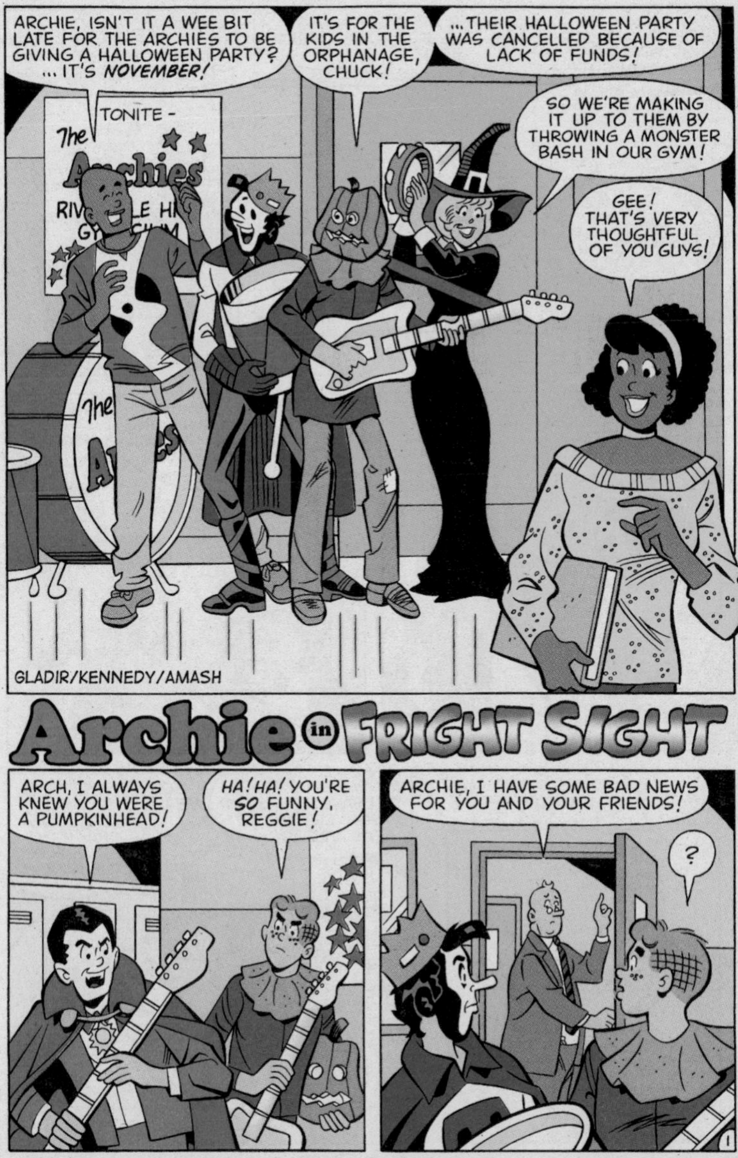
ARCHIE, ISN'T IT A WEE BIT LATE FOR THE ARCHIES TO BE GIVING A HALLOWEEN PARTY? ... IT'S NOVEMBER!
IT'S FOR THE KIDS IN THE ORPHANAGE, CHUCK!
...THEIR HALLOWEEN PARTY WAS CANCELLED BECAUSE OF LACK OF FUNDS!
SO WE'RE MAKING IT UP TO THEM BY THROWING A MONSTER BASH IN OUR GYM!
GEE! THAT'S VERY THOUGHTFUL OF YOU GUYS!
TONITE -
The Archies
GLADIR/KENNEDY/AMASH
Archie in FRIGHT SIGHT
ARCH, I ALWAYS KNEW YOU WERE A PUMPKINHEAD!
HA! HA! YOU'RE SO FUNNY, REGGIE!
ARCHIE, I HAVE SOME BAD NEWS FOR YOU AND YOUR FRIENDS!
?
1

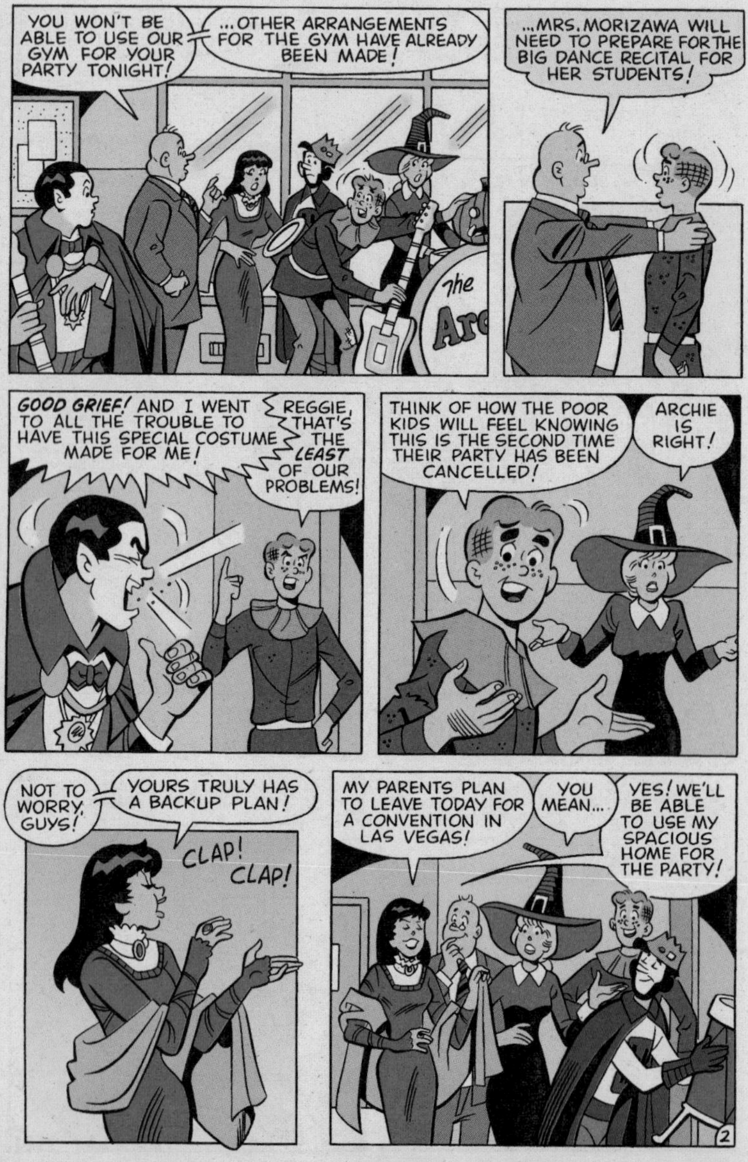
YOU WON'T BE ABLE TO USE OUR GYM FOR YOUR PARTY TONIGHT!
...OTHER ARRANGEMENTS FOR THE GYM HAVE ALREADY BEEN MADE!
...MRS. MORIZAWA WILL NEED TO PREPARE FOR THE BIG DANCE RECITAL FOR HER STUDENTS!
GOOD GRIEF! AND I WENT TO ALL THE TROUBLE TO HAVE THIS SPECIAL COSTUME MADE FOR ME!
REGGIE, THAT'S THE LEAST OF OUR PROBLEMS!
THINK OF HOW THE POOR KIDS WILL FEEL KNOWING THIS IS THE SECOND TIME THEIR PARTY HAS BEEN CANCELLED!
ARCHIE IS RIGHT!
NOT TO WORRY, GUYS!
YOURS TRULY HAS A BACKUP PLAN!
CLAP! CLAP!
MY PARENTS PLAN TO LEAVE TODAY FOR A CONVENTION IN LAS VEGAS!
YOU MEAN...
YES! WE'LL BE ABLE TO USE MY SPACIOUS HOME FOR THE PARTY!
2

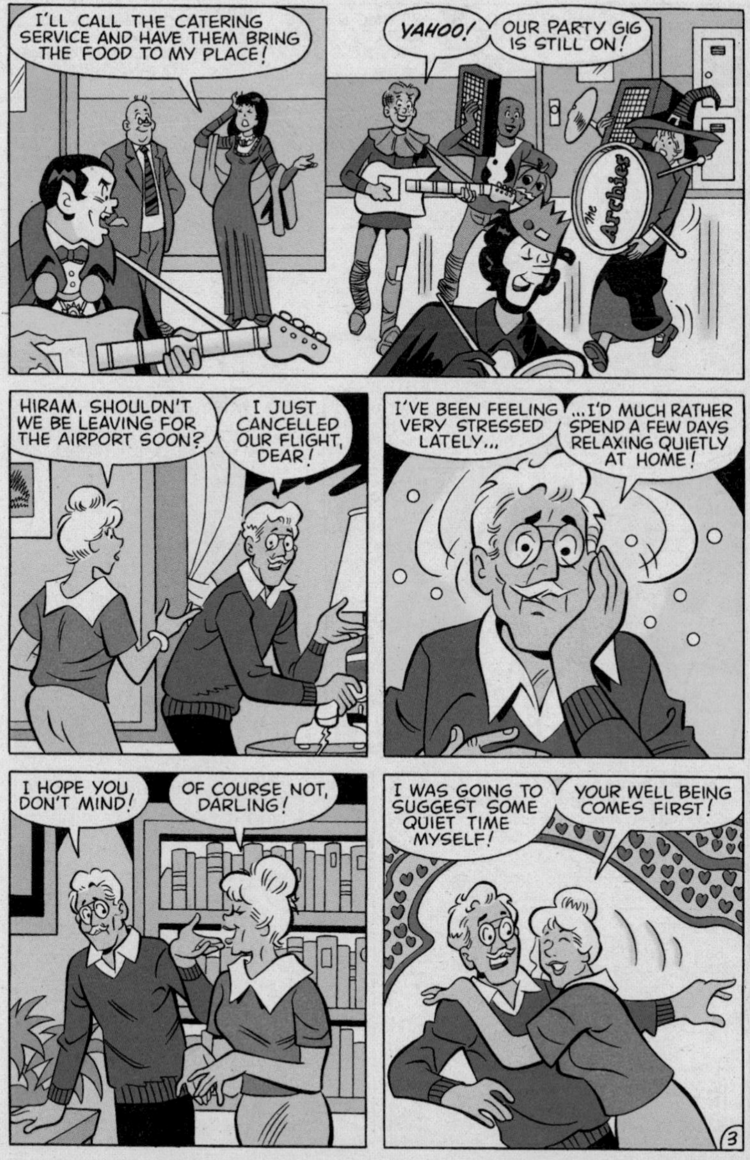
I'LL CALL THE CATERING SERVICE AND HAVE THEM BRING THE FOOD TO MY PLACE!
YAHOO!
OUR PARTY GIG IS STILL ON!
The Archies
HIRAM, SHOULDN'T WE BE LEAVING FOR THE AIRPORT SOON?
I JUST CANCELLED OUR FLIGHT, DEAR!
I'VE BEEN FEELING VERY STRESSED LATELY...
...I'D MUCH RATHER SPEND A FEW DAYS RELAXING QUIETLY AT HOME!
I HOPE YOU DON'T MIND!
OF COURSE NOT, DARLING!
I WAS GOING TO SUGGEST SOME QUIET TIME MYSELF!
YOUR WELL BEING COMES FIRST!
3

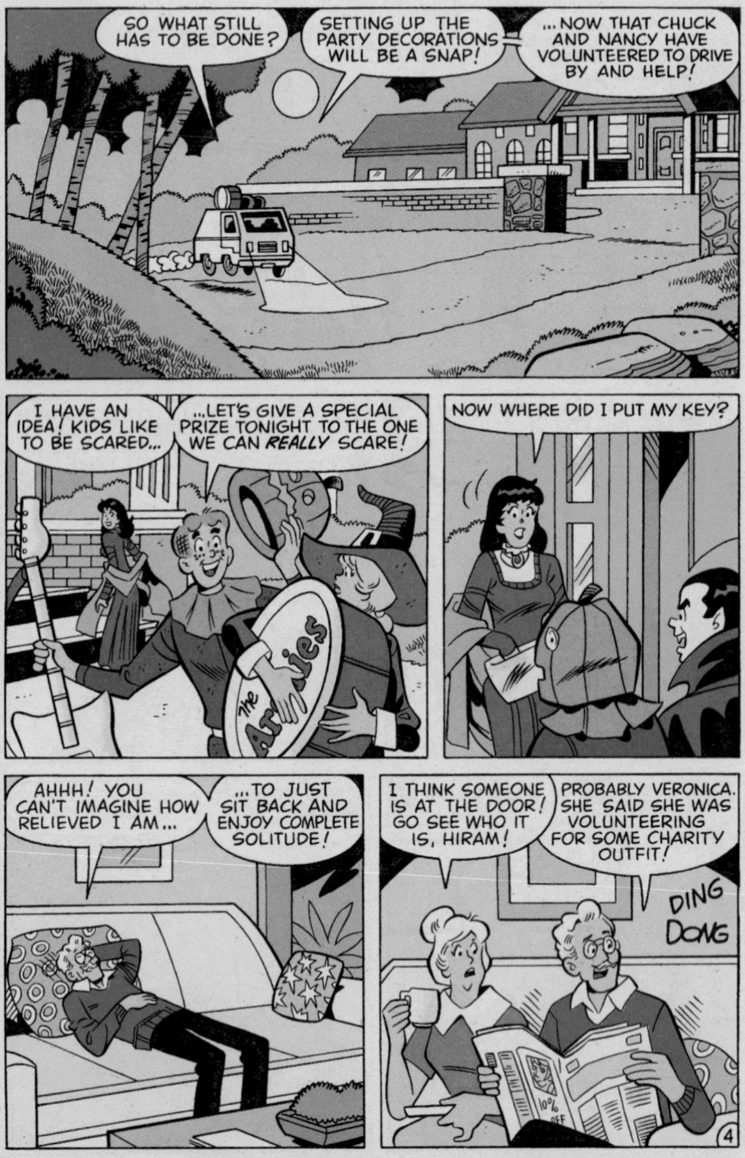
SO WHAT STILL HAS TO BE DONE?
SETTING UP THE PARTY DECORATIONS WILL BE A SNAP!
...NOW THAT CHUCK AND NANCY HAVE VOLUNTEERED TO DRIVE BY AND HELP!
I HAVE AN IDEA! KIDS LIKE TO BE SCARED...
...LET'S GIVE A SPECIAL PRIZE TONIGHT TO THE ONE WE CAN REALLY SCARE!
The Archies
NOW WHERE DID I PUT MY KEY?
AHHH! YOU CAN'T IMAGINE HOW RELIEVED I AM...
...TO JUST SIT BACK AND ENJOY COMPLETE SOLITUDE!
I THINK SOMEONE IS AT THE DOOR! GO SEE WHO IT IS, HIRAM!
PROBABLY VERONICA. SHE SAID SHE WAS VOLUNTEERING FOR SOME CHARITY OUTFIT!
DING DONG
10% OFF
4

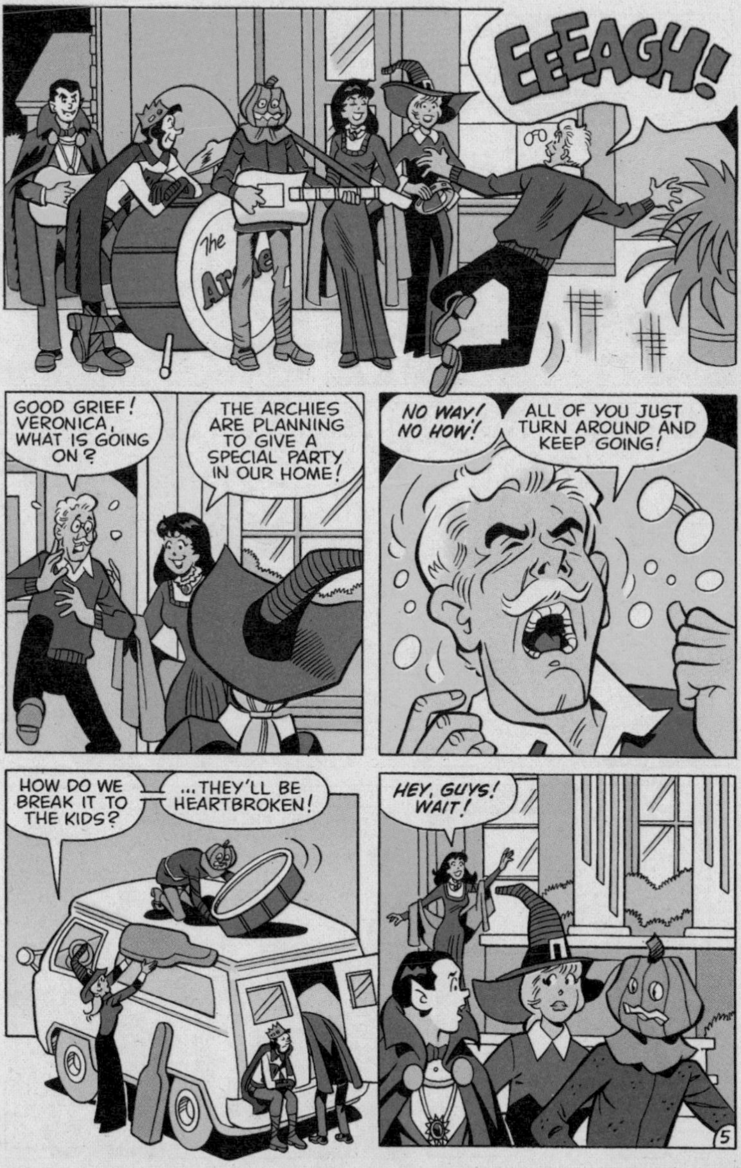

EEEAGH!
GOOD GRIEF! VERONICA, WHAT IS GOING ON?
THE ARCHIES ARE PLANNING TO GIVE A SPECIAL PARTY IN OUR HOME!
NO WAY! NO HOW!
ALL OF YOU JUST TURN AROUND AND KEEP GOING!
HOW DO WE BREAK IT TO THE KIDS?
...THEY'LL BE HEARTBROKEN!
HEY, GUYS! WAIT!

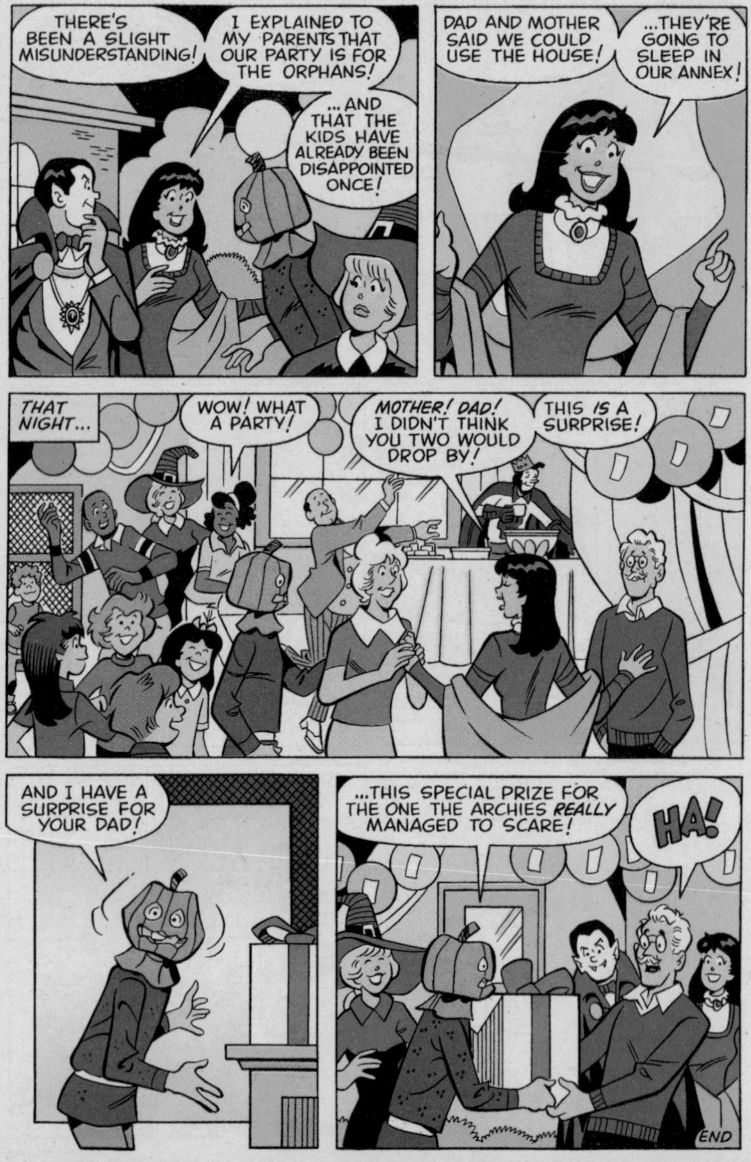
THERE'S BEEN A SLIGHT MISUNDERSTANDING!
I EXPLAINED TO MY PARENTS THAT OUR PARTY IS FOR THE ORPHANS!
...AND THAT THE KIDS HAVE ALREADY BEEN DISAPPOINTED ONCE!
DAD AND MOTHER SAID WE COULD USE THE HOUSE!
...THEY'RE GOING TO SLEEP IN OUR ANNEX!
THAT NIGHT...
WOW! WHAT A PARTY!
MOTHER! DAD! I DIDN'T THINK YOU TWO WOULD DROP BY!
THIS IS A SURPRISE!
AND I HAVE A SURPRISE FOR YOUR DAD!
...THIS SPECIAL PRIZE FOR THE ONE THE ARCHIES REALLY MANAGED TO SCARE!
HA!
END

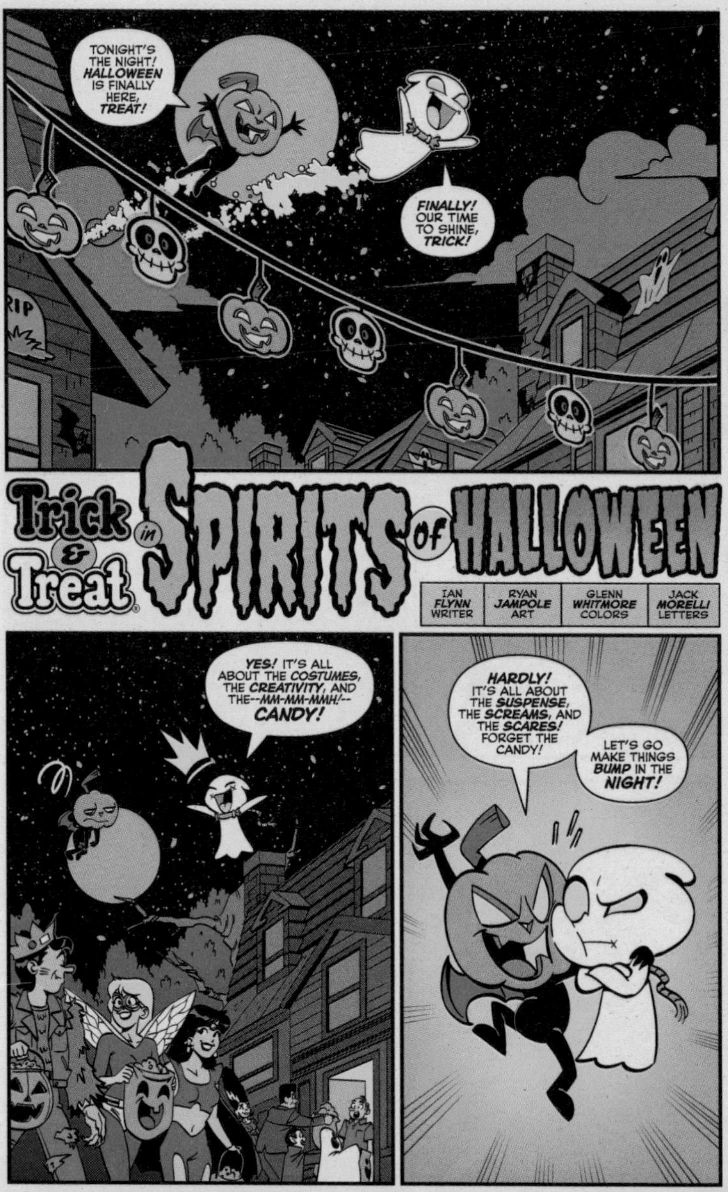
TONIGHT'S THE NIGHT! HALLOWEEN IS FINALLY HERE, TREAT!
FINALLY! OUR TIME TO SHINE, TRICK!
Trick & Treat in SPIRITS of HALLOWEEN
IAN FLYNN WRITER
RYAN JAMPOLE ART
GLENN WHITMORE COLORS
JACK MORELLI LETTERS
YES! IT'S ALL ABOUT THE COSTUMES, THE CREATIVITY, AND THE--MM-MM-MMH!-- CANDY!
HARDLY! IT'S ALL ABOUT THE SUSPENSE, THE SCREAMS, AND THE SCARES! FORGET THE CANDY!
LET'S GO MAKE THINGS BUMP IN THE NIGHT!
RIP

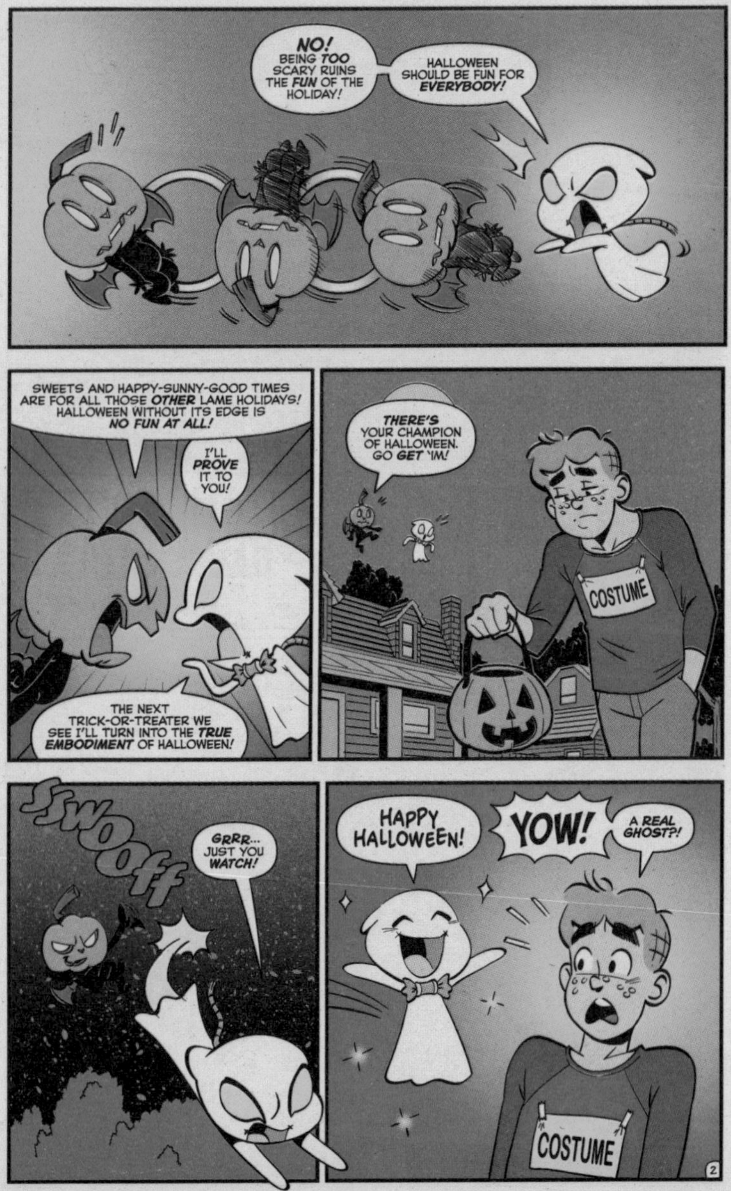
NO! BEING TOO SCARY RUINS THE FUN OF THE HOLIDAY!
HALLOWEEN SHOULD BE FUN FOR EVERYBODY!
SWEETS AND HAPPY-SUNNY-GOOD TIMES ARE FOR ALL THOSE OTHER LAME HOLIDAYS! HALLOWEEN WITHOUT ITS EDGE IS NO FUN AT ALL!
I'LL PROVE IT TO YOU!
THE NEXT TRICK-OR-TREATER WE SEE I'LL TURN INTO THE TRUE EMBODIMENT OF HALLOWEEN!
THERE'S YOUR CHAMPION OF HALLOWEEN. GO GET 'IM!
COSTUME
SWOOFF
GRRR... JUST YOU WATCH!
HAPPY HALLOWEEN!
YOW!
A REAL GHOST?!
COSTUME
2

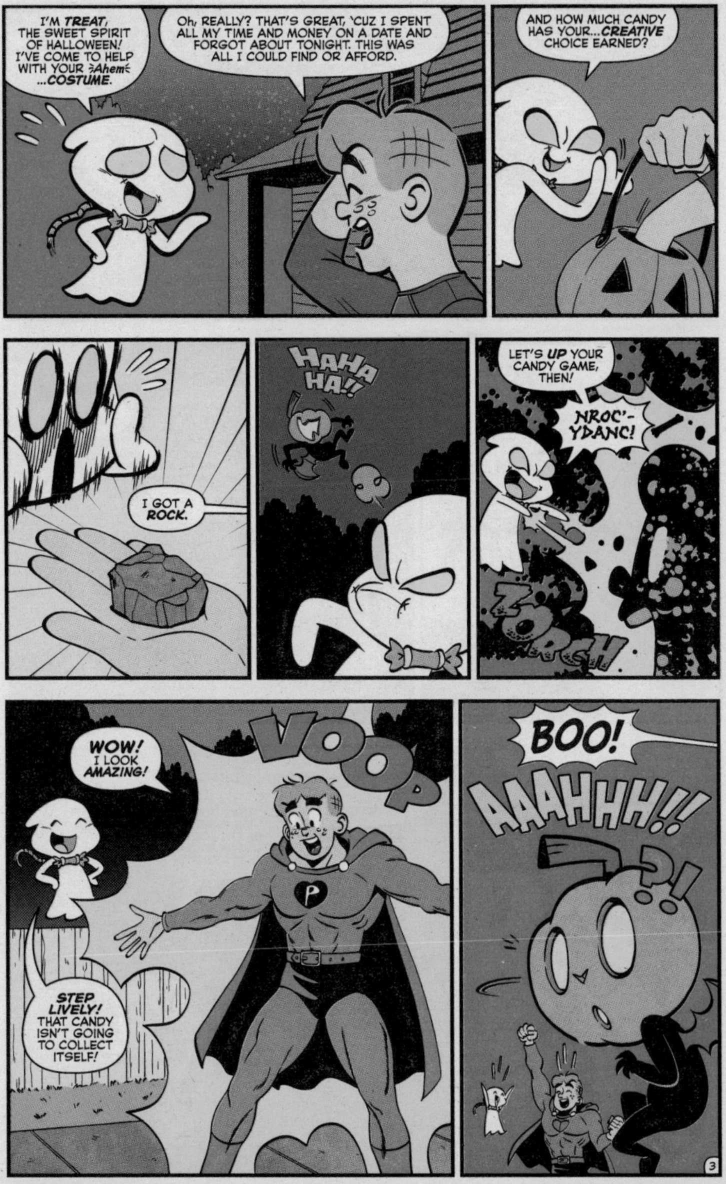
I'M TREAT, THE SWEET SPIRIT OF HALLOWEEN! I'VE COME TO HELP WITH YOUR ≷Ahem≶ ...COSTUME.
Oh, REALLY? THAT'S GREAT, 'CUZ I SPENT ALL MY TIME AND MONEY ON A DATE AND FORGOT ABOUT TONIGHT. THIS WAS ALL I COULD FIND OR AFFORD.
AND HOW MUCH CANDY HAS YOUR...CREATIVE CHOICE EARNED?
I GOT A ROCK.
HAHAHA!!
LET'S UP YOUR CANDY GAME, THEN!
NROC'-YDANC!
ZORCH
VOOP
WOW! I LOOK AMAZING!
STEP LIVELY! THAT CANDY ISN'T GOING TO COLLECT ITSELF!
BOO!
AAAHHH!!
?!
3

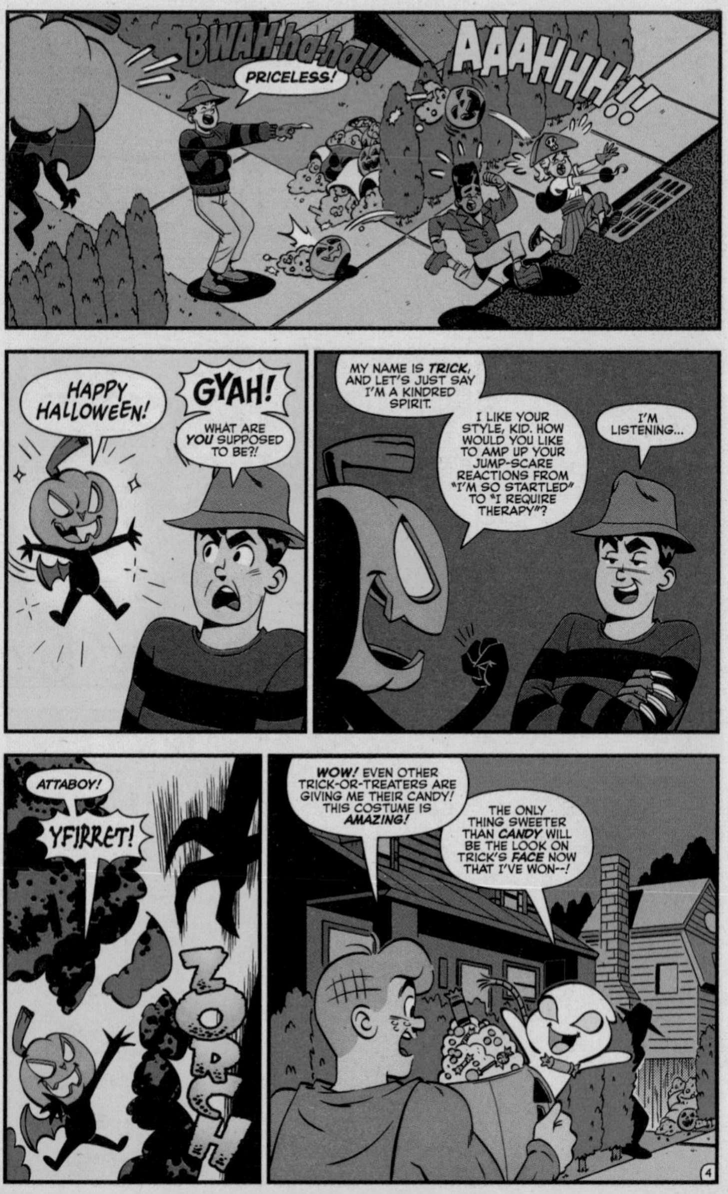
BWAH-ha-ha!!
PRICELESS!
AAAHHH!!
HAPPY HALLOWEEN!
GYAH!
WHAT ARE YOU SUPPOSED TO BE?!
MY NAME IS TRICK, AND LET'S JUST SAY I'M A KINDRED SPIRIT.
I LIKE YOUR STYLE, KID. HOW WOULD YOU LIKE TO AMP UP YOUR JUMP-SCARE REACTIONS FROM "I'M SO STARTLED" TO "I REQUIRE THERAPY"?
I'M LISTENING...
ATTABOY!
YFIRRET!
ZORCH
WOW! EVEN OTHER TRICK-OR-TREATERS ARE GIVING ME THEIR CANDY! THIS COSTUME IS AMAZING!
THE ONLY THING SWEETER THAN CANDY WILL BE THE LOOK ON TRICK'S FACE NOW THAT I'VE WON--!

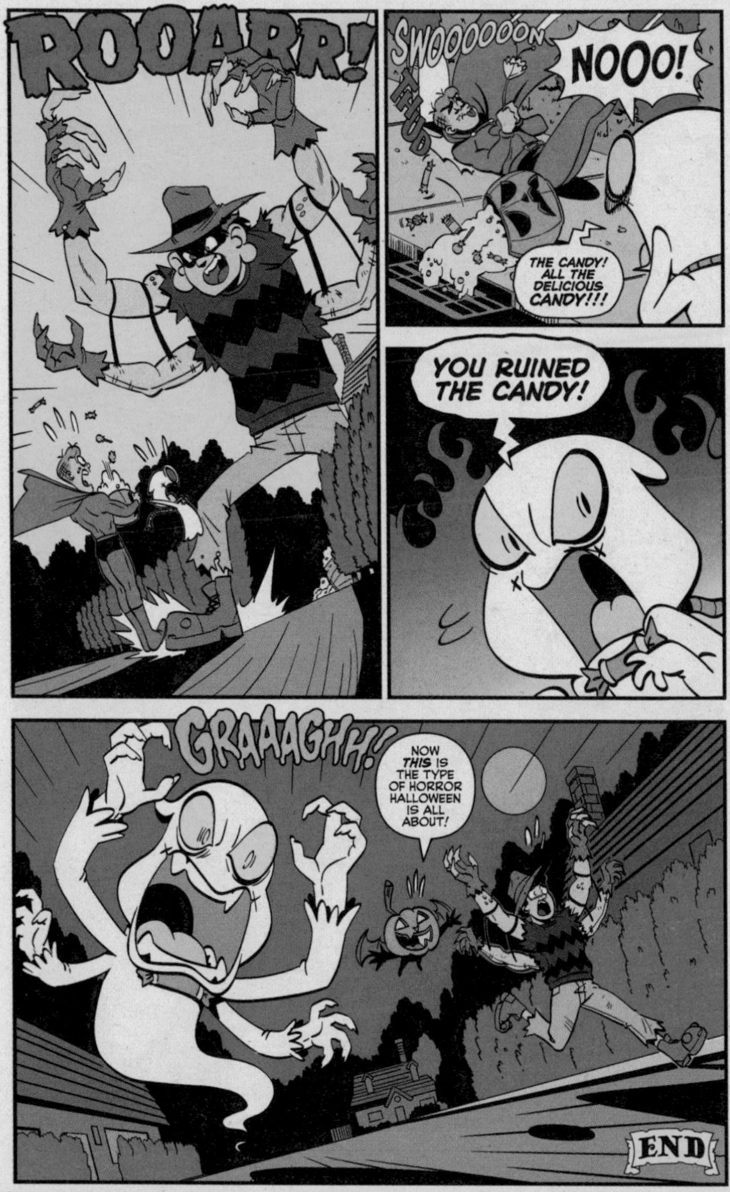
ROOARR!
SWOOOOOON
THUD
NOOO!
THE CANDY! ALL THE DELICIOUS CANDY!!!
YOU RUINED THE CANDY!
GRAAAGHH!
NOW THIS IS THE TYPE OF HORROR HALLOWEEN IS ALL ABOUT!
END

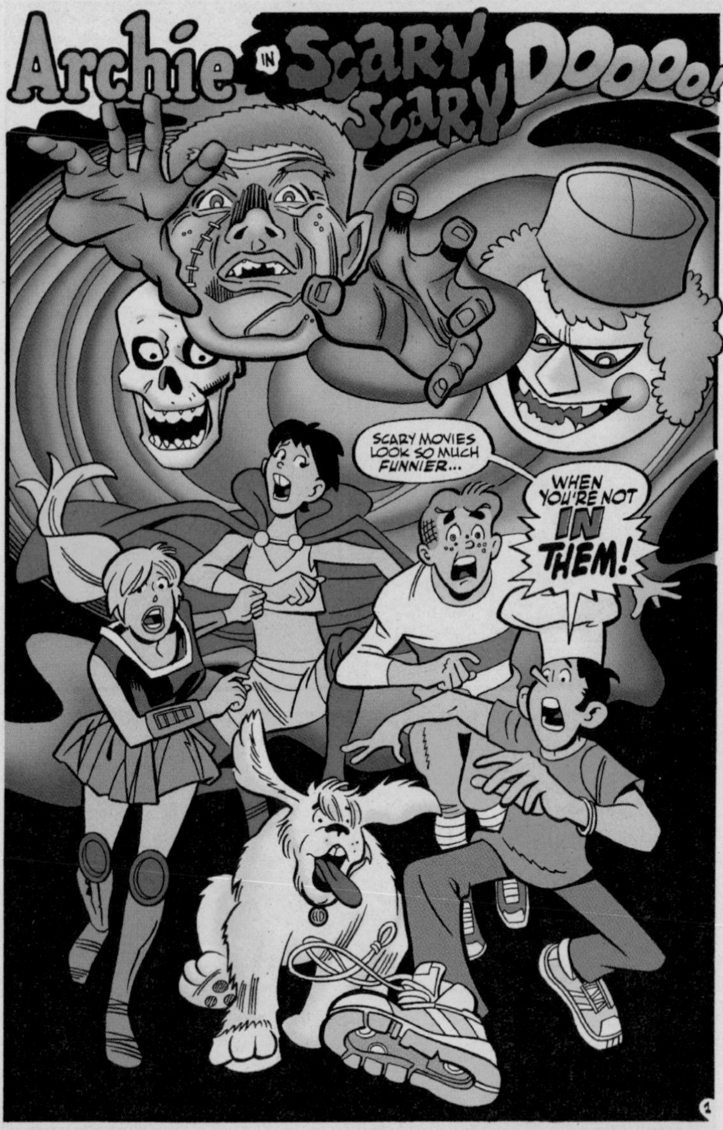
Archie in Scary Scary Doooo!
SCARY MOVIES LOOK SO MUCH FUNNIER...
WHEN YOU'RE NOT IN THEM!
1

SCRIPT:	PENCILS:	INKS:	LETTERS:	COLORS:
ALEX SIMMONS	PAT & TIM KENNEDY	JIM AMASH	JACK MORELLI	DIGIKORE STUDIOS

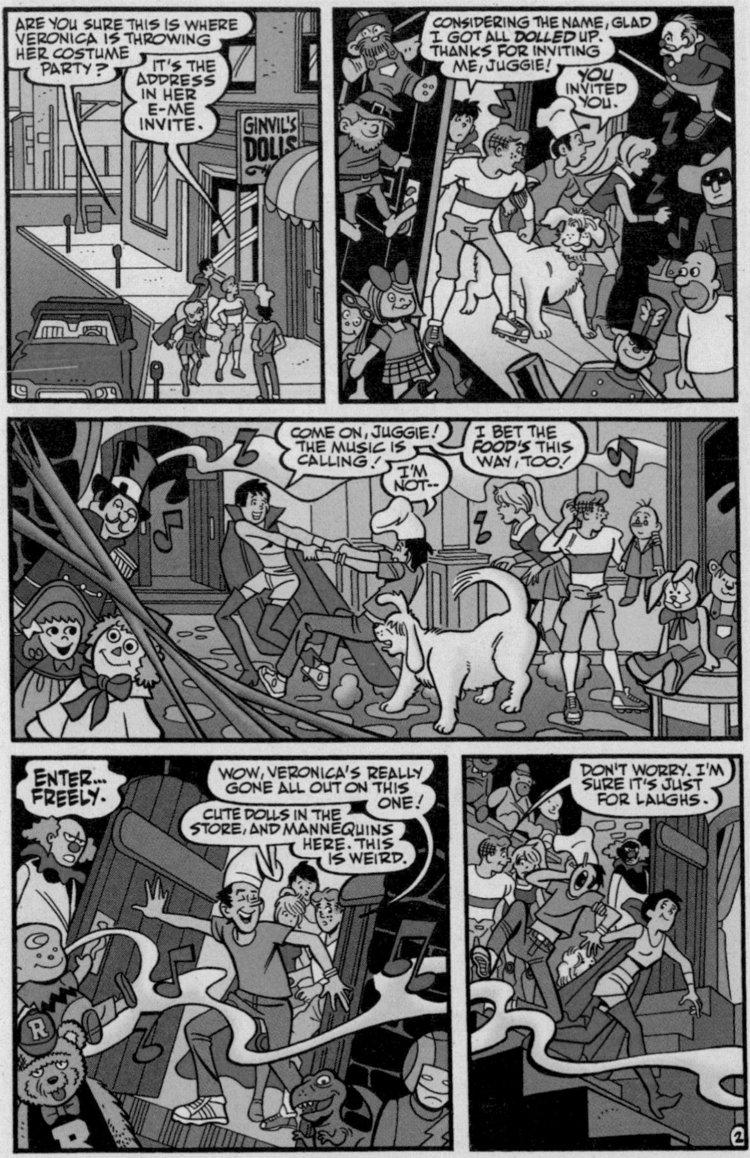
ARE YOU SURE THIS IS WHERE VERONICA IS THROWING HER COSTUME PARTY?
IT'S THE ADDRESS IN HER E-ME INVITE.
GINVIL'S DOLLS
CONSIDERING THE NAME, GLAD I GOT ALL DOLLED UP. THANKS FOR INVITING ME, JUGGIE!
YOU INVITED YOU.
COME ON, JUGGIE! THE MUSIC IS CALLING!
I'M NOT--
I BET THE FOOD'S THIS WAY, TOO!
ENTER... FREELY.
WOW, VERONICA'S REALLY GONE ALL OUT ON THIS ONE!
CUTE DOLLS IN THE STORE, AND MANNEQUINS HERE. THIS IS WEIRD.
DON'T WORRY. I'M SURE IT'S JUST FOR LAUGHS.
2

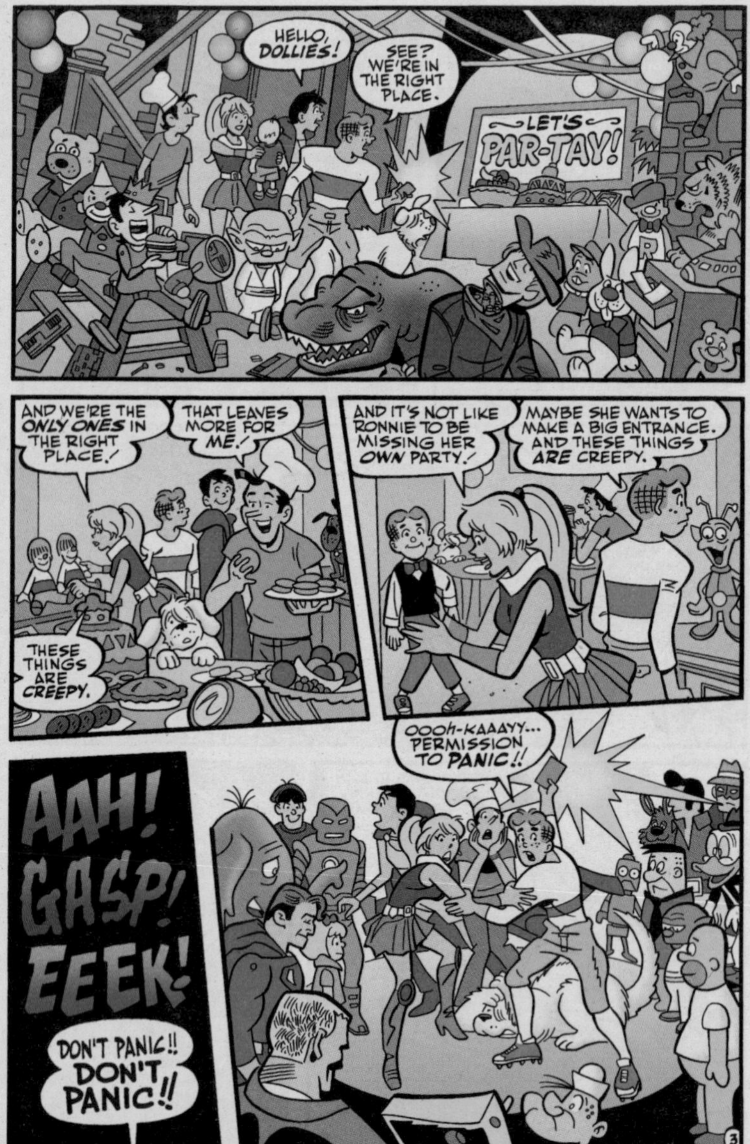
HELLO, DOLLIES!
SEE? WE'RE IN THE RIGHT PLACE.
LET'S PAR-TAY!
AND WE'RE THE ONLY ONES IN THE RIGHT PLACE.!
THAT LEAVES MORE FOR ME.!
THESE THINGS ARE CREEPY.
AND IT'S NOT LIKE RONNIE TO BE MISSING HER OWN PARTY.!
MAYBE SHE WANTS TO MAKE A BIG ENTRANCE. AND THESE THINGS ARE CREEPY.
OOOH-KAAAYY... PERMISSION TO PANIC!!
AAH! GASP! EEEK!
DON'T PANIC!! DON'T PANIC!!
3

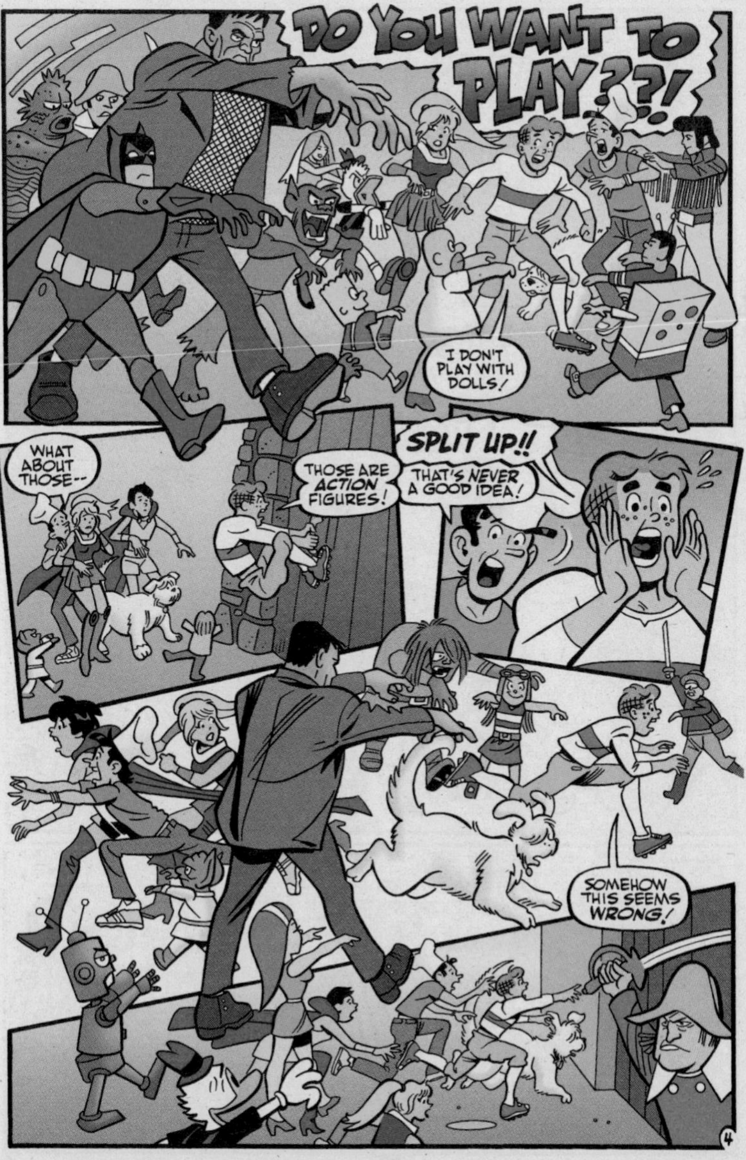
DO YOU WANT TO PLAY???!
I DON'T PLAY WITH DOLLS!
WHAT ABOUT THOSE--
THOSE ARE ACTION FIGURES!
SPLIT UP!!
THAT'S NEVER A GOOD IDEA!
SOMEHOW THIS SEEMS WRONG!
4

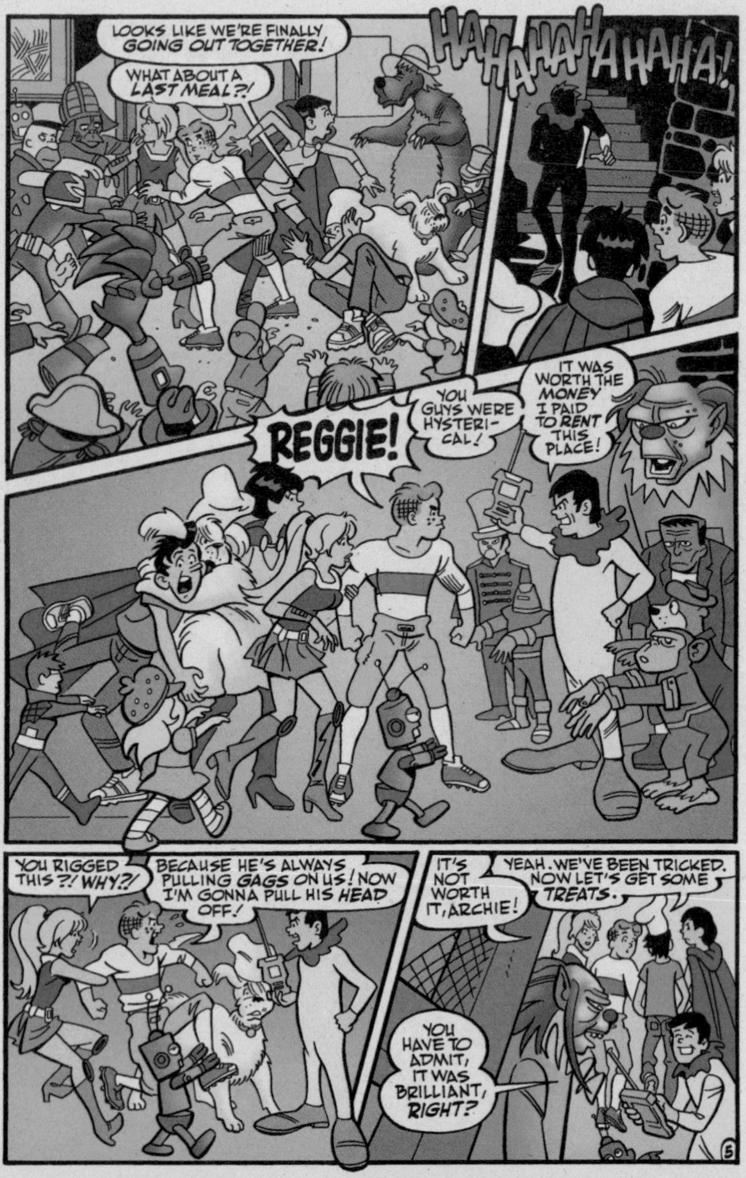
LOOKS LIKE WE'RE FINALLY GOING OUT TOGETHER!
WHAT ABOUT A LAST MEAL?!
HAHAHAHAHAHAHAHA!
REGGIE!
YOU GUYS WERE HYSTERICAL!
IT WAS WORTH THE MONEY I PAID TO RENT THIS PLACE!
YOU RIGGED THIS?! WHY?!
BECAUSE HE'S ALWAYS PULLING GAGS ON US! NOW I'M GONNA PULL HIS HEAD OFF!
IT'S NOT WORTH IT, ARCHIE!
YEAH. WE'VE BEEN TRICKED. NOW LET'S GET SOME TREATS.
YOU HAVE TO ADMIT, IT WAS BRILLIANT, RIGHT?
5

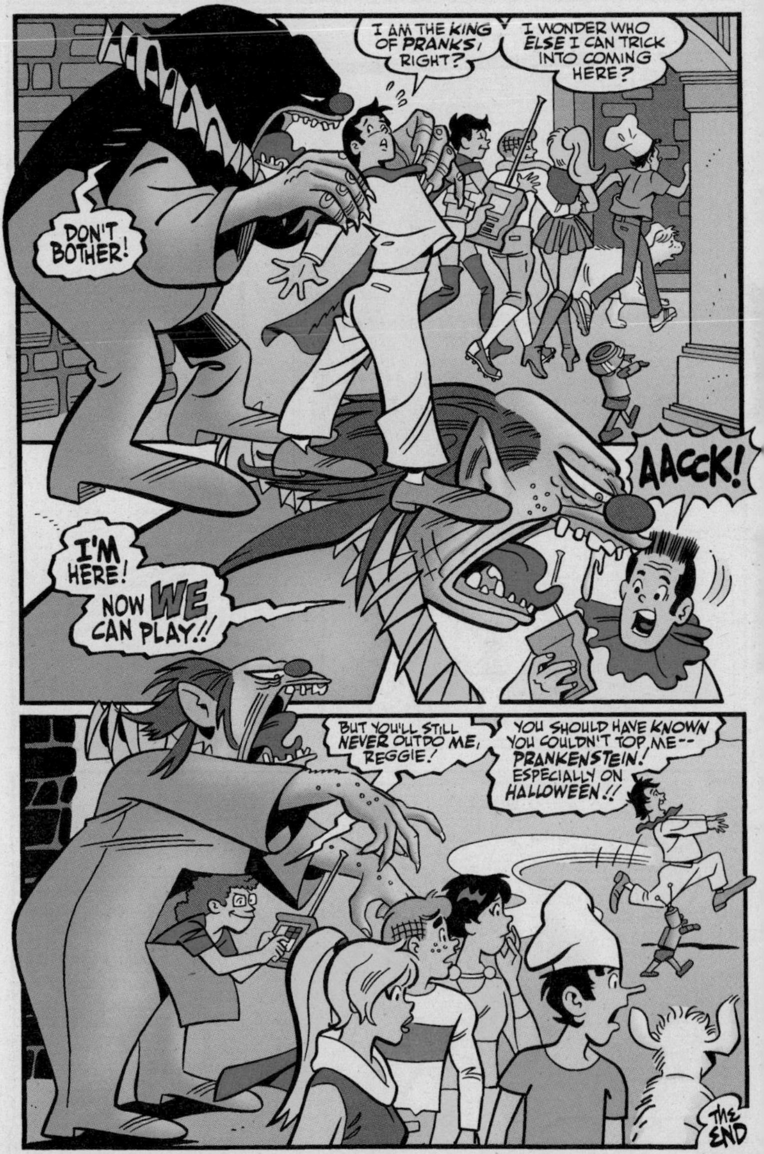
I AM THE KING OF PRANKS, RIGHT?
I WONDER WHO ELSE I CAN TRICK INTO COMING HERE?
DON'T BOTHER!
AACCK!
I'M HERE! NOW WE CAN PLAY!!
BUT YOU'LL STILL NEVER OUTDO ME, REGGIE!
YOU SHOULD HAVE KNOWN YOU COULDN'T TOP ME-- PRANKENSTEIN! ESPECIALLY ON HALLOWEEN!!
THE END

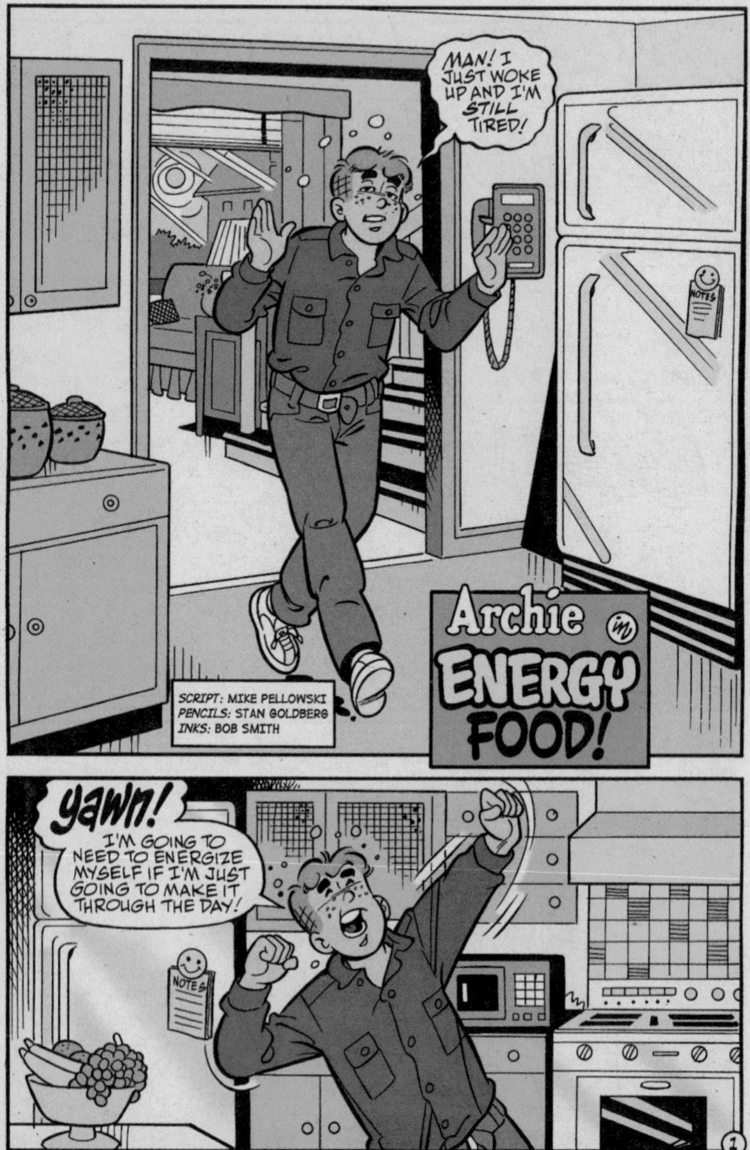

MAN! I JUST WOKE UP AND I'M STILL TIRED!
NOTES
Archie in ENERGY FOOD!
SCRIPT: MIKE PELLOWSKI
PENCILS: STAN GOLDBERG
INKS: BOB SMITH
yawn!
I'M GOING TO NEED TO ENERGIZE MYSELF IF I'M JUST GOING TO MAKE IT THROUGH THE DAY!
NOTES

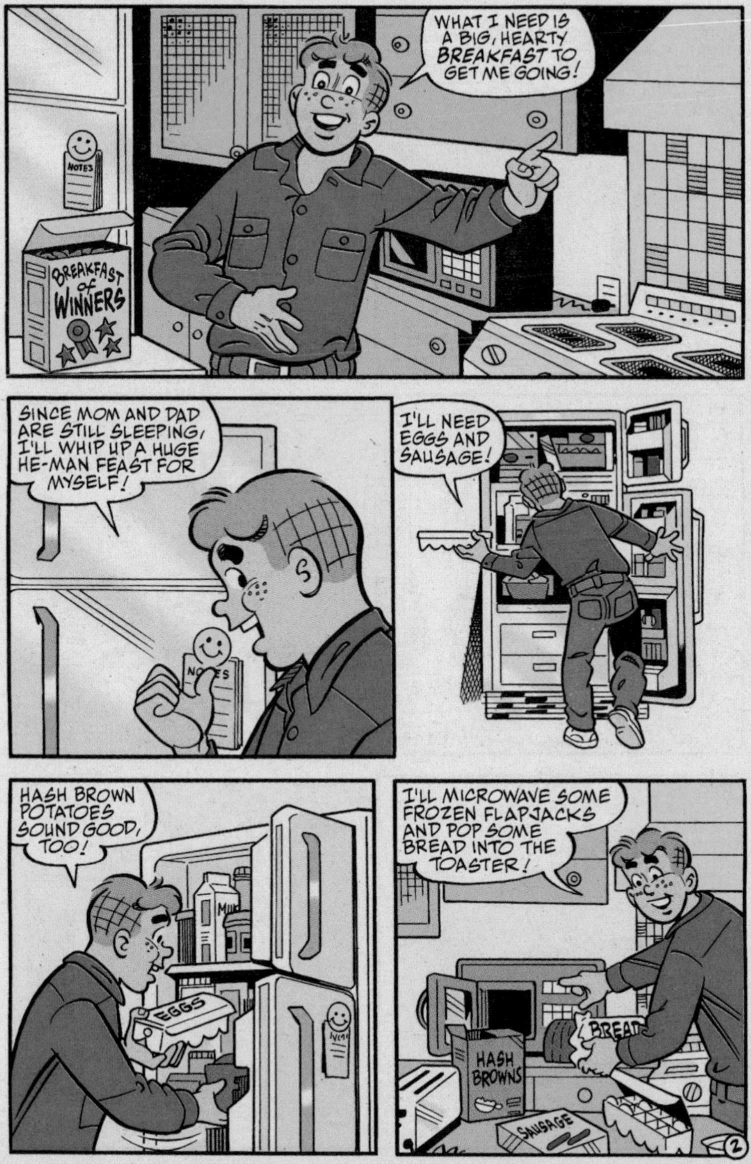
WHAT I NEED IS A BIG, HEARTY BREAKFAST TO GET ME GOING!
NOTES
BREAKFAST of WINNERS
SINCE MOM AND DAD ARE STILL SLEEPING, I'LL WHIP UP A HUGE HE-MAN FEAST FOR MYSELF!
I'LL NEED EGGS AND SAUSAGE!
HASH BROWN POTATOES SOUND GOOD, TOO!
EGGS
I'LL MICROWAVE SOME FROZEN FLAPJACKS AND POP SOME BREAD INTO THE TOASTER!
HASH BROWNS
SAUSAGE
2

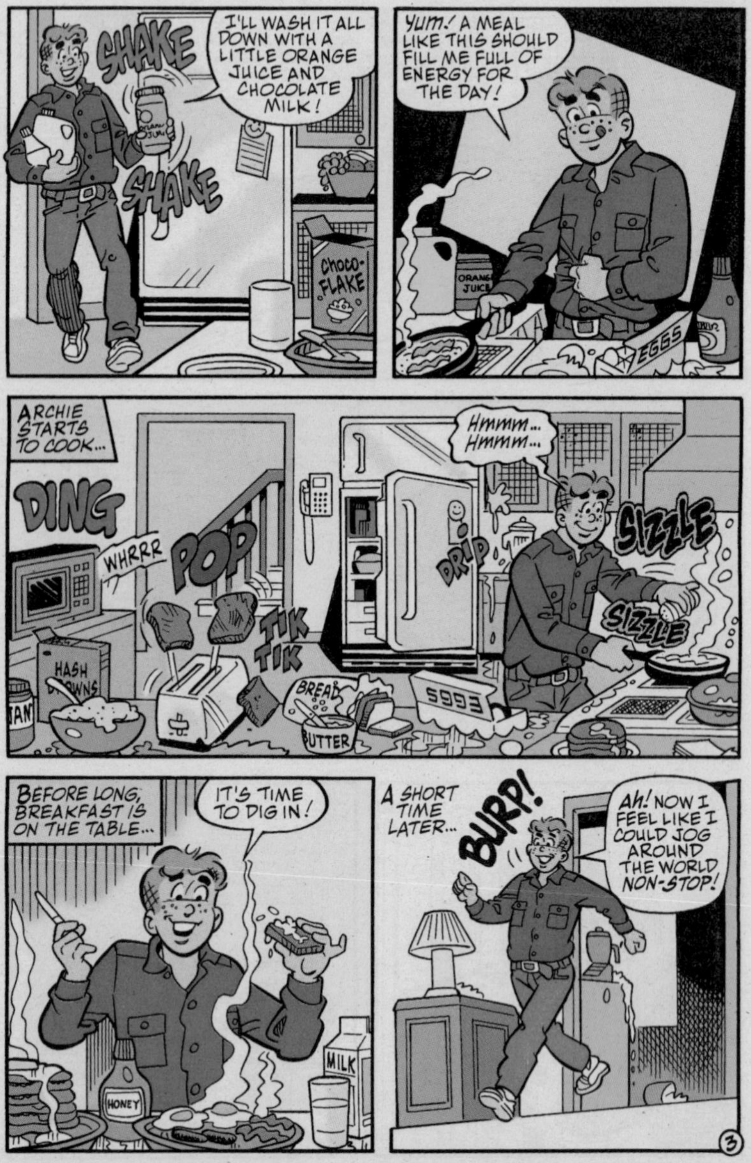
SHAKE
SHAKE
I'LL WASH IT ALL DOWN WITH A LITTLE ORANGE JUICE AND CHOCOLATE MILK!
CHOCO-FLAKE
YUM! A MEAL LIKE THIS SHOULD FILL ME FULL OF ENERGY FOR THE DAY!
ORANGE JUICE
EGGS
ARCHIE STARTS TO COOK...
DING
WHRRR
POP
TIK TIK
Hmmm... Hmmm...
DRIP
SIZZLE
SIZZLE
HASH BROWNS
JAM
BREAD
BUTTER
EGGS
BEFORE LONG, BREAKFAST IS ON THE TABLE...
IT'S TIME TO DIG IN!
HONEY
MILK
A SHORT TIME LATER...
BURP!
AH! NOW I FEEL LIKE I COULD JOG AROUND THE WORLD NON-STOP!

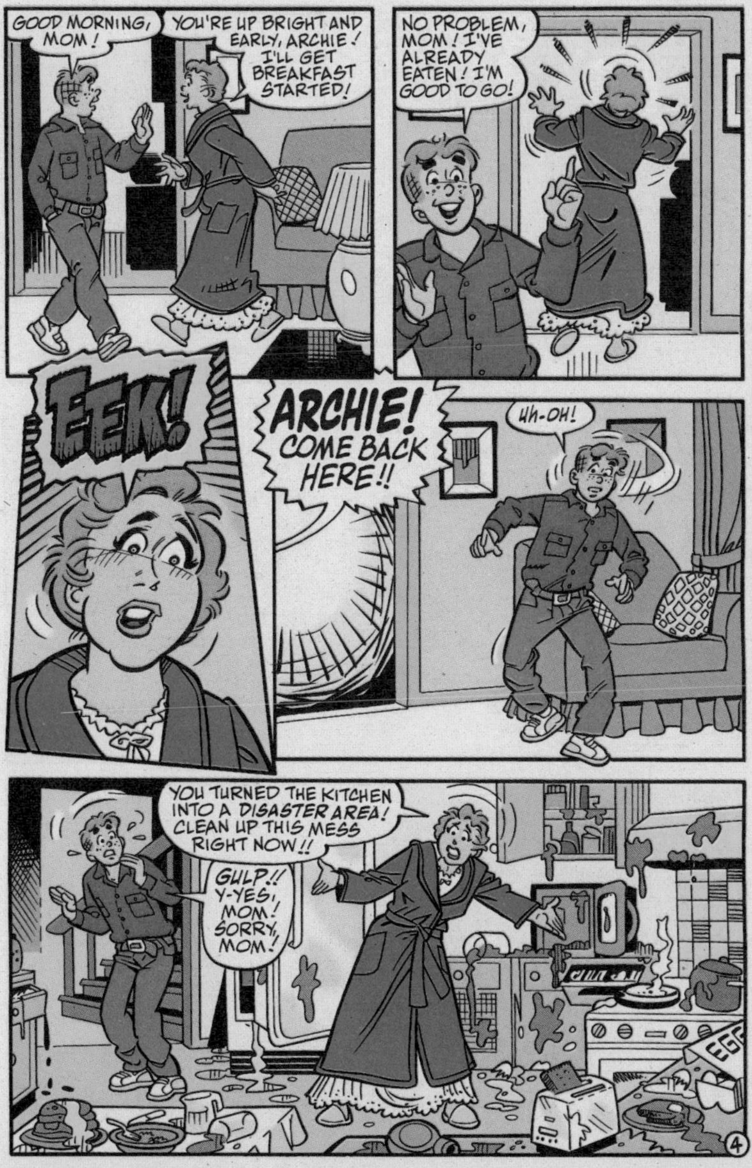
GOOD MORNING, MOM!
YOU'RE UP BRIGHT AND EARLY, ARCHIE! I'LL GET BREAKFAST STARTED!
NO PROBLEM, MOM! I'VE ALREADY EATEN! I'M GOOD TO GO!
EEK!
ARCHIE! COME BACK HERE!!
UH-OH!
YOU TURNED THE KITCHEN INTO A DISASTER AREA! CLEAN UP THIS MESS RIGHT NOW!!
GULP!! Y-YES, MOM! SORRY, MOM!
4

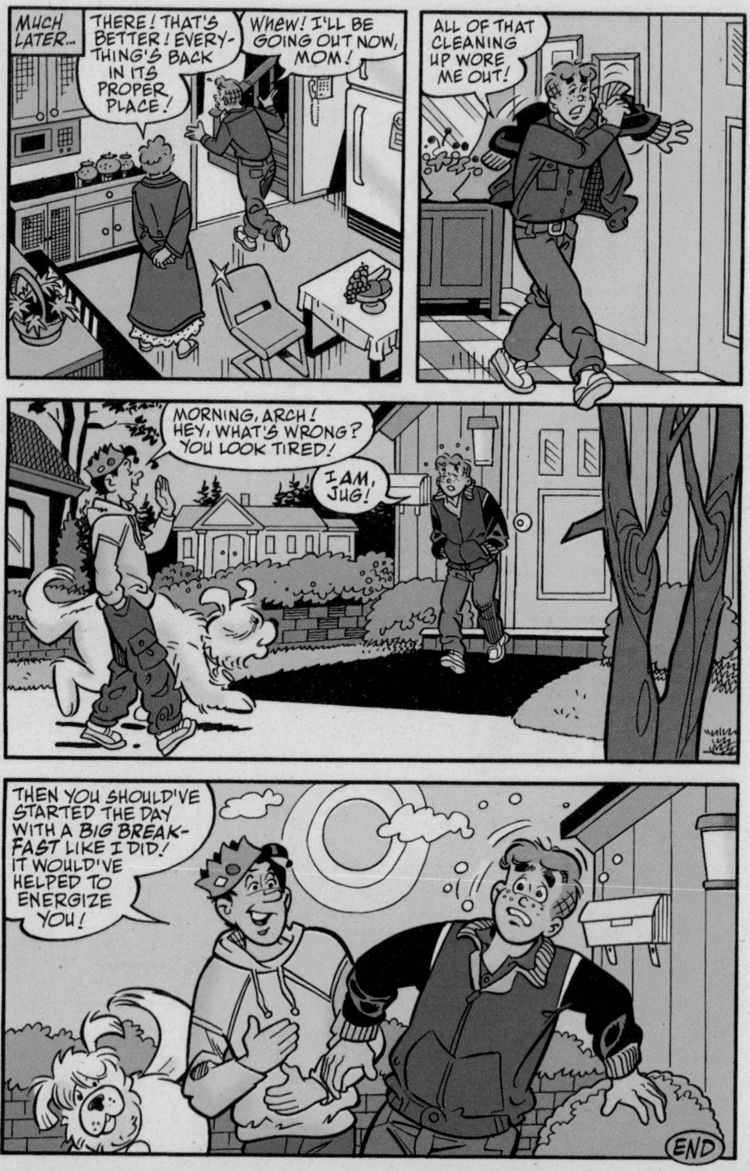
MUCH LATER...
THERE! THAT'S BETTER! EVERYTHING'S BACK IN ITS PROPER PLACE!
WHEW! I'LL BE GOING OUT NOW, MOM!
ALL OF THAT CLEANING UP WORE ME OUT!
MORNING, ARCH! HEY, WHAT'S WRONG? YOU LOOK TIRED!
I AM, JUG!
THEN YOU SHOULD'VE STARTED THE DAY WITH A BIG BREAKFAST LIKE I DID! IT WOULD'VE HELPED TO ENERGIZE YOU!
END

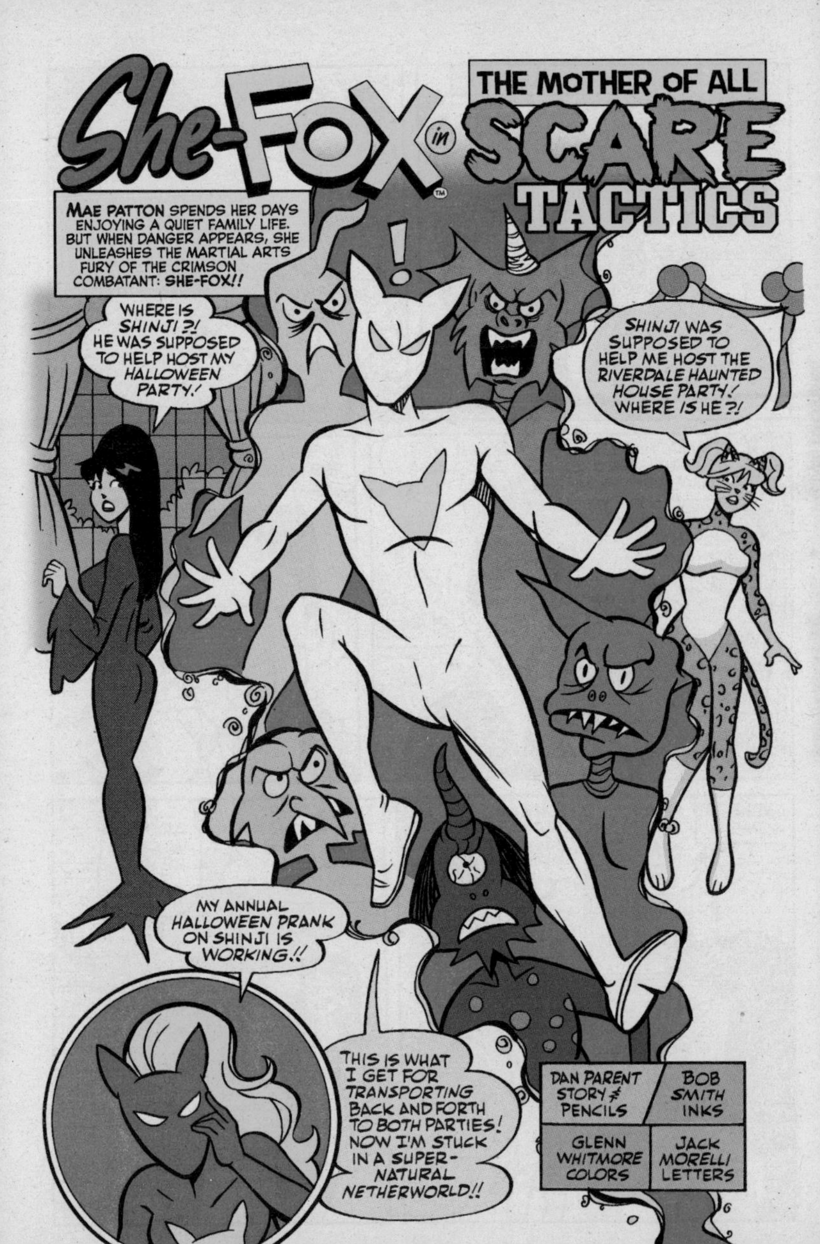
She-Fox in
THE MOTHER OF ALL
SCARE TACTICS
MAE PATTON SPENDS HER DAYS ENJOYING A QUIET FAMILY LIFE. BUT WHEN DANGER APPEARS, SHE UNLEASHES THE MARTIAL ARTS FURY OF THE CRIMSON COMBATANT: SHE-FOX!!
WHERE IS SHINJI ?! HE WAS SUPPOSED TO HELP HOST MY HALLOWEEN PARTY!
!
SHINJI WAS SUPPOSED TO HELP ME HOST THE RIVERDALE HAUNTED HOUSE PARTY! WHERE IS HE ?!
MY ANNUAL HALLOWEEN PRANK ON SHINJI IS WORKING!!
THIS IS WHAT I GET FOR TRANSPORTING BACK AND FORTH TO BOTH PARTIES! NOW I'M STUCK IN A SUPER-NATURAL NETHERWORLD!!
DAN PARENT STORY & PENCILS
BOB SMITH INKS
GLENN WHITMORE COLORS
JACK MORELLI LETTERS

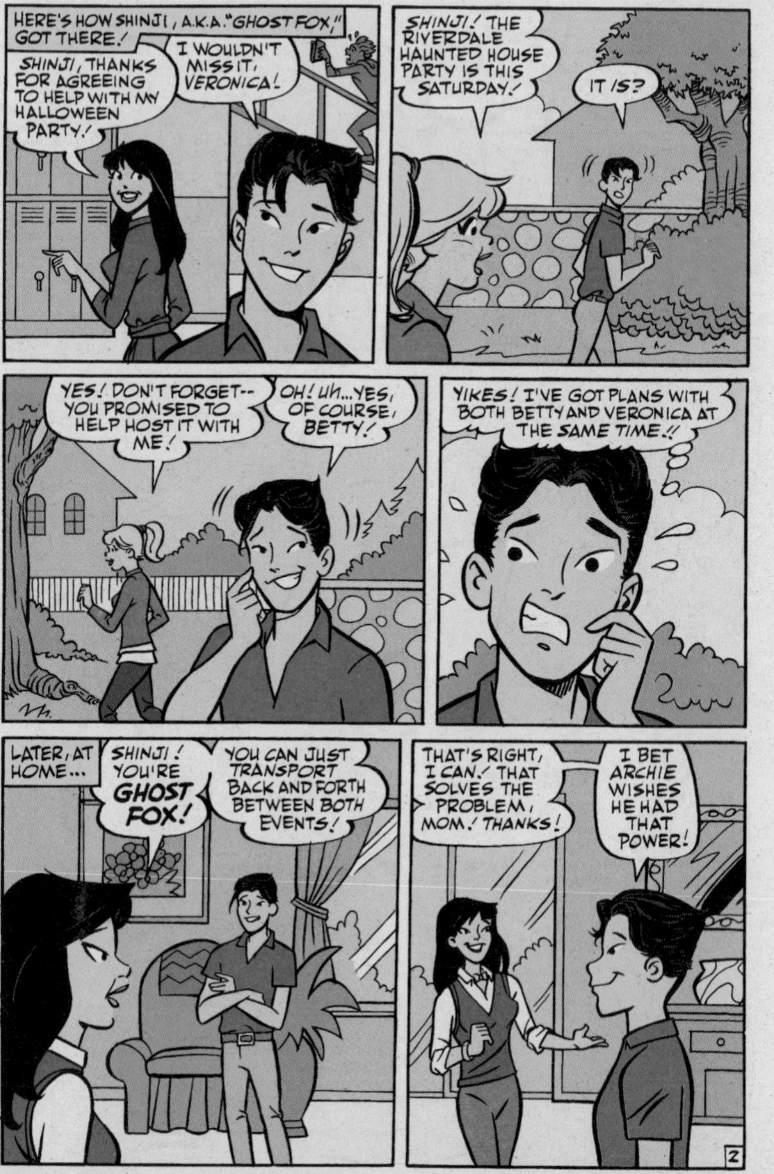
HERE'S HOW SHINJI, A.K.A. "GHOST FOX," GOT THERE!
SHINJI, THANKS FOR AGREEING TO HELP WITH MY HALLOWEEN PARTY!
I WOULDN'T MISS IT, VERONICA!
SHINJI! THE RIVERDALE HAUNTED HOUSE PARTY IS THIS SATURDAY!
IT IS?
YES! DON'T FORGET-- YOU PROMISED TO HELP HOST IT WITH ME!
OH! UH... YES, OF COURSE, BETTY!
YIKES! I'VE GOT PLANS WITH BOTH BETTY AND VERONICA AT THE SAME TIME!!
LATER, AT HOME...
SHINJI! YOU'RE GHOST FOX!
YOU CAN JUST TRANSPORT BACK AND FORTH BETWEEN BOTH EVENTS!
THAT'S RIGHT, I CAN! THAT SOLVES THE PROBLEM, MOM! THANKS!
I BET ARCHIE WISHES HE HAD THAT POWER!
2

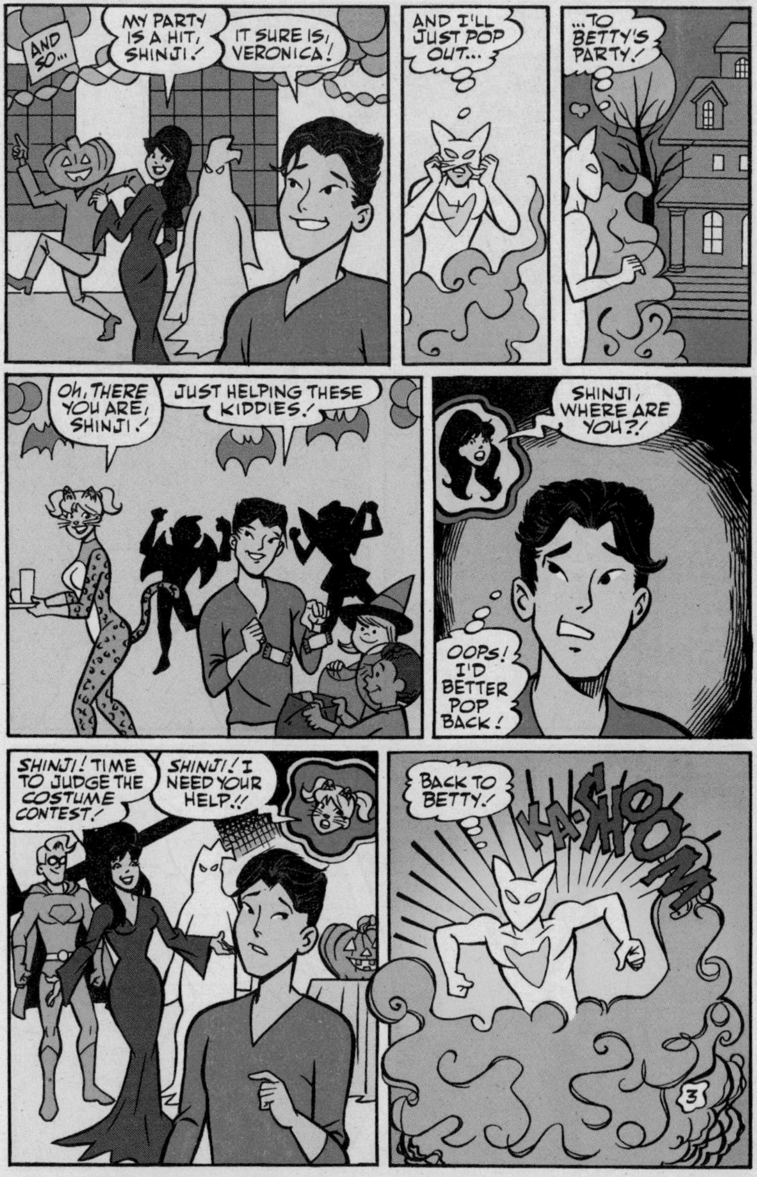
AND SO...
MY PARTY IS A HIT, SHINJI!
IT SURE IS, VERONICA!
AND I'LL JUST POP OUT...
...TO BETTY'S PARTY!
Oh, THERE YOU ARE, SHINJI!
JUST HELPING THESE KIDDIES!
SHINJI, WHERE ARE YOU?!
OOPS! I'D BETTER POP BACK!
SHINJI! TIME TO JUDGE THE COSTUME CONTEST!
SHINJI! I NEED YOUR HELP!!
BACK TO BETTY!
KA-SHOOM
3

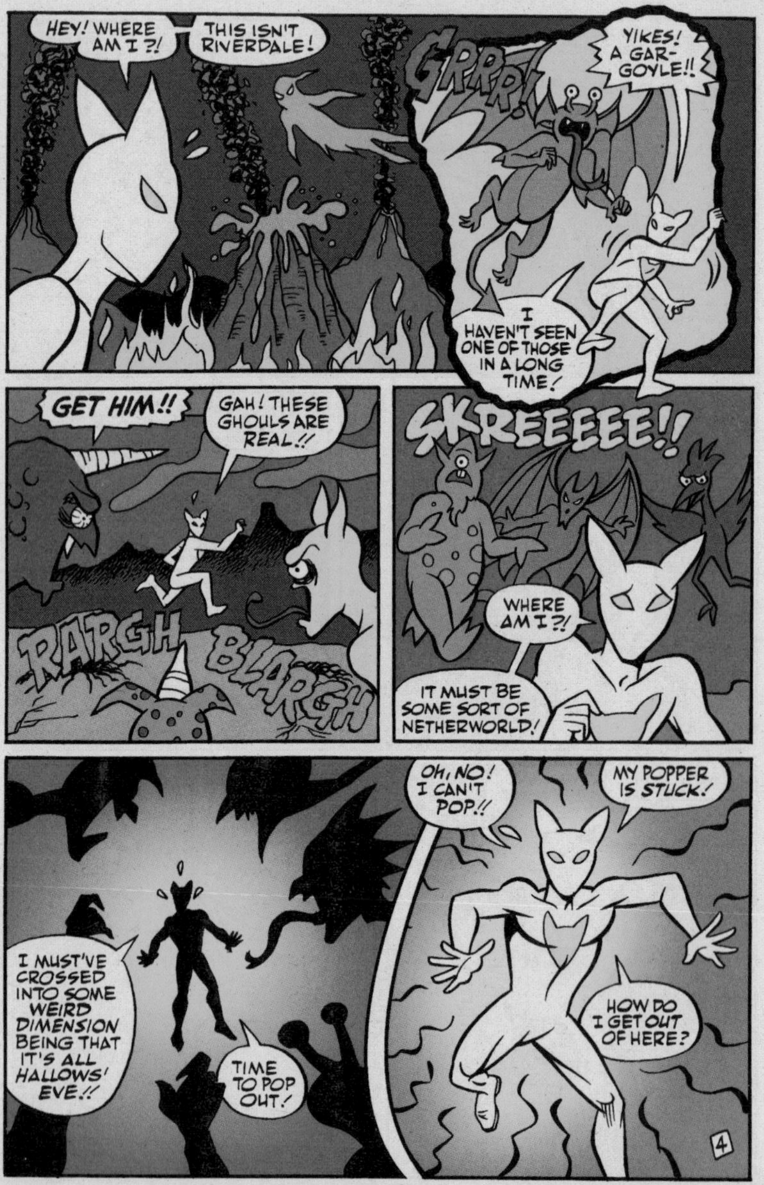
HEY! WHERE AM I?!
THIS ISN'T RIVERDALE!
GRRR!
YIKES! A GAR-GOYLE!!
I HAVEN'T SEEN ONE OF THOSE IN A LONG TIME!
GET HIM!!
GAH! THESE GHOULS ARE REAL!!
RARGH
BLARGH
SKREEEEEE!!
WHERE AM I?!
IT MUST BE SOME SORT OF NETHERWORLD!
I MUST'VE CROSSED INTO SOME WEIRD DIMENSION BEING THAT IT'S ALL HALLOWS' EVE!!
TIME TO POP OUT!
OH, NO! I CAN'T POP!!
MY POPPER IS STUCK!
HOW DO I GET OUT OF HERE?
4

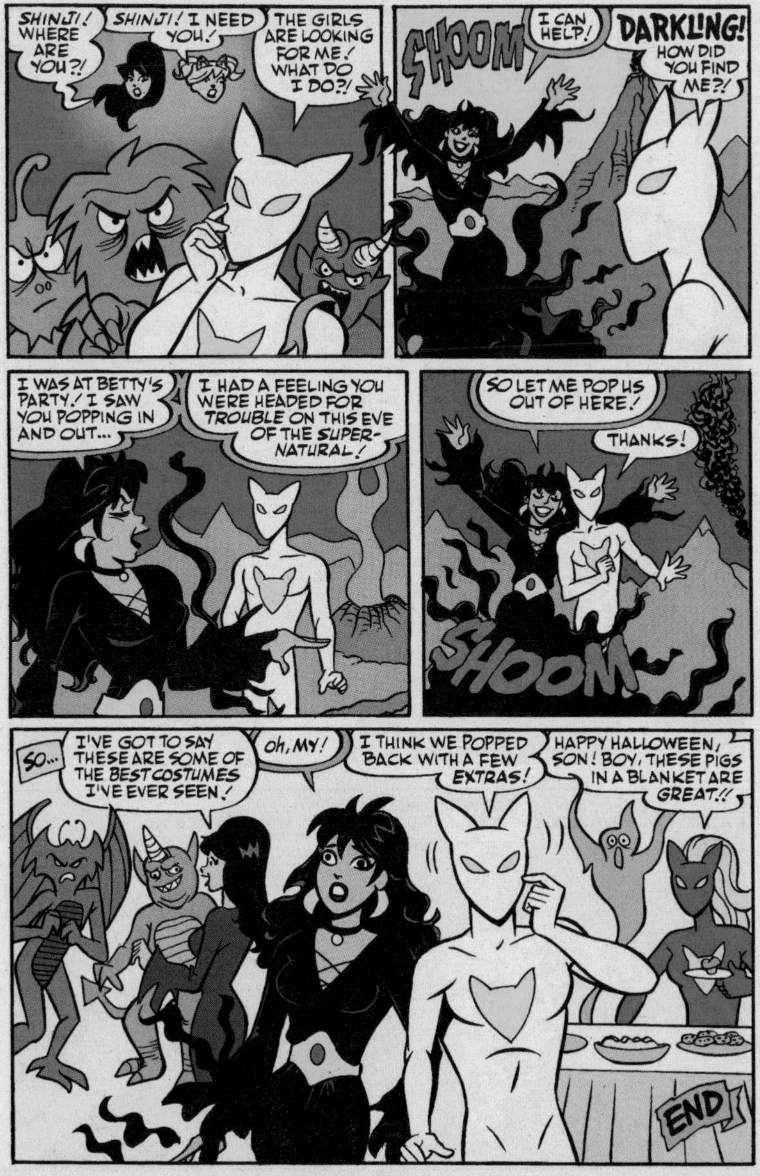
SHINJI! WHERE ARE YOU?!
SHINJI! I NEED YOU!
THE GIRLS ARE LOOKING FOR ME! WHAT DO I DO?!
SHOOM
I CAN HELP!
DARKLING! HOW DID YOU FIND ME?!
I WAS AT BETTY'S PARTY! I SAW YOU POPPING IN AND OUT...
I HAD A FEELING YOU WERE HEADED FOR TROUBLE ON THIS EVE OF THE SUPER-NATURAL!
SO LET ME POP US OUT OF HERE!
THANKS!
SHOOM
SO...
I'VE GOT TO SAY THESE ARE SOME OF THE BEST COSTUMES I'VE EVER SEEN!
oh, MY!
I THINK WE POPPED BACK WITH A FEW EXTRAS!
HAPPY HALLOWEEN, SON! BOY, THESE PIGS IN A BLANKET ARE GREAT!!
END

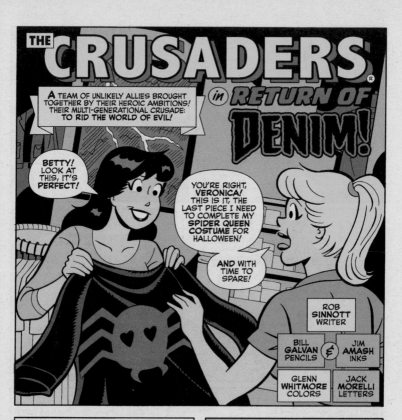

THE CRUSADERS in RETURN OF DENIM!

A TEAM OF UNLIKELY ALLIES BROUGHT TOGETHER BY THEIR HEROIC AMBITIONS! THEIR MULTI-GENERATIONAL CRUSADE: TO RID THE WORLD OF EVIL!

BETTY! LOOK AT THIS, IT'S PERFECT!

YOU'RE RIGHT, VERONICA! THIS IS IT, THE LAST PIECE I NEED TO COMPLETE MY SPIDER QUEEN COSTUME FOR HALLOWEEN!

AND WITH TIME TO SPARE!

ROB SINNOTT
WRITER

BILL GALVAN
PENCILS

JIM AMASH
INKS

GLENN WHITMORE
COLORS

JACK MORELLI
LETTERS

I TOLD YOU THE THRIFT STORE WOULD BE A GREAT PLACE TO LOOK FOR THE JACKET.

FASHION ALWAYS COMES BACK IN STYLE.

I CAN'T WAIT TO GET HOME AND TRY ON MY FINISHED COSTUME!

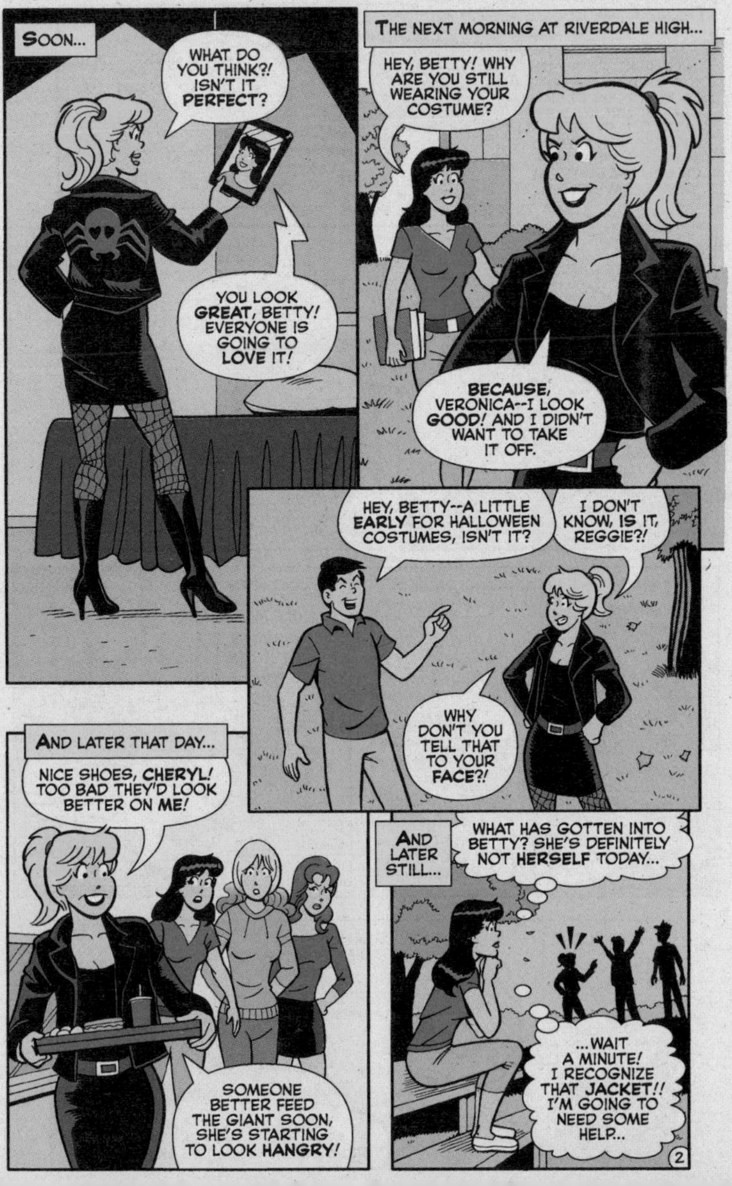
SOON...
WHAT DO YOU THINK?! ISN'T IT PERFECT?
YOU LOOK GREAT, BETTY! EVERYONE IS GOING TO LOVE IT!
THE NEXT MORNING AT RIVERDALE HIGH...
HEY, BETTY! WHY ARE YOU STILL WEARING YOUR COSTUME?
BECAUSE, VERONICA--I LOOK GOOD! AND I DIDN'T WANT TO TAKE IT OFF.
HEY, BETTY--A LITTLE EARLY FOR HALLOWEEN COSTUMES, ISN'T IT?
I DON'T KNOW, IS IT, REGGIE?!
WHY DON'T YOU TELL THAT TO YOUR FACE?!
AND LATER THAT DAY...
NICE SHOES, CHERYL! TOO BAD THEY'D LOOK BETTER ON ME!
SOMEONE BETTER FEED THE GIANT SOON, SHE'S STARTING TO LOOK HANGRY!
AND LATER STILL...
WHAT HAS GOTTEN INTO BETTY? SHE'S DEFINITELY NOT HERSELF TODAY...
...WAIT A MINUTE! I RECOGNIZE THAT JACKET!! I'M GOING TO NEED SOME HELP...
2

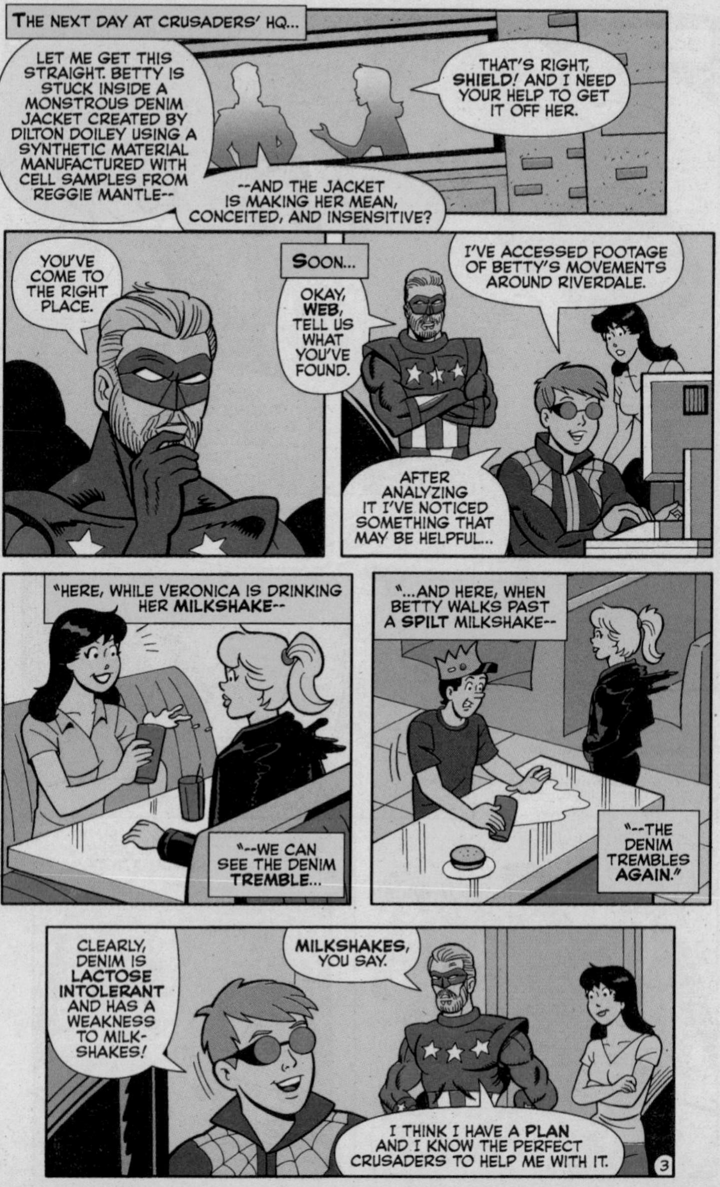
THE NEXT DAY AT CRUSADERS' HQ...
LET ME GET THIS STRAIGHT. BETTY IS STUCK INSIDE A MONSTROUS DENIM JACKET CREATED BY DILTON DOILEY USING A SYNTHETIC MATERIAL MANUFACTURED WITH CELL SAMPLES FROM REGGIE MANTLE--
THAT'S RIGHT, SHIELD! AND I NEED YOUR HELP TO GET IT OFF HER.
--AND THE JACKET IS MAKING HER MEAN, CONCEITED, AND INSENSITIVE?
YOU'VE COME TO THE RIGHT PLACE.
SOON...
OKAY, WEB, TELL US WHAT YOU'VE FOUND.
I'VE ACCESSED FOOTAGE OF BETTY'S MOVEMENTS AROUND RIVERDALE.
AFTER ANALYZING IT I'VE NOTICED SOMETHING THAT MAY BE HELPFUL...
"HERE, WHILE VERONICA IS DRINKING HER MILKSHAKE--
"--WE CAN SEE THE DENIM TREMBLE...
"...AND HERE, WHEN BETTY WALKS PAST A SPILT MILKSHAKE--
"--THE DENIM TREMBLES AGAIN."
CLEARLY, DENIM IS LACTOSE INTOLERANT AND HAS A WEAKNESS TO MILK-SHAKES!
MILKSHAKES, YOU SAY.
I THINK I HAVE A PLAN AND I KNOW THE PERFECT CRUSADERS TO HELP ME WITH IT.
3

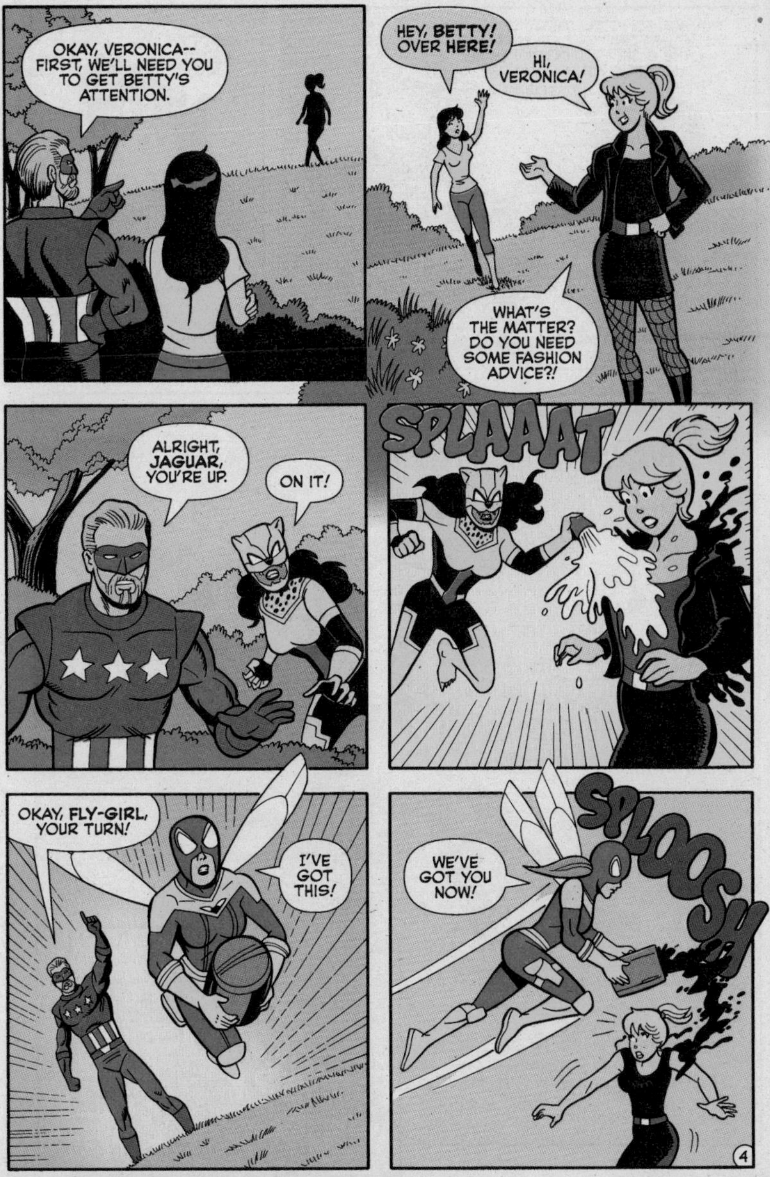
OKAY, VERONICA-- FIRST, WE'LL NEED YOU TO GET BETTY'S ATTENTION.
HEY, BETTY! OVER HERE!
HI, VERONICA!
WHAT'S THE MATTER? DO YOU NEED SOME FASHION ADVICE?!
ALRIGHT, JAGUAR, YOU'RE UP.
ON IT!
SPLAAAT
OKAY, FLY-GIRL, YOUR TURN!
I'VE GOT THIS!
WE'VE GOT YOU NOW!
SPLOOSH

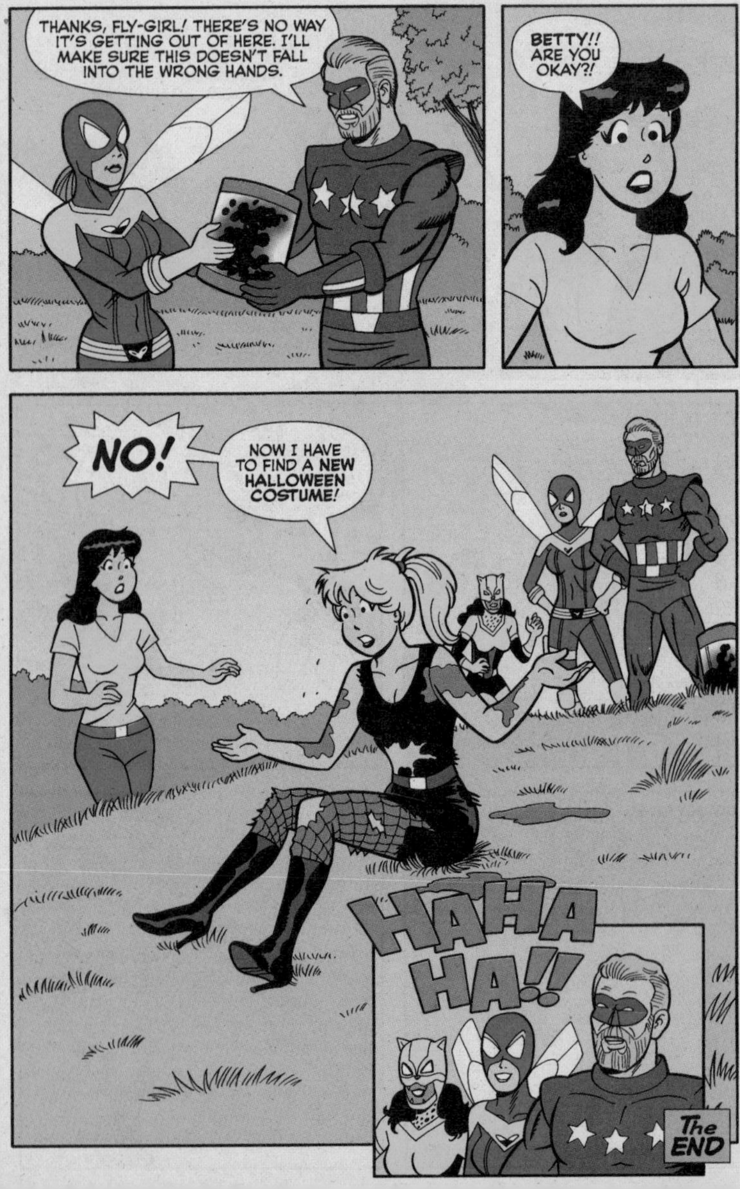
THANKS, FLY-GIRL! THERE'S NO WAY IT'S GETTING OUT OF HERE. I'LL MAKE SURE THIS DOESN'T FALL INTO THE WRONG HANDS.
BETTY!! ARE YOU OKAY?!
NO!
NOW I HAVE TO FIND A NEW HALLOWEEN COSTUME!
HAHA HA!!
The END

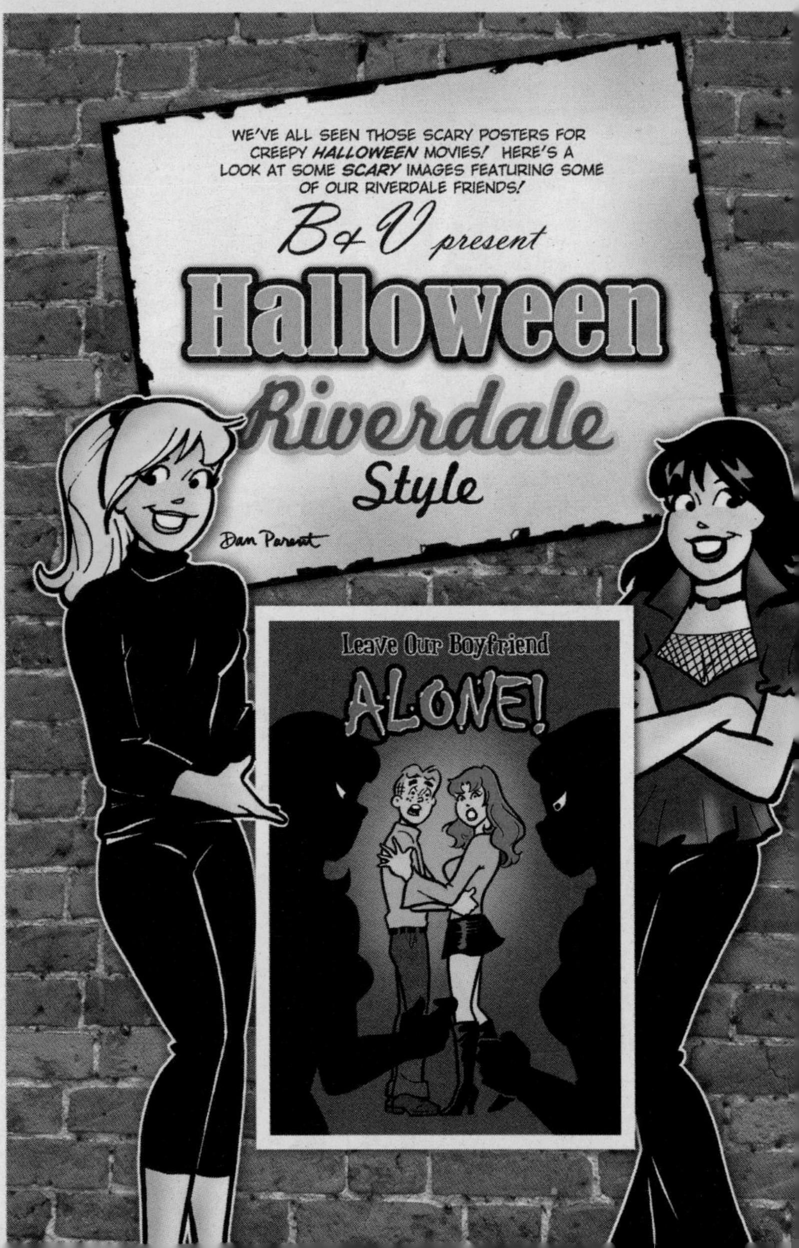

WE'VE ALL SEEN THOSE SCARY POSTERS FOR CREEPY HALLOWEEN MOVIES! HERE'S A LOOK AT SOME SCARY IMAGES FEATURING SOME OF OUR RIVERDALE FRIENDS!
B&V present
Halloween
Riverdale
Style
Dan Parent
Leave Our Boyfriend
ALONE!

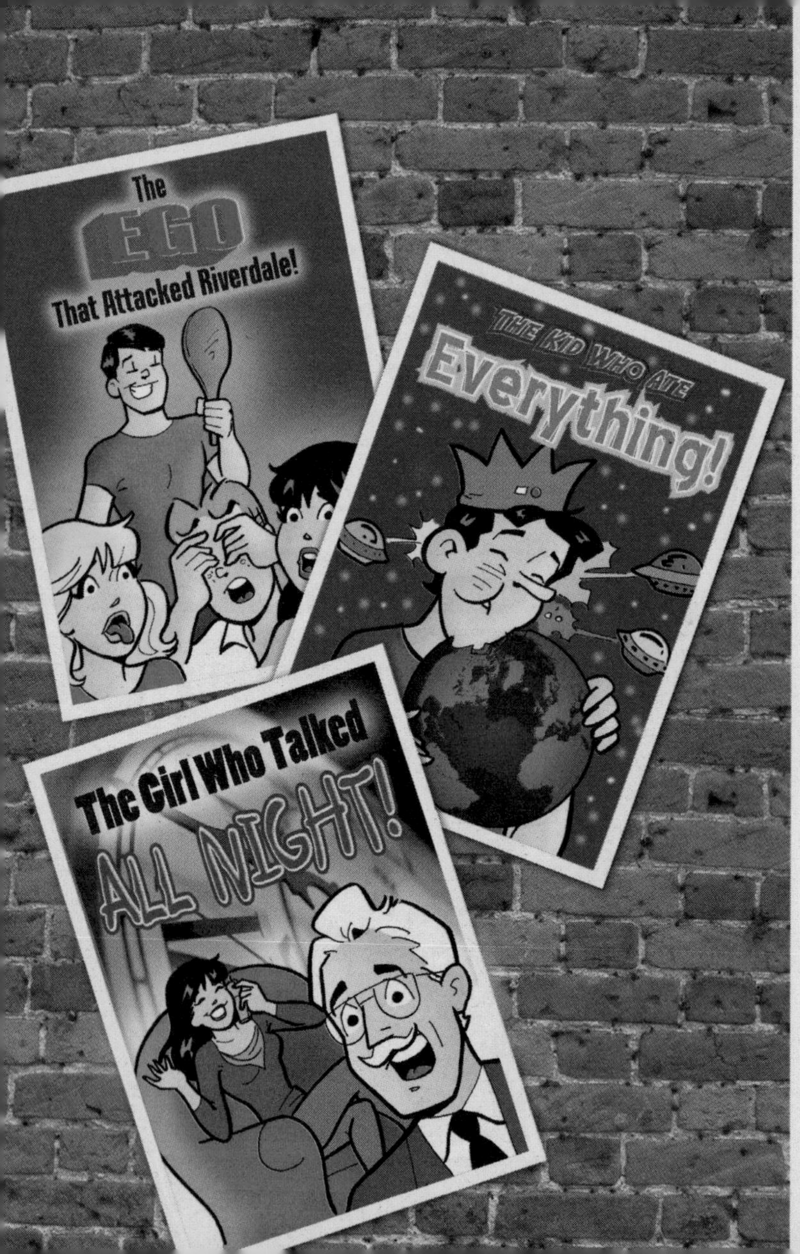
The EGO That Attacked Riverdale!
THE KID WHO ATE Everything!
The Girl Who Talked ALL NIGHT!

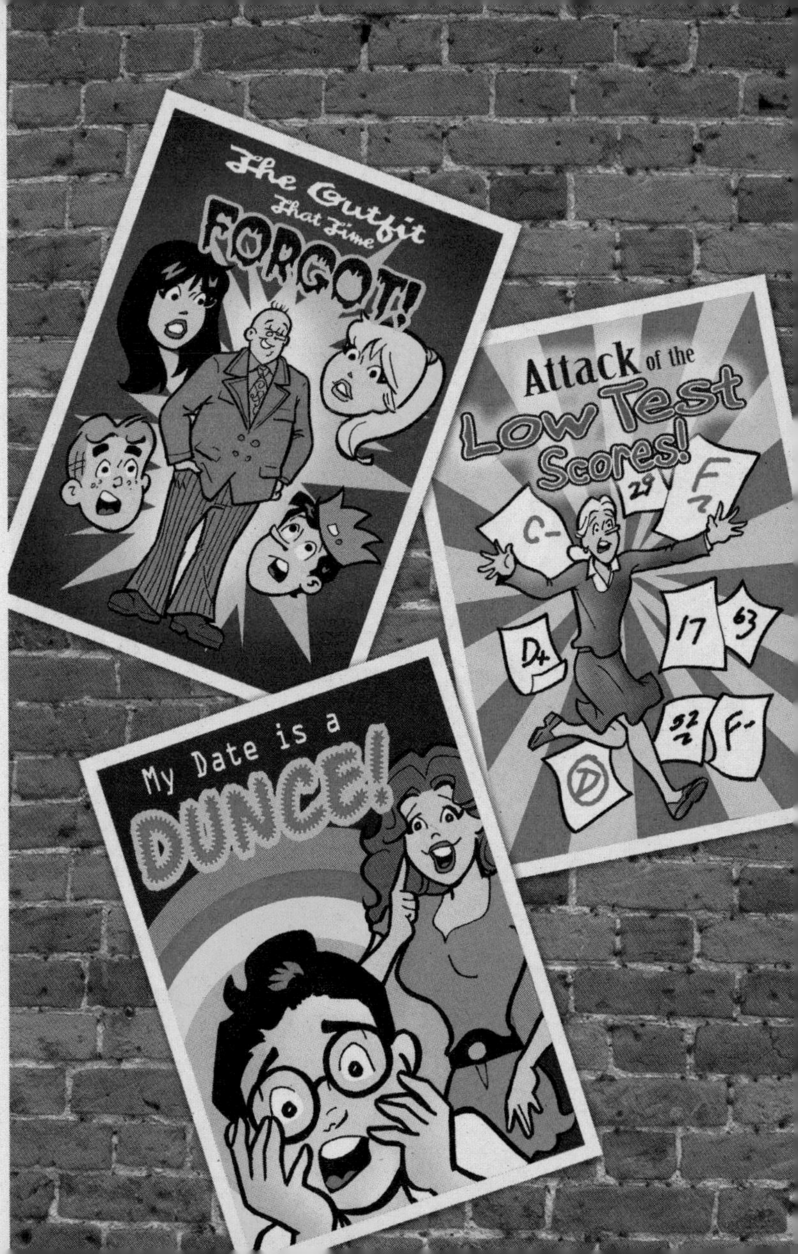
The Outfit That Time FORGOT!
Attack of the Low Test Scores!
C-
29
F
17
63
F-
My Date is a DUNCE!

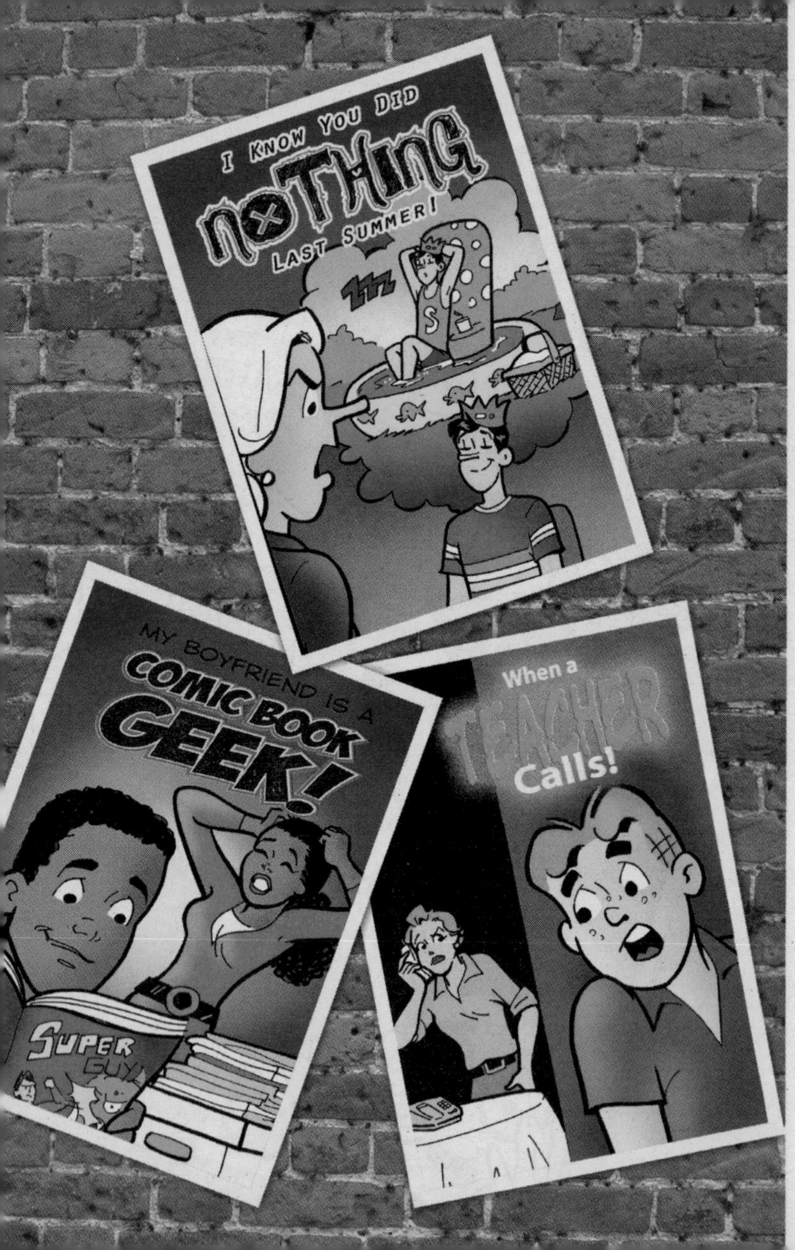

I KNOW YOU DID
NOTHING
LAST SUMMER!
ZZZ
MY BOYFRIEND IS A
COMIC BOOK
GEEK!
SUPER
GUY
When a
TEACHER
Calls!

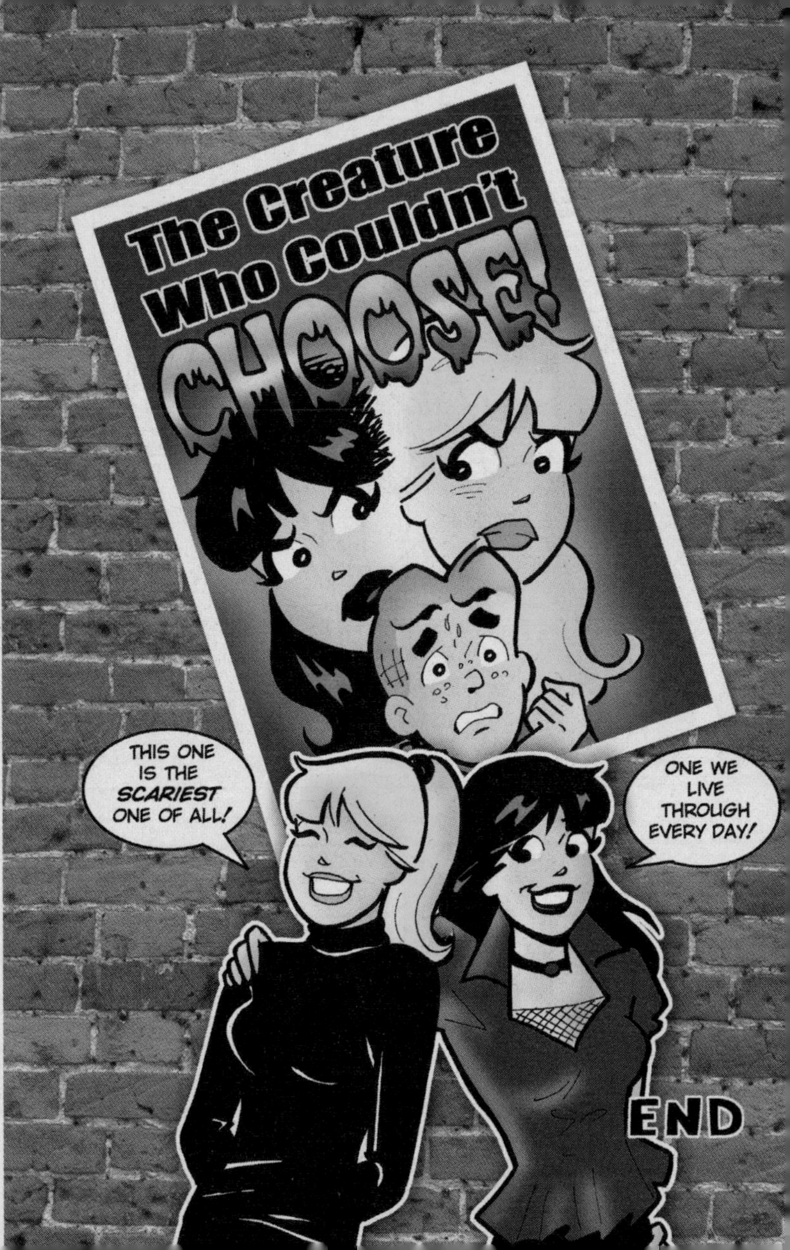
The Creature Who Couldn't CHOOSE!
THIS ONE IS THE *SCARIEST* ONE OF ALL!
ONE WE LIVE THROUGH EVERY DAY!
END

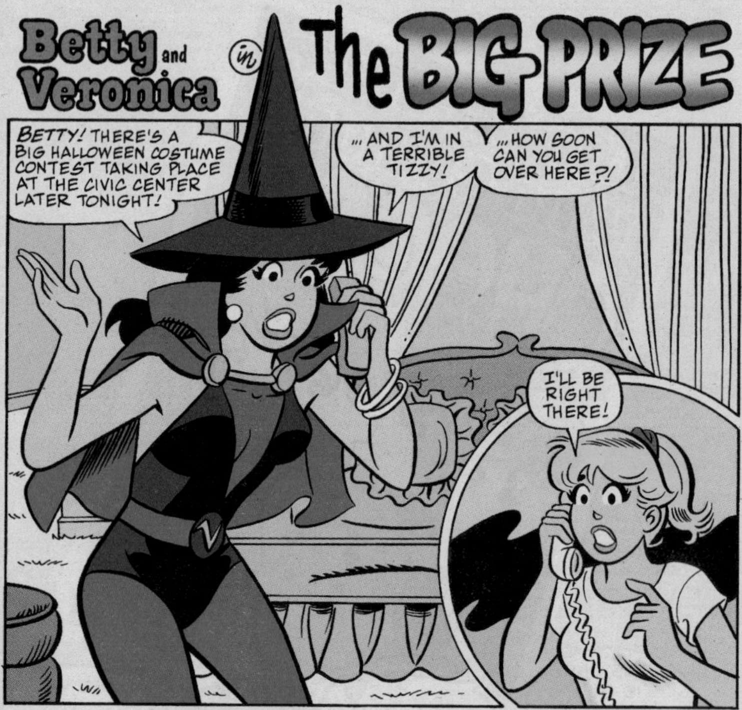
Betty and Veronica in The BIG PRIZE
BETTY! THERE'S A BIG HALLOWEEN COSTUME CONTEST TAKING PLACE AT THE CIVIC CENTER LATER TONIGHT!
...AND I'M IN A TERRIBLE TIZZY!
...HOW SOON CAN YOU GET OVER HERE?!
I'LL BE RIGHT THERE!

SCRIPT: GEORGE GLADIR PENCILS: JEFF SHULTZ INKING: AL MILGROM LETTERING: JACK MORELLI COLORING: BARRY GROSSMAN

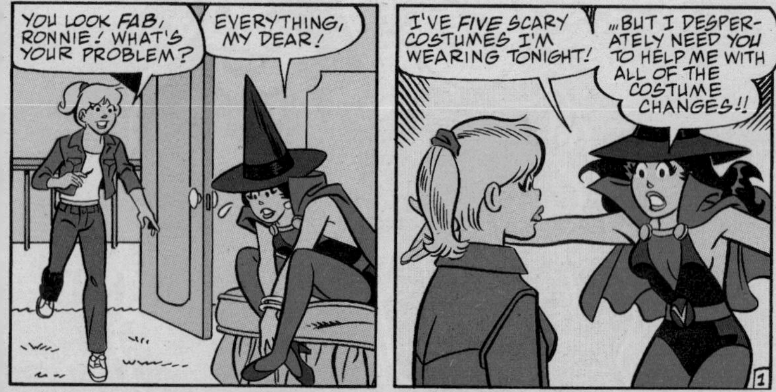
YOU LOOK FAB, RONNIE! WHAT'S YOUR PROBLEM?
EVERYTHING, MY DEAR!
I'VE FIVE SCARY COSTUMES I'M WEARING TONIGHT!
...BUT I DESPERATELY NEED YOU TO HELP ME WITH ALL OF THE COSTUME CHANGES!!
1

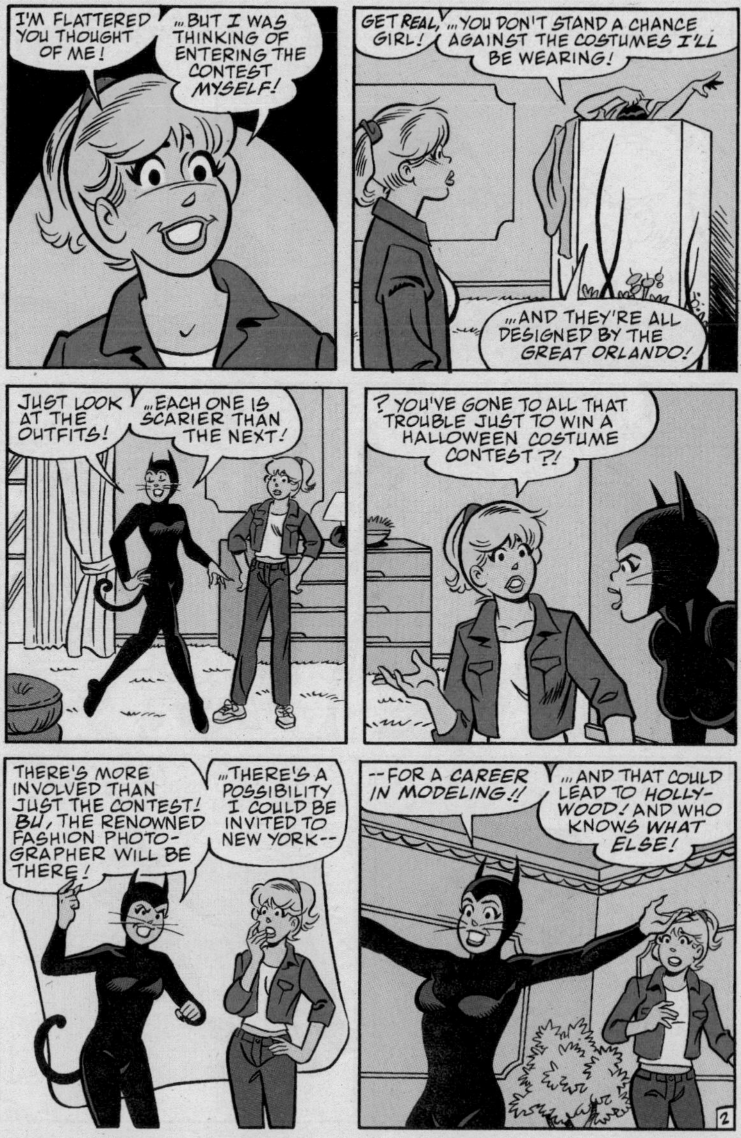
I'M FLATTERED YOU THOUGHT OF ME!
...BUT I WAS THINKING OF ENTERING THE CONTEST MYSELF!
GET REAL, GIRL!
...YOU DON'T STAND A CHANCE AGAINST THE COSTUMES I'LL BE WEARING!
...AND THEY'RE ALL DESIGNED BY THE GREAT ORLANDO!
JUST LOOK AT THE OUTFITS!
...EACH ONE IS SCARIER THAN THE NEXT!
? YOU'VE GONE TO ALL THAT TROUBLE JUST TO WIN A HALLOWEEN COSTUME CONTEST ?!
THERE'S MORE INVOLVED THAN JUST THE CONTEST! BU, THE RENOWNED FASHION PHOTOGRAPHER WILL BE THERE!
...THERE'S A POSSIBILITY I COULD BE INVITED TO NEW YORK--
--FOR A CAREER IN MODELING!!
...AND THAT COULD LEAD TO HOLLYWOOD! AND WHO KNOWS WHAT ELSE!
2

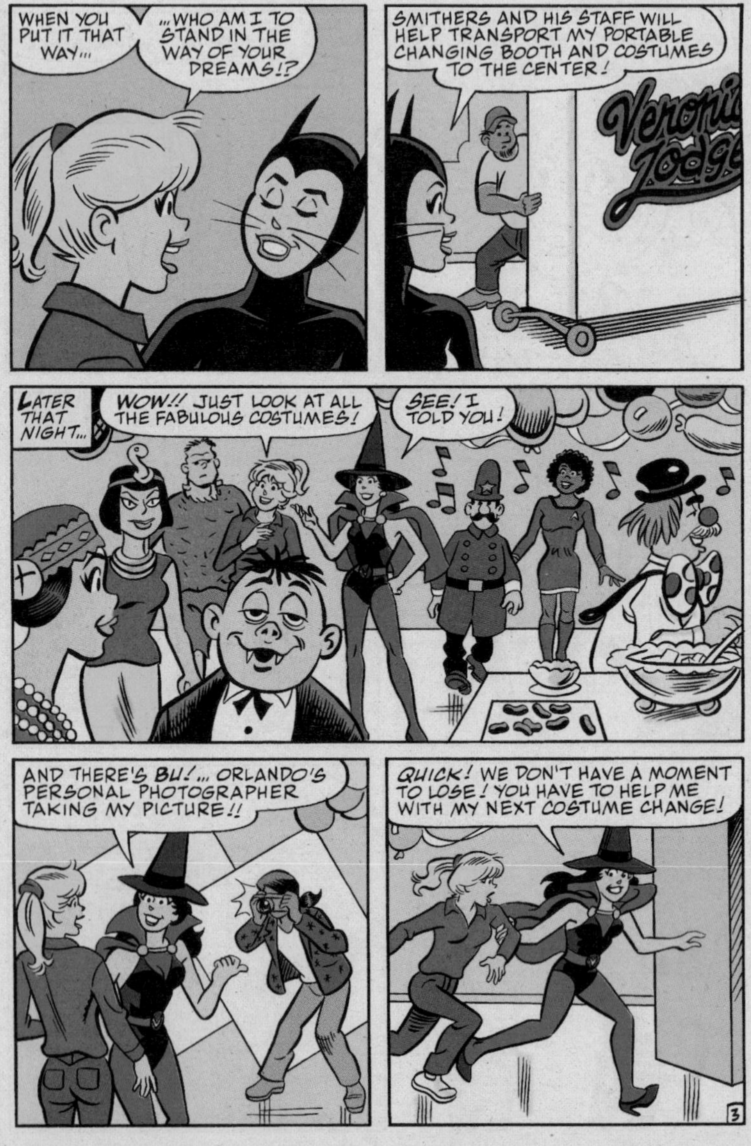
WHEN YOU PUT IT THAT WAY...
...WHO AM I TO STAND IN THE WAY OF YOUR DREAMS!?
SMITHERS AND HIS STAFF WILL HELP TRANSPORT MY PORTABLE CHANGING BOOTH AND COSTUMES TO THE CENTER!
LATER THAT NIGHT...
WOW!! JUST LOOK AT ALL THE FABULOUS COSTUMES!
SEE! I TOLD YOU!
AND THERE'S BU!... ORLANDO'S PERSONAL PHOTOGRAPHER TAKING MY PICTURE!!
QUICK! WE DON'T HAVE A MOMENT TO LOSE! YOU HAVE TO HELP ME WITH MY NEXT COSTUME CHANGE!
3

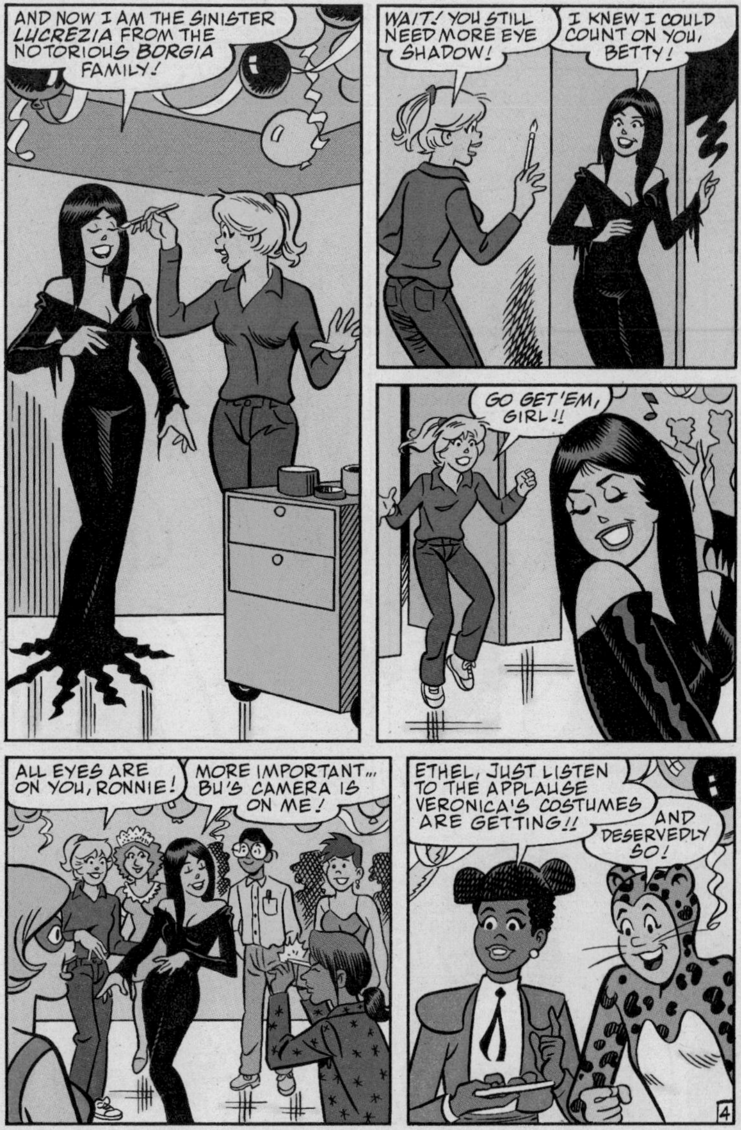
AND NOW I AM THE SINISTER LUCREZIA FROM THE NOTORIOUS BORGIA FAMILY!
WAIT! YOU STILL NEED MORE EYE SHADOW!
I KNEW I COULD COUNT ON YOU, BETTY!
GO GET 'EM, GIRL!!
ALL EYES ARE ON YOU, RONNIE!
MORE IMPORTANT... BU'S CAMERA IS ON ME!
ETHEL, JUST LISTEN TO THE APPLAUSE VERONICA'S COSTUMES ARE GETTING!!
AND DESERVEDLY SO!
4

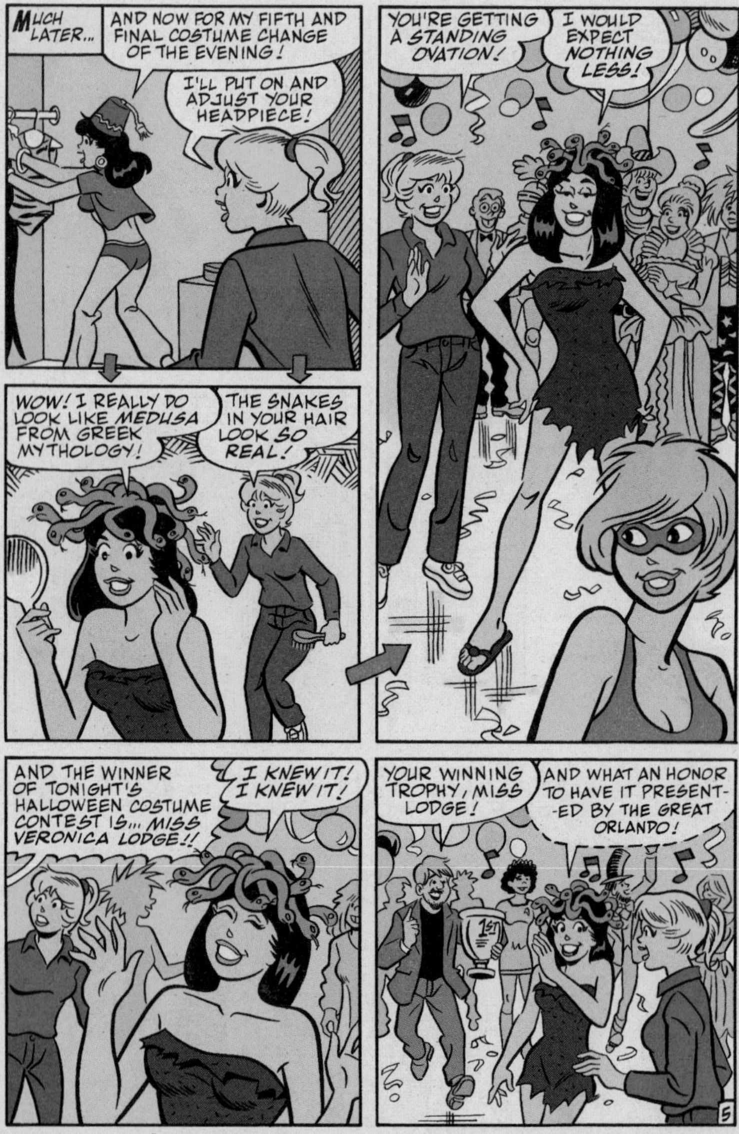

MUCH LATER...
AND NOW FOR MY FIFTH AND FINAL COSTUME CHANGE OF THE EVENING!
I'LL PUT ON AND ADJUST YOUR HEADPIECE!
WOW! I REALLY DO LOOK LIKE MEDUSA FROM GREEK MYTHOLOGY!
THE SNAKES IN YOUR HAIR LOOK SO REAL!
YOU'RE GETTING A STANDING OVATION!
I WOULD EXPECT NOTHING LESS!
AND THE WINNER OF TONIGHT'S HALLOWEEN COSTUME CONTEST IS... MISS VERONICA LODGE!!
I KNEW IT! I KNEW IT!
YOUR WINNING TROPHY, MISS LODGE!
AND WHAT AN HONOR TO HAVE IT PRESENT-ED BY THE GREAT ORLANDO!
1ST

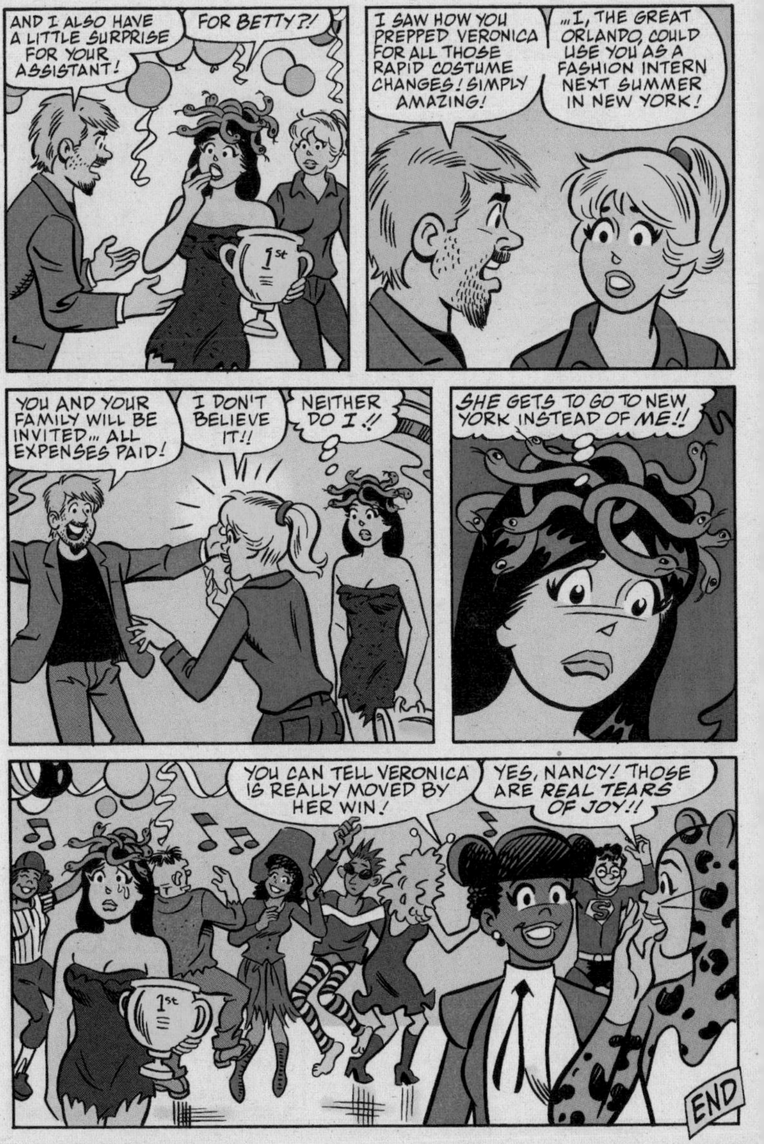
AND I ALSO HAVE A LITTLE SURPRISE FOR YOUR ASSISTANT!
FOR BETTY?!
I SAW HOW YOU PREPPED VERONICA FOR ALL THOSE RAPID COSTUME CHANGES! SIMPLY AMAZING!
...I, THE GREAT ORLANDO, COULD USE YOU AS A FASHION INTERN NEXT SUMMER IN NEW YORK!
1st
YOU AND YOUR FAMILY WILL BE INVITED... ALL EXPENSES PAID!
I DON'T BELIEVE IT!!
NEITHER DO I!!
SHE GETS TO GO TO NEW YORK INSTEAD OF ME!!
YOU CAN TELL VERONICA IS REALLY MOVED BY HER WIN!
YES, NANCY! THOSE ARE REAL TEARS OF JOY!!
1st
END

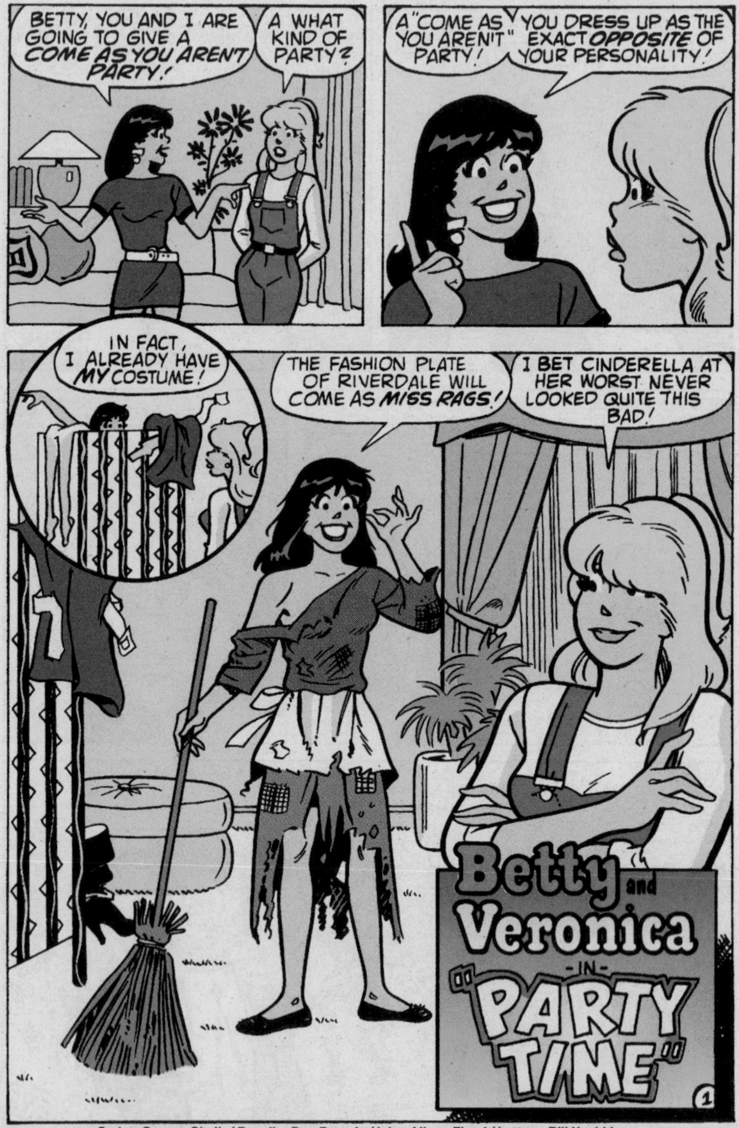
BETTY, YOU AND I ARE GOING TO GIVE A COME AS YOU AREN'T PARTY!
A WHAT KIND OF PARTY?
A "COME AS YOU AREN'T" PARTY!
YOU DRESS UP AS THE EXACT OPPOSITE OF YOUR PERSONALITY!
IN FACT, I ALREADY HAVE MY COSTUME!
THE FASHION PLATE OF RIVERDALE WILL COME AS MISS RAGS!
I BET CINDERELLA AT HER WORST NEVER LOOKED QUITE THIS BAD!
Betty and Veronica
-IN-
"PARTY TIME"
1

Script: George Gladir / Pencils: Dan Decarlo / Inks: Alison Flood / Letters: Bill Yoshida

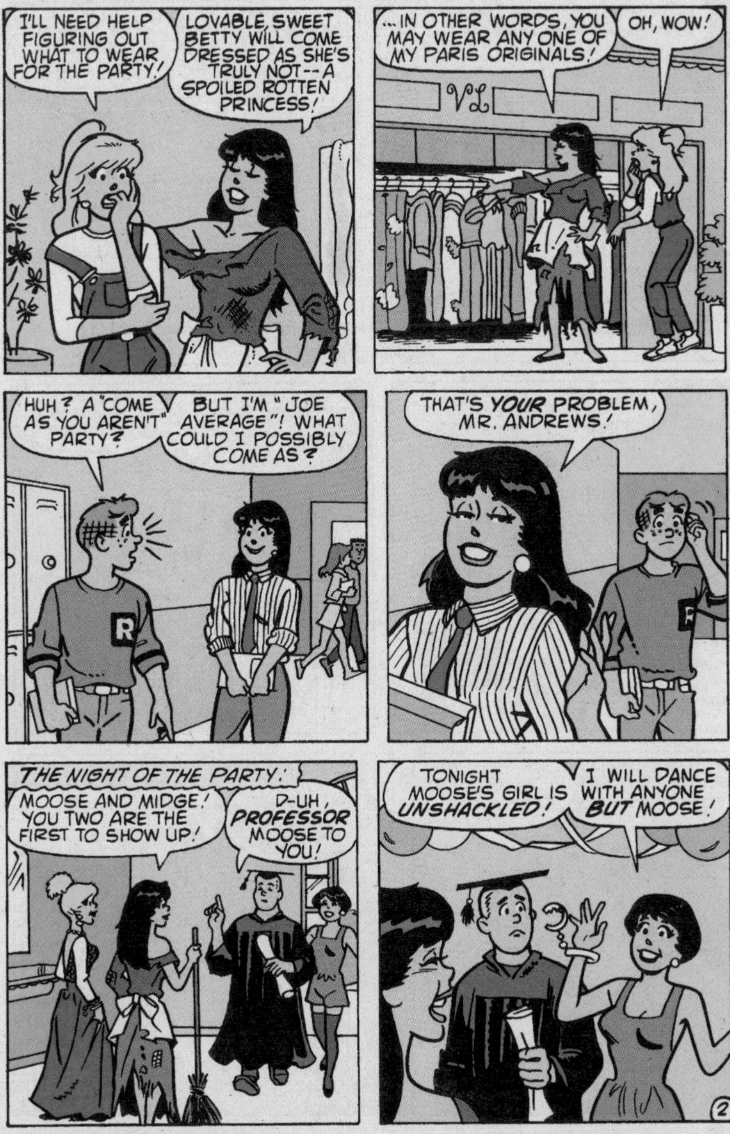
I'LL NEED HELP FIGURING OUT WHAT TO WEAR FOR THE PARTY!
LOVABLE, SWEET BETTY WILL COME DRESSED AS SHE'S TRULY NOT -- A SPOILED ROTTEN PRINCESS!
...IN OTHER WORDS, YOU MAY WEAR ANY ONE OF MY PARIS ORIGINALS!
OH, WOW!
VL
HUH? A "COME AS YOU AREN'T" PARTY?
BUT I'M "JOE AVERAGE"! WHAT COULD I POSSIBLY COME AS?
THAT'S YOUR PROBLEM, MR. ANDREWS!
THE NIGHT OF THE PARTY:
MOOSE AND MIDGE! YOU TWO ARE THE FIRST TO SHOW UP!
D-UH, PROFESSOR MOOSE TO YOU!
TONIGHT MOOSE'S GIRL IS UNSHACKLED!
I WILL DANCE WITH ANYONE BUT MOOSE!
2

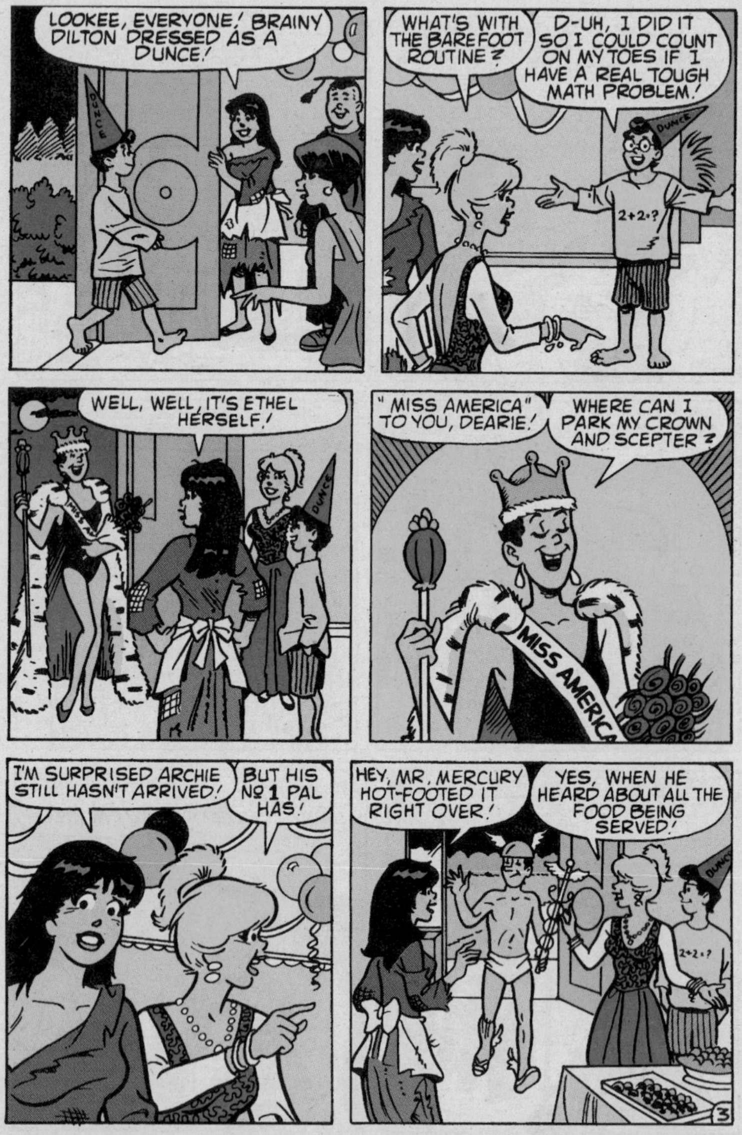
LOOKEE, EVERYONE! BRAINY DILTON DRESSED AS A DUNCE!
DUNCE
WHAT'S WITH THE BAREFOOT ROUTINE?
D-UH, I DID IT SO I COULD COUNT ON MY TOES IF I HAVE A REAL TOUGH MATH PROBLEM!
DUNCE
2+2=?
WELL, WELL, IT'S ETHEL HERSELF!
DUNCE
"MISS AMERICA" TO YOU, DEARIE!
WHERE CAN I PARK MY CROWN AND SCEPTER?
MISS AMERICA
I'M SURPRISED ARCHIE STILL HASN'T ARRIVED!
BUT HIS № 1 PAL HAS!
HEY, MR. MERCURY HOT-FOOTED IT RIGHT OVER!
YES, WHEN HE HEARD ABOUT ALL THE FOOD BEING SERVED!
2+2=?
3

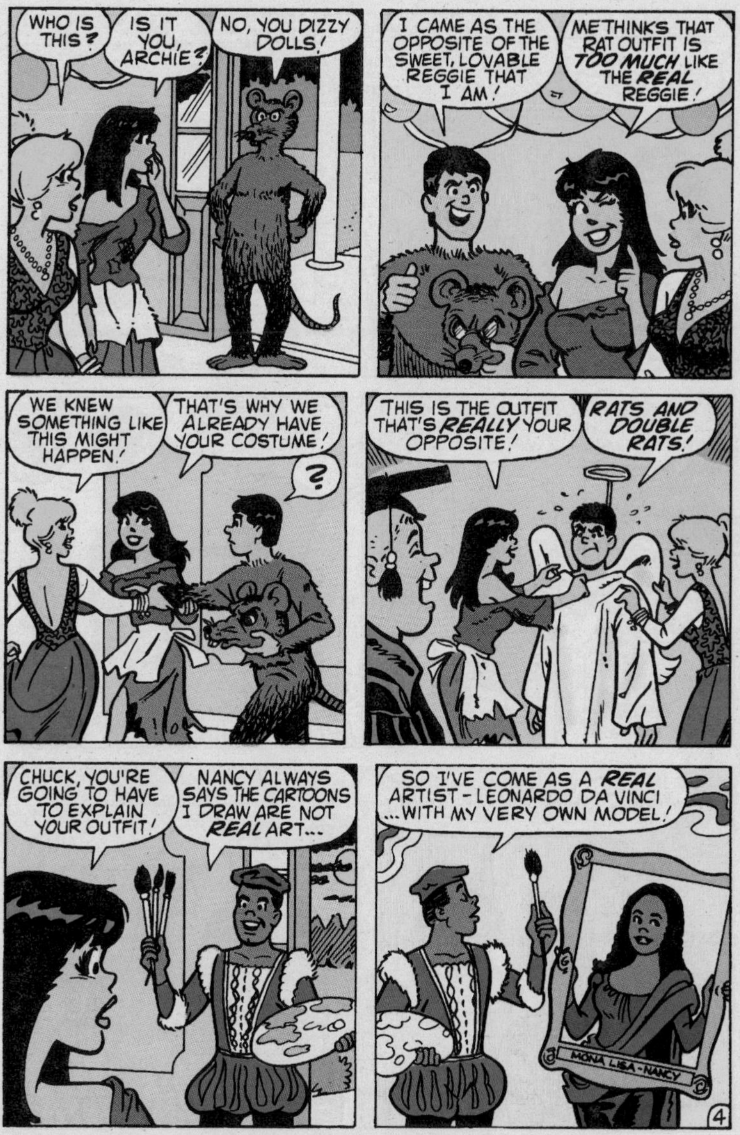
WHO IS THIS?
IS IT YOU, ARCHIE?
NO, YOU DIZZY DOLLS!
I CAME AS THE OPPOSITE OF THE SWEET, LOVABLE REGGIE THAT I AM!
METHINKS THAT RAT OUTFIT IS TOO MUCH LIKE THE REAL REGGIE!
WE KNEW SOMETHING LIKE THIS MIGHT HAPPEN!
THAT'S WHY WE ALREADY HAVE YOUR COSTUME!
?
THIS IS THE OUTFIT THAT'S REALLY YOUR OPPOSITE!
RATS AND DOUBLE RATS!
CHUCK, YOU'RE GOING TO HAVE TO EXPLAIN YOUR OUTFIT!
NANCY ALWAYS SAYS THE CARTOONS I DRAW ARE NOT REAL ART...
SO I'VE COME AS A REAL ARTIST - LEONARDO DA VINCI ...WITH MY VERY OWN MODEL!
MONA LISA-NANCY
4

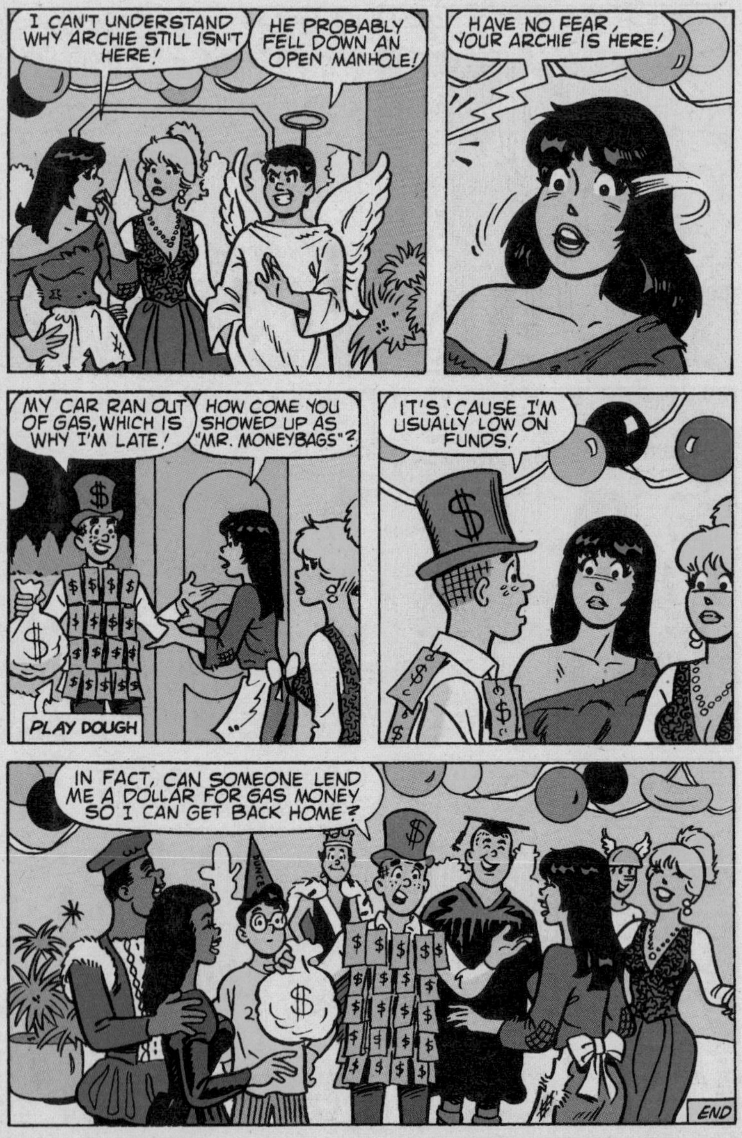
I CAN'T UNDERSTAND WHY ARCHIE STILL ISN'T HERE!
HE PROBABLY FELL DOWN AN OPEN MANHOLE!
HAVE NO FEAR, YOUR ARCHIE IS HERE!
MY CAR RAN OUT OF GAS, WHICH IS WHY I'M LATE!
HOW COME YOU SHOWED UP AS "MR. MONEYBAGS"?
PLAY DOUGH
IT'S 'CAUSE I'M USUALLY LOW ON FUNDS!
IN FACT, CAN SOMEONE LEND ME A DOLLAR FOR GAS MONEY SO I CAN GET BACK HOME?
END

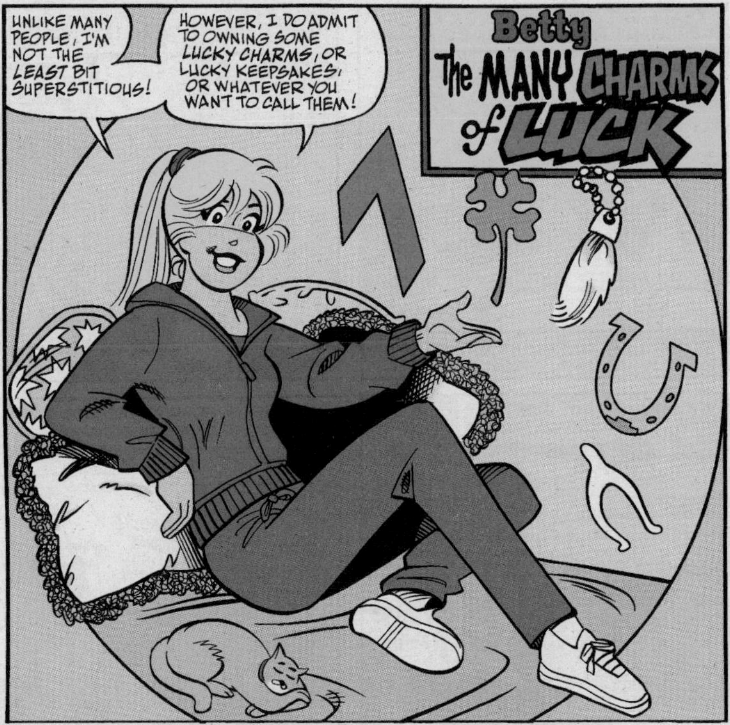
Betty
The MANY CHARMS of LUCK
UNLIKE MANY PEOPLE, I'M NOT THE LEAST BIT SUPERSTITIOUS!
HOWEVER, I DO ADMIT TO OWNING SOME LUCKY CHARMS, OR LUCKY KEEPSAKES, OR WHATEVER YOU WANT TO CALL THEM!

SCRIPT: GEORGE GLADIR PENCILS: STAN GOLDBERG INKING: JOHN LOWE LETTERING: JACK MORELLI COLORING: BARRY GROSSMAN

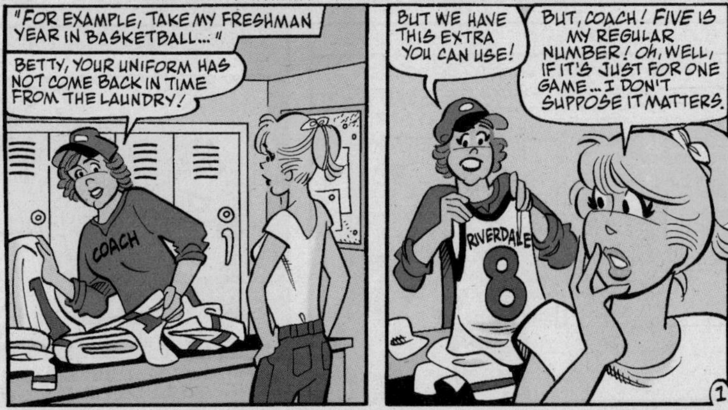
"FOR EXAMPLE, TAKE MY FRESHMAN YEAR IN BASKETBALL..."
BETTY, YOUR UNIFORM HAS NOT COME BACK IN TIME FROM THE LAUNDRY!
COACH
BUT WE HAVE THIS EXTRA YOU CAN USE!
BUT, COACH! FIVE IS MY REGULAR NUMBER! Oh, WELL, IF IT'S JUST FOR ONE GAME... I DON'T SUPPOSE IT MATTERS.
RIVERDALE
8

"THAT NIGHT OUR COACH SAID I PLAYED A BRILLIANT DEFENSIVE GAME..."

"BLOCKING 8 SHOTS AND MAKING 8 REBOUNDS AND 8 STEALS..."

"I ALSO SCORED 8 POINTS IN EACH HALF, AND HAD 8 ASSISTS!"

| RIVERDALE JV | 10 | 12 | 8 | 8 | 38 |
| CENTRAL JV | 2 | 4 | 2 | 8 | 16 |

"NEEDLESS TO SAY, EIGHT HAS BEEN MY LUCKY NUMBER EVER SINCE!"

| RIVERDALE | 16 | 8 | 10 | 12 | 46 |
| MIDVILLE | 4 | 2 | 6 | 7 | 19 |

"AND THEN THERE WAS THE TIME I DID QUITE WELL ON MY TRIGONOMETRY EXAM..."

BETTY COOPER A+

TEST RESULTS TODAY

"BUT ARCHIE POINTED OUT SOMETHING TO ME..."

I KNOW WHY YOU ALWAYS DO SO WELL ON YOUR TESTS!

BECAUSE I STUDY HARD?

NO! IT'S BECAUSE YOU ALWAYS WEAR YOUR LUCKY BRACELET!

"I NEVER THOUGHT OF IT THAT WAY... WAS ARCHIE RIGHT?"

"...MAYBE MY BRACELET DID HAVE SOMETHING TO DO WITH IT!"

2

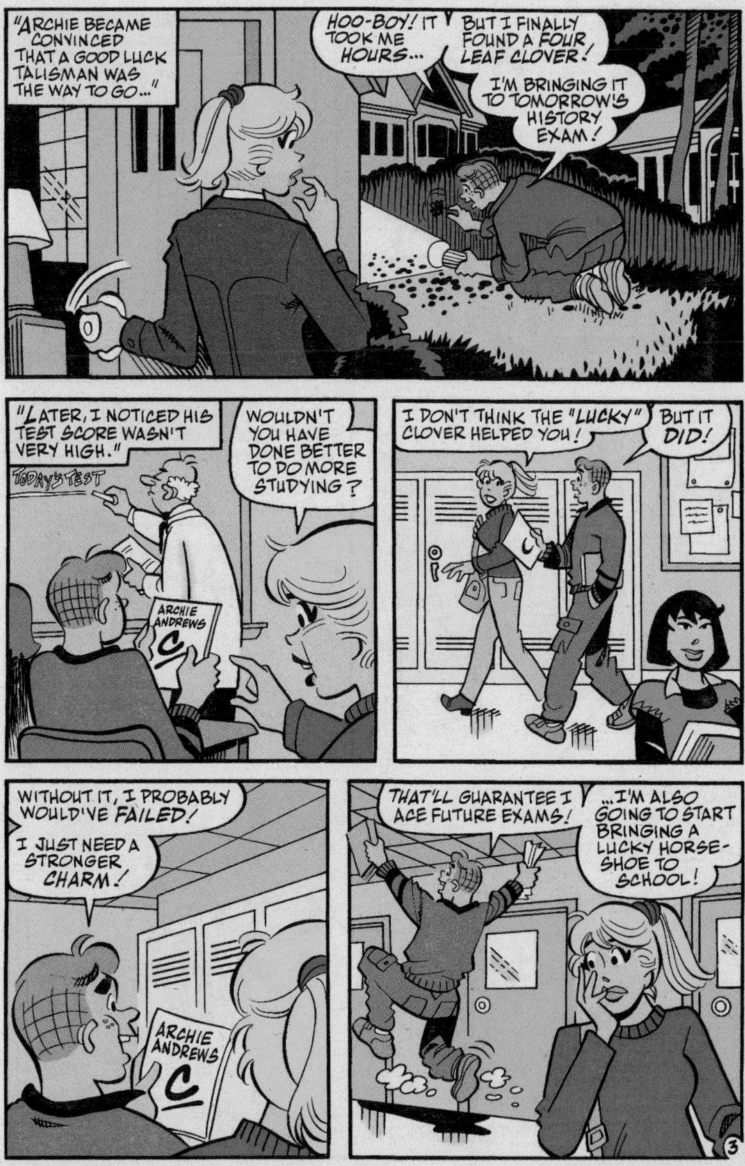
"ARCHIE BECAME CONVINCED THAT A GOOD LUCK TALISMAN WAS THE WAY TO GO..."
HOO-BOY! IT TOOK ME HOURS...
BUT I FINALLY FOUND A FOUR LEAF CLOVER!
I'M BRINGING IT TO TOMORROW'S HISTORY EXAM!
"LATER, I NOTICED HIS TEST SCORE WASN'T VERY HIGH."
TODAY'S TEST
ARCHIE ANDREWS C
WOULDN'T YOU HAVE DONE BETTER TO DO MORE STUDYING?
I DON'T THINK THE "LUCKY" CLOVER HELPED YOU!
BUT IT DID!
WITHOUT IT, I PROBABLY WOULD'VE FAILED!
I JUST NEED A STRONGER CHARM!
ARCHIE ANDREWS C
...I'M ALSO GOING TO START BRINGING A LUCKY HORSE-SHOE TO SCHOOL!
THAT'LL GUARANTEE I ACE FUTURE EXAMS!

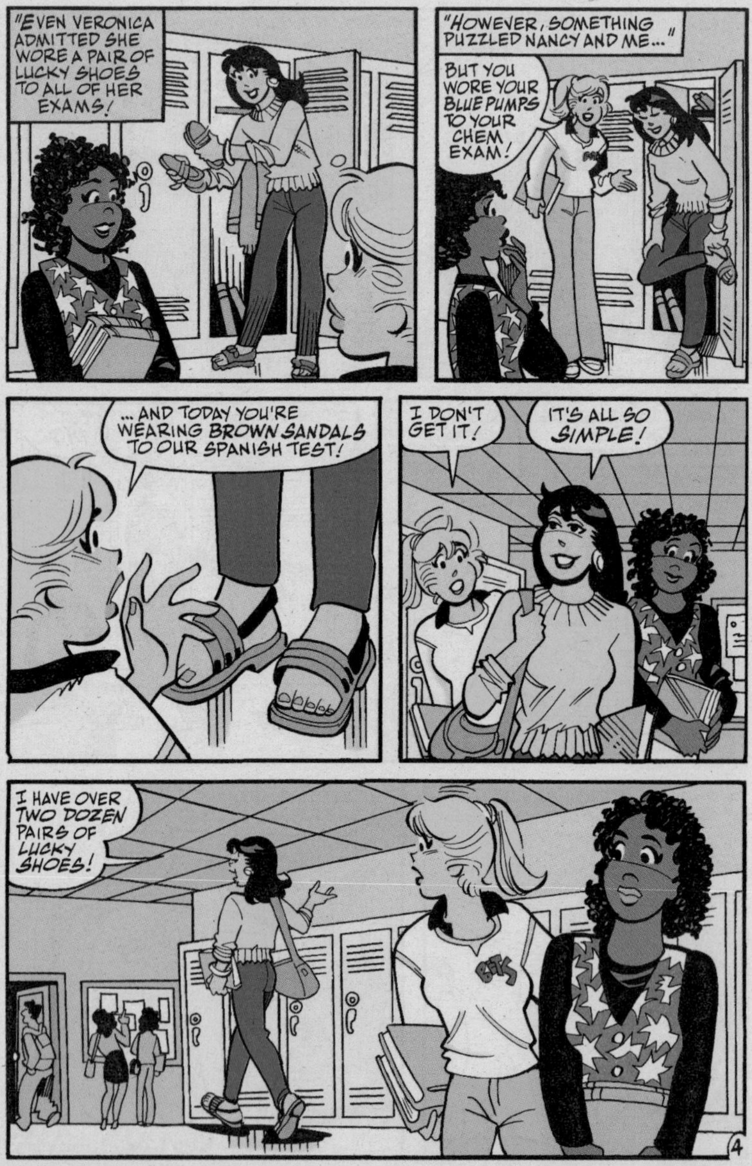
"EVEN VERONICA ADMITTED SHE WORE A PAIR OF LUCKY SHOES TO ALL OF HER EXAMS!
"HOWEVER, SOMETHING PUZZLED NANCY AND ME..."
BUT YOU WORE YOUR BLUE PUMPS TO YOUR CHEM EXAM!
...AND TODAY YOU'RE WEARING BROWN SANDALS TO OUR SPANISH TEST!
I DON'T GET IT!
IT'S ALL SO SIMPLE!
I HAVE OVER TWO DOZEN PAIRS OF LUCKY SHOES!
4

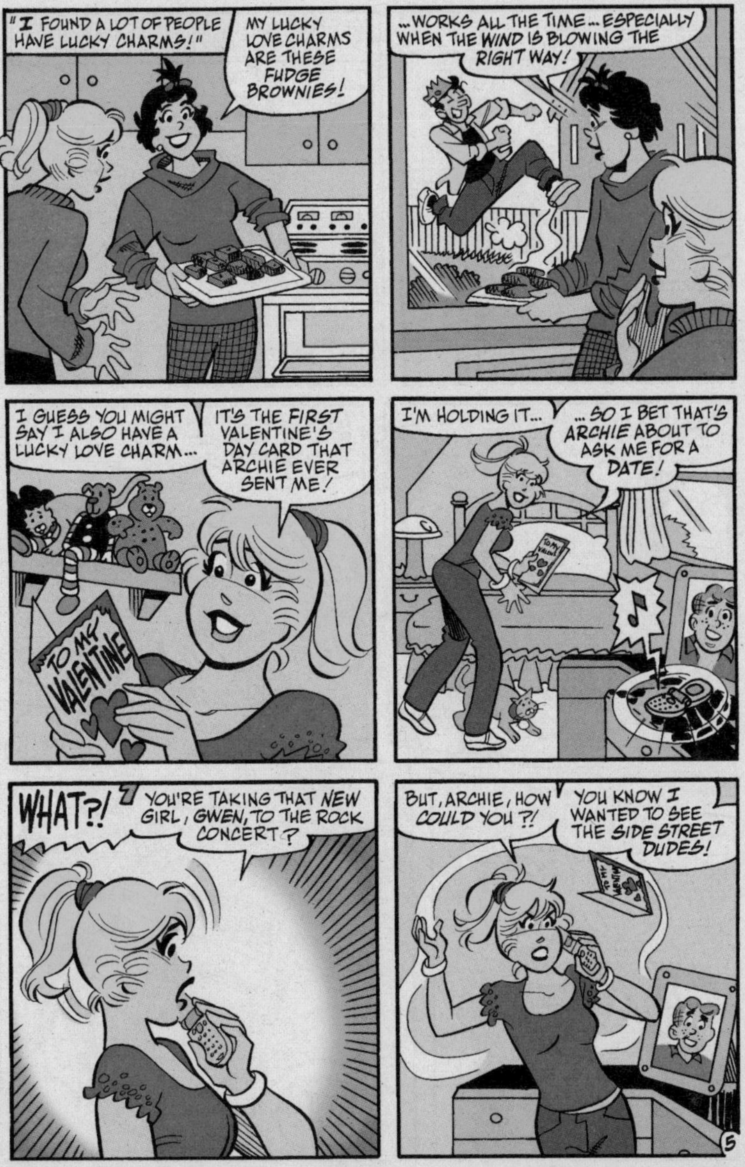
"I FOUND A LOT OF PEOPLE HAVE LUCKY CHARMS!"
MY LUCKY LOVE CHARMS ARE THESE FUDGE BROWNIES!
...WORKS ALL THE TIME... ESPECIALLY WHEN THE WIND IS BLOWING THE RIGHT WAY!
I GUESS YOU MIGHT SAY I ALSO HAVE A LUCKY LOVE CHARM...
IT'S THE FIRST VALENTINE'S DAY CARD THAT ARCHIE EVER SENT ME!
TO MY VALENTINE
I'M HOLDING IT...
...SO I BET THAT'S ARCHIE ABOUT TO ASK ME FOR A DATE!
WHAT?!
YOU'RE TAKING THAT NEW GIRL, GWEN, TO THE ROCK CONCERT?
BUT, ARCHIE, HOW COULD YOU?!
YOU KNOW I WANTED TO SEE THE SIDE STREET DUDES!

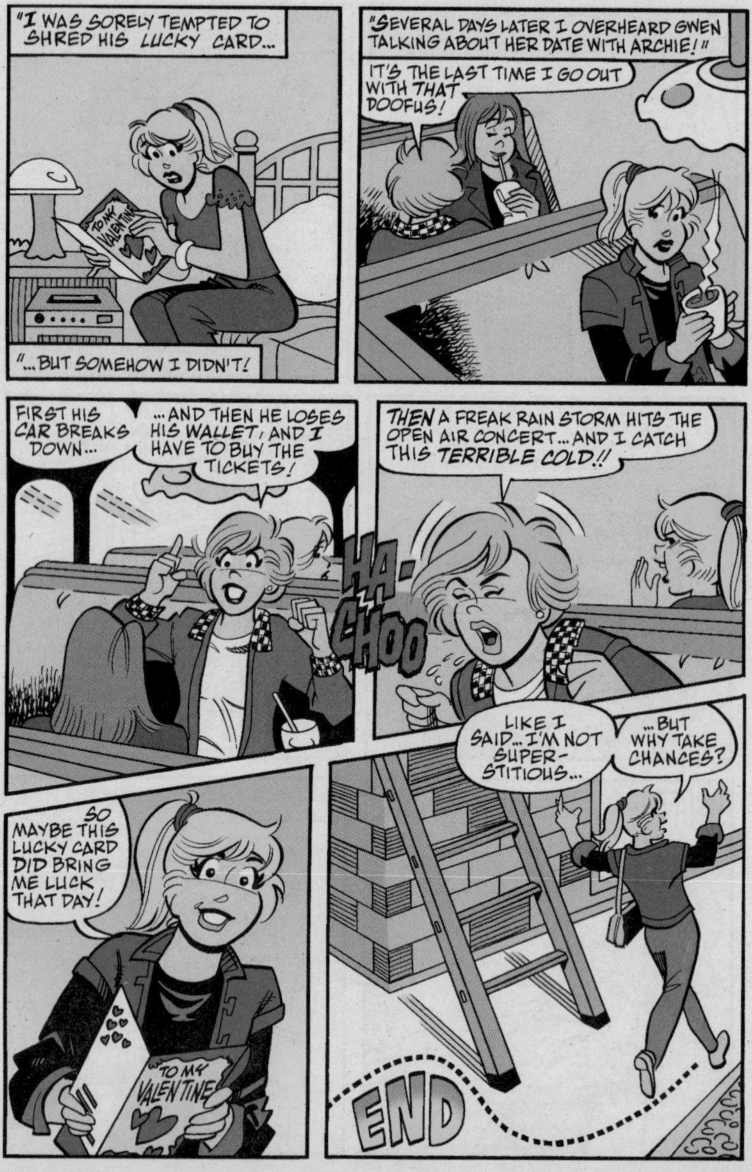

"I WAS SORELY TEMPTED TO SHRED HIS LUCKY CARD...
TO MY VALENTINE
"...BUT SOMEHOW I DIDN'T!
"SEVERAL DAYS LATER I OVERHEARD GWEN TALKING ABOUT HER DATE WITH ARCHIE!"
IT'S THE LAST TIME I GO OUT WITH THAT DOOFUS!
FIRST HIS CAR BREAKS DOWN...
...AND THEN HE LOSES HIS WALLET, AND I HAVE TO BUY THE TICKETS!
THEN A FREAK RAIN STORM HITS THE OPEN AIR CONCERT... AND I CATCH THIS TERRIBLE COLD!!
HA-CHOO
SO MAYBE THIS LUCKY CARD DID BRING ME LUCK THAT DAY!
TO MY VALENTINE
LIKE I SAID... I'M NOT SUPER-STITIOUS...
...BUT WHY TAKE CHANCES?
END

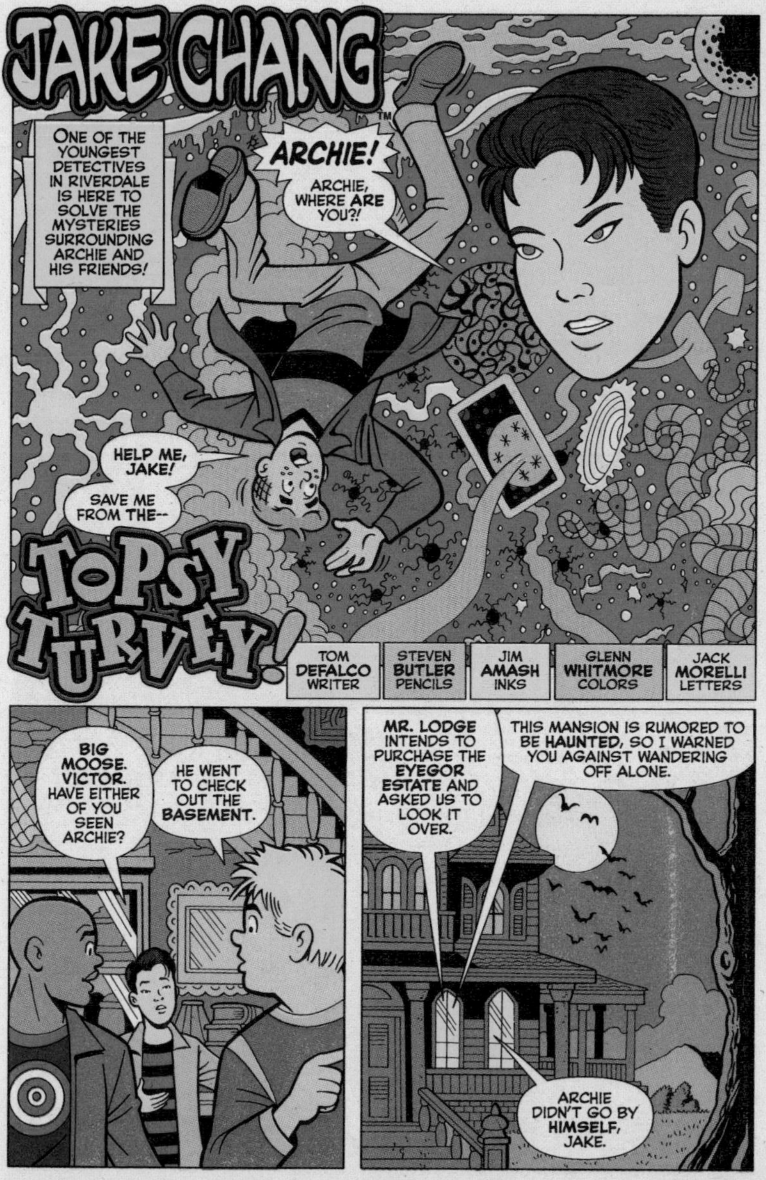
JAKE CHANG™
ONE OF THE YOUNGEST DETECTIVES IN RIVERDALE IS HERE TO SOLVE THE MYSTERIES SURROUNDING ARCHIE AND HIS FRIENDS!
ARCHIE!
ARCHIE, WHERE ARE YOU?!
HELP ME, JAKE!
SAVE ME FROM THE--
TOPSY TURVEY!
TOM DEFALCO WRITER
STEVEN BUTLER PENCILS
JIM AMASH INKS
GLENN WHITMORE COLORS
JACK MORELLI LETTERS
BIG MOOSE. VICTOR. HAVE EITHER OF YOU SEEN ARCHIE?
HE WENT TO CHECK OUT THE BASEMENT.
MR. LODGE INTENDS TO PURCHASE THE EYEGOR ESTATE AND ASKED US TO LOOK IT OVER.
THIS MANSION IS RUMORED TO BE HAUNTED, SO I WARNED YOU AGAINST WANDERING OFF ALONE.
ARCHIE DIDN'T GO BY HIMSELF, JAKE.

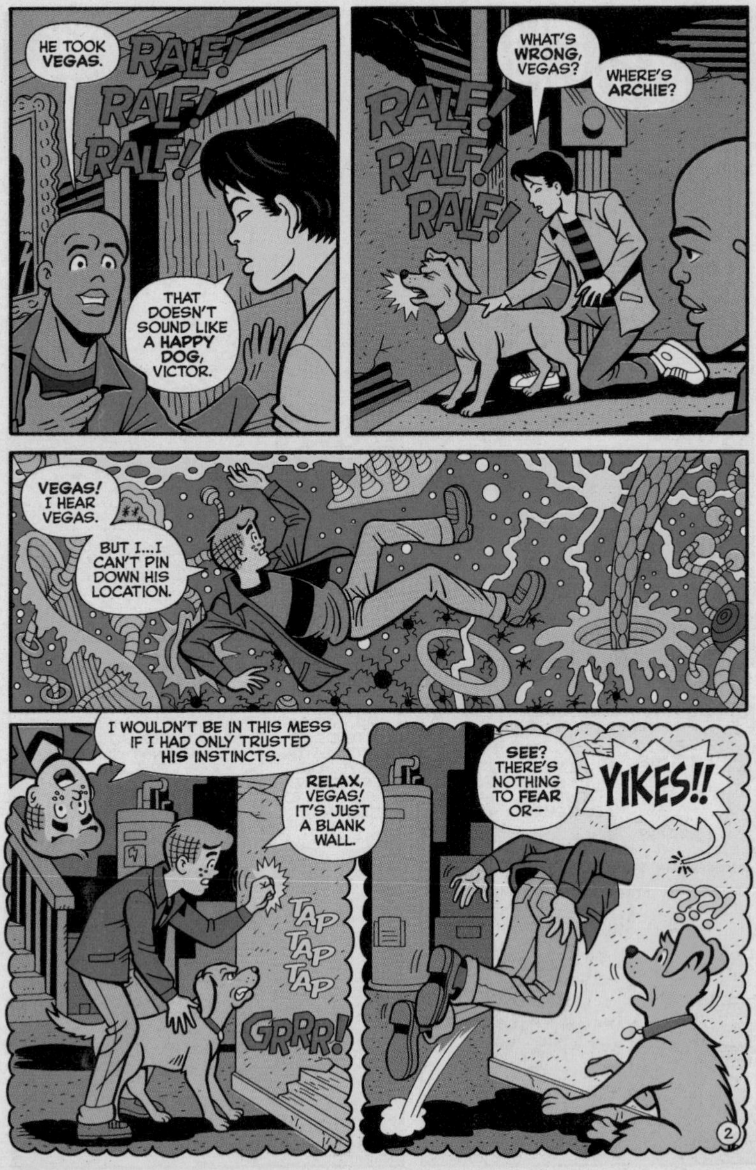
HE TOOK VEGAS.
RALF! RALF! RALF!
THAT DOESN'T SOUND LIKE A HAPPY DOG, VICTOR.
WHAT'S WRONG, VEGAS?
WHERE'S ARCHIE?
RALF! RALF! RALF!
VEGAS! I HEAR VEGAS.
BUT I...I CAN'T PIN DOWN HIS LOCATION.
I WOULDN'T BE IN THIS MESS IF I HAD ONLY TRUSTED HIS INSTINCTS.
RELAX, VEGAS! IT'S JUST A BLANK WALL.
TAP TAP TAP
GRRR!
SEE? THERE'S NOTHING TO FEAR OR--
YIKES!!
???
2

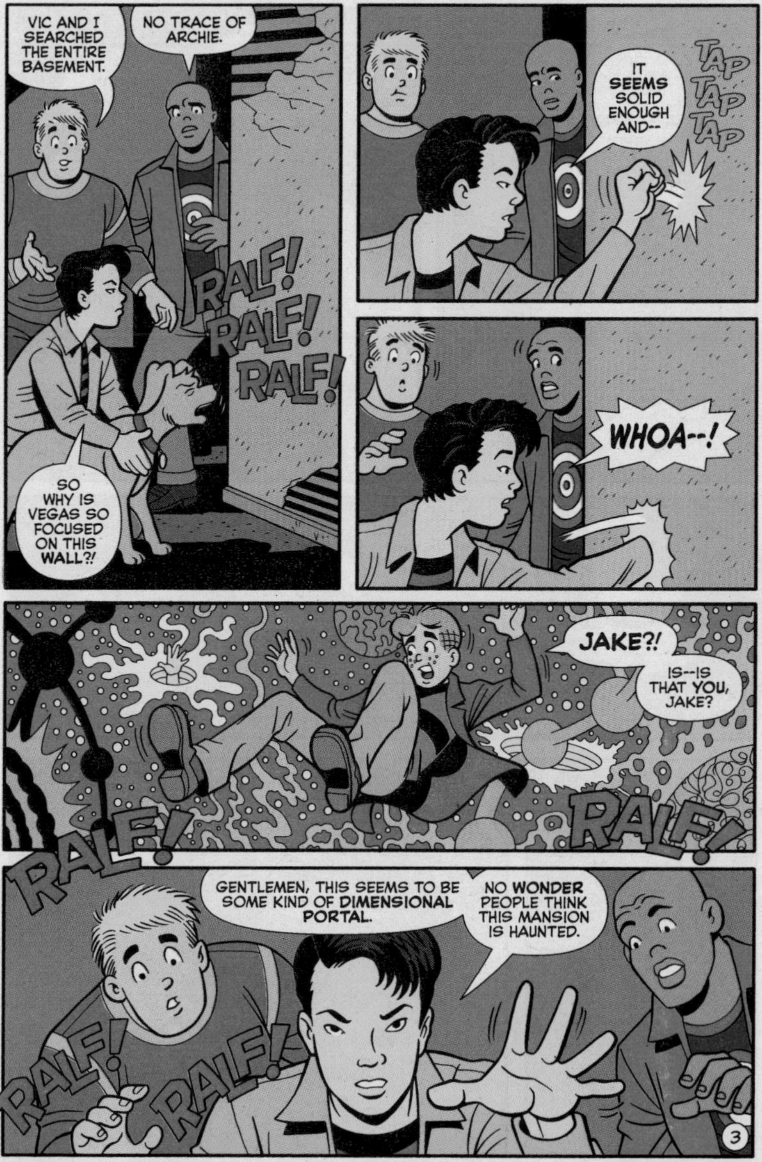
VIC AND I SEARCHED THE ENTIRE BASEMENT.
NO TRACE OF ARCHIE.
RALF! RALF! RALF!
SO WHY IS VEGAS SO FOCUSED ON THIS WALL?!
IT SEEMS SOLID ENOUGH AND--
TAP TAP TAP
WHOA--!
JAKE?!
IS--IS THAT YOU, JAKE?
RALF! RALF!
RALF!
GENTLEMEN, THIS SEEMS TO BE SOME KIND OF DIMENSIONAL PORTAL.
NO WONDER PEOPLE THINK THIS MANSION IS HAUNTED.
RALF! RALF!
3

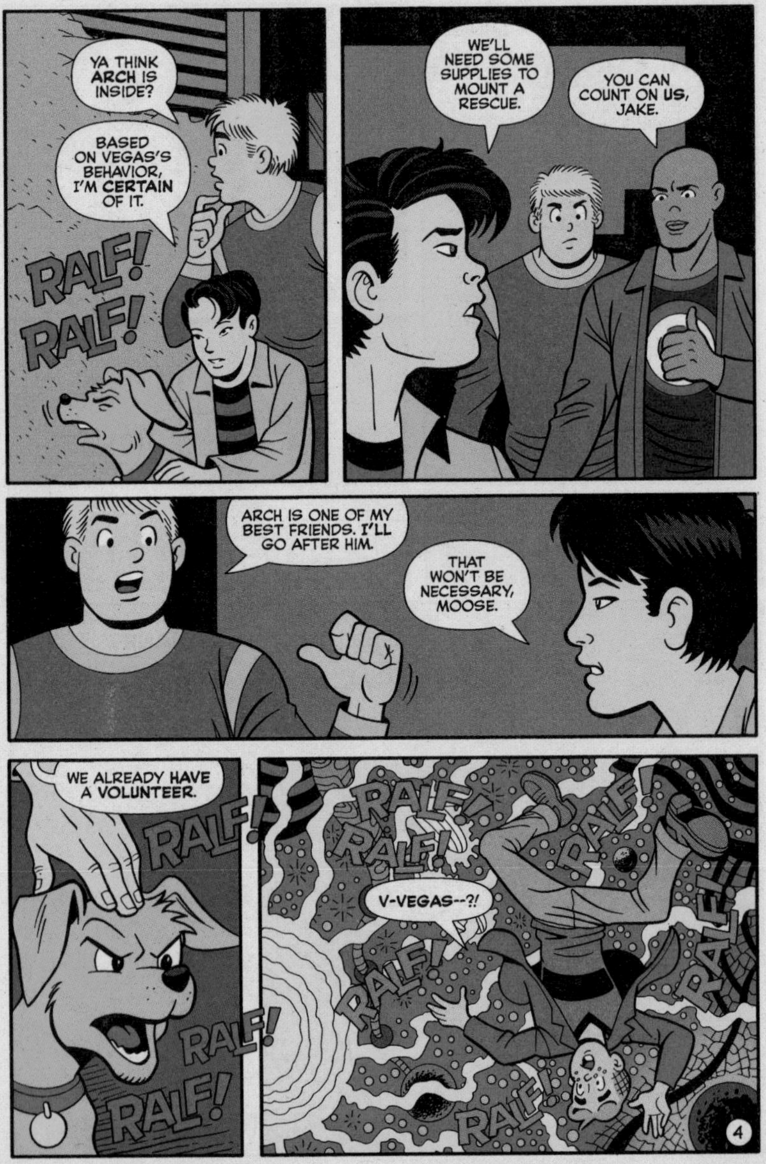
YA THINK ARCH IS INSIDE?
BASED ON VEGAS'S BEHAVIOR, I'M CERTAIN OF IT.
RALF! RALF!
WE'LL NEED SOME SUPPLIES TO MOUNT A RESCUE.
YOU CAN COUNT ON US, JAKE.
ARCH IS ONE OF MY BEST FRIENDS. I'LL GO AFTER HIM.
THAT WON'T BE NECESSARY, MOOSE.
WE ALREADY HAVE A VOLUNTEER.
RALF! RALF! RALF!
RALF! RALF! RALF!
V-VEGAS--?!
RALF! RALF! RALF! RALF!
4

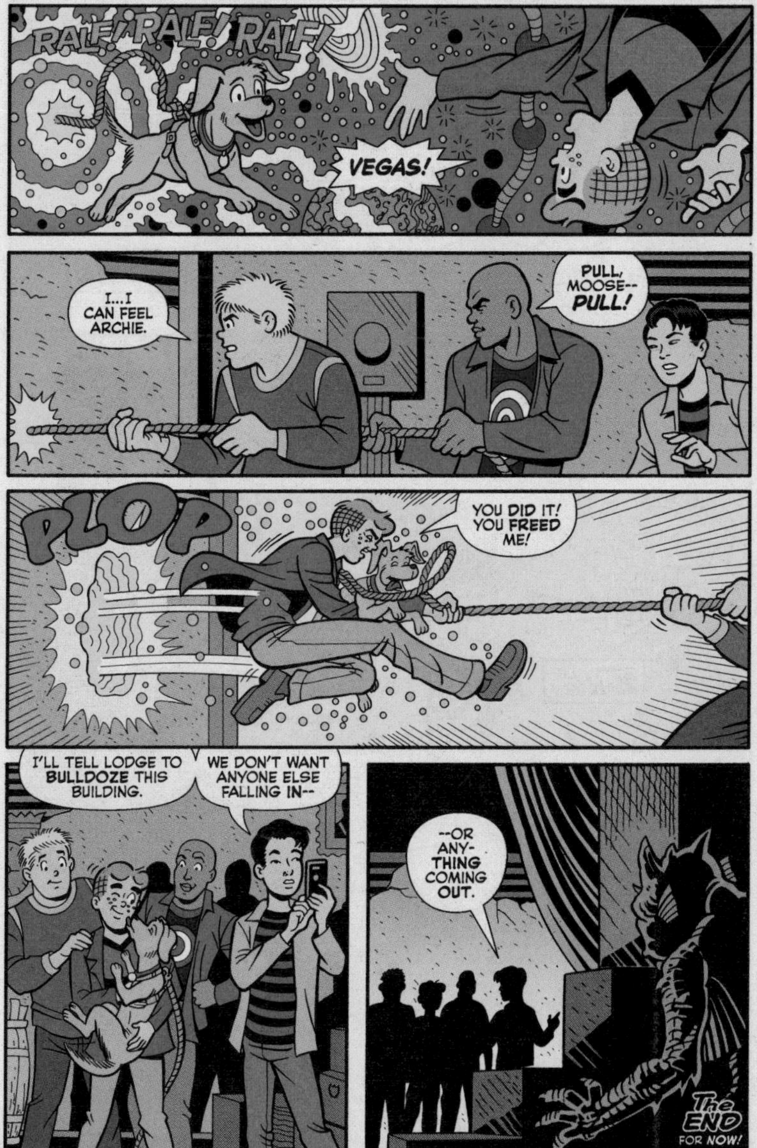
RALF! RALF! RALF!
VEGAS!
I...I CAN FEEL ARCHIE.
PULL, MOOSE-- PULL!
PLOP
YOU DID IT! YOU FREED ME!
I'LL TELL LODGE TO BULLDOZE THIS BUILDING.
WE DON'T WANT ANYONE ELSE FALLING IN--
--OR ANY-THING COMING OUT.
The END FOR NOW!

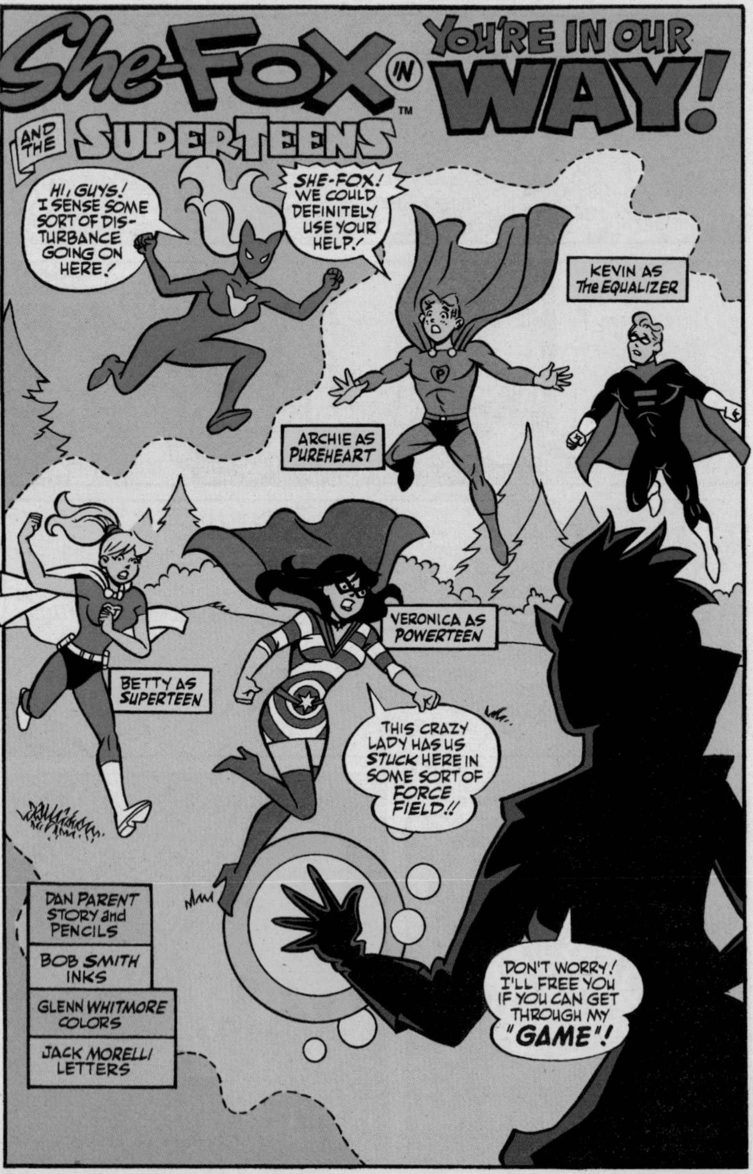
She-Fox™ in YOU'RE IN OUR WAY!
AND THE SUPERTEENS
HI, GUYS! I SENSE SOME SORT OF DIS-TURBANCE GOING ON HERE!
SHE-FOX! WE COULD DEFINITELY USE YOUR HELP!
KEVIN AS The EQUALIZER
ARCHIE AS PUREHEART
VERONICA AS POWERTEEN
BETTY AS SUPERTEEN
THIS CRAZY LADY HAS US STUCK HERE IN SOME SORT OF FORCE FIELD!!
DAN PARENT STORY and PENCILS
BOB SMITH INKS
GLENN WHITMORE COLORS
JACK MORELLI LETTERS
DON'T WORRY! I'LL FREE YOU IF YOU CAN GET THROUGH MY "GAME"!

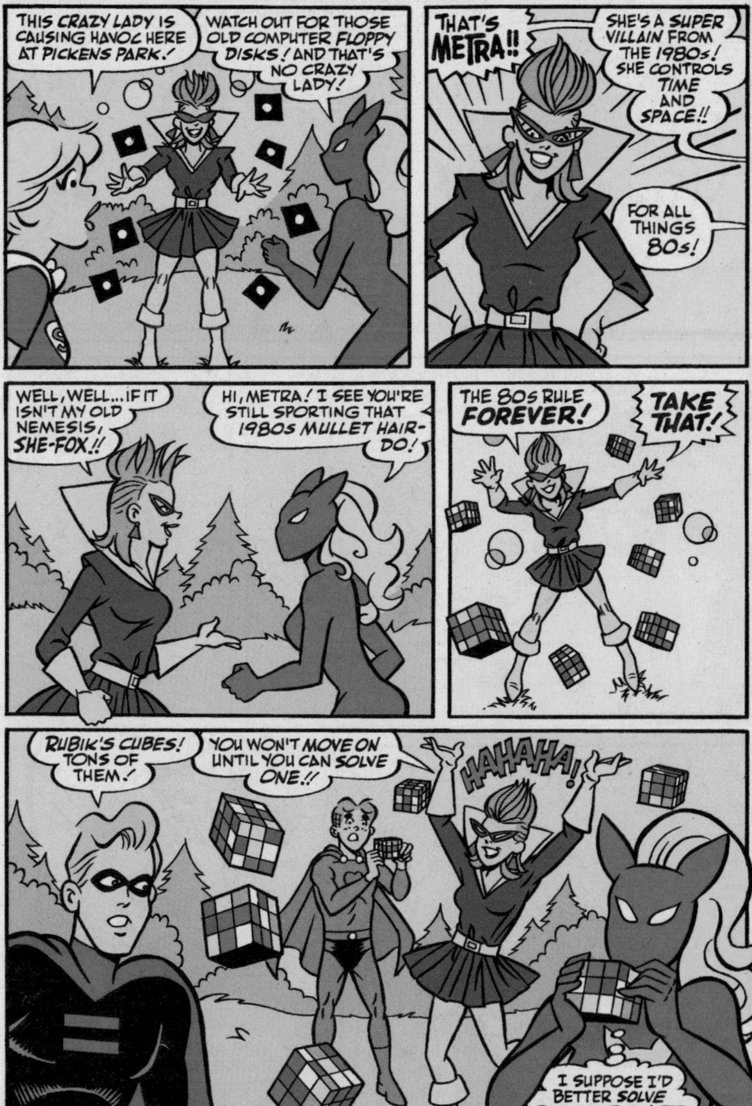
THIS CRAZY LADY IS CAUSING HAVOC HERE AT PICKENS PARK.!
WATCH OUT FOR THOSE OLD COMPUTER FLOPPY DISKS! AND THAT'S NO CRAZY LADY!
THAT'S METRA!!
SHE'S A SUPER VILLAIN FROM THE 1980s! SHE CONTROLS TIME AND SPACE!!
FOR ALL THINGS 80s!
WELL, WELL... IF IT ISN'T MY OLD NEMESIS, SHE-FOX!!
HI, METRA! I SEE YOU'RE STILL SPORTING THAT 1980s MULLET HAIR-DO!
THE 80s RULE FOREVER!
TAKE THAT!
RUBIK'S CUBES! TONS OF THEM!
YOU WON'T MOVE ON UNTIL YOU CAN SOLVE ONE!!
HAHAHA!
I SUPPOSE I'D BETTER SOLVE THIS SO WE CAN GET OUT OF THIS SILLY TRAP!
2

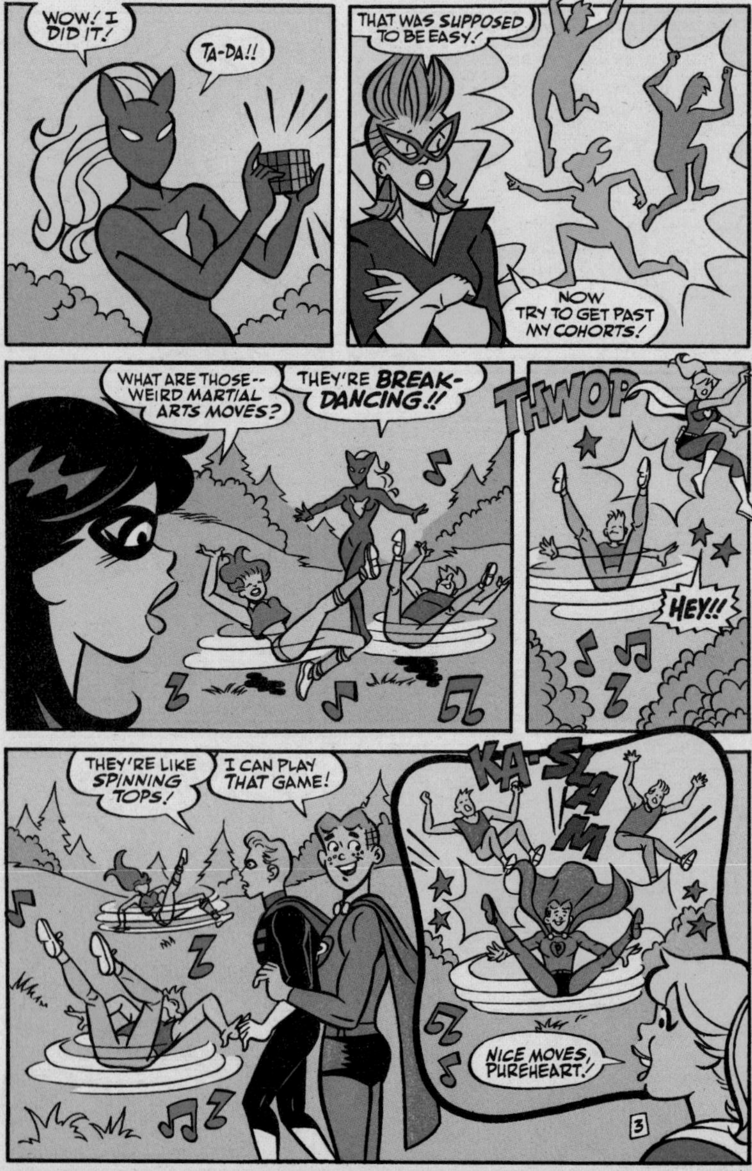
WOW! I DID IT!
TA-DA!!
THAT WAS SUPPOSED TO BE EASY!
NOW TRY TO GET PAST MY COHORTS!
WHAT ARE THOSE-- WEIRD MARTIAL ARTS MOVES?
THEY'RE BREAK-DANCING!!
THWOP
HEY!!
THEY'RE LIKE SPINNING TOPS!
I CAN PLAY THAT GAME!
KA-SLAM
NICE MOVES, PUREHEART!
3

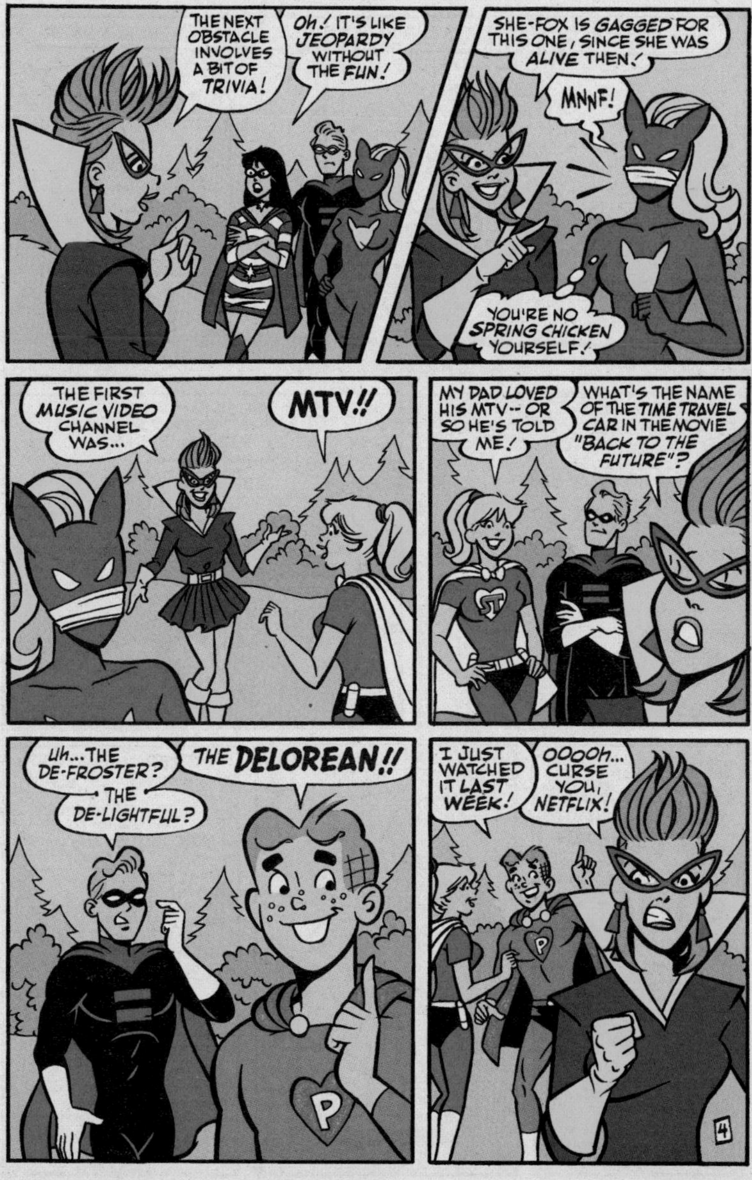
THE NEXT OBSTACLE INVOLVES A BIT OF TRIVIA!
Oh! IT'S LIKE JEOPARDY WITHOUT THE FUN!
SHE-FOX IS GAGGED FOR THIS ONE, SINCE SHE WAS ALIVE THEN!
MNNF!
YOU'RE NO SPRING CHICKEN YOURSELF!
THE FIRST MUSIC VIDEO CHANNEL WAS...
MTV!!
MY DAD LOVED HIS MTV-- OR SO HE'S TOLD ME!
WHAT'S THE NAME OF THE TIME TRAVEL CAR IN THE MOVIE "BACK TO THE FUTURE"?
Uh... THE DE-FROSTER?
THE DE-LIGHTFUL?
THE DELOREAN!!
I JUST WATCHED IT LAST WEEK!
OOOOh... CURSE YOU, NETFLIX!
4

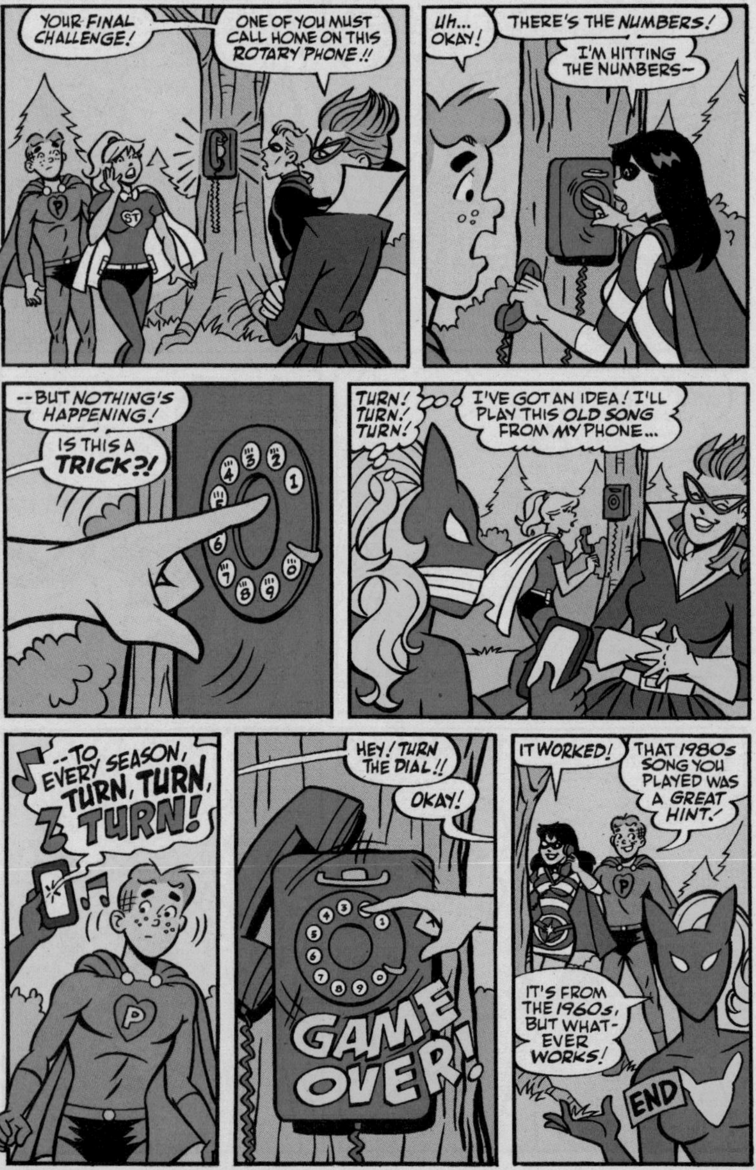
YOUR FINAL CHALLENGE!
ONE OF YOU MUST CALL HOME ON THIS ROTARY PHONE!!
UH... OKAY!
THERE'S THE NUMBERS!
I'M HITTING THE NUMBERS--
--BUT NOTHING'S HAPPENING!
IS THIS A TRICK?!
TURN! TURN! TURN!
I'VE GOT AN IDEA! I'LL PLAY THIS OLD SONG FROM MY PHONE...
--TO EVERY SEASON, TURN, TURN, TURN!
HEY! TURN THE DIAL!!
OKAY!
GAME OVER!
IT WORKED!
THAT 1980s SONG YOU PLAYED WAS A GREAT HINT!
IT'S FROM THE 1960s, BUT WHAT-EVER WORKS!
END

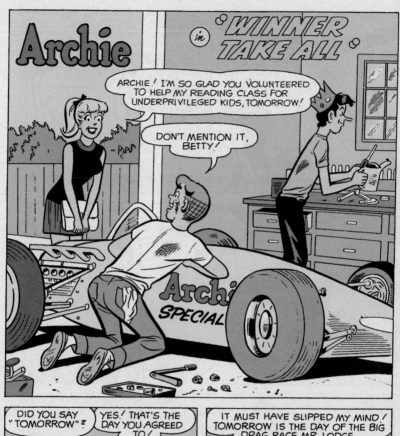

Archie in "WINNER TAKE ALL"

ARCHIE! I'M SO GLAD YOU VOLUNTEERED TO HELP MY READING CLASS FOR UNDERPRIVILEGED KIDS, TOMORROW!

DON'T MENTION IT, BETTY!

Archie
SPECIAL

DID YOU SAY "TOMORROW"?

YES! THAT'S THE DAY YOU AGREED TO!

IT MUST HAVE SLIPPED MY MIND! TOMORROW IS THE DAY OF THE BIG DRAG RACE MR. LODGE IS SPONSORING!

SEPT. 16 SATURDAY

Script: GEORGE GLADIR   Pencils: BILL VIGODA   Inks: MARIO ACQUAVIVA   Letters: BILL YOSHIDA

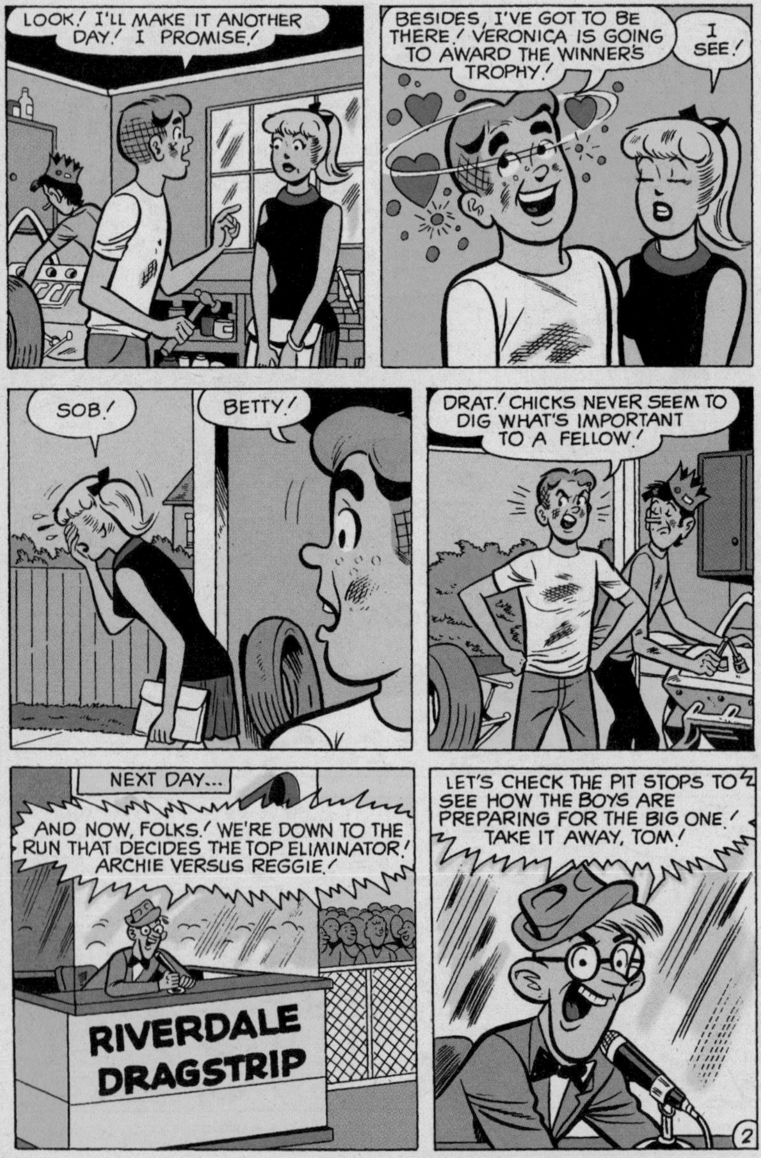
LOOK! I'LL MAKE IT ANOTHER DAY! I PROMISE!
BESIDES, I'VE GOT TO BE THERE! VERONICA IS GOING TO AWARD THE WINNER'S TROPHY!
I SEE!
SOB!
BETTY!
DRAT! CHICKS NEVER SEEM TO DIG WHAT'S IMPORTANT TO A FELLOW!
NEXT DAY...
AND NOW, FOLKS! WE'RE DOWN TO THE RUN THAT DECIDES THE TOP ELIMINATOR! ARCHIE VERSUS REGGIE!
RIVERDALE DRAGSTRIP
LET'S CHECK THE PIT STOPS TO SEE HOW THE BOYS ARE PREPARING FOR THE BIG ONE! TAKE IT AWAY, TOM!
2

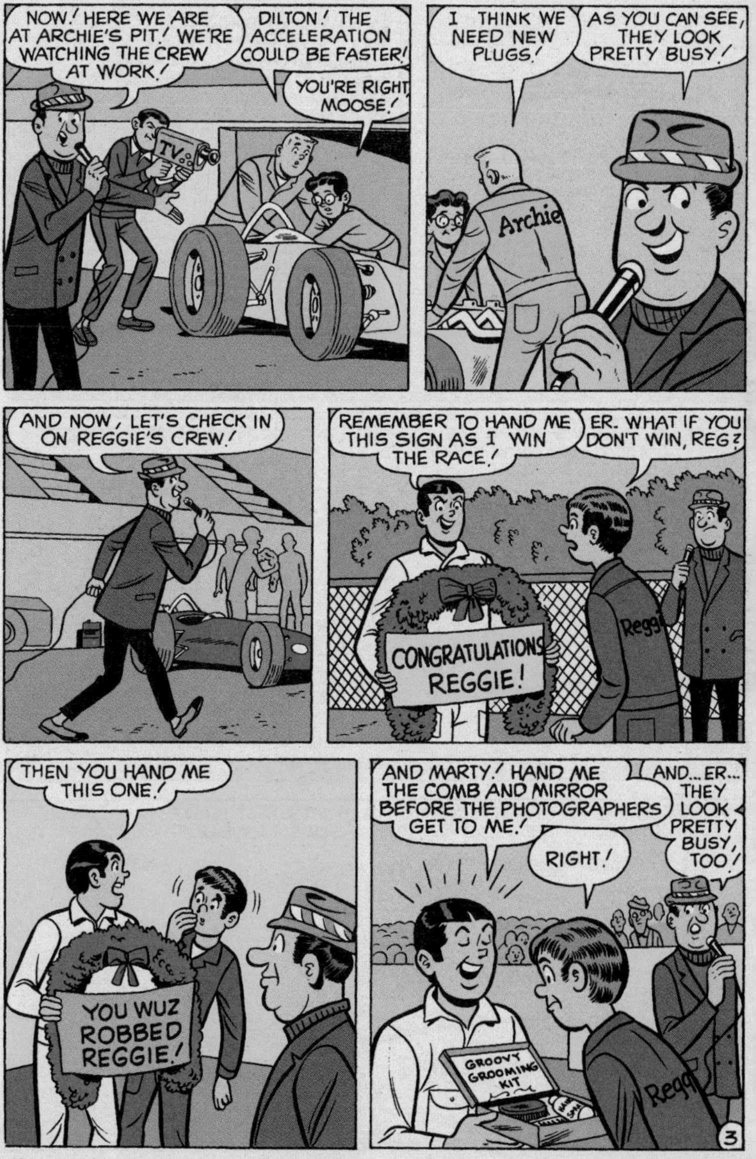
NOW! HERE WE ARE AT ARCHIE'S PIT! WE'RE WATCHING THE CREW AT WORK!
TV
DILTON! THE ACCELERATION COULD BE FASTER!
YOU'RE RIGHT, MOOSE!
I THINK WE NEED NEW PLUGS!
AS YOU CAN SEE, THEY LOOK PRETTY BUSY!
Archie
AND NOW, LET'S CHECK IN ON REGGIE'S CREW!
REMEMBER TO HAND ME THIS SIGN AS I WIN THE RACE!
ER. WHAT IF YOU DON'T WIN, REG?
CONGRATULATIONS REGGIE!
THEN YOU HAND ME THIS ONE!
YOU WUZ ROBBED REGGIE!
AND MARTY! HAND ME THE COMB AND MIRROR BEFORE THE PHOTOGRAPHERS GET TO ME!
RIGHT!
AND... ER... THEY LOOK PRETTY BUSY, TOO!
GROOVY GROOMING KIT
3

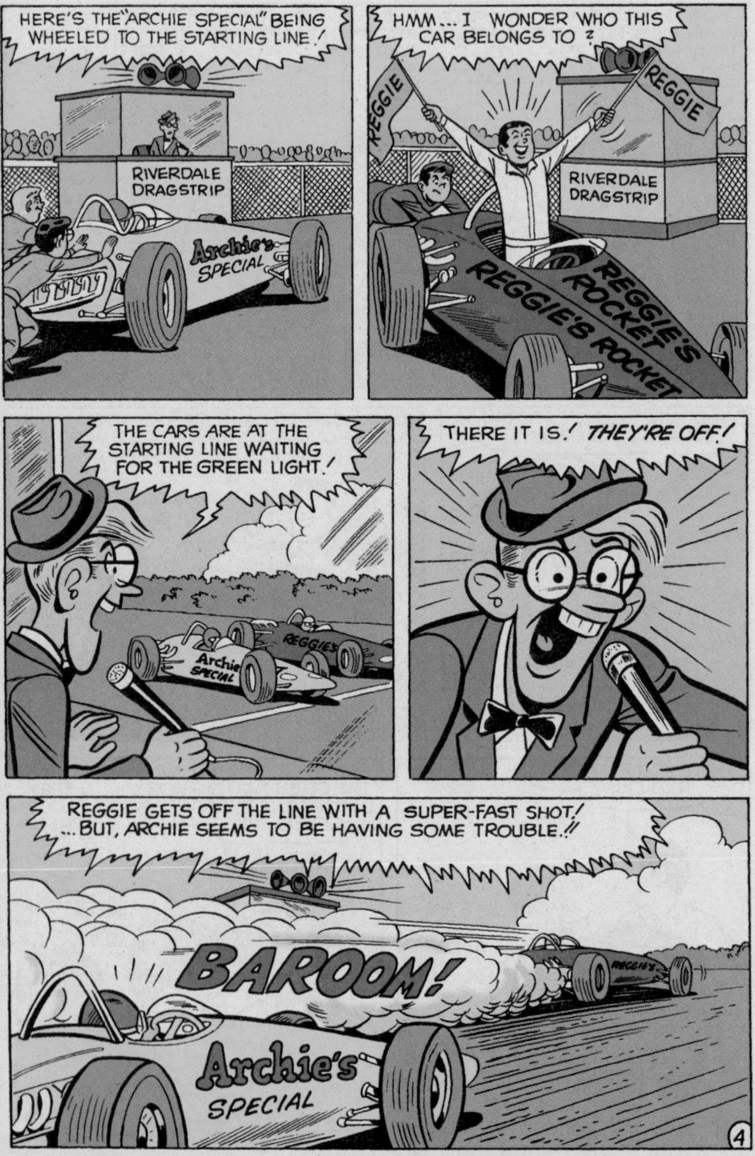

HERE'S THE "ARCHIE SPECIAL" BEING WHEELED TO THE STARTING LINE!
RIVERDALE DRAGSTRIP
Archie's SPECIAL
HMM... I WONDER WHO THIS CAR BELONGS TO ?
REGGIE
REGGIE
RIVERDALE DRAGSTRIP
REGGIE'S ROCKET
REGGIE'S ROCKET
THE CARS ARE AT THE STARTING LINE WAITING FOR THE GREEN LIGHT!
Archie SPECIAL
REGGIES
THERE IT IS! THEY'RE OFF!
REGGIE GETS OFF THE LINE WITH A SUPER-FAST SHOT! ...BUT, ARCHIE SEEMS TO BE HAVING SOME TROUBLE.!!
BAROOM!
REGGIE'S
Archie's SPECIAL
4

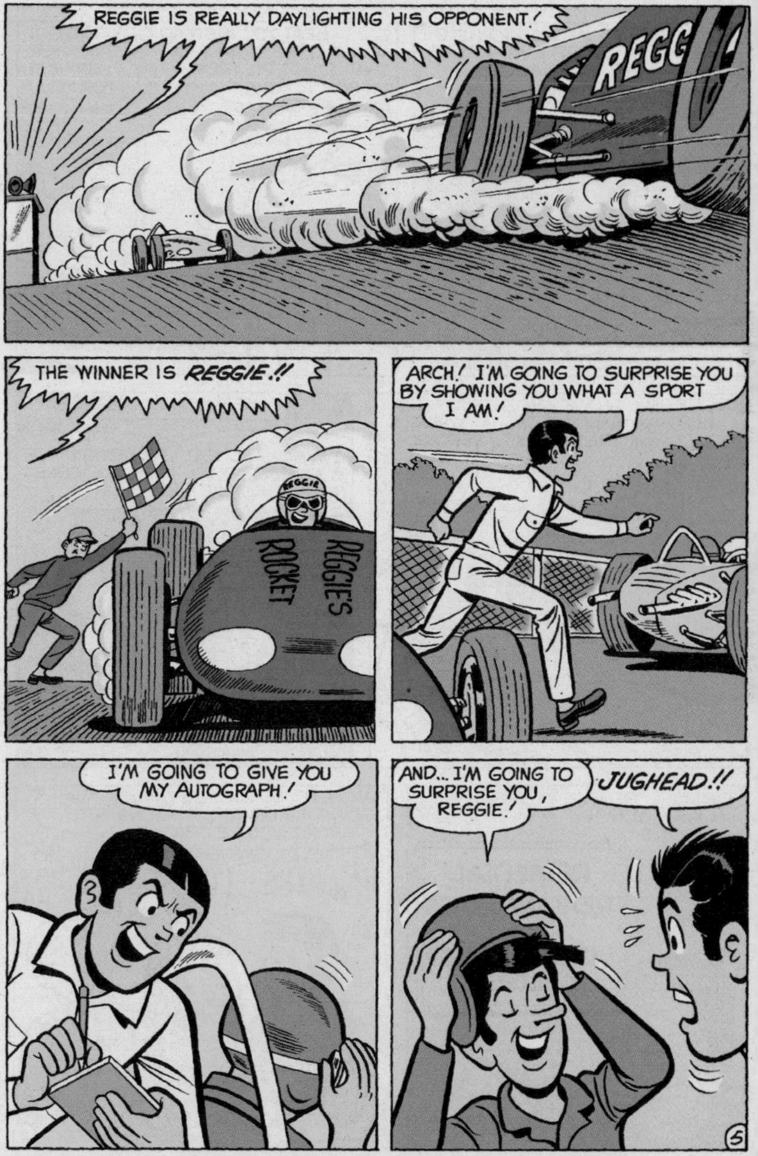
REGGIE IS REALLY DAYLIGHTING HIS OPPONENT!
REGG
THE WINNER IS REGGIE!!
REGGIE
REGGIE'S ROCKET
ARCH! I'M GOING TO SURPRISE YOU BY SHOWING YOU WHAT A SPORT I AM!
I'M GOING TO GIVE YOU MY AUTOGRAPH!
AND... I'M GOING TO SURPRISE YOU, REGGIE!
JUGHEAD!!
5

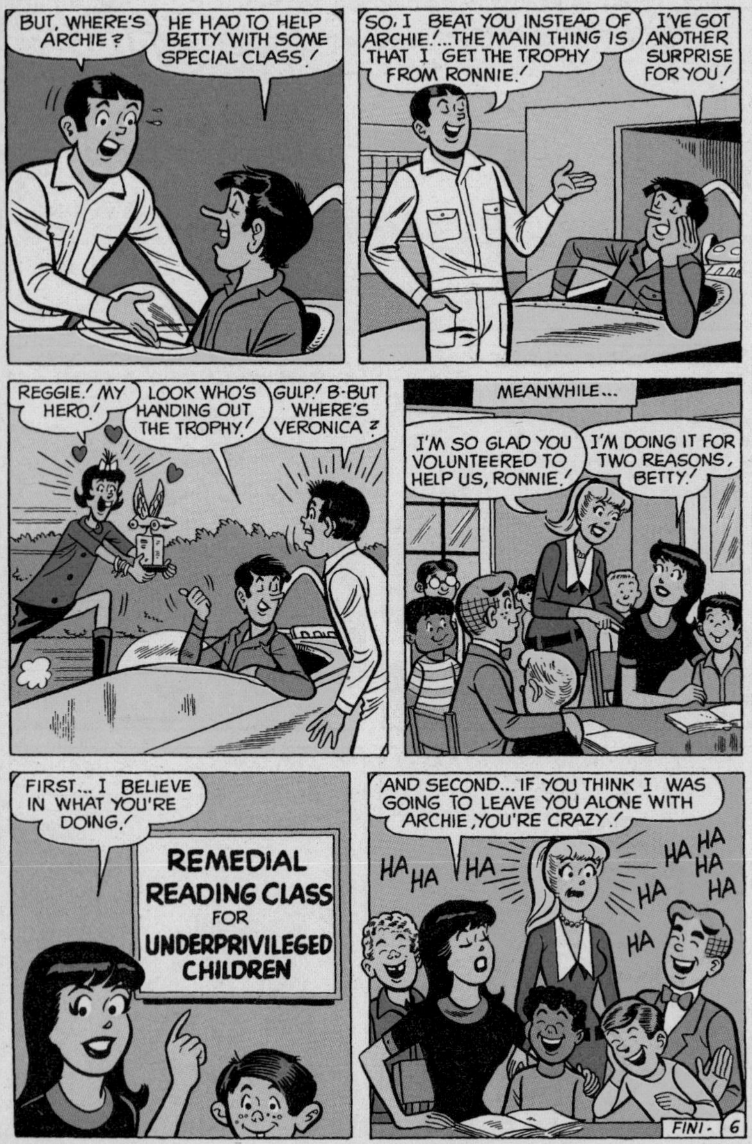
BUT, WHERE'S ARCHIE?
HE HAD TO HELP BETTY WITH SOME SPECIAL CLASS!
SO, I BEAT YOU INSTEAD OF ARCHIE!...THE MAIN THING IS THAT I GET THE TROPHY FROM RONNIE!
I'VE GOT ANOTHER SURPRISE FOR YOU!
REGGIE! MY HERO!
LOOK WHO'S HANDING OUT THE TROPHY!
GULP! B-BUT WHERE'S VERONICA?
MEANWHILE...
I'M SO GLAD YOU VOLUNTEERED TO HELP US, RONNIE!
I'M DOING IT FOR TWO REASONS, BETTY!
FIRST... I BELIEVE IN WHAT YOU'RE DOING!
REMEDIAL READING CLASS FOR UNDERPRIVILEGED CHILDREN
AND SECOND... IF YOU THINK I WAS GOING TO LEAVE YOU ALONE WITH ARCHIE, YOU'RE CRAZY!
HA HA HA
HA HA HA HA HA
HA
FINI-
6

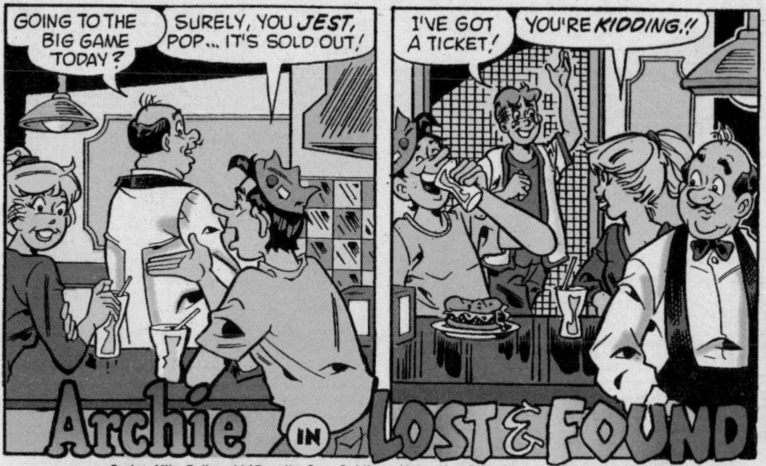
GOING TO THE BIG GAME TODAY?
SURELY, YOU JEST, POP... IT'S SOLD OUT!
I'VE GOT A TICKET!
YOU'RE KIDDING!!
Archie IN LOST & FOUND

Script: Mike Pellowski / Pencils: Stan Goldberg / Inks: Ken Selig / Letters: Bill Yoshida

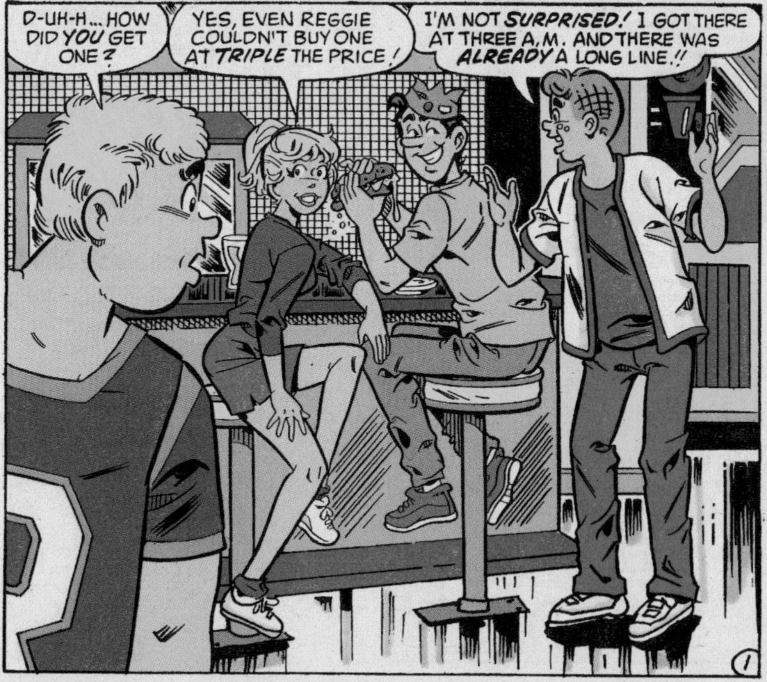
D-UH-H... HOW DID YOU GET ONE?
YES, EVEN REGGIE COULDN'T BUY ONE AT TRIPLE THE PRICE!
I'M NOT SURPRISED! I GOT THERE AT THREE A.M. AND THERE WAS ALREADY A LONG LINE!!
1

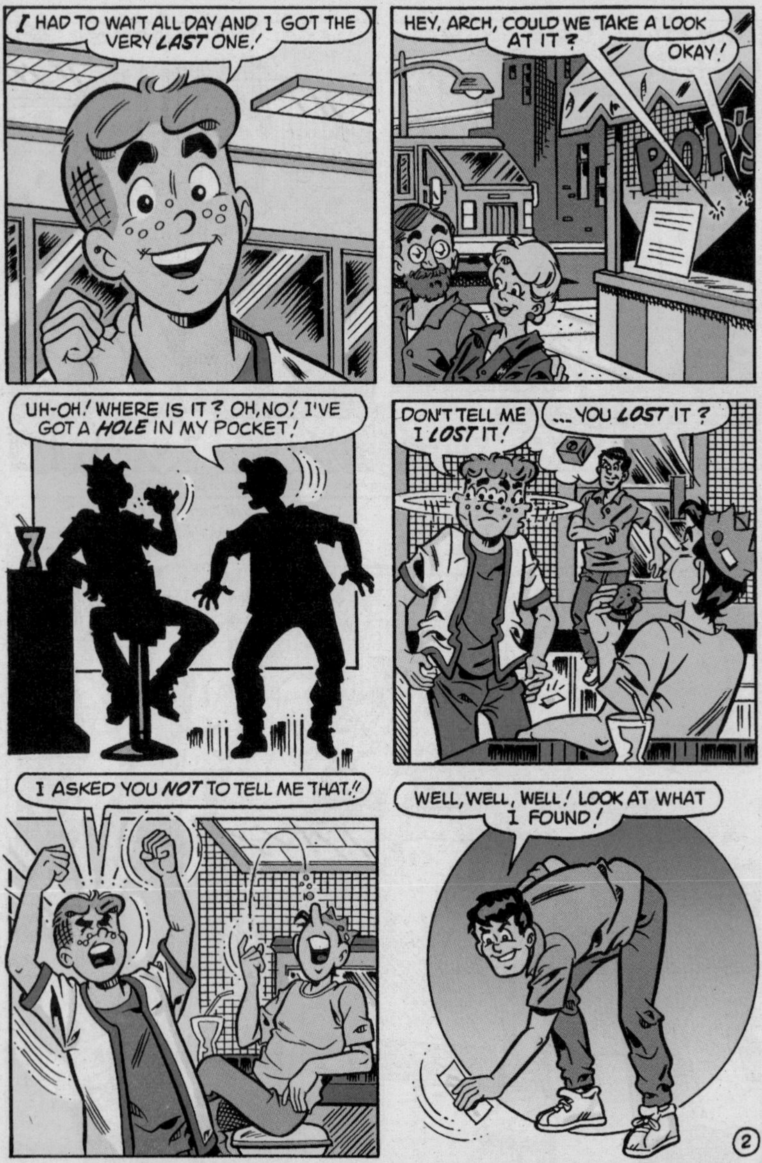
I HAD TO WAIT ALL DAY AND I GOT THE VERY *LAST* ONE!
HEY, ARCH, COULD WE TAKE A LOOK AT IT?
OKAY!
POP'S
UH-OH! WHERE IS IT? OH, NO! I'VE GOT A *HOLE* IN MY POCKET!
DON'T TELL ME I *LOST* IT!
... YOU *LOST* IT?
I ASKED YOU *NOT* TO TELL ME THAT!!
WELL, WELL, WELL! LOOK AT WHAT I FOUND!
2

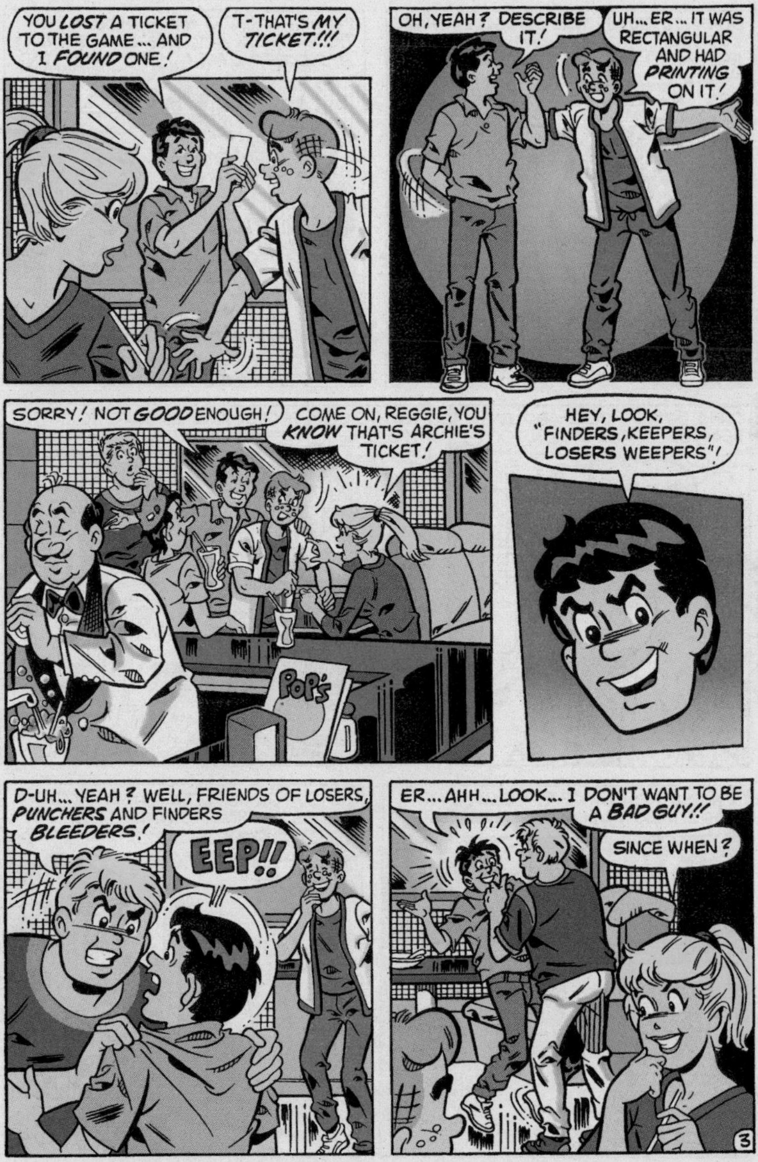
YOU LOST A TICKET TO THE GAME ... AND I FOUND ONE!
T-THAT'S MY TICKET!!!
OH, YEAH? DESCRIBE IT!
UH... ER... IT WAS RECTANGULAR AND HAD PRINTING ON IT!
SORRY! NOT GOOD ENOUGH!
COME ON, REGGIE, YOU KNOW THAT'S ARCHIE'S TICKET!
POP'S
HEY, LOOK, "FINDERS, KEEPERS, LOSERS WEEPERS"!
D-UH... YEAH? WELL, FRIENDS OF LOSERS, PUNCHERS AND FINDERS BLEEDERS!
EEP!!
ER... AHH... LOOK... I DON'T WANT TO BE A BAD GUY!!
SINCE WHEN?
3

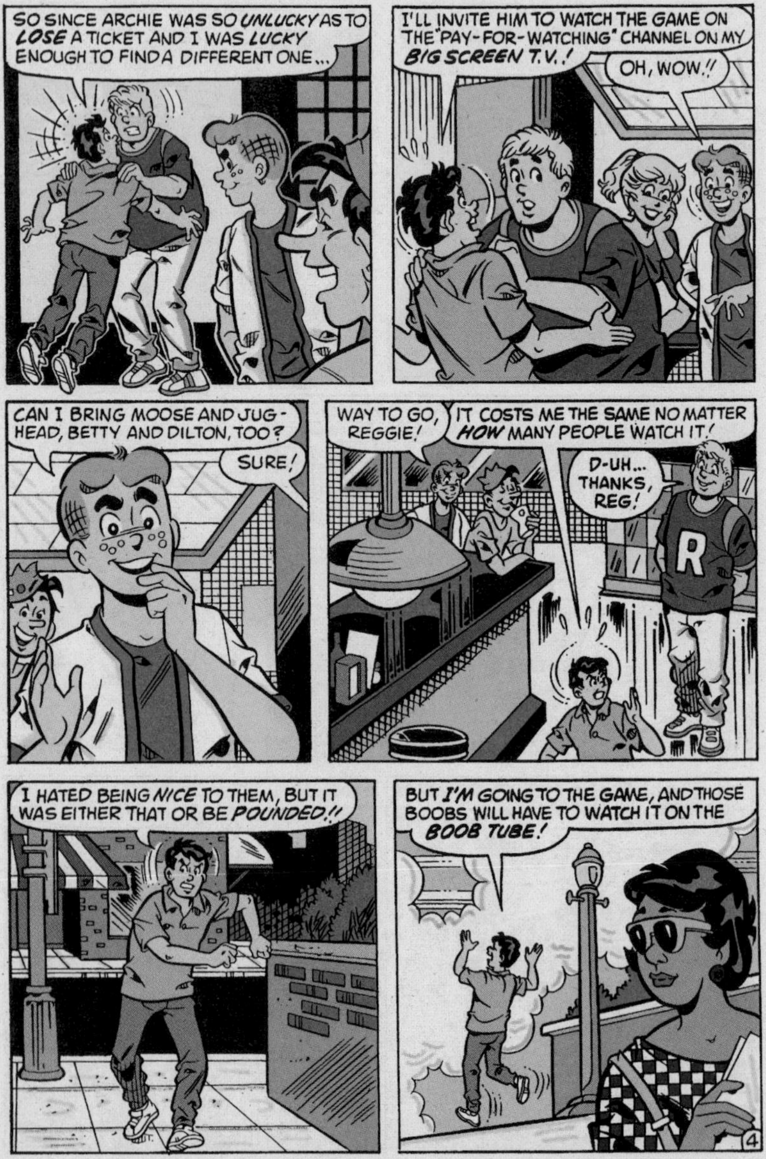
SO SINCE ARCHIE WAS SO UNLUCKY AS TO LOSE A TICKET AND I WAS LUCKY ENOUGH TO FIND A DIFFERENT ONE...
I'LL INVITE HIM TO WATCH THE GAME ON THE "PAY-FOR-WATCHING" CHANNEL ON MY BIG SCREEN T.V.!
OH, WOW!!
CAN I BRING MOOSE AND JUG-HEAD, BETTY AND DILTON, TOO?
SURE!
WAY TO GO, REGGIE!
IT COSTS ME THE SAME NO MATTER HOW MANY PEOPLE WATCH IT!
D-UH... THANKS, REG!
R
I HATED BEING NICE TO THEM, BUT IT WAS EITHER THAT OR BE POUNDED!!
BUT I'M GOING TO THE GAME, AND THOSE BOOBS WILL HAVE TO WATCH IT ON THE BOOB TUBE!
4

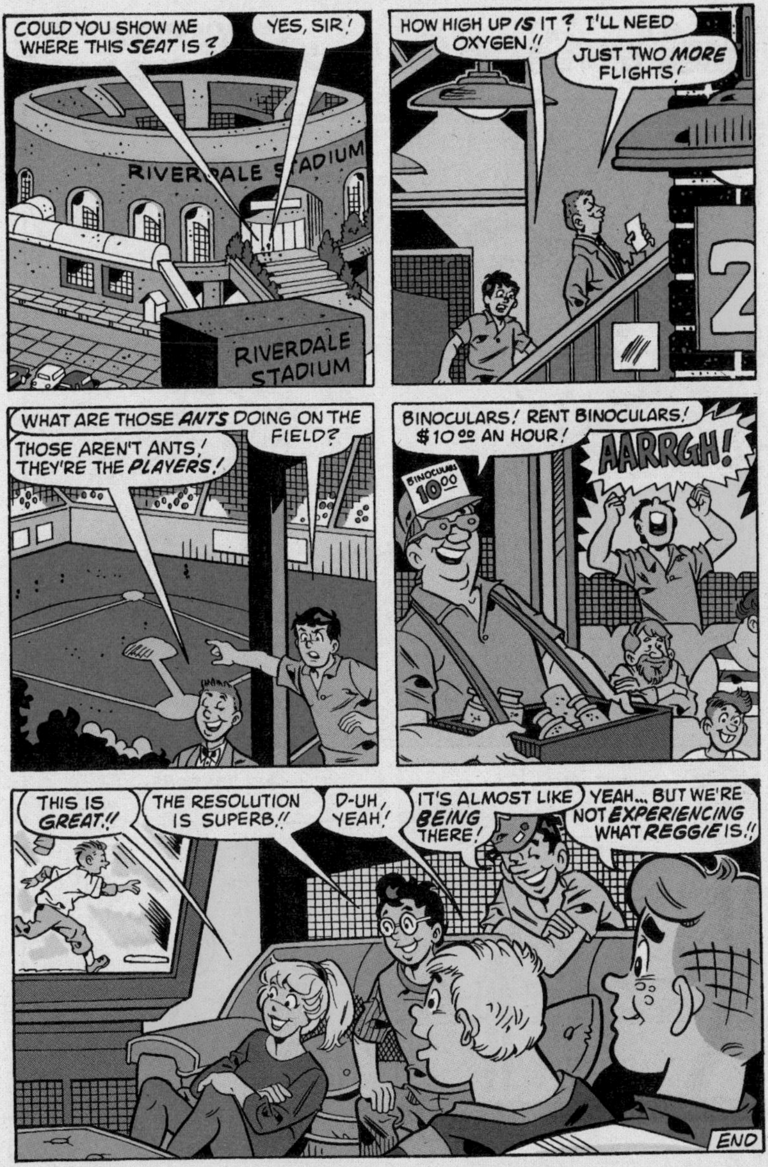
COULD YOU SHOW ME WHERE THIS SEAT IS?
YES, SIR!
RIVERDALE STADIUM
RIVERDALE STADIUM
HOW HIGH UP IS IT? I'LL NEED OXYGEN!!
JUST TWO MORE FLIGHTS!
WHAT ARE THOSE ANTS DOING ON THE FIELD?
THOSE AREN'T ANTS! THEY'RE THE PLAYERS!
BINOCULARS! RENT BINOCULARS! $10.00 AN HOUR!
BINOCULARS 10.00
AARRGH!
THIS IS GREAT!!
THE RESOLUTION IS SUPERB!!
D-UH, YEAH!
IT'S ALMOST LIKE BEING THERE!
YEAH... BUT WE'RE NOT EXPERIENCING WHAT REGGIE IS!!
END

Archie and the Gang in 'Just a Perfect Friendship'

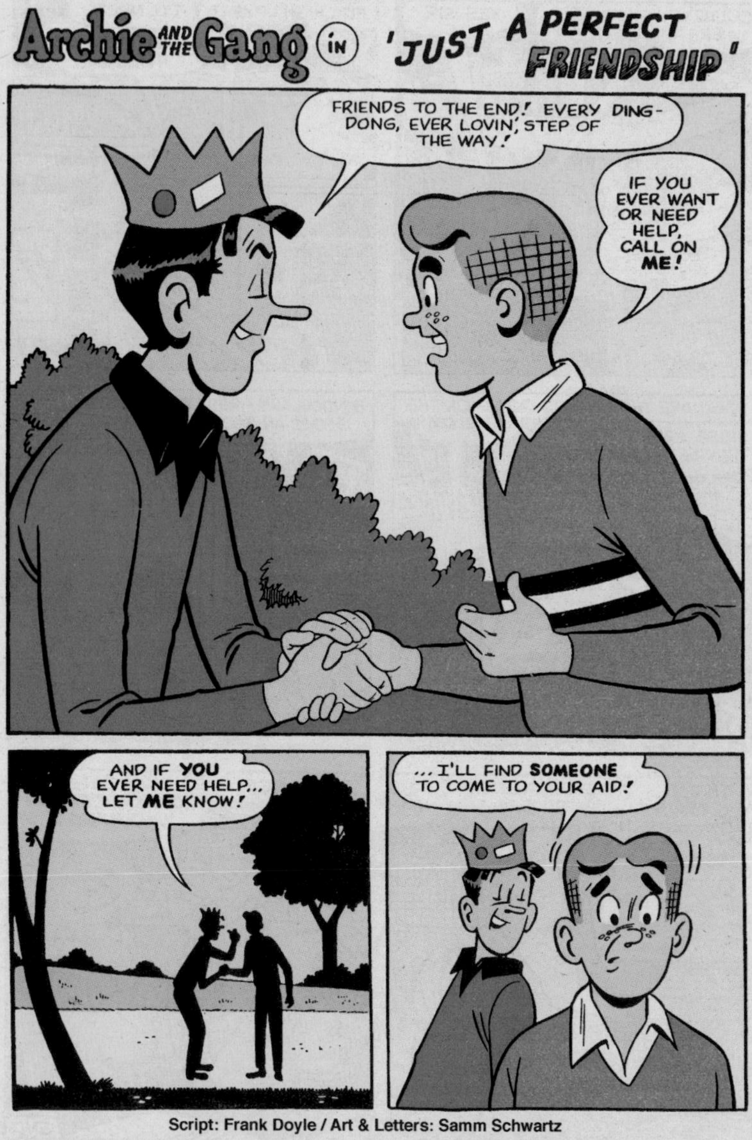

FRIENDS TO THE END! EVERY DING-DONG, EVER LOVIN', STEP OF THE WAY!
IF YOU EVER WANT OR NEED HELP, CALL ON ME!
AND IF YOU EVER NEED HELP... LET ME KNOW!
... I'LL FIND SOMEONE TO COME TO YOUR AID!

Script: Frank Doyle / Art & Letters: Samm Schwartz

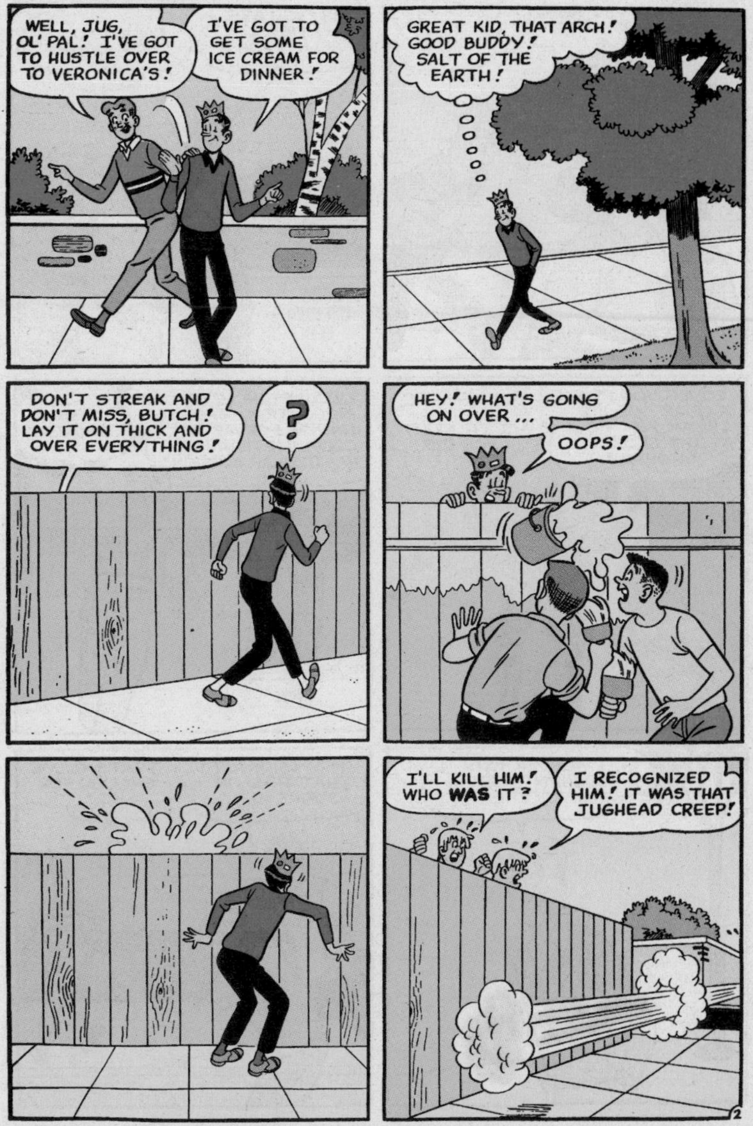
WELL, JUG, OL' PAL! I'VE GOT TO HUSTLE OVER TO VERONICA'S!
I'VE GOT TO GET SOME ICE CREAM FOR DINNER!
GREAT KID, THAT ARCH! GOOD BUDDY! SALT OF THE EARTH!
DON'T STREAK AND DON'T MISS, BUTCH! LAY IT ON THICK AND OVER EVERYTHING!
?
HEY! WHAT'S GOING ON OVER...
OOPS!
I'LL KILL HIM! WHO WAS IT?
I RECOGNIZED HIM! IT WAS THAT JUGHEAD CREEP!

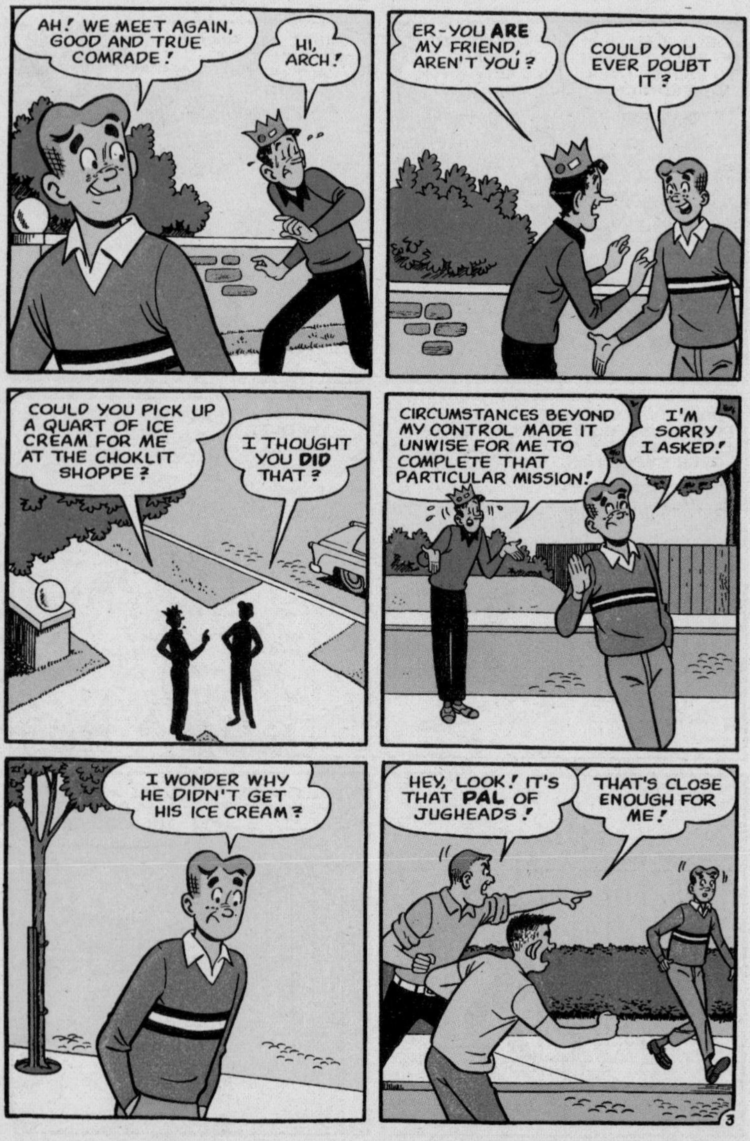
AH! WE MEET AGAIN, GOOD AND TRUE COMRADE!
HI, ARCH!
ER-YOU ARE MY FRIEND, AREN'T YOU?
COULD YOU EVER DOUBT IT?
COULD YOU PICK UP A QUART OF ICE CREAM FOR ME AT THE CHOKLIT SHOPPE?
I THOUGHT YOU DID THAT?
CIRCUMSTANCES BEYOND MY CONTROL MADE IT UNWISE FOR ME TO COMPLETE THAT PARTICULAR MISSION!
I'M SORRY I ASKED!
I WONDER WHY HE DIDN'T GET HIS ICE CREAM?
HEY, LOOK! IT'S THAT PAL OF JUGHEADS!
THAT'S CLOSE ENOUGH FOR ME!

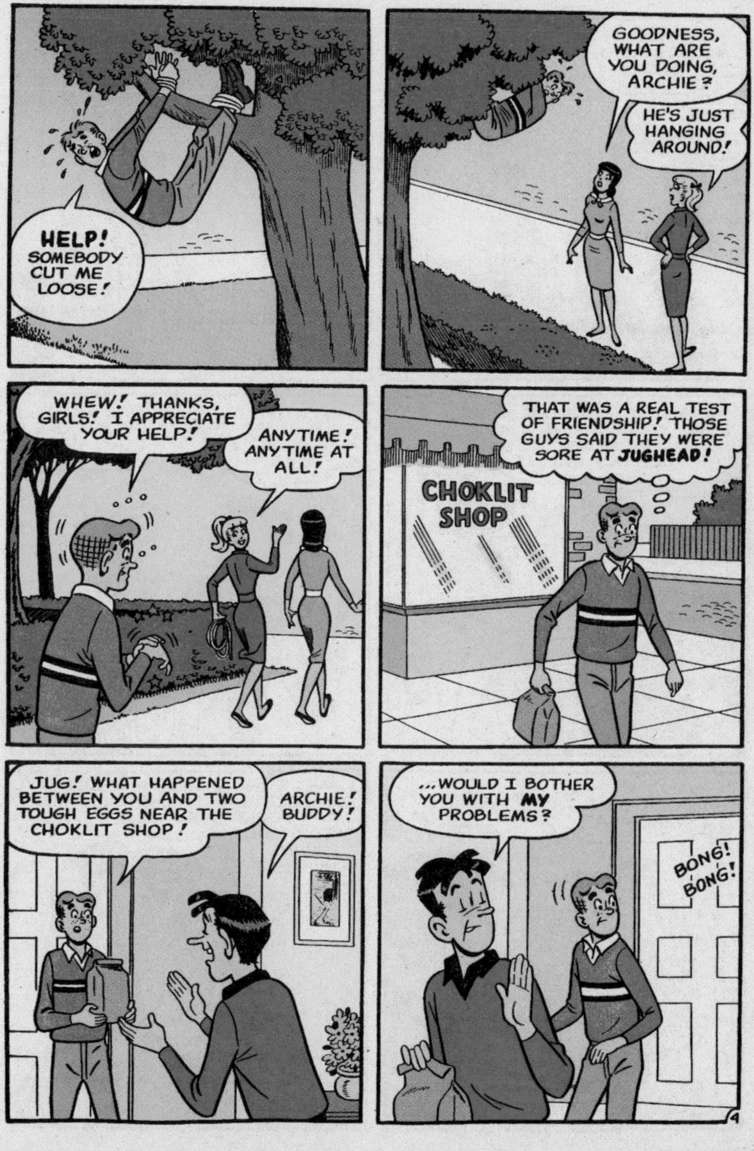
HELP! SOMEBODY CUT ME LOOSE!
GOODNESS, WHAT ARE YOU DOING, ARCHIE?
HE'S JUST HANGING AROUND!
WHEW! THANKS, GIRLS! I APPRECIATE YOUR HELP!
ANYTIME! ANYTIME AT ALL!
THAT WAS A REAL TEST OF FRIENDSHIP! THOSE GUYS SAID THEY WERE SORE AT JUGHEAD!
CHOKLIT SHOP
JUG! WHAT HAPPENED BETWEEN YOU AND TWO TOUGH EGGS NEAR THE CHOKLIT SHOP!
ARCHIE! BUDDY!
...WOULD I BOTHER YOU WITH MY PROBLEMS?
BONG! BONG!
4

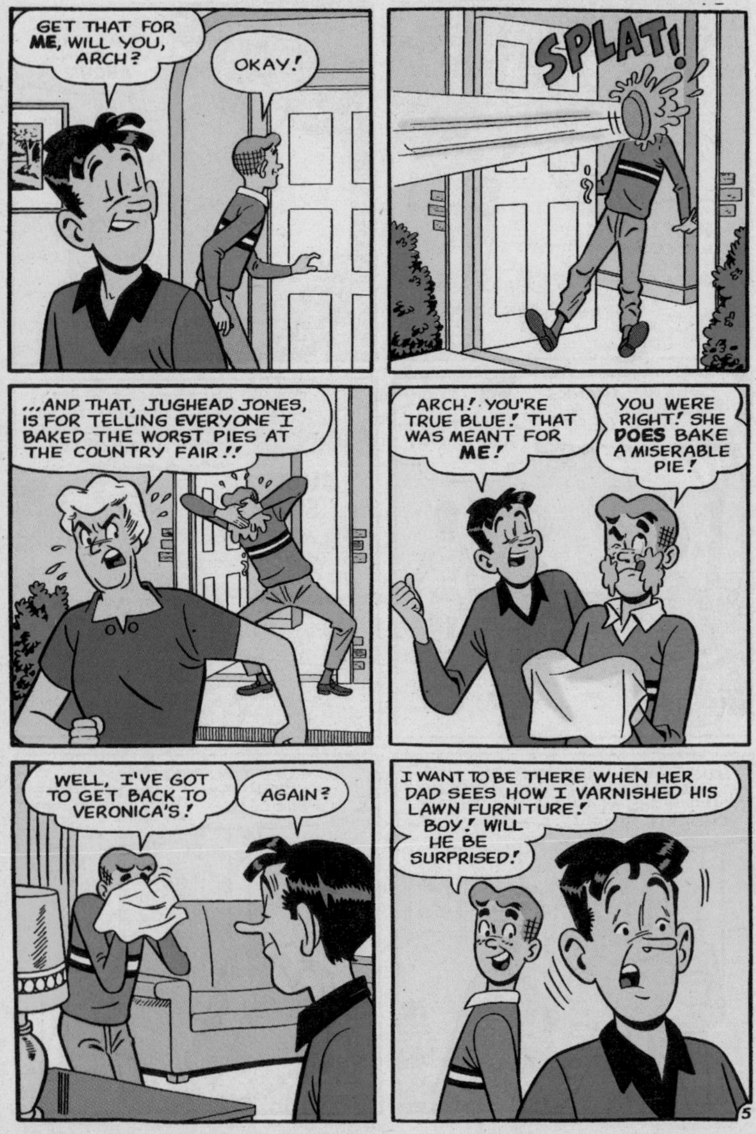

GET THAT FOR ME, WILL YOU, ARCH?
OKAY!
SPLAT!
...AND THAT, JUGHEAD JONES, IS FOR TELLING EVERYONE I BAKED THE WORST PIES AT THE COUNTRY FAIR!!
ARCH! YOU'RE TRUE BLUE! THAT WAS MEANT FOR ME!
YOU WERE RIGHT! SHE DOES BAKE A MISERABLE PIE!
WELL, I'VE GOT TO GET BACK TO VERONICA'S!
AGAIN?
I WANT TO BE THERE WHEN HER DAD SEES HOW I VARNISHED HIS LAWN FURNITURE!
BOY! WILL HE BE SURPRISED!

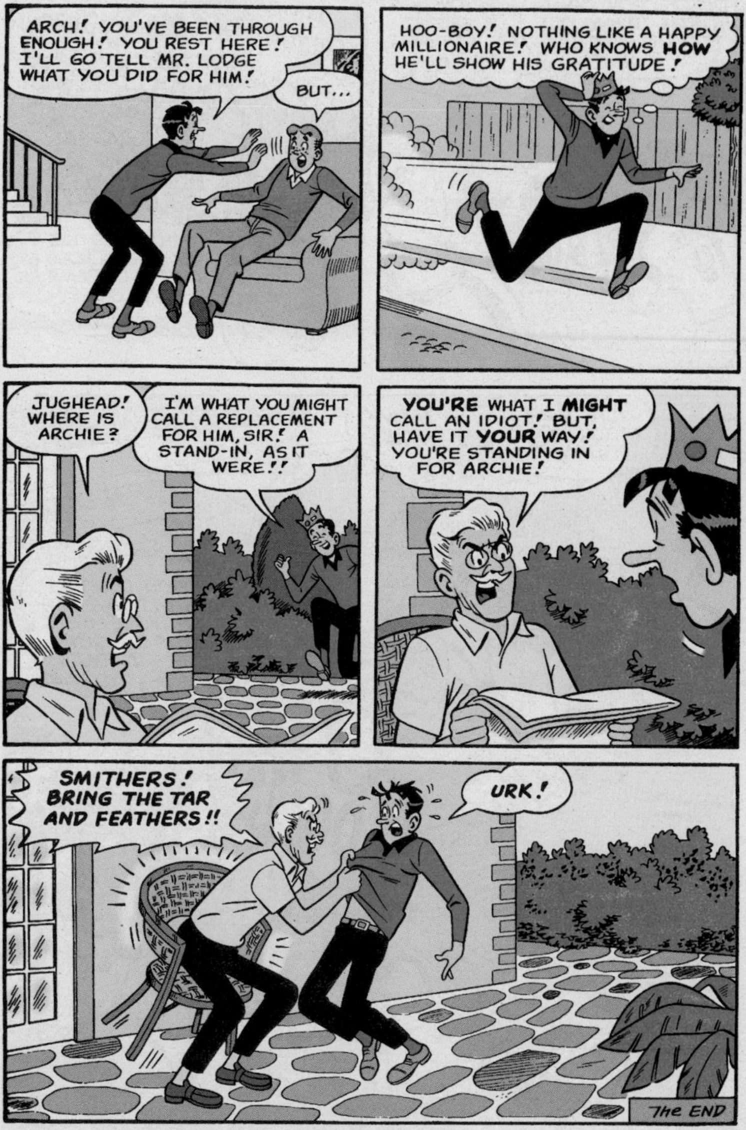
ARCH! YOU'VE BEEN THROUGH ENOUGH! YOU REST HERE! I'LL GO TELL MR. LODGE WHAT YOU DID FOR HIM!
BUT...
HOO-BOY! NOTHING LIKE A HAPPY MILLIONAIRE! WHO KNOWS HOW HE'LL SHOW HIS GRATITUDE!
JUGHEAD! WHERE IS ARCHIE?
I'M WHAT YOU MIGHT CALL A REPLACEMENT FOR HIM, SIR! A STAND-IN, AS IT WERE!!
YOU'RE WHAT I MIGHT CALL AN IDIOT! BUT, HAVE IT YOUR WAY! YOU'RE STANDING IN FOR ARCHIE!
SMITHERS! BRING THE TAR AND FEATHERS!!
URK!
The END

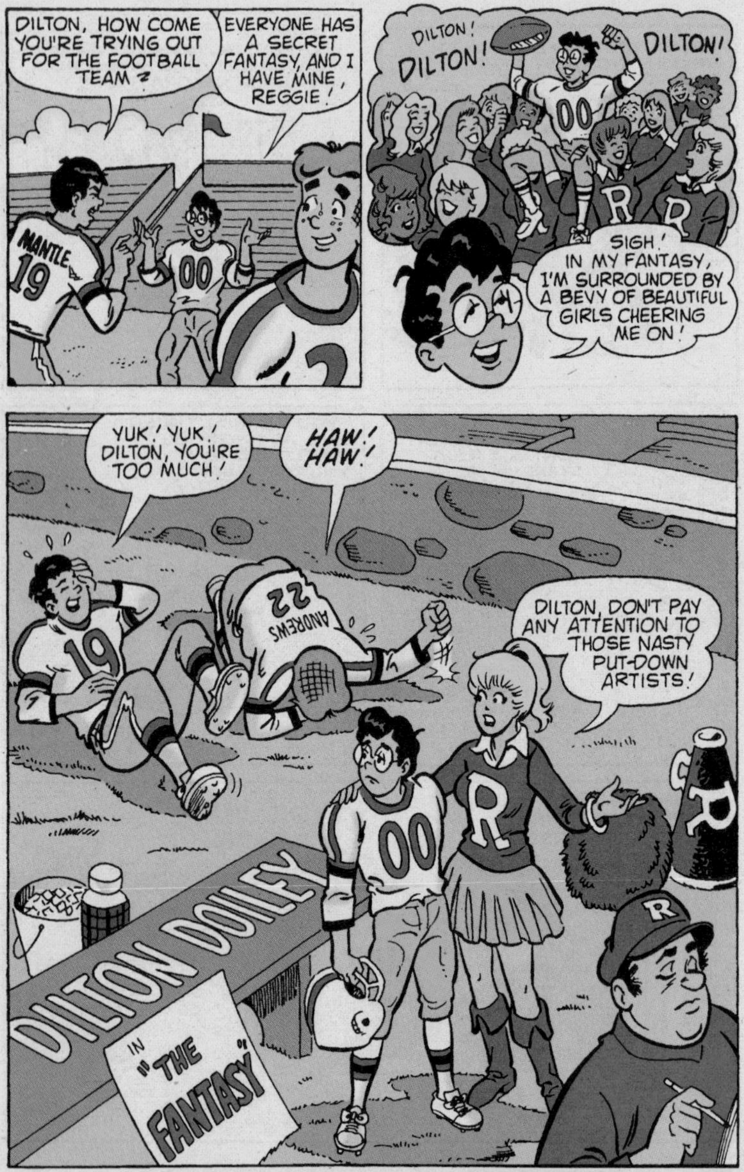
DILTON, HOW COME YOU'RE TRYING OUT FOR THE FOOTBALL TEAM?
EVERYONE HAS A SECRET FANTASY, AND I HAVE MINE, REGGIE!
DILTON! DILTON!
DILTON!
SIGH! IN MY FANTASY, I'M SURROUNDED BY A BEVY OF BEAUTIFUL GIRLS CHEERING ME ON!
YUK! YUK! DILTON, YOU'RE TOO MUCH!
HAW! HAW!
DILTON, DON'T PAY ANY ATTENTION TO THOSE NASTY PUT-DOWN ARTISTS!
DILTON DOILEY
IN "THE FANTASY"

Script: George Gladir / Pencils: Doug Crane / Inks: Mike Esposito / Letters: Bill Yoshida

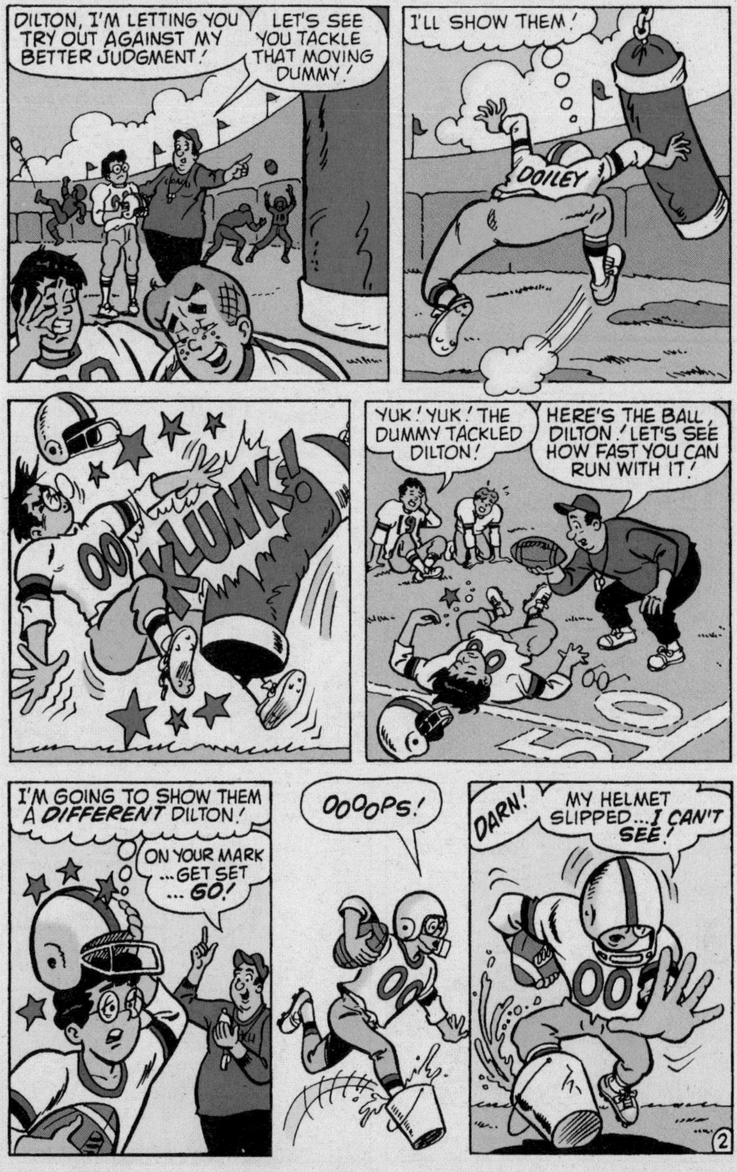
DILTON, I'M LETTING YOU TRY OUT AGAINST MY BETTER JUDGMENT!
LET'S SEE YOU TACKLE THAT MOVING DUMMY!
I'LL SHOW THEM!
DOILEY
KLUNK!
YUK! YUK! THE DUMMY TACKLED DILTON!
HERE'S THE BALL, DILTON! LET'S SEE HOW FAST YOU CAN RUN WITH IT!
I'M GOING TO SHOW THEM A *DIFFERENT* DILTON!
ON YOUR MARK ...GET SET ... *GO!*
OOOOPS!
DARN!
MY HELMET SLIPPED... *I CAN'T SEE!*

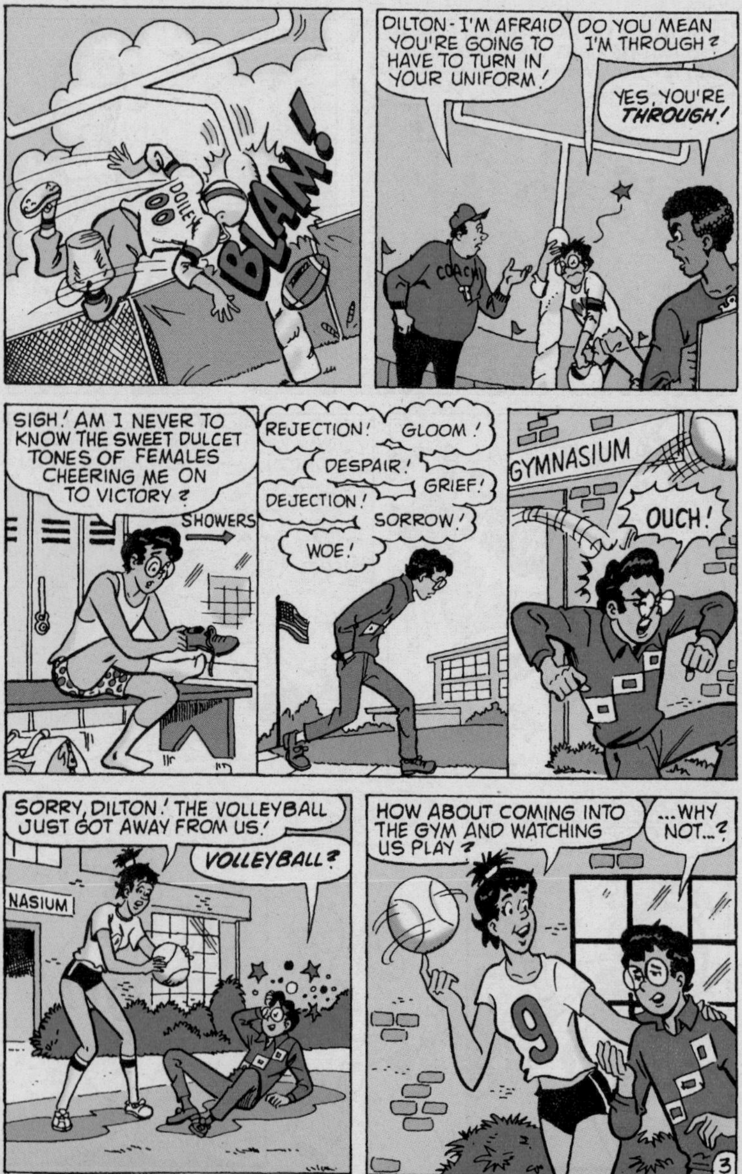
DOILEY
00
BLAM!
DILTON - I'M AFRAID YOU'RE GOING TO HAVE TO TURN IN YOUR UNIFORM!
DO YOU MEAN I'M THROUGH?
YES, YOU'RE THROUGH!
COACH
SIGH! AM I NEVER TO KNOW THE SWEET DULCET TONES OF FEMALES CHEERING ME ON TO VICTORY?
SHOWERS
REJECTION! GLOOM! DESPAIR! GRIEF! DEJECTION! SORROW! WOE!
GYMNASIUM
OUCH!
SORRY, DILTON! THE VOLLEYBALL JUST GOT AWAY FROM US!
VOLLEYBALL?
NASIUM
HOW ABOUT COMING INTO THE GYM AND WATCHING US PLAY?
...WHY NOT...?
9
3

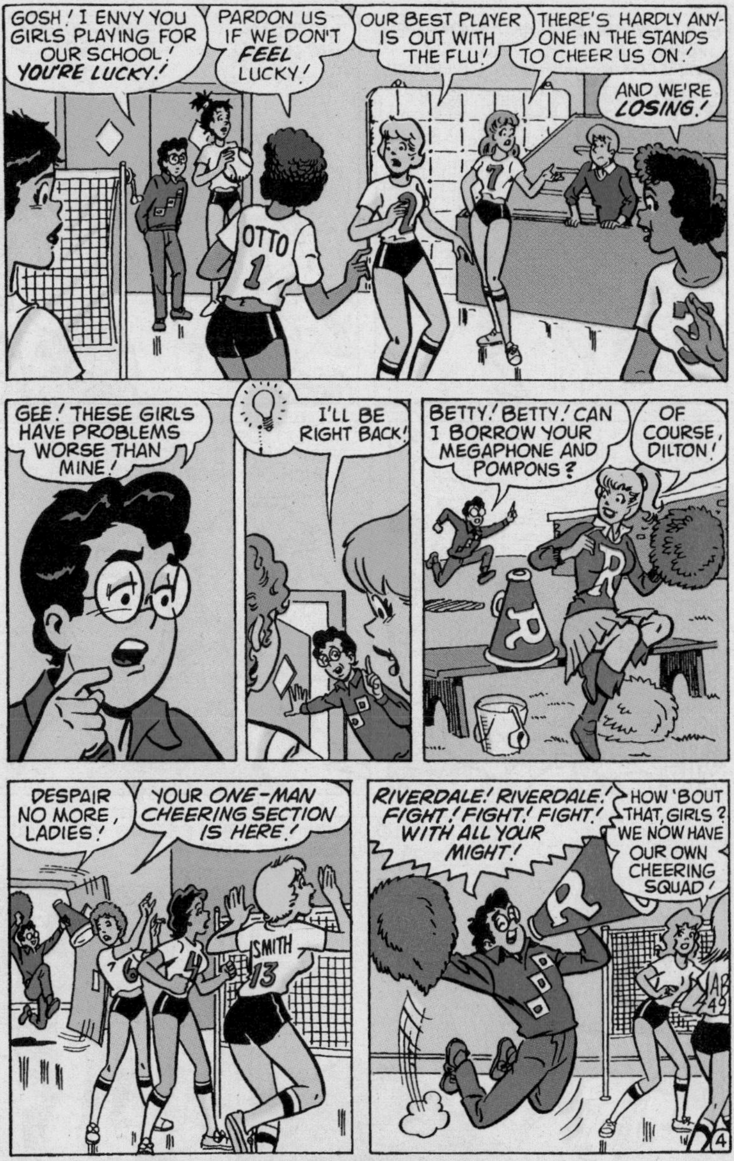

GOSH! I ENVY YOU GIRLS PLAYING FOR OUR SCHOOL! YOU'RE LUCKY!
PARDON US IF WE DON'T FEEL LUCKY!
OUR BEST PLAYER IS OUT WITH THE FLU!
THERE'S HARDLY ANYONE IN THE STANDS TO CHEER US ON!
AND WE'RE LOSING!
OTTO 1
GEE! THESE GIRLS HAVE PROBLEMS WORSE THAN MINE!
I'LL BE RIGHT BACK!
BETTY! BETTY! CAN I BORROW YOUR MEGAPHONE AND POMPONS?
OF COURSE, DILTON!
DESPAIR NO MORE, LADIES!
YOUR ONE-MAN CHEERING SECTION IS HERE!
SMITH 13
RIVERDALE! RIVERDALE! FIGHT! FIGHT! FIGHT! WITH ALL YOUR MIGHT!
HOW 'BOUT THAT, GIRLS? WE NOW HAVE OUR OWN CHEERING SQUAD!
4

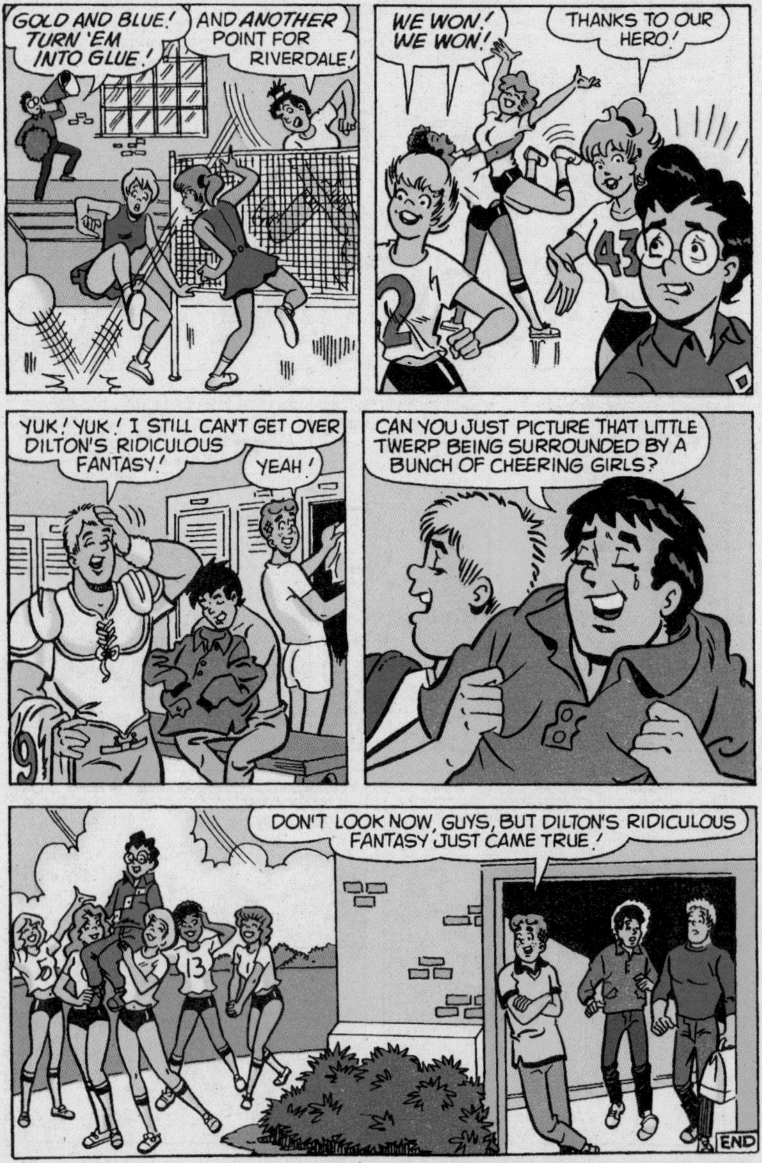
GOLD AND BLUE! TURN 'EM INTO GLUE!
AND ANOTHER POINT FOR RIVERDALE!
WE WON! WE WON!
THANKS TO OUR HERO!
YUK! YUK! I STILL CAN'T GET OVER DILTON'S RIDICULOUS FANTASY!
YEAH!
CAN YOU JUST PICTURE THAT LITTLE TWERP BEING SURROUNDED BY A BUNCH OF CHEERING GIRLS?
DON'T LOOK NOW, GUYS, BUT DILTON'S RIDICULOUS FANTASY JUST CAME TRUE!
END

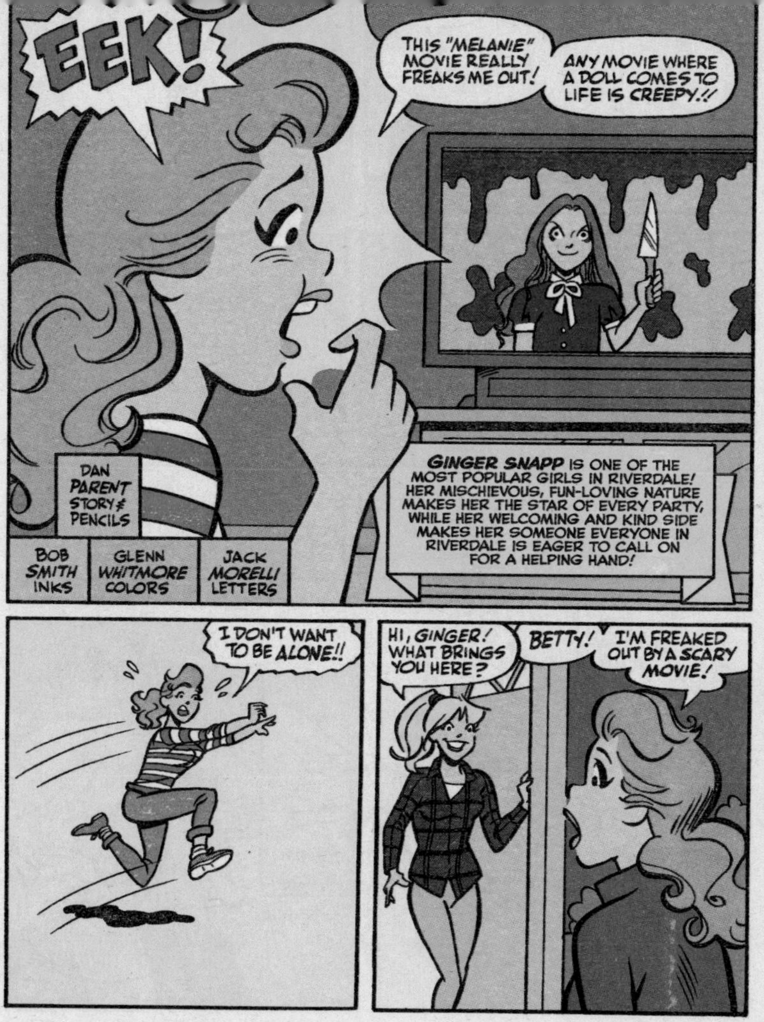
EEK!
THIS "MELANIE" MOVIE REALLY FREAKS ME OUT!
ANY MOVIE WHERE A DOLL COMES TO LIFE IS CREEPY!!
DAN PARENT STORY & PENCILS
BOB SMITH INKS
GLENN WHITMORE COLORS
JACK MORELLI LETTERS
GINGER SNAPP IS ONE OF THE MOST POPULAR GIRLS IN RIVERDALE! HER MISCHIEVOUS, FUN-LOVING NATURE MAKES HER THE STAR OF EVERY PARTY, WHILE HER WELCOMING AND KIND SIDE MAKES HER SOMEONE EVERYONE IN RIVERDALE IS EAGER TO CALL ON FOR A HELPING HAND!
I DON'T WANT TO BE ALONE!!
HI, GINGER! WHAT BRINGS YOU HERE?
BETTY!
I'M FREAKED OUT BY A SCARY MOVIE!

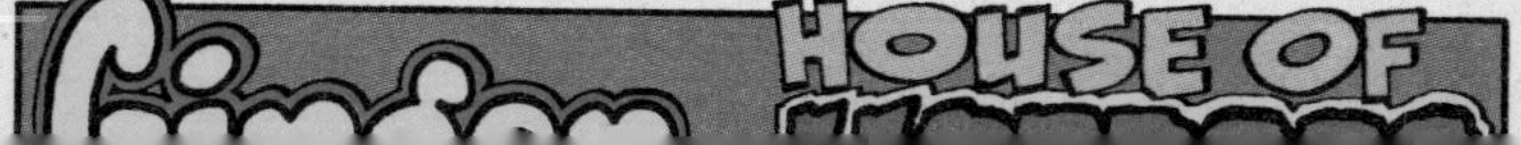
HOUSE OF

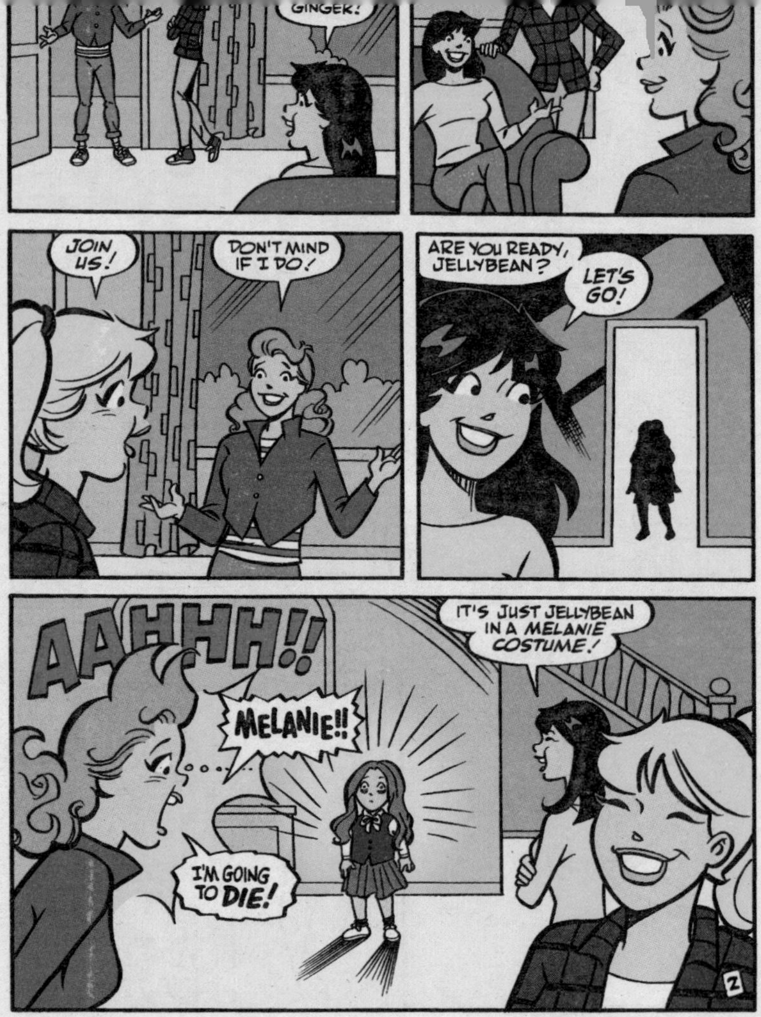
GINGER!
JOIN US!
DON'T MIND IF I DO!
ARE YOU READY, JELLYBEAN?
LET'S GO!
AAHHH!!
MELANIE!!
I'M GOING TO DIE!
IT'S JUST JELLYBEAN IN A MELANIE COSTUME!
2

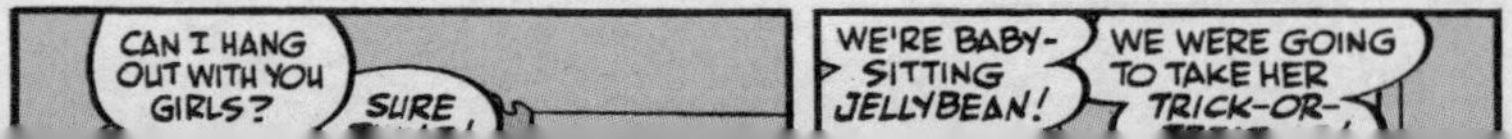
CAN I HANG OUT WITH YOU GIRLS?
SURE
WE'RE BABY-SITTING JELLYBEAN!
WE WERE GOING TO TAKE HER TRICK-OR-

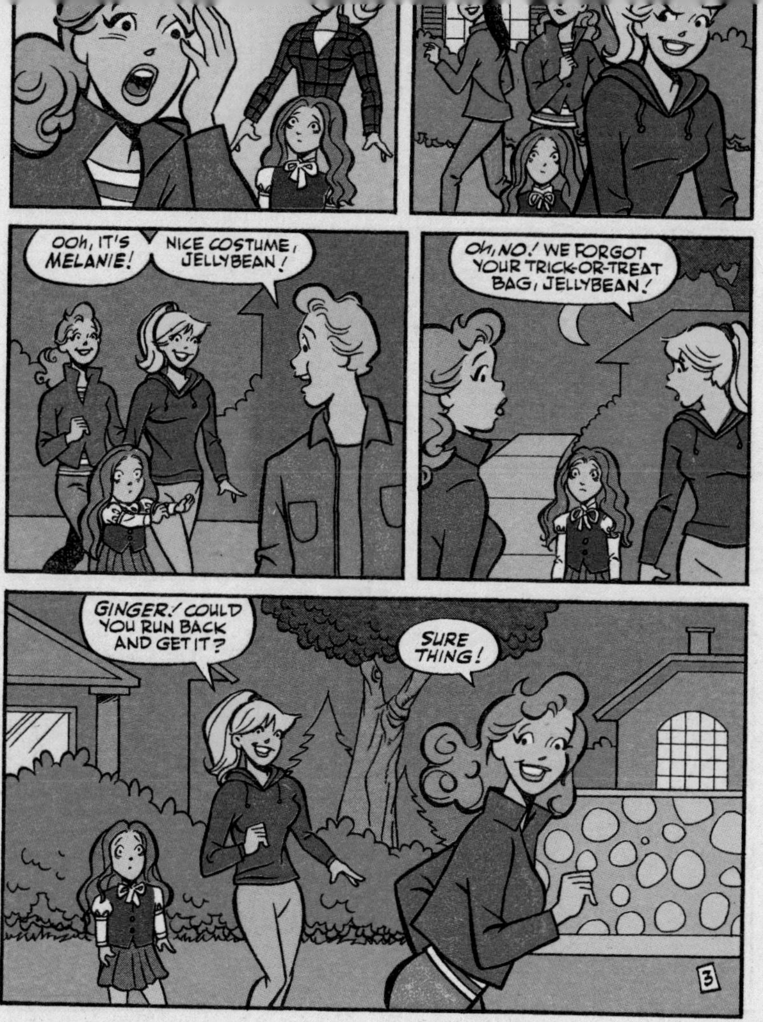
OOH, IT'S MELANIE!
NICE COSTUME, JELLYBEAN!
OH, NO! WE FORGOT YOUR TRICK-OR-TREAT BAG, JELLYBEAN!
GINGER! COULD YOU RUN BACK AND GET IT?
SURE THING!
3

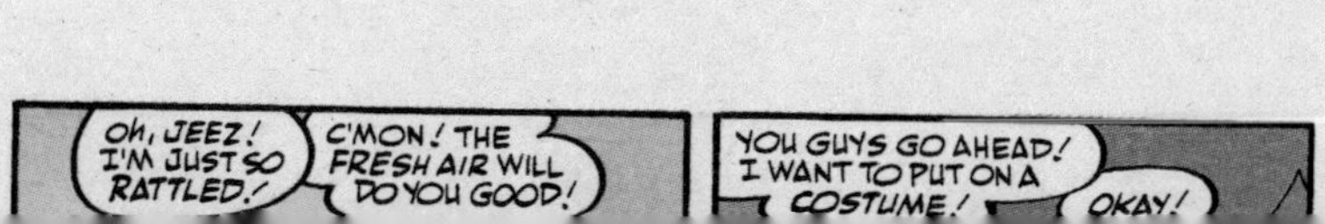
OH, JEEZ! I'M JUST SO RATTLED!
C'MON! THE FRESH AIR WILL DO YOU GOOD!
YOU GUYS GO AHEAD! I WANT TO PUT ON A COSTUME!
OKAY!

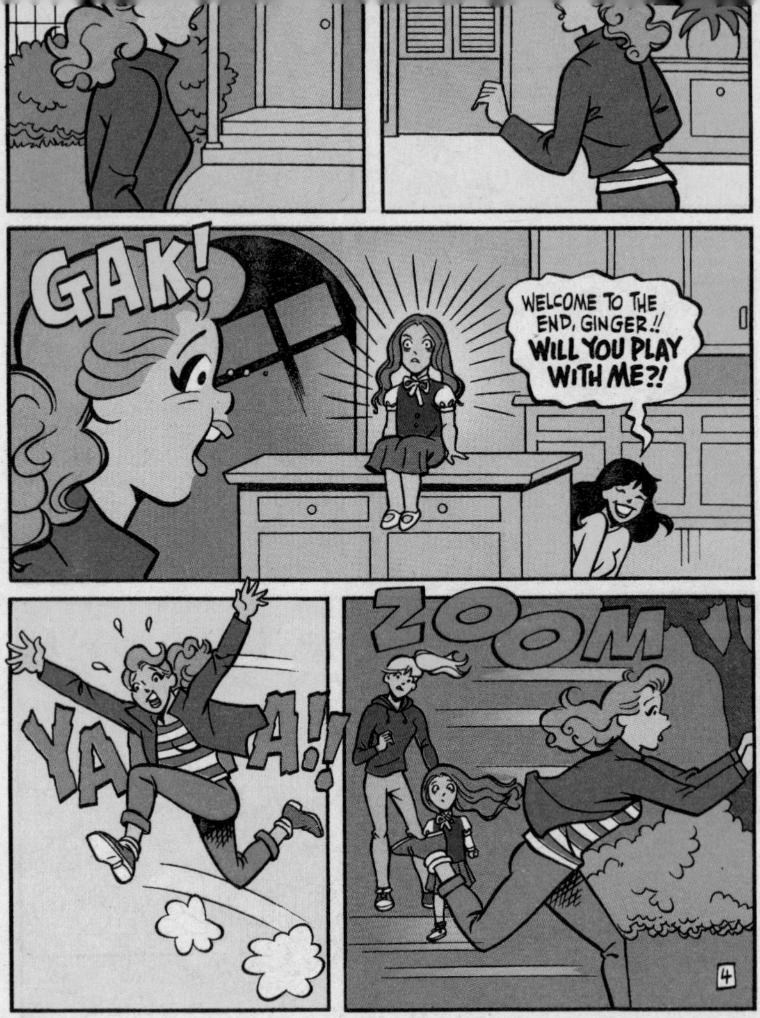
GAK!
WELCOME TO THE END, GINGER!! WILL YOU PLAY WITH ME?!
YAAA!!
ZOOM
4

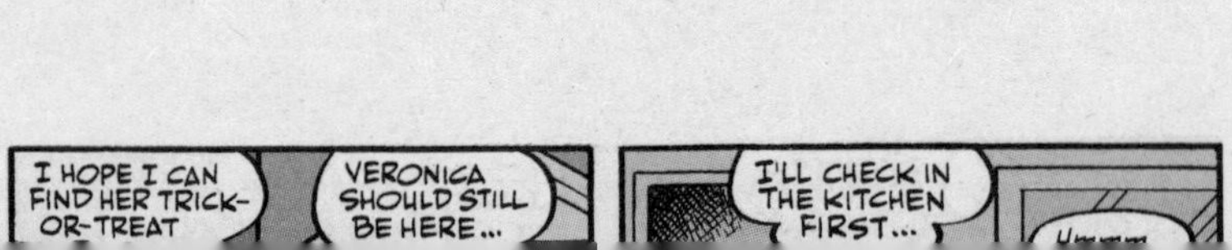
I HOPE I CAN FIND HER TRICK-OR-TREAT
VERONICA SHOULD STILL BE HERE...
I'LL CHECK IN THE KITCHEN FIRST...

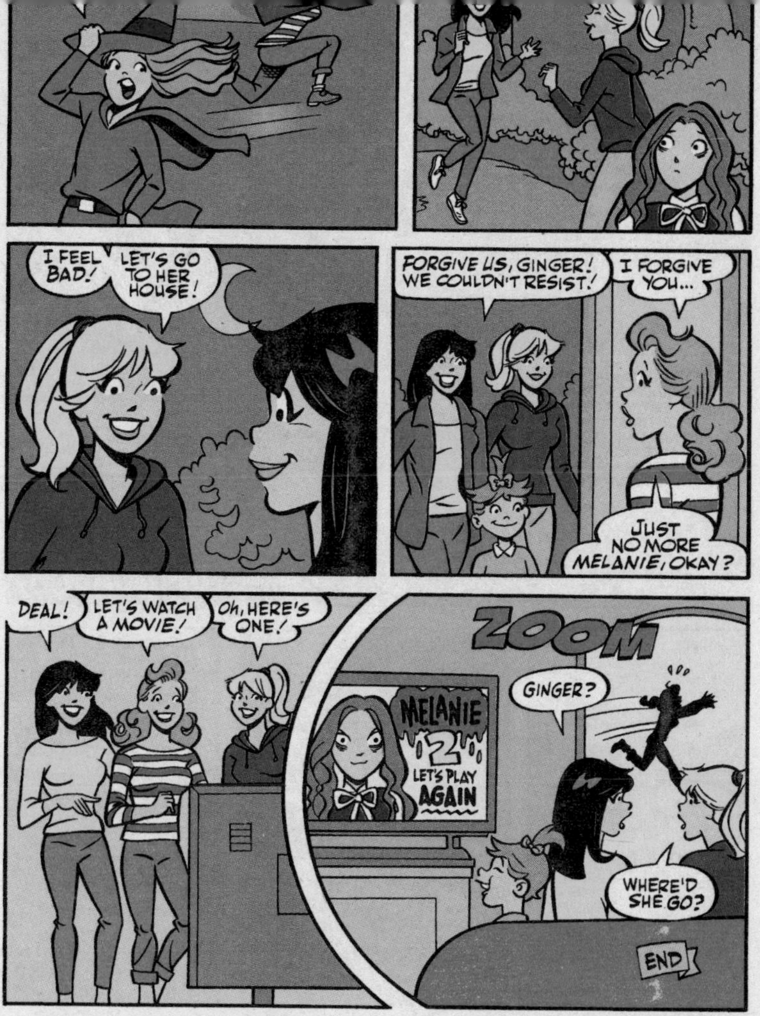
I FEEL BAD!
LET'S GO TO HER HOUSE!
FORGIVE US, GINGER! WE COULDN'T RESIST!
I FORGIVE YOU...
JUST NO MORE MELANIE, OKAY?
DEAL!
LET'S WATCH A MOVIE!
Oh, HERE'S ONE!
ZOOM
MELANIE 2 LET'S PLAY AGAIN
GINGER?
WHERE'D SHE GO?
END

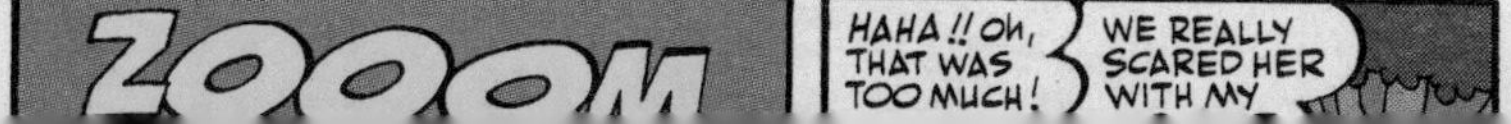
ZOOOM
HAHA!! Oh, THAT WAS TOO MUCH!
WE REALLY SCARED HER WITH MY

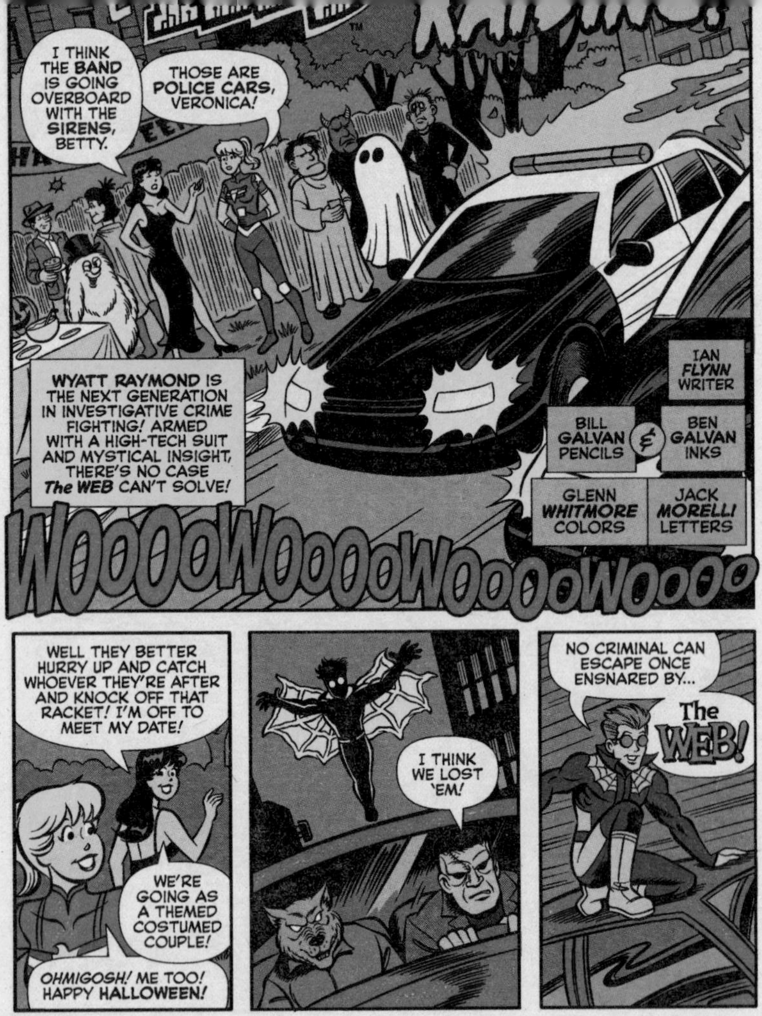
I THINK THE BAND IS GOING OVERBOARD WITH THE SIRENS, BETTY.
THOSE ARE POLICE CARS, VERONICA!
WYATT RAYMOND IS THE NEXT GENERATION IN INVESTIGATIVE CRIME FIGHTING! ARMED WITH A HIGH-TECH SUIT AND MYSTICAL INSIGHT, THERE'S NO CASE The WEB CAN'T SOLVE!
IAN FLYNN WRITER
BILL GALVAN PENCILS
&
BEN GALVAN INKS
GLENN WHITMORE COLORS
JACK MORELLI LETTERS
WOOOOWOOOOWOOOOWOOOO
WELL THEY BETTER HURRY UP AND CATCH WHOEVER THEY'RE AFTER AND KNOCK OFF THAT RACKET! I'M OFF TO MEET MY DATE!
WE'RE GOING AS A THEMED COSTUMED COUPLE!
OHMIGOSH! ME TOO! HAPPY HALLOWEEN!
I THINK WE LOST 'EM!
NO CRIMINAL CAN ESCAPE ONCE ENSNARED BY...
The WEB!

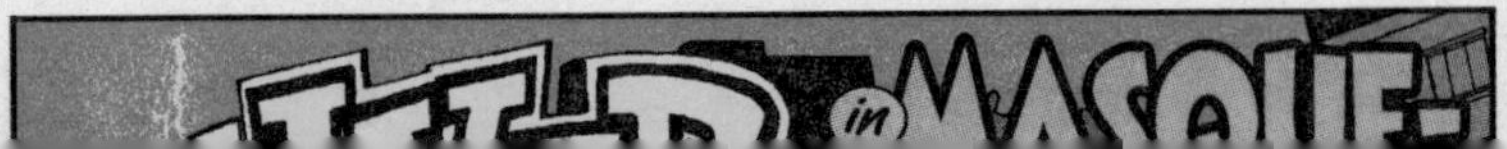
in

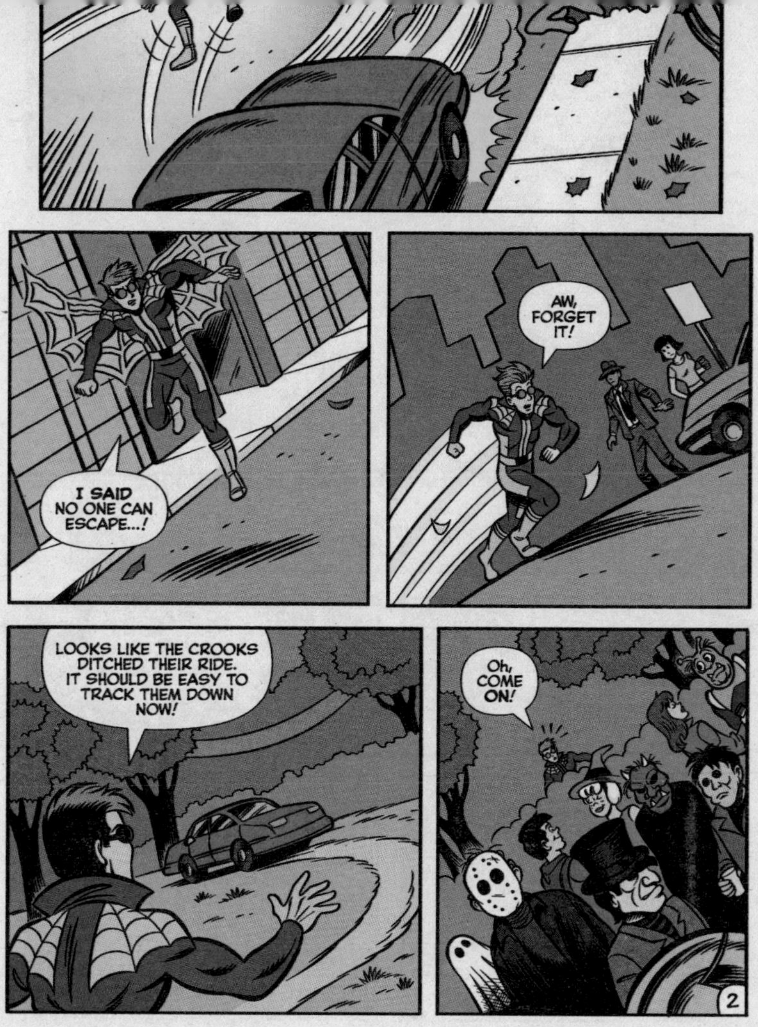
I SAID NO ONE CAN ESCAPE...!
AW, FORGET IT!
LOOKS LIKE THE CROOKS DITCHED THEIR RIDE. IT SHOULD BE EASY TO TRACK THEM DOWN NOW!
Oh, COME ON!
2

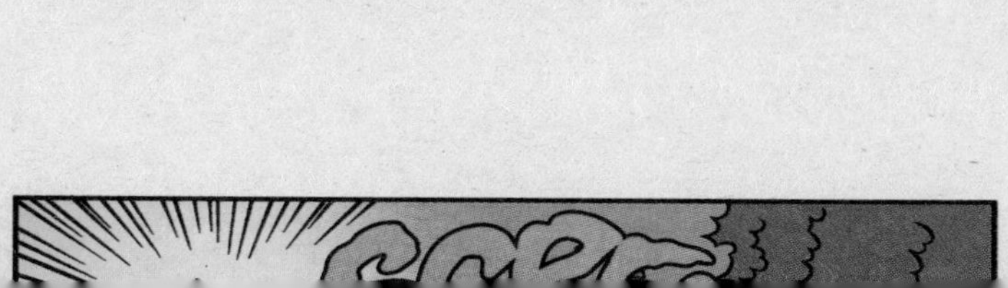

...NOPE. THERE'S TOO MANY PEOPLE AND TOO MANY CONNECTIONS!

UGH! THIS IS AMATEUR HOUR! I'M A DISGRACE!

WEB! ARE YOU OKAY?

A COUPLE OF MASK-WEARING GOONS GAVE ME THE SLIP AND DISAPPEARED INTO THE CROWD!

YIKES!

I DON'T THINK I CAN LEND MUCH HELP WITH JUST THAT...

...AND ARCHIE IS NO HELP AT ALL! WE WERE SUPPOSED TO GO AS THE TWO SHIELDS!

VWWWWW VWVWWWW VWWVWWWW VWWWWW

I CAN'T UNDERSTAND A WORD YOU SAY IN THAT AWFUL MASK!

3

IF I USE MY STRAND SENSE

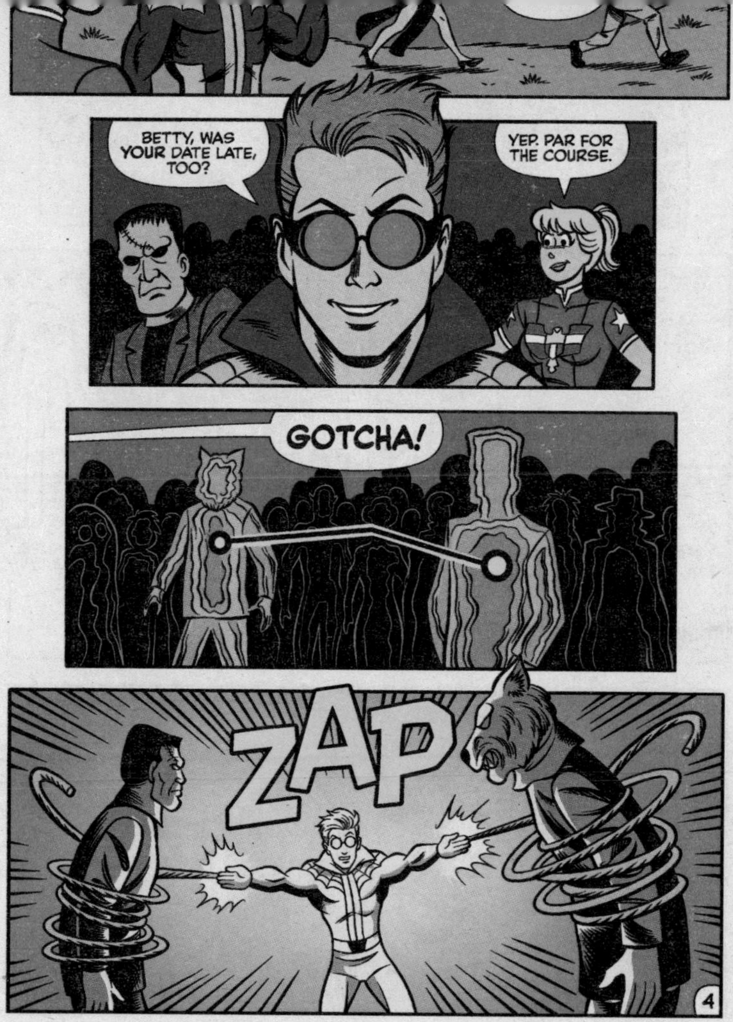
BETTY, WAS YOUR DATE LATE, TOO?
YEP. PAR FOR THE COURSE.
GOTCHA!
ZAP

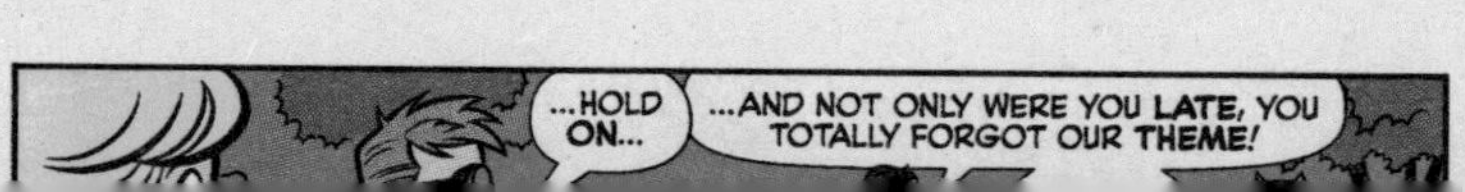
...HOLD ON...
...AND NOT ONLY WERE YOU LATE, YOU TOTALLY FORGOT OUR THEME!

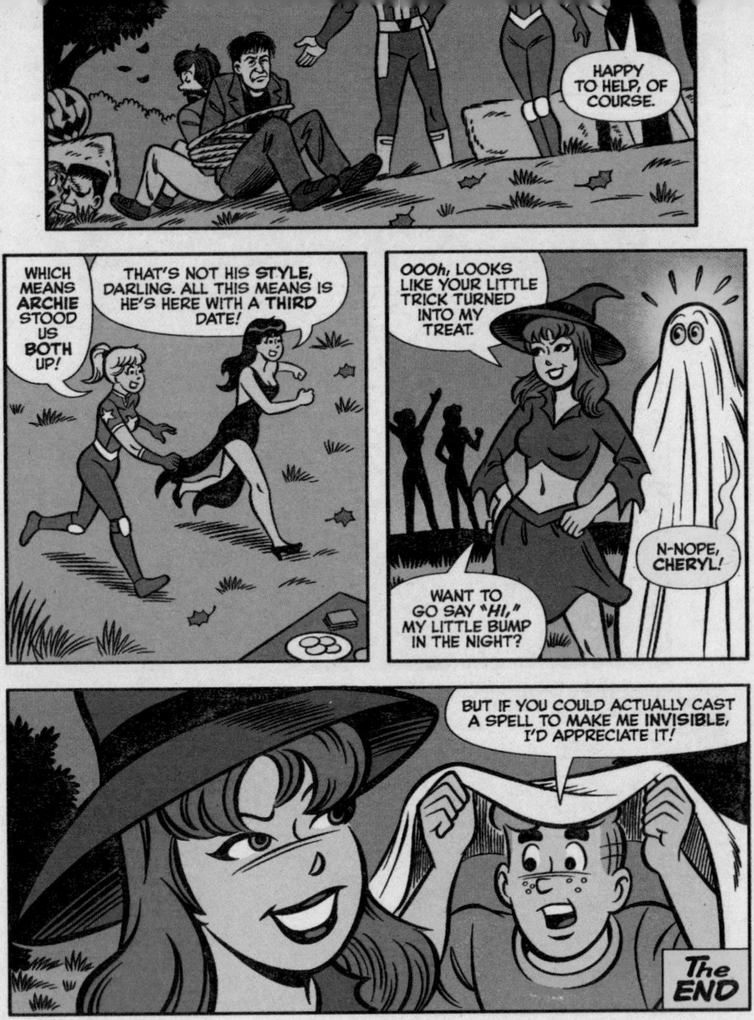
HAPPY TO HELP, OF COURSE.
WHICH MEANS ARCHIE STOOD US BOTH UP!
THAT'S NOT HIS STYLE, DARLING. ALL THIS MEANS IS HE'S HERE WITH A THIRD DATE!
OOOh, LOOKS LIKE YOUR LITTLE TRICK TURNED INTO MY TREAT.
WANT TO GO SAY "HI," MY LITTLE BUMP IN THE NIGHT?
N-NOPE, CHERYL!
BUT IF YOU COULD ACTUALLY CAST A SPELL TO MAKE ME INVISIBLE, I'D APPRECIATE IT!
The END

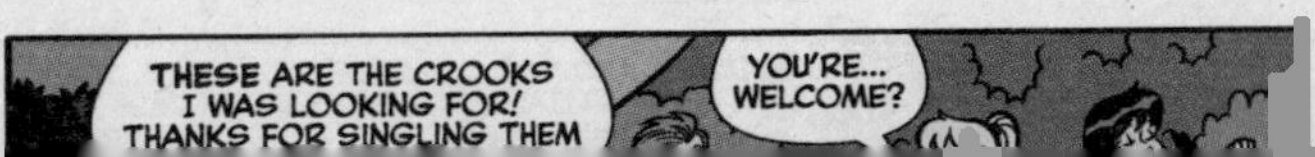
THESE ARE THE CROOKS I WAS LOOKING FOR! THANKS FOR SINGLING THEM
YOU'RE... WELCOME?

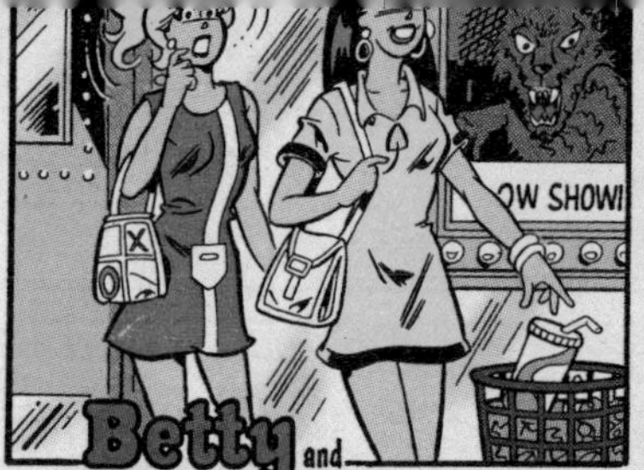
OW SHOWI

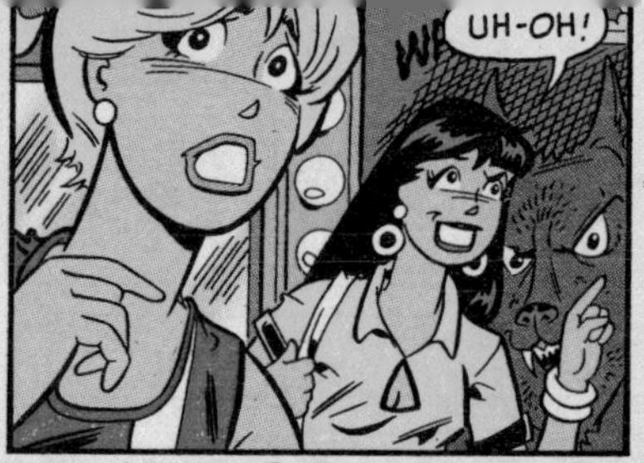
UH-OH!

Betty and Veronica in WHERE'S THE WEREWOLF?

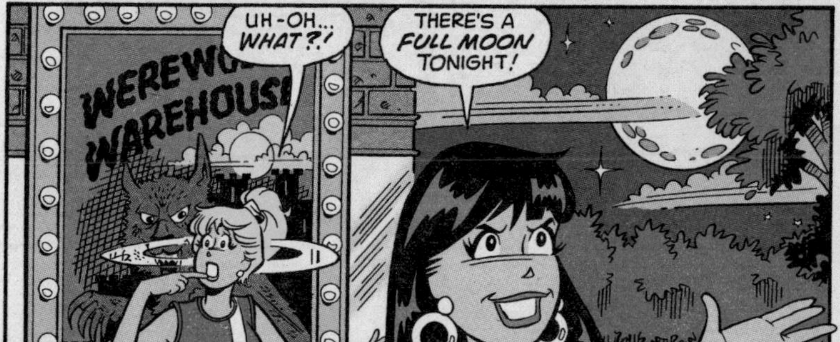
UH-OH... WHAT?!
THERE'S A FULL MOON TONIGHT!
WEREWO
WAREHOUSE
OW
WING

Script: Hal Smith / Pencils: Holly G! / Inks: Ken Selig / Letters: Bill Yoshida

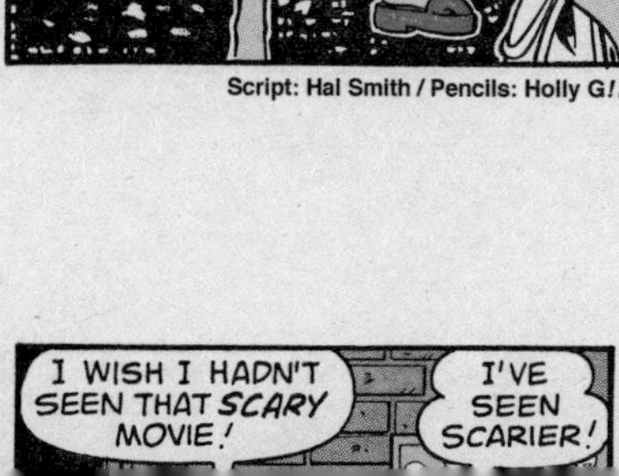
I WISH I HADN'T SEEN THAT SCARY MOVIE!
I'VE SEEN SCARIER!

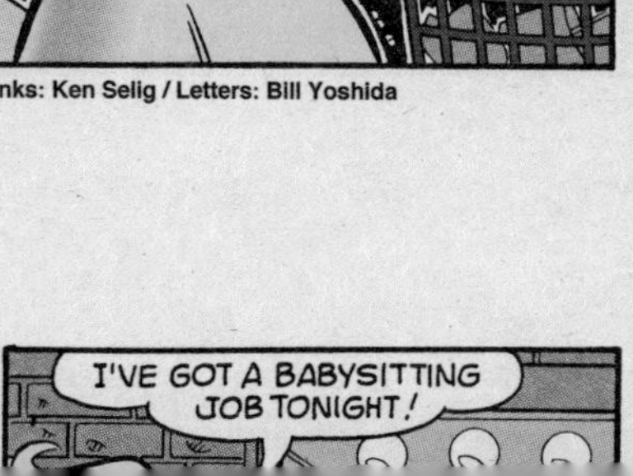
I'VE GOT A BABYSITTING JOB TONIGHT!

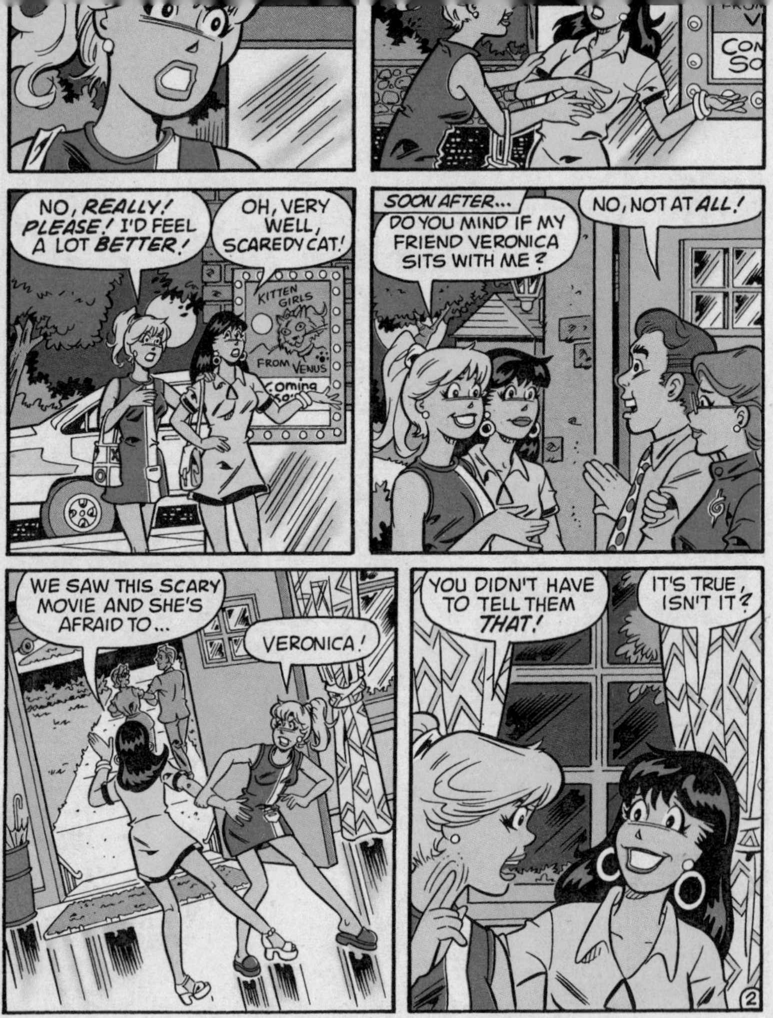
NO, REALLY! PLEASE! I'D FEEL A LOT BETTER!
OH, VERY WELL, SCAREDY CAT!
KITTEN GIRLS FROM VENUS
SOON AFTER...
DO YOU MIND IF MY FRIEND VERONICA SITS WITH ME?
NO, NOT AT ALL!
WE SAW THIS SCARY MOVIE AND SHE'S AFRAID TO...
VERONICA!
YOU DIDN'T HAVE TO TELL THEM THAT!
IT'S TRUE, ISN'T IT?
2

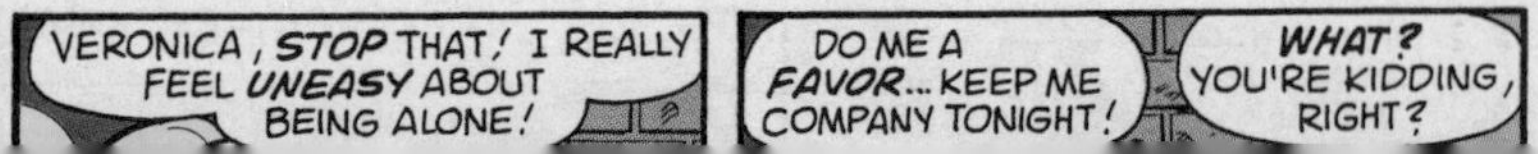
VERONICA, STOP THAT! I REALLY FEEL UNEASY ABOUT BEING ALONE!
DO ME A FAVOR... KEEP ME COMPANY TONIGHT!
WHAT? YOU'RE KIDDING, RIGHT?

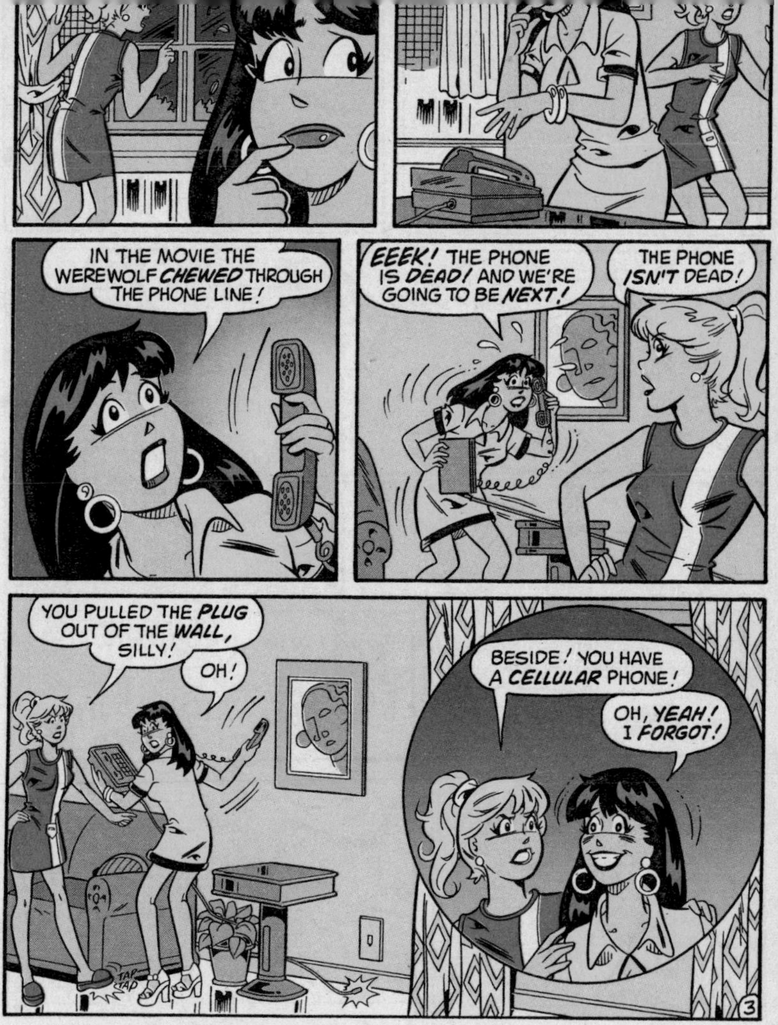
IN THE MOVIE THE WEREWOLF CHEWED THROUGH THE PHONE LINE!
EEEK! THE PHONE IS DEAD! AND WE'RE GOING TO BE NEXT!
THE PHONE ISN'T DEAD!
YOU PULLED THE PLUG OUT OF THE WALL, SILLY!
OH!
TAP TAP
BESIDE! YOU HAVE A CELLULAR PHONE!
OH, YEAH! I FORGOT!
3

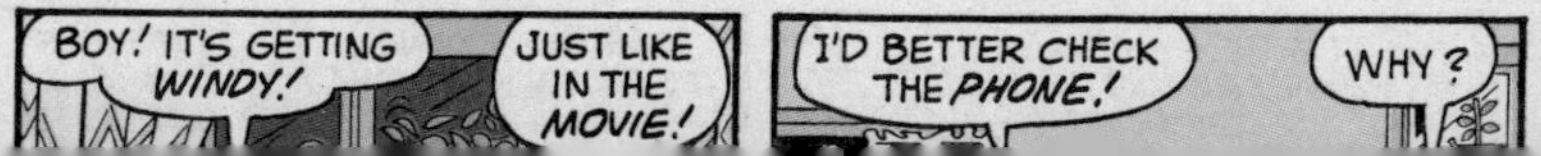
BOY! IT'S GETTING WINDY!
JUST LIKE IN THE MOVIE!
I'D BETTER CHECK THE PHONE!
WHY?

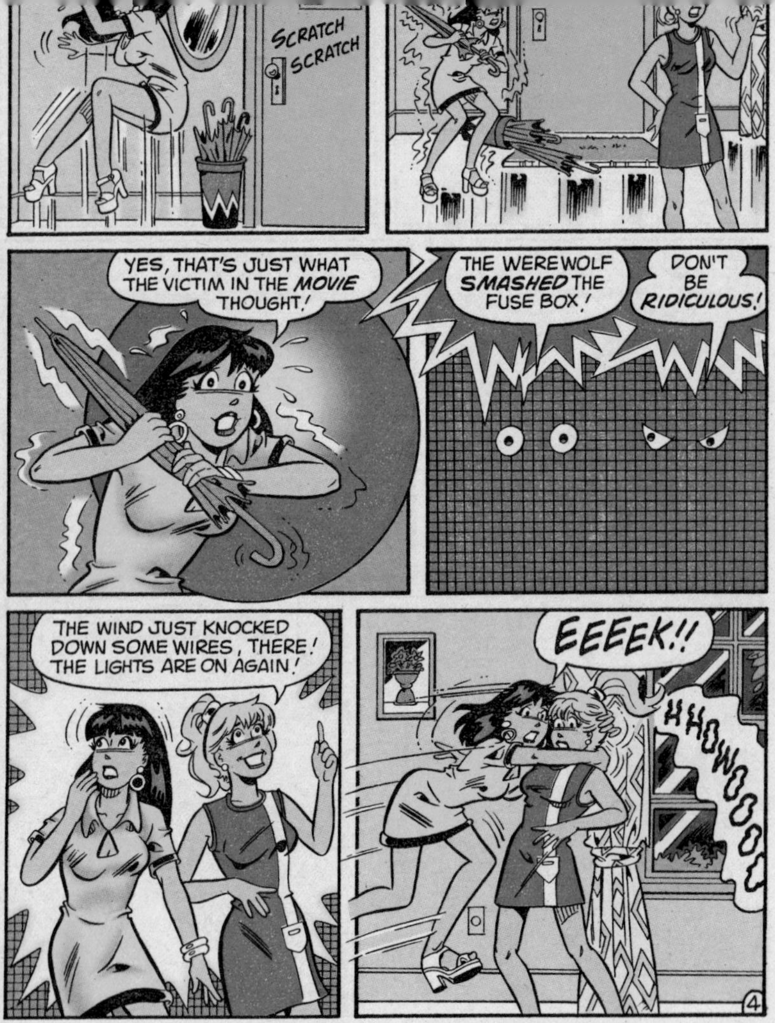
SCRATCH
SCRATCH
YES, THAT'S JUST WHAT THE VICTIM IN THE MOVIE THOUGHT!
THE WEREWOLF SMASHED THE FUSE BOX!
DON'T BE RIDICULOUS!
THE WIND JUST KNOCKED DOWN SOME WIRES, THERE! THE LIGHTS ARE ON AGAIN!
EEEEK!!
HHOWOOOOO
4

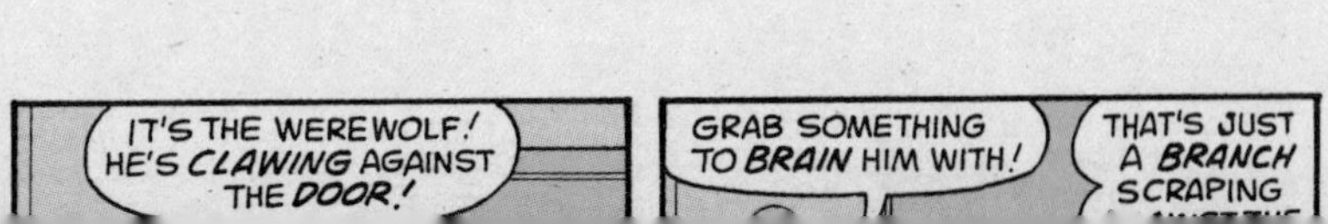
IT'S THE WEREWOLF! HE'S CLAWING AGAINST THE DOOR!
GRAB SOMETHING TO BRAIN HIM WITH!
THAT'S JUST A BRANCH SCRAPING

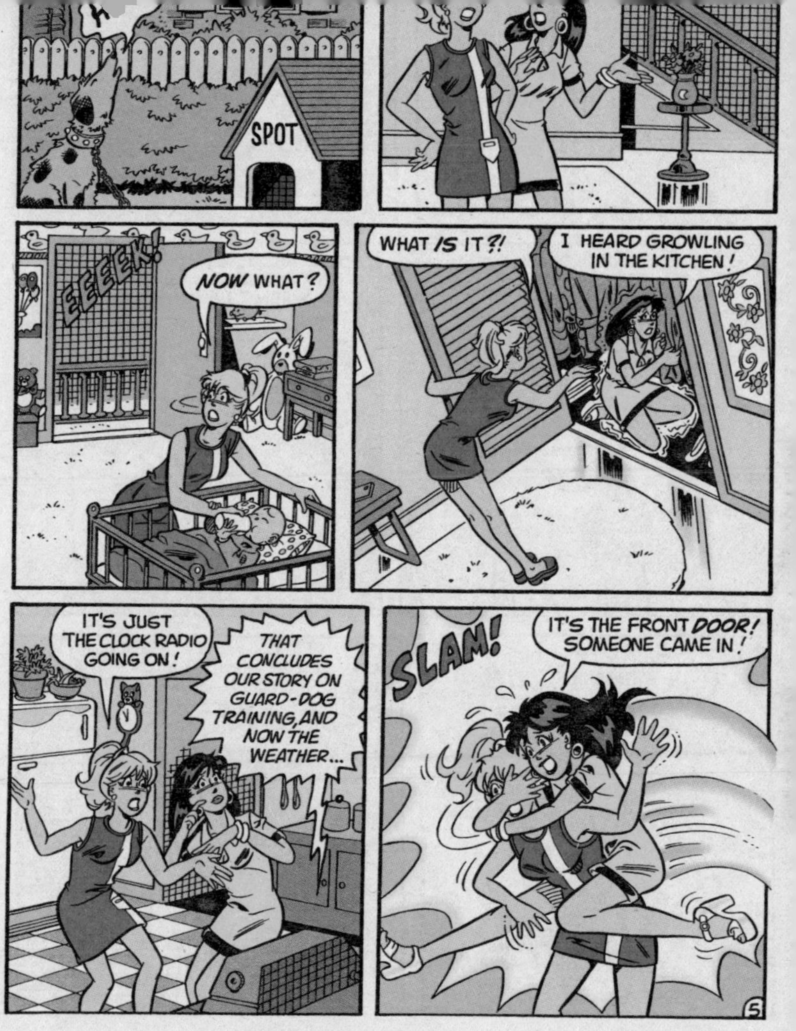
SPOT
EEEEK!
NOW WHAT?
WHAT IS IT?!
I HEARD GROWLING IN THE KITCHEN!
IT'S JUST THE CLOCK RADIO GOING ON!
THAT CONCLUDES OUR STORY ON GUARD-DOG TRAINING, AND NOW THE WEATHER...
SLAM!
IT'S THE FRONT DOOR! SOMEONE CAME IN!
5

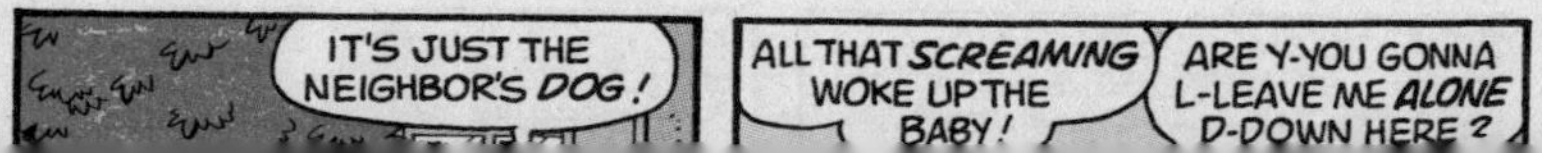
IT'S JUST THE NEIGHBOR'S DOG!
ALL THAT SCREAMING WOKE UP THE BABY!
ARE Y-YOU GONNA L-LEAVE ME ALONE D-DOWN HERE?

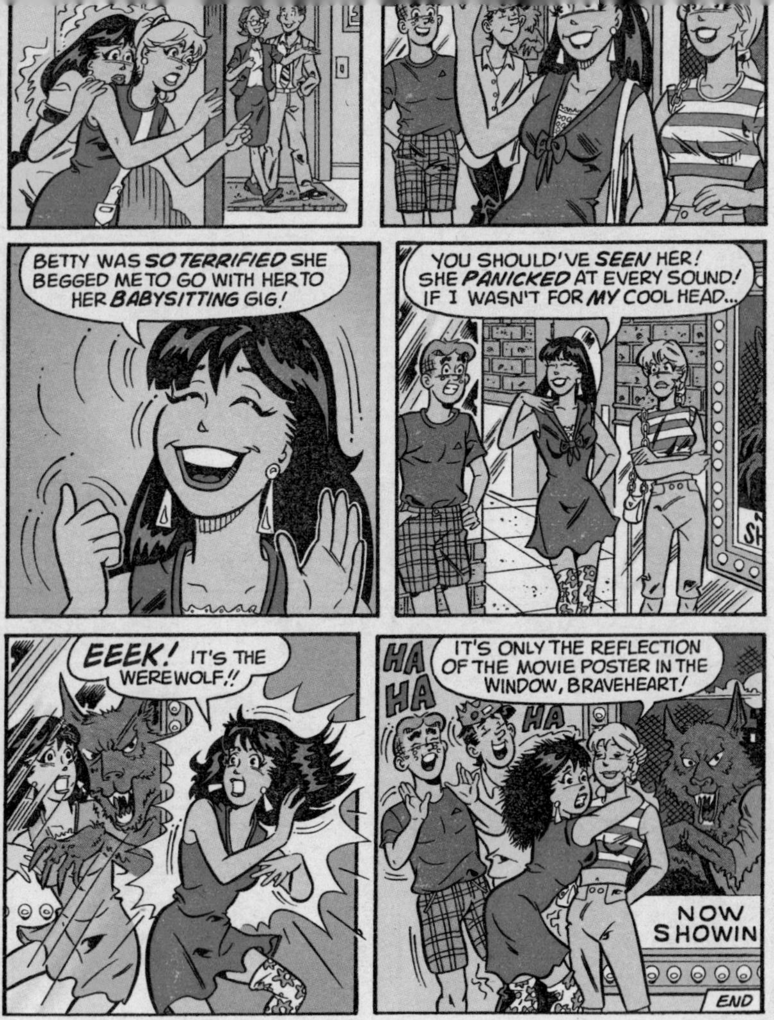
BETTY WAS SO TERRIFIED SHE BEGGED ME TO GO WITH HER TO HER BABYSITTING GIG!
YOU SHOULD'VE SEEN HER! SHE PANICKED AT EVERY SOUND! IF I WASN'T FOR MY COOL HEAD...
EEEK! IT'S THE WEREWOLF!!
HA HA
IT'S ONLY THE REFLECTION OF THE MOVIE POSTER IN THE WINDOW, BRAVEHEART!
HA
NOW SHOWIN
END

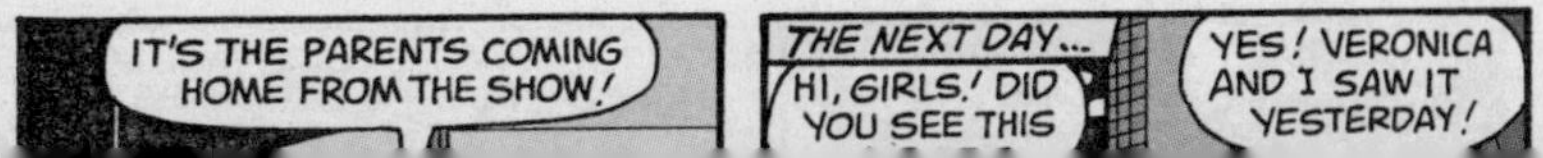
IT'S THE PARENTS COMING HOME FROM THE SHOW!
THE NEXT DAY...
HI, GIRLS! DID YOU SEE THIS
YES! VERONICA AND I SAW IT YESTERDAY!

HEY, *LOOK!* THE PET STORE IS HAVING A *COSTUME* CONTEST!

IT'S JUST FOR *PETS!* ISN'T THAT THE SILLIEST THING YOU EVER HEARD OF, BETTS?

McFLEASON'S PRESENTS THE **1st** ANNUAL **HOWL-OWEEN** COSTUME CONTEST *for* **PETS!** OCT. 31st @ 3PM **GRAND PRIZE:** THE WINNER WILL APPEAR ON THE POPULAR TELEVISION SHOW *"WAKE UP RIVERDALE!"*

SCRIPT: ANGELO DECESARE
PENCILS: JEFF SHULTZ
INKS: JIM AMASH
LETTERS: JACK MORELLI
COLORS: DIGIKORE STUDIOS

RONNIE, I WOULD *NEVER* PUT A COSTUME ON MY CAT *CARAMEL!* SHE'D LOOK RIDICULOUS!

AND WORST OF ALL, THE WINNER IS GOING ON *TV!* IF I DID THAT TO MY *FIFI,* SHE'D HAVE TO SEE A DOGGIE PSYCHIATRIST!

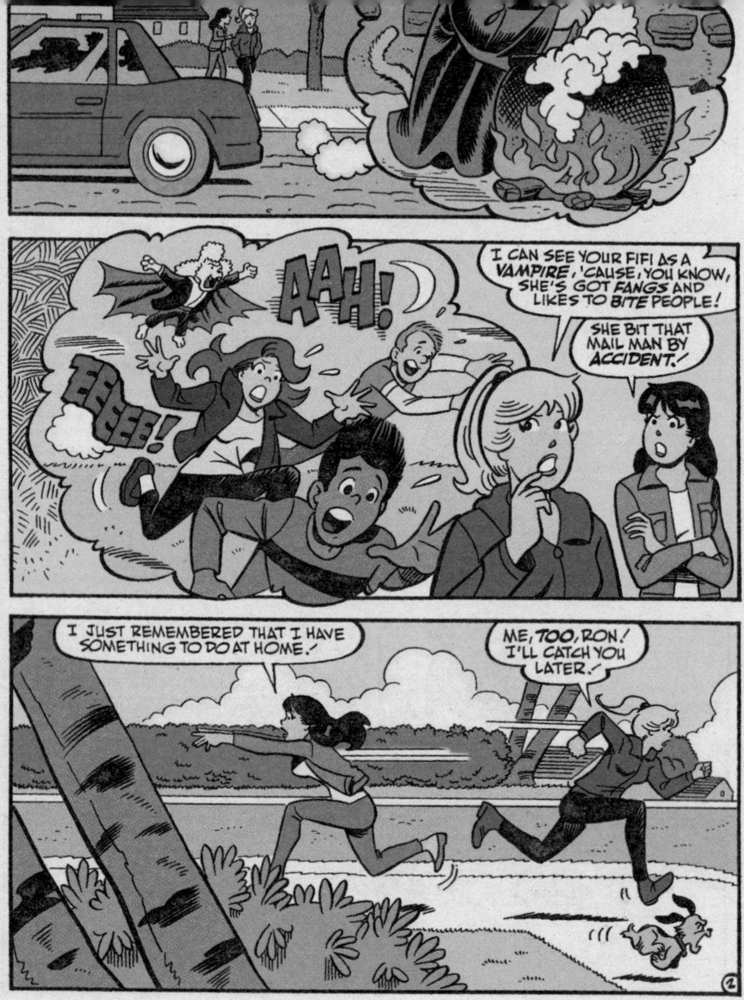

AAH!
EEEEE!
I CAN SEE YOUR FIFI AS A VAMPIRE, 'CAUSE, YOU KNOW, SHE'S GOT FANGS AND LIKES TO BITE PEOPLE!
SHE BIT THAT MAIL MAN BY ACCIDENT!
I JUST REMEMBERED THAT I HAVE SOMETHING TO DO AT HOME!
ME, TOO, RON! I'LL CATCH YOU LATER!
2

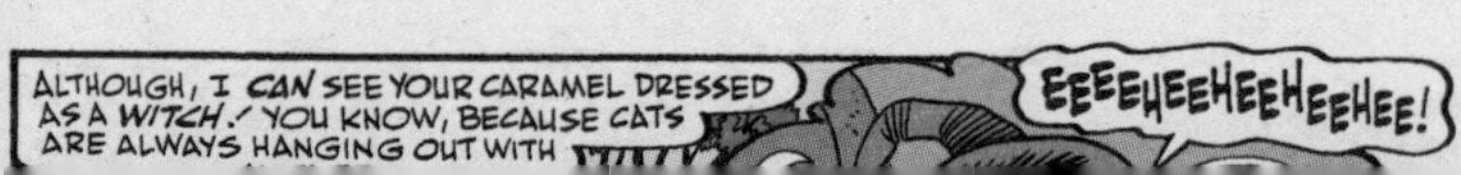

ALTHOUGH, I CAN SEE YOUR CARAMEL DRESSED AS A WITCH! YOU KNOW, BECAUSE CATS ARE ALWAYS HANGING OUT WITH
EEEEHEEHEEHEEHEE!

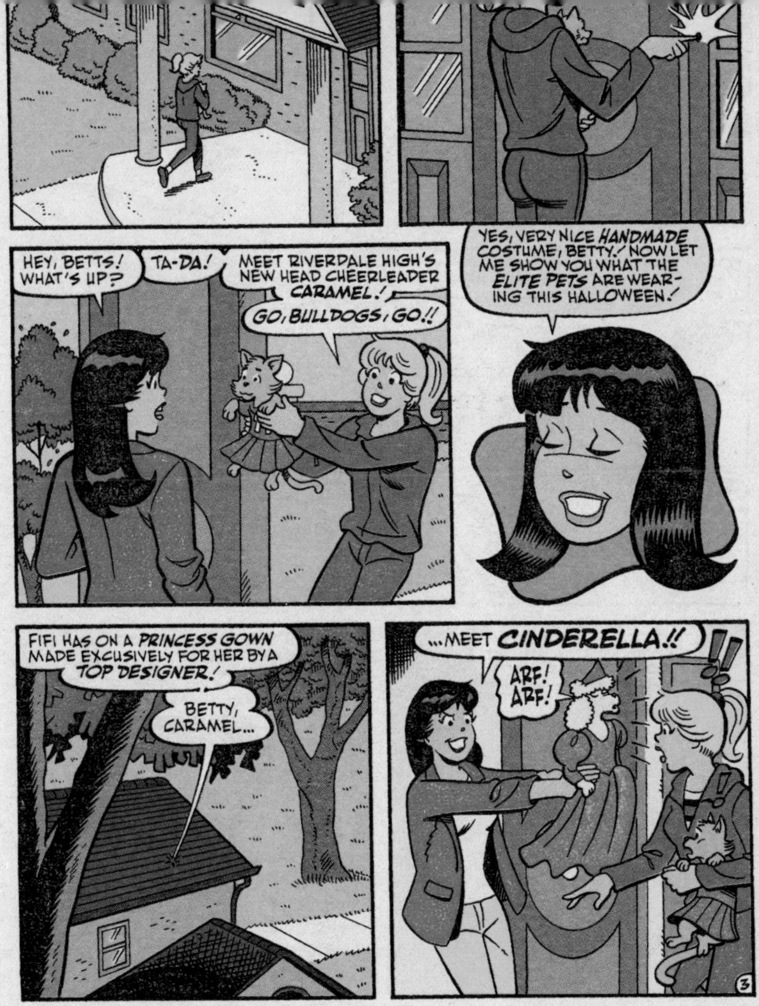
HEY, BETTS! WHAT'S UP?
TA-DA!
MEET RIVERDALE HIGH'S NEW HEAD CHEERLEADER CARAMEL!
GO, BULLDOGS, GO!!
YES, VERY NICE HANDMADE COSTUME, BETTY! NOW LET ME SHOW YOU WHAT THE ELITE PETS ARE WEARING THIS HALLOWEEN!
FIFI HAS ON A PRINCESS GOWN MADE EXCUSIVELY FOR HER BY A TOP DESIGNER!
BETTY, CARAMEL...
...MEET CINDERELLA!!
ARF! ARF!
3

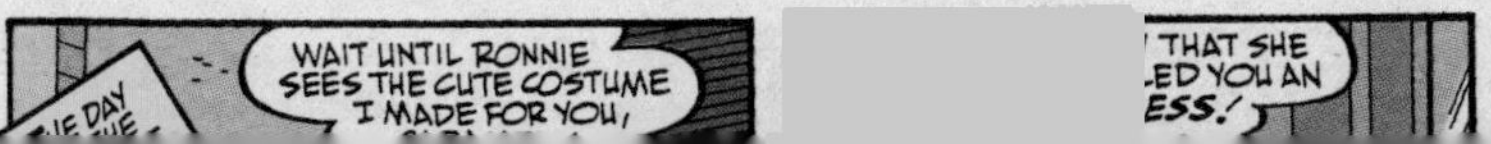
WAIT UNTIL RONNIE SEES THE CUTE COSTUME I MADE FOR YOU,
THAT SHE
YOU AN

SOON!!

WHAT IF RONNIE IS *RIGHT?* I MEAN, PRINCESSES *ARE* MORE POPULAR THAN CHEERLEADERS!

WHAT IF BETTY IS *RIGHT?* THE JUDGES MIGHT PREFER A COSTUME THAT WAS MADE BY HAND...THE IDIOTS!

WE'VE GOT TO MAKE YOU LOOK *REALLY* SPECIAL! LET'S GO VISIT THE SCHOOL ATHLETIC FIELD!

IT'S TIME TO TAKE THIS TO THE *NEXT LEVEL!* LET'S CALL THE OWNERS OF THE "FAIRY TALE VILLAGE" AMUSEMENT PARK!

4

LISTEN, RON! ANYBODY CAN *BUY* A COSTUME! THE JUDGES WILL BE MORE

IN WHAT UNIVERSE? A PRINCESS IS *WAY* MORE POPULAR THAN A

Hmph!

WE'LL SEE ABOUT THAT!

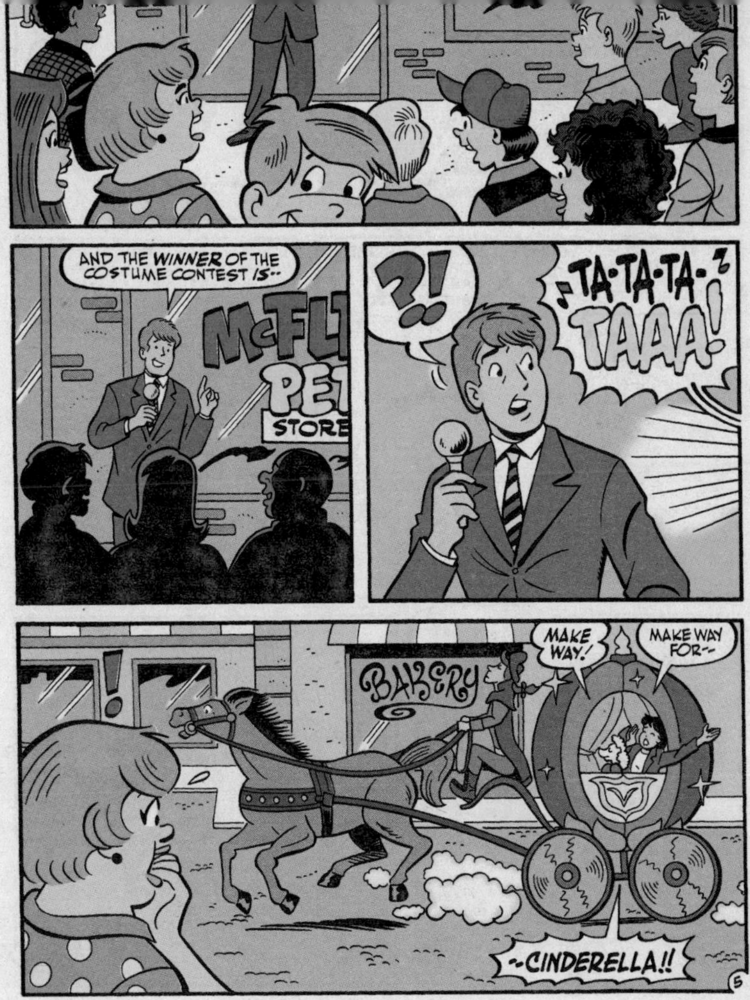
AND THE WINNER OF THE COSTUME CONTEST IS--
McFL
PET
STORE
?!
TA-TA-TA-TAAA!
BAKERY
MAKE WAY!
MAKE WAY FOR--
--CINDERELLA!!

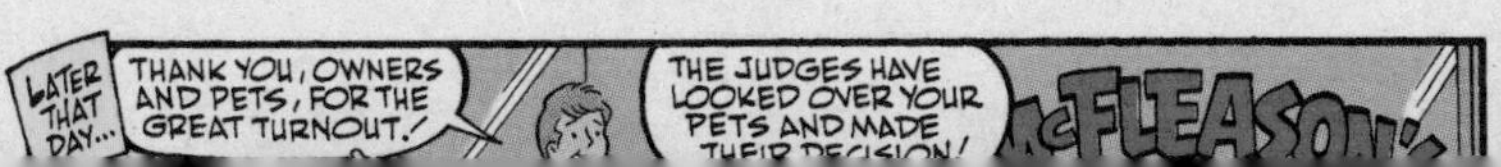
LATER THAT DAY...
THANK YOU, OWNERS AND PETS, FOR THE GREAT TURNOUT!
THE JUDGES HAVE LOOKED OVER YOUR PETS AND MADE
McFLEASON

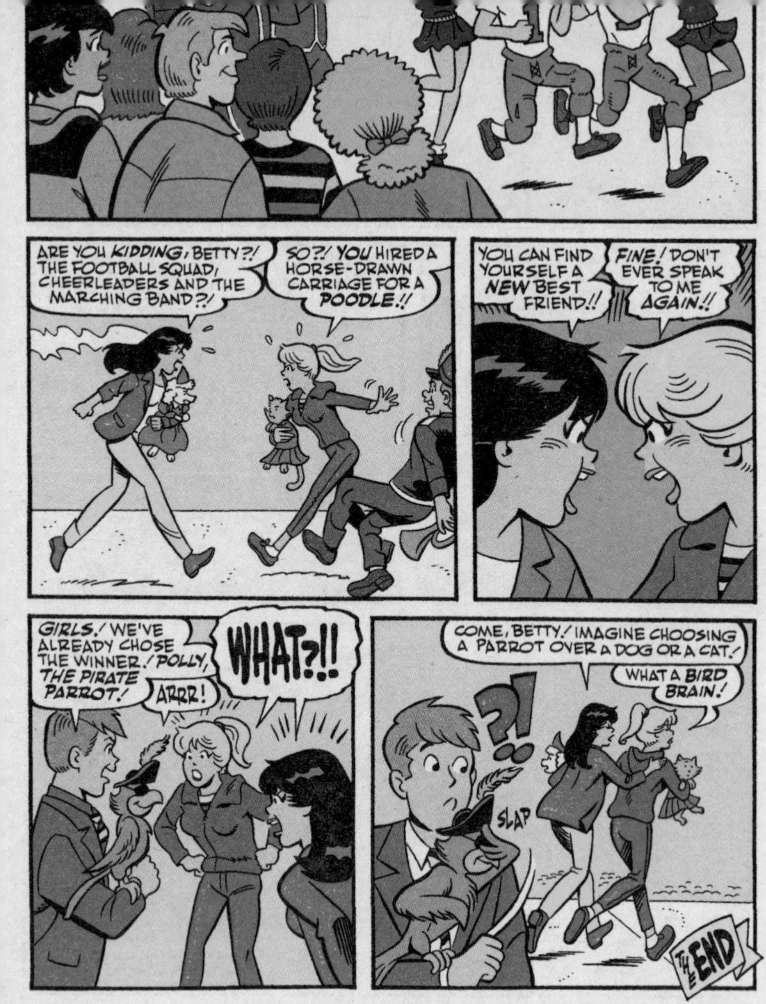
ARE YOU KIDDING, BETTY?! THE FOOTBALL SQUAD, CHEERLEADERS AND THE MARCHING BAND?!
SO?! YOU HIRED A HORSE-DRAWN CARRIAGE FOR A POODLE!!
YOU CAN FIND YOURSELF A NEW BEST FRIEND!!
FINE! DON'T EVER SPEAK TO ME AGAIN!!
GIRLS! WE'VE ALREADY CHOSE THE WINNER! POLLY, THE PIRATE PARROT!
ARRR!
WHAT?!!
COME, BETTY! IMAGINE CHOOSING A PARROT OVER A DOG OR A CAT!
WHAT A BIRD BRAIN!
?!
SLAP
THE END

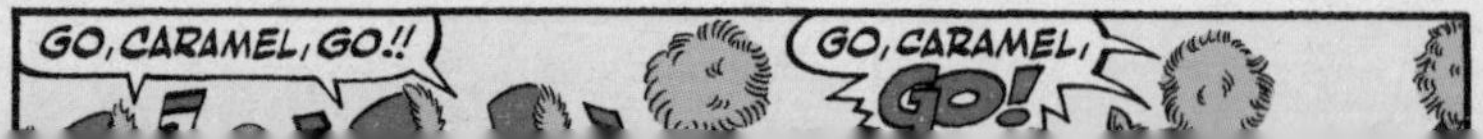
GO, CARAMEL, GO!!
GO, CARAMEL, GO!

Betty in... "ODE TO BE A DOLLY"

YOU'RE *LUCKY, DOLLY!* WHILE I'M PUSHING *MOP* AND *BROOM* YOU'RE UP HERE *SMILING* IN MY *ROOM!*

Script: Hal Smith
Pencils: Stan Goldberg
Inks: Mike Esposito
Letters: Bill Yoshida

BOY! CLEANING MY ROOM IS

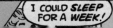

I COULD *SLEEP* FOR A *WEEK!*

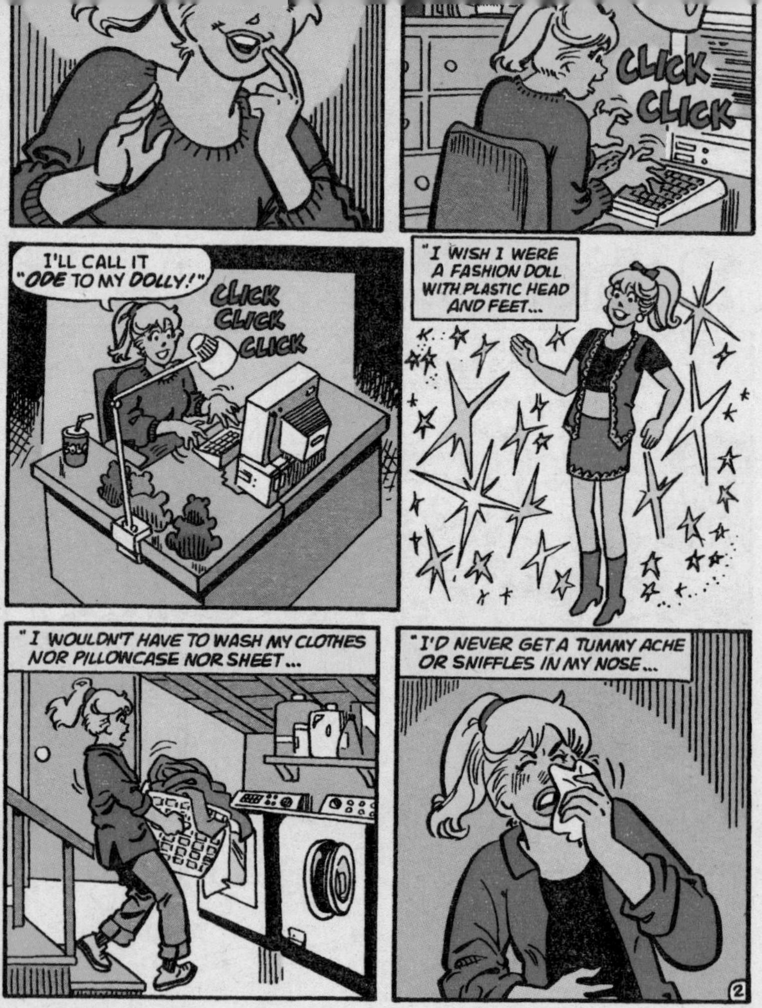
CLICK CLICK
I'LL CALL IT "ODE TO MY DOLLY!"
CLICK CLICK CLICK
"I WISH I WERE A FASHION DOLL WITH PLASTIC HEAD AND FEET...
"I WOULDN'T HAVE TO WASH MY CLOTHES NOR PILLOWCASE NOR SHEET...
"I'D NEVER GET A TUMMY ACHE OR SNIFFLES IN MY NOSE...
2

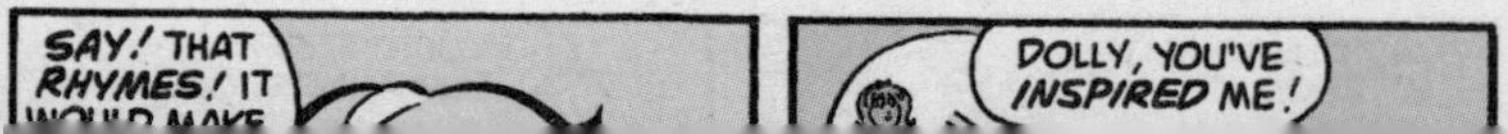
SAY! THAT RHYMES! IT
DOLLY, YOU'VE INSPIRED ME!

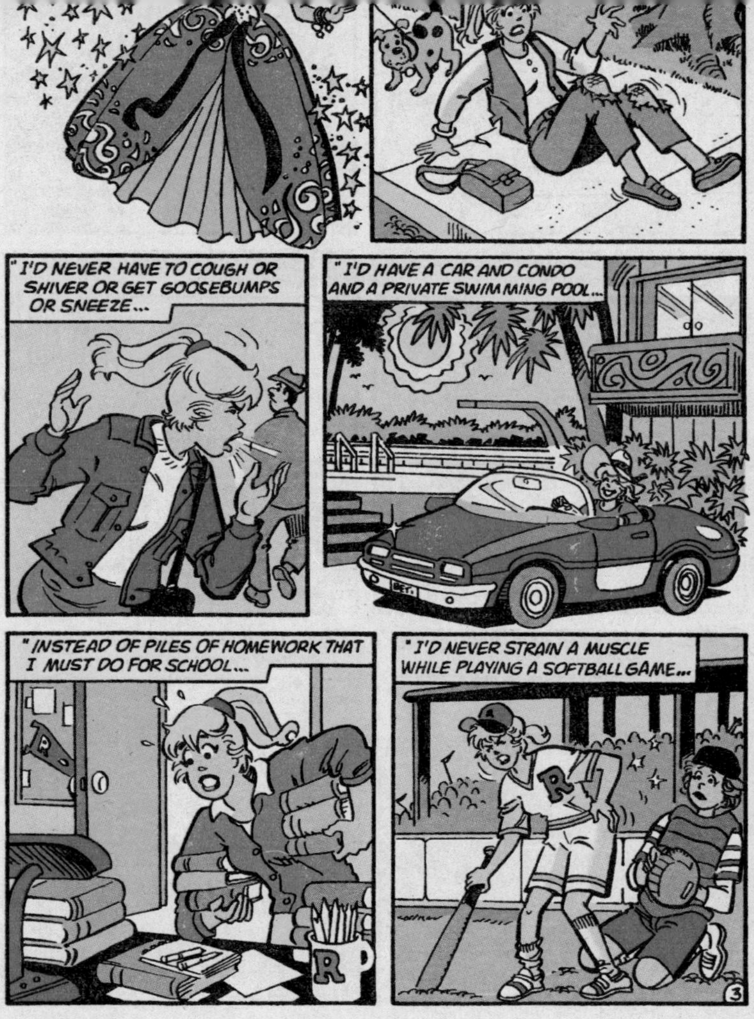
"I'D NEVER HAVE TO COUGH OR SHIVER OR GET GOOSEBUMPS OR SNEEZE...
"I'D HAVE A CAR AND CONDO AND A PRIVATE SWIMMING POOL...
"INSTEAD OF PILES OF HOMEWORK THAT I MUST DO FOR SCHOOL...
"I'D NEVER STRAIN A MUSCLE WHILE PLAYING A SOFTBALL GAME...
3

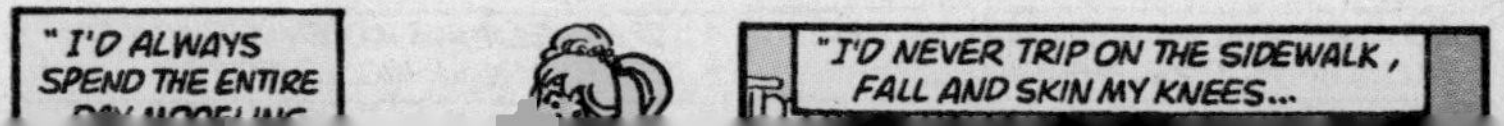
"I'D ALWAYS SPEND THE ENTIRE
"I'D NEVER TRIP ON THE SIDEWALK, FALL AND SKIN MY KNEES...

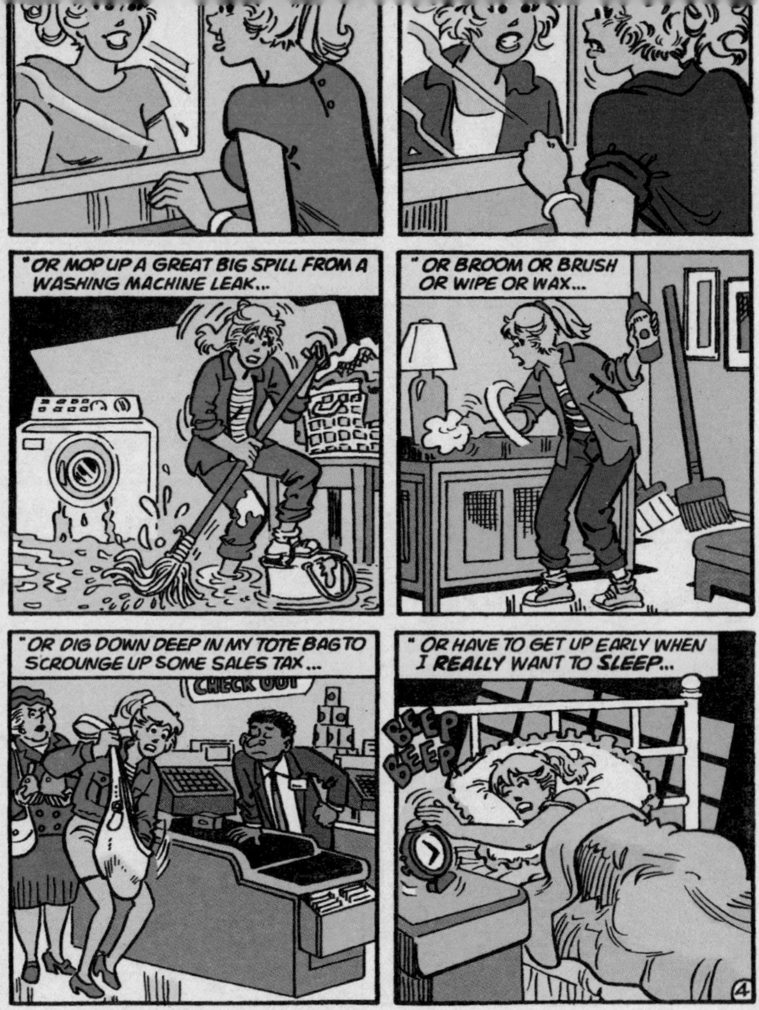

"OR MOP UP A GREAT BIG SPILL FROM A WASHING MACHINE LEAK...
"OR BROOM OR BRUSH OR WIPE OR WAX...
"OR DIG DOWN DEEP IN MY TOTE BAG TO SCROUNGE UP SOME SALES TAX...
CHECK OUT
"OR HAVE TO GET UP EARLY WHEN I REALLY WANT TO SLEEP...
BEEP BEEP
4

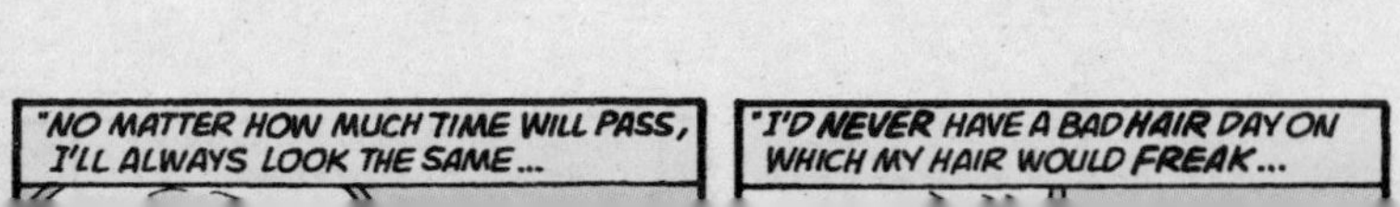

"NO MATTER HOW MUCH TIME WILL PASS, I'LL ALWAYS LOOK THE SAME...
"I'D NEVER HAVE A BAD HAIR DAY ON WHICH MY HAIR WOULD FREAK...

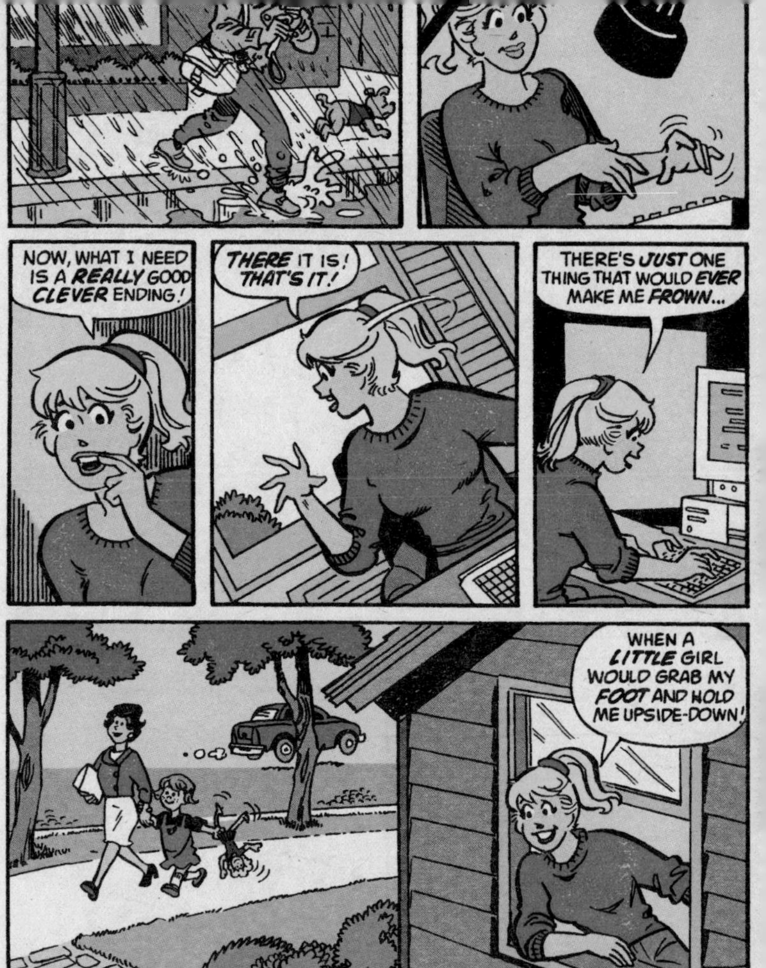
NOW, WHAT I NEED IS A REALLY GOOD CLEVER ENDING!
THERE IT IS! THAT'S IT!
THERE'S JUST ONE THING THAT WOULD EVER MAKE ME FROWN...
WHEN A LITTLE GIRL WOULD GRAB MY FOOT AND HOLD ME UPSIDE-DOWN!
END

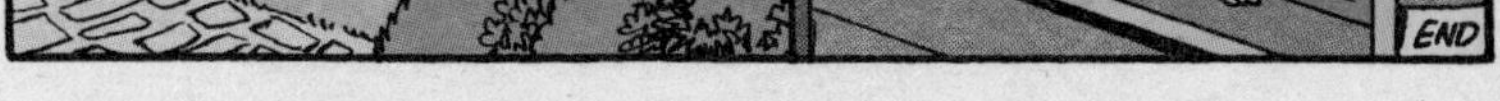
"OR NEGOTIATE A PUDDLE, WHEN RAIN MAKES WATER DEEP...
I'D SMILE ALL DAY AND NEVER HAVE A CARE! WITH PERFECT SKIN AND A PERFECT SMILE AND PERFECT

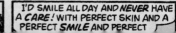

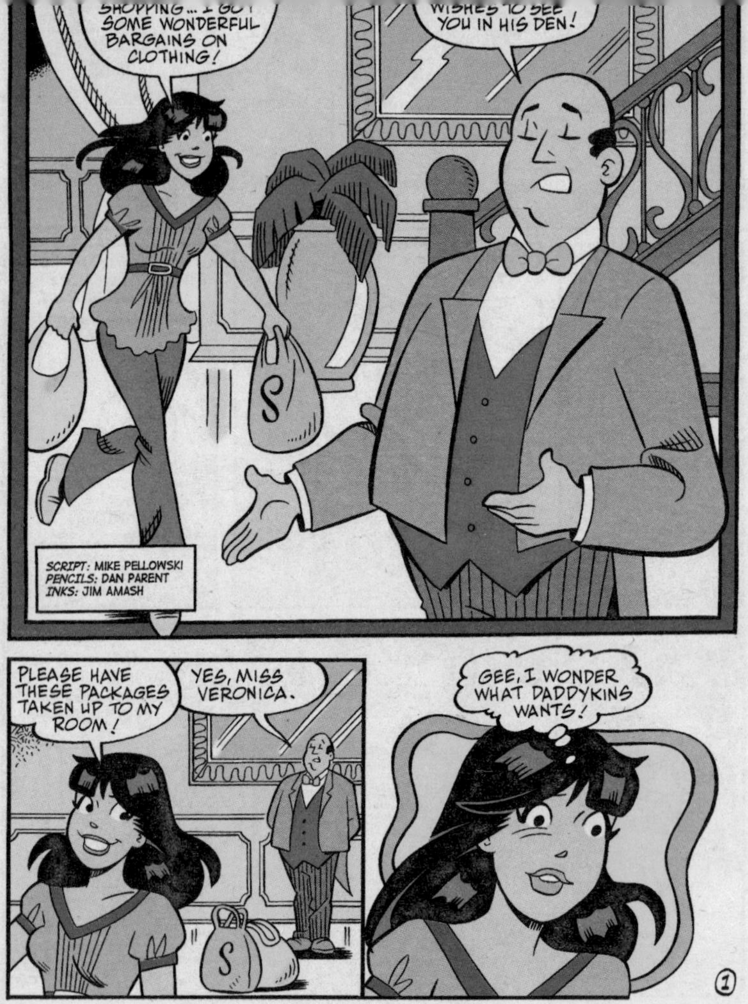
SHOPPING... I GOT SOME WONDERFUL BARGAINS ON CLOTHING!
WISHES TO SEE YOU IN HIS DEN!
SCRIPT: MIKE PELLOWSKI
PENCILS: DAN PARENT
INKS: JIM AMASH
PLEASE HAVE THESE PACKAGES TAKEN UP TO MY ROOM!
YES, MISS VERONICA.
GEE, I WONDER WHAT DADDYKINS WANTS!
S
1

Veronica in SPORTS WEAR

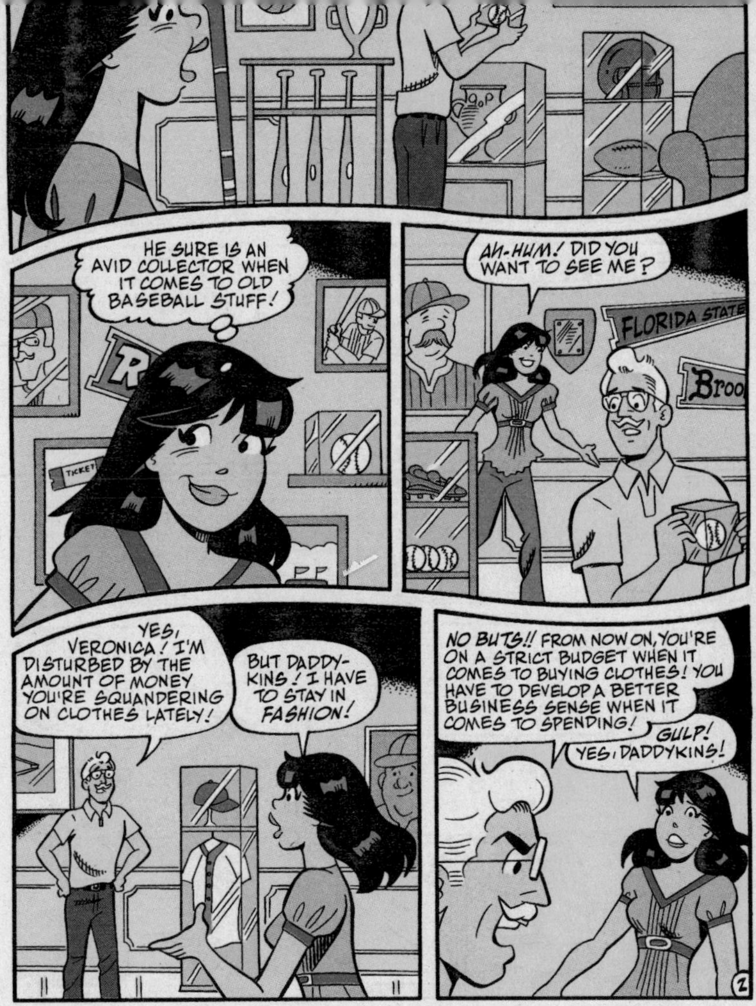
HE SURE IS AN AVID COLLECTOR WHEN IT COMES TO OLD BASEBALL STUFF!
AH-HUM! DID YOU WANT TO SEE ME?
FLORIDA STATE
YES, VERONICA! I'M DISTURBED BY THE AMOUNT OF MONEY YOU'RE SQUANDERING ON CLOTHES LATELY!
BUT DADDY-KINS! I HAVE TO STAY IN FASHION!
NO BUTS!! FROM NOW ON, YOU'RE ON A STRICT BUDGET WHEN IT COMES TO BUYING CLOTHES! YOU HAVE TO DEVELOP A BETTER BUSINESS SENSE WHEN IT COMES TO SPENDING!
GULP! YES, DADDYKINS!
2

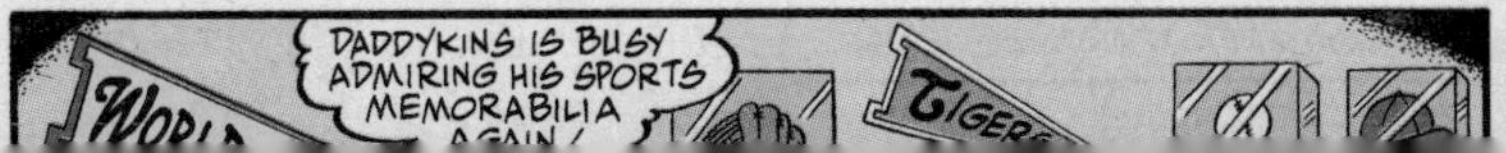
DADDYKINS IS BUSY ADMIRING HIS SPORTS MEMORABILIA

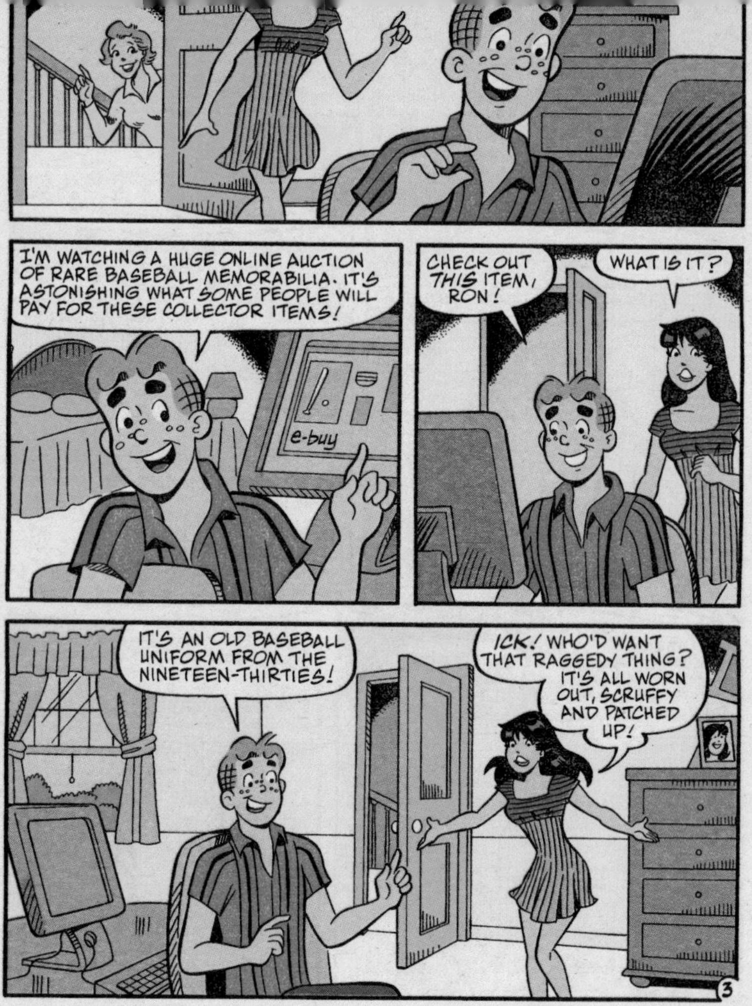

I'M WATCHING A HUGE ONLINE AUCTION OF RARE BASEBALL MEMORABILIA. IT'S ASTONISHING WHAT SOME PEOPLE WILL PAY FOR THESE COLLECTOR ITEMS!
e-buy
CHECK OUT THIS ITEM, RON!
WHAT IS IT?
IT'S AN OLD BASEBALL UNIFORM FROM THE NINETEEN-THIRTIES!
ICK! WHO'D WANT THAT RAGGEDY THING? IT'S ALL WORN OUT, SCRUFFY AND PATCHED UP!
3

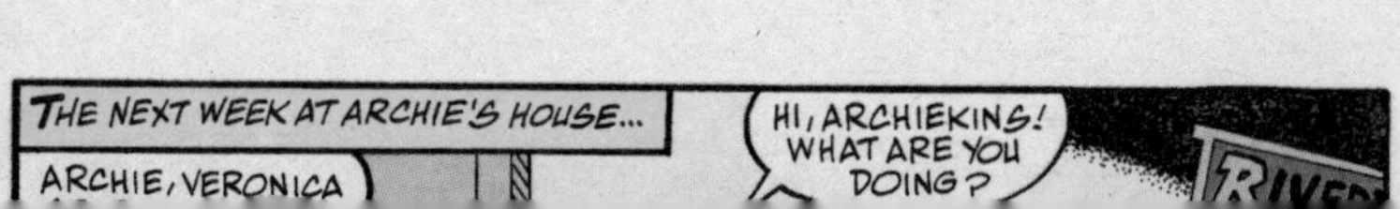

THE NEXT WEEK AT ARCHIE'S HOUSE...
ARCHIE, VERONICA
HI, ARCHIEKINS! WHAT ARE YOU DOING?

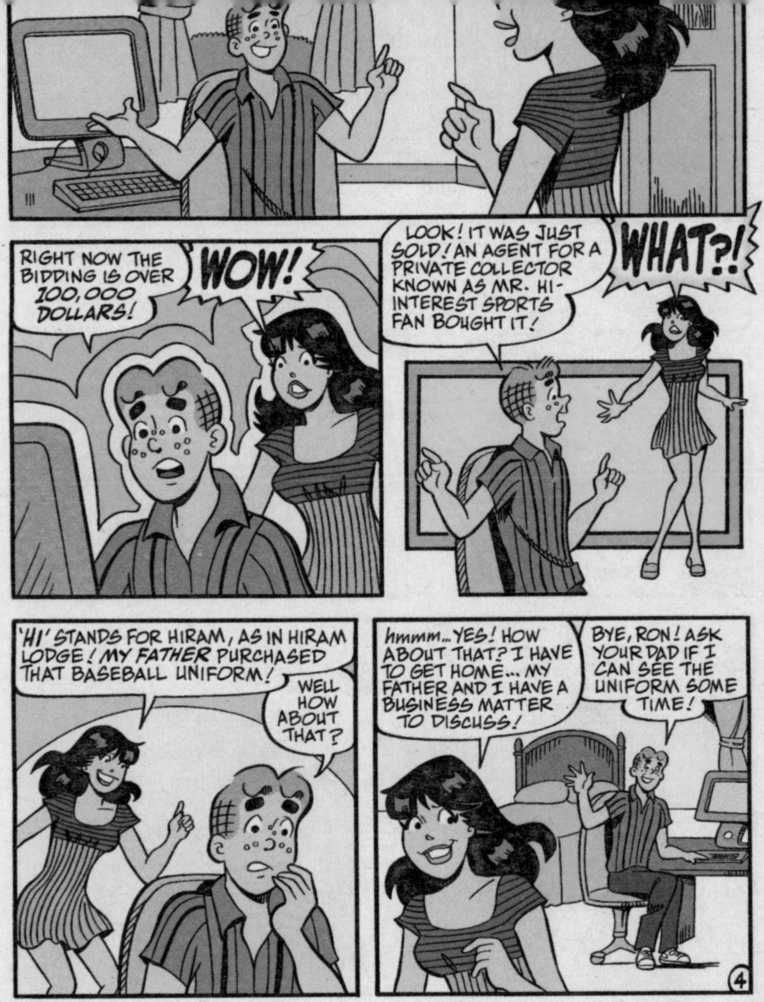
RIGHT NOW THE BIDDING IS OVER 100,000 DOLLARS!
WOW!
LOOK! IT WAS JUST SOLD! AN AGENT FOR A PRIVATE COLLECTOR KNOWN AS MR. HI-INTEREST SPORTS FAN BOUGHT IT!
WHAT?!
'HI' STANDS FOR HIRAM, AS IN HIRAM LODGE! MY FATHER PURCHASED THAT BASEBALL UNIFORM!
WELL HOW ABOUT THAT?
hmmm... YES! HOW ABOUT THAT? I HAVE TO GET HOME... MY FATHER AND I HAVE A BUSINESS MATTER TO DISCUSS!
BYE, RON! ASK YOUR DAD IF I CAN SEE THE UNIFORM SOME TIME!
4

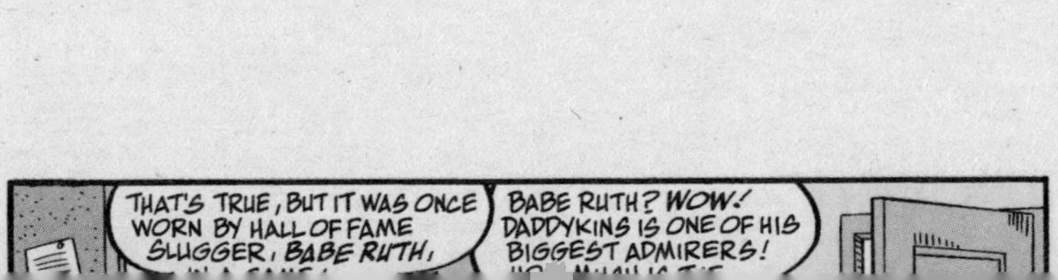
THAT'S TRUE, BUT IT WAS ONCE WORN BY HALL OF FAME SLUGGER, BABE RUTH,
BABE RUTH? WOW! DADDYKINS IS ONE OF HIS BIGGEST ADMIRERS!

THEN I GUESS YOU SAW ME PURCHASE THAT BASEBALL UNIFORM! IT WAS A WISE INVESTMENT!

I NEVER REALIZED BUYING OLD, USED CLOTHING COULD BE SO PROFITABLE!

IT'S *VERY* PROFIT-ABLE! THE VALUE OF THESE RARE COLLECTORS' ITEMS ALMOST ALWAYS *RISES!*

IN FACT, NEXT MONTH THERE IS AN AUCTION OF CLASSIC MOVIE COSTUME MEMORABILIA. PERHAPS WE COULD WATCH IT TOGETHER!

I DON'T HAVE MUCH OF A MIND FOR BUSINESS, DADDYKINS, BUT *THAT'S* THE KIND OF INVESTING THAT REALLY EXCITES ME!

The END

LATER AT THE LODGE MANSION...

HELLO, VERONICA! WHERE HAVE YOU BEEN?

I WAS AT ARCHIE'S HOUSE WATCHING AN ONLINE AUCTION OF SPORTS MEMOR...

Archie -in- "DREAM SCENE"

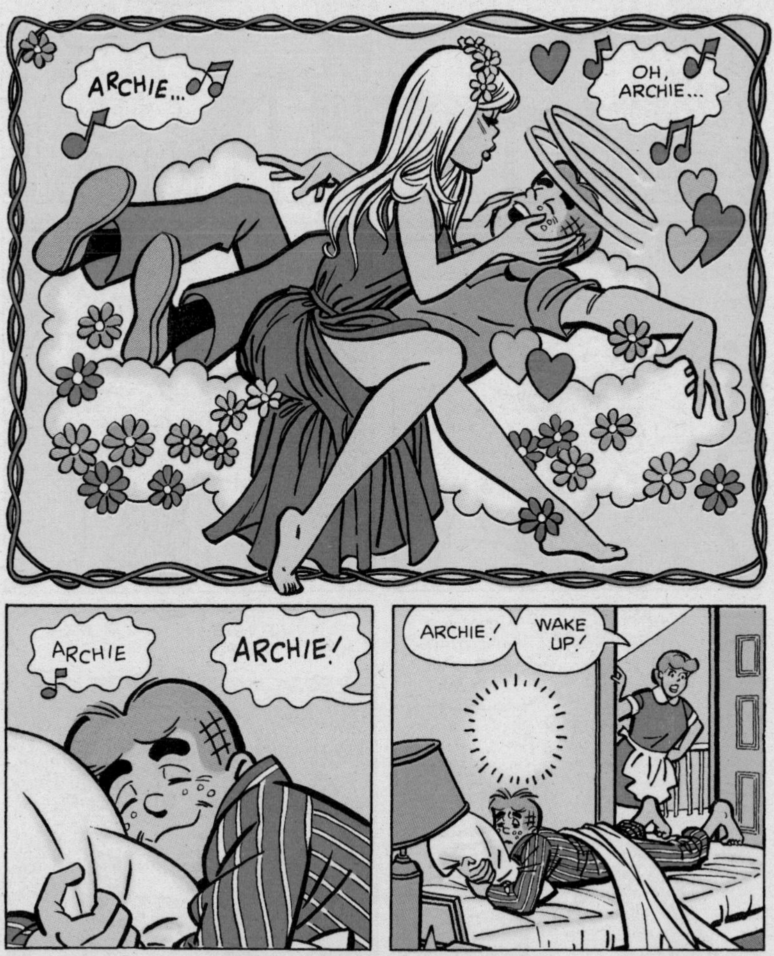

ARCHIE...
OH, ARCHIE...
ARCHIE
ARCHIE!
ARCHIE!
WAKE UP!

Script & Art: Al Hartley / Letters: Bill Yoshida

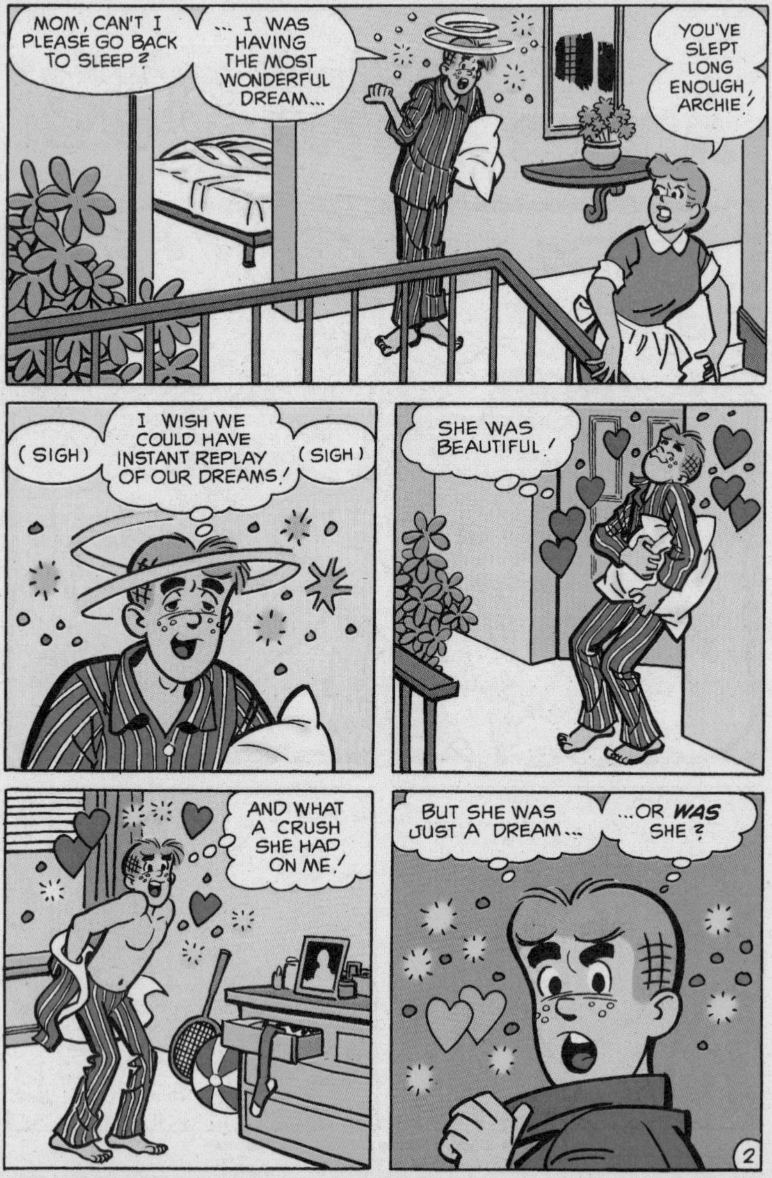
MOM, CAN'T I PLEASE GO BACK TO SLEEP?
... I WAS HAVING THE MOST WONDERFUL DREAM...
YOU'VE SLEPT LONG ENOUGH, ARCHIE!
(SIGH)
I WISH WE COULD HAVE INSTANT REPLAY OF OUR DREAMS!
(SIGH)
SHE WAS BEAUTIFUL!
AND WHAT A CRUSH SHE HAD ON ME!
BUT SHE WAS JUST A DREAM...
...OR *WAS* SHE?
2

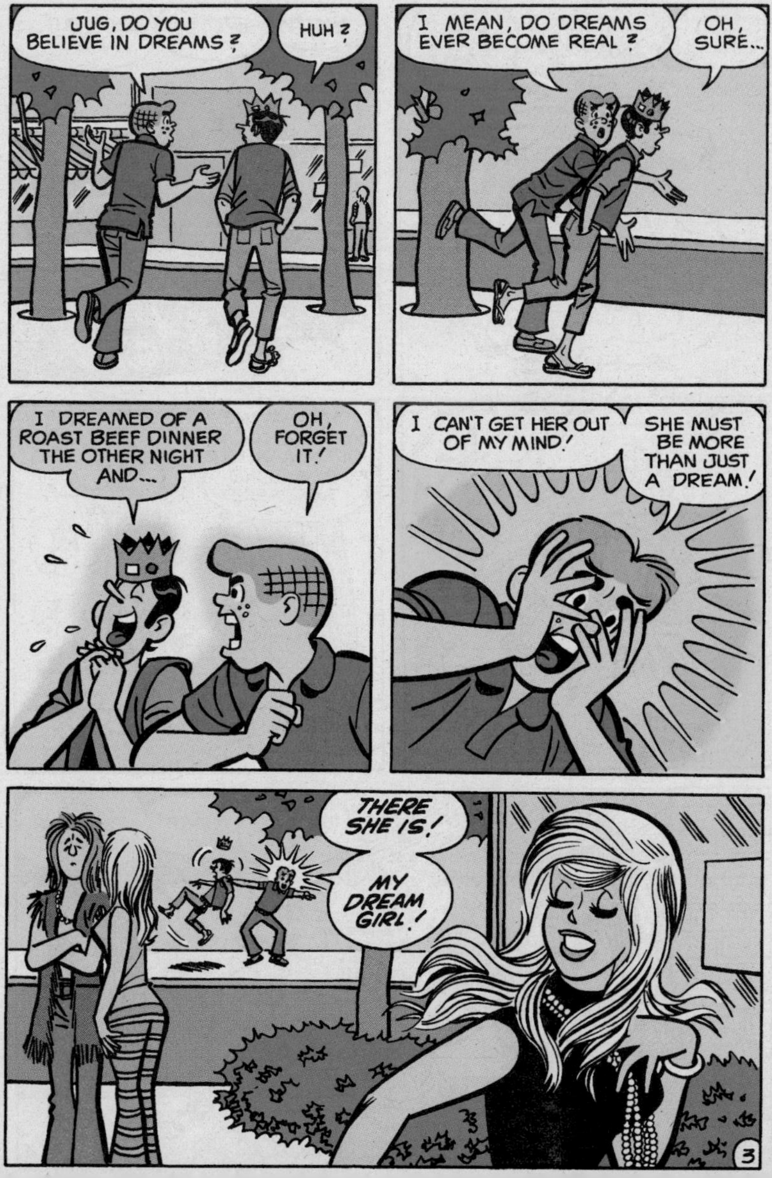
JUG, DO YOU BELIEVE IN DREAMS?
HUH?
I MEAN, DO DREAMS EVER BECOME REAL?
OH, SURE...
I DREAMED OF A ROAST BEEF DINNER THE OTHER NIGHT AND...
OH, FORGET IT!
I CAN'T GET HER OUT OF MY MIND!
SHE MUST BE MORE THAN JUST A DREAM!
THERE SHE IS!
MY DREAM GIRL!
3

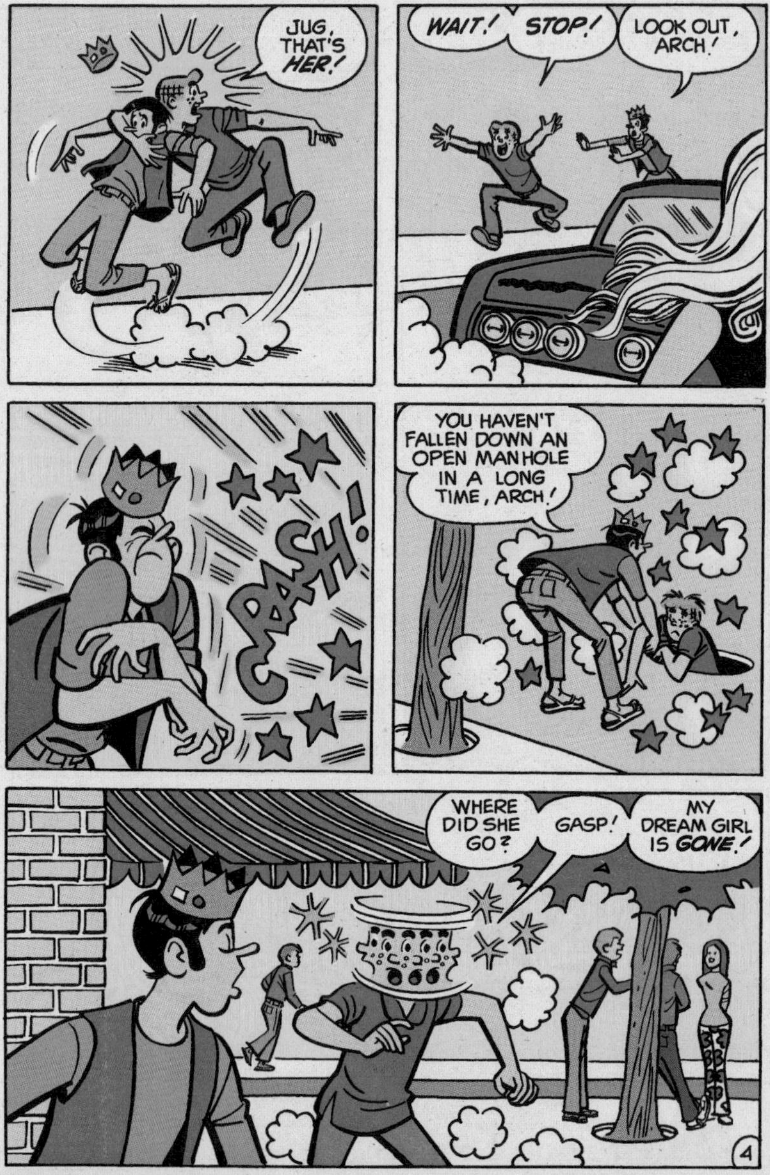
JUG, THAT'S *HER!*
WAIT!
STOP!
LOOK OUT, ARCH!
CRASH!
YOU HAVEN'T FALLEN DOWN AN OPEN MANHOLE IN A LONG TIME, ARCH!
WHERE DID SHE GO?
GASP!
MY DREAM GIRL IS *GONE!*

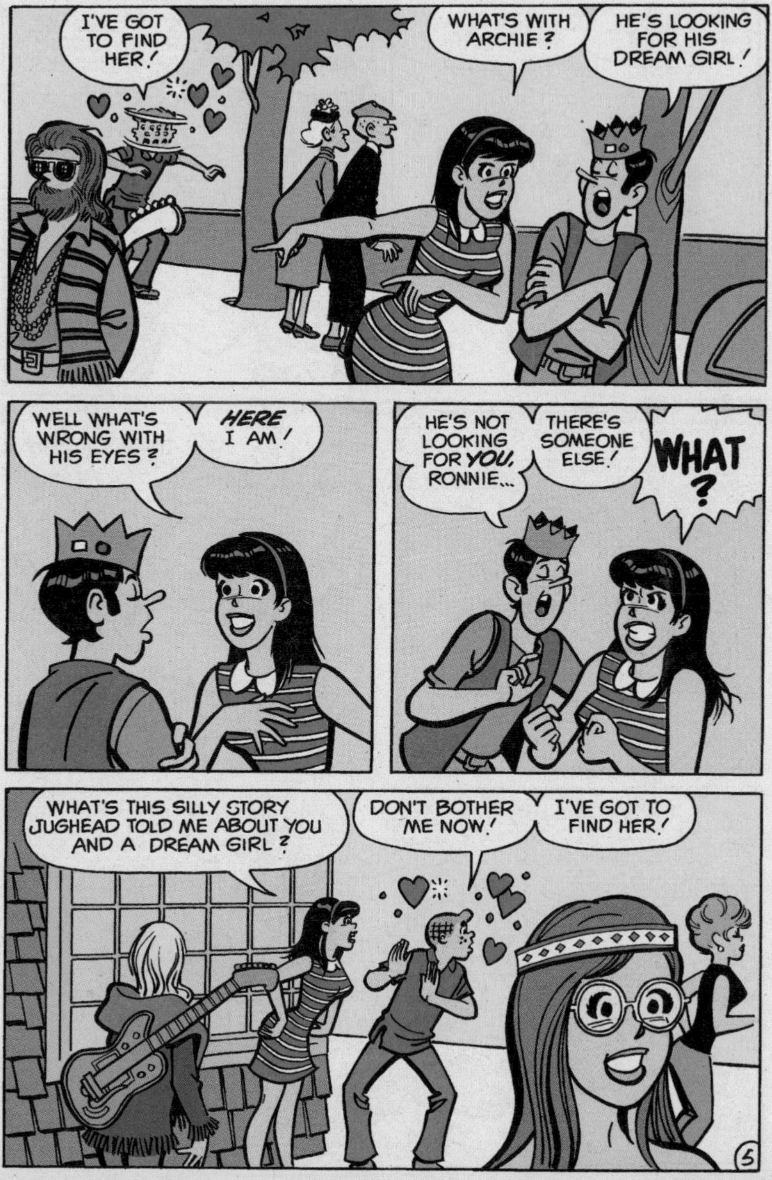
I'VE GOT TO FIND HER!
WHAT'S WITH ARCHIE?
HE'S LOOKING FOR HIS DREAM GIRL!
WELL WHAT'S WRONG WITH HIS EYES?
HERE I AM!
HE'S NOT LOOKING FOR YOU, RONNIE...
THERE'S SOMEONE ELSE!
WHAT?
WHAT'S THIS SILLY STORY JUGHEAD TOLD ME ABOUT YOU AND A DREAM GIRL?
DON'T BOTHER ME NOW!
I'VE GOT TO FIND HER!
5

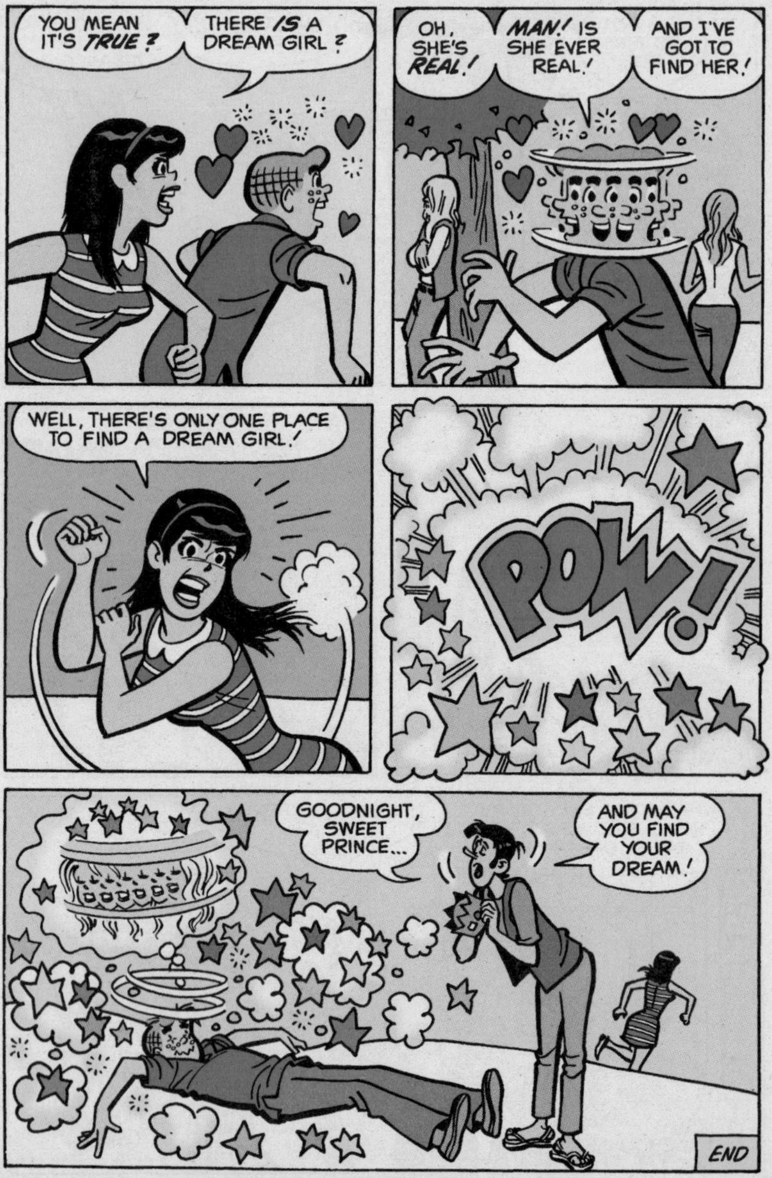
YOU MEAN IT'S TRUE?
THERE IS A DREAM GIRL?
OH, SHE'S REAL!
MAN! IS SHE EVER REAL!
AND I'VE GOT TO FIND HER!
WELL, THERE'S ONLY ONE PLACE TO FIND A DREAM GIRL!
POW!
GOODNIGHT, SWEET PRINCE...
AND MAY YOU FIND YOUR DREAM!
END

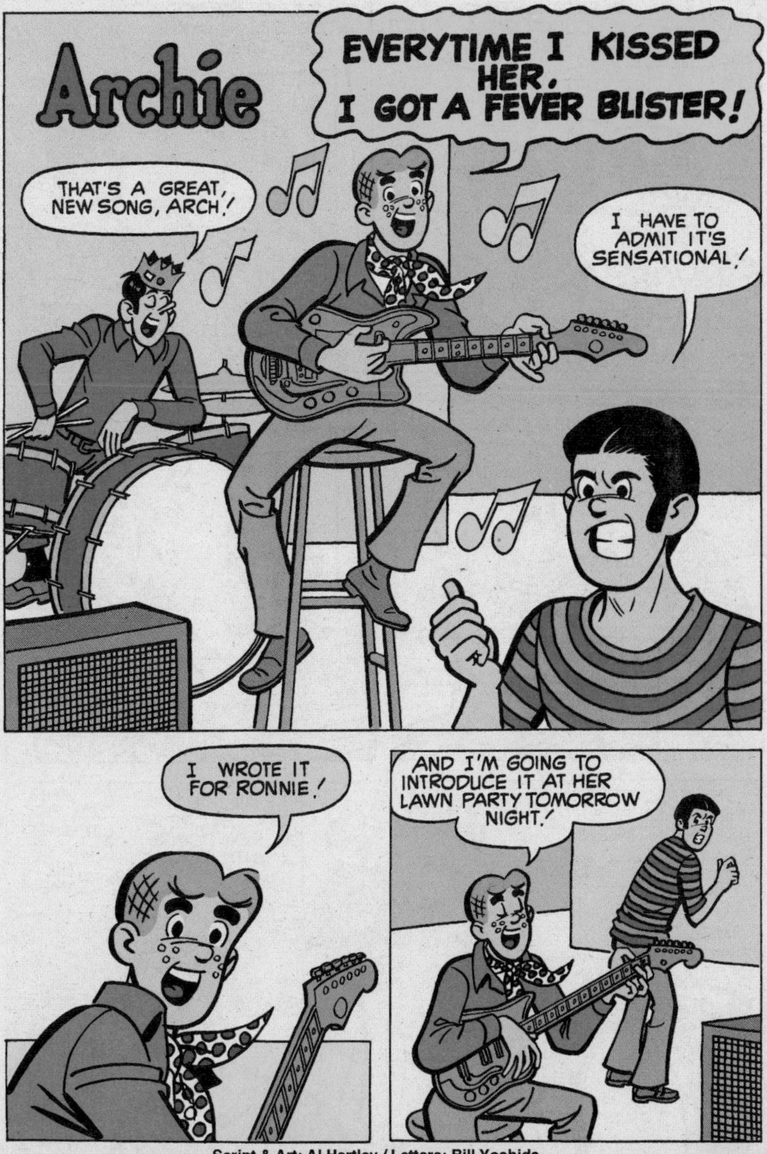
Archie
EVERYTIME I KISSED HER. I GOT A FEVER BLISTER!
THAT'S A GREAT, NEW SONG, ARCH!
I HAVE TO ADMIT IT'S SENSATIONAL!
I WROTE IT FOR RONNIE!
AND I'M GOING TO INTRODUCE IT AT HER LAWN PARTY TOMORROW NIGHT!

Script & Art: Al Hartley / Letters: Bill Yoshida

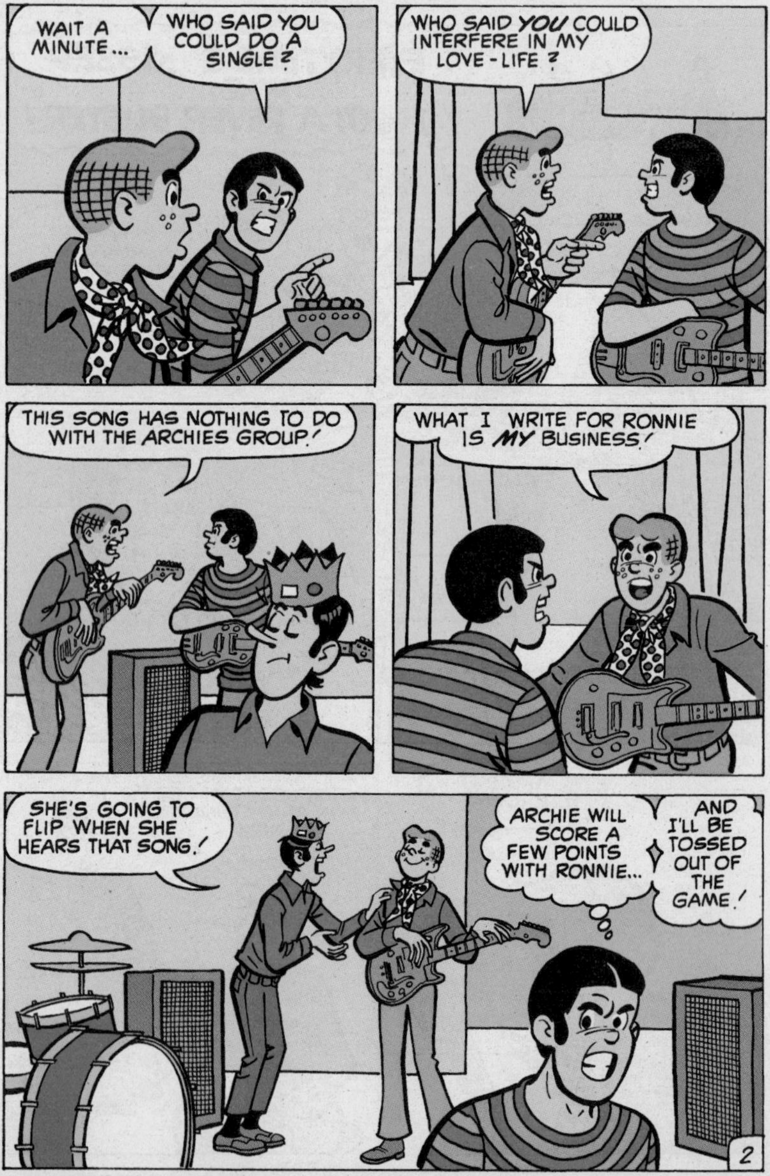
WAIT A MINUTE...
WHO SAID YOU COULD DO A SINGLE?
WHO SAID YOU COULD INTERFERE IN MY LOVE-LIFE?
THIS SONG HAS NOTHING TO DO WITH THE ARCHIES GROUP!
WHAT I WRITE FOR RONNIE IS MY BUSINESS!
SHE'S GOING TO FLIP WHEN SHE HEARS THAT SONG!
ARCHIE WILL SCORE A FEW POINTS WITH RONNIE...
AND I'LL BE TOSSED OUT OF THE GAME!
2

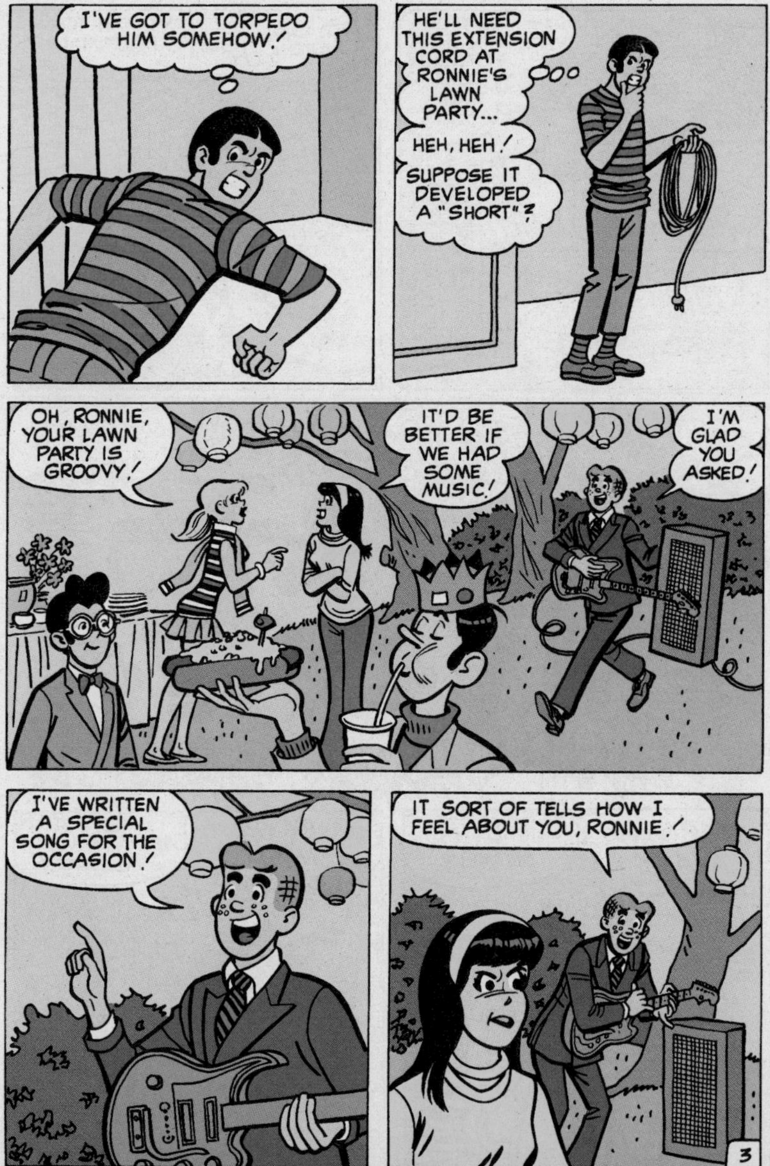
I'VE GOT TO TORPEDO HIM SOMEHOW!
HE'LL NEED THIS EXTENSION CORD AT RONNIE'S LAWN PARTY...
HEH, HEH!
SUPPOSE IT DEVELOPED A "SHORT"?
OH, RONNIE, YOUR LAWN PARTY IS GROOVY!
IT'D BE BETTER IF WE HAD SOME MUSIC!
I'M GLAD YOU ASKED!
I'VE WRITTEN A SPECIAL SONG FOR THE OCCASION!
IT SORT OF TELLS HOW I FEEL ABOUT YOU, RONNIE!
3

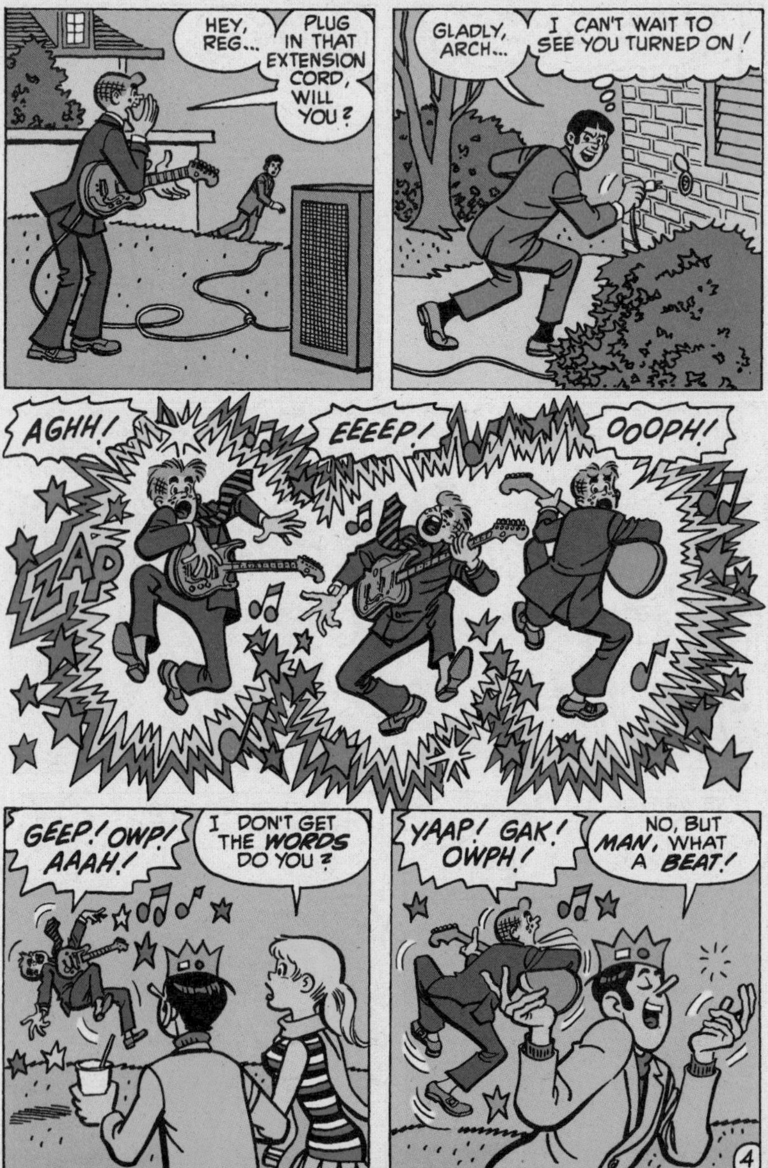
HEY, REG...
PLUG IN THAT EXTENSION CORD, WILL YOU?
GLADLY, ARCH...
I CAN'T WAIT TO SEE YOU TURNED ON!
AGHH!
EEEEP!
OOOPH!
ZAP
GEEP! OWP! AAAH!
I DON'T GET THE WORDS DO YOU?
YAAP! GAK! OWPH!
NO, BUT MAN, WHAT A BEAT!

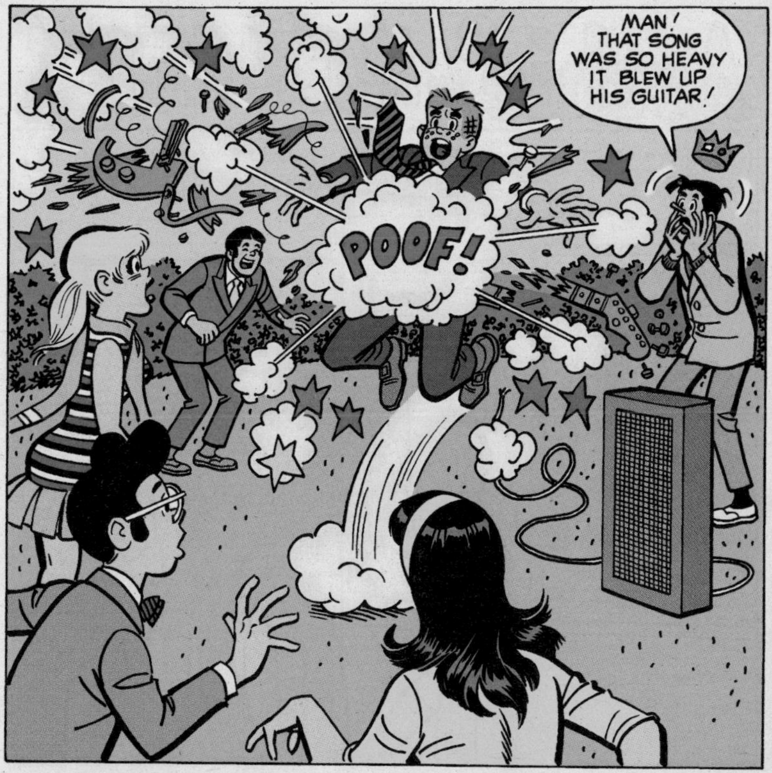
POOF!
MAN! THAT SONG WAS SO HEAVY IT BLEW UP HIS GUITAR!

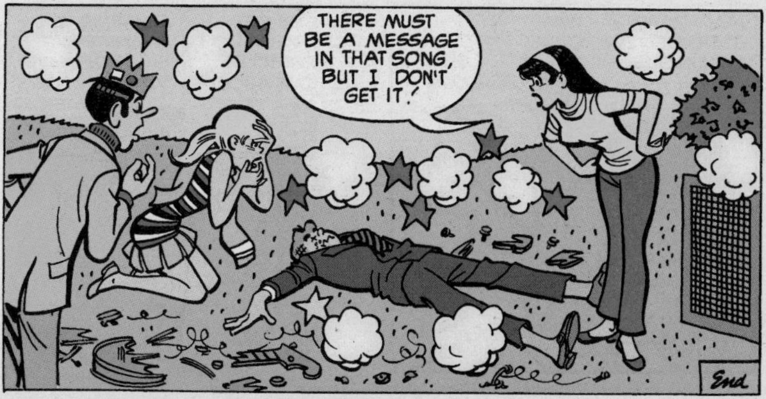
THERE MUST BE A MESSAGE IN THAT SONG, BUT I DON'T GET IT!
End

Archie in The Music Critics

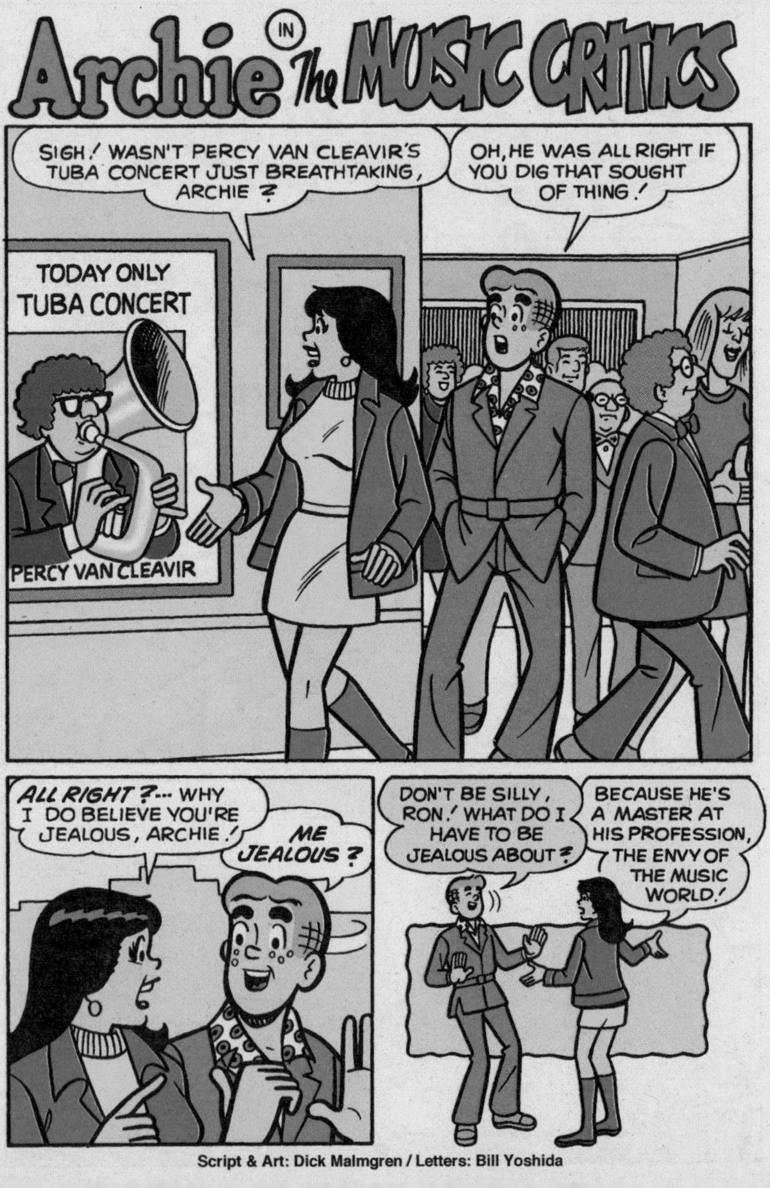
SIGH! WASN'T PERCY VAN CLEAVIR'S TUBA CONCERT JUST BREATHTAKING, ARCHIE ?
OH, HE WAS ALL RIGHT IF YOU DIG THAT SOUGHT OF THING!
TODAY ONLY TUBA CONCERT
PERCY VAN CLEAVIR
ALL RIGHT ?--- WHY I DO BELIEVE YOU'RE JEALOUS, ARCHIE!
ME JEALOUS ?
DON'T BE SILLY, RON! WHAT DO I HAVE TO BE JEALOUS ABOUT ?
BECAUSE HE'S A MASTER AT HIS PROFESSION, THE ENVY OF THE MUSIC WORLD!

Script & Art: Dick Malmgren / Letters: Bill Yoshida

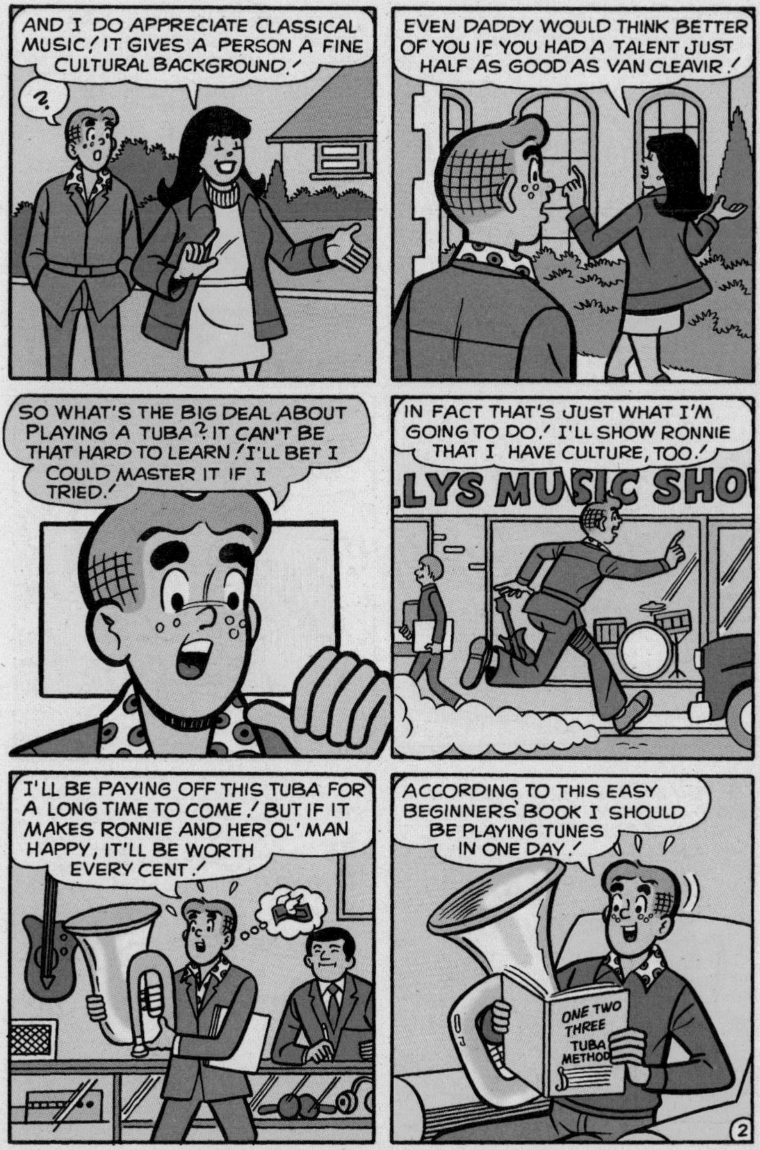
AND I DO APPRECIATE CLASSICAL MUSIC! IT GIVES A PERSON A FINE CULTURAL BACKGROUND!
?
EVEN DADDY WOULD THINK BETTER OF YOU IF YOU HAD A TALENT JUST HALF AS GOOD AS VAN CLEAVIR!
SO WHAT'S THE BIG DEAL ABOUT PLAYING A TUBA? IT CAN'T BE THAT HARD TO LEARN! I'LL BET I COULD MASTER IT IF I TRIED!
IN FACT THAT'S JUST WHAT I'M GOING TO DO! I'LL SHOW RONNIE THAT I HAVE CULTURE, TOO!
LYS MUSIC SHO
I'LL BE PAYING OFF THIS TUBA FOR A LONG TIME TO COME! BUT IF IT MAKES RONNIE AND HER OL' MAN HAPPY, IT'LL BE WORTH EVERY CENT!
ACCORDING TO THIS EASY BEGINNERS' BOOK I SHOULD BE PLAYING TUNES IN ONE DAY!
ONE TWO THREE TUBA METHOD
2

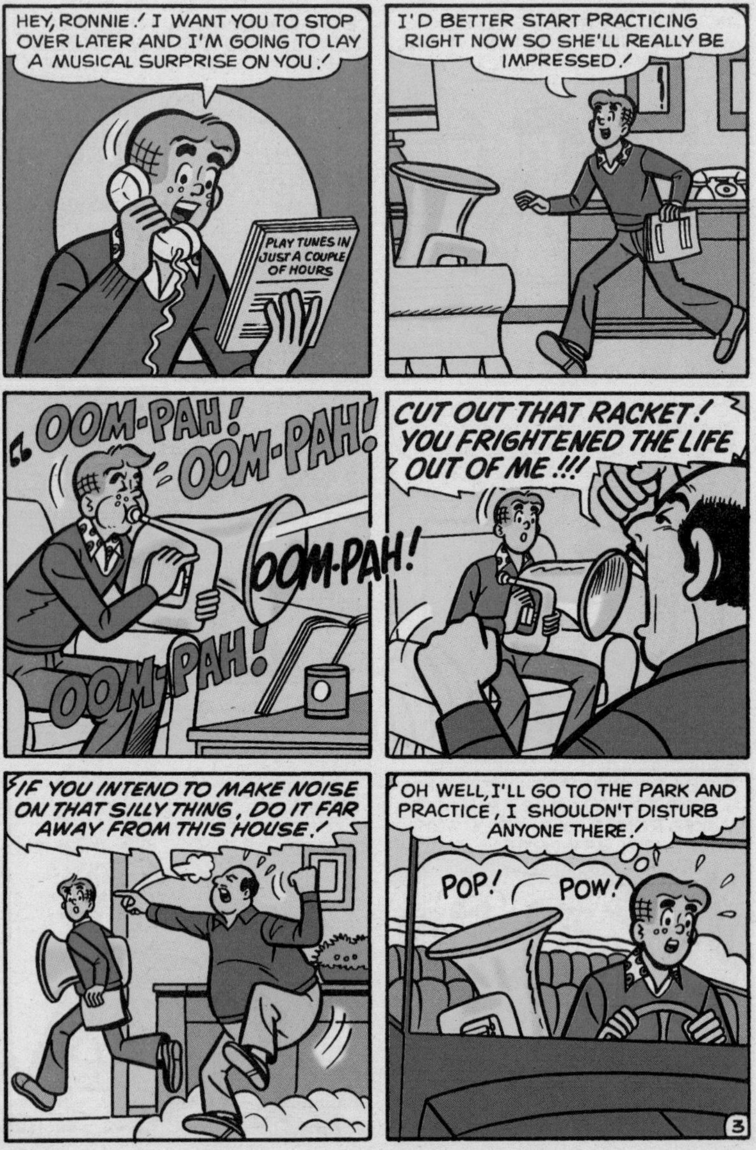
HEY, RONNIE! I WANT YOU TO STOP OVER LATER AND I'M GOING TO LAY A MUSICAL SURPRISE ON YOU!
PLAY TUNES IN JUST A COUPLE OF HOURS
I'D BETTER START PRACTICING RIGHT NOW SO SHE'LL REALLY BE IMPRESSED!
OOM-PAH! OOM-PAH!
OOM-PAH!
OOM-PAH!
CUT OUT THAT RACKET! YOU FRIGHTENED THE LIFE OUT OF ME!!!
IF YOU INTEND TO MAKE NOISE ON THAT SILLY THING, DO IT FAR AWAY FROM THIS HOUSE!
OH WELL, I'LL GO TO THE PARK AND PRACTICE, I SHOULDN'T DISTURB ANYONE THERE!
POP! POW!
3

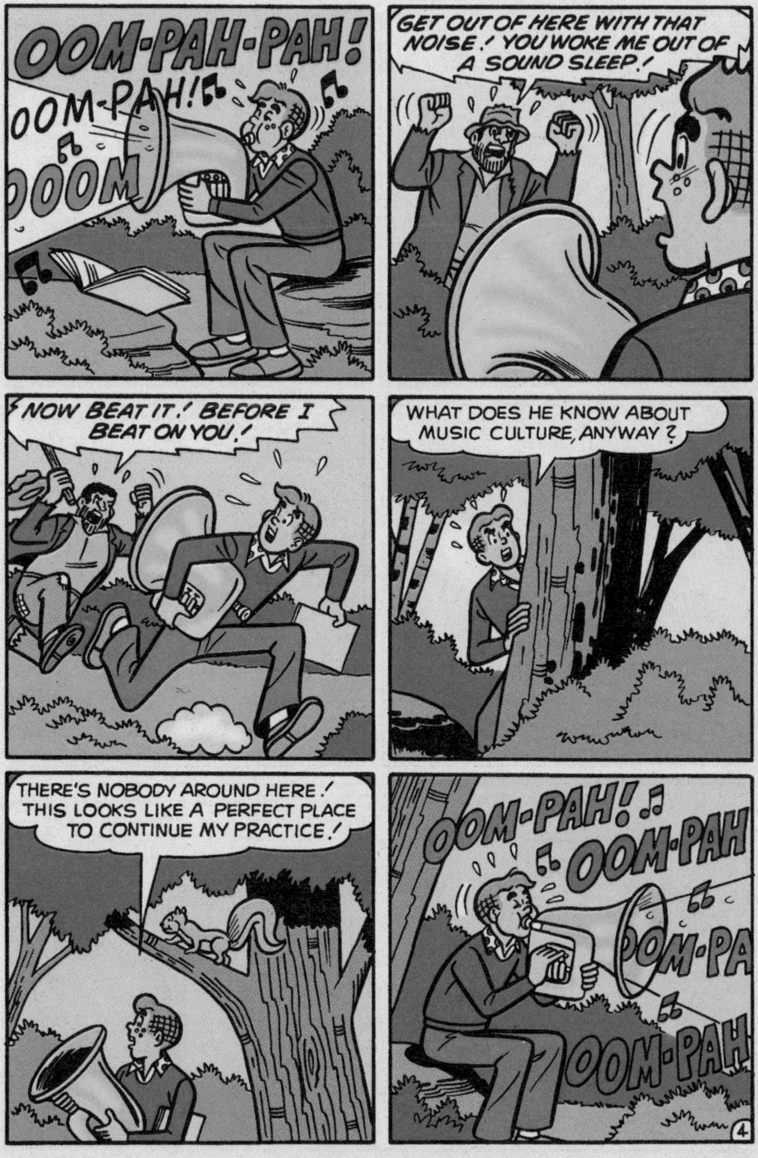
OOM-PAH-PAH!
OOM-PAH!
OOOM
GET OUT OF HERE WITH THAT NOISE! YOU WOKE ME OUT OF A SOUND SLEEP!
NOW BEAT IT! BEFORE I BEAT ON YOU!
WHAT DOES HE KNOW ABOUT MUSIC CULTURE, ANYWAY?
THERE'S NOBODY AROUND HERE! THIS LOOKS LIKE A PERFECT PLACE TO CONTINUE MY PRACTICE!
OOM-PAH!
OOM-PAH
OOM-PA
OOM-PAH
4

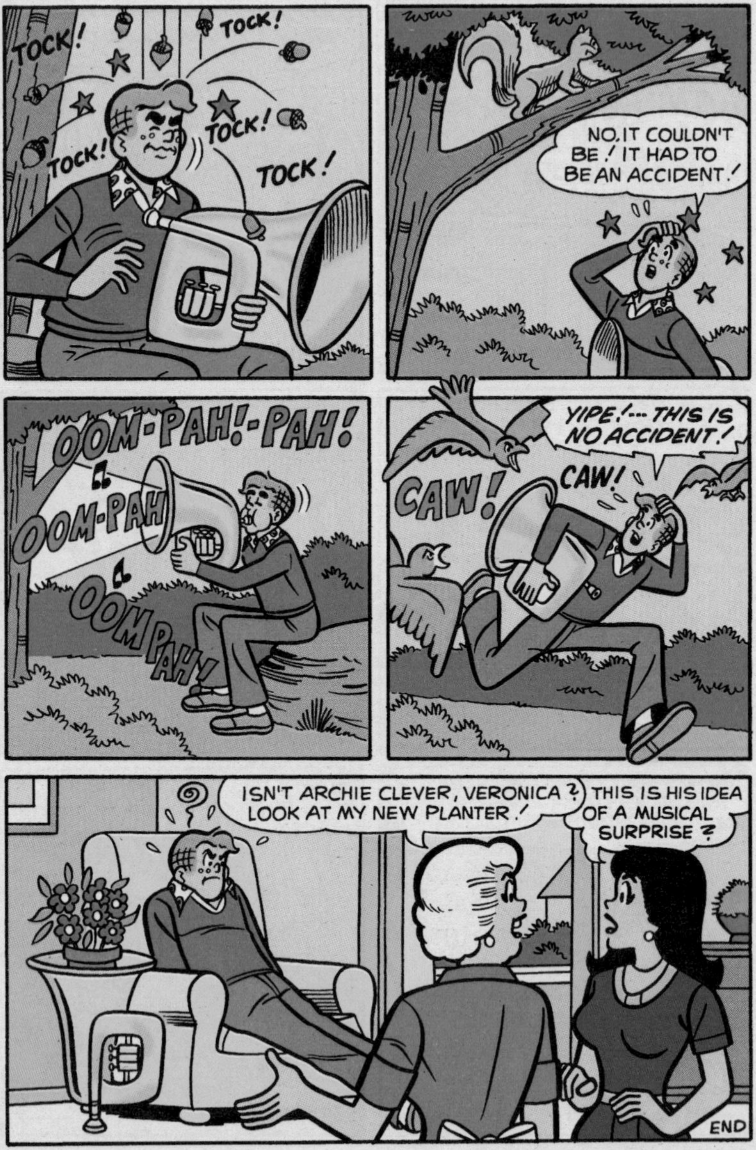
TOCK!
TOCK!
TOCK!
TOCK!
TOCK!
NO, IT COULDN'T BE! IT HAD TO BE AN ACCIDENT!
OOM-PAH!-PAH!
OOM-PAH
OOMPAH!
YIPE!--- THIS IS NO ACCIDENT!
CAW!
CAW!
ISN'T ARCHIE CLEVER, VERONICA? LOOK AT MY NEW PLANTER!
THIS IS HIS IDEA OF A MUSICAL SURPRISE?
END

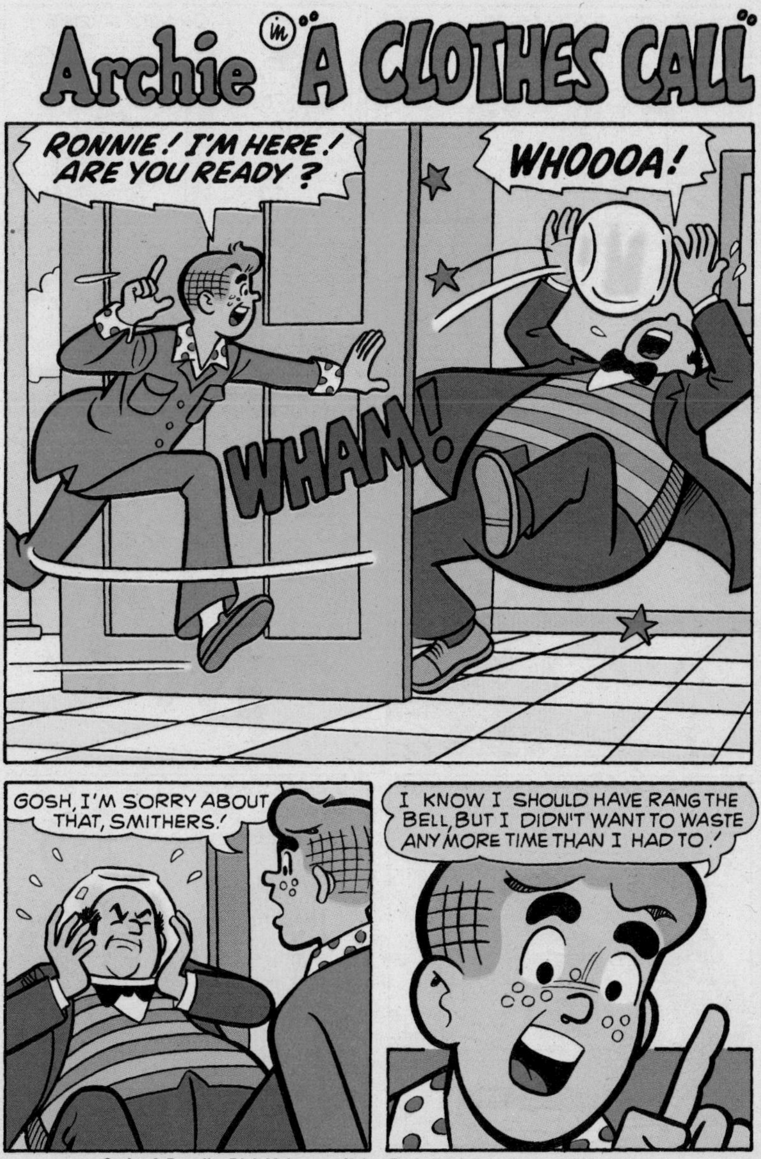
Archie in "A CLOTHES CALL"
RONNIE! I'M HERE! ARE YOU READY?
WHOOOA!
WHAM!
GOSH, I'M SORRY ABOUT THAT, SMITHERS!
I KNOW I SHOULD HAVE RANG THE BELL, BUT I DIDN'T WANT TO WASTE ANY MORE TIME THAN I HAD TO!

Script & Pencils: Dick Malmgren / Inks: Rudy Lapick / Letters: Bill Yoshida

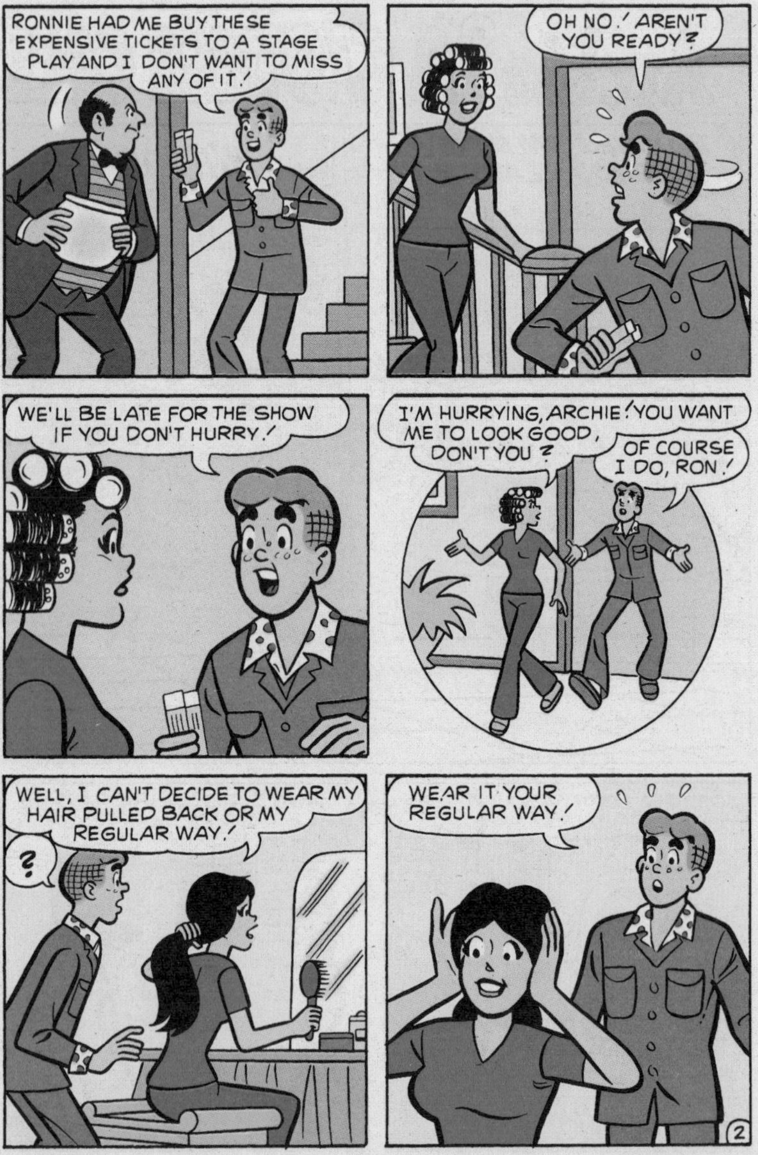
RONNIE HAD ME BUY THESE EXPENSIVE TICKETS TO A STAGE PLAY AND I DON'T WANT TO MISS ANY OF IT!
OH NO! AREN'T YOU READY?
WE'LL BE LATE FOR THE SHOW IF YOU DON'T HURRY!
I'M HURRYING, ARCHIE! YOU WANT ME TO LOOK GOOD, DON'T YOU?
OF COURSE I DO, RON!
WELL, I CAN'T DECIDE TO WEAR MY HAIR PULLED BACK OR MY REGULAR WAY!
?
WEAR IT YOUR REGULAR WAY!
2

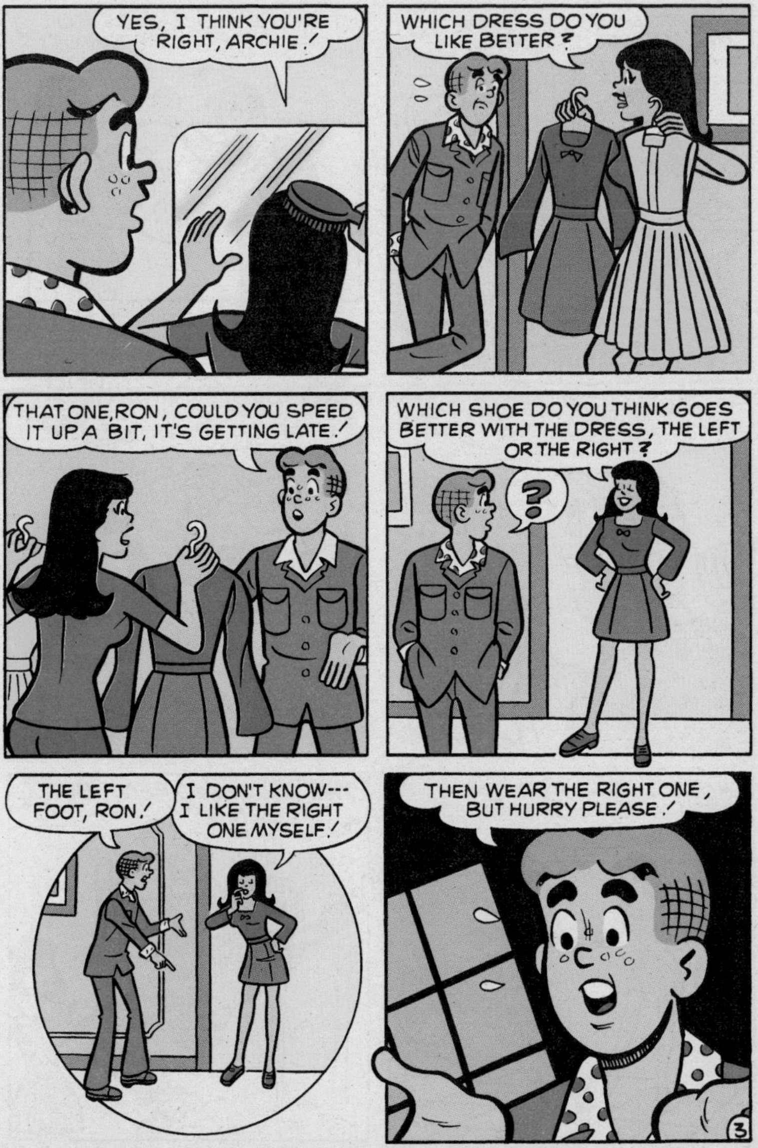
YES, I THINK YOU'RE RIGHT, ARCHIE.!
WHICH DRESS DO YOU LIKE BETTER?
THAT ONE, RON, COULD YOU SPEED IT UP A BIT, IT'S GETTING LATE.!
WHICH SHOE DO YOU THINK GOES BETTER WITH THE DRESS, THE LEFT OR THE RIGHT?
?
THE LEFT FOOT, RON.!
I DON'T KNOW--- I LIKE THE RIGHT ONE MYSELF.!
THEN WEAR THE RIGHT ONE, BUT HURRY PLEASE.!
3

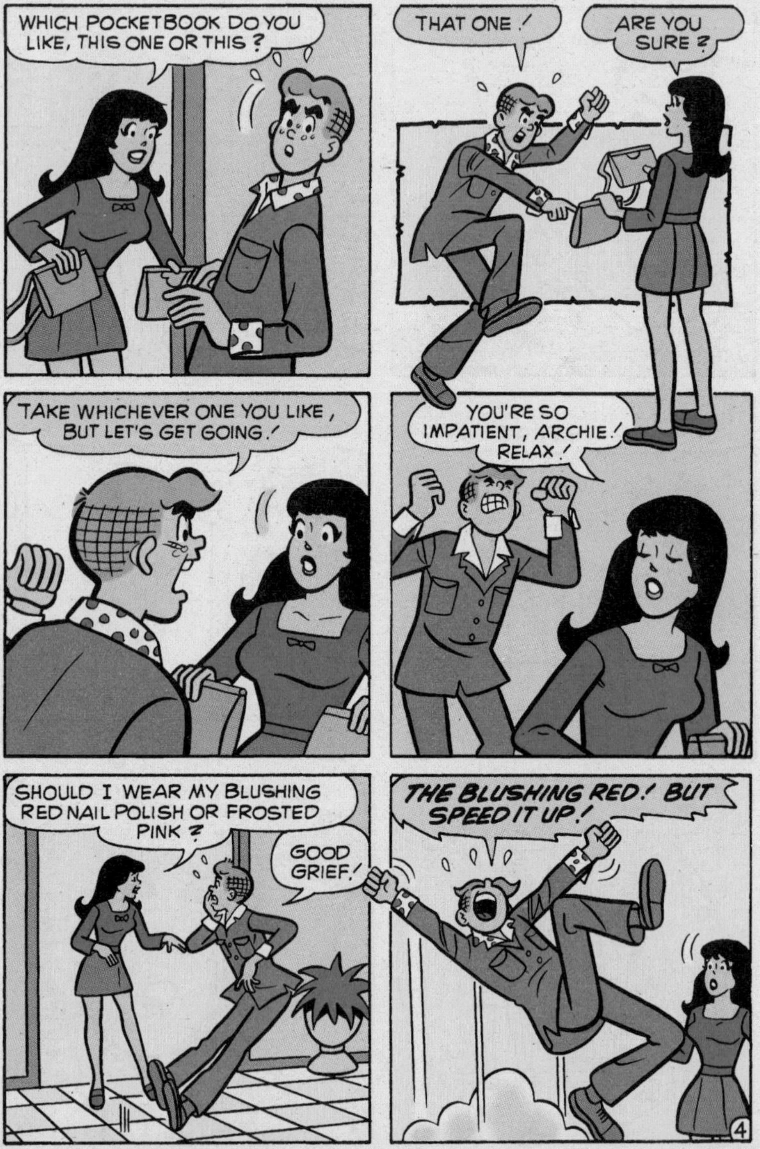
WHICH POCKETBOOK DO YOU LIKE, THIS ONE OR THIS ?
THAT ONE !
ARE YOU SURE ?
TAKE WHICHEVER ONE YOU LIKE, BUT LET'S GET GOING !
YOU'RE SO IMPATIENT, ARCHIE ! RELAX !
SHOULD I WEAR MY BLUSHING RED NAIL POLISH OR FROSTED PINK ?
GOOD GRIEF !
THE BLUSHING RED ! BUT SPEED IT UP !
4

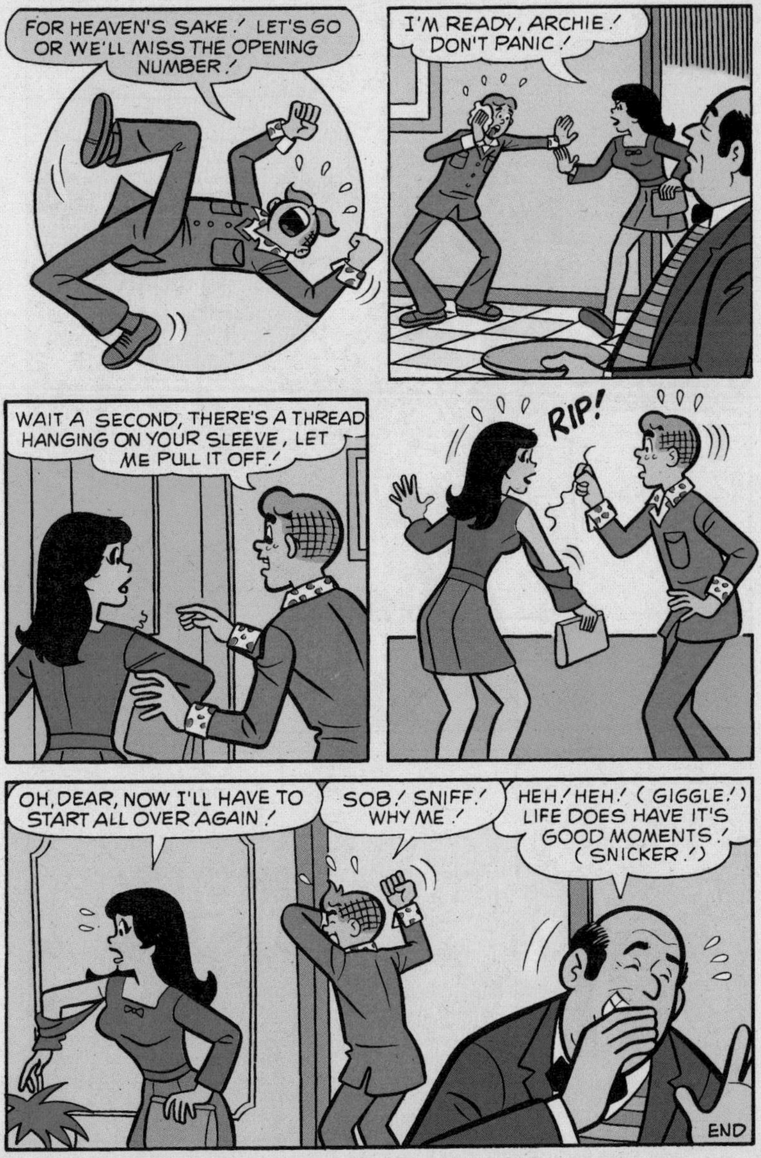
FOR HEAVEN'S SAKE! LET'S GO OR WE'LL MISS THE OPENING NUMBER!
I'M READY, ARCHIE! DON'T PANIC!
WAIT A SECOND, THERE'S A THREAD HANGING ON YOUR SLEEVE, LET ME PULL IT OFF!
RIP!
OH, DEAR, NOW I'LL HAVE TO START ALL OVER AGAIN!
SOB! SNIFF! WHY ME!
HEH! HEH! (GIGGLE!) LIFE DOES HAVE IT'S GOOD MOMENTS! (SNICKER!)
END

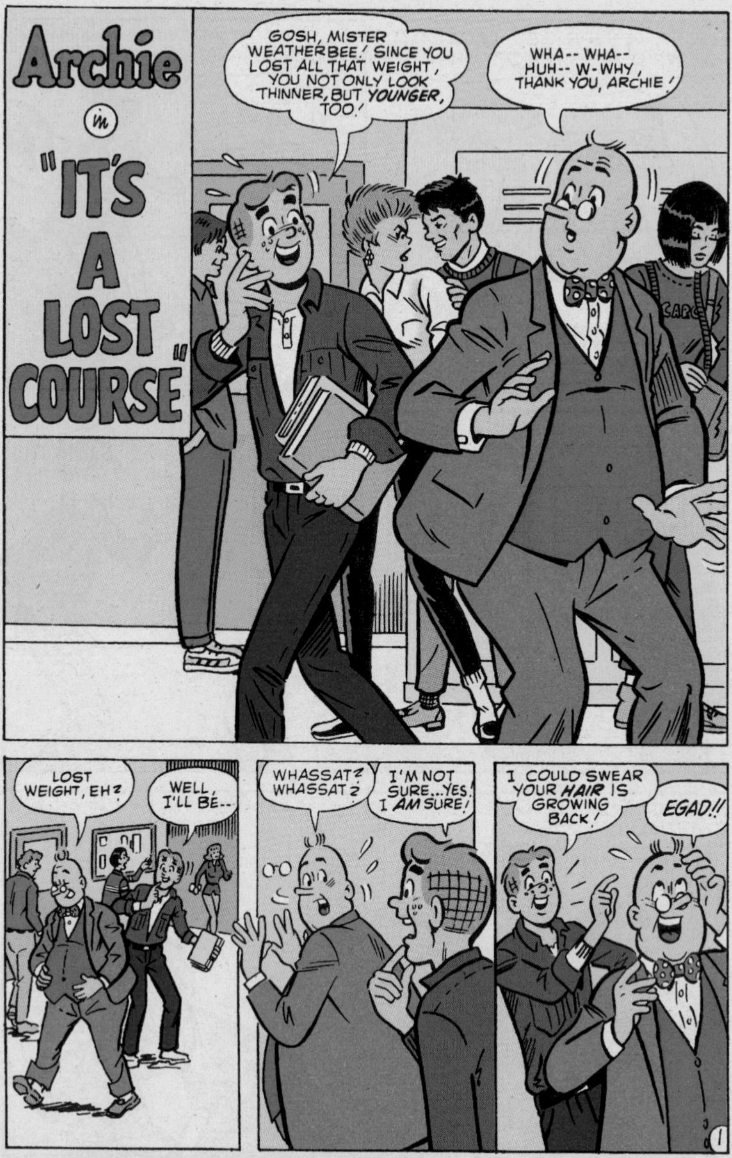
Archie
in
"IT'S A LOST COURSE"
GOSH, MISTER WEATHERBEE! SINCE YOU LOST ALL THAT WEIGHT, YOU NOT ONLY LOOK THINNER, BUT YOUNGER, TOO!
WHA-- WHA-- HUH-- W-WHY, THANK YOU, ARCHIE!
LOST WEIGHT, EH?
WELL, I'LL BE--
WHASSAT? WHASSAT?
I'M NOT SURE...YES! I AM SURE!
I COULD SWEAR YOUR HAIR IS GROWING BACK!
EGAD!!
1

Script: Frank Doyle / Pencils: Nate Butler / Inks: Rudy Lapick / Letters: Bill Yoshida

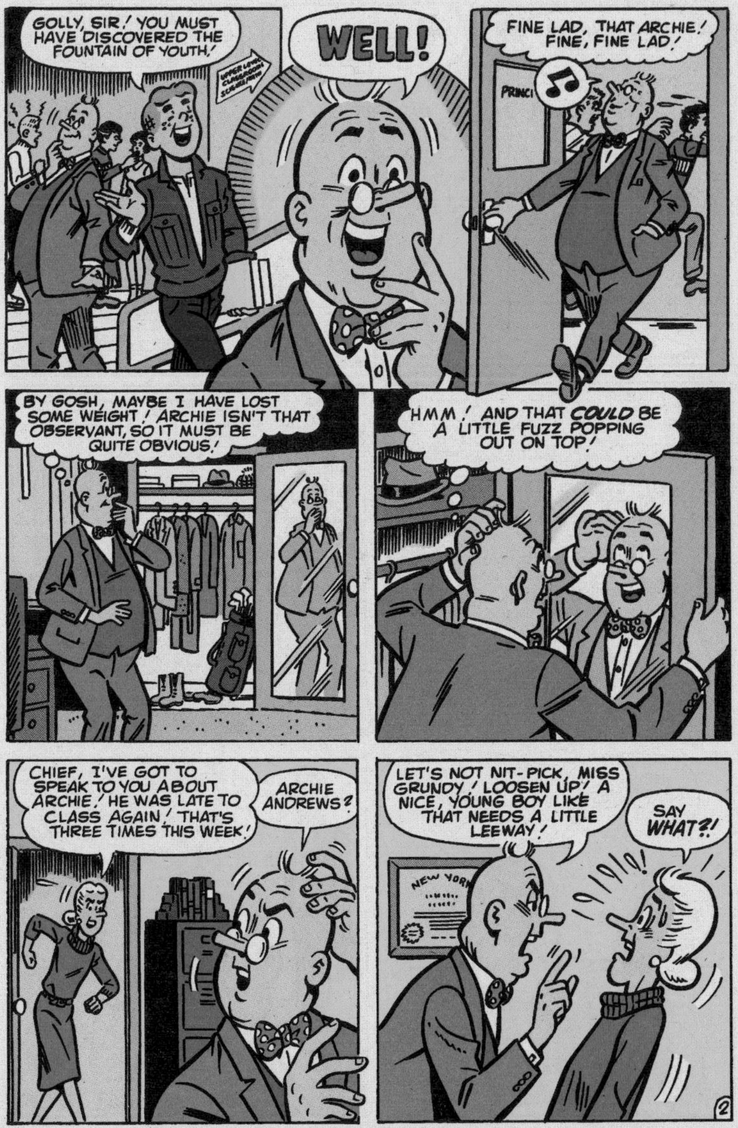
GOLLY, SIR! YOU MUST HAVE DISCOVERED THE FOUNTAIN OF YOUTH!
WELL!
FINE LAD, THAT ARCHIE! FINE, FINE LAD!
PRINCI
BY GOSH, MAYBE I HAVE LOST SOME WEIGHT! ARCHIE ISN'T THAT OBSERVANT, SO IT MUST BE QUITE OBVIOUS!
HMM! AND THAT COULD BE A LITTLE FUZZ POPPING OUT ON TOP!
CHIEF, I'VE GOT TO SPEAK TO YOU ABOUT ARCHIE! HE WAS LATE TO CLASS AGAIN! THAT'S THREE TIMES THIS WEEK!
ARCHIE ANDREWS?
LET'S NOT NIT-PICK, MISS GRUNDY! LOOSEN UP! A NICE, YOUNG BOY LIKE THAT NEEDS A LITTLE LEEWAY!
SAY WHAT?!
NEW YORK

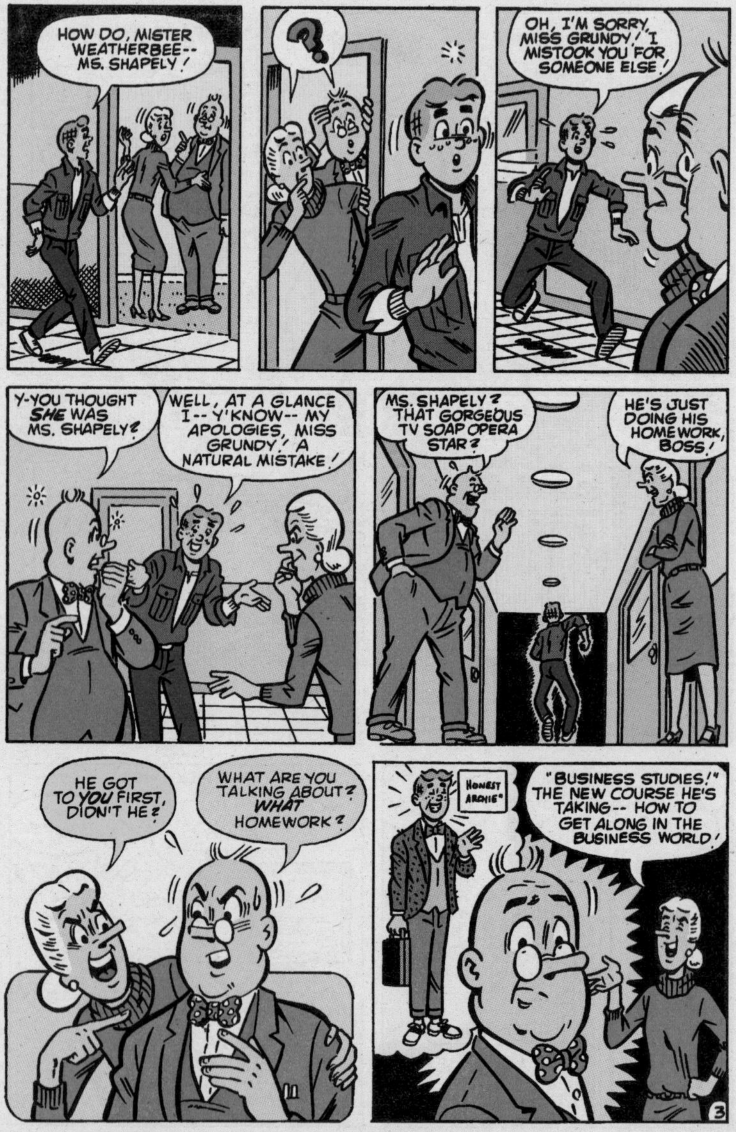
HOW DO, MISTER WEATHERBEE-- MS. SHAPELY!
?
OH, I'M SORRY, MISS GRUNDY! I MISTOOK YOU FOR SOMEONE ELSE!
Y-YOU THOUGHT SHE WAS MS. SHAPELY?
WELL, AT A GLANCE I-- Y'KNOW-- MY APOLOGIES, MISS GRUNDY! A NATURAL MISTAKE!
MS. SHAPELY? THAT GORGEOUS TV SOAP OPERA STAR?
HE'S JUST DOING HIS HOMEWORK, BOSS!
HE GOT TO YOU FIRST, DIDN'T HE?
WHAT ARE YOU TALKING ABOUT? WHAT HOMEWORK?
HONEST ARCHIE"
"BUSINESS STUDIES!" THE NEW COURSE HE'S TAKING-- HOW TO GET ALONG IN THE BUSINESS WORLD!
3

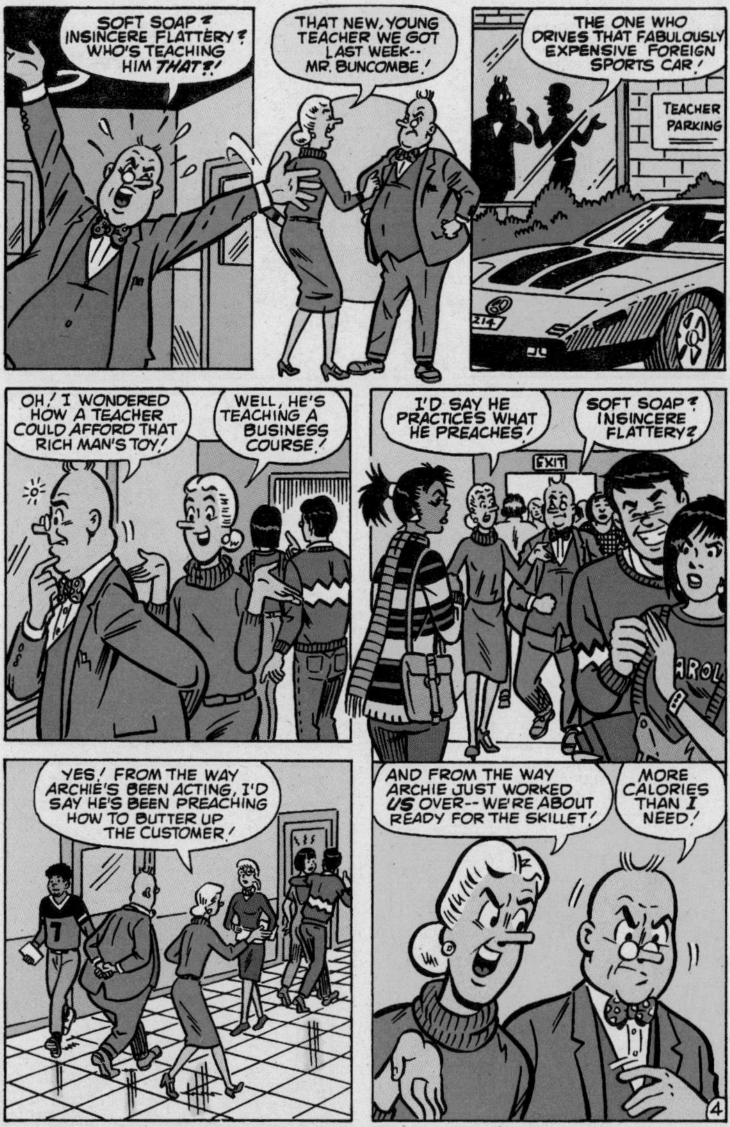
SOFT SOAP? INSINCERE FLATTERY? WHO'S TEACHING HIM THAT?!
THAT NEW, YOUNG TEACHER WE GOT LAST WEEK-- MR. BUNCOMBE!
THE ONE WHO DRIVES THAT FABULOUSLY EXPENSIVE FOREIGN SPORTS CAR!
TEACHER PARKING
OH! I WONDERED HOW A TEACHER COULD AFFORD THAT RICH MAN'S TOY!
WELL, HE'S TEACHING A BUSINESS COURSE!
I'D SAY HE PRACTICES WHAT HE PREACHES!
EXIT
SOFT SOAP? INSINCERE FLATTERY?
YES! FROM THE WAY ARCHIE'S BEEN ACTING, I'D SAY HE'S BEEN PREACHING HOW TO BUTTER UP THE CUSTOMER!
AND FROM THE WAY ARCHIE JUST WORKED US OVER-- WE'RE ABOUT READY FOR THE SKILLET!
MORE CALORIES THAN I NEED!
4

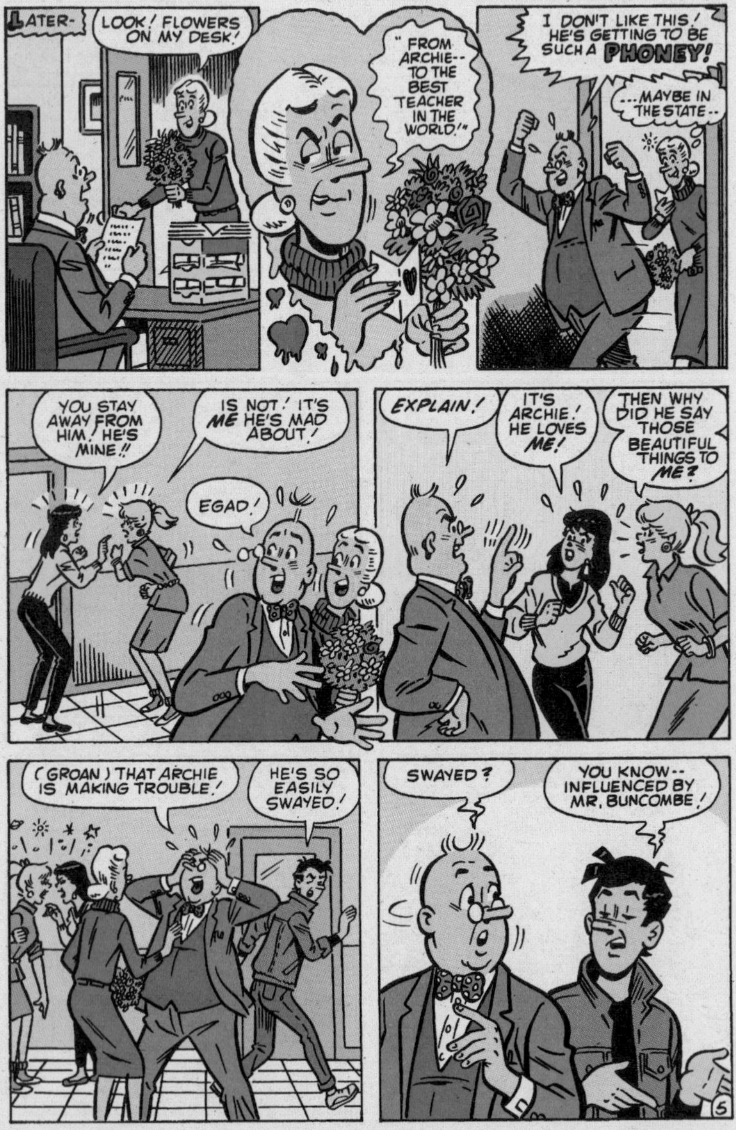
LATER-
LOOK! FLOWERS ON MY DESK!
" FROM ARCHIE-- TO THE BEST TEACHER IN THE WORLD!"
I DON'T LIKE THIS! HE'S GETTING TO BE SUCH A PHONEY!
...MAYBE IN THE STATE--
YOU STAY AWAY FROM HIM! HE'S MINE!!
IS NOT! IT'S ME HE'S MAD ABOUT!
EGAD!
EXPLAIN!
IT'S ARCHIE! HE LOVES ME!
THEN WHY DID HE SAY THOSE BEAUTIFUL THINGS TO ME?
(GROAN) THAT ARCHIE IS MAKING TROUBLE!
HE'S SO EASILY SWAYED!
SWAYED?
YOU KNOW-- INFLUENCED BY MR. BUNCOMBE!
5

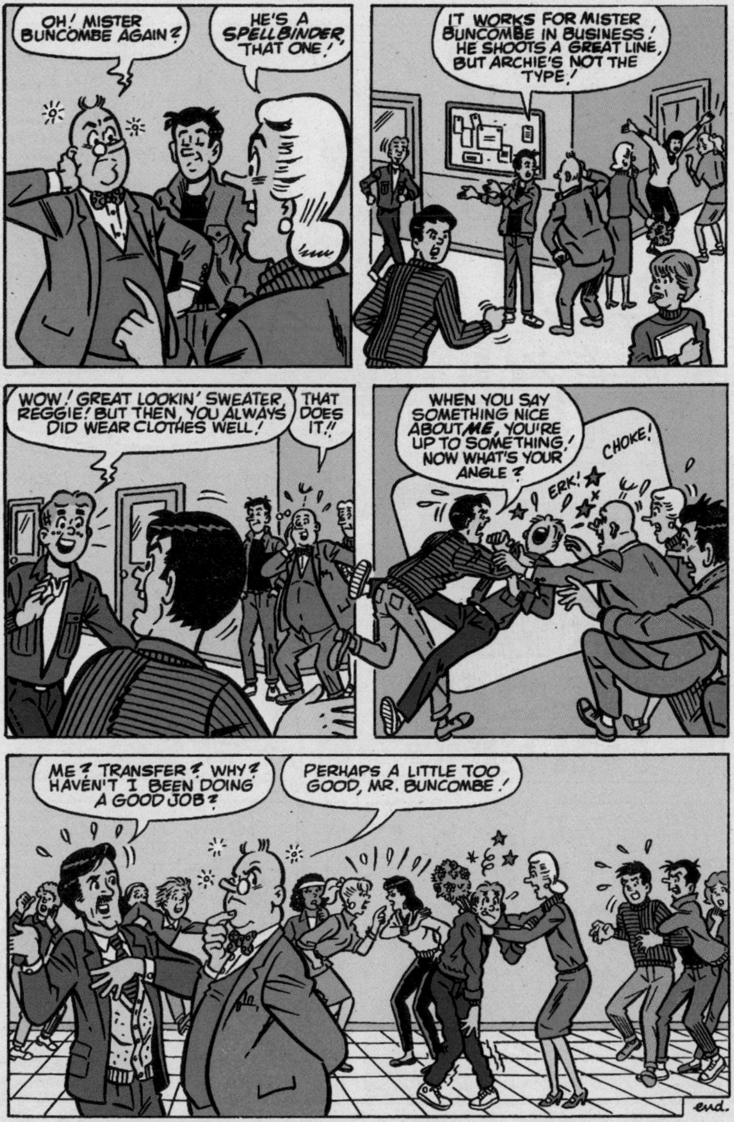

OH! MISTER BUNCOMBE AGAIN?
HE'S A SPELLBINDER, THAT ONE!
IT WORKS FOR MISTER BUNCOMBE IN BUSINESS! HE SHOOTS A GREAT LINE, BUT ARCHIE'S NOT THE TYPE!
WOW! GREAT LOOKIN' SWEATER, REGGIE! BUT THEN, YOU ALWAYS DID WEAR CLOTHES WELL!
THAT DOES IT!!
WHEN YOU SAY SOMETHING NICE ABOUT ME, YOU'RE UP TO SOMETHING! NOW WHAT'S YOUR ANGLE?
CHOKE!
ERK!
ME? TRANSFER? WHY? HAVEN'T I BEEN DOING A GOOD JOB?
PERHAPS A LITTLE TOO GOOD, MR. BUNCOMBE!
end.

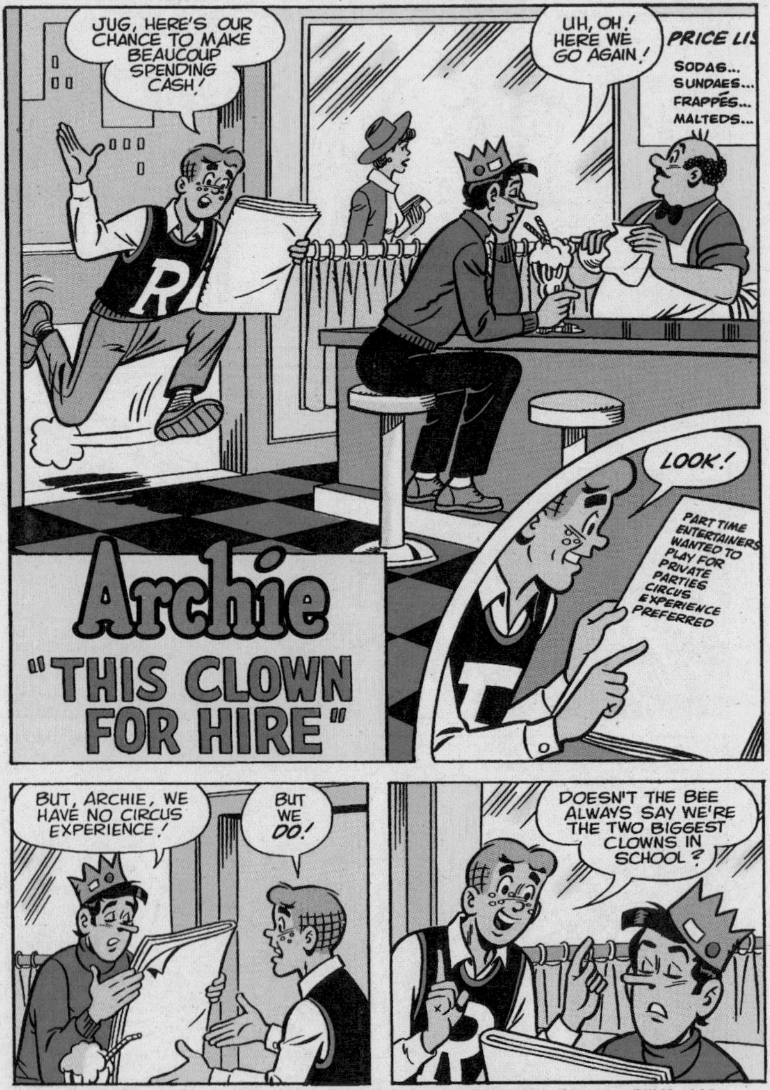
JUG, HERE'S OUR CHANCE TO MAKE BEAUCOUP SPENDING CASH!
UH, OH! HERE WE GO AGAIN!
PRICE LIS
SODAS... SUNDAES... FRAPPÉS... MALTEDS...
LOOK!
PART TIME ENTERTAINERS WANTED TO PLAY FOR PRIVATE PARTIES CIRCUS EXPERIENCE PREFERRED
Archie
"THIS CLOWN FOR HIRE"
BUT, ARCHIE, WE HAVE NO CIRCUS EXPERIENCE!
BUT WE DO!
DOESN'T THE BEE ALWAYS SAY WE'RE THE TWO BIGGEST CLOWNS IN SCHOOL?

Script: George Gladir / Pencils: Hy Eisman / Inks: Jon D'Agostino / Letters: Bill Yoshida

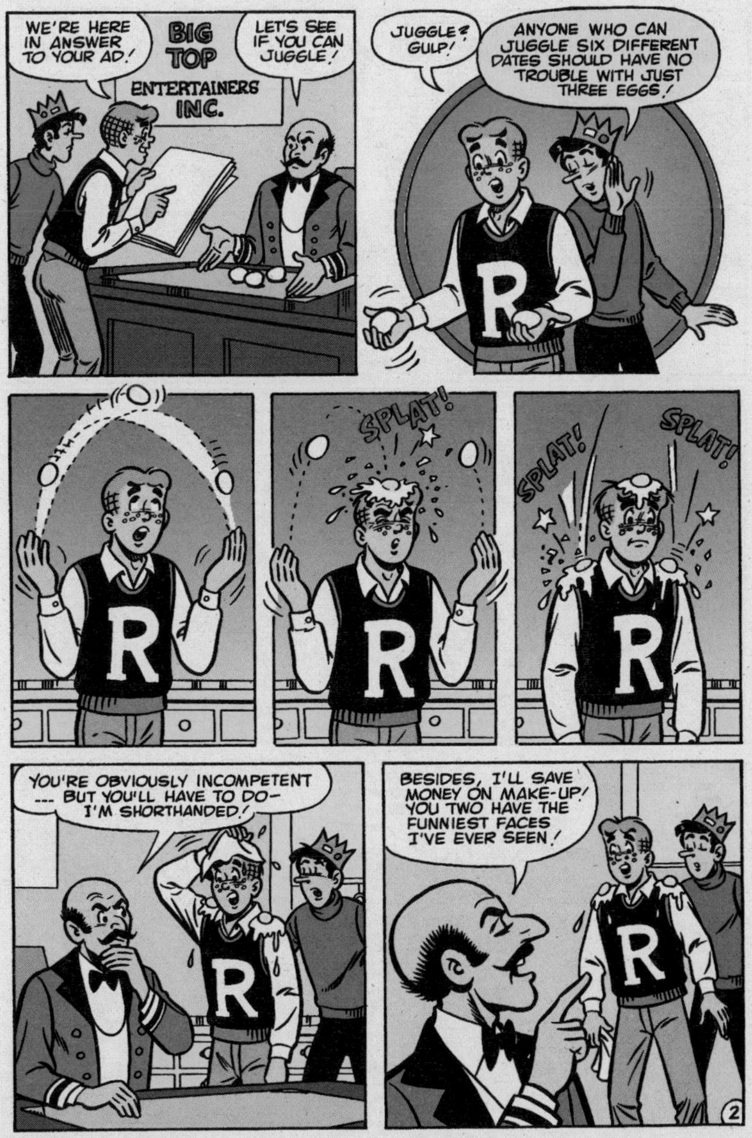
WE'RE HERE IN ANSWER TO YOUR AD!
BIG TOP ENTERTAINERS INC.
LET'S SEE IF YOU CAN JUGGLE!
JUGGLE? GULP!
ANYONE WHO CAN JUGGLE SIX DIFFERENT DATES SHOULD HAVE NO TROUBLE WITH JUST THREE EGGS!
SPLAT!
SPLAT!
SPLAT!
YOU'RE OBVIOUSLY INCOMPETENT --- BUT YOU'LL HAVE TO DO- I'M SHORTHANDED!
BESIDES, I'LL SAVE MONEY ON MAKE-UP! YOU TWO HAVE THE FUNNIEST FACES I'VE EVER SEEN!
2

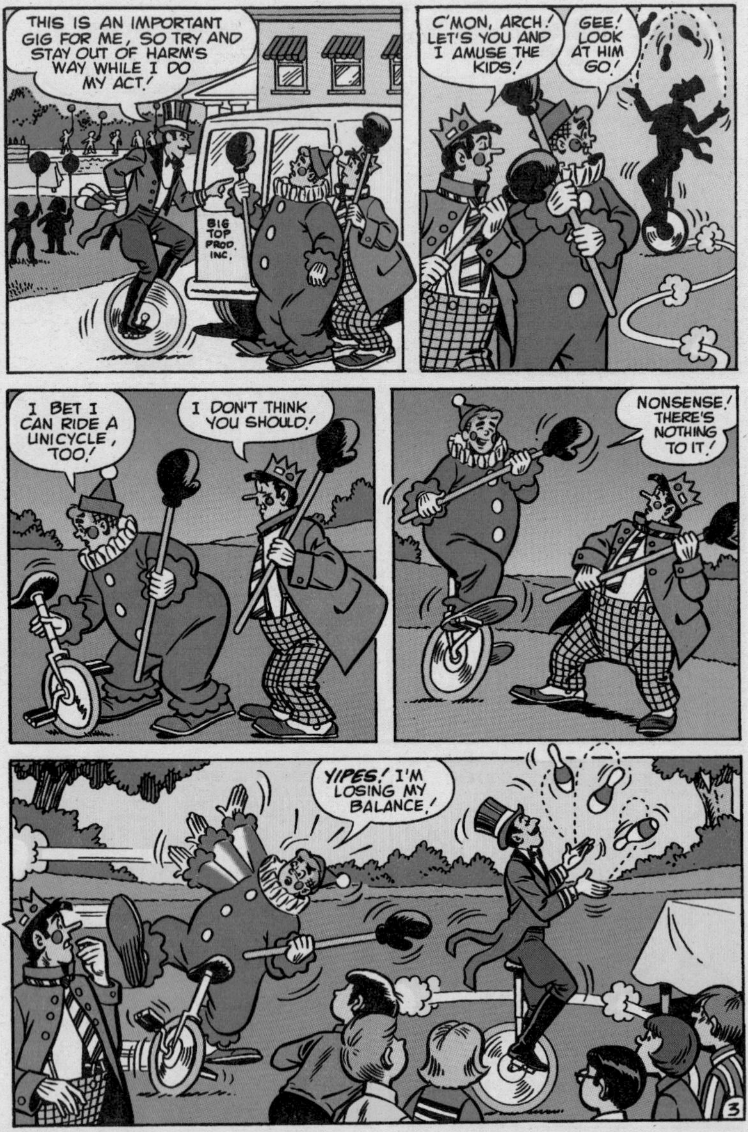
THIS IS AN IMPORTANT GIG FOR ME, SO TRY AND STAY OUT OF HARM'S WAY WHILE I DO MY ACT!
BIG TOP PROD. INC.
C'MON, ARCH! LET'S YOU AND I AMUSE THE KIDS!
GEE! LOOK AT HIM GO!
I BET I CAN RIDE A UNICYCLE, TOO!
I DON'T THINK YOU SHOULD!
NONSENSE! THERE'S NOTHING TO IT!
YIPES! I'M LOSING MY BALANCE!
3

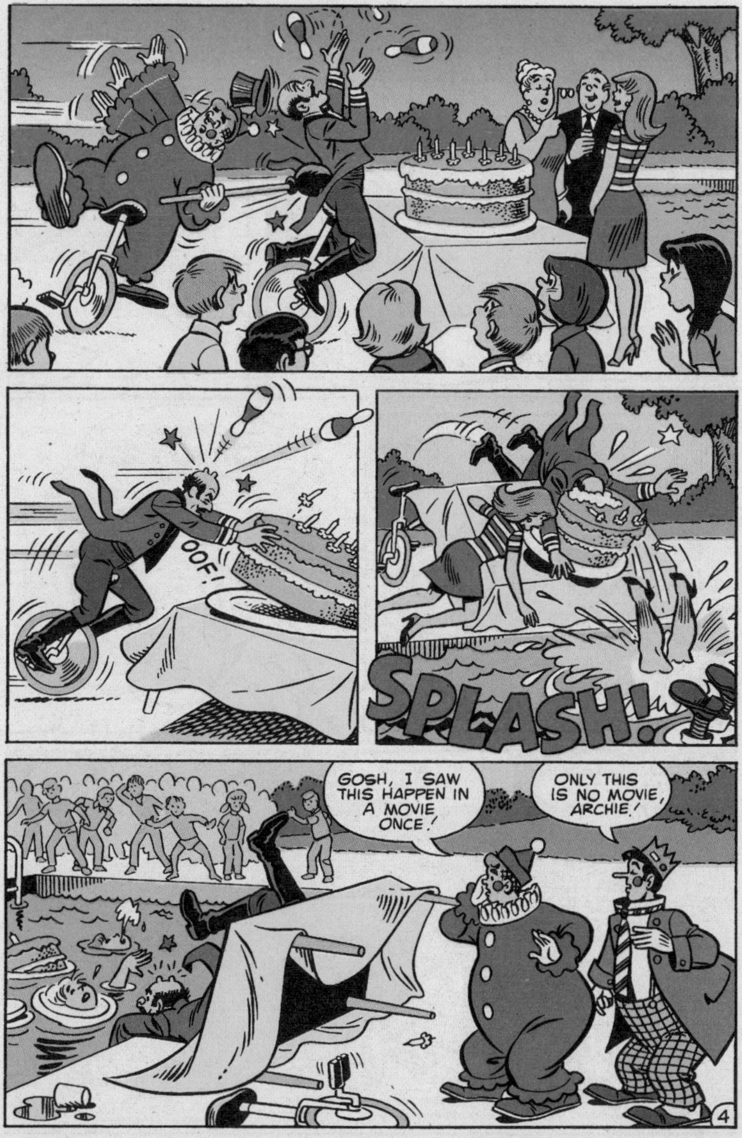

OOF!
SPLASH!
GOSH, I SAW THIS HAPPEN IN A MOVIE ONCE!
ONLY THIS IS NO MOVIE, ARCHIE!

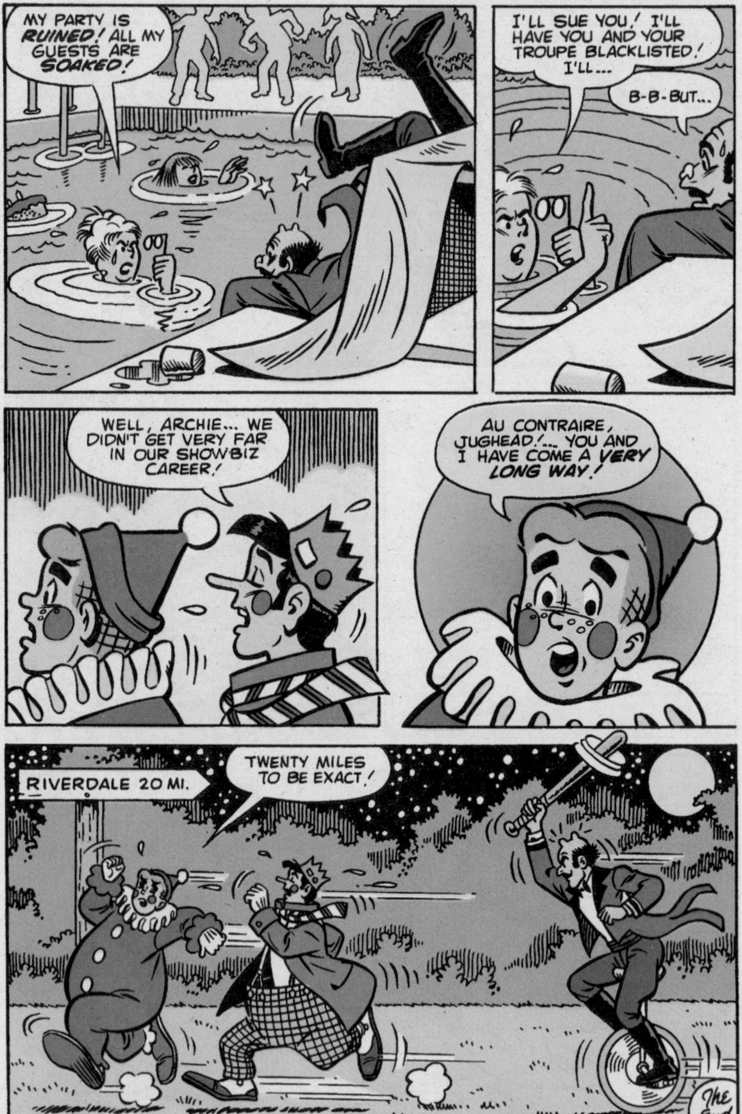
MY PARTY IS RUINED! ALL MY GUESTS ARE SOAKED!
I'LL SUE YOU! I'LL HAVE YOU AND YOUR TROUPE BLACKLISTED! I'LL...
B-B-BUT...
WELL, ARCHIE... WE DIDN'T GET VERY FAR IN OUR SHOWBIZ CAREER!
AU CONTRAIRE, JUGHEAD!... YOU AND I HAVE COME A VERY LONG WAY!
RIVERDALE 20 MI.
TWENTY MILES TO BE EXACT!
The End

Betty and Veronica in "The First 100 Years"

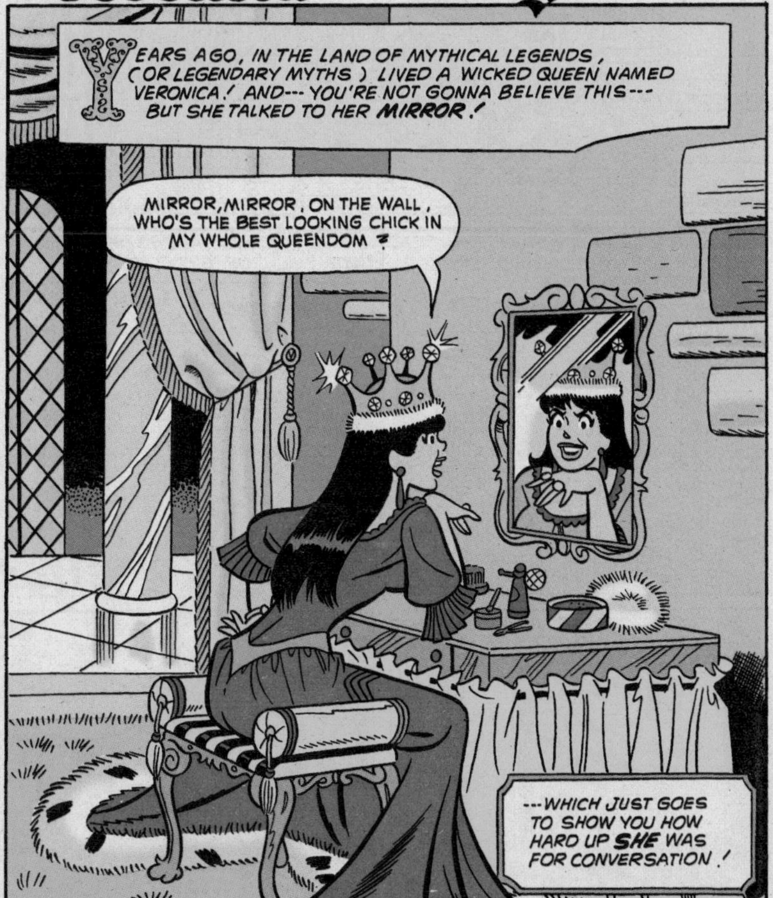

YEARS AGO, IN THE LAND OF MYTHICAL LEGENDS, (OR LEGENDARY MYTHS) LIVED A WICKED QUEEN NAMED VERONICA! AND--- YOU'RE NOT GONNA BELIEVE THIS--- BUT SHE TALKED TO HER MIRROR!
MIRROR, MIRROR, ON THE WALL, WHO'S THE BEST LOOKING CHICK IN MY WHOLE QUEENDOM?
---WHICH JUST GOES TO SHOW YOU HOW HARD UP SHE WAS FOR CONVERSATION!

Script: Frank Doyle / Pencils: Dan DeCarlo / Inks: Jim DeCarlo / Letters: Bill Yoshida

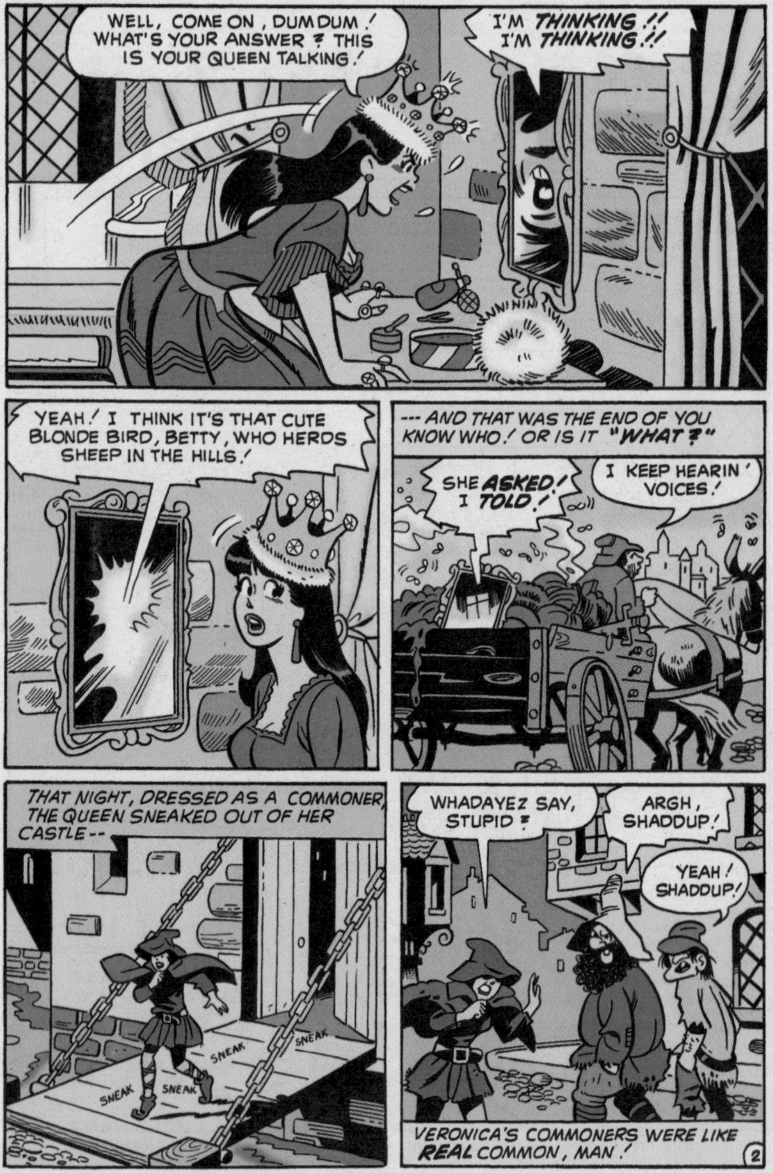
WELL, COME ON, DUMDUM! WHAT'S YOUR ANSWER? THIS IS YOUR QUEEN TALKING!
I'M THINKING!! I'M THINKING!!
YEAH! I THINK IT'S THAT CUTE BLONDE BIRD, BETTY, WHO HERDS SHEEP IN THE HILLS!
--- AND THAT WAS THE END OF YOU KNOW WHO! OR IS IT "WHAT?"
SHE ASKED! I TOLD!
I KEEP HEARIN' VOICES!
THAT NIGHT, DRESSED AS A COMMONER, THE QUEEN SNEAKED OUT OF HER CASTLE --
SNEAK
SNEAK
SNEAK
SNEAK
WHADAYEZ SAY, STUPID?
ARGH, SHADDUP!
YEAH! SHADDUP!
VERONICA'S COMMONERS WERE LIKE REAL COMMON, MAN!
2

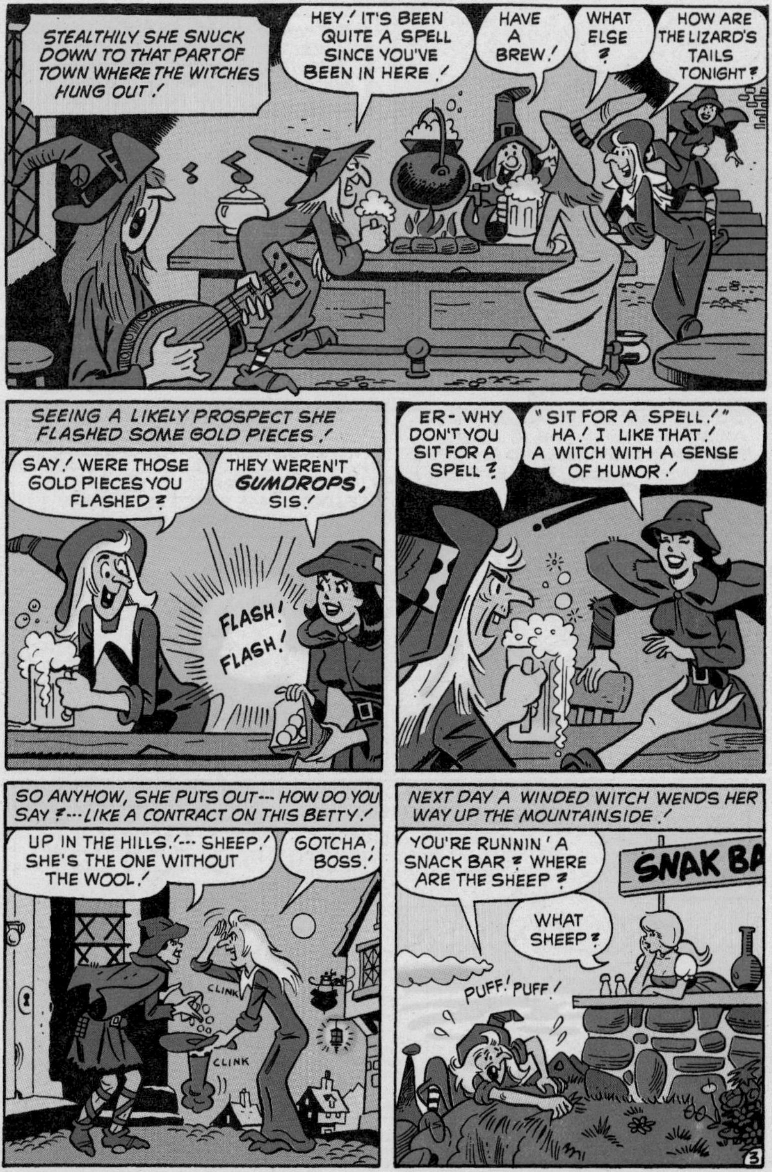
STEALTHILY SHE SNUCK DOWN TO THAT PART OF TOWN WHERE THE WITCHES HUNG OUT!
HEY! IT'S BEEN QUITE A SPELL SINCE YOU'VE BEEN IN HERE!
HAVE A BREW!
WHAT ELSE?
HOW ARE THE LIZARD'S TAILS TONIGHT?
SEEING A LIKELY PROSPECT SHE FLASHED SOME GOLD PIECES!
SAY! WERE THOSE GOLD PIECES YOU FLASHED?
THEY WEREN'T GUMDROPS, SIS!
FLASH! FLASH!
ER- WHY DON'T YOU SIT FOR A SPELL?
"SIT FOR A SPELL!" HA! I LIKE THAT! A WITCH WITH A SENSE OF HUMOR!
SO ANYHOW, SHE PUTS OUT--- HOW DO YOU SAY?--- LIKE A CONTRACT ON THIS BETTY!
UP IN THE HILLS!--- SHEEP! SHE'S THE ONE WITHOUT THE WOOL!
GOTCHA, BOSS!
CLINK
CLINK
NEXT DAY A WINDED WITCH WENDS HER WAY UP THE MOUNTAINSIDE!
SNAK BA
YOU'RE RUNNIN' A SNACK BAR? WHERE ARE THE SHEEP?
WHAT SHEEP?
PUFF! PUFF!
3

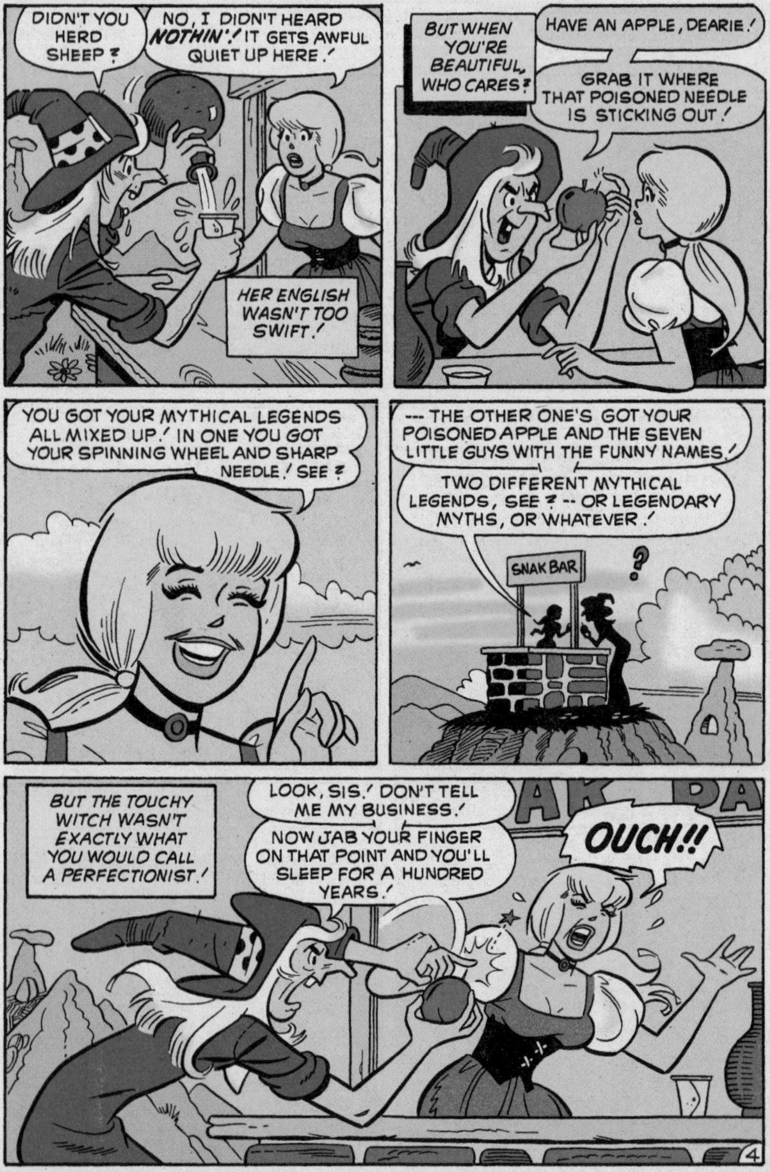
DIDN'T YOU HERD SHEEP ?
NO, I DIDN'T HEARD NOTHIN'! IT GETS AWFUL QUIET UP HERE!
HER ENGLISH WASN'T TOO SWIFT!
BUT WHEN YOU'RE BEAUTIFUL, WHO CARES?
HAVE AN APPLE, DEARIE!
GRAB IT WHERE THAT POISONED NEEDLE IS STICKING OUT!
YOU GOT YOUR MYTHICAL LEGENDS ALL MIXED UP! IN ONE YOU GOT YOUR SPINNING WHEEL AND SHARP NEEDLE! SEE ?
--- THE OTHER ONE'S GOT YOUR POISONED APPLE AND THE SEVEN LITTLE GUYS WITH THE FUNNY NAMES!
TWO DIFFERENT MYTHICAL LEGENDS, SEE ? -- OR LEGENDARY MYTHS, OR WHATEVER!
SNAK BAR
?
BUT THE TOUCHY WITCH WASN'T EXACTLY WHAT YOU WOULD CALL A PERFECTIONIST!
LOOK, SIS! DON'T TELL ME MY BUSINESS!
NOW JAB YOUR FINGER ON THAT POINT AND YOU'LL SLEEP FOR A HUNDRED YEARS!
OUCH!!
4

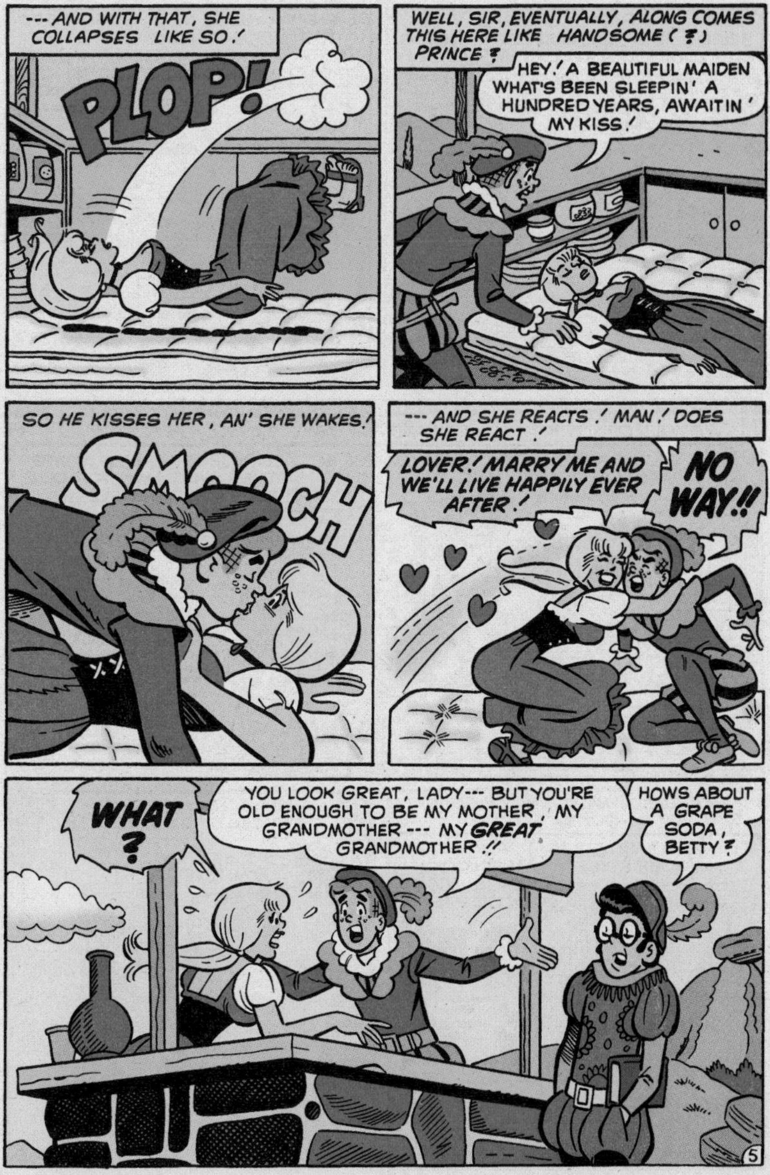
--- AND WITH THAT, SHE COLLAPSES LIKE SO.!
PLOP!
WELL, SIR, EVENTUALLY, ALONG COMES THIS HERE LIKE HANDSOME (?) PRINCE?
HEY.! A BEAUTIFUL MAIDEN WHAT'S BEEN SLEEPIN' A HUNDRED YEARS, AWAITIN' MY KISS.!
SO HE KISSES HER, AN' SHE WAKES.!
SMOOCH
--- AND SHE REACTS.! MAN.! DOES SHE REACT.!
LOVER.! MARRY ME AND WE'LL LIVE HAPPILY EVER AFTER.!
NO WAY.!!
WHAT?
YOU LOOK GREAT, LADY--- BUT YOU'RE OLD ENOUGH TO BE MY MOTHER, MY GRANDMOTHER --- MY GREAT GRANDMOTHER.!!
HOWS ABOUT A GRAPE SODA, BETTY?
5

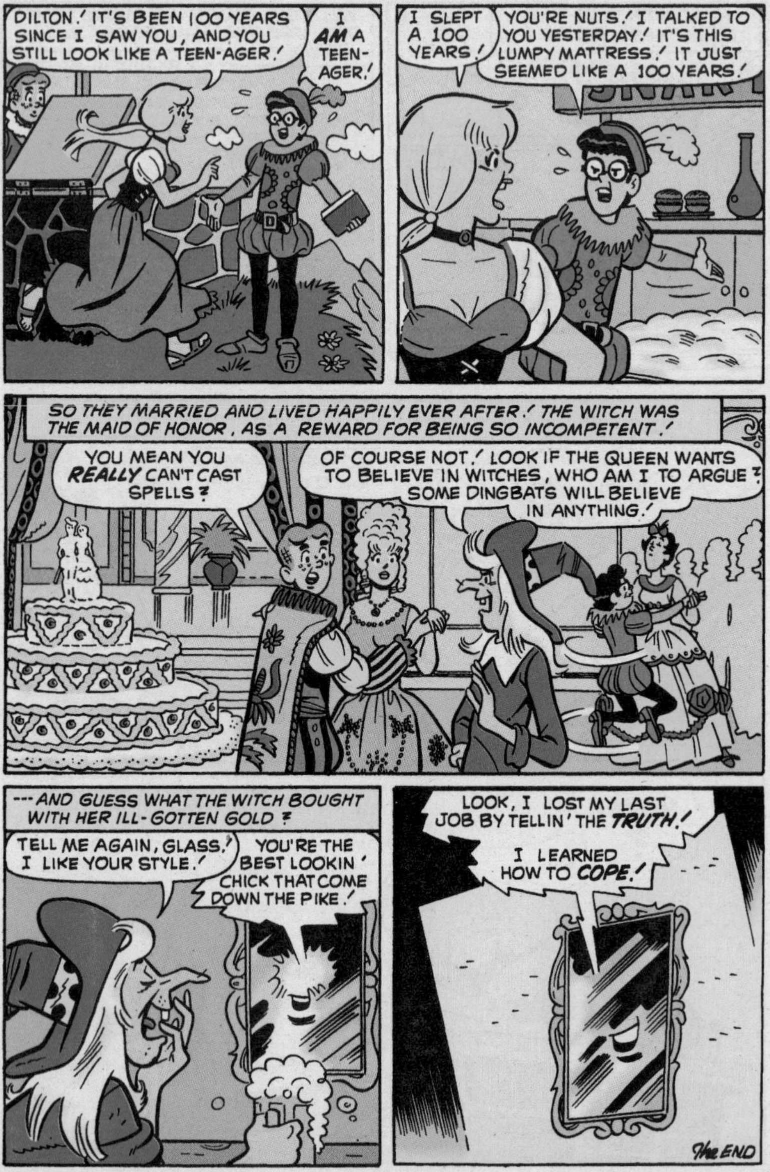

DILTON! IT'S BEEN 100 YEARS SINCE I SAW YOU, AND YOU STILL LOOK LIKE A TEEN-AGER!
I AM A TEEN-AGER!
I SLEPT A 100 YEARS!
YOU'RE NUTS! I TALKED TO YOU YESTERDAY! IT'S THIS LUMPY MATTRESS! IT JUST SEEMED LIKE A 100 YEARS!
SO THEY MARRIED AND LIVED HAPPILY EVER AFTER! THE WITCH WAS THE MAID OF HONOR, AS A REWARD FOR BEING SO INCOMPETENT!
YOU MEAN YOU REALLY CAN'T CAST SPELLS?
OF COURSE NOT! LOOK IF THE QUEEN WANTS TO BELIEVE IN WITCHES, WHO AM I TO ARGUE? SOME DINGBATS WILL BELIEVE IN ANYTHING!
---AND GUESS WHAT THE WITCH BOUGHT WITH HER ILL-GOTTEN GOLD?
TELL ME AGAIN, GLASS! I LIKE YOUR STYLE!
YOU'RE THE BEST LOOKIN' CHICK THAT COME DOWN THE PIKE!
LOOK, I LOST MY LAST JOB BY TELLIN' THE TRUTH!
I LEARNED HOW TO COPE!
The END

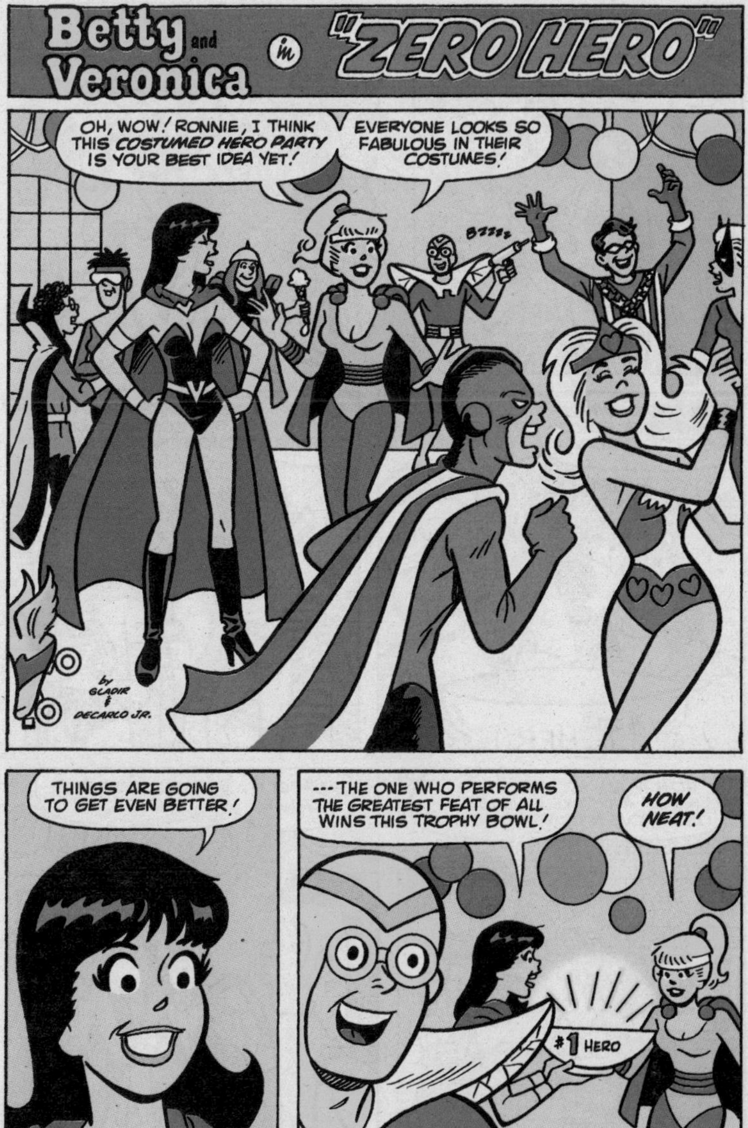
Betty and Veronica
in
"ZERO HERO"
OH, WOW! RONNIE, I THINK THIS COSTUMED HERO PARTY IS YOUR BEST IDEA YET!
EVERYONE LOOKS SO FABULOUS IN THEIR COSTUMES!
BZZZZ
by GLADIR & DECARLO JR.
THINGS ARE GOING TO GET EVEN BETTER!
---THE ONE WHO PERFORMS THE GREATEST FEAT OF ALL WINS THIS TROPHY BOWL!
HOW NEAT!
#1 HERO

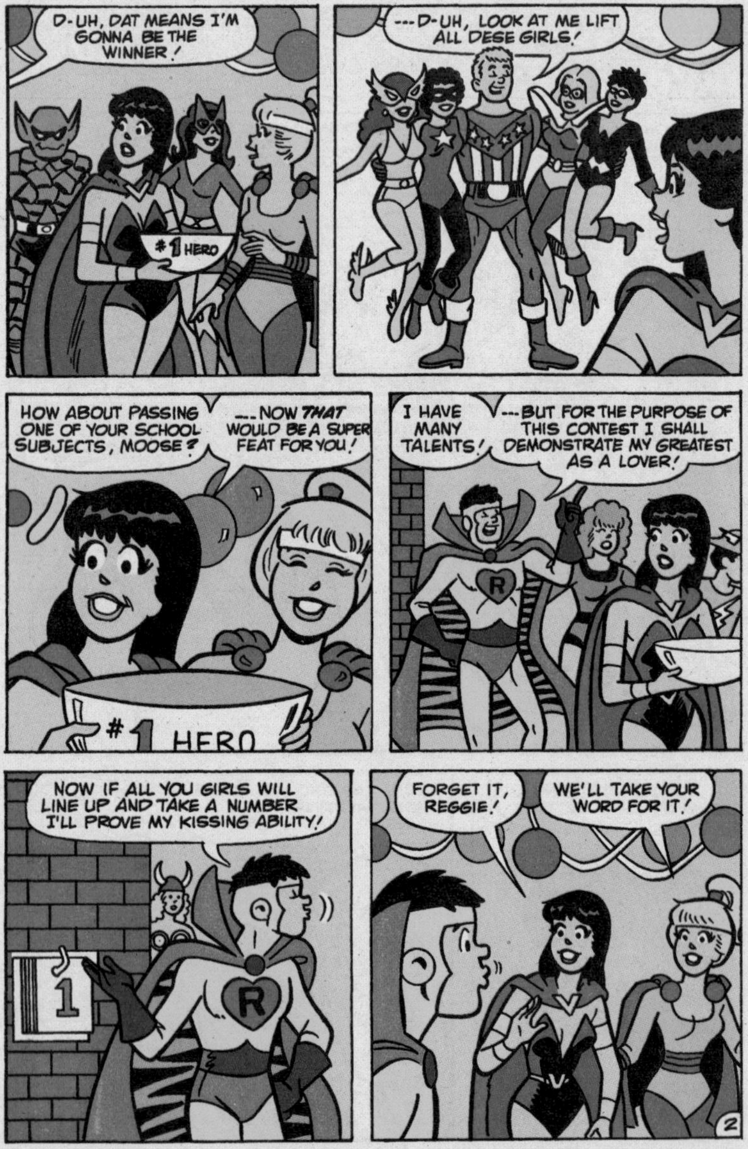
D-UH, DAT MEANS I'M GONNA BE THE WINNER!
#1 HERO
---D-UH, LOOK AT ME LIFT ALL DESE GIRLS!
HOW ABOUT PASSING ONE OF YOUR SCHOOL SUBJECTS, MOOSE?
---NOW THAT WOULD BE A SUPER FEAT FOR YOU!
#1 HERO
I HAVE MANY TALENTS!
---BUT FOR THE PURPOSE OF THIS CONTEST I SHALL DEMONSTRATE MY GREATEST AS A LOVER!
NOW IF ALL YOU GIRLS WILL LINE UP AND TAKE A NUMBER I'LL PROVE MY KISSING ABILITY!
1
FORGET IT, REGGIE!
WE'LL TAKE YOUR WORD FOR IT!
2

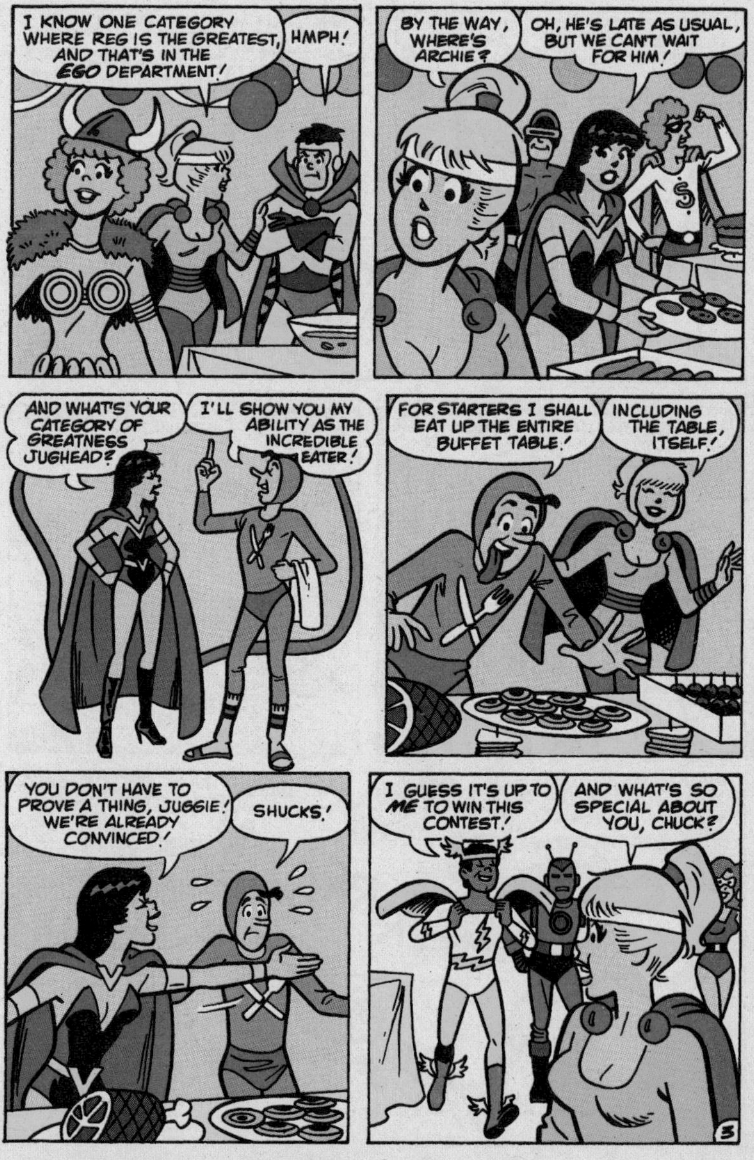

I KNOW ONE CATEGORY WHERE REG IS THE GREATEST, AND THAT'S IN THE EGO DEPARTMENT!
HMPH!
BY THE WAY, WHERE'S ARCHIE?
OH, HE'S LATE AS USUAL, BUT WE CAN'T WAIT FOR HIM!
AND WHAT'S YOUR CATEGORY OF GREATNESS JUGHEAD?
I'LL SHOW YOU MY ABILITY AS THE INCREDIBLE EATER!
FOR STARTERS I SHALL EAT UP THE ENTIRE BUFFET TABLE!
INCLUDING THE TABLE, ITSELF!
YOU DON'T HAVE TO PROVE A THING, JUGGIE! WE'RE ALREADY CONVINCED!
SHUCKS!
I GUESS IT'S UP TO ME TO WIN THIS CONTEST!
AND WHAT'S SO SPECIAL ABOUT YOU, CHUCK?
3

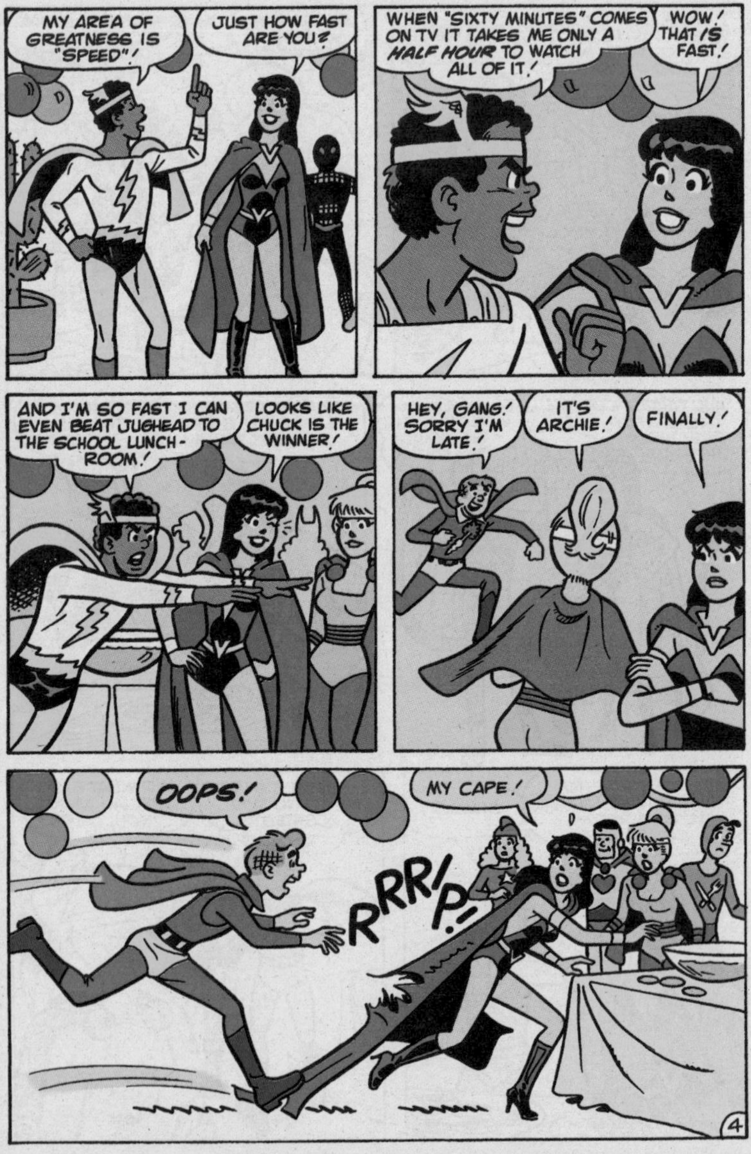
MY AREA OF GREATNESS IS "SPEED"!
JUST HOW FAST ARE YOU?
WHEN "SIXTY MINUTES" COMES ON TV IT TAKES ME ONLY A HALF HOUR TO WATCH ALL OF IT!
WOW! THAT IS FAST!
AND I'M SO FAST I CAN EVEN BEAT JUGHEAD TO THE SCHOOL LUNCH-ROOM!
LOOKS LIKE CHUCK IS THE WINNER!
HEY, GANG! SORRY I'M LATE!
IT'S ARCHIE!
FINALLY!
OOPS!
MY CAPE!
RRRIP!
4

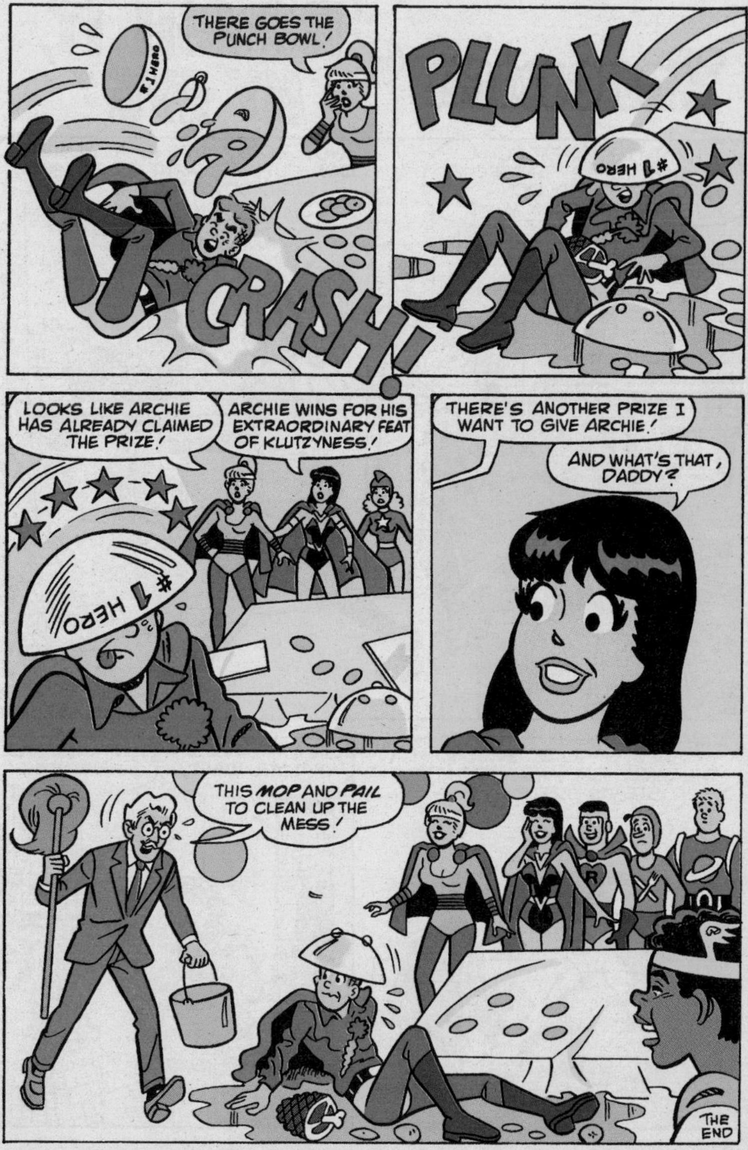
THERE GOES THE PUNCH BOWL!
#1 HERO
CRASH!
PLUNK
#1 HERO
LOOKS LIKE ARCHIE HAS ALREADY CLAIMED THE PRIZE!
ARCHIE WINS FOR HIS EXTRAORDINARY FEAT OF KLUTZYNESS!
#1 HERO
THERE'S ANOTHER PRIZE I WANT TO GIVE ARCHIE!
AND WHAT'S THAT, DADDY?
THIS MOP AND PAIL TO CLEAN UP THE MESS!
THE END

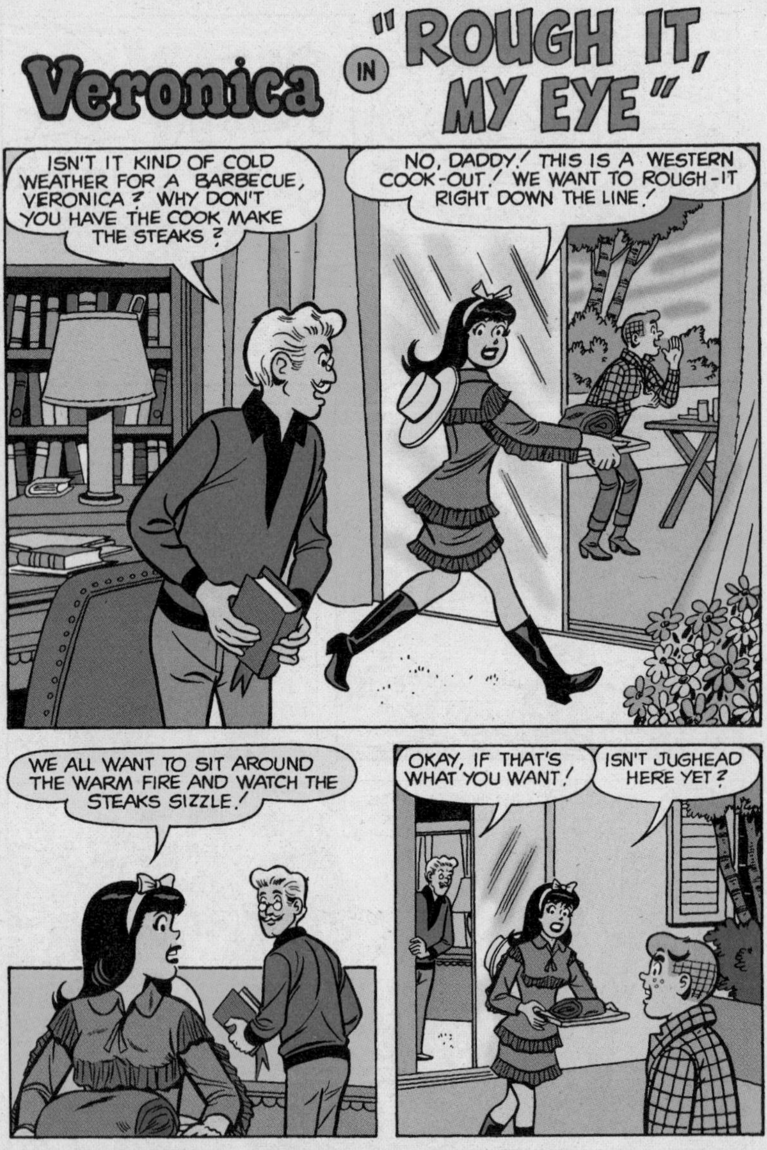
Veronica IN "ROUGH IT, MY EYE"
ISN'T IT KIND OF COLD WEATHER FOR A BARBECUE, VERONICA? WHY DON'T YOU HAVE THE COOK MAKE THE STEAKS?
NO, DADDY! THIS IS A WESTERN COOK-OUT! WE WANT TO ROUGH-IT RIGHT DOWN THE LINE!
WE ALL WANT TO SIT AROUND THE WARM FIRE AND WATCH THE STEAKS SIZZLE!
OKAY, IF THAT'S WHAT YOU WANT!
ISN'T JUGHEAD HERE YET?

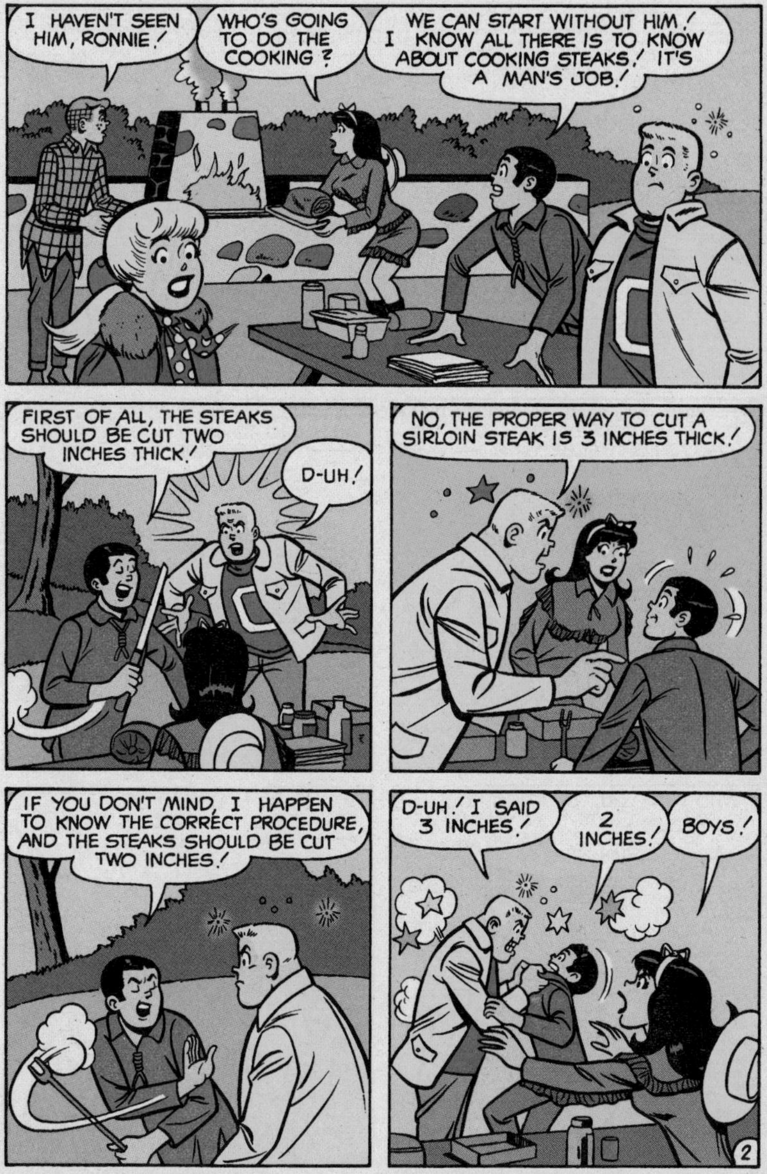
I HAVEN'T SEEN HIM, RONNIE!
WHO'S GOING TO DO THE COOKING?
WE CAN START WITHOUT HIM! I KNOW ALL THERE IS TO KNOW ABOUT COOKING STEAKS! IT'S A MAN'S JOB!
FIRST OF ALL, THE STEAKS SHOULD BE CUT TWO INCHES THICK!
D-UH!
NO, THE PROPER WAY TO CUT A SIRLOIN STEAK IS 3 INCHES THICK!
IF YOU DON'T MIND, I HAPPEN TO KNOW THE CORRECT PROCEDURE, AND THE STEAKS SHOULD BE CUT TWO INCHES!
D-UH! I SAID 3 INCHES!
2 INCHES!
BOYS!
2

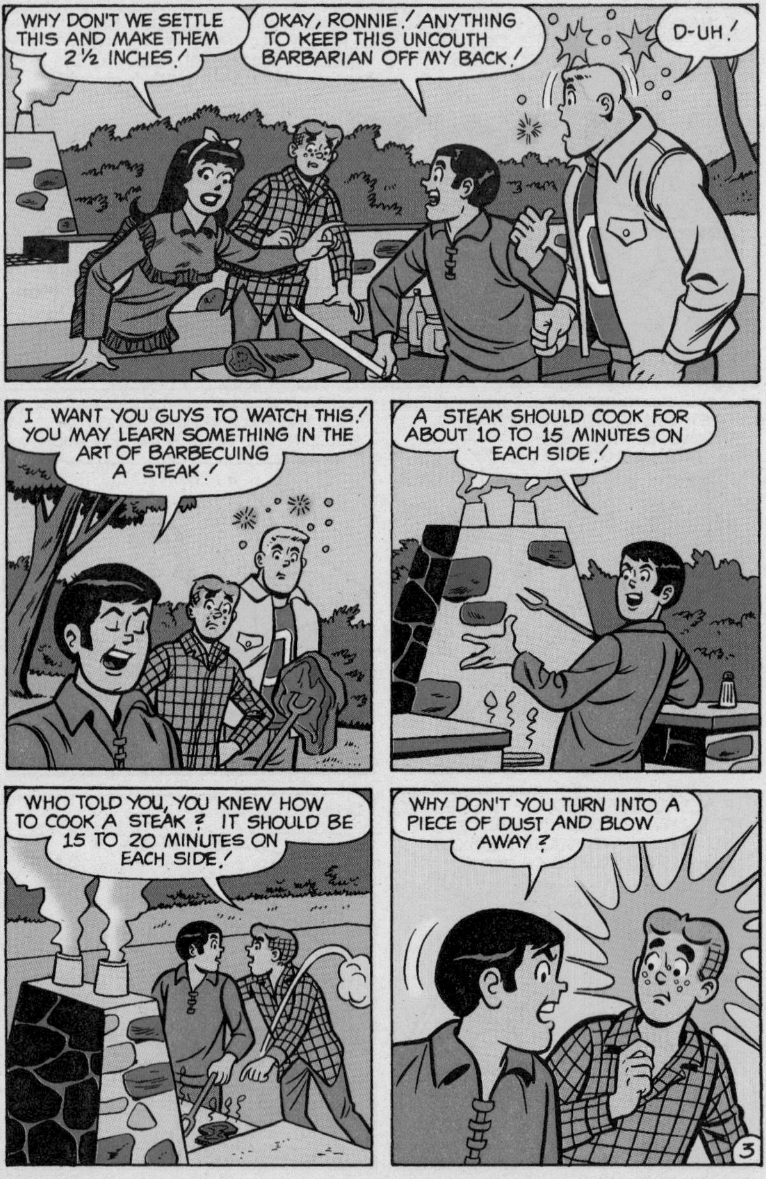
WHY DON'T WE SETTLE THIS AND MAKE THEM 2½ INCHES!
OKAY, RONNIE! ANYTHING TO KEEP THIS UNCOUTH BARBARIAN OFF MY BACK!
D-UH!
I WANT YOU GUYS TO WATCH THIS! YOU MAY LEARN SOMETHING IN THE ART OF BARBECUING A STEAK!
A STEAK SHOULD COOK FOR ABOUT 10 TO 15 MINUTES ON EACH SIDE!
WHO TOLD YOU, YOU KNEW HOW TO COOK A STEAK? IT SHOULD BE 15 TO 20 MINUTES ON EACH SIDE!
WHY DON'T YOU TURN INTO A PIECE OF DUST AND BLOW AWAY?
3

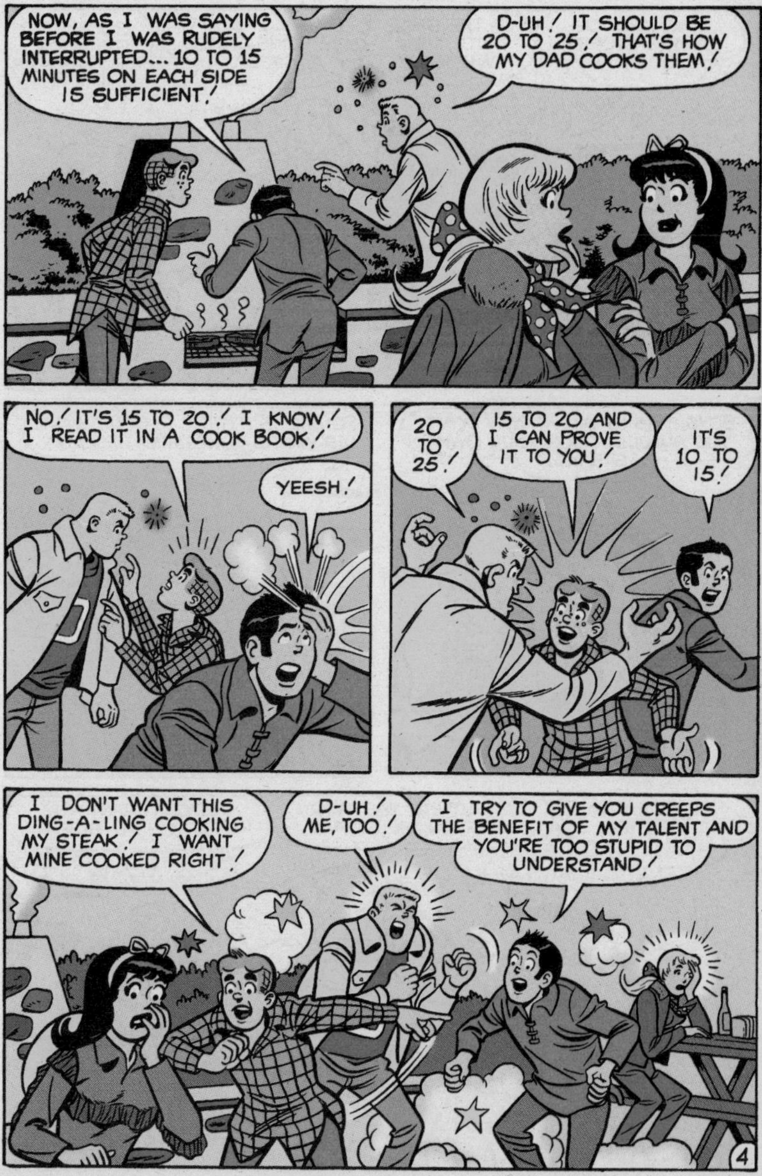
NOW, AS I WAS SAYING BEFORE I WAS RUDELY INTERRUPTED... 10 TO 15 MINUTES ON EACH SIDE IS SUFFICIENT!
D-UH! IT SHOULD BE 20 TO 25! THAT'S HOW MY DAD COOKS THEM!
NO! IT'S 15 TO 20! I KNOW! I READ IT IN A COOK BOOK!
YEESH!
20 TO 25!
15 TO 20 AND I CAN PROVE IT TO YOU!
IT'S 10 TO 15!
I DON'T WANT THIS DING-A-LING COOKING MY STEAK! I WANT MINE COOKED RIGHT!
D-UH! ME, TOO!
I TRY TO GIVE YOU CREEPS THE BENEFIT OF MY TALENT AND YOU'RE TOO STUPID TO UNDERSTAND!
4

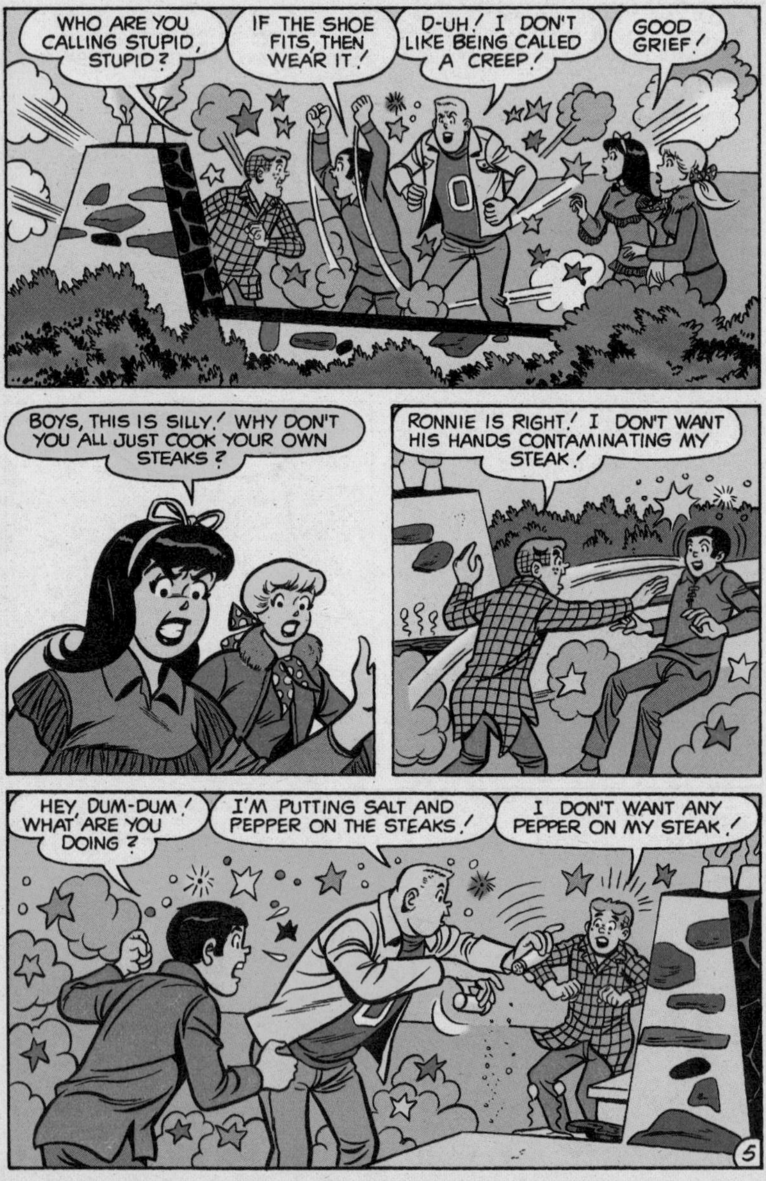
WHO ARE YOU CALLING STUPID, STUPID?
IF THE SHOE FITS, THEN WEAR IT!
D-UH! I DON'T LIKE BEING CALLED A CREEP!
GOOD GRIEF!
BOYS, THIS IS SILLY! WHY DON'T YOU ALL JUST COOK YOUR OWN STEAKS?
RONNIE IS RIGHT! I DON'T WANT HIS HANDS CONTAMINATING MY STEAK!
HEY, DUM-DUM! WHAT ARE YOU DOING?
I'M PUTTING SALT AND PEPPER ON THE STEAKS!
I DON'T WANT ANY PEPPER ON MY STEAK!
5

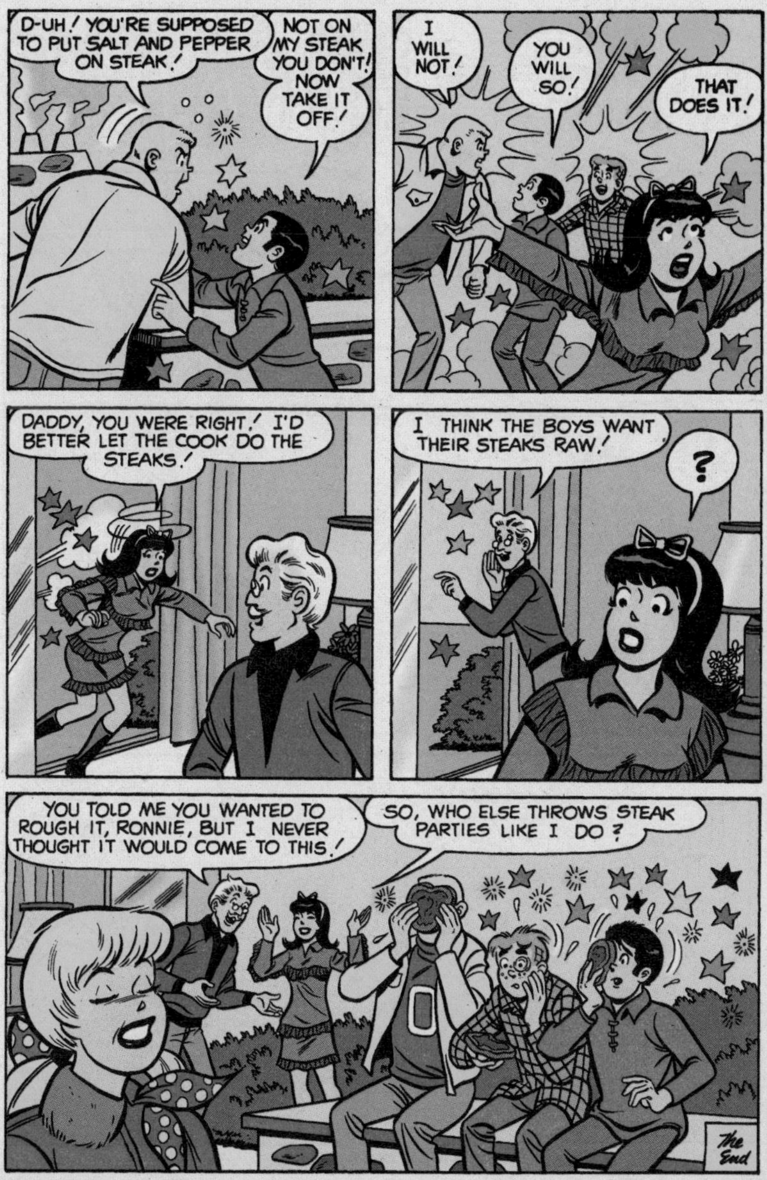
D-UH! YOU'RE SUPPOSED TO PUT SALT AND PEPPER ON STEAK!
NOT ON MY STEAK YOU DON'T! NOW TAKE IT OFF!
I WILL NOT!
YOU WILL SO!
THAT DOES IT!
DADDY, YOU WERE RIGHT! I'D BETTER LET THE COOK DO THE STEAKS!
I THINK THE BOYS WANT THEIR STEAKS RAW!
?
YOU TOLD ME YOU WANTED TO ROUGH IT, RONNIE, BUT I NEVER THOUGHT IT WOULD COME TO THIS!
SO, WHO ELSE THROWS STEAK PARTIES LIKE I DO?
The End

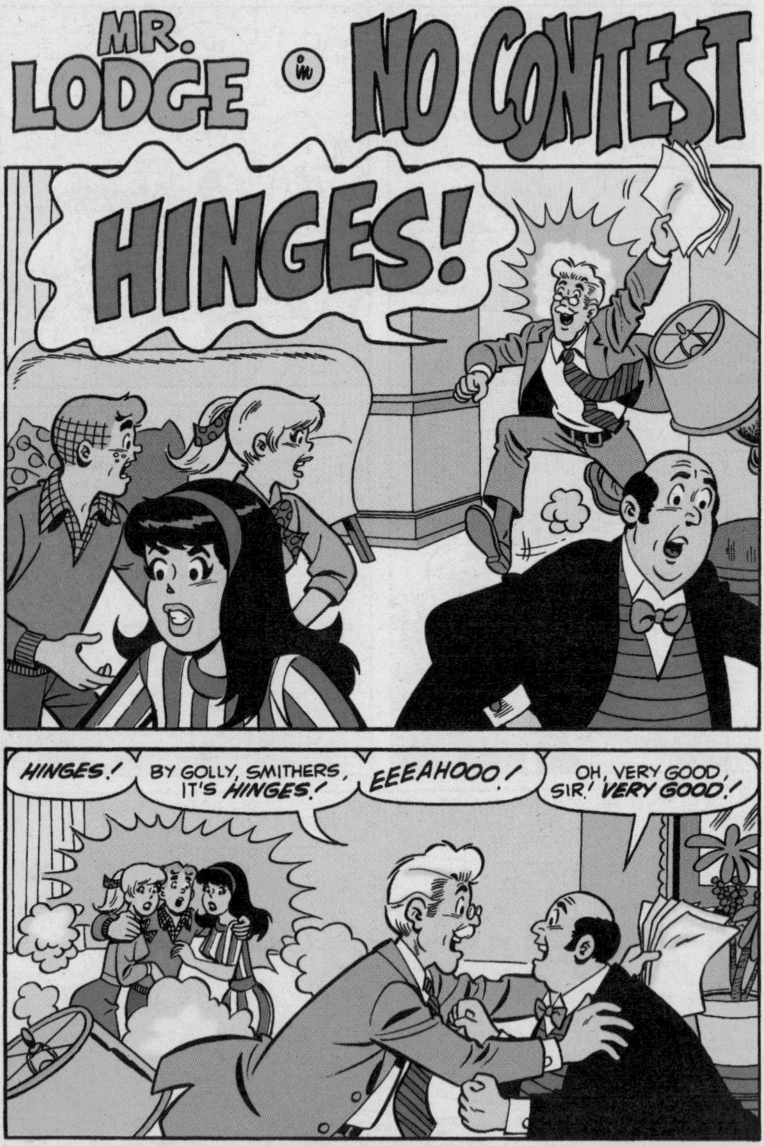
MR. LODGE in NO CONTEST
HINGES!
HINGES!
BY GOLLY, SMITHERS, IT'S HINGES!
EEEAHOOO!
OH, VERY GOOD, SIR! VERY GOOD!

Script, Art & Letters: Al Hartley

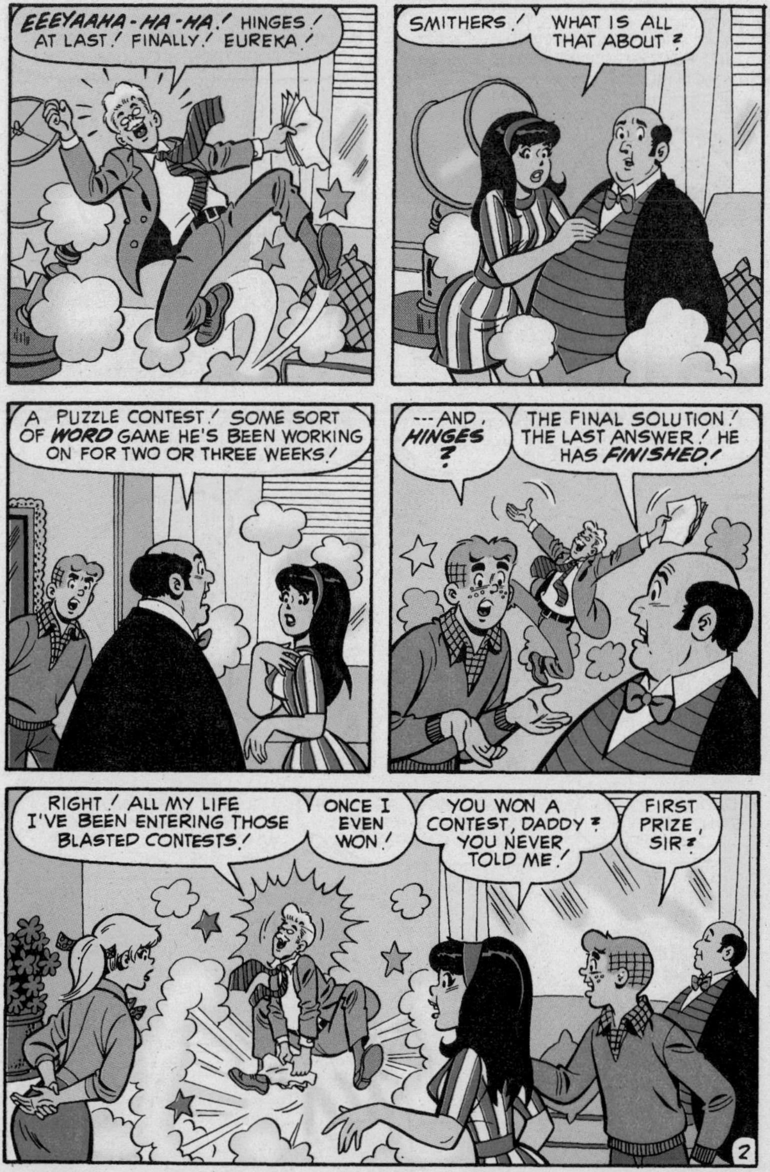
EEEYAAHA-HA-HA! HINGES! AT LAST! FINALLY! EUREKA!
SMITHERS!
WHAT IS ALL THAT ABOUT?
A PUZZLE CONTEST! SOME SORT OF WORD GAME HE'S BEEN WORKING ON FOR TWO OR THREE WEEKS!
---AND, HINGES?
THE FINAL SOLUTION! THE LAST ANSWER! HE HAS FINISHED!
RIGHT! ALL MY LIFE I'VE BEEN ENTERING THOSE BLASTED CONTESTS!
ONCE I EVEN WON!
YOU WON A CONTEST, DADDY? YOU NEVER TOLD ME!
FIRST PRIZE, SIR?
2

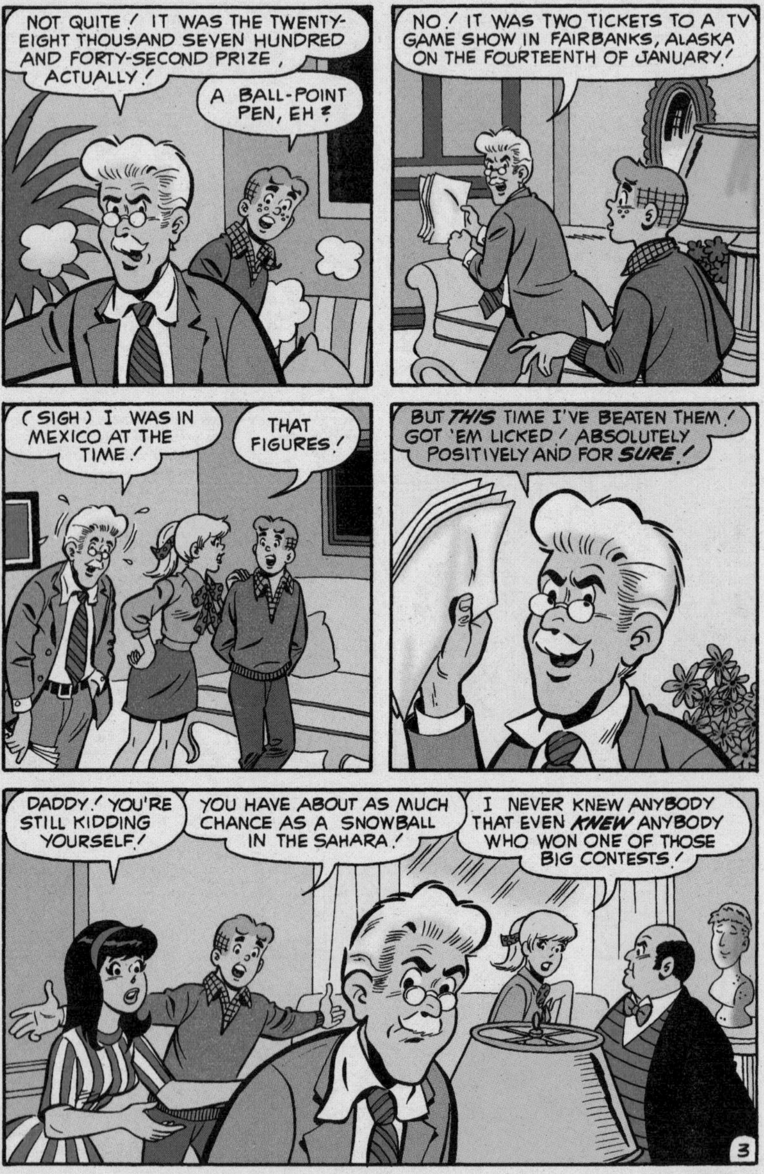
NOT QUITE! IT WAS THE TWENTY-EIGHT THOUSAND SEVEN HUNDRED AND FORTY-SECOND PRIZE, ACTUALLY!
A BALL-POINT PEN, EH?
NO! IT WAS TWO TICKETS TO A TV GAME SHOW IN FAIRBANKS, ALASKA ON THE FOURTEENTH OF JANUARY!
(SIGH) I WAS IN MEXICO AT THE TIME!
THAT FIGURES!
BUT THIS TIME I'VE BEATEN THEM! GOT 'EM LICKED! ABSOLUTELY POSITIVELY AND FOR SURE!
DADDY! YOU'RE STILL KIDDING YOURSELF!
YOU HAVE ABOUT AS MUCH CHANCE AS A SNOWBALL IN THE SAHARA!
I NEVER KNEW ANYBODY THAT EVEN KNEW ANYBODY WHO WON ONE OF THOSE BIG CONTESTS!
3

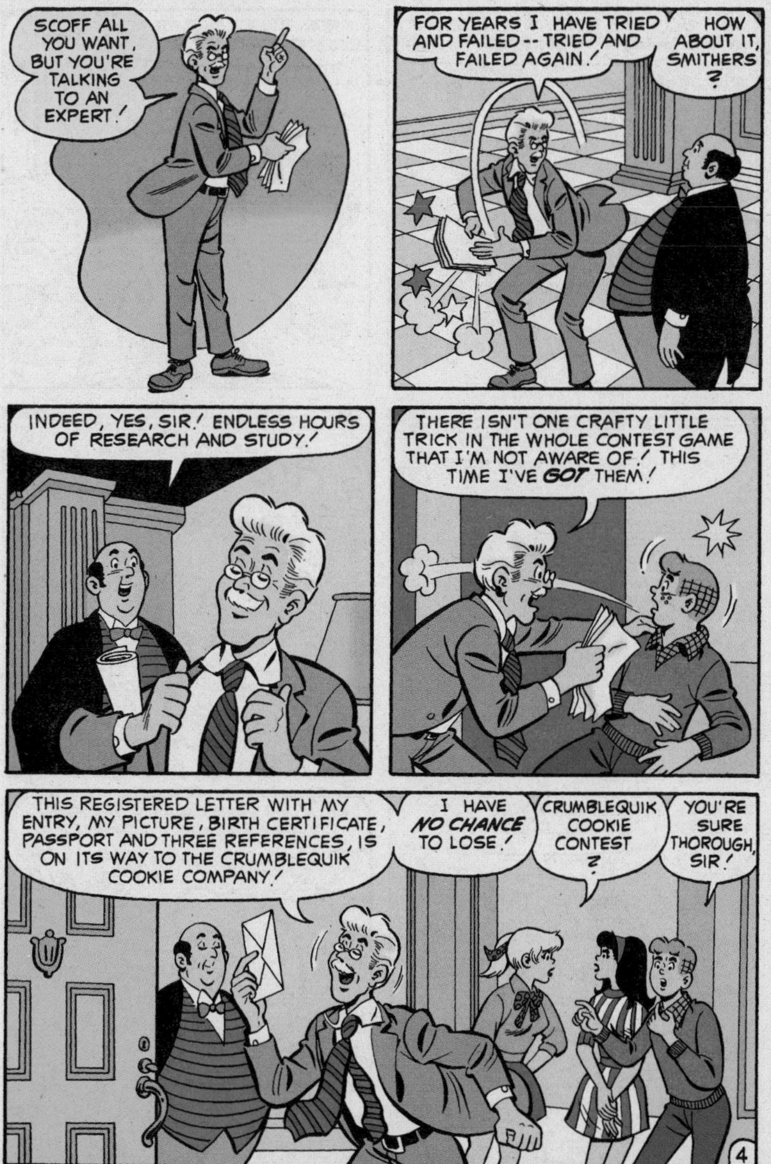

SCOFF ALL YOU WANT, BUT YOU'RE TALKING TO AN EXPERT!
FOR YEARS I HAVE TRIED AND FAILED -- TRIED AND FAILED AGAIN!
HOW ABOUT IT, SMITHERS?
INDEED, YES, SIR! ENDLESS HOURS OF RESEARCH AND STUDY!
THERE ISN'T ONE CRAFTY LITTLE TRICK IN THE WHOLE CONTEST GAME THAT I'M NOT AWARE OF! THIS TIME I'VE GOT THEM!
THIS REGISTERED LETTER WITH MY ENTRY, MY PICTURE, BIRTH CERTIFICATE, PASSPORT AND THREE REFERENCES, IS ON ITS WAY TO THE CRUMBLEQUIK COOKIE COMPANY!
I HAVE NO CHANCE TO LOSE!
CRUMBLEQUIK COOKIE CONTEST?
YOU'RE SURE THOROUGH, SIR!
4

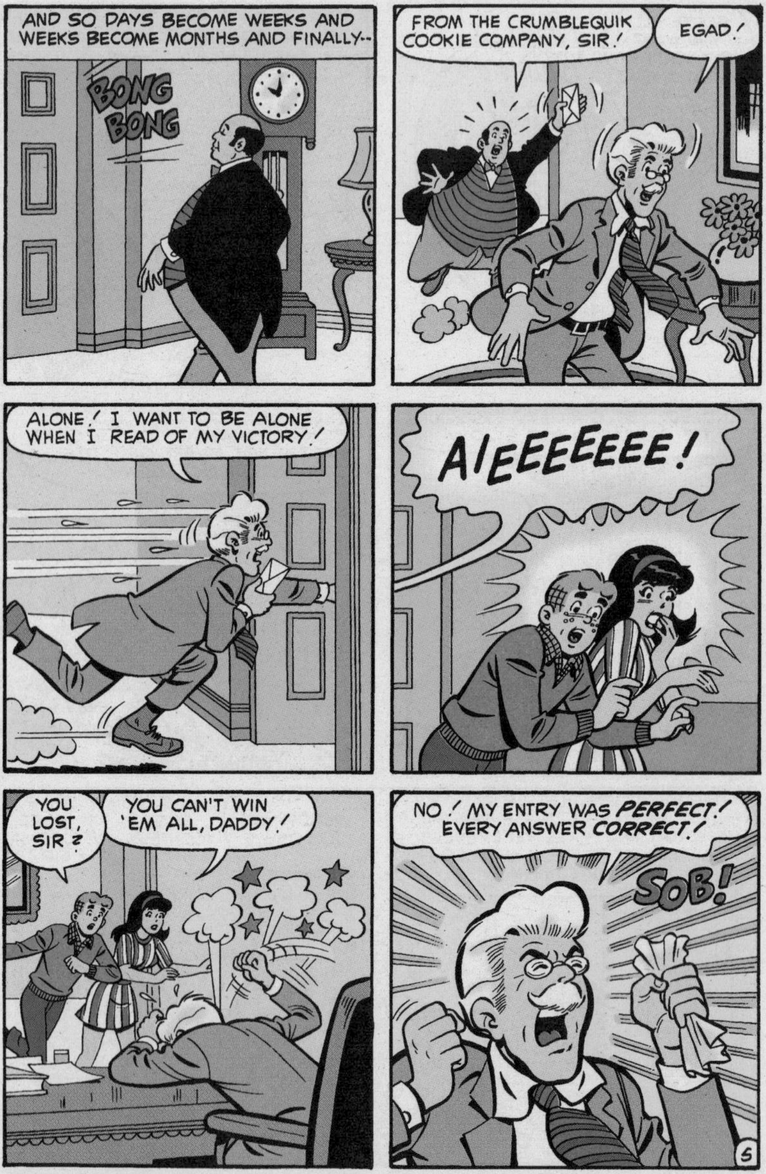
AND SO DAYS BECOME WEEKS AND WEEKS BECOME MONTHS AND FINALLY--
BONG BONG
FROM THE CRUMBLEQUIK COOKIE COMPANY, SIR!
EGAD!
ALONE! I WANT TO BE ALONE WHEN I READ OF MY VICTORY!
AIEEEEEEE!
YOU LOST, SIR?
YOU CAN'T WIN 'EM ALL, DADDY!
NO! MY ENTRY WAS PERFECT! EVERY ANSWER CORRECT!
SOB!
5

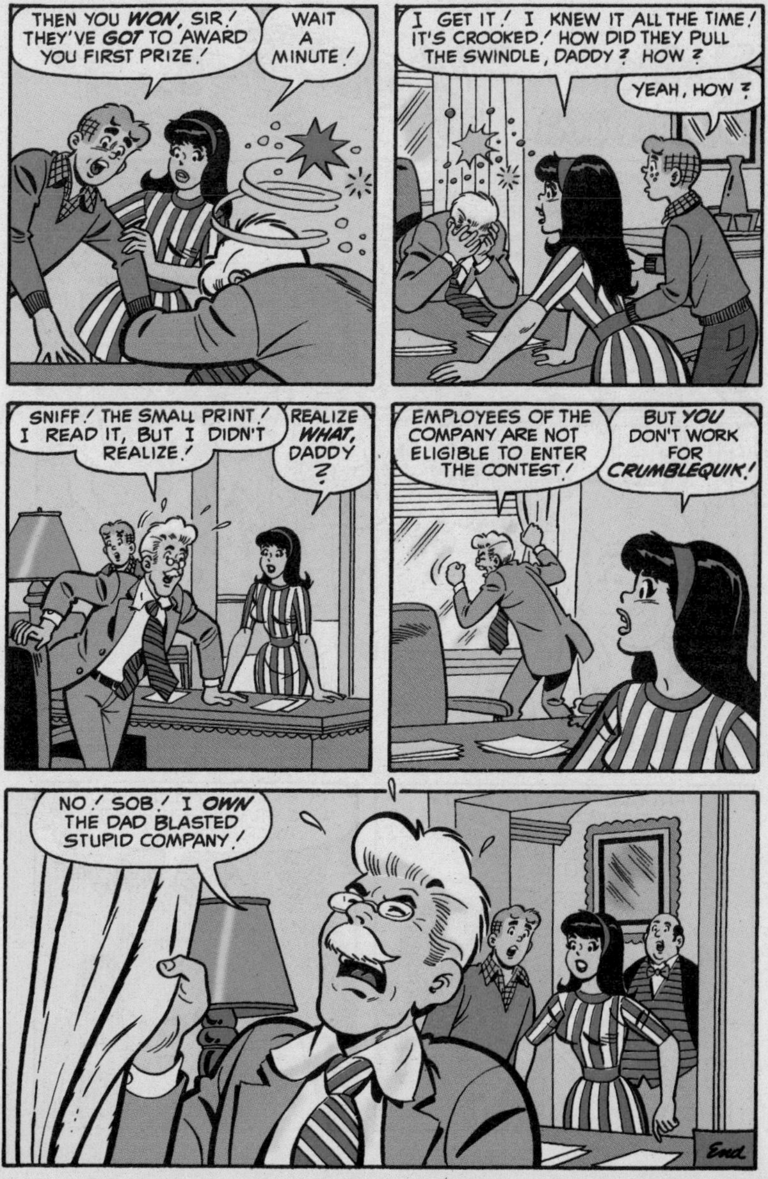
THEN YOU WON, SIR! THEY'VE GOT TO AWARD YOU FIRST PRIZE!
WAIT A MINUTE!
I GET IT! I KNEW IT ALL THE TIME! IT'S CROOKED! HOW DID THEY PULL THE SWINDLE, DADDY? HOW?
YEAH, HOW?
SNIFF! THE SMALL PRINT! I READ IT, BUT I DIDN'T REALIZE!
REALIZE WHAT, DADDY?
EMPLOYEES OF THE COMPANY ARE NOT ELIGIBLE TO ENTER THE CONTEST!
BUT YOU DON'T WORK FOR CRUMBLEQUIK!
NO! SOB! I OWN THE DAD BLASTED STUPID COMPANY!
End

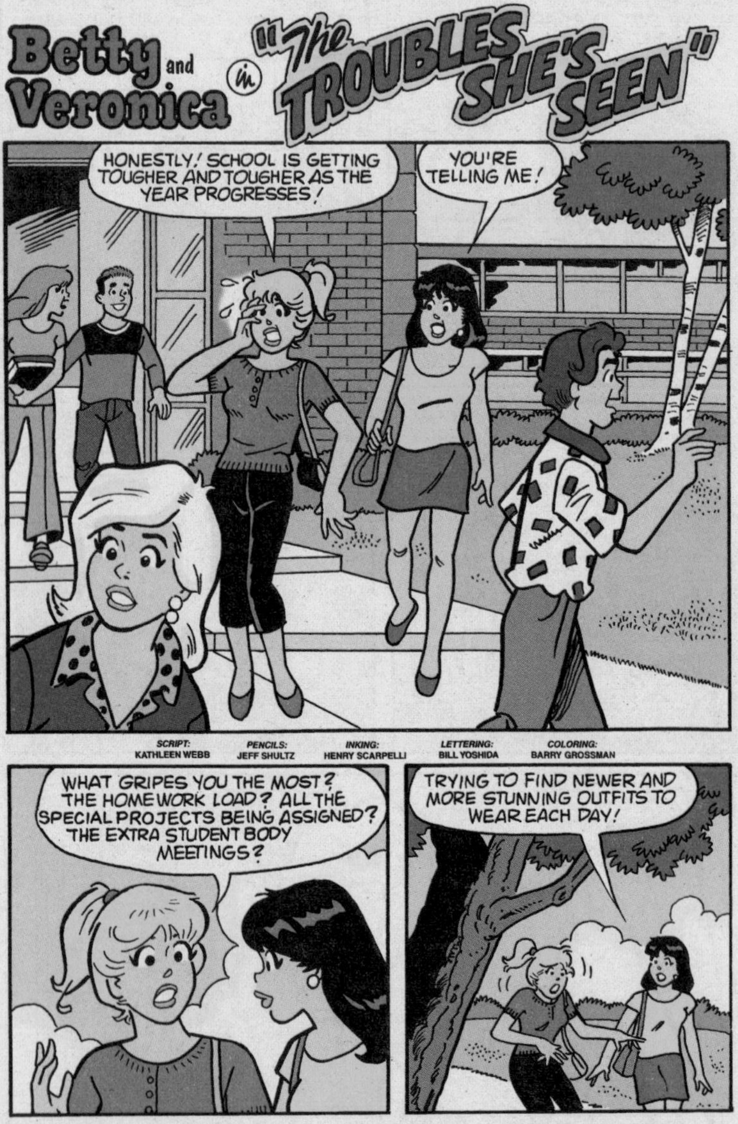
Betty and Veronica in "The TROUBLES SHE'S SEEN"
HONESTLY! SCHOOL IS GETTING TOUGHER AND TOUGHER AS THE YEAR PROGRESSES!
YOU'RE TELLING ME!
SCRIPT: KATHLEEN WEBB
PENCILS: JEFF SHULTZ
INKING: HENRY SCARPELLI
LETTERING: BILL YOSHIDA
COLORING: BARRY GROSSMAN
WHAT GRIPES YOU THE MOST? THE HOMEWORK LOAD? ALL THE SPECIAL PROJECTS BEING ASSIGNED? THE EXTRA STUDENT BODY MEETINGS?
TRYING TO FIND NEWER AND MORE STUNNING OUTFITS TO WEAR EACH DAY!

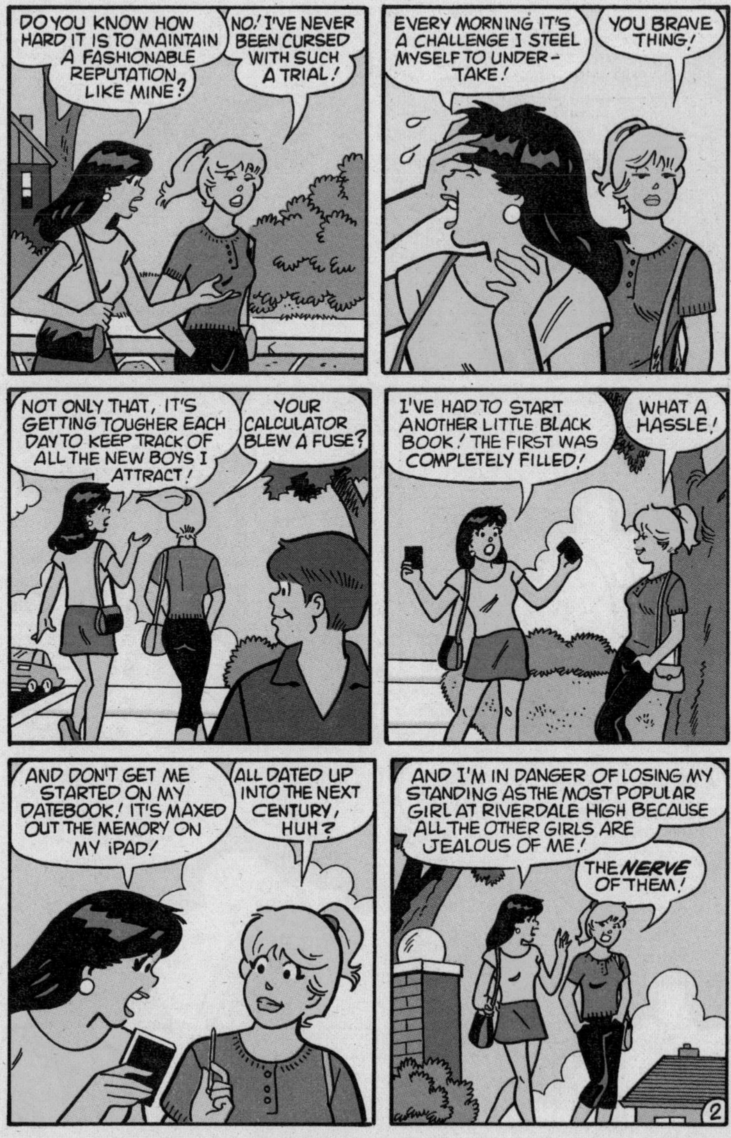
DO YOU KNOW HOW HARD IT IS TO MAINTAIN A FASHIONABLE REPUTATION LIKE MINE?
NO! I'VE NEVER BEEN CURSED WITH SUCH A TRIAL!
EVERY MORNING IT'S A CHALLENGE I STEEL MYSELF TO UNDER-TAKE!
YOU BRAVE THING!
NOT ONLY THAT, IT'S GETTING TOUGHER EACH DAY TO KEEP TRACK OF ALL THE NEW BOYS I ATTRACT!
YOUR CALCULATOR BLEW A FUSE?
I'VE HAD TO START ANOTHER LITTLE BLACK BOOK! THE FIRST WAS COMPLETELY FILLED!
WHAT A HASSLE!
AND DON'T GET ME STARTED ON MY DATEBOOK! IT'S MAXED OUT THE MEMORY ON MY iPAD!
ALL DATED UP INTO THE NEXT CENTURY, HUH?
AND I'M IN DANGER OF LOSING MY STANDING AS THE MOST POPULAR GIRL AT RIVERDALE HIGH BECAUSE ALL THE OTHER GIRLS ARE JEALOUS OF ME!
THE ***NERVE*** OF THEM!
2

I AGREE, BETTY! SCHOOL IS GETTING MORE DIFFICULT! I'LL JUST HAVE TO BUCKLE DOWN AND PERSEVERE!

YOU GO, GIRL!

Y'KNOW... I'M GLAD I'M AWARE THAT SCHOOL IS MORE THAN JUST A HUGE POPULARITY CONTEST!

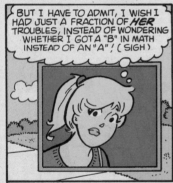

BUT I HAVE TO ADMIT, I WISH I HAD JUST A FRACTION OF *HER* TROUBLES, INSTEAD OF WONDERING WHETHER I GOT A "B" IN MATH INSTEAD OF AN "A"! (SIGH)

NEXT DAY...

BETTY, HONEY, AREN'T YOU READY FOR SCHOOL YET?

I CAN'T FIND ANYTHING TO WEAR!

I FORGOT TO WASH MY DIRTY LAUNDRY LAST NIGHT! I DON'T HAVE ANY CLEAN CLOTHES!

WEAR SOMETHING OF MINE!

AND LOOK LIKE I'M OVER FORTY? MOM!!

OH, THE HORROR! HEAVEN FORBID YOU SHOULD EVER GET OLD!

3

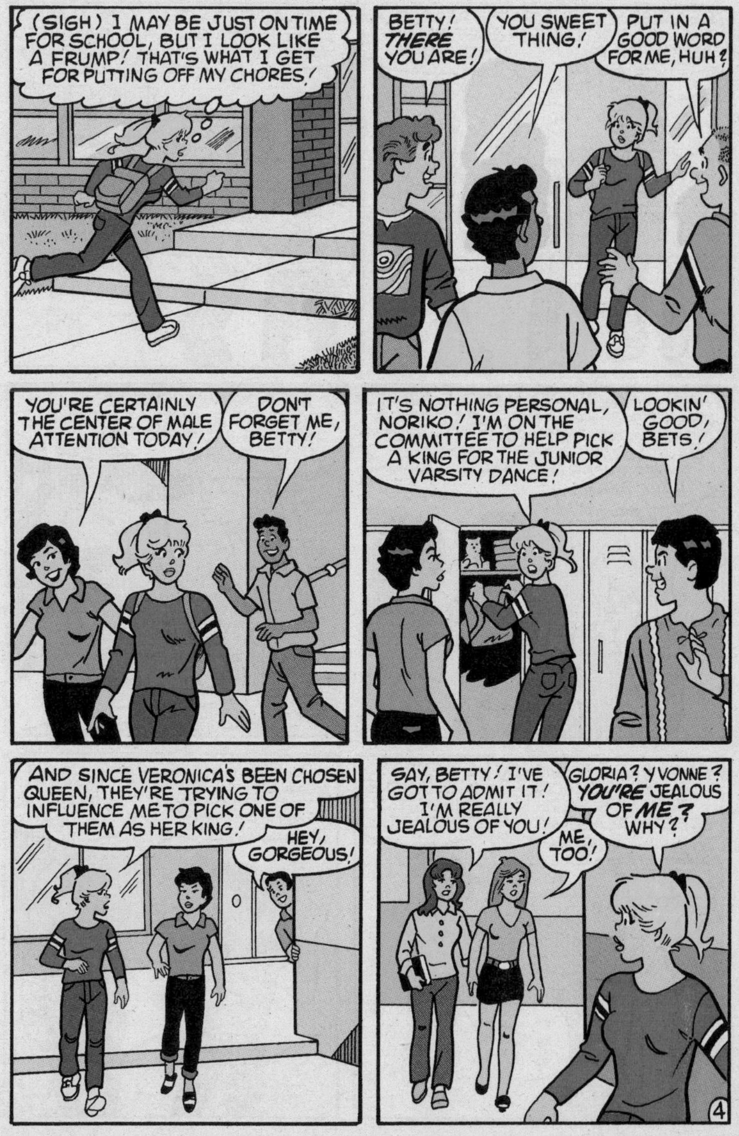
(SIGH) I MAY BE JUST ON TIME FOR SCHOOL, BUT I LOOK LIKE A FRUMP! THAT'S WHAT I GET FOR PUTTING OFF MY CHORES!
BETTY! THERE YOU ARE!
YOU SWEET THING!
PUT IN A GOOD WORD FOR ME, HUH?
YOU'RE CERTAINLY THE CENTER OF MALE ATTENTION TODAY!
DON'T FORGET ME, BETTY!
IT'S NOTHING PERSONAL, NORIKO! I'M ON THE COMMITTEE TO HELP PICK A KING FOR THE JUNIOR VARSITY DANCE!
LOOKIN' GOOD, BETS!
AND SINCE VERONICA'S BEEN CHOSEN QUEEN, THEY'RE TRYING TO INFLUENCE ME TO PICK ONE OF THEM AS HER KING!
HEY, GORGEOUS!
SAY, BETTY! I'VE GOT TO ADMIT IT! I'M REALLY JEALOUS OF YOU!
ME, TOO!
GLORIA? YVONNE? YOU'RE JEALOUS OF ME? WHY?
4

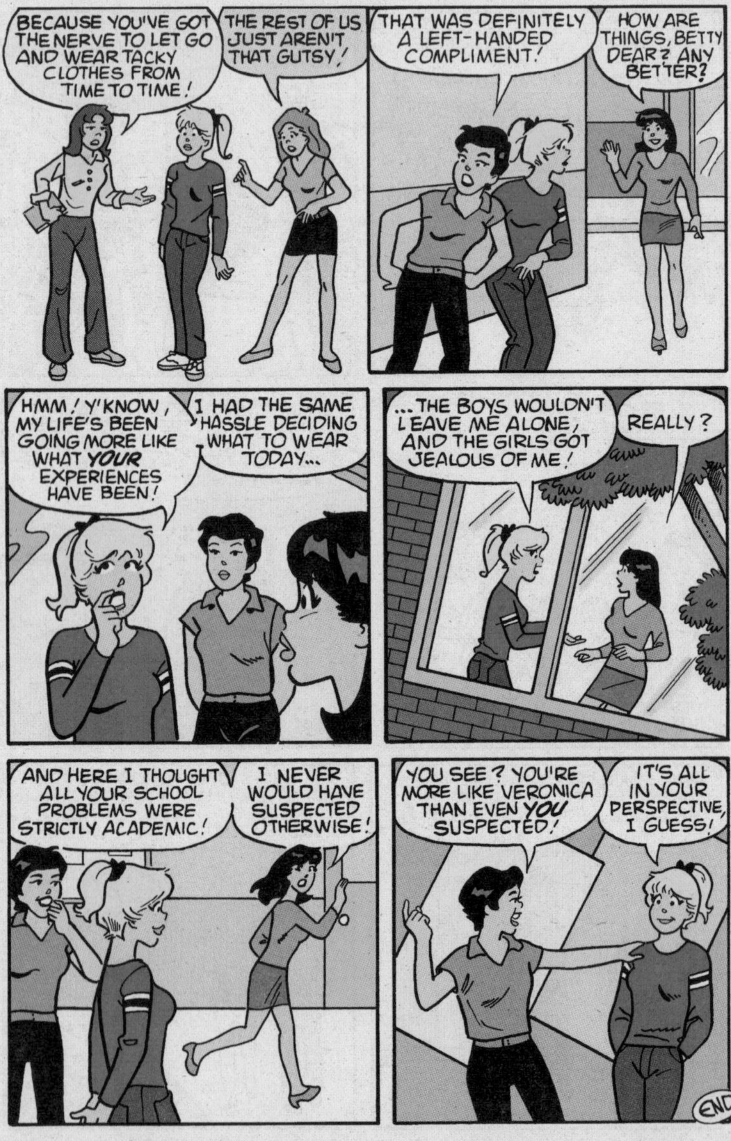
BECAUSE YOU'VE GOT THE NERVE TO LET GO AND WEAR TACKY CLOTHES FROM TIME TO TIME!
THE REST OF US JUST AREN'T THAT GUTSY!
THAT WAS DEFINITELY A LEFT-HANDED COMPLIMENT!
HOW ARE THINGS, BETTY DEAR? ANY BETTER?
HMM! Y'KNOW, MY LIFE'S BEEN GOING MORE LIKE WHAT YOUR EXPERIENCES HAVE BEEN!
I HAD THE SAME HASSLE DECIDING WHAT TO WEAR TODAY...
...THE BOYS WOULDN'T LEAVE ME ALONE, AND THE GIRLS GOT JEALOUS OF ME!
REALLY?
AND HERE I THOUGHT ALL YOUR SCHOOL PROBLEMS WERE STRICTLY ACADEMIC!
I NEVER WOULD HAVE SUSPECTED OTHERWISE!
YOU SEE? YOU'RE MORE LIKE VERONICA THAN EVEN YOU SUSPECTED!
IT'S ALL IN YOUR PERSPECTIVE, I GUESS!
END

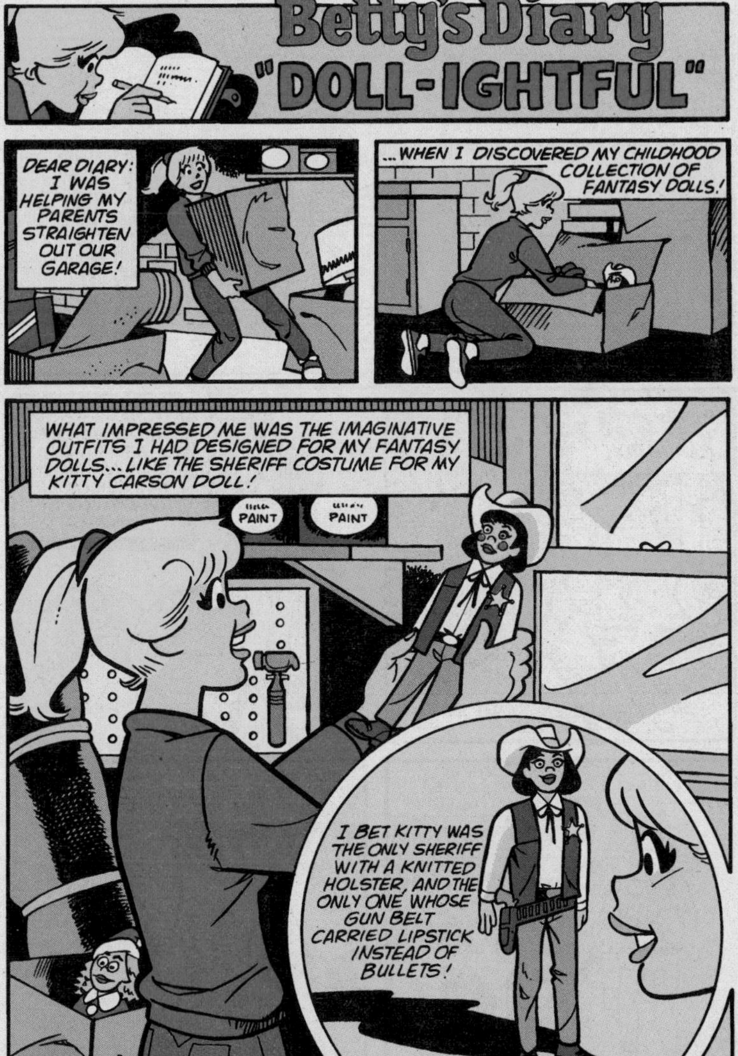

Betty's Diary
"DOLL-IGHTFUL"
DEAR DIARY: I WAS HELPING MY PARENTS STRAIGHTEN OUT OUR GARAGE!
...WHEN I DISCOVERED MY CHILDHOOD COLLECTION OF FANTASY DOLLS!
WHAT IMPRESSED ME WAS THE IMAGINATIVE OUTFITS I HAD DESIGNED FOR MY FANTASY DOLLS... LIKE THE SHERIFF COSTUME FOR MY KITTY CARSON DOLL!
PAINT
PAINT
I BET KITTY WAS THE ONLY SHERIFF WITH A KNITTED HOLSTER, AND THE ONLY ONE WHOSE GUN BELT CARRIED LIPSTICK INSTEAD OF BULLETS!
1

Script: George Gladir / Art: Henry Scarpelli / Letters: Bill Yoshida

I EVEN DISCOVERED A SPECIAL LARIAT I MADE FOR MY KITTY DOLL!

...IT WAS USED MOSTLY TO HELP CATCH SHY COWBOY DOLLS FOR DATES!

I EVEN MADE A **SANDRA** CLAUS DOLL!

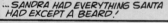
...SANDRA HAD EVERYTHING SANTA HAD EXCEPT A BEARD!

SANDRA'S SLIM FIGURE ENABLED HER TO SLIDE DOWN CHIMNEYS THAT HER CHUBBY HUSBAND COULDN'T MANAGE!

SANDRA WAS VERY GENEROUS IN DISPENSING TOYS TO BOTH LITTLE BOYS AND LITTLE GIRLS!

...BUT SHE HAD A SPECIAL BAG OF LUMPY COAL FOR NAUGHTY BOYS WHO TUGGED ON THE PIGTAILS OF LITTLE GIRLS!

BAD LIST

2

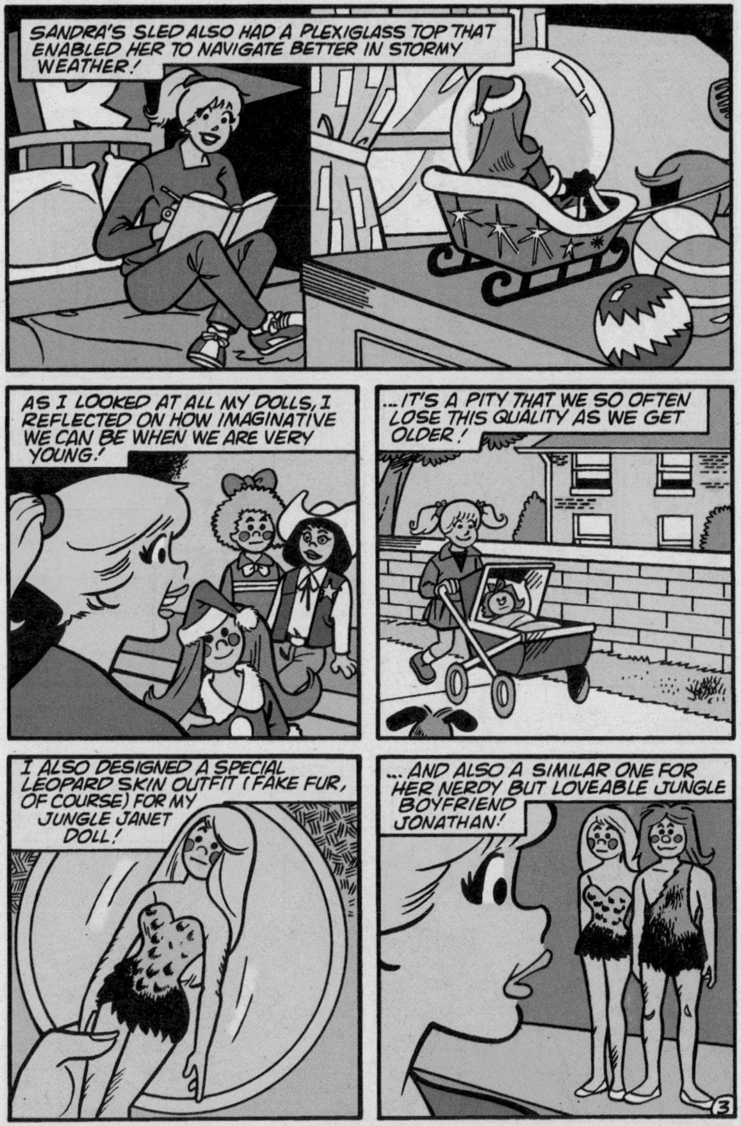
SANDRA'S SLED ALSO HAD A PLEXIGLASS TOP THAT ENABLED HER TO NAVIGATE BETTER IN STORMY WEATHER!
AS I LOOKED AT ALL MY DOLLS, I REFLECTED ON HOW IMAGINATIVE WE CAN BE WHEN WE ARE VERY YOUNG!
...IT'S A PITY THAT WE SO OFTEN LOSE THIS QUALITY AS WE GET OLDER!
I ALSO DESIGNED A SPECIAL LEOPARD SKIN OUTFIT (FAKE FUR, OF COURSE) FOR MY JUNGLE JANET DOLL!
...AND ALSO A SIMILAR ONE FOR HER NERDY BUT LOVEABLE JUNGLE BOYFRIEND JONATHAN!
3

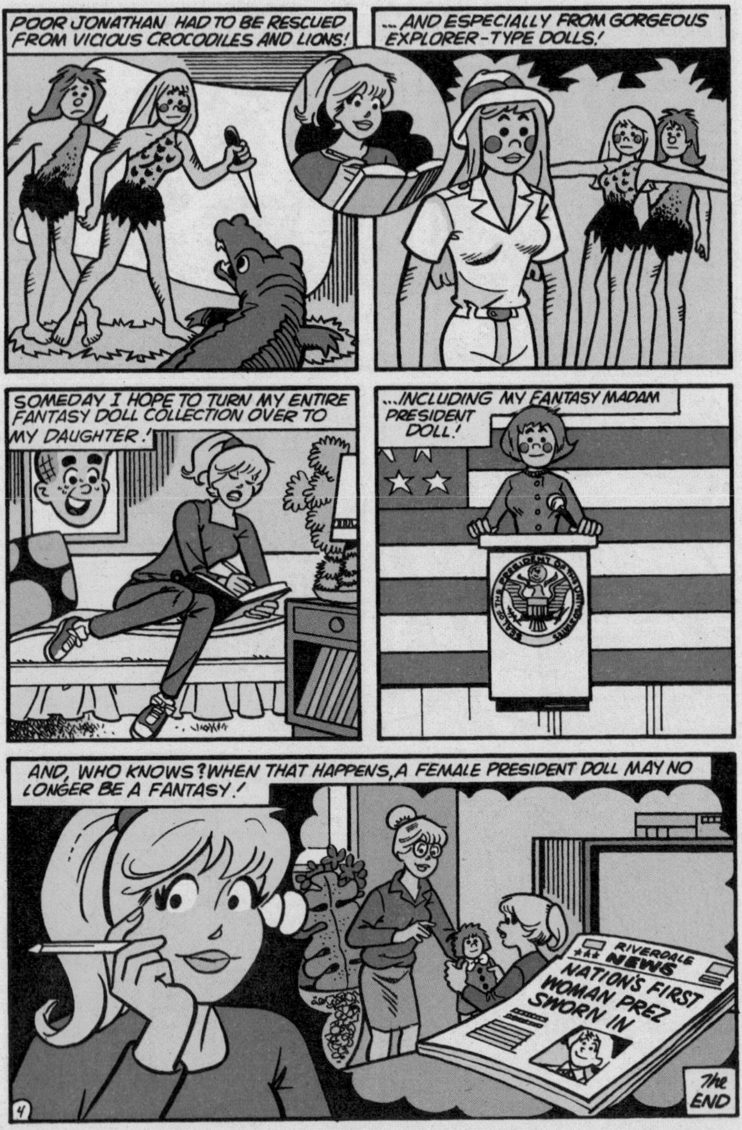
POOR JONATHAN HAD TO BE RESCUED FROM VICIOUS CROCODILES AND LIONS!
...AND ESPECIALLY FROM GORGEOUS EXPLORER-TYPE DOLLS!
SOMEDAY I HOPE TO TURN MY ENTIRE FANTASY DOLL COLLECTION OVER TO MY DAUGHTER!
...INCLUDING MY FANTASY MADAM PRESIDENT DOLL!
SEAL OF THE PRESIDENT OF THE UNITED STATES
AND, WHO KNOWS? WHEN THAT HAPPENS, A FEMALE PRESIDENT DOLL MAY NO LONGER BE A FANTASY!
RIVERDALE NEWS
NATION'S FIRST WOMAN PREZ SWORN IN
The END
4

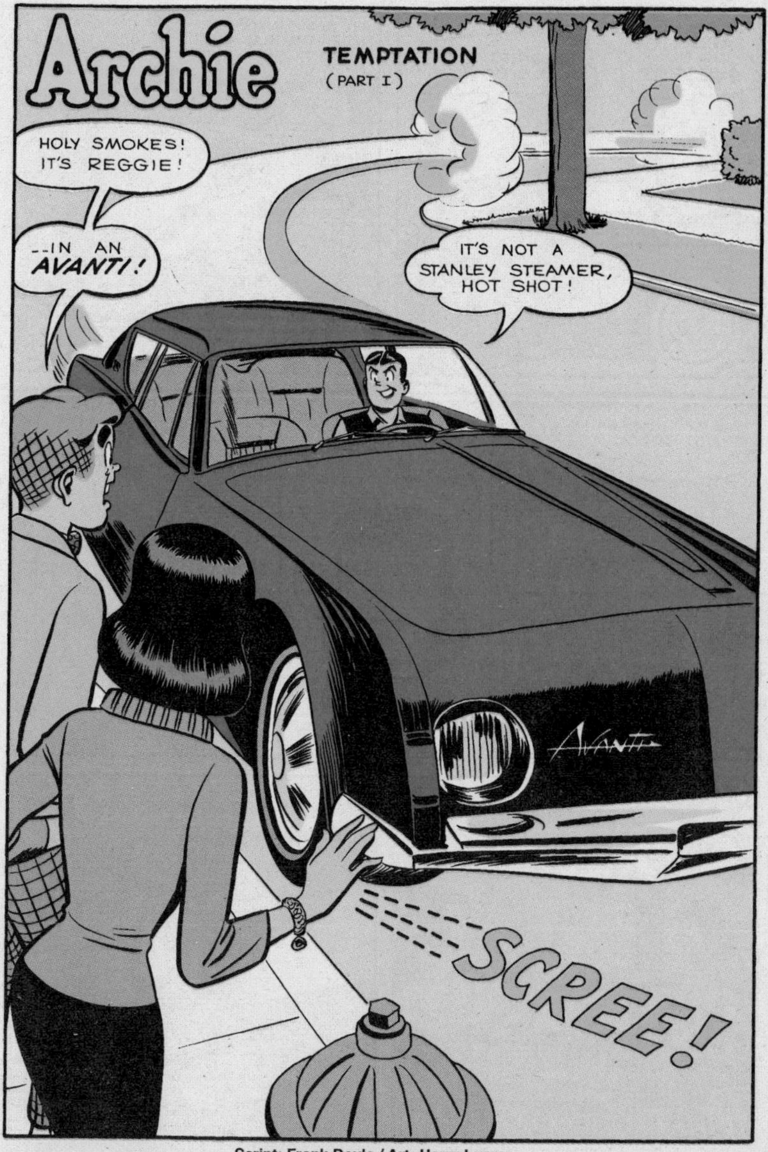
Archie
TEMPTATION
(PART I)
HOLY SMOKES! IT'S REGGIE!
--IN AN AVANTI!
IT'S NOT A STANLEY STEAMER, HOT SHOT!
AVANTI
SCREEE!

Script: Frank Doyle / Art: Harry Lucey

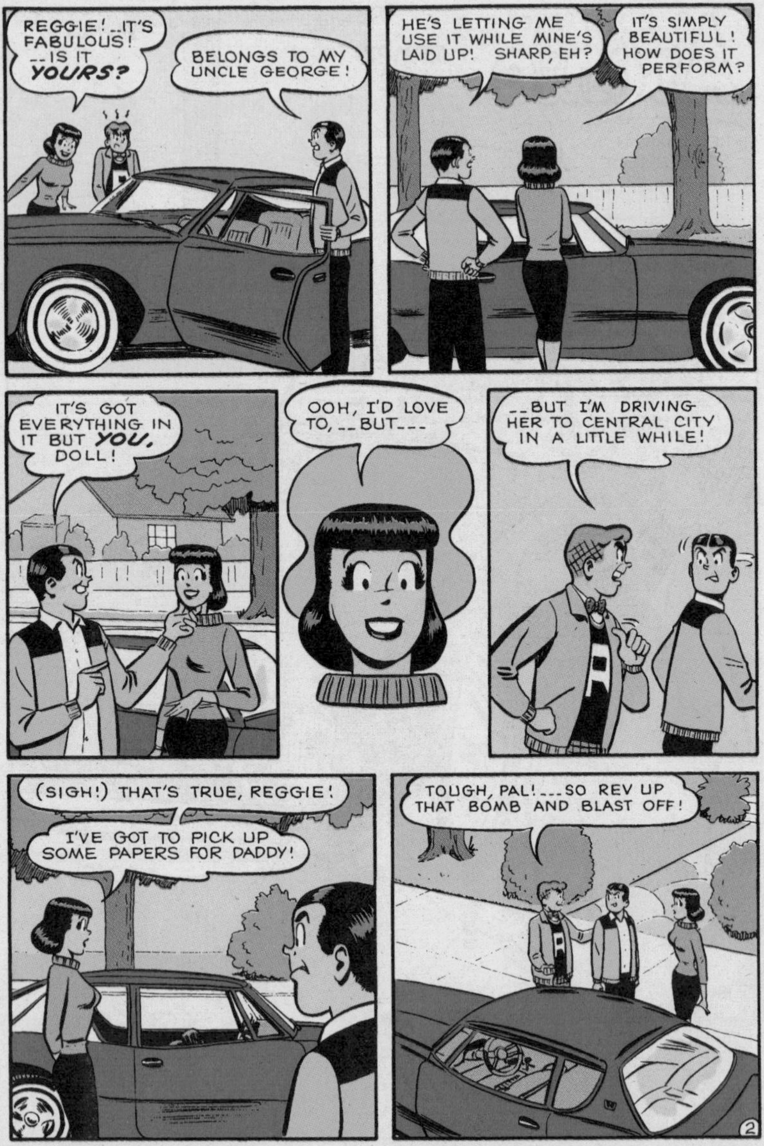
REGGIE! --IT'S FABULOUS! --IS IT *YOURS?*
BELONGS TO MY UNCLE GEORGE!
HE'S LETTING ME USE IT WHILE MINE'S LAID UP! SHARP, EH?
IT'S SIMPLY BEAUTIFUL! HOW DOES IT PERFORM?
IT'S GOT EVERYTHING IN IT BUT *YOU,* DOLL!
OOH, I'D LOVE TO, --BUT---
--BUT I'M DRIVING HER TO CENTRAL CITY IN A LITTLE WHILE!
(SIGH!) THAT'S TRUE, REGGIE!
I'VE GOT TO PICK UP SOME PAPERS FOR DADDY!
TOUGH, PAL! ---SO REV UP THAT BOMB AND BLAST OFF!
2

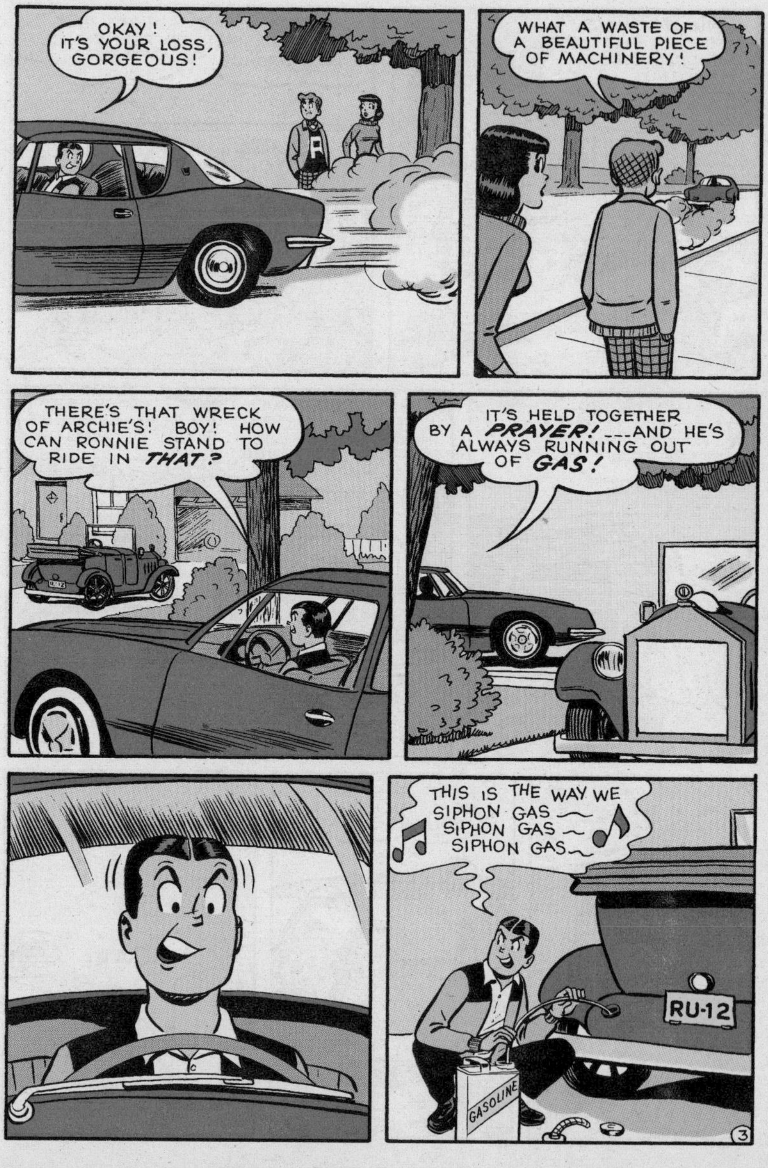
OKAY! IT'S YOUR LOSS, GORGEOUS!
WHAT A WASTE OF A BEAUTIFUL PIECE OF MACHINERY!
THERE'S THAT WRECK OF ARCHIE'S! BOY! HOW CAN RONNIE STAND TO RIDE IN THAT?
IT'S HELD TOGETHER BY A PRAYER! ---AND HE'S ALWAYS RUNNING OUT OF GAS!
THIS IS THE WAY WE SIPHON GAS~ SIPHON GAS~ SIPHON GAS~
RU-12
GASOLINE
3

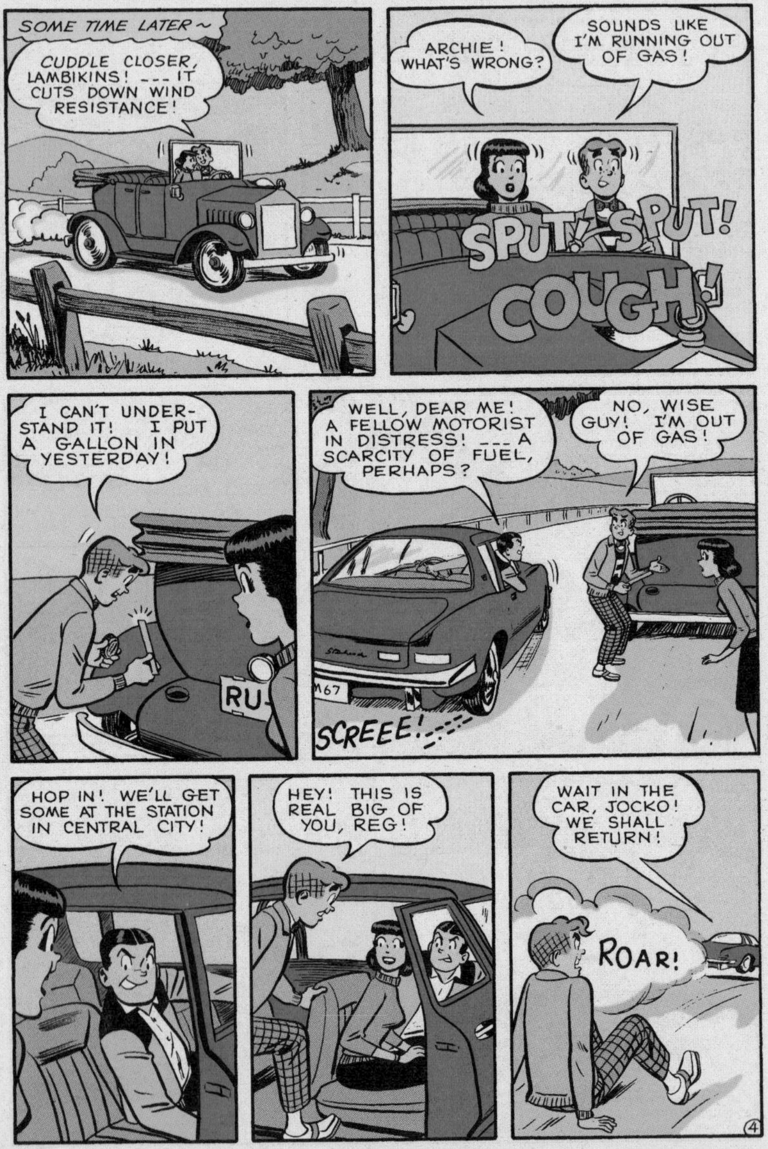
SOME TIME LATER~
CUDDLE CLOSER, LAMBIKINS! --- IT CUTS DOWN WIND RESISTANCE!
ARCHIE! WHAT'S WRONG?
SOUNDS LIKE I'M RUNNING OUT OF GAS!
SPUT! SPUT!
COUGH!
I CAN'T UNDERSTAND IT! I PUT A GALLON IN YESTERDAY!
RU-
WELL, DEAR ME! A FELLOW MOTORIST IN DISTRESS! --- A SCARCITY OF FUEL, PERHAPS?
NO, WISE GUY! I'M OUT OF GAS!
M67
SCREEE!
HOP IN! WE'LL GET SOME AT THE STATION IN CENTRAL CITY!
HEY! THIS IS REAL BIG OF YOU, REG!
WAIT IN THE CAR, JOCKO! WE SHALL RETURN!
ROAR!
4

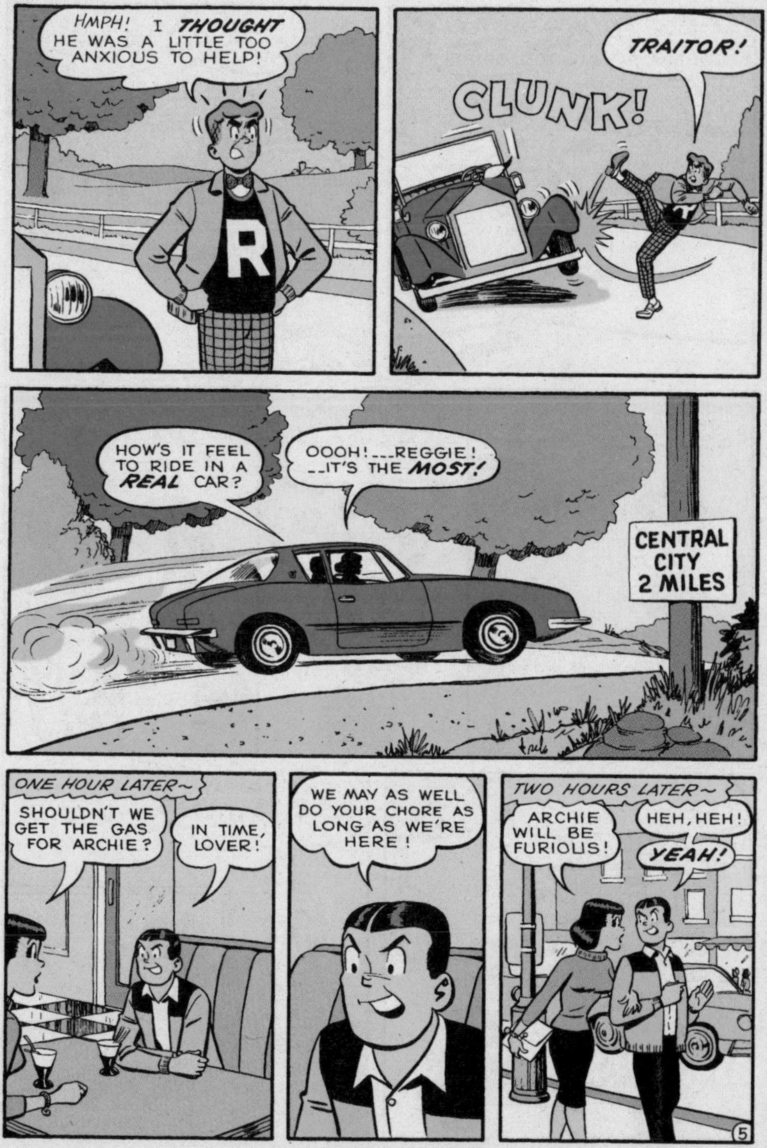

HMPH! I THOUGHT HE WAS A LITTLE TOO ANXIOUS TO HELP!
CLUNK!
TRAITOR!
HOW'S IT FEEL TO RIDE IN A REAL CAR?
OOOH! ---REGGIE! --IT'S THE MOST!
CENTRAL CITY 2 MILES
ONE HOUR LATER~
SHOULDN'T WE GET THE GAS FOR ARCHIE?
IN TIME, LOVER!
WE MAY AS WELL DO YOUR CHORE AS LONG AS WE'RE HERE!
TWO HOURS LATER~
ARCHIE WILL BE FURIOUS!
HEH, HEH!
YEAH!
5

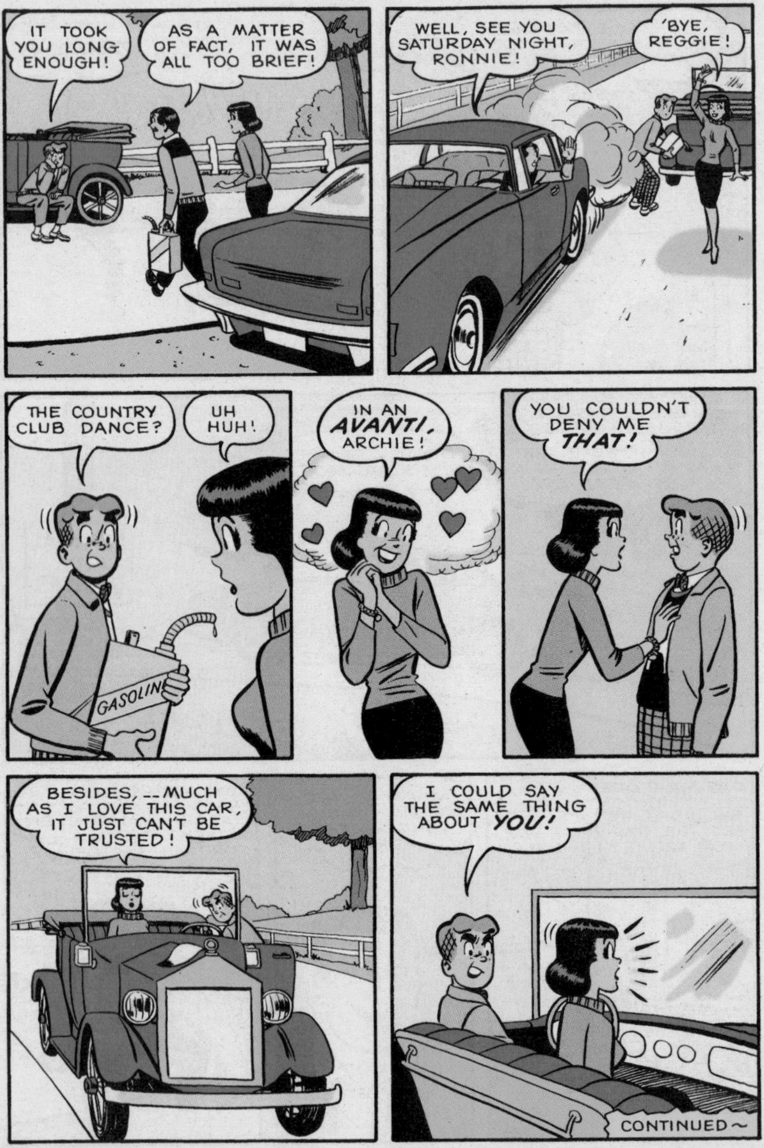
IT TOOK YOU LONG ENOUGH!
AS A MATTER OF FACT, IT WAS ALL TOO BRIEF!
WELL, SEE YOU SATURDAY NIGHT, RONNIE!
'BYE, REGGIE!
THE COUNTRY CLUB DANCE?
UH HUH!
GASOLIN
IN AN AVANTI, ARCHIE!
YOU COULDN'T DENY ME THAT!
BESIDES, -- MUCH AS I LOVE THIS CAR, IT JUST CAN'T BE TRUSTED!
I COULD SAY THE SAME THING ABOUT YOU!
CONTINUED ~

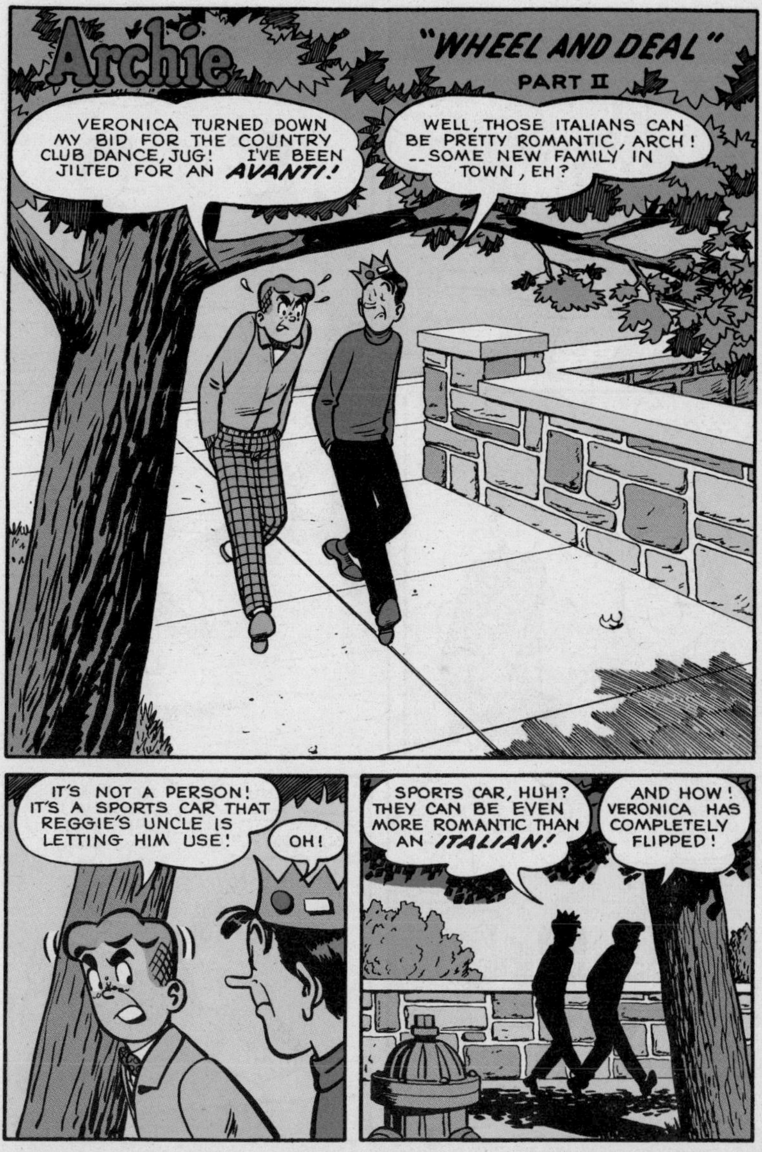
Archie
"WHEEL AND DEAL"
PART II
VERONICA TURNED DOWN MY BID FOR THE COUNTRY CLUB DANCE, JUG! I'VE BEEN JILTED FOR AN AVANTI!
WELL, THOSE ITALIANS CAN BE PRETTY ROMANTIC, ARCH! --SOME NEW FAMILY IN TOWN, EH?
IT'S NOT A PERSON! IT'S A SPORTS CAR THAT REGGIE'S UNCLE IS LETTING HIM USE!
OH!
SPORTS CAR, HUH? THEY CAN BE EVEN MORE ROMANTIC THAN AN ITALIAN!
AND HOW! VERONICA HAS COMPLETELY FLIPPED!

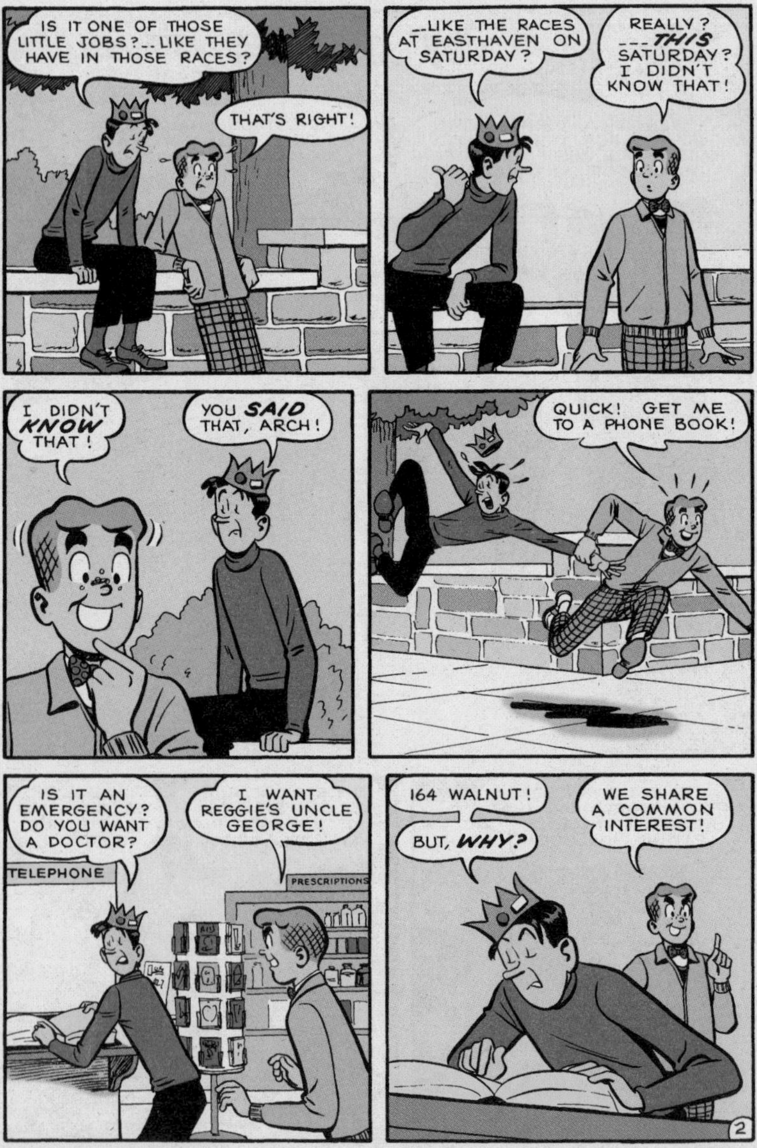
IS IT ONE OF THOSE LITTLE JOBS?.. LIKE THEY HAVE IN THOSE RACES?
THAT'S RIGHT!
..LIKE THE RACES AT EASTHAVEN ON SATURDAY?
REALLY? ---THIS SATURDAY? I DIDN'T KNOW THAT!
I DIDN'T KNOW THAT!
YOU SAID THAT, ARCH!
QUICK! GET ME TO A PHONE BOOK!
IS IT AN EMERGENCY? DO YOU WANT A DOCTOR?
I WANT REGGIE'S UNCLE GEORGE!
TELEPHONE
PRESCRIPTIONS
164 WALNUT!
BUT, WHY?
WE SHARE A COMMON INTEREST!
2

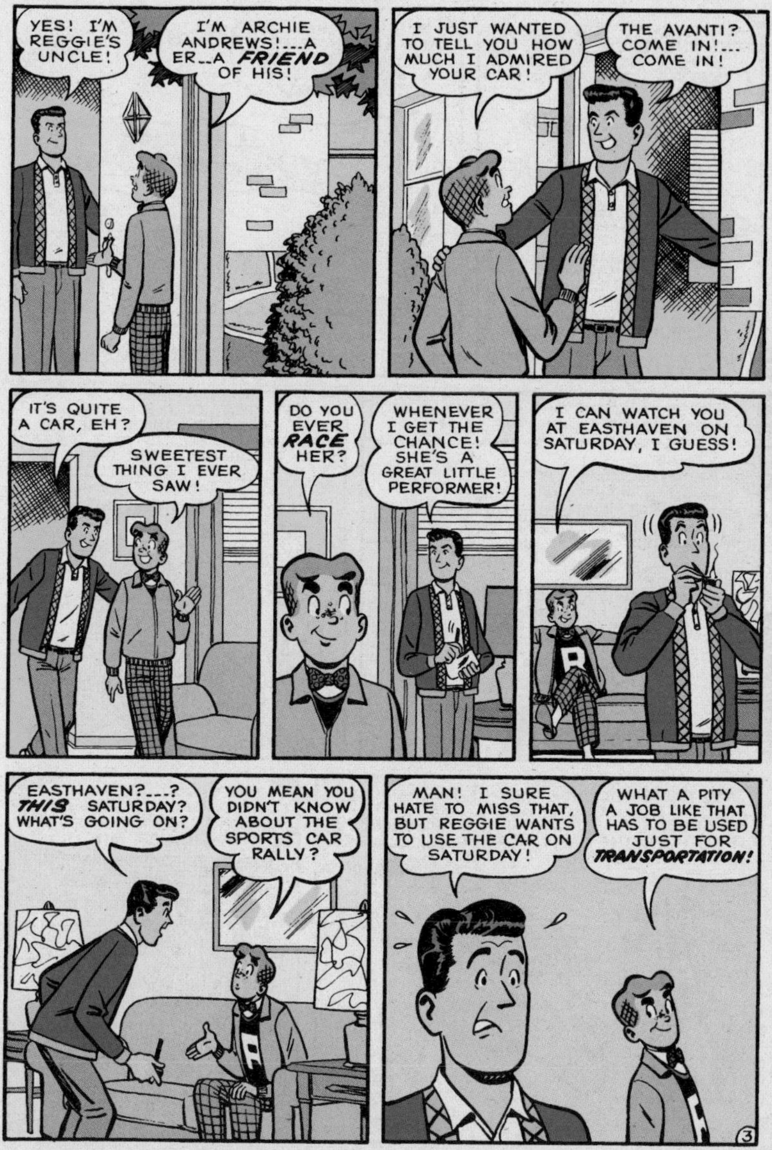
YES! I'M REGGIE'S UNCLE!
I'M ARCHIE ANDREWS!...A ER..A FRIEND OF HIS!
I JUST WANTED TO TELL YOU HOW MUCH I ADMIRED YOUR CAR!
THE AVANTI? COME IN!... COME IN!
IT'S QUITE A CAR, EH?
SWEETEST THING I EVER SAW!
DO YOU EVER RACE HER?
WHENEVER I GET THE CHANCE! SHE'S A GREAT LITTLE PERFORMER!
I CAN WATCH YOU AT EASTHAVEN ON SATURDAY, I GUESS!
EASTHAVEN?...? THIS SATURDAY? WHAT'S GOING ON?
YOU MEAN YOU DIDN'T KNOW ABOUT THE SPORTS CAR RALLY?
MAN! I SURE HATE TO MISS THAT, BUT REGGIE WANTS TO USE THE CAR ON SATURDAY!
WHAT A PITY A JOB LIKE THAT HAS TO BE USED JUST FOR TRANSPORTATION!
3

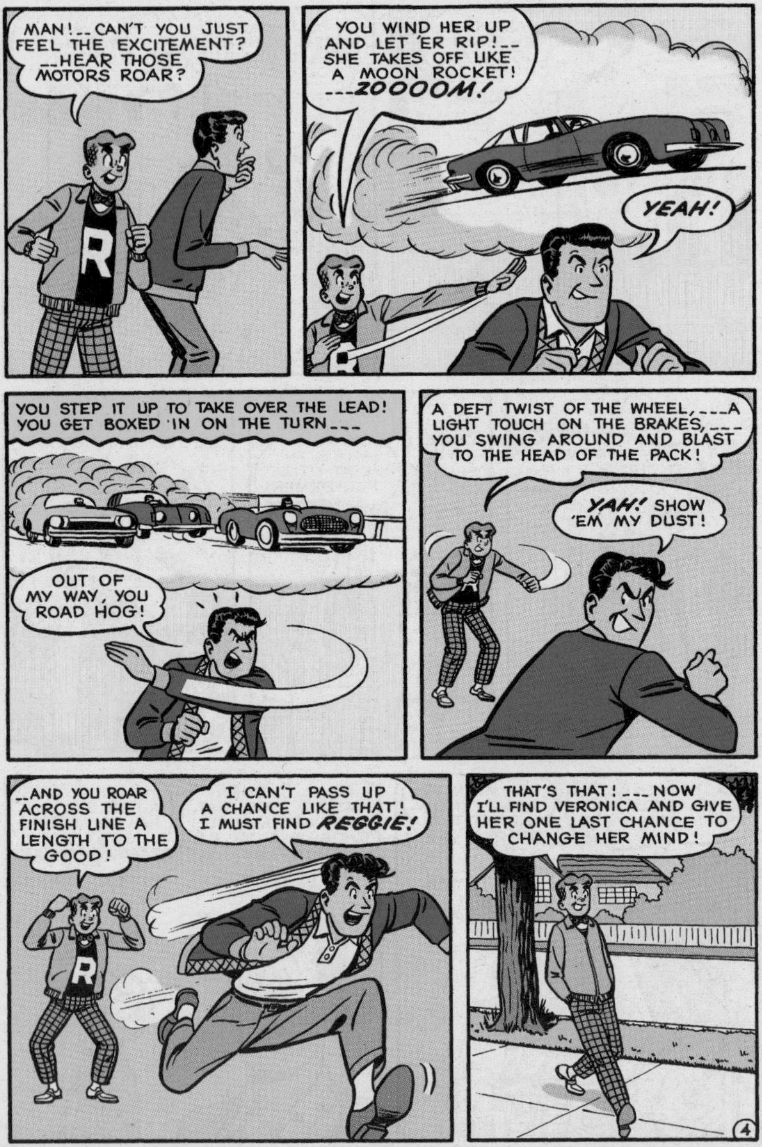
MAN! -- CAN'T YOU JUST FEEL THE EXCITEMENT? -- HEAR THOSE MOTORS ROAR?
YOU WIND HER UP AND LET 'ER RIP! -- SHE TAKES OFF LIKE A MOON ROCKET! --- ZOOOOM!
YEAH!
YOU STEP IT UP TO TAKE OVER THE LEAD! YOU GET BOXED IN ON THE TURN ---
OUT OF MY WAY, YOU ROAD HOG!
A DEFT TWIST OF THE WHEEL, --- A LIGHT TOUCH ON THE BRAKES, --- YOU SWING AROUND AND BLAST TO THE HEAD OF THE PACK!
YAH! SHOW 'EM MY DUST!
-- AND YOU ROAR ACROSS THE FINISH LINE A LENGTH TO THE GOOD!
I CAN'T PASS UP A CHANCE LIKE THAT! I MUST FIND REGGIE!
THAT'S THAT! --- NOW I'LL FIND VERONICA AND GIVE HER ONE LAST CHANCE TO CHANGE HER MIND!
4

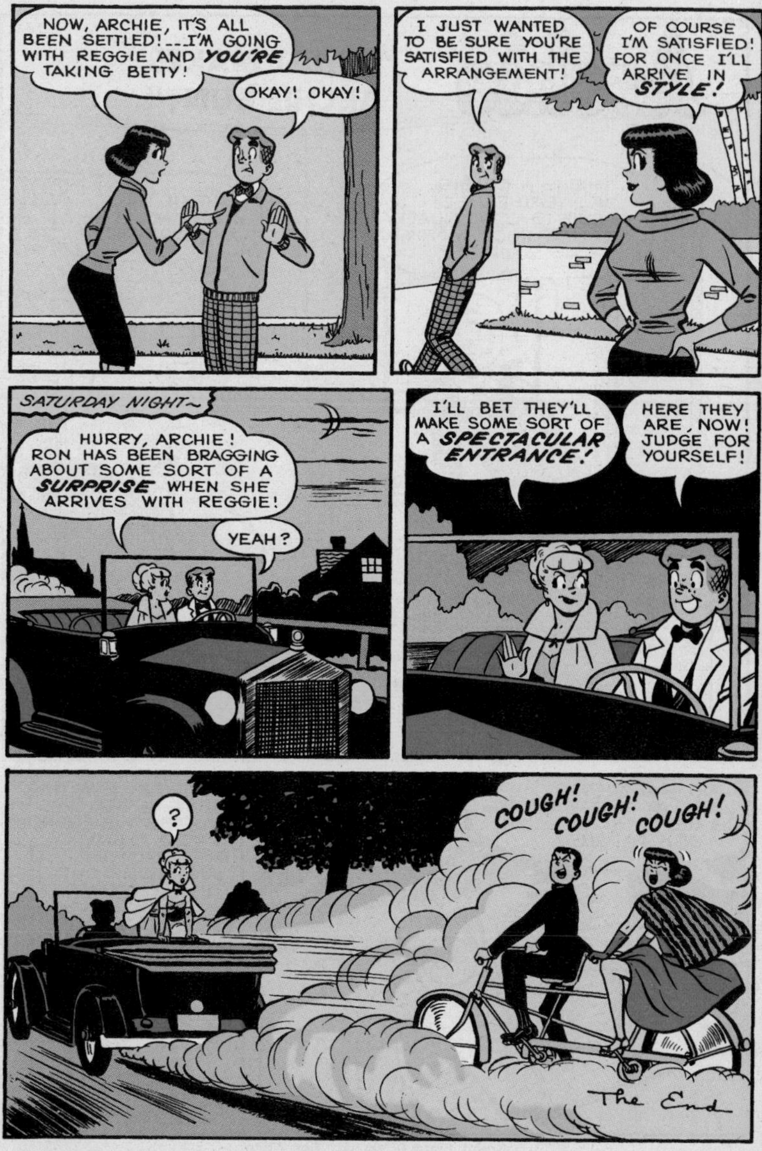
NOW, ARCHIE, IT'S ALL BEEN SETTLED!...I'M GOING WITH REGGIE AND YOU'RE TAKING BETTY!
OKAY! OKAY!
I JUST WANTED TO BE SURE YOU'RE SATISFIED WITH THE ARRANGEMENT!
OF COURSE I'M SATISFIED! FOR ONCE I'LL ARRIVE IN STYLE!
SATURDAY NIGHT~
HURRY, ARCHIE! RON HAS BEEN BRAGGING ABOUT SOME SORT OF A SURPRISE WHEN SHE ARRIVES WITH REGGIE!
YEAH?
I'LL BET THEY'LL MAKE SOME SORT OF A SPECTACULAR ENTRANCE!
HERE THEY ARE, NOW! JUDGE FOR YOURSELF!
?
COUGH! COUGH! COUGH!
The End

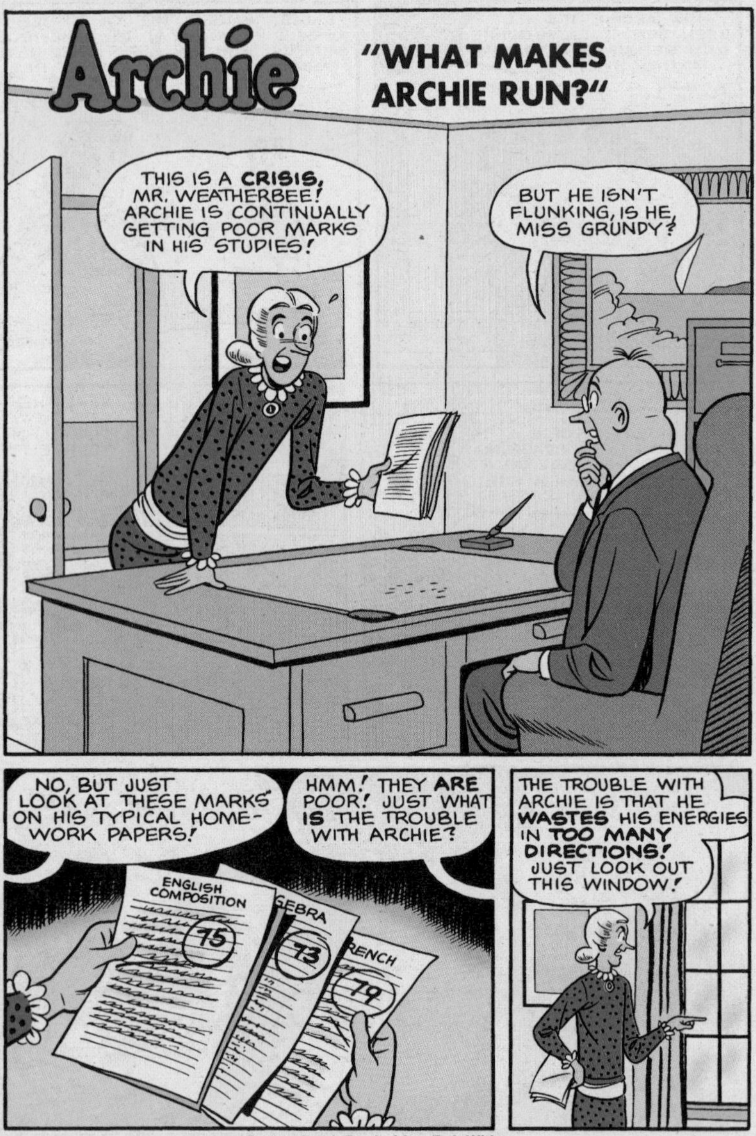
Archie
"WHAT MAKES ARCHIE RUN?"
THIS IS A CRISIS, MR. WEATHERBEE! ARCHIE IS CONTINUALLY GETTING POOR MARKS IN HIS STUDIES!
BUT HE ISN'T FLUNKING, IS HE, MISS GRUNDY?
NO, BUT JUST LOOK AT THESE MARKS ON HIS TYPICAL HOME-WORK PAPERS!
HMM! THEY ARE POOR! JUST WHAT IS THE TROUBLE WITH ARCHIE?
ENGLISH COMPOSITION
75
GEBRA
73
RENCH
79
THE TROUBLE WITH ARCHIE IS THAT HE WASTES HIS ENERGIES IN TOO MANY DIRECTIONS! JUST LOOK OUT THIS WINDOW!

Script: Frank Doyle / Art: Bob White

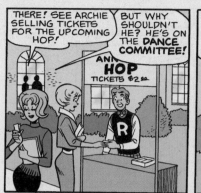

THERE! SEE ARCHIE SELLING TICKETS FOR THE UPCOMING HOP!

BUT WHY SHOULDN'T HE? HE'S ON THE **DANCE** COMMITTEE!

HOP TICKETS $2.00

AND **NOW** LOOK AT HIM! HE'S GOING OFF WITH VERONICA LODGE TO WASTE MORE TIME!

BUT SHE'S HIS **GIRL!**

ARCHIE ANDREWS, REPORT TO THE TRACK COACH!

AND LISTEN TO THAT!

BUT, MISS GRUNDY, ARCHIE'S ON THE TRACK TEAM!

YES, AND ON THE **GLEE CLUB,** THE **TENNIS TEAM,** THE **SCHOOL NEWSPAPER,** THE **DEBATING TEAM,** AND HEAVEN KNOWS WHAT ELSE!

HE IS SO BUSY RUNNING AROUND WITH THESE EXTRA-CURRICULAR ACTIVITIES THAT HE HAS NO TIME TO CONCENTRATE ON HIS **SCHOOL WORK!** IT'S POSSIBLE THAT ARCHIE MAY NOT GRADUATE WITH HIS CLASS!

ARCHIE! NOT GRADUATE!

2

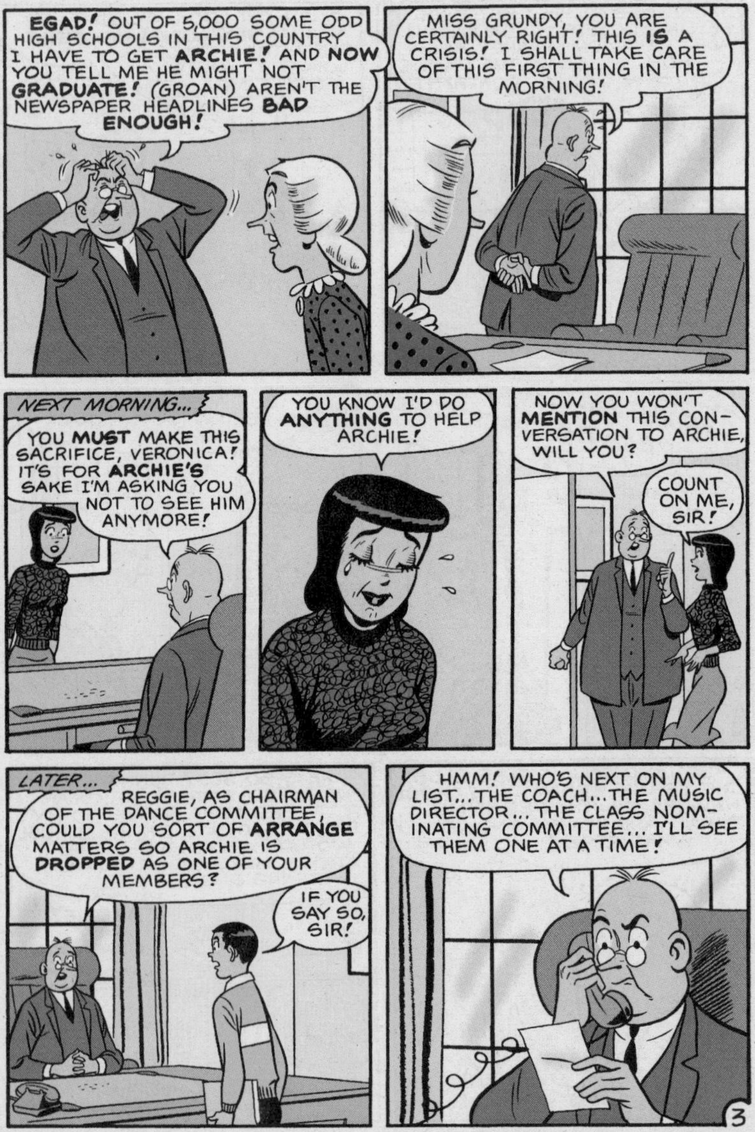

EGAD! OUT OF 5,000 SOME ODD HIGH SCHOOLS IN THIS COUNTRY I HAVE TO GET ARCHIE! AND NOW YOU TELL ME HE MIGHT NOT GRADUATE! (GROAN) AREN'T THE NEWSPAPER HEADLINES BAD ENOUGH!
MISS GRUNDY, YOU ARE CERTAINLY RIGHT! THIS IS A CRISIS! I SHALL TAKE CARE OF THIS FIRST THING IN THE MORNING!
NEXT MORNING...
YOU MUST MAKE THIS SACRIFICE, VERONICA! IT'S FOR ARCHIE'S SAKE I'M ASKING YOU NOT TO SEE HIM ANYMORE!
YOU KNOW I'D DO ANYTHING TO HELP ARCHIE!
NOW YOU WON'T MENTION THIS CON-VERSATION TO ARCHIE, WILL YOU?
COUNT ON ME, SIR!
LATER...
REGGIE, AS CHAIRMAN OF THE DANCE COMMITTEE, COULD YOU SORT OF ARRANGE MATTERS SO ARCHIE IS DROPPED AS ONE OF YOUR MEMBERS?
IF YOU SAY SO, SIR!
HMM! WHO'S NEXT ON MY LIST... THE COACH... THE MUSIC DIRECTOR... THE CLASS NOM-INATING COMMITTEE... I'LL SEE THEM ONE AT A TIME!
3

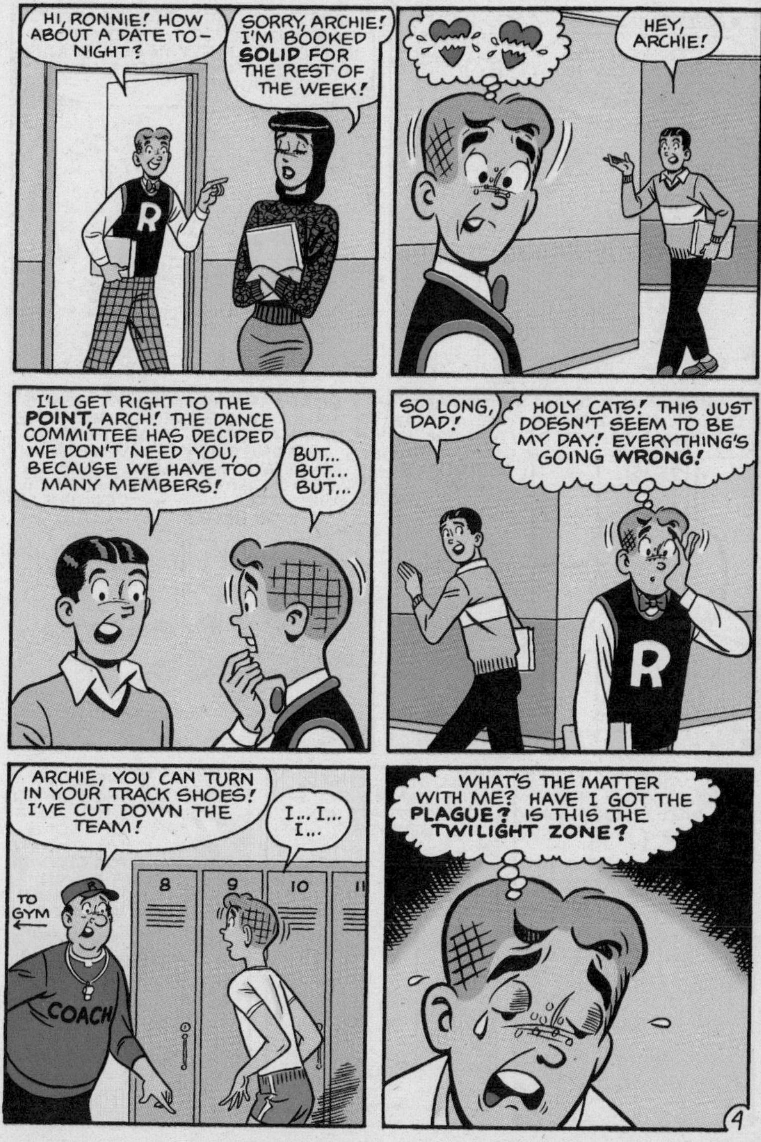
HI, RONNIE! HOW ABOUT A DATE TO-NIGHT?
SORRY, ARCHIE! I'M BOOKED SOLID FOR THE REST OF THE WEEK!
HEY, ARCHIE!
I'LL GET RIGHT TO THE POINT, ARCH! THE DANCE COMMITTEE HAS DECIDED WE DON'T NEED YOU, BECAUSE WE HAVE TOO MANY MEMBERS!
BUT... BUT... BUT...
SO LONG, DAD!
HOLY CATS! THIS JUST DOESN'T SEEM TO BE MY DAY! EVERYTHING'S GOING WRONG!
ARCHIE, YOU CAN TURN IN YOUR TRACK SHOES! I'VE CUT DOWN THE TEAM!
I... I... I...
TO GYM
8
9
10
COACH
WHAT'S THE MATTER WITH ME? HAVE I GOT THE PLAGUE? IS THIS THE TWILIGHT ZONE?

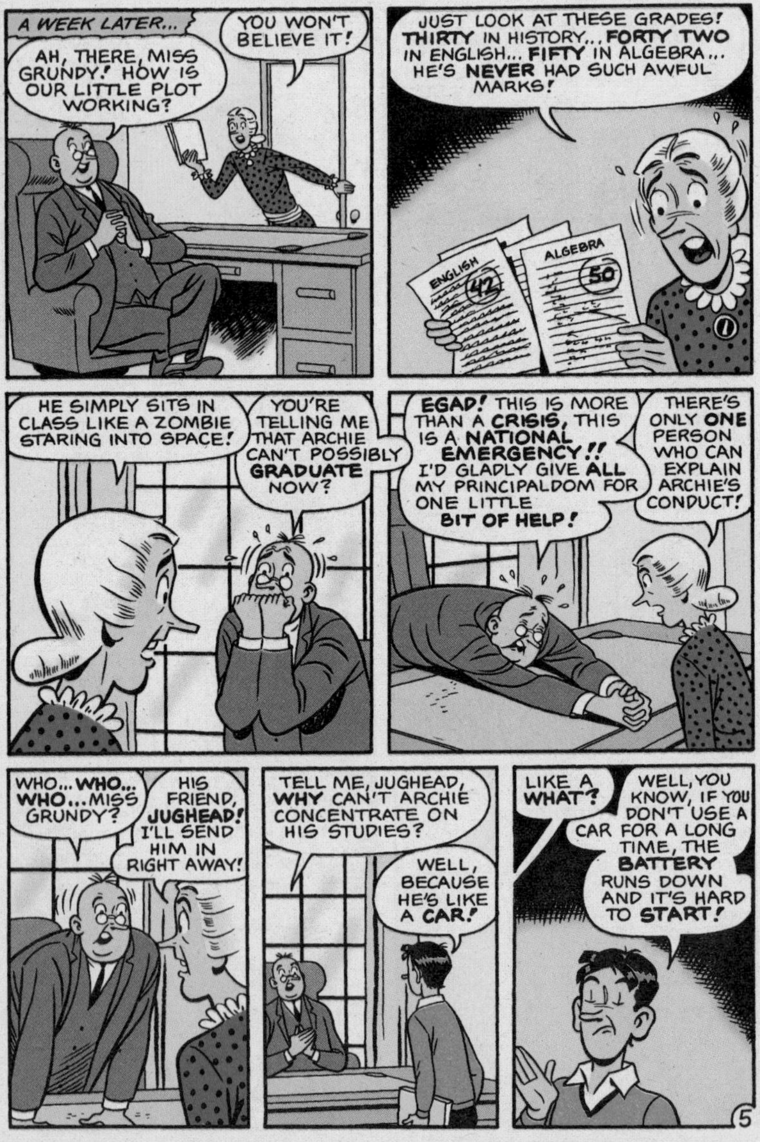
A WEEK LATER...
AH, THERE, MISS GRUNDY! HOW IS OUR LITTLE PLOT WORKING?
YOU WON'T BELIEVE IT!
JUST LOOK AT THESE GRADES! THIRTY IN HISTORY... FORTY TWO IN ENGLISH... FIFTY IN ALGEBRA... HE'S NEVER HAD SUCH AWFUL MARKS!
ENGLISH
42
ALGEBRA
50
HE SIMPLY SITS IN CLASS LIKE A ZOMBIE STARING INTO SPACE!
YOU'RE TELLING ME THAT ARCHIE CAN'T POSSIBLY GRADUATE NOW?
EGAD! THIS IS MORE THAN A CRISIS, THIS IS A NATIONAL EMERGENCY!! I'D GLADLY GIVE ALL MY PRINCIPALDOM FOR ONE LITTLE BIT OF HELP!
THERE'S ONLY ONE PERSON WHO CAN EXPLAIN ARCHIE'S CONDUCT!
WHO... WHO... WHO... MISS GRUNDY?
HIS FRIEND, JUGHEAD! I'LL SEND HIM IN RIGHT AWAY!
TELL ME, JUGHEAD, WHY CAN'T ARCHIE CONCENTRATE ON HIS STUDIES?
WELL, BECAUSE HE'S LIKE A CAR!
LIKE A WHAT?
WELL, YOU KNOW, IF YOU DON'T USE A CAR FOR A LONG TIME, THE BATTERY RUNS DOWN AND IT'S HARD TO START!

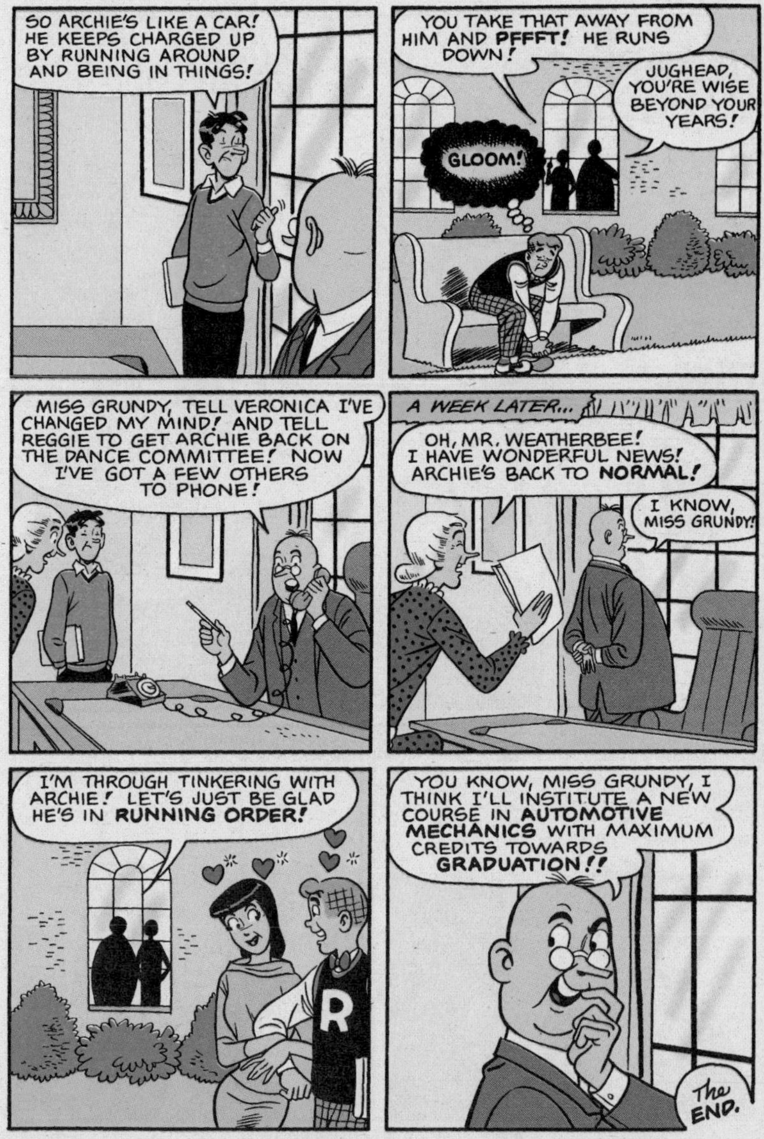
SO ARCHIE'S LIKE A CAR! HE KEEPS CHARGED UP BY RUNNING AROUND AND BEING IN THINGS!
YOU TAKE THAT AWAY FROM HIM AND PFFFT! HE RUNS DOWN!
JUGHEAD, YOU'RE WISE BEYOND YOUR YEARS!
GLOOM!
MISS GRUNDY, TELL VERONICA I'VE CHANGED MY MIND! AND TELL REGGIE TO GET ARCHIE BACK ON THE DANCE COMMITTEE! NOW I'VE GOT A FEW OTHERS TO PHONE!
A WEEK LATER...
OH, MR. WEATHERBEE! I HAVE WONDERFUL NEWS! ARCHIE'S BACK TO NORMAL!
I KNOW, MISS GRUNDY!
I'M THROUGH TINKERING WITH ARCHIE! LET'S JUST BE GLAD HE'S IN RUNNING ORDER!
YOU KNOW, MISS GRUNDY, I THINK I'LL INSTITUTE A NEW COURSE IN AUTOMOTIVE MECHANICS WITH MAXIMUM CREDITS TOWARDS GRADUATION!!
The END.

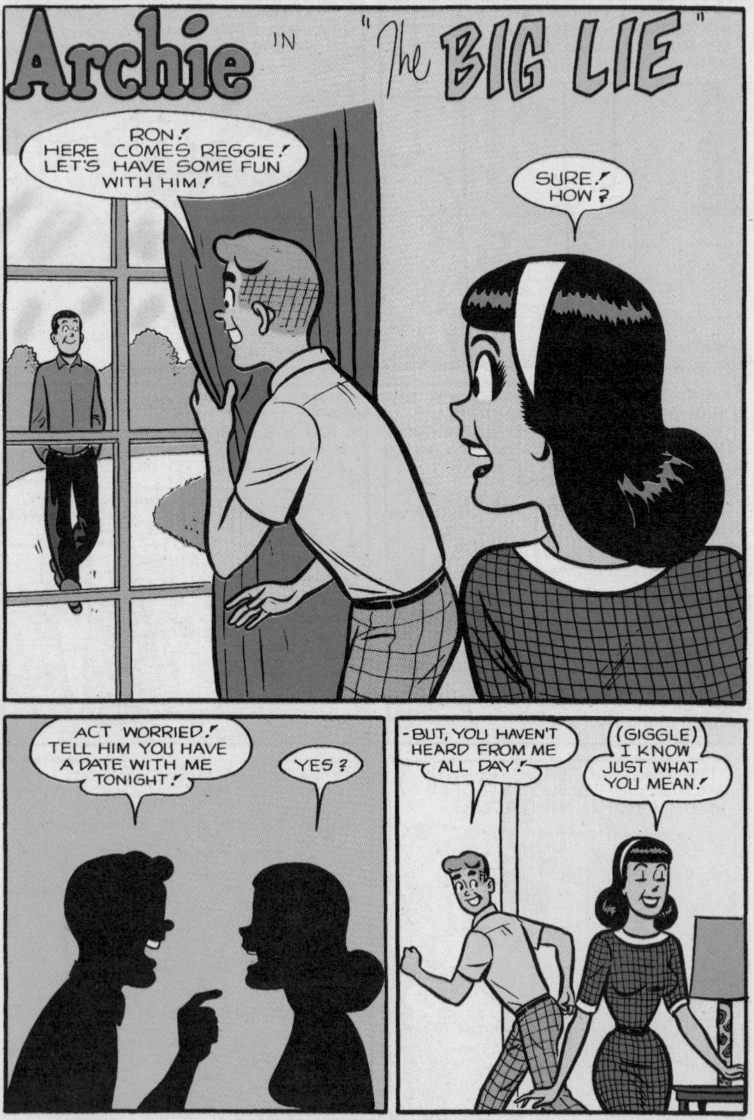
Archie IN "The BIG LIE"
RON! HERE COMES REGGIE! LET'S HAVE SOME FUN WITH HIM!
SURE! HOW?
ACT WORRIED! TELL HIM YOU HAVE A DATE WITH ME TONIGHT!
YES?
-BUT, YOU HAVEN'T HEARD FROM ME ALL DAY!
(GIGGLE) I KNOW JUST WHAT YOU MEAN!

Script: Frank Doyle / Art: Bill Vigoda

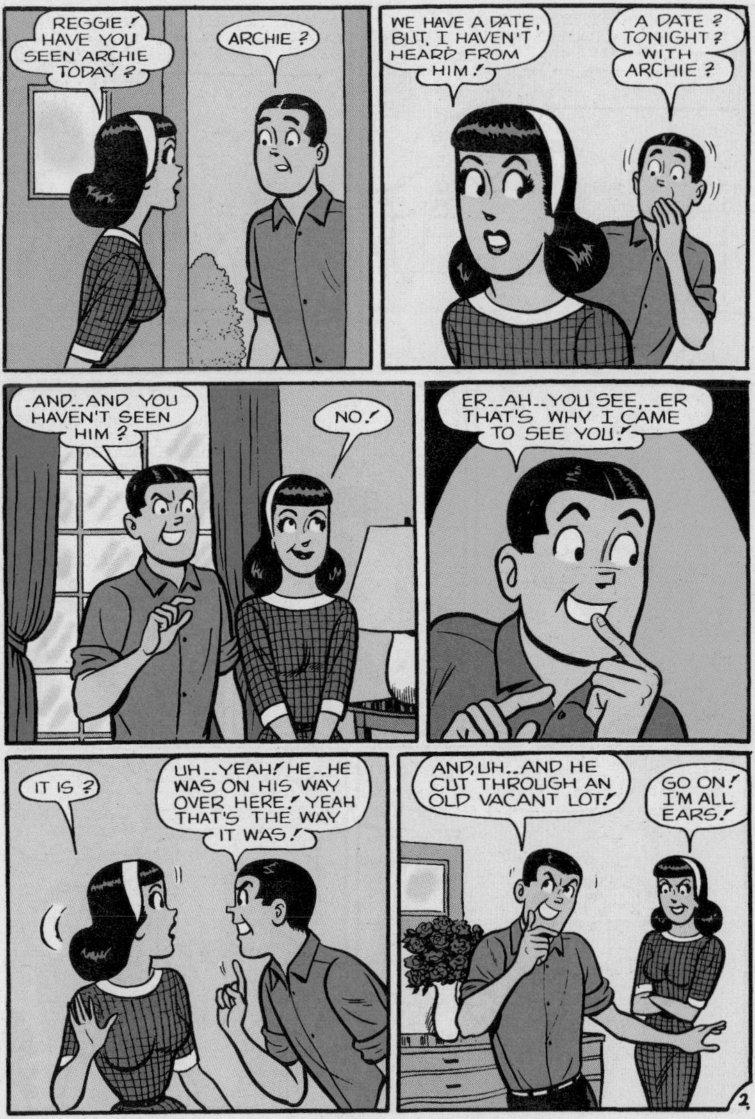
REGGIE! HAVE YOU SEEN ARCHIE TODAY?
ARCHIE?
WE HAVE A DATE, BUT, I HAVEN'T HEARD FROM HIM!
A DATE? TONIGHT? WITH ARCHIE?
..AND..AND YOU HAVEN'T SEEN HIM?
NO!
ER..AH..YOU SEE,..ER THAT'S WHY I CAME TO SEE YOU!
IT IS?
UH..YEAH! HE..HE WAS ON HIS WAY OVER HERE! YEAH THAT'S THE WAY IT WAS!
AND, UH..AND HE CUT THROUGH AN OLD VACANT LOT!
GO ON! I'M ALL EARS!
2.

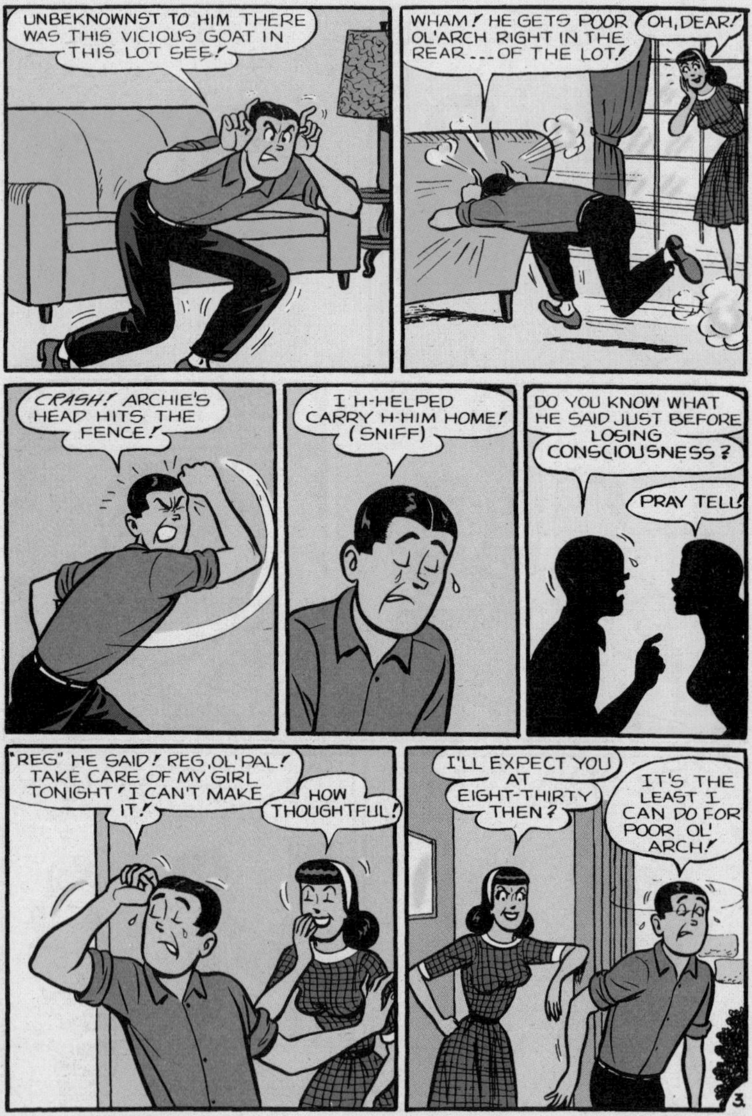
UNBEKNOWNST TO HIM THERE WAS THIS VICIOUS GOAT IN THIS LOT SEE!
WHAM! HE GETS POOR OL'ARCH RIGHT IN THE REAR ... OF THE LOT!
OH, DEAR!
CRASH! ARCHIE'S HEAD HITS THE FENCE!
I H-HELPED CARRY H-HIM HOME! (SNIFF)
DO YOU KNOW WHAT HE SAID JUST BEFORE LOSING CONSCIOUSNESS?
PRAY TELL!
"REG" HE SAID! REG, OL' PAL! TAKE CARE OF MY GIRL TONIGHT! I CAN'T MAKE IT!
HOW THOUGHTFUL!
I'LL EXPECT YOU AT EIGHT-THIRTY THEN?
IT'S THE LEAST I CAN DO FOR POOR OL' ARCH!
3

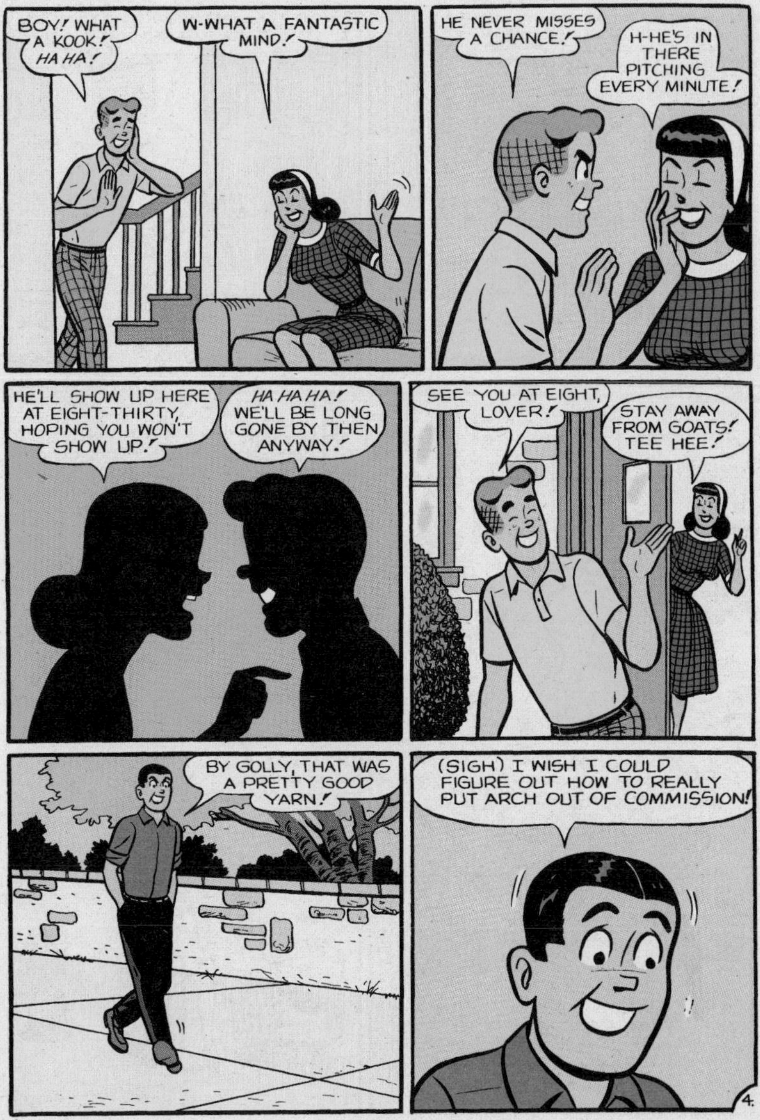

BOY! WHAT A KOOK! HA HA!
W-WHAT A FANTASTIC MIND!
HE NEVER MISSES A CHANCE!
H-HE'S IN THERE PITCHING EVERY MINUTE!
HE'LL SHOW UP HERE AT EIGHT-THIRTY, HOPING YOU WON'T SHOW UP!
HA HA HA! WE'LL BE LONG GONE BY THEN ANYWAY!
SEE YOU AT EIGHT, LOVER!
STAY AWAY FROM GOATS! TEE HEE!
BY GOLLY, THAT WAS A PRETTY GOOD YARN!
(SIGH) I WISH I COULD FIGURE OUT HOW TO REALLY PUT ARCH OUT OF COMMISSION!

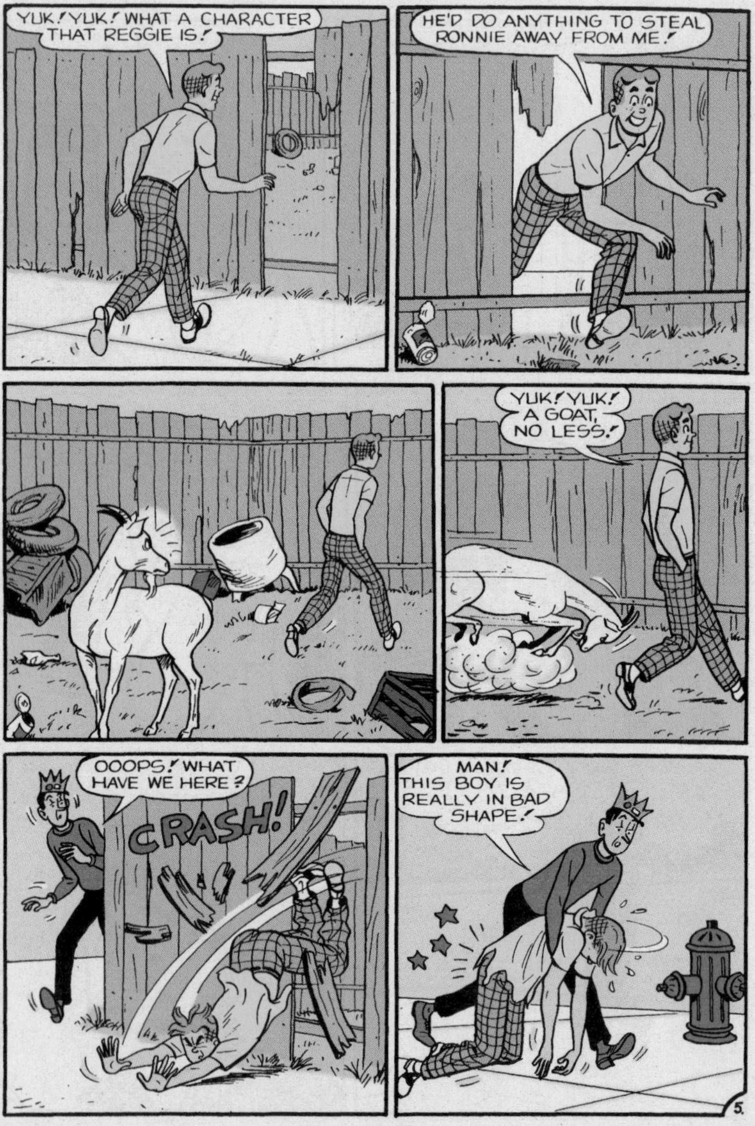
YUK! YUK! WHAT A CHARACTER THAT REGGIE IS!
HE'D DO ANYTHING TO STEAL RONNIE AWAY FROM ME!
YUK! YUK! A GOAT, NO LESS!
OOOPS! WHAT HAVE WE HERE?
CRASH!
MAN! THIS BOY IS REALLY IN BAD SHAPE!

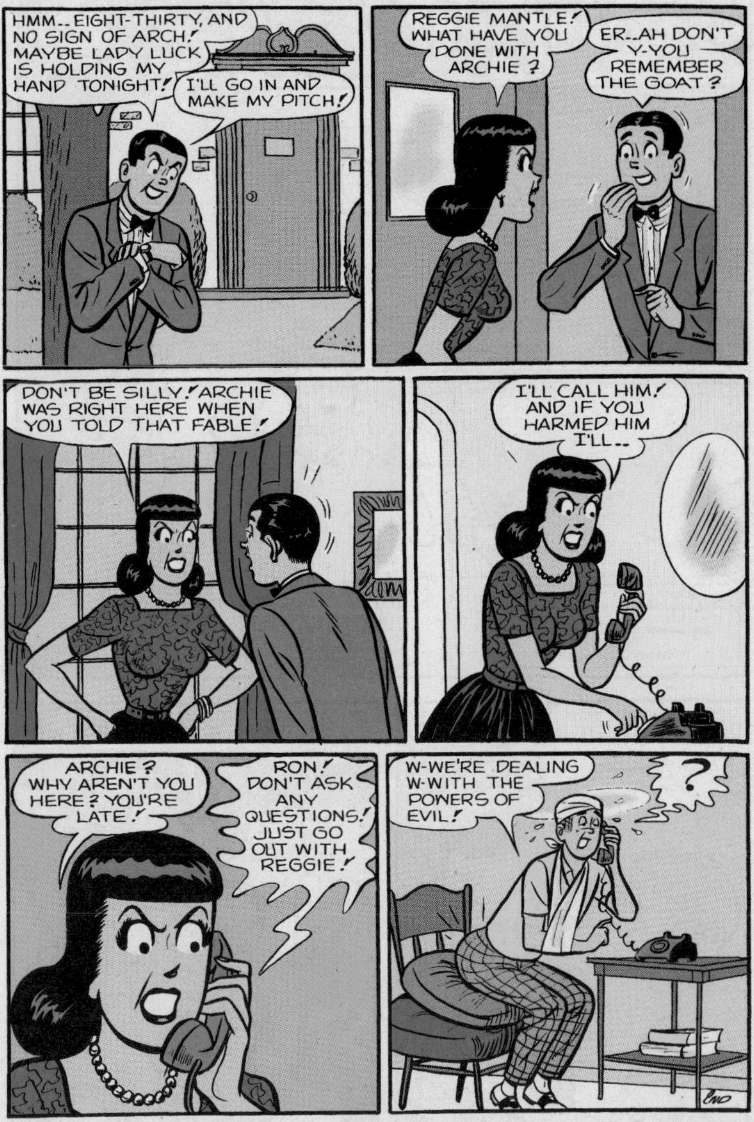
HMM.. EIGHT-THIRTY, AND NO SIGN OF ARCH! MAYBE LADY LUCK IS HOLDING MY HAND TONIGHT!
I'LL GO IN AND MAKE MY PITCH!
REGGIE MANTLE! WHAT HAVE YOU DONE WITH ARCHIE ?
ER..AH DON'T Y-YOU REMEMBER THE GOAT ?
DON'T BE SILLY! ARCHIE WAS RIGHT HERE WHEN YOU TOLD THAT FABLE!
I'LL CALL HIM! AND IF YOU HARMED HIM I'LL..
ARCHIE ? WHY AREN'T YOU HERE ? YOU'RE LATE!
RON! DON'T ASK ANY QUESTIONS! JUST GO OUT WITH REGGIE!
W-WE'RE DEALING W-WITH THE POWERS OF EVIL!
?
END

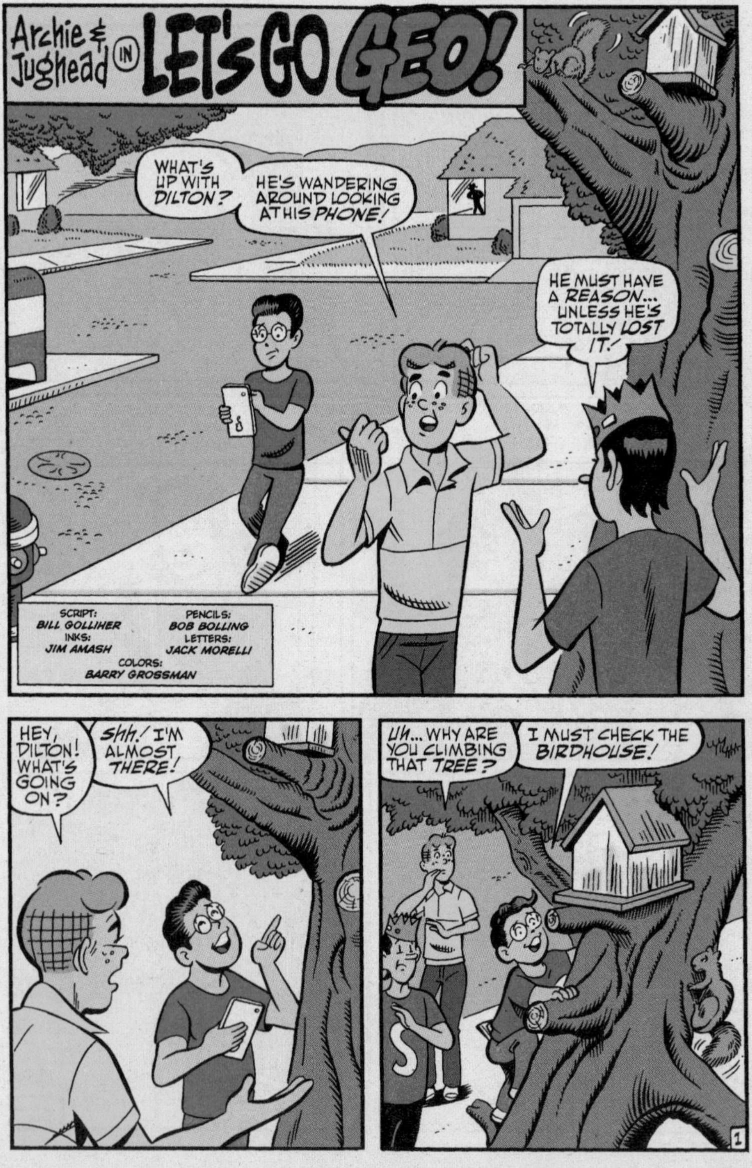
Archie & Jughead IN LET'S GO GEO!
WHAT'S UP WITH DILTON?
HE'S WANDERING AROUND LOOKING AT HIS PHONE!
HE MUST HAVE A REASON... UNLESS HE'S TOTALLY LOST IT!
SCRIPT: BILL GOLLIHER
PENCILS: BOB BOLLING
INKS: JIM AMASH
LETTERS: JACK MORELLI
COLORS: BARRY GROSSMAN
HEY, DILTON! WHAT'S GOING ON?
SHH! I'M ALMOST THERE!
UH... WHY ARE YOU CLIMBING THAT TREE?
I MUST CHECK THE BIRDHOUSE!
1

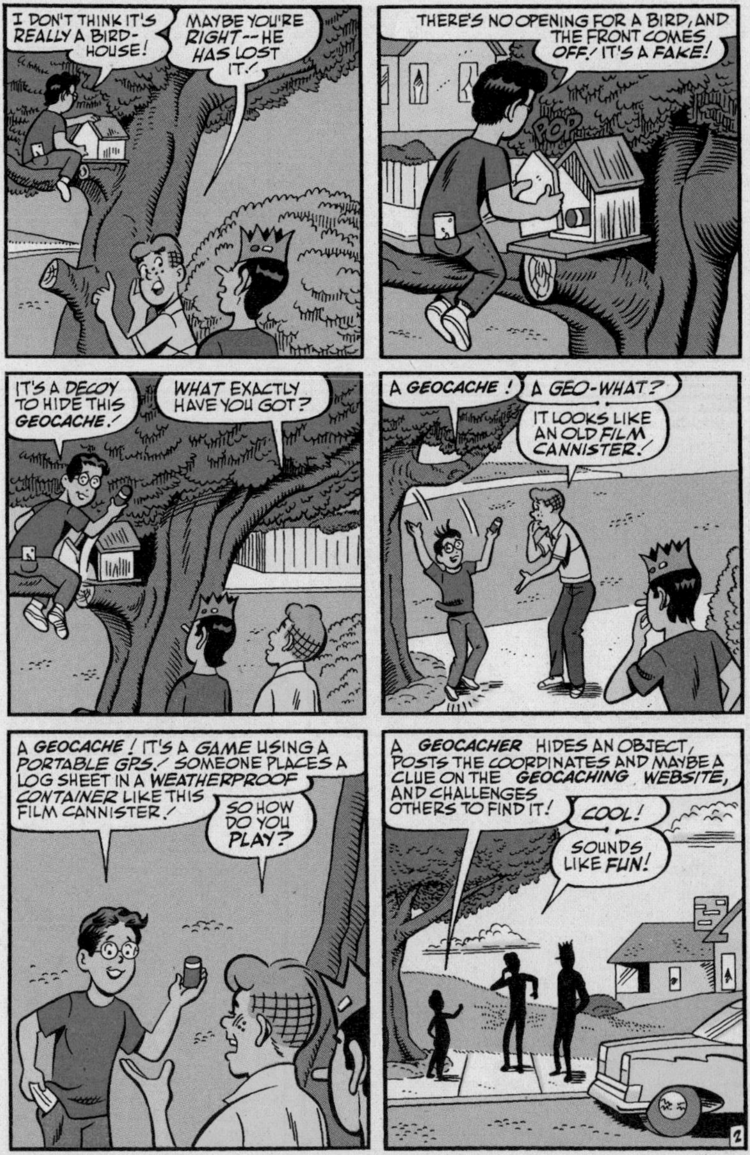

I DON'T THINK IT'S REALLY A BIRD-HOUSE!
MAYBE YOU'RE RIGHT--HE HAS LOST IT!
THERE'S NO OPENING FOR A BIRD, AND THE FRONT COMES OFF! IT'S A FAKE!
POP
IT'S A DECOY TO HIDE THIS GEOCACHE!
WHAT EXACTLY HAVE YOU GOT?
A GEOCACHE!
A GEO-WHAT?
IT LOOKS LIKE AN OLD FILM CANNISTER!
A GEOCACHE! IT'S A GAME USING A PORTABLE GPS! SOMEONE PLACES A LOG SHEET IN A WEATHERPROOF CONTAINER LIKE THIS FILM CANNISTER!
SO HOW DO YOU PLAY?
A GEOCACHER HIDES AN OBJECT, POSTS THE COORDINATES AND MAYBE A CLUE ON THE GEOCACHING WEBSITE, AND CHALLENGES OTHERS TO FIND IT!
COOL!
SOUNDS LIKE FUN!
2

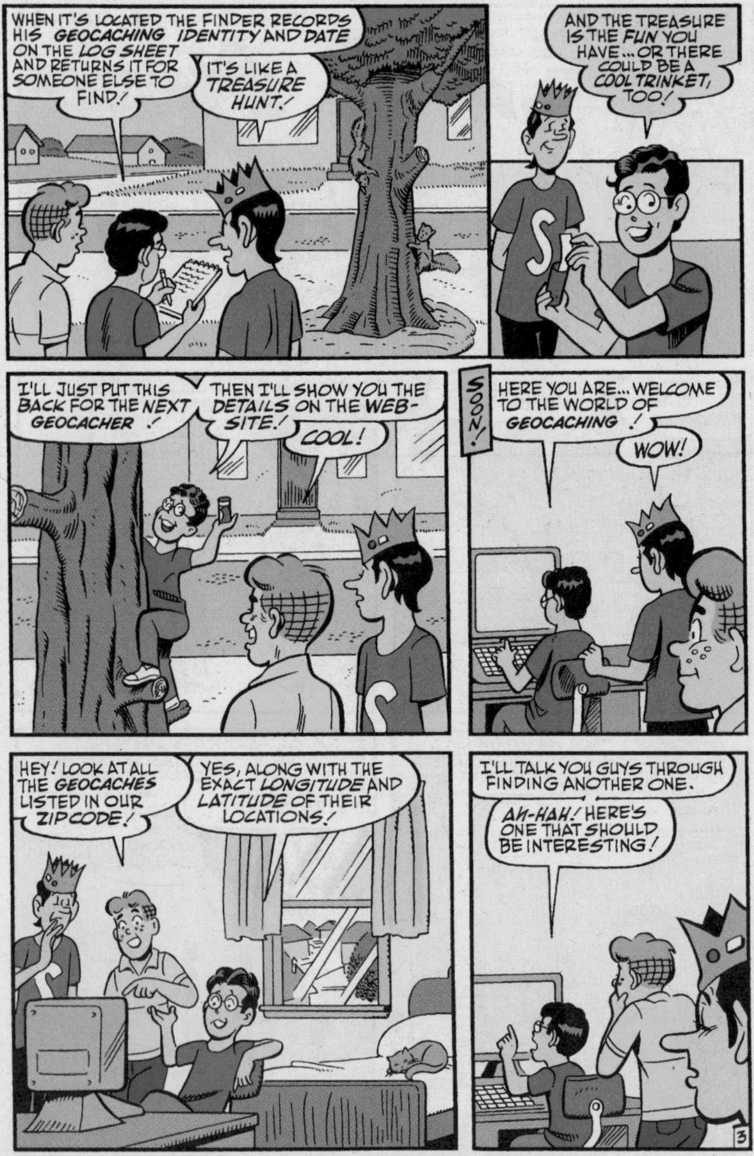

WHEN IT'S LOCATED THE FINDER RECORDS HIS GEOCACHING IDENTITY AND DATE ON THE LOG SHEET AND RETURNS IT FOR SOMEONE ELSE TO FIND!
IT'S LIKE A TREASURE HUNT!
AND THE TREASURE IS THE FUN YOU HAVE... OR THERE COULD BE A COOL TRINKET, TOO!
I'LL JUST PUT THIS BACK FOR THE NEXT GEOCACHER!
THEN I'LL SHOW YOU THE DETAILS ON THE WEB-SITE!
COOL!
SOON!
HERE YOU ARE... WELCOME TO THE WORLD OF GEOCACHING!
WOW!
HEY! LOOK AT ALL THE GEOCACHES LISTED IN OUR ZIP CODE!
YES, ALONG WITH THE EXACT LONGITUDE AND LATITUDE OF THEIR LOCATIONS!
I'LL TALK YOU GUYS THROUGH FINDING ANOTHER ONE.
AH-HAH! HERE'S ONE THAT SHOULD BE INTERESTING!
3

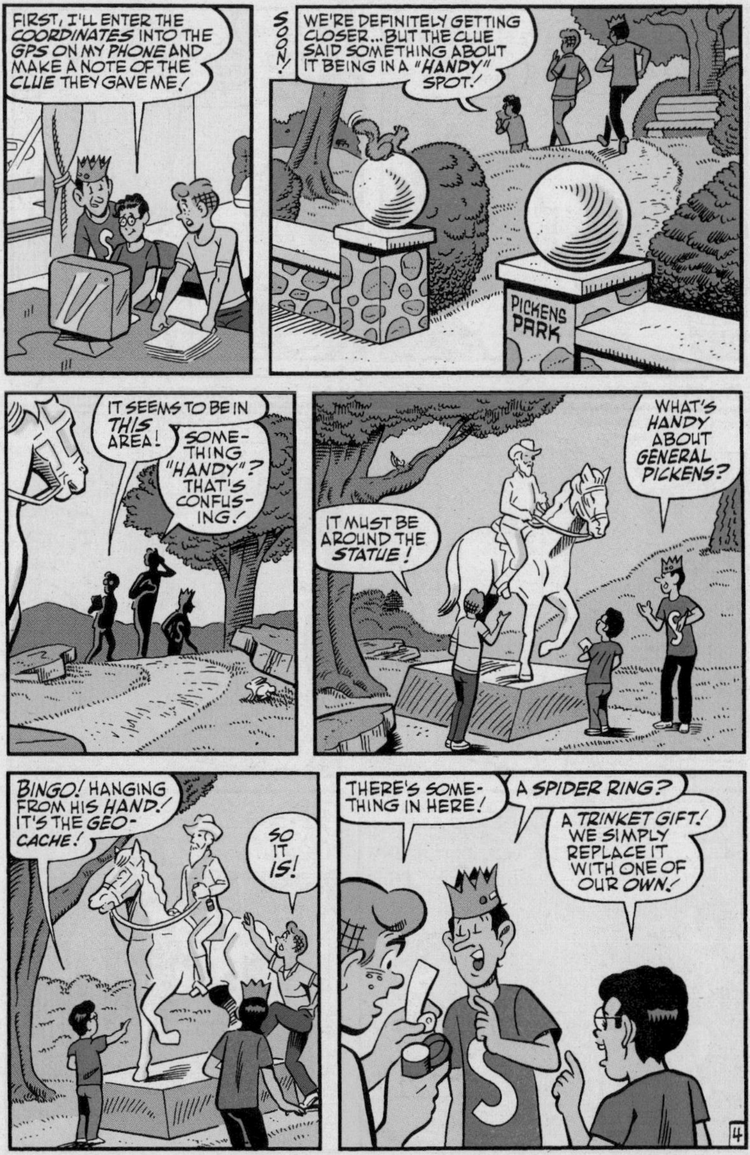
FIRST, I'LL ENTER THE COORDINATES INTO THE GPS ON MY PHONE AND MAKE A NOTE OF THE CLUE THEY GAVE ME!
SOON!
WE'RE DEFINITELY GETTING CLOSER... BUT THE CLUE SAID SOMETHING ABOUT IT BEING IN A "HANDY" SPOT!
PICKENS PARK
IT SEEMS TO BE IN THIS AREA!
SOMETHING "HANDY"? THAT'S CONFUSING!
IT MUST BE AROUND THE STATUE!
WHAT'S HANDY ABOUT GENERAL PICKENS?
BINGO! HANGING FROM HIS HAND! IT'S THE GEOCACHE!
SO IT IS!
THERE'S SOMETHING IN HERE!
A SPIDER RING?
A TRINKET GIFT! WE SIMPLY REPLACE IT WITH ONE OF OUR OWN!
4

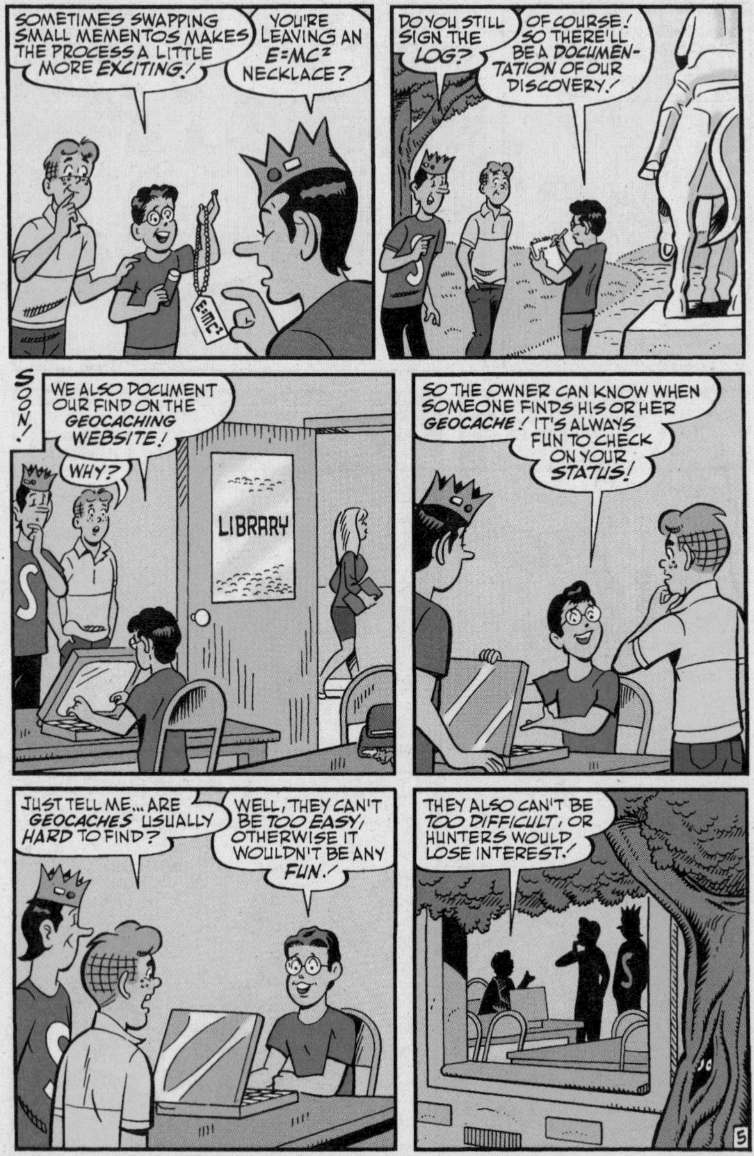
SOMETIMES SWAPPING SMALL MEMENTOS MAKES THE PROCESS A LITTLE MORE EXCITING!
YOU'RE LEAVING AN E=MC² NECKLACE?
E=MC²
DO YOU STILL SIGN THE LOG?
OF COURSE! SO THERE'LL BE A DOCUMENTATION OF OUR DISCOVERY!
SOON,!
WE ALSO DOCUMENT OUR FIND ON THE GEOCACHING WEBSITE!
WHY?
LIBRARY
SO THE OWNER CAN KNOW WHEN SOMEONE FINDS HIS OR HER GEOCACHE! IT'S ALWAYS FUN TO CHECK ON YOUR STATUS!
JUST TELL ME... ARE GEOCACHES USUALLY HARD TO FIND?
WELL, THEY CAN'T BE TOO EASY, OTHERWISE IT WOULDN'T BE ANY FUN!
THEY ALSO CAN'T BE TOO DIFFICULT, OR HUNTERS WOULD LOSE INTEREST!
5

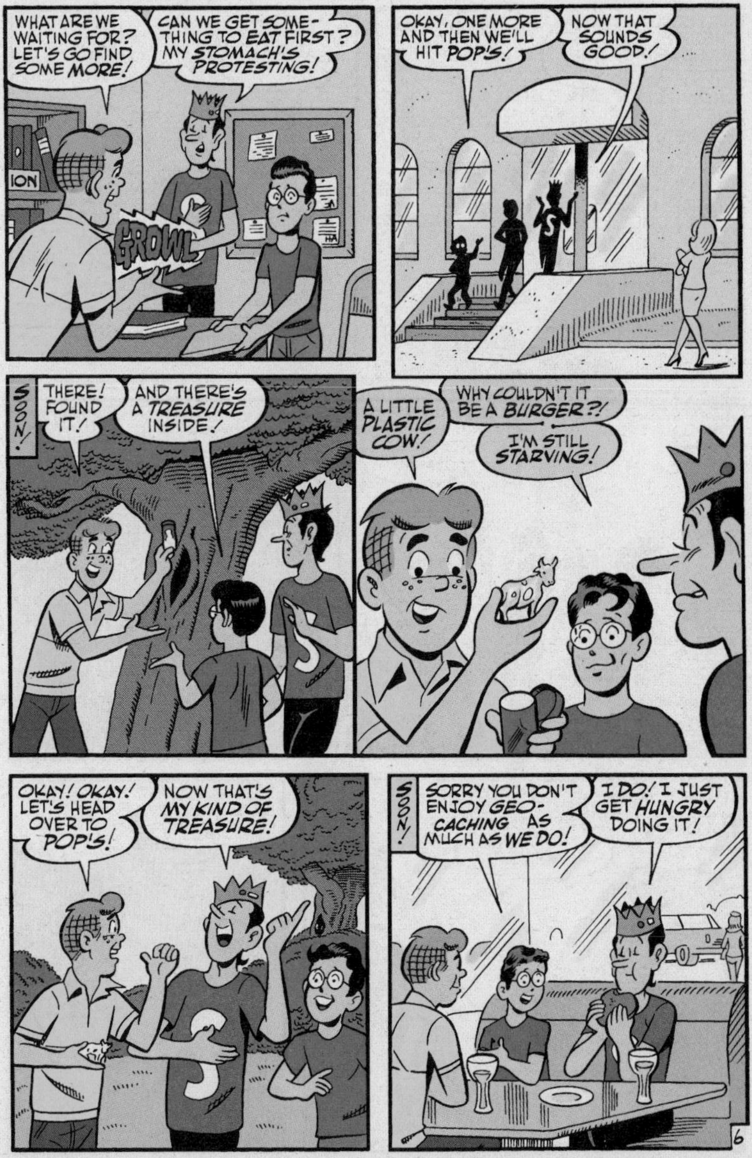
WHAT ARE WE WAITING FOR? LET'S GO FIND SOME MORE!
CAN WE GET SOME-THING TO EAT FIRST? MY STOMACH'S PROTESTING!
GROWL
ION
HA
OKAY, ONE MORE AND THEN WE'LL HIT POP'S!
NOW THAT SOUNDS GOOD!
SOON!
THERE! FOUND IT!
AND THERE'S A TREASURE INSIDE!
A LITTLE PLASTIC COW!
WHY COULDN'T IT BE A BURGER?!
I'M STILL STARVING!
OKAY! OKAY! LET'S HEAD OVER TO POP'S!
NOW THAT'S MY KIND OF TREASURE!
SOON!
SORRY YOU DON'T ENJOY GEO-CACHING AS MUCH AS WE DO!
I DO! I JUST GET HUNGRY DOING IT!

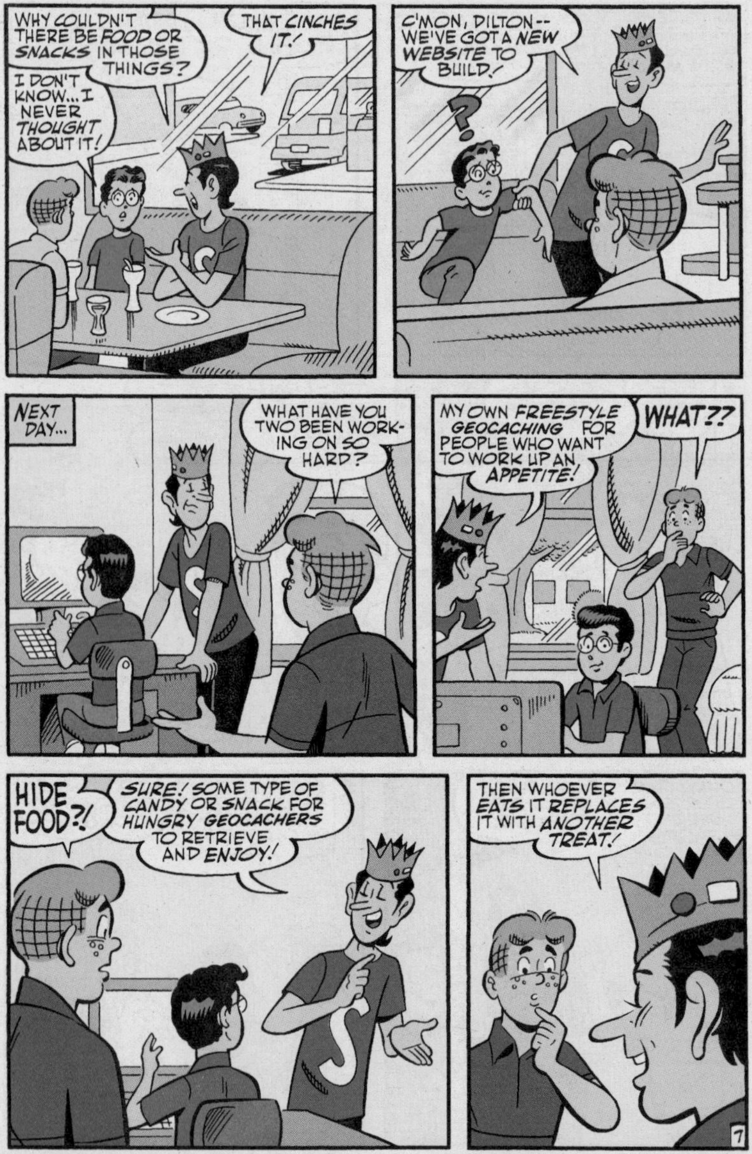
WHY COULDN'T THERE BE FOOD OR SNACKS IN THOSE THINGS?
I DON'T KNOW... I NEVER THOUGHT ABOUT IT!
THAT CINCHES IT!
C'MON, DILTON-- WE'VE GOT A NEW WEBSITE TO BUILD!
?
NEXT DAY...
WHAT HAVE YOU TWO BEEN WORKING ON SO HARD?
MY OWN FREESTYLE GEOCACHING FOR PEOPLE WHO WANT TO WORK UP AN APPETITE!
WHAT??
HIDE FOOD?!
SURE! SOME TYPE OF CANDY OR SNACK FOR HUNGRY GEOCACHERS TO RETRIEVE AND ENJOY!
THEN WHOEVER EATS IT REPLACES IT WITH ANOTHER TREAT!
7

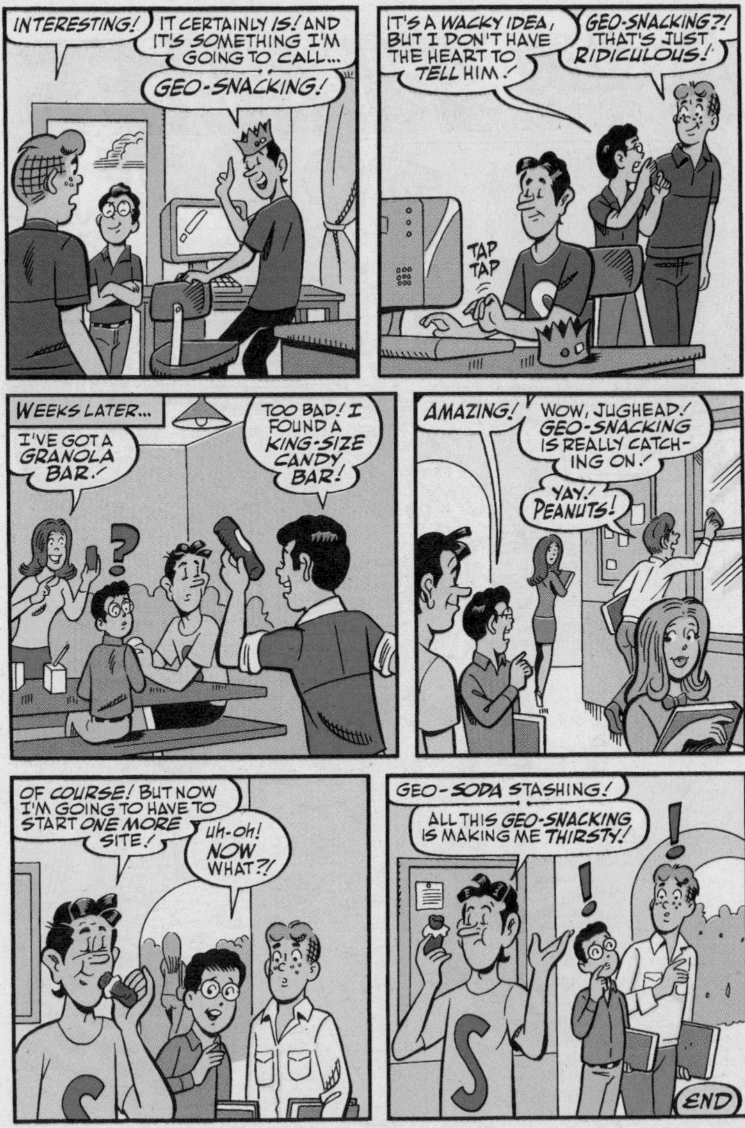

INTERESTING!
IT CERTAINLY IS! AND IT'S SOMETHING I'M GOING TO CALL...
GEO-SNACKING!
IT'S A WACKY IDEA, BUT I DON'T HAVE THE HEART TO TELL HIM!
GEO-SNACKING?! THAT'S JUST RIDICULOUS!
TAP TAP
WEEKS LATER...
I'VE GOT A GRANOLA BAR!
TOO BAD! I FOUND A KING-SIZE CANDY BAR!
AMAZING!
WOW, JUGHEAD! GEO-SNACKING IS REALLY CATCHING ON!
YAY! PEANUTS!
OF COURSE! BUT NOW I'M GOING TO HAVE TO START ONE MORE SITE!
uh-oh! NOW WHAT?!
GEO-SODA STASHING!
ALL THIS GEO-SNACKING IS MAKING ME THIRSTY!
END

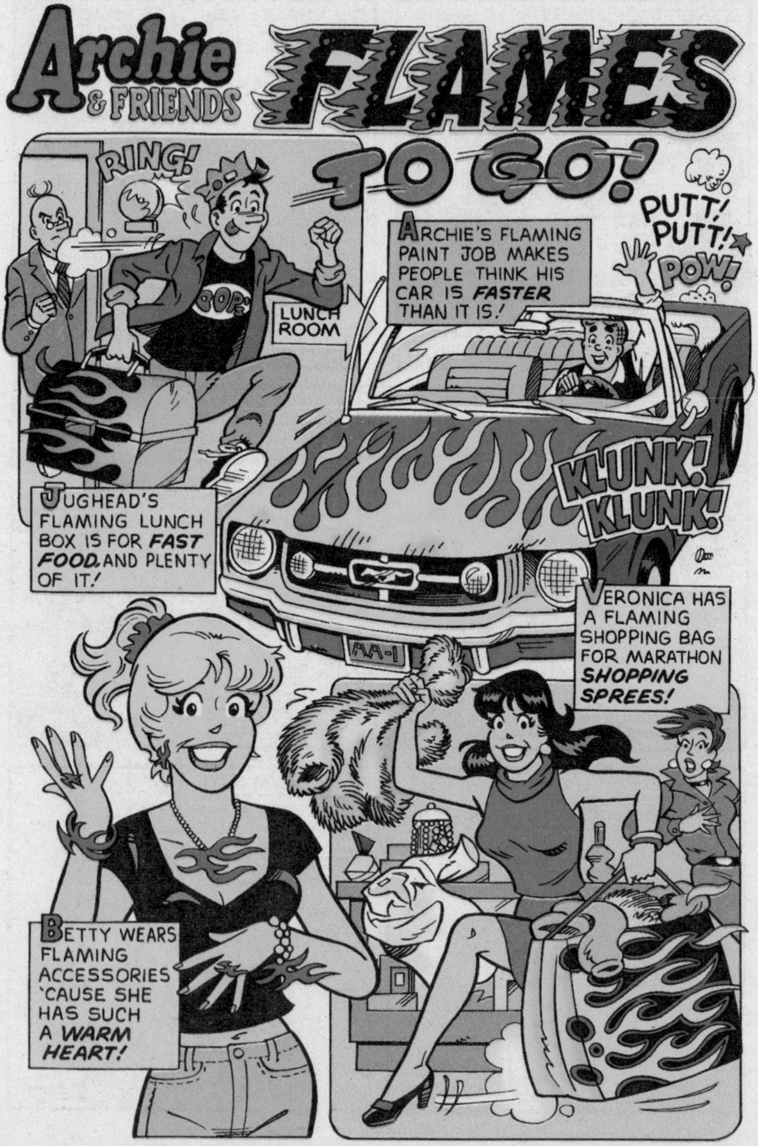
Archie & FRIENDS
FLAMES TO GO!
RING!
LUNCH ROOM
POP'S
ARCHIE'S FLAMING PAINT JOB MAKES PEOPLE THINK HIS CAR IS FASTER THAN IT IS!
PUTT! PUTT! POW!
KLUNK! KLUNK!
JUGHEAD'S FLAMING LUNCH BOX IS FOR FAST FOOD, AND PLENTY OF IT!
AA-1
VERONICA HAS A FLAMING SHOPPING BAG FOR MARATHON SHOPPING SPREES!
BETTY WEARS FLAMING ACCESSORIES 'CAUSE SHE HAS SUCH A WARM HEART!

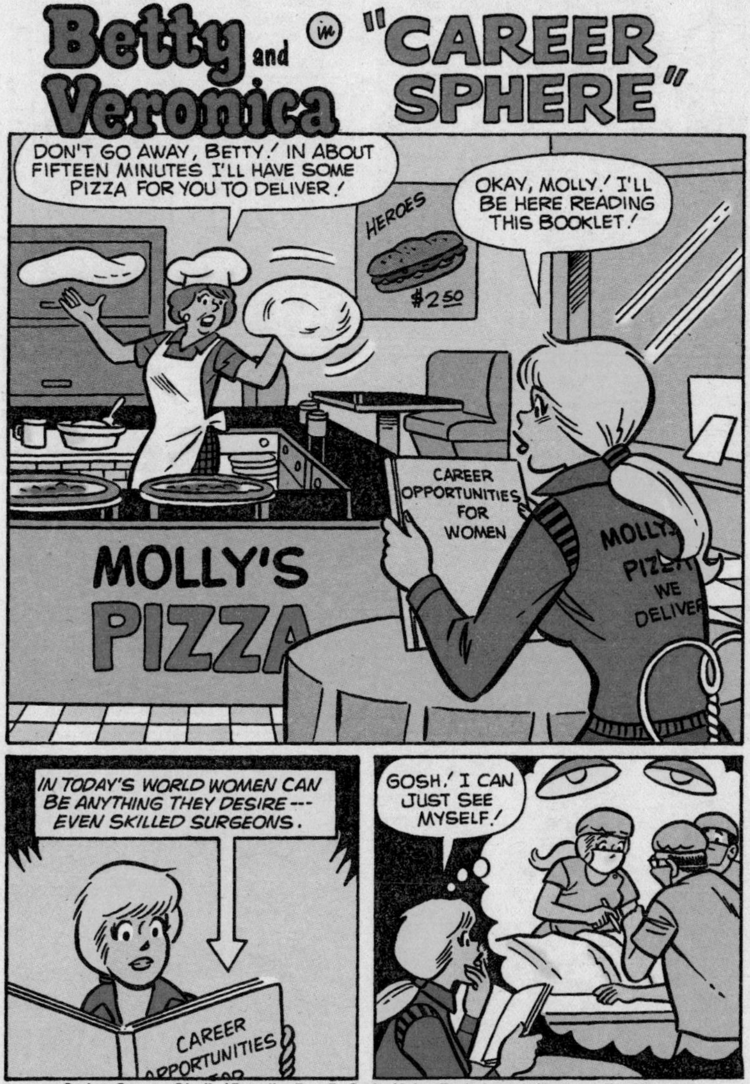
Betty and Veronica in "CAREER SPHERE"
DON'T GO AWAY, BETTY! IN ABOUT FIFTEEN MINUTES I'LL HAVE SOME PIZZA FOR YOU TO DELIVER!
OKAY, MOLLY! I'LL BE HERE READING THIS BOOKLET!
HEROES
$2.50
CAREER OPPORTUNITIES FOR WOMEN
MOLLY'S PIZZA
MOLLY'S PIZZA WE DELIVER
IN TODAY'S WORLD WOMEN CAN BE ANYTHING THEY DESIRE--- EVEN SKILLED SURGEONS.
CAREER OPPORTUNITIES
GOSH! I CAN JUST SEE MYSELF!

Script: George Gladir / Pencils: Dan DeCarlo / Inks: Rudy Lapick / Letters: Bill Yoshida

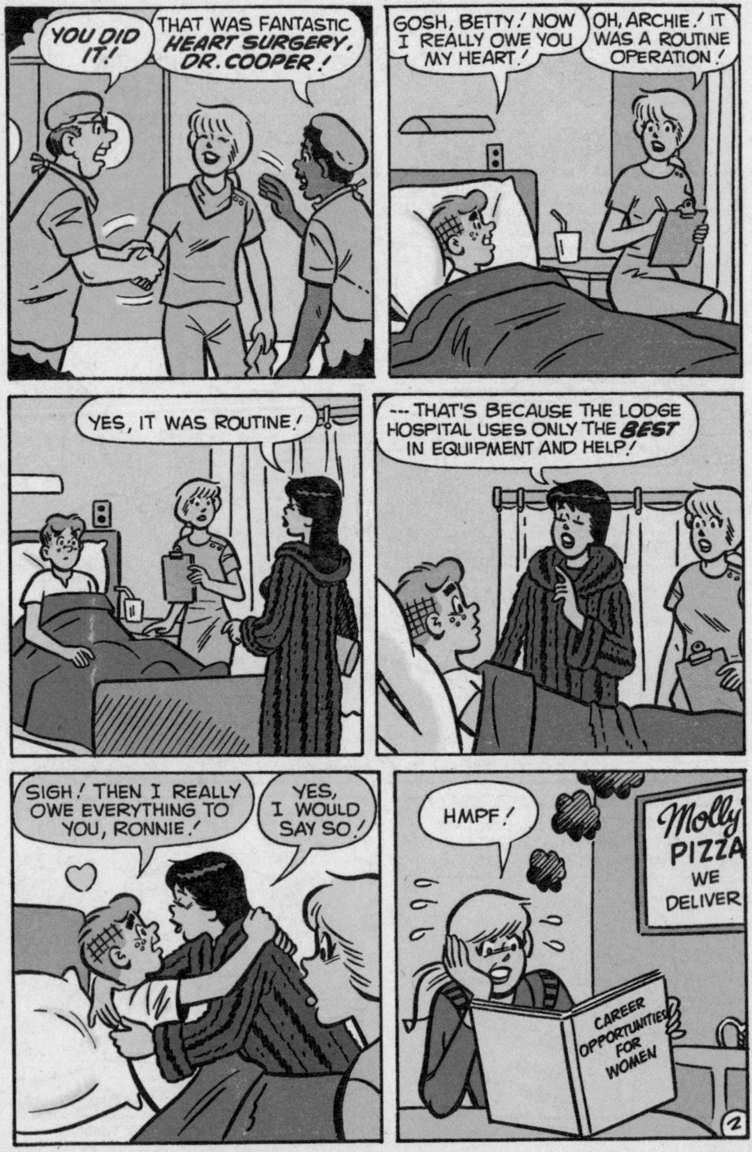
YOU DID IT!
THAT WAS FANTASTIC HEART SURGERY, DR. COOPER!
GOSH, BETTY! NOW I REALLY OWE YOU MY HEART!
OH, ARCHIE! IT WAS A ROUTINE OPERATION!
YES, IT WAS ROUTINE!
--- THAT'S BECAUSE THE LODGE HOSPITAL USES ONLY THE BEST IN EQUIPMENT AND HELP!
SIGH! THEN I REALLY OWE EVERYTHING TO YOU, RONNIE!
YES, I WOULD SAY SO!
HMPF!
MOLLY'S PIZZA WE DELIVER
CAREER OPPORTUNITIES FOR WOMEN
2

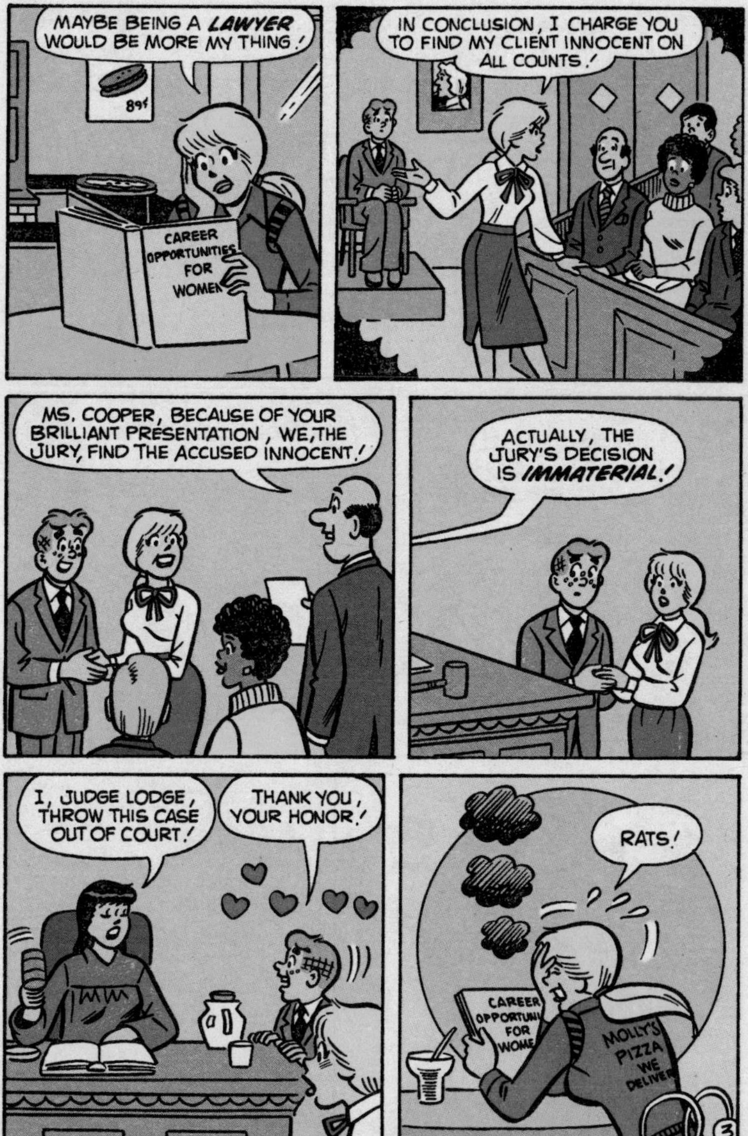
MAYBE BEING A LAWYER WOULD BE MORE MY THING!
89¢
CAREER OPPORTUNITIES FOR WOMEN
IN CONCLUSION, I CHARGE YOU TO FIND MY CLIENT INNOCENT ON ALL COUNTS!
MS. COOPER, BECAUSE OF YOUR BRILLIANT PRESENTATION, WE, THE JURY, FIND THE ACCUSED INNOCENT!
ACTUALLY, THE JURY'S DECISION IS IMMATERIAL!
I, JUDGE LODGE, THROW THIS CASE OUT OF COURT!
THANK YOU, YOUR HONOR!
RATS!
CAREER OPPORTUNI FOR WOME
MOLLY'S PIZZA WE DELIVER
3

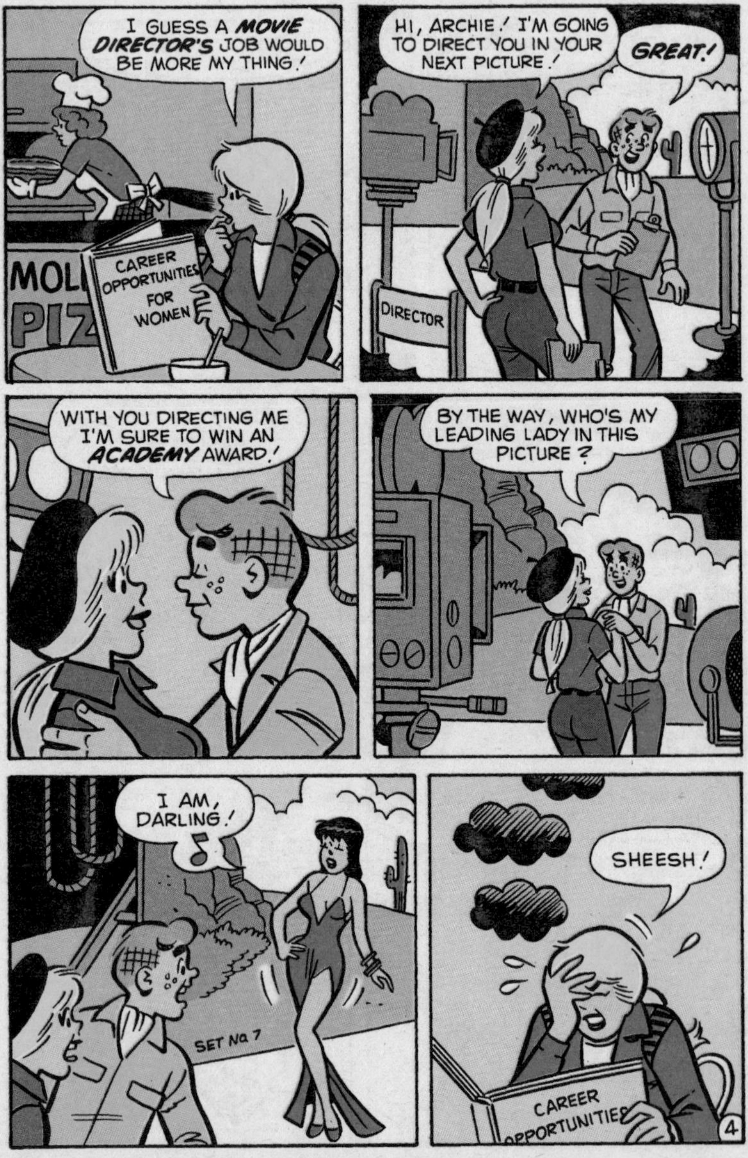
I GUESS A MOVIE DIRECTOR'S JOB WOULD BE MORE MY THING!
MOL
PIZ
CAREER OPPORTUNITIES FOR WOMEN
HI, ARCHIE! I'M GOING TO DIRECT YOU IN YOUR NEXT PICTURE!
GREAT!
DIRECTOR
WITH YOU DIRECTING ME I'M SURE TO WIN AN ACADEMY AWARD!
BY THE WAY, WHO'S MY LEADING LADY IN THIS PICTURE?
I AM, DARLING!
SET No. 7
SHEESH!
CAREER OPPORTUNITIES
4

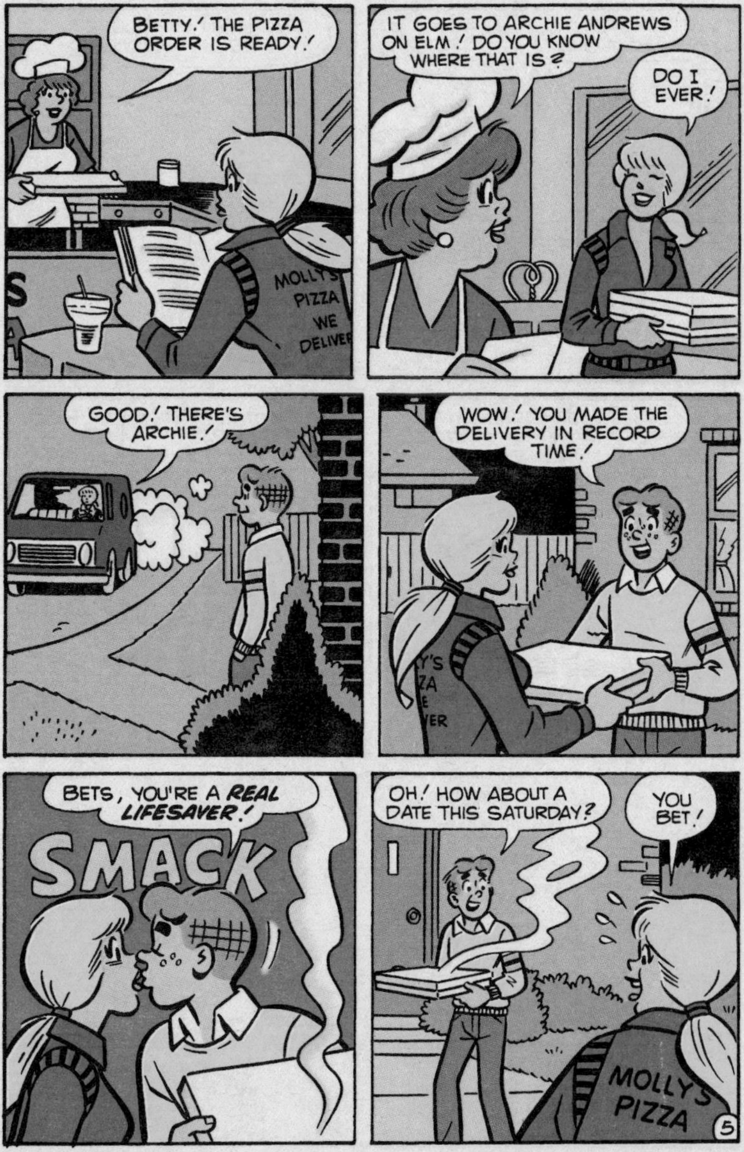
BETTY! THE PIZZA ORDER IS READY!
MOLLY'S PIZZA WE DELIVER
IT GOES TO ARCHIE ANDREWS ON ELM! DO YOU KNOW WHERE THAT IS?
DO I EVER!
GOOD! THERE'S ARCHIE!
WOW! YOU MADE THE DELIVERY IN RECORD TIME!
BETS, YOU'RE A *REAL LIFESAVER!*
SMACK
OH! HOW ABOUT A DATE THIS SATURDAY?
YOU BET!
MOLLY'S PIZZA

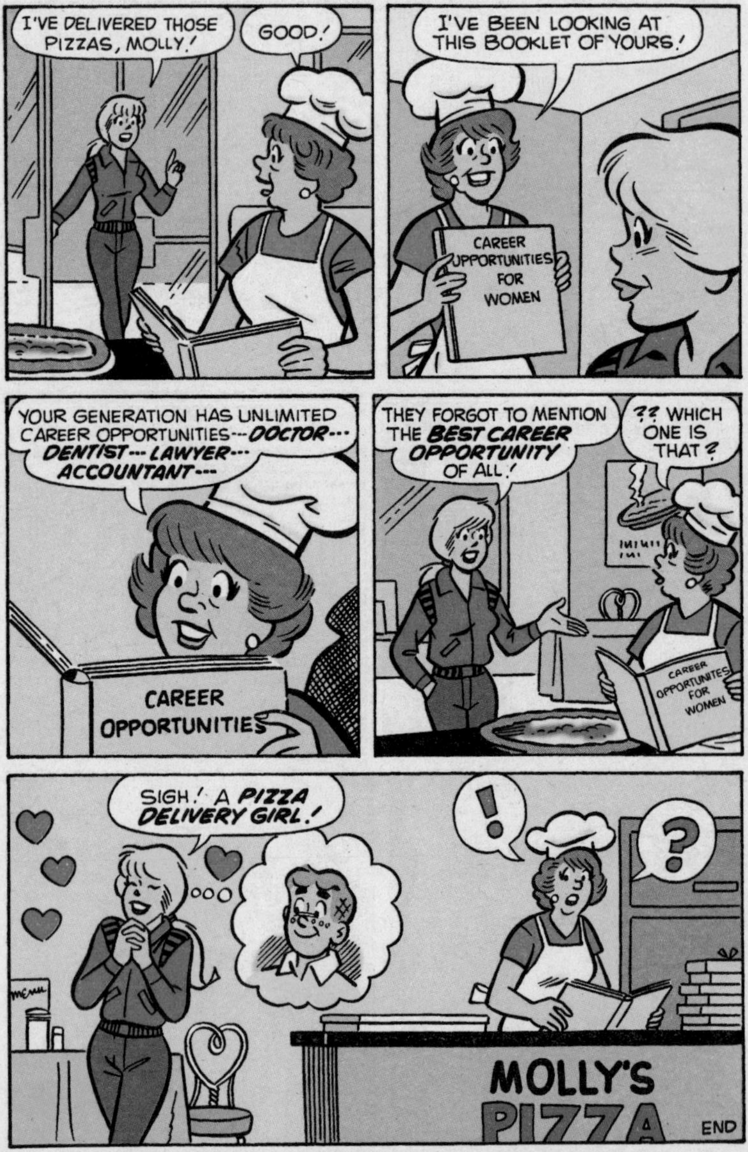
I'VE DELIVERED THOSE PIZZAS, MOLLY!
GOOD!
I'VE BEEN LOOKING AT THIS BOOKLET OF YOURS!
CAREER OPPORTUNITIES FOR WOMEN
YOUR GENERATION HAS UNLIMITED CAREER OPPORTUNITIES---DOCTOR--- DENTIST--- LAWYER--- ACCOUNTANT---
CAREER OPPORTUNITIES
THEY FORGOT TO MENTION THE BEST CAREER OPPORTUNITY OF ALL!
?? WHICH ONE IS THAT?
CAREER OPPORTUNITES FOR WOMEN
SIGH! A PIZZA DELIVERY GIRL!
!
?
MOLLY'S PIZZA
END

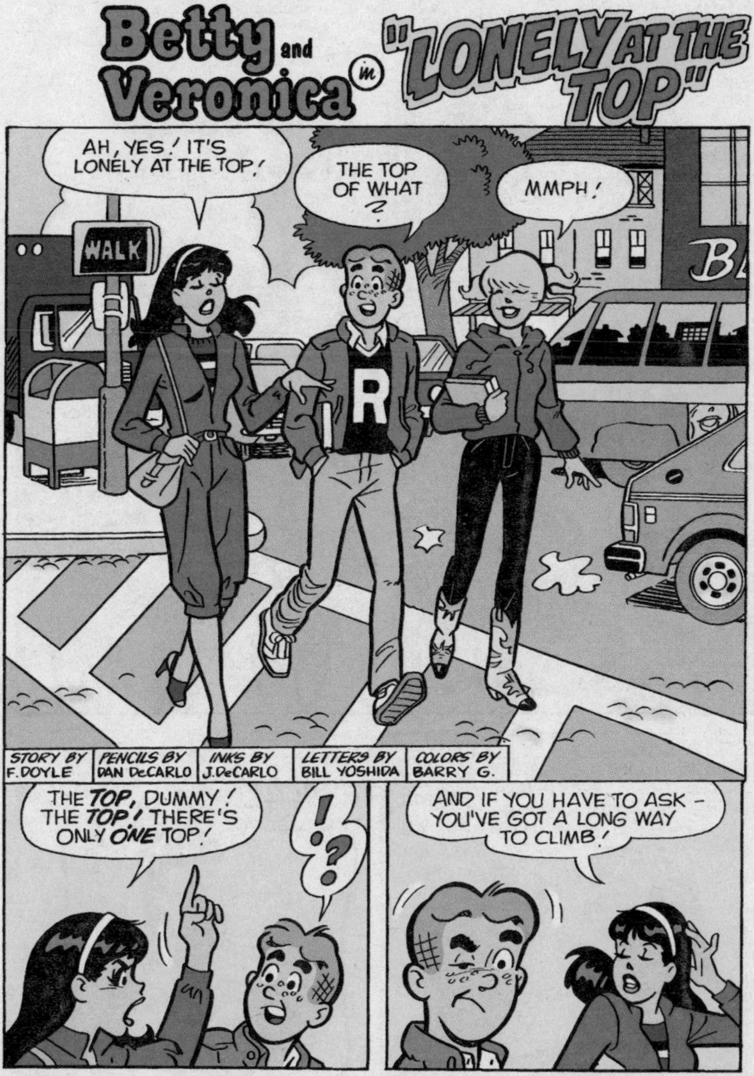
Betty and Veronica in
"LONELY AT THE TOP"
AH, YES! IT'S LONELY AT THE TOP!
THE TOP OF WHAT ?
MMPH!
WALK
STORY BY F. DOYLE
PENCILS BY DAN DeCARLO
INKS BY J. DeCARLO
LETTERS BY BILL YOSHIDA
COLORS BY BARRY G.
THE TOP, DUMMY! THE TOP! THERE'S ONLY ONE TOP!
!?
AND IF YOU HAVE TO ASK - YOU'VE GOT A LONG WAY TO CLIMB!

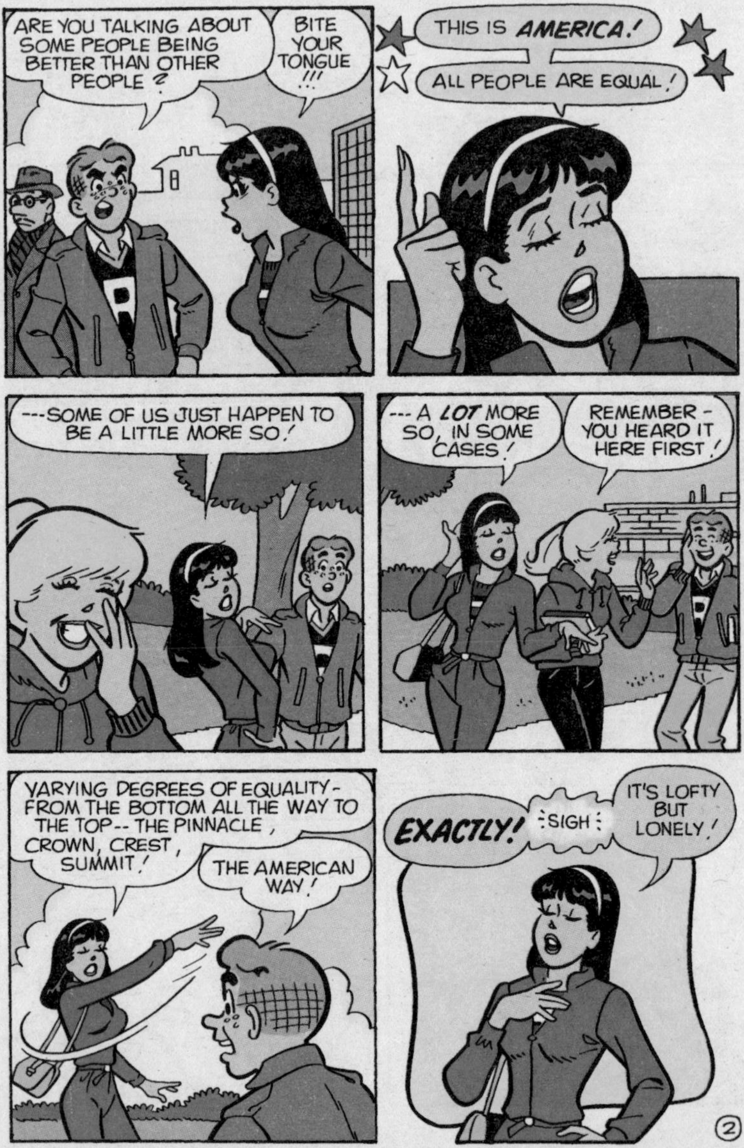
ARE YOU TALKING ABOUT SOME PEOPLE BEING BETTER THAN OTHER PEOPLE ?
BITE YOUR TONGUE !!!
THIS IS AMERICA!
ALL PEOPLE ARE EQUAL!
---SOME OF US JUST HAPPEN TO BE A LITTLE MORE SO!
---A LOT MORE SO, IN SOME CASES!
REMEMBER - YOU HEARD IT HERE FIRST!
YARYING DEGREES OF EQUALITY - FROM THE BOTTOM ALL THE WAY TO THE TOP-- THE PINNACLE, CROWN, CREST, SUMMIT!
THE AMERICAN WAY!
EXACTLY!
SIGH
IT'S LOFTY BUT LONELY!

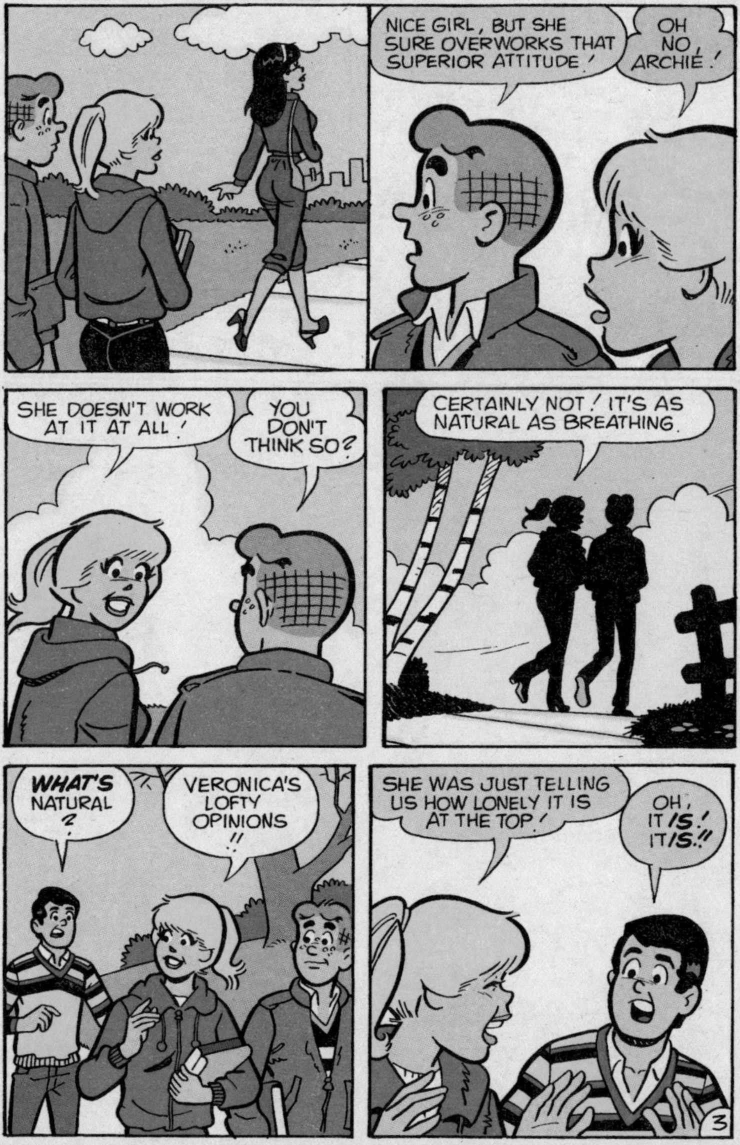
NICE GIRL, BUT SHE SURE OVERWORKS THAT SUPERIOR ATTITUDE!
OH NO, ARCHIE!
SHE DOESN'T WORK AT IT AT ALL!
YOU DON'T THINK SO?
CERTAINLY NOT! IT'S AS NATURAL AS BREATHING.
WHAT'S NATURAL?
VERONICA'S LOFTY OPINIONS!!
SHE WAS JUST TELLING US HOW LONELY IT IS AT THE TOP!
OH, IT IS! IT IS!!
3

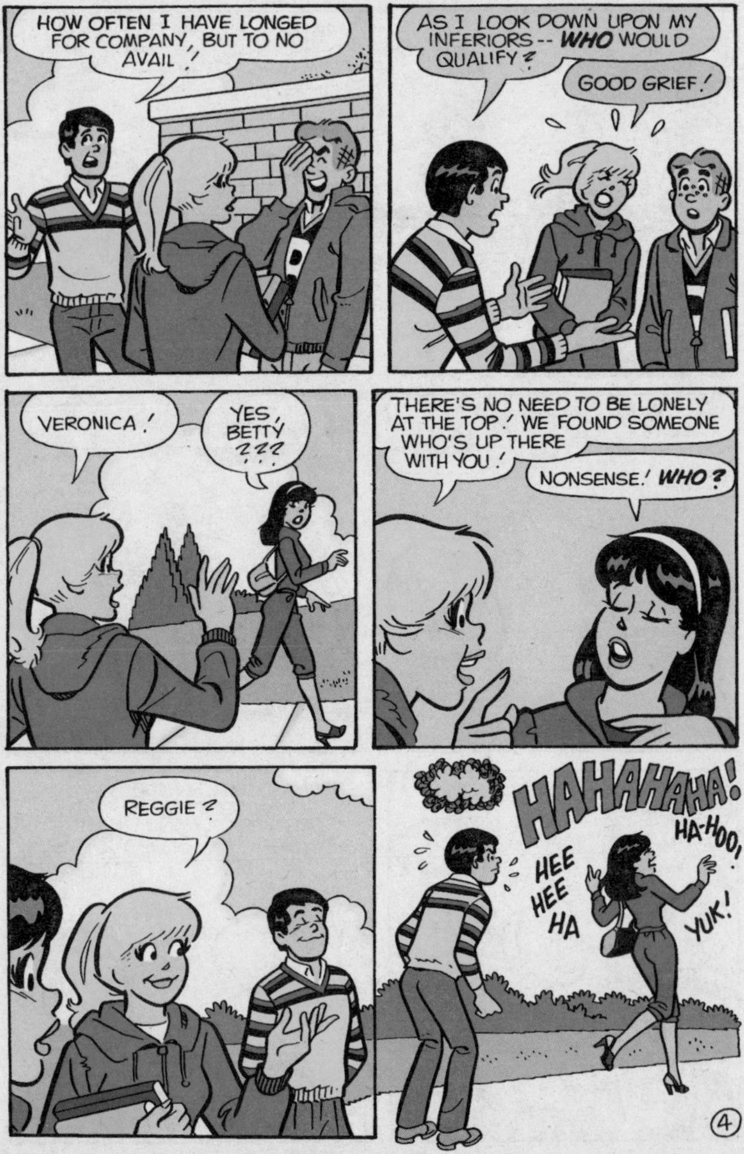
HOW OFTEN I HAVE LONGED FOR COMPANY, BUT TO NO AVAIL!
AS I LOOK DOWN UPON MY INFERIORS -- WHO WOULD QUALIFY?
GOOD GRIEF!
VERONICA!
YES, BETTY ???
THERE'S NO NEED TO BE LONELY AT THE TOP! WE FOUND SOMEONE WHO'S UP THERE WITH YOU!
NONSENSE! WHO?
REGGIE?
HAHAHAHAHA!
HA-HOO!
HEE HEE HA
YUK!

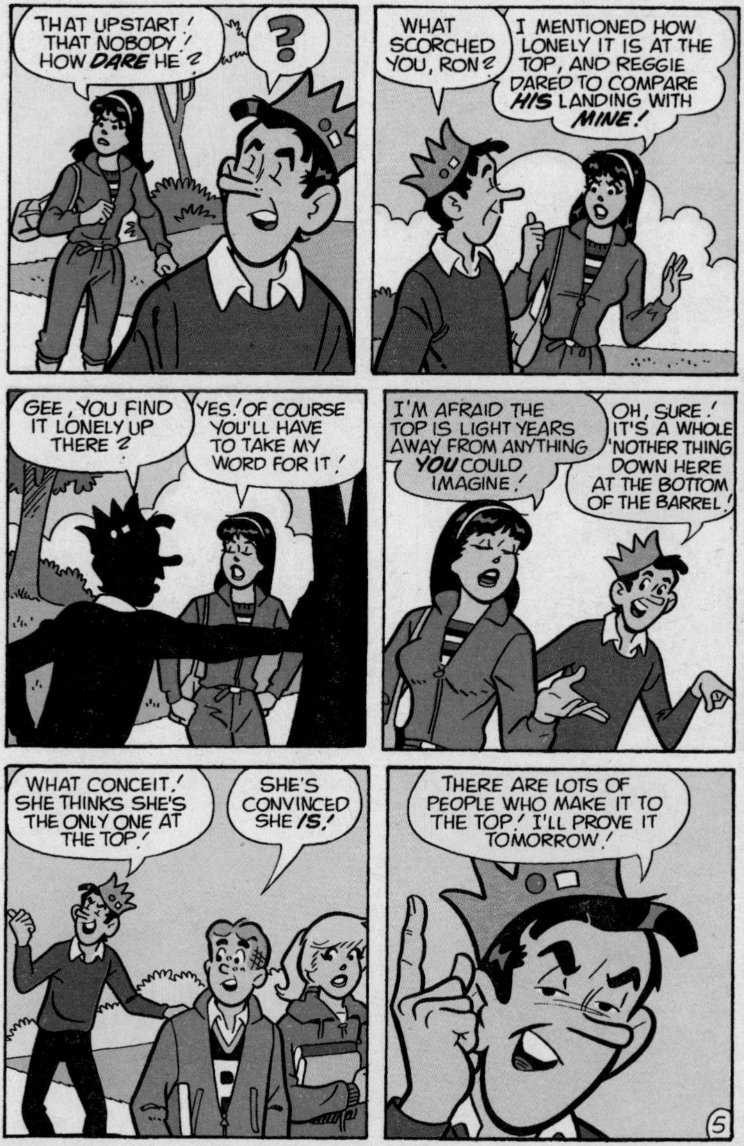
THAT UPSTART! THAT NOBODY! HOW DARE HE?
?
WHAT SCORCHED YOU, RON?
I MENTIONED HOW LONELY IT IS AT THE TOP, AND REGGIE DARED TO COMPARE HIS LANDING WITH MINE!
GEE, YOU FIND IT LONELY UP THERE?
YES! OF COURSE YOU'LL HAVE TO TAKE MY WORD FOR IT!
I'M AFRAID THE TOP IS LIGHT YEARS AWAY FROM ANYTHING YOU COULD IMAGINE!
OH, SURE! IT'S A WHOLE 'NOTHER THING DOWN HERE AT THE BOTTOM OF THE BARREL!
WHAT CONCEIT! SHE THINKS SHE'S THE ONLY ONE AT THE TOP!
SHE'S CONVINCED SHE IS!
THERE ARE LOTS OF PEOPLE WHO MAKE IT TO THE TOP! I'LL PROVE IT TOMORROW!
5

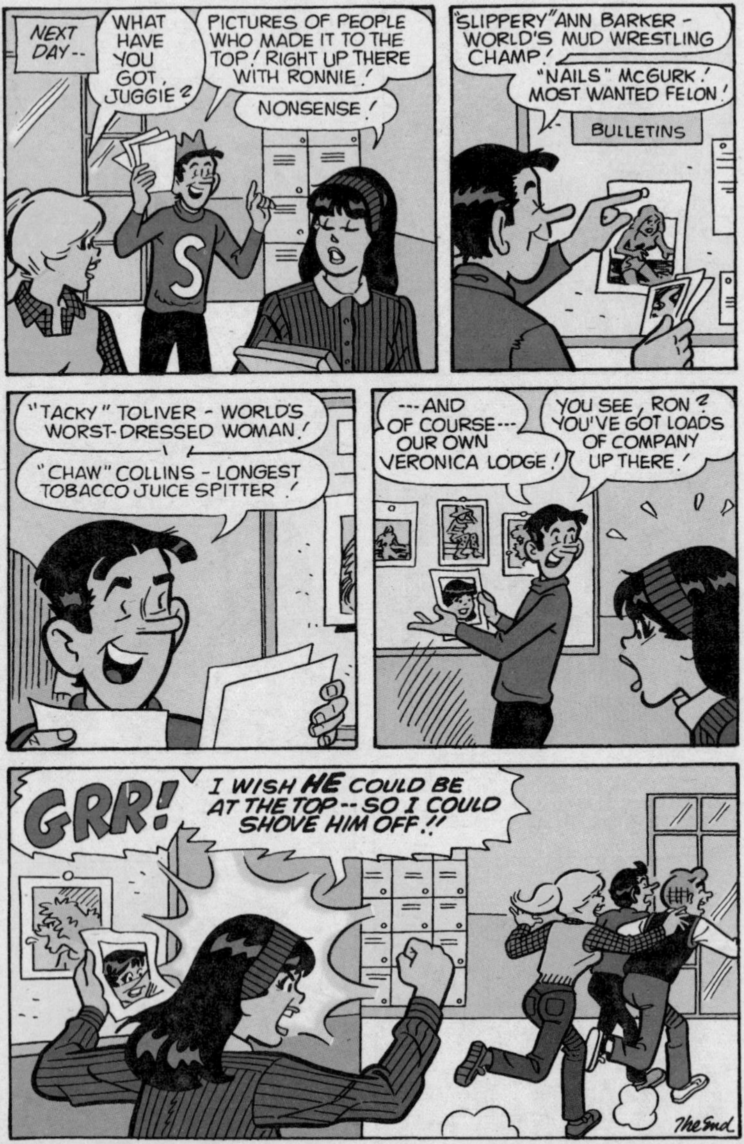
NEXT DAY--
WHAT HAVE YOU GOT, JUGGIE?
PICTURES OF PEOPLE WHO MADE IT TO THE TOP! RIGHT UP THERE WITH RONNIE!
NONSENSE!
"SLIPPERY" ANN BARKER - WORLD'S MUD WRESTLING CHAMP!
"NAILS" McGURK! MOST WANTED FELON!
BULLETINS
"TACKY" TOLIVER - WORLD'S WORST-DRESSED WOMAN!
"CHAW" COLLINS - LONGEST TOBACCO JUICE SPITTER!
---AND OF COURSE--- OUR OWN VERONICA LODGE!
YOU SEE, RON? YOU'VE GOT LOADS OF COMPANY UP THERE!
GRR!
I WISH HE COULD BE AT THE TOP-- SO I COULD SHOVE HIM OFF!!
The End

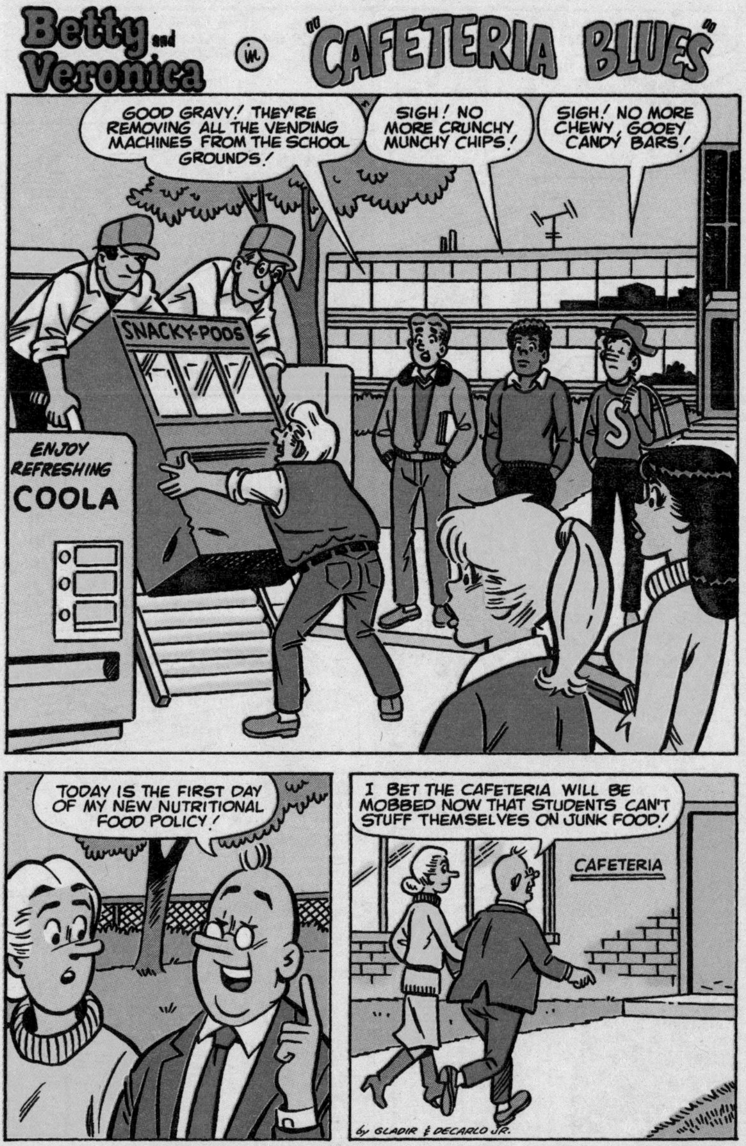
Betty and Veronica in "CAFETERIA BLUES"
GOOD GRAVY! THEY'RE REMOVING ALL THE VENDING MACHINES FROM THE SCHOOL GROUNDS!
SIGH! NO MORE CRUNCHY MUNCHY CHIPS!
SIGH! NO MORE CHEWY, GOOEY CANDY BARS!
SNACKY-POOS
ENJOY REFRESHING COOLA
TODAY IS THE FIRST DAY OF MY NEW NUTRITIONAL FOOD POLICY!
I BET THE CAFETERIA WILL BE MOBBED NOW THAT STUDENTS CAN'T STUFF THEMSELVES ON JUNK FOOD!
CAFETERIA
by GLADIR & DECARLO JR.

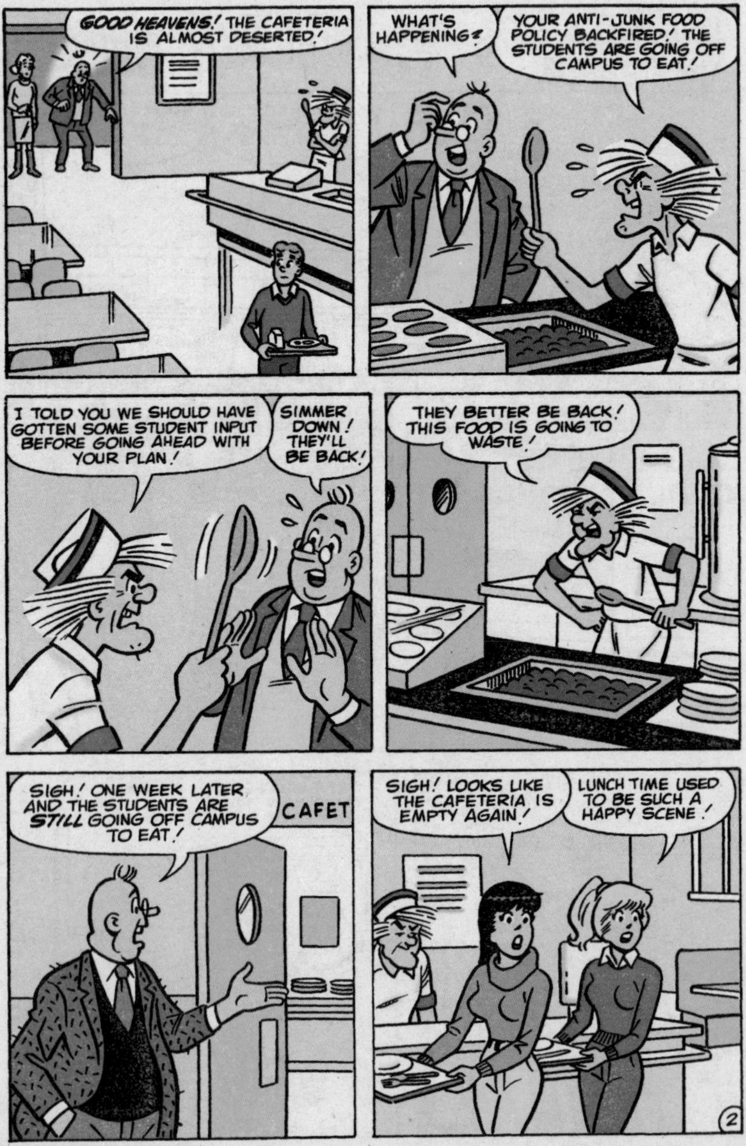
GOOD HEAVENS! THE CAFETERIA IS ALMOST DESERTED!
WHAT'S HAPPENING?
YOUR ANTI-JUNK FOOD POLICY BACKFIRED! THE STUDENTS ARE GOING OFF CAMPUS TO EAT!
I TOLD YOU WE SHOULD HAVE GOTTEN SOME STUDENT INPUT BEFORE GOING AHEAD WITH YOUR PLAN!
SIMMER DOWN! THEY'LL BE BACK!
THEY BETTER BE BACK! THIS FOOD IS GOING TO WASTE!
SIGH! ONE WEEK LATER AND THE STUDENTS ARE STILL GOING OFF CAMPUS TO EAT!
CAFET
SIGH! LOOKS LIKE THE CAFETERIA IS EMPTY AGAIN!
LUNCH TIME USED TO BE SUCH A HAPPY SCENE!
2

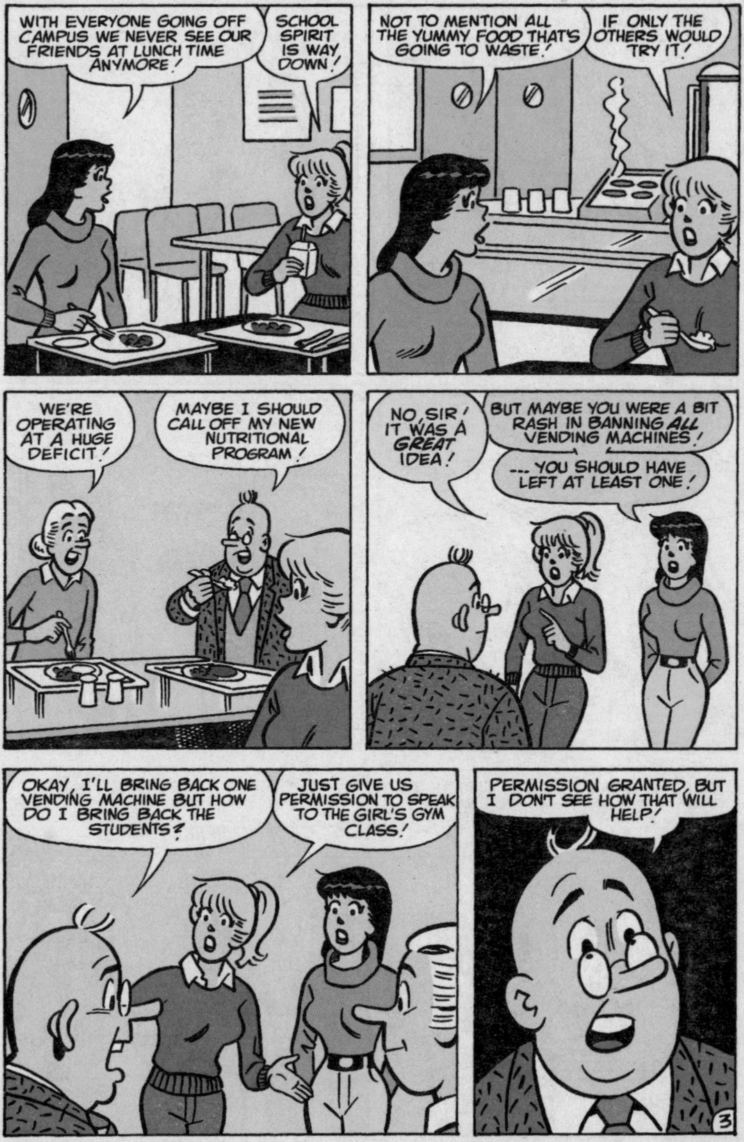
WITH EVERYONE GOING OFF CAMPUS WE NEVER SEE OUR FRIENDS AT LUNCH TIME ANYMORE!
SCHOOL SPIRIT IS WAY DOWN!
NOT TO MENTION ALL THE YUMMY FOOD THAT'S GOING TO WASTE!
IF ONLY THE OTHERS WOULD TRY IT!
WE'RE OPERATING AT A HUGE DEFICIT!
MAYBE I SHOULD CALL OFF MY NEW NUTRITIONAL PROGRAM!
NO, SIR! IT WAS A GREAT IDEA!
BUT MAYBE YOU WERE A BIT RASH IN BANNING ALL VENDING MACHINES!
--- YOU SHOULD HAVE LEFT AT LEAST ONE!
OKAY, I'LL BRING BACK ONE VENDING MACHINE BUT HOW DO I BRING BACK THE STUDENTS?
JUST GIVE US PERMISSION TO SPEAK TO THE GIRL'S GYM CLASS!
PERMISSION GRANTED, BUT I DON'T SEE HOW THAT WILL HELP!
3

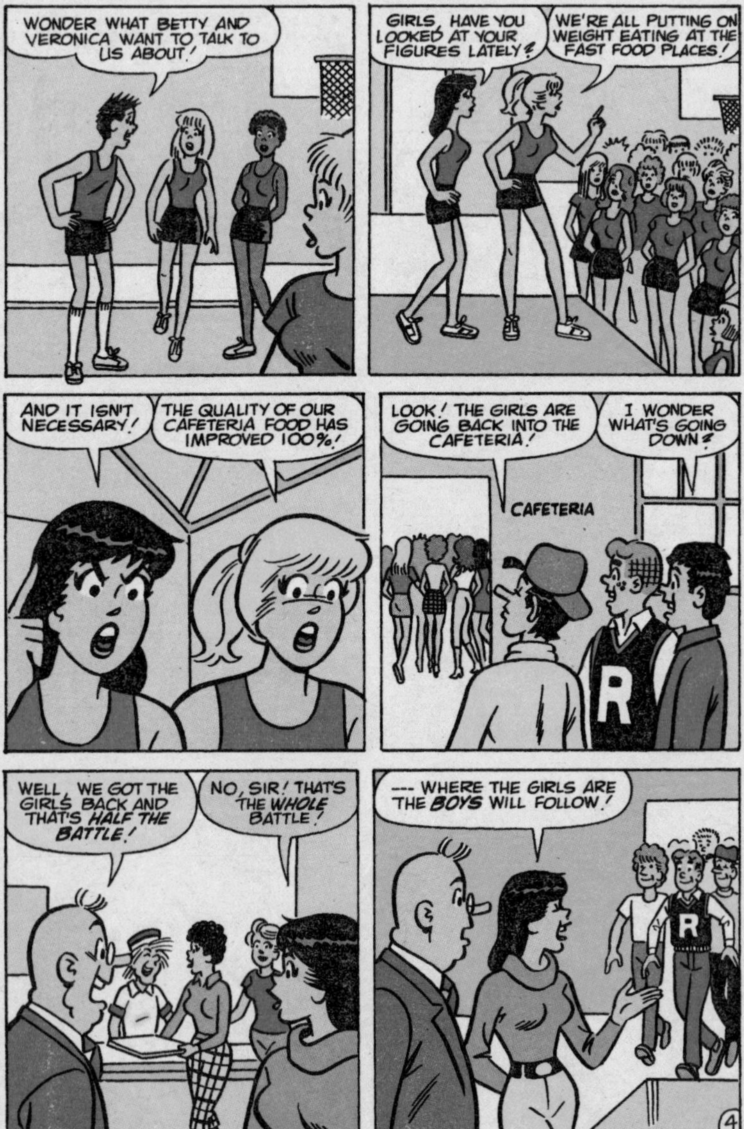
WONDER WHAT BETTY AND VERONICA WANT TO TALK TO US ABOUT!
GIRLS, HAVE YOU LOOKED AT YOUR FIGURES LATELY?
WE'RE ALL PUTTING ON WEIGHT EATING AT THE FAST FOOD PLACES!
AND IT ISN'T NECESSARY!
THE QUALITY OF OUR CAFETERIA FOOD HAS IMPROVED 100%!
LOOK! THE GIRLS ARE GOING BACK INTO THE CAFETERIA!
CAFETERIA
I WONDER WHAT'S GOING DOWN?
WELL, WE GOT THE GIRLS BACK AND THAT'S HALF THE BATTLE!
NO, SIR! THAT'S THE WHOLE BATTLE!
--- WHERE THE GIRLS ARE THE BOYS WILL FOLLOW!
4

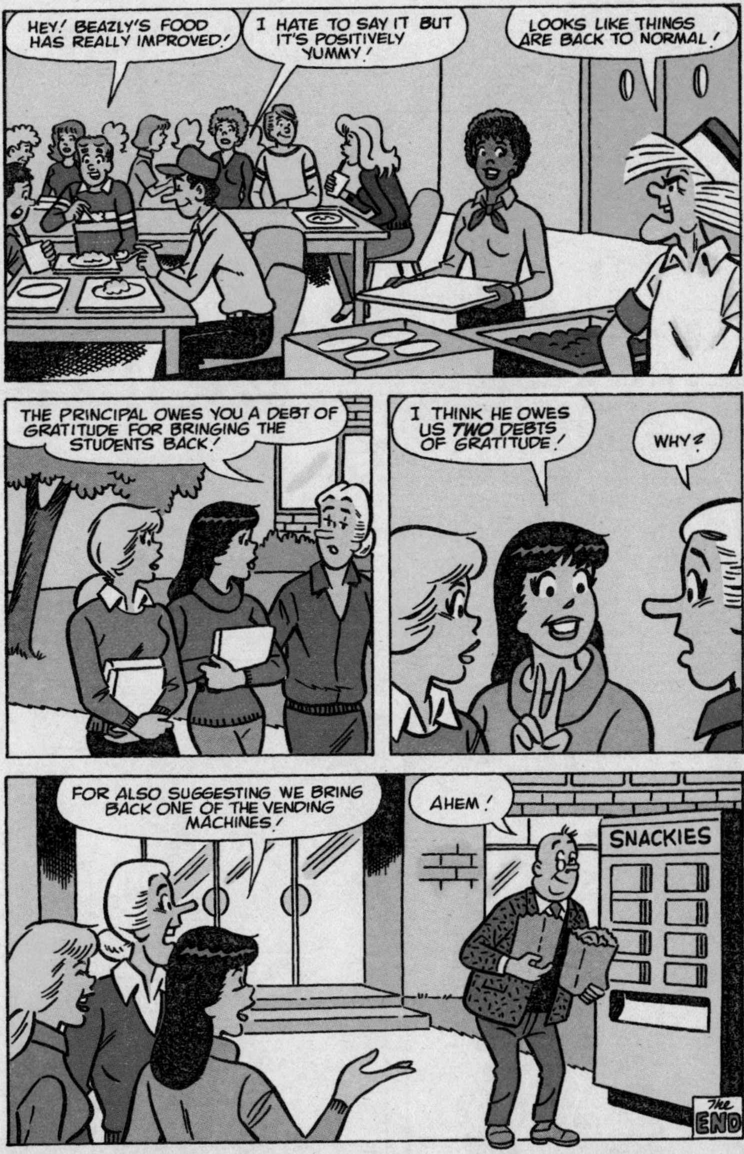
HEY! BEAZLY'S FOOD HAS REALLY IMPROVED!
I HATE TO SAY IT BUT IT'S POSITIVELY YUMMY!
LOOKS LIKE THINGS ARE BACK TO NORMAL!
THE PRINCIPAL OWES YOU A DEBT OF GRATITUDE FOR BRINGING THE STUDENTS BACK!
I THINK HE OWES US *TWO* DEBTS OF GRATITUDE!
WHY?
FOR ALSO SUGGESTING WE BRING BACK ONE OF THE VENDING MACHINES!
AHEM!
SNACKIES
The END

Betty and Veronica in "IS THIS PLACE A ZOO?"

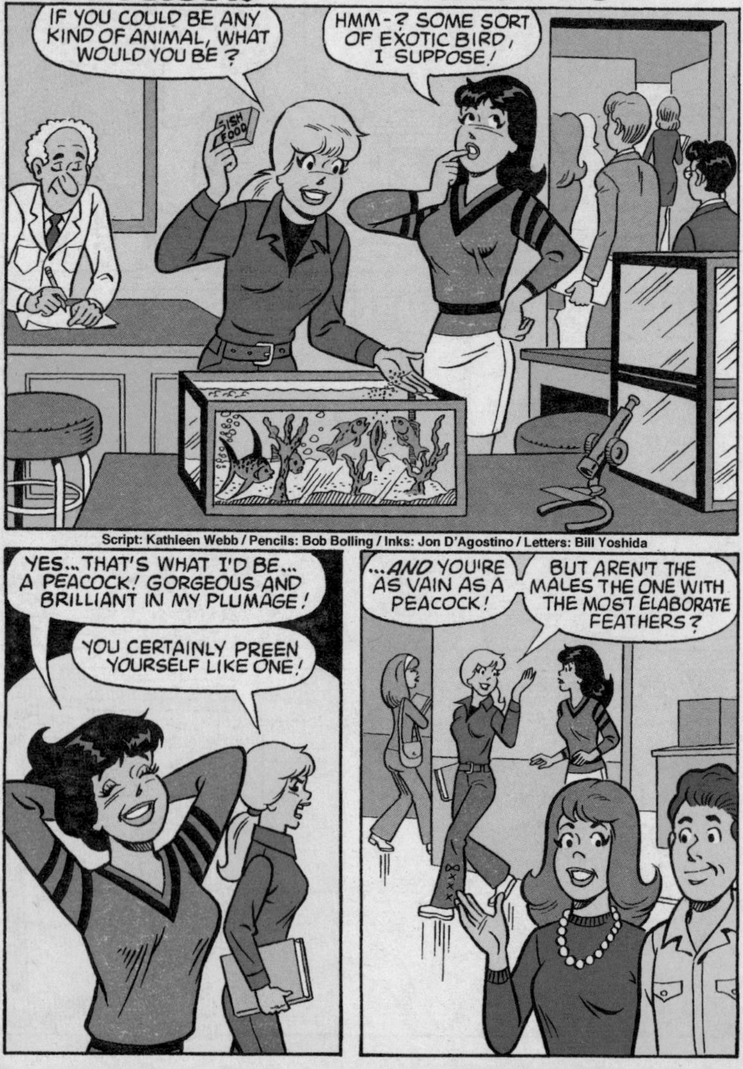

IF YOU COULD BE ANY KIND OF ANIMAL, WHAT WOULD YOU BE ?
HMM-? SOME SORT OF EXOTIC BIRD, I SUPPOSE!
FISH FOOD
YES... THAT'S WHAT I'D BE... A PEACOCK! GORGEOUS AND BRILLIANT IN MY PLUMAGE!
YOU CERTAINLY PREEN YOURSELF LIKE ONE!
...AND YOU'RE AS VAIN AS A PEACOCK!
BUT AREN'T THE MALES THE ONE WITH THE MOST ELABORATE FEATHERS ?

Script: Kathleen Webb / Pencils: Bob Bolling / Inks: Jon D'Agostino / Letters: Bill Yoshida

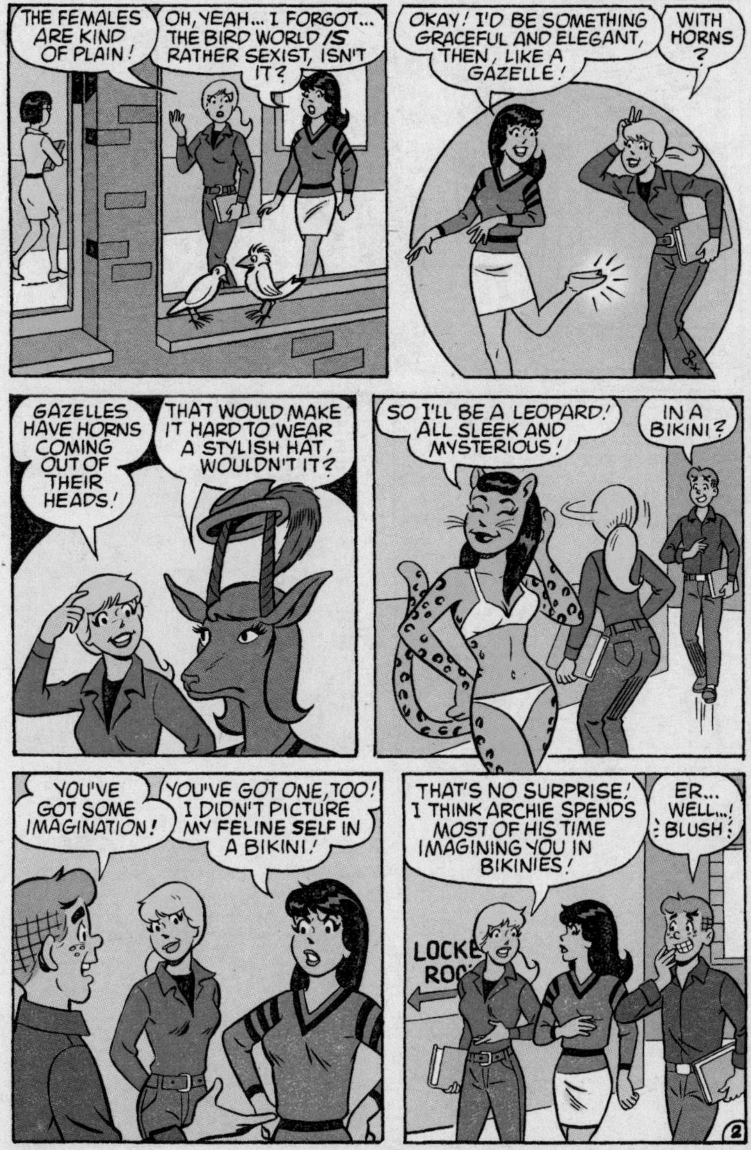
THE FEMALES ARE KIND OF PLAIN!
OH, YEAH... I FORGOT... THE BIRD WORLD IS RATHER SEXIST, ISN'T IT?
OKAY! I'D BE SOMETHING GRACEFUL AND ELEGANT, THEN, LIKE A GAZELLE!
WITH HORNS?
GAZELLES HAVE HORNS COMING OUT OF THEIR HEADS!
THAT WOULD MAKE IT HARD TO WEAR A STYLISH HAT, WOULDN'T IT?
SO I'LL BE A LEOPARD! ALL SLEEK AND MYSTERIOUS!
IN A BIKINI?
YOU'VE GOT SOME IMAGINATION!
YOU'VE GOT ONE, TOO! I DIDN'T PICTURE MY FELINE SELF IN A BIKINI!
THAT'S NO SURPRISE! I THINK ARCHIE SPENDS MOST OF HIS TIME IMAGINING YOU IN BIKINIES!
ER... WELL...! BLUSH
LOCKE
ROO
2

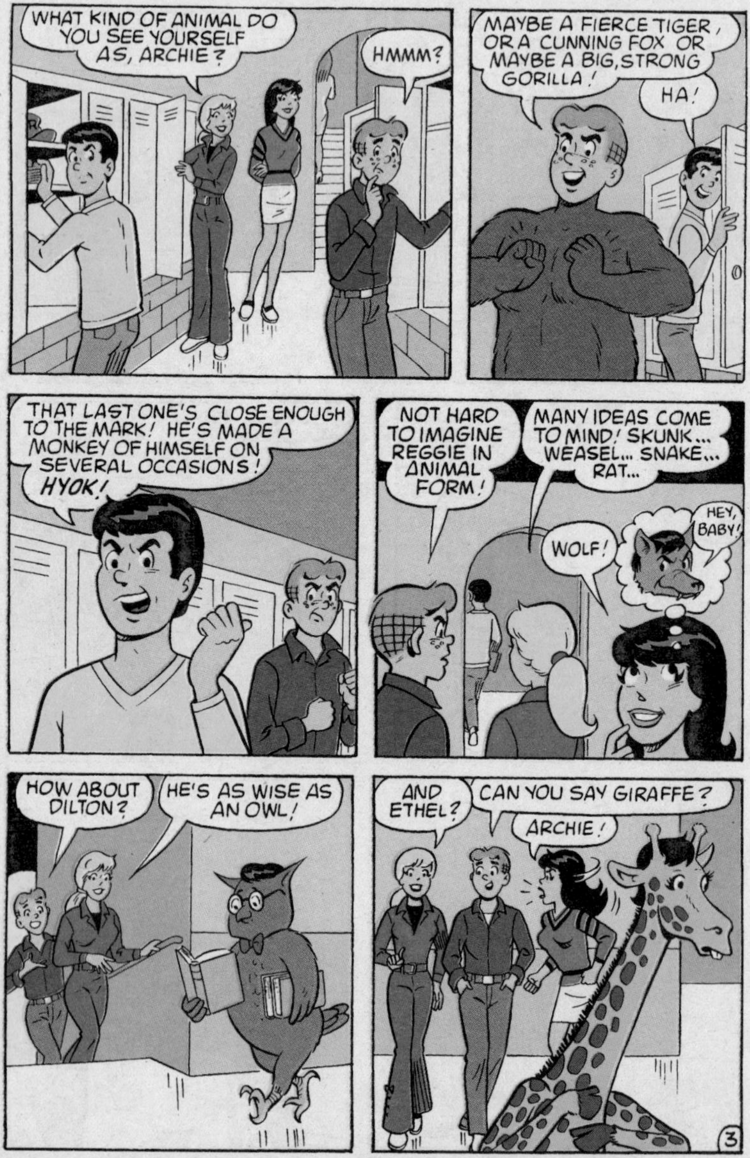
WHAT KIND OF ANIMAL DO YOU SEE YOURSELF AS, ARCHIE?
HMMM?
MAYBE A FIERCE TIGER, OR A CUNNING FOX OR MAYBE A BIG, STRONG GORILLA!
HA!
THAT LAST ONE'S CLOSE ENOUGH TO THE MARK! HE'S MADE A MONKEY OF HIMSELF ON SEVERAL OCCASIONS! HYOK!
NOT HARD TO IMAGINE REGGIE IN ANIMAL FORM!
MANY IDEAS COME TO MIND! SKUNK... WEASEL... SNAKE... RAT...
WOLF!
HEY, BABY!
HOW ABOUT DILTON?
HE'S AS WISE AS AN OWL!
AND ETHEL?
CAN YOU SAY GIRAFFE?
ARCHIE!
3

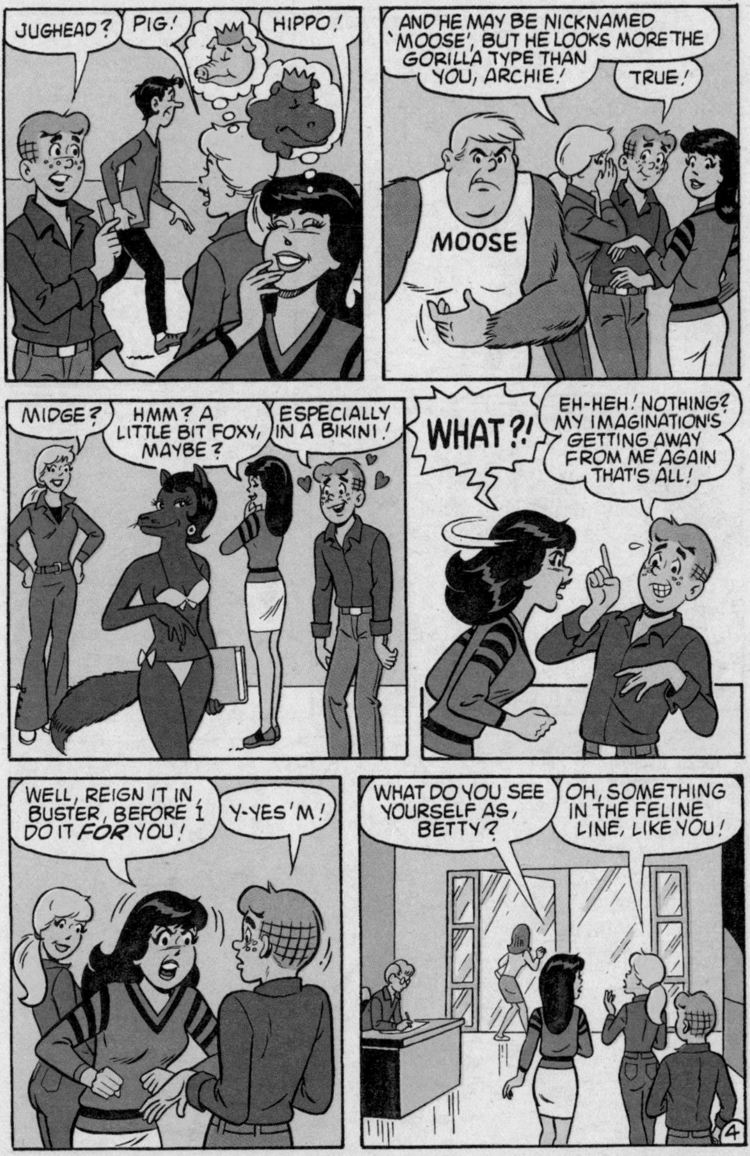
JUGHEAD?
PIG!
HIPPO!
AND HE MAY BE NICKNAMED 'MOOSE', BUT HE LOOKS MORE THE GORILLA TYPE THAN YOU, ARCHIE!
TRUE!
MOOSE
MIDGE?
HMM? A LITTLE BIT FOXY, MAYBE?
ESPECIALLY IN A BIKINI!
WHAT?!
EH-HEH! NOTHING? MY IMAGINATION'S GETTING AWAY FROM ME AGAIN THAT'S ALL!
WELL, REIGN IT IN, BUSTER, BEFORE I DO IT FOR YOU!
Y-YES'M!
WHAT DO YOU SEE YOURSELF AS, BETTY?
OH, SOMETHING IN THE FELINE LINE, LIKE YOU!
4

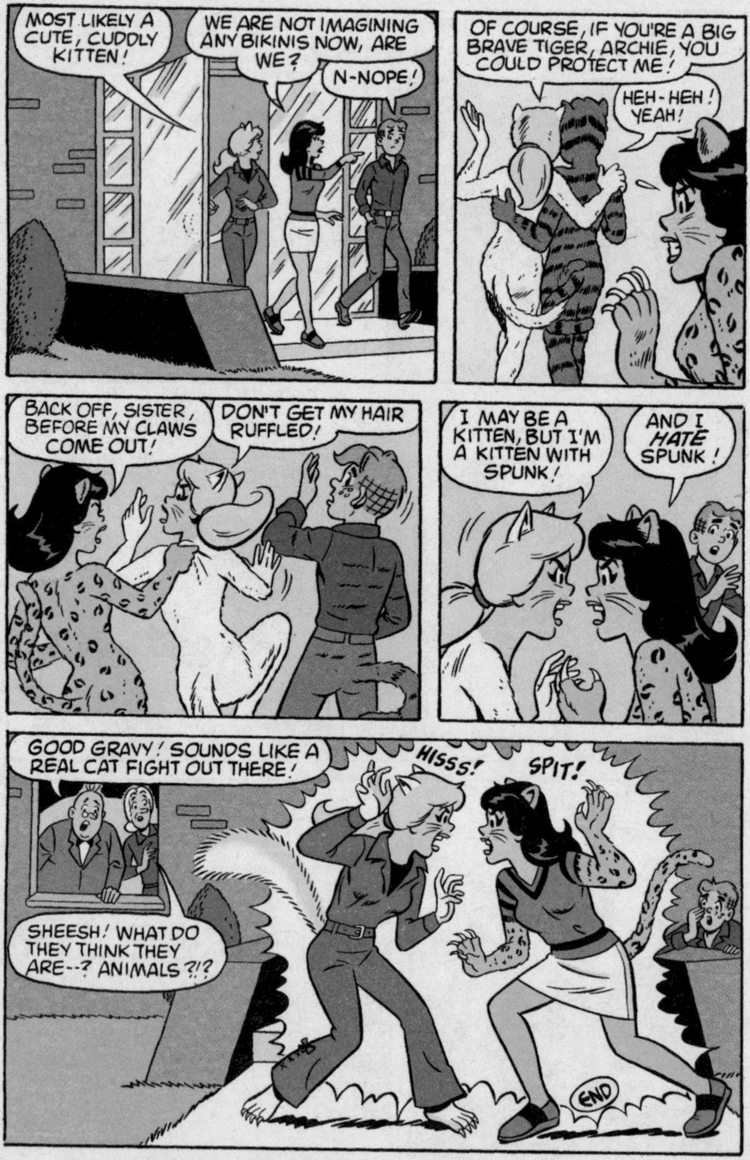
MOST LIKELY A CUTE, CUDDLY KITTEN!
WE ARE NOT IMAGINING ANY BIKINIS NOW, ARE WE?
N-NOPE!
OF COURSE, IF YOU'RE A BIG BRAVE TIGER, ARCHIE, YOU COULD PROTECT ME!
HEH-HEH! YEAH!
BACK OFF, SISTER, BEFORE MY CLAWS COME OUT!
DON'T GET MY HAIR RUFFLED!
I MAY BE A KITTEN, BUT I'M A KITTEN WITH SPUNK!
AND I HATE SPUNK!
GOOD GRAVY! SOUNDS LIKE A REAL CAT FIGHT OUT THERE!
HISSS!
SPIT!
SHEESH! WHAT DO THEY THINK THEY ARE--? ANIMALS?!?
END

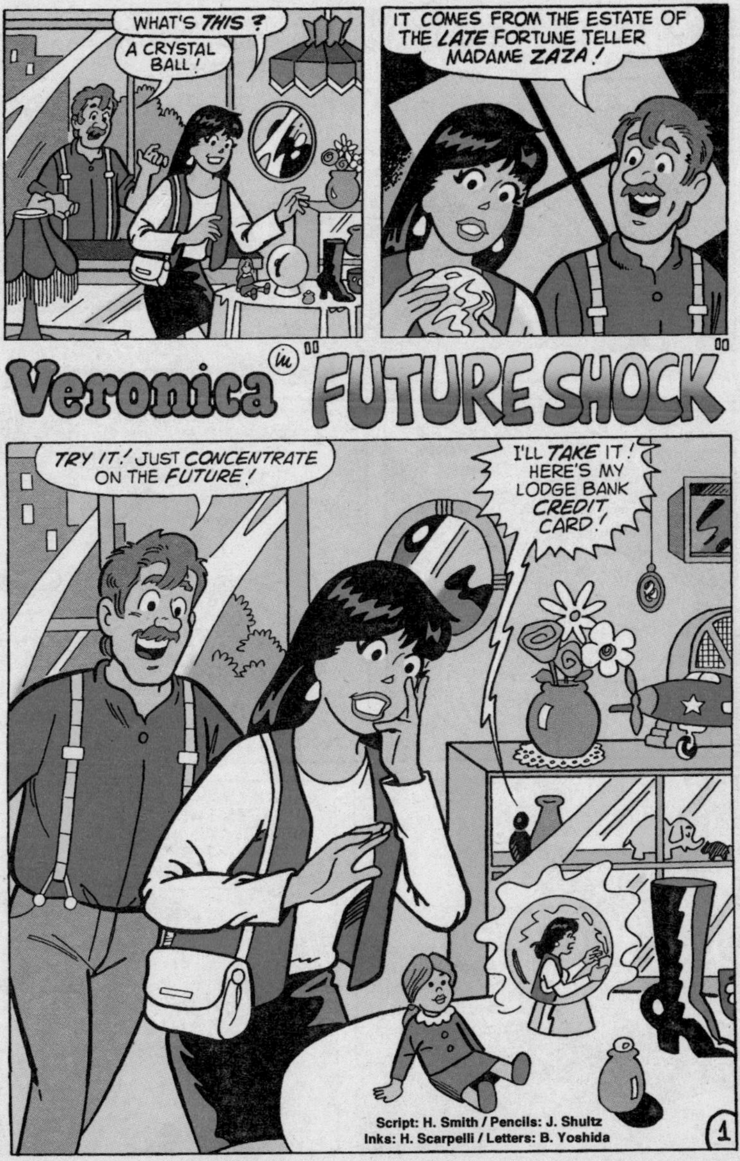
WHAT'S THIS ?
A CRYSTAL BALL !
IT COMES FROM THE ESTATE OF THE LATE FORTUNE TELLER MADAME ZAZA !
Veronica in "FUTURE SHOCK"
TRY IT! JUST CONCENTRATE ON THE FUTURE!
I'LL TAKE IT! HERE'S MY LODGE BANK CREDIT CARD!
Script: H. Smith / Pencils: J. Shultz
Inks: H. Scarpelli / Letters: B. Yoshida
1

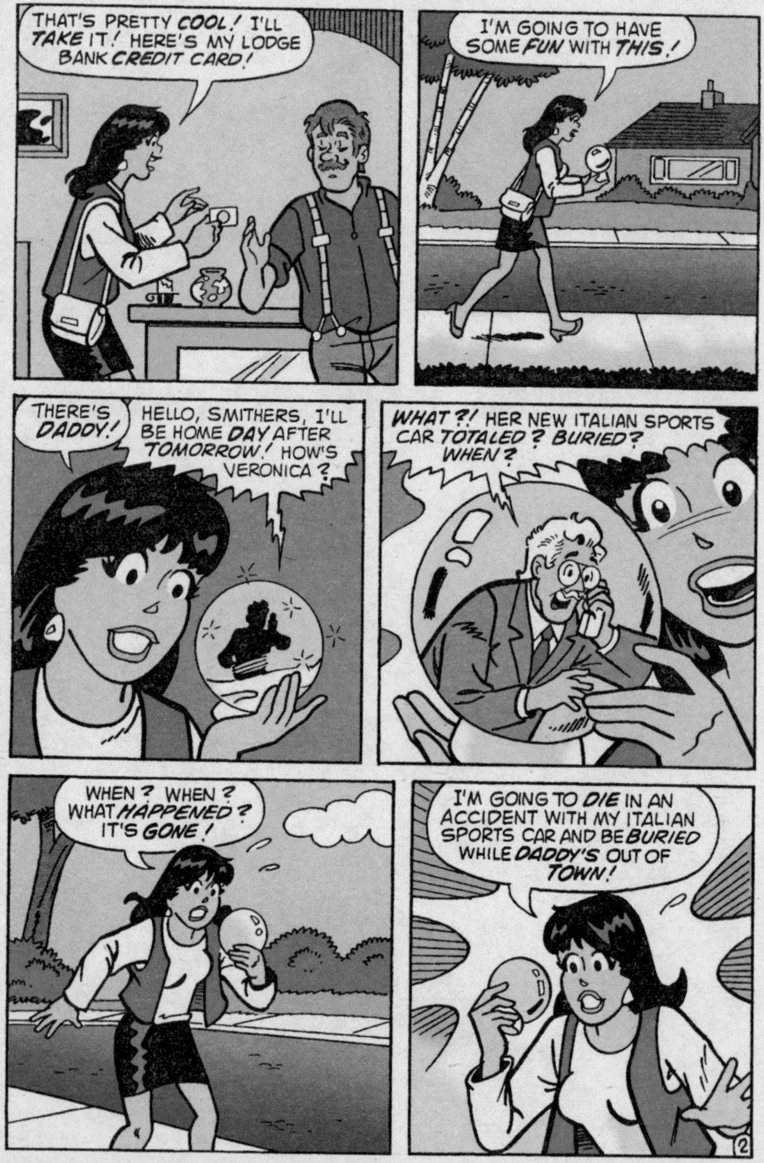
THAT'S PRETTY COOL! I'LL TAKE IT! HERE'S MY LODGE BANK CREDIT CARD!
I'M GOING TO HAVE SOME FUN WITH THIS!
THERE'S DADDY!
HELLO, SMITHERS, I'LL BE HOME DAY AFTER TOMORROW! HOW'S VERONICA?
WHAT?! HER NEW ITALIAN SPORTS CAR TOTALED? BURIED? WHEN?
WHEN? WHEN? WHAT HAPPENED? IT'S GONE!
I'M GOING TO DIE IN AN ACCIDENT WITH MY ITALIAN SPORTS CAR AND BE BURIED WHILE DADDY'S OUT OF TOWN!
2

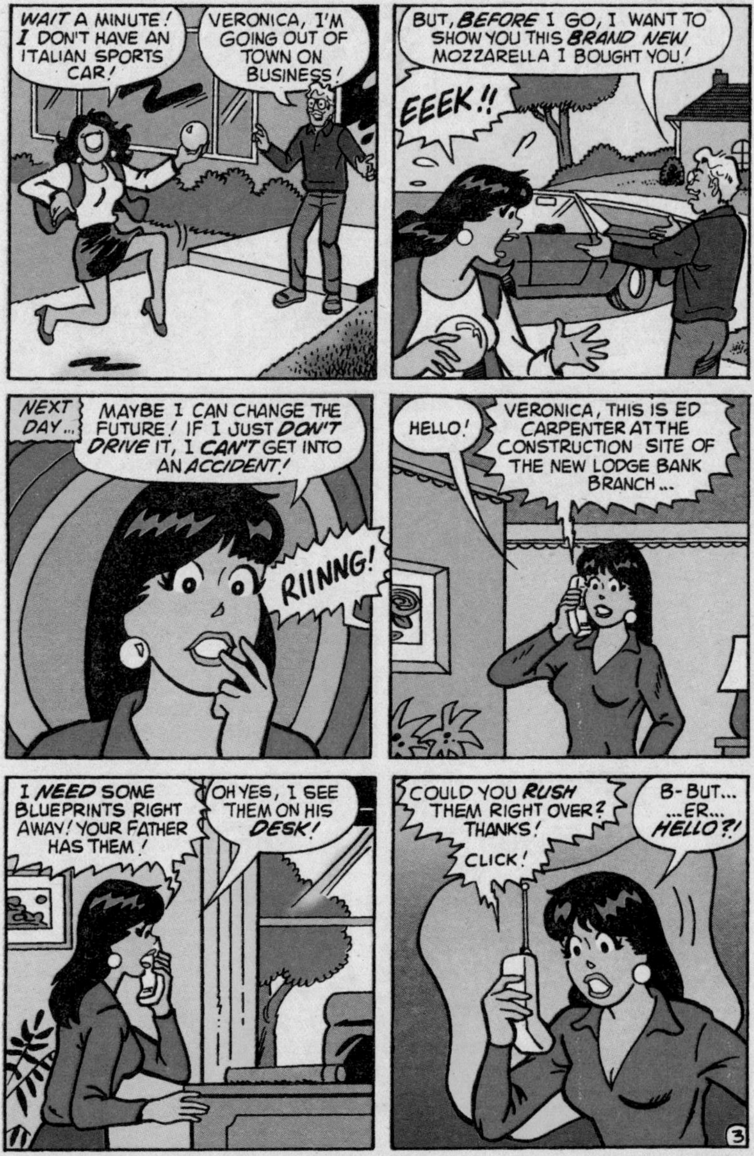
WAIT A MINUTE! I DON'T HAVE AN ITALIAN SPORTS CAR!
VERONICA, I'M GOING OUT OF TOWN ON BUSINESS!
BUT, BEFORE I GO, I WANT TO SHOW YOU THIS BRAND NEW MOZZARELLA I BOUGHT YOU!
EEEK!!
NEXT DAY...
MAYBE I CAN CHANGE THE FUTURE! IF I JUST DON'T DRIVE IT, I CAN'T GET INTO AN ACCIDENT!
RIINNG!
HELLO!
VERONICA, THIS IS ED CARPENTER AT THE CONSTRUCTION SITE OF THE NEW LODGE BANK BRANCH...
I NEED SOME BLUEPRINTS RIGHT AWAY! YOUR FATHER HAS THEM!
OH YES, I SEE THEM ON HIS DESK!
COULD YOU RUSH THEM RIGHT OVER? THANKS!
CLICK!
B-BUT... ...ER... HELLO?!
3

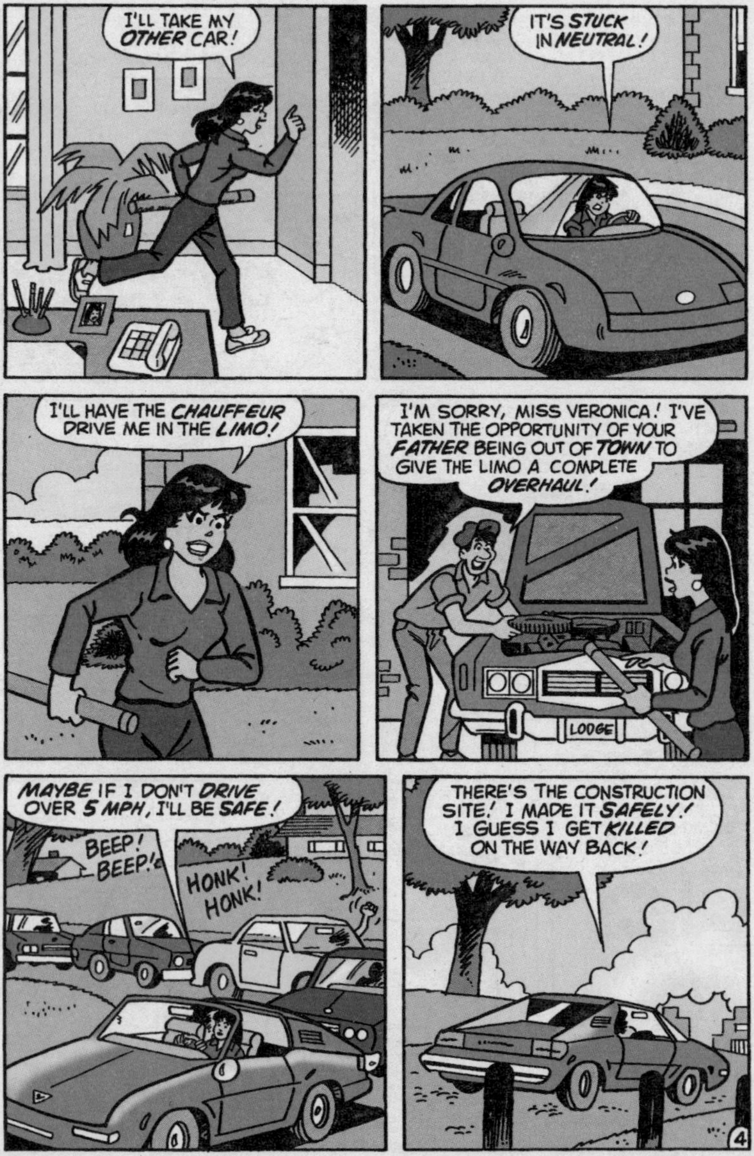

I'LL TAKE MY OTHER CAR!
IT'S STUCK IN NEUTRAL!
I'LL HAVE THE CHAUFFEUR DRIVE ME IN THE LIMO!
I'M SORRY, MISS VERONICA! I'VE TAKEN THE OPPORTUNITY OF YOUR FATHER BEING OUT OF TOWN TO GIVE THE LIMO A COMPLETE OVERHAUL!
LODGE
MAYBE IF I DON'T DRIVE OVER 5 MPH, I'LL BE SAFE!
BEEP! BEEP!
HONK! HONK!
THERE'S THE CONSTRUCTION SITE! I MADE IT SAFELY! I GUESS I GET KILLED ON THE WAY BACK!
4

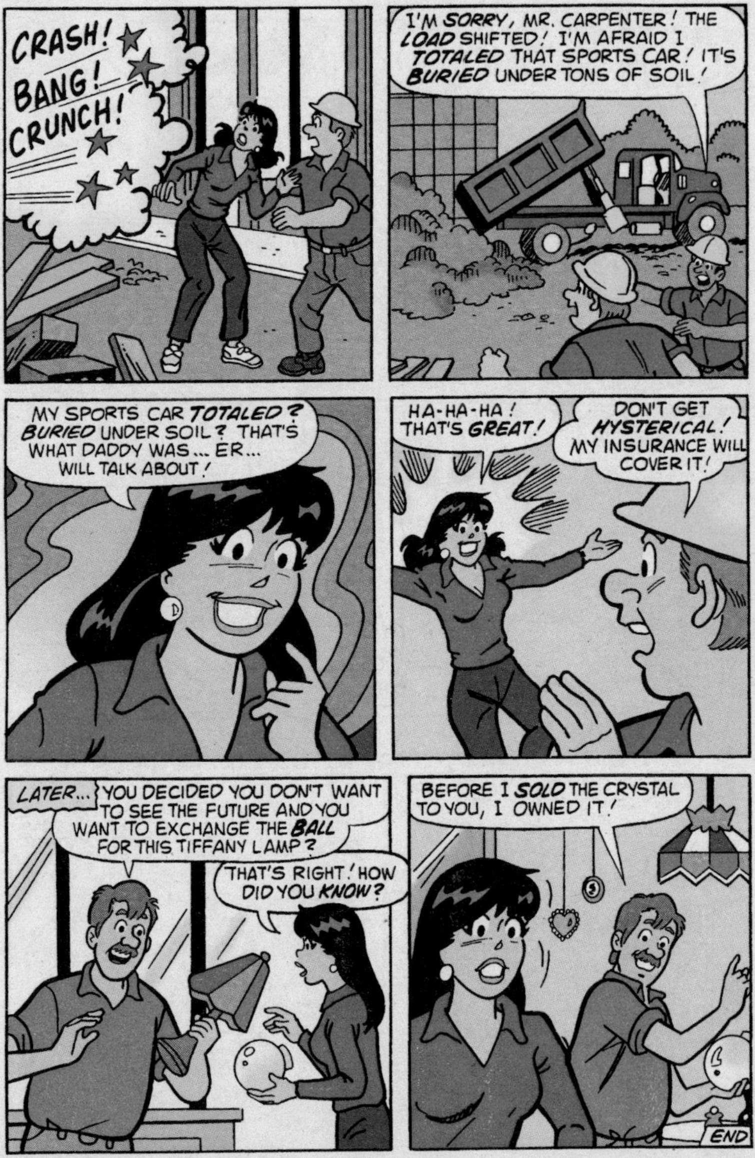
CRASH!
BANG!
CRUNCH!
I'M SORRY, MR. CARPENTER! THE LOAD SHIFTED! I'M AFRAID I TOTALED THAT SPORTS CAR! IT'S BURIED UNDER TONS OF SOIL!
MY SPORTS CAR TOTALED? BURIED UNDER SOIL? THAT'S WHAT DADDY WAS... ER... WILL TALK ABOUT!
HA-HA-HA! THAT'S GREAT!
DON'T GET HYSTERICAL! MY INSURANCE WILL COVER IT!
LATER...
YOU DECIDED YOU DON'T WANT TO SEE THE FUTURE AND YOU WANT TO EXCHANGE THE BALL FOR THIS TIFFANY LAMP?
THAT'S RIGHT! HOW DID YOU KNOW?
BEFORE I SOLD THE CRYSTAL TO YOU, I OWNED IT!
END

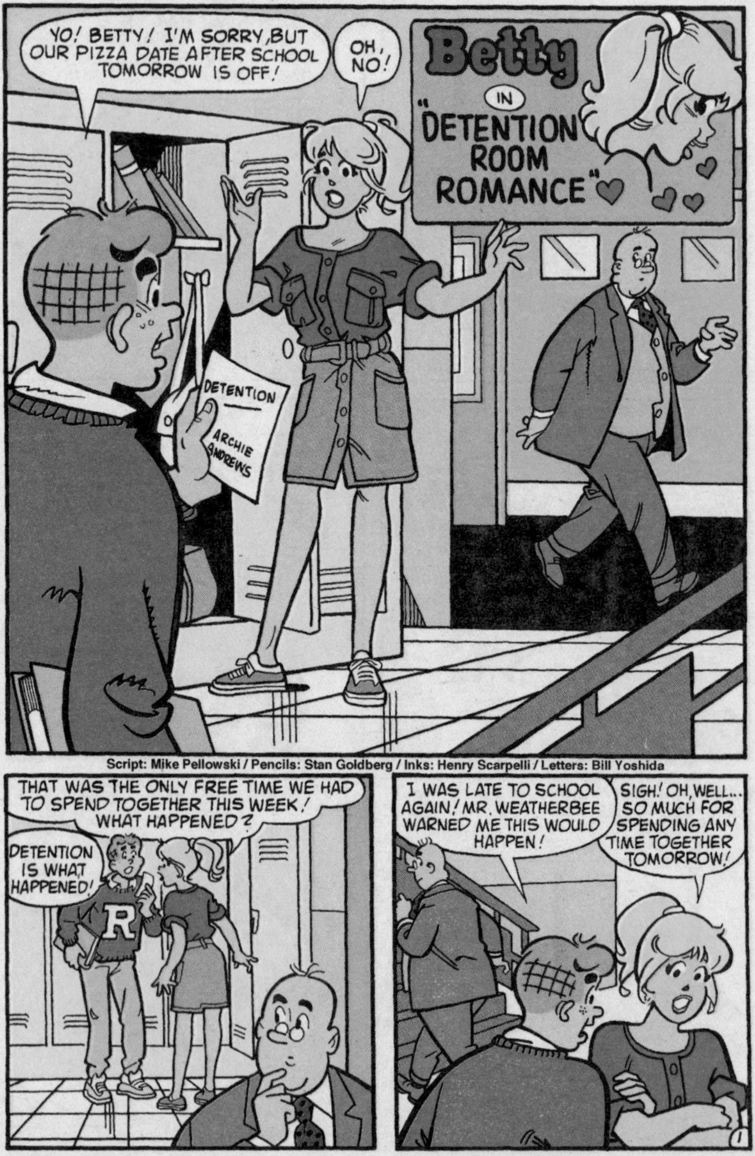
YO! BETTY! I'M SORRY, BUT OUR PIZZA DATE AFTER SCHOOL TOMORROW IS OFF!
OH, NO!
Betty
IN
"DETENTION ROOM ROMANCE"
DETENTION
ARCHIE ANDREWS
Script: Mike Pellowski / Pencils: Stan Goldberg / Inks: Henry Scarpelli / Letters: Bill Yoshida
THAT WAS THE ONLY FREE TIME WE HAD TO SPEND TOGETHER THIS WEEK! WHAT HAPPENED?
DETENTION IS WHAT HAPPENED!
R
I WAS LATE TO SCHOOL AGAIN! MR. WEATHERBEE WARNED ME THIS WOULD HAPPEN!
SIGH! OH, WELL... SO MUCH FOR SPENDING ANY TIME TOGETHER TOMORROW!
1

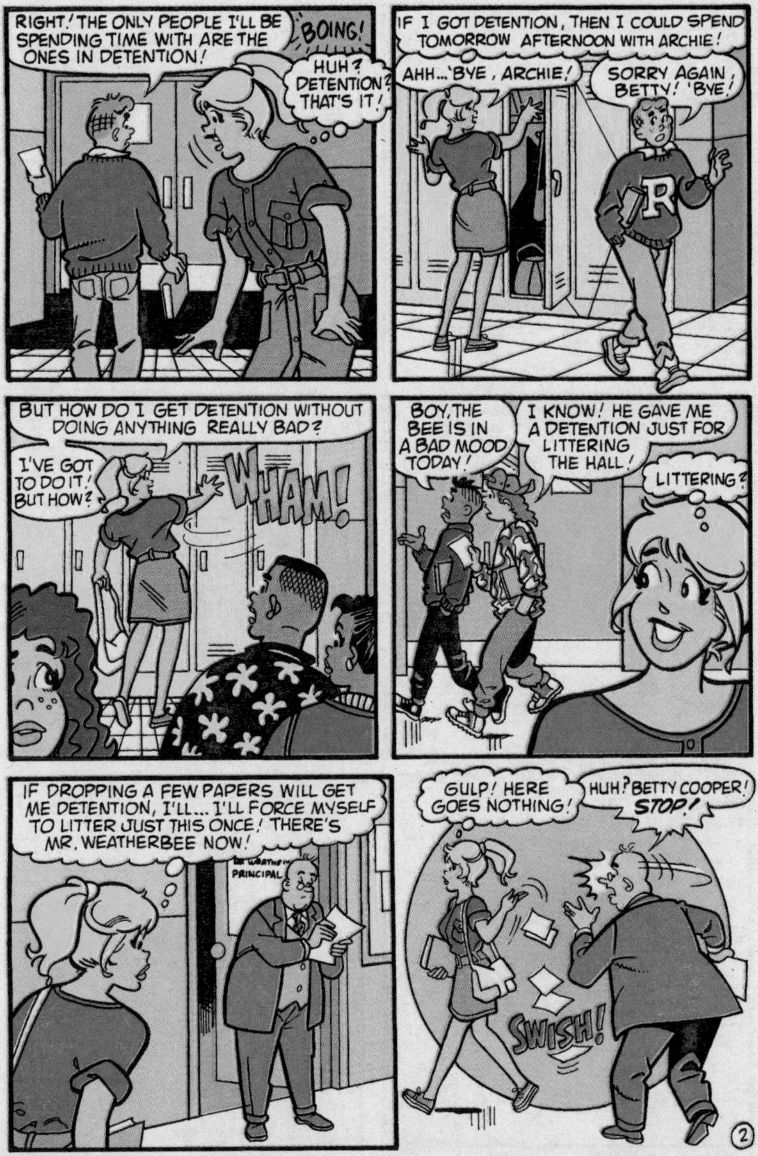
RIGHT! THE ONLY PEOPLE I'LL BE SPENDING TIME WITH ARE THE ONES IN DETENTION!
BOING!
HUH? DETENTION? THAT'S IT!
IF I GOT DETENTION, THEN I COULD SPEND TOMORROW AFTERNOON WITH ARCHIE!
AHH...'BYE, ARCHIE!
SORRY AGAIN, BETTY! 'BYE!
BUT HOW DO I GET DETENTION WITHOUT DOING ANYTHING REALLY BAD?
I'VE GOT TO DO IT! BUT HOW?
WHAM!
BOY, THE BEE IS IN A BAD MOOD TODAY!
I KNOW! HE GAVE ME A DETENTION JUST FOR LITTERING THE HALL!
LITTERING?
IF DROPPING A FEW PAPERS WILL GET ME DETENTION, I'LL... I'LL FORCE MYSELF TO LITTER JUST THIS ONCE! THERE'S MR. WEATHERBEE NOW!
PRINCIPAL
GULP! HERE GOES NOTHING!
HUH? BETTY COOPER! STOP!
SWISH!

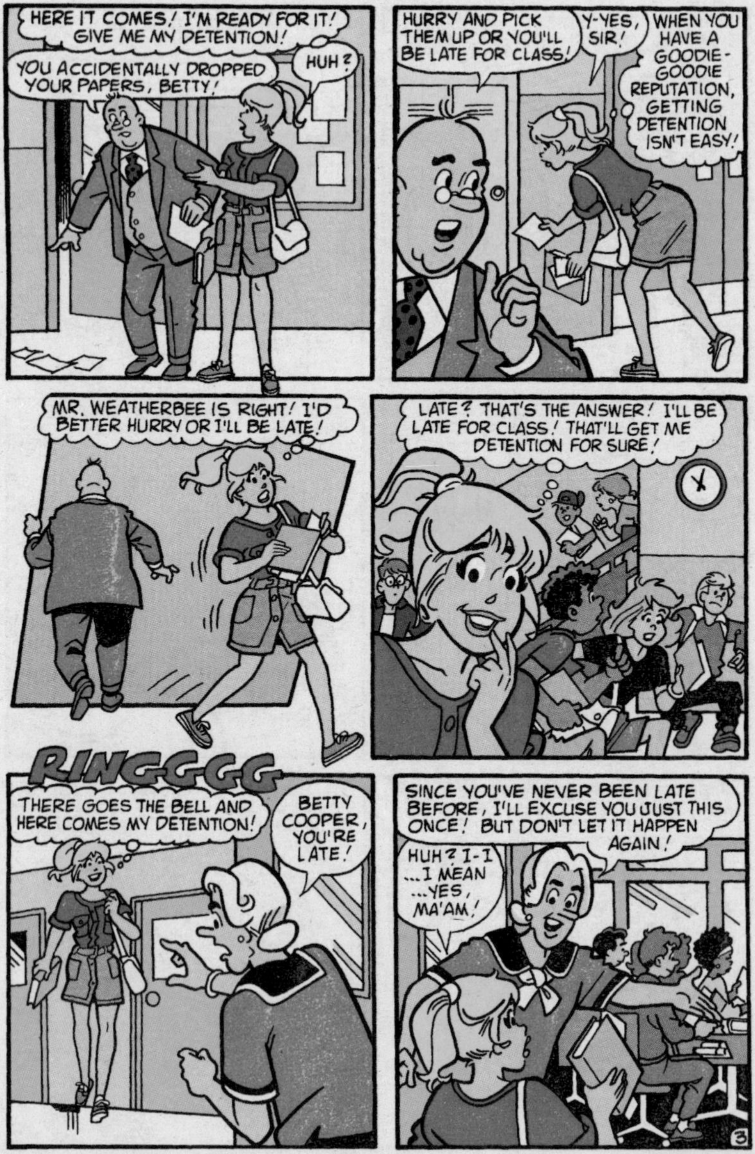
HERE IT COMES! I'M READY FOR IT! GIVE ME MY DETENTION!
YOU ACCIDENTALLY DROPPED YOUR PAPERS, BETTY!
HUH?
HURRY AND PICK THEM UP OR YOU'LL BE LATE FOR CLASS!
Y-YES, SIR!
WHEN YOU HAVE A GOODIE-GOODIE REPUTATION, GETTING DETENTION ISN'T EASY!
MR. WEATHERBEE IS RIGHT! I'D BETTER HURRY OR I'LL BE LATE!
LATE? THAT'S THE ANSWER! I'LL BE LATE FOR CLASS! THAT'LL GET ME DETENTION FOR SURE!
RINGGGG
THERE GOES THE BELL AND HERE COMES MY DETENTION!
BETTY COOPER, YOU'RE LATE!
SINCE YOU'VE NEVER BEEN LATE BEFORE, I'LL EXCUSE YOU JUST THIS ONCE! BUT DON'T LET IT HAPPEN AGAIN!
HUH? I-I ...I MEAN ...YES, MA'AM!

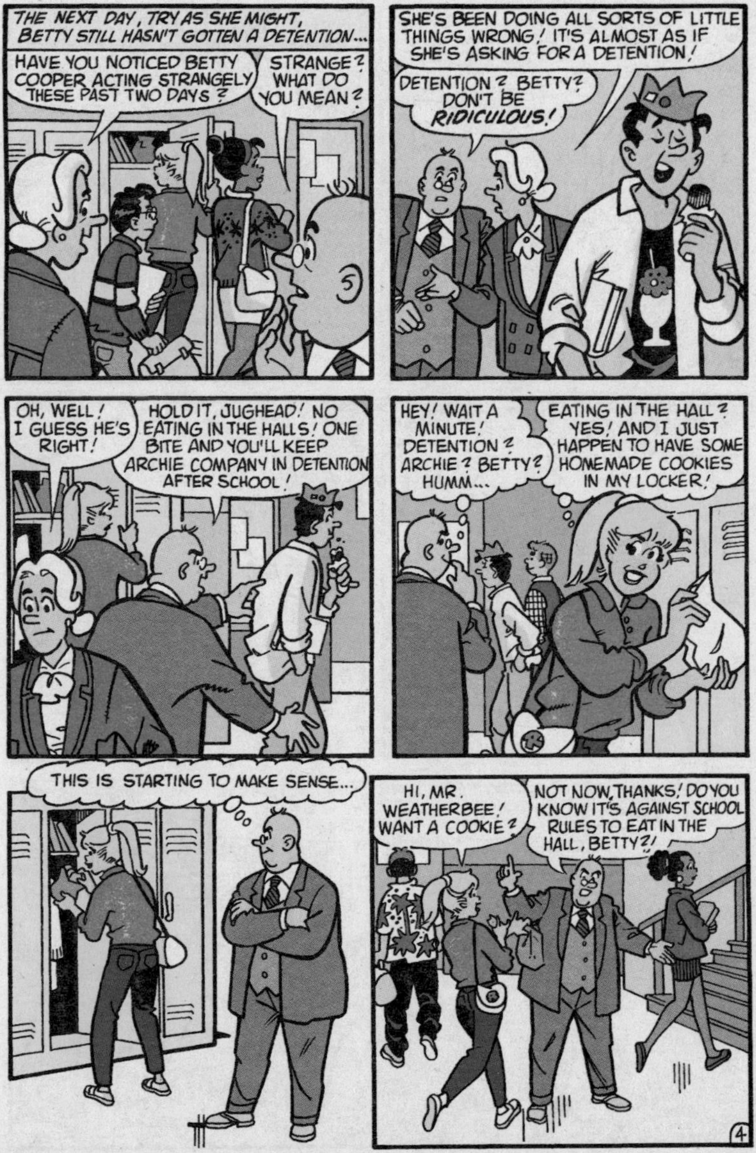
THE NEXT DAY, TRY AS SHE MIGHT, BETTY STILL HASN'T GOTTEN A DETENTION...
HAVE YOU NOTICED BETTY COOPER ACTING STRANGELY THESE PAST TWO DAYS?
STRANGE? WHAT DO YOU MEAN?
SHE'S BEEN DOING ALL SORTS OF LITTLE THINGS WRONG! IT'S ALMOST AS IF SHE'S ASKING FOR A DETENTION!
DETENTION? BETTY? DON'T BE RIDICULOUS!
OH, WELL! I GUESS HE'S RIGHT!
HOLD IT, JUGHEAD! NO EATING IN THE HALLS! ONE BITE AND YOU'LL KEEP ARCHIE COMPANY IN DETENTION AFTER SCHOOL!
HEY! WAIT A MINUTE! DETENTION? ARCHIE? BETTY? HUMM...
EATING IN THE HALL? YES! AND I JUST HAPPEN TO HAVE SOME HOMEMADE COOKIES IN MY LOCKER!
THIS IS STARTING TO MAKE SENSE...
HI, MR. WEATHERBEE! WANT A COOKIE?
NOT NOW, THANKS! DO YOU KNOW IT'S AGAINST SCHOOL RULES TO EAT IN THE HALL, BETTY?!
4

YES, SIR, BUT I WAS SO HUNGRY I JUST COULDN'T HELP MYSELF!

WELL, I GUESS I HAVE NO CHOICE BUT TO LET YOU JOIN ARCHIE IN DETENTION!

YES! DETENTION!

HUM... NOT THE TYPICAL RESPONSE TO DETENTION I NORMALLY SEE, BUT IN THIS CASE IT'S THE ONE I EXPECTED!

AFTER SCHOOL IN THE DETENTION ROOM...

BETTY, TAKE THE SEAT ACROSS FROM ARCHIE!

DETENTION ROOM

ARCHIE
BETTY

B-BETTY? YOU HAVE DETENTION?

I GUESS WE'LL BE SPENDING THE AFTERNOON TOGETHER AFTER ALL, ARCHIE!

NOW THAT'S DEFINITELY NOT A TYPICAL HIGH SCHOOL LOVE STORY! IT'S MORE LIKE A DETENTION ROOM ROMANCE!

5

END

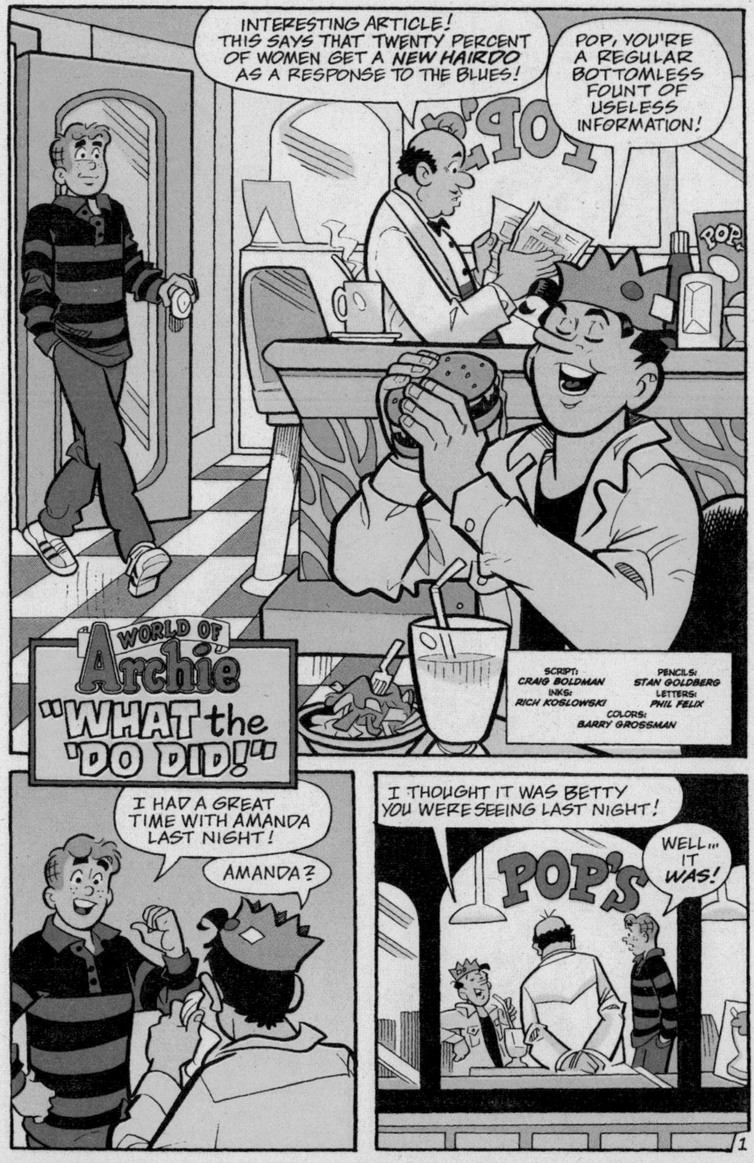
INTERESTING ARTICLE! THIS SAYS THAT TWENTY PERCENT OF WOMEN GET A NEW HAIRDO AS A RESPONSE TO THE BLUES!
POP, YOU'RE A REGULAR BOTTOMLESS FOUNT OF USELESS INFORMATION!
POP'S
WORLD OF Archie
"WHAT the 'DO DID!"
SCRIPT: CRAIG BOLDMAN
PENCILS: STAN GOLDBERG
INKS: RICH KOSLOWSKI
LETTERS: PHIL FELIX
COLORS: BARRY GROSSMAN
I HAD A GREAT TIME WITH AMANDA LAST NIGHT!
AMANDA?
I THOUGHT IT WAS BETTY YOU WERE SEEING LAST NIGHT!
POP'S
WELL... IT WAS!

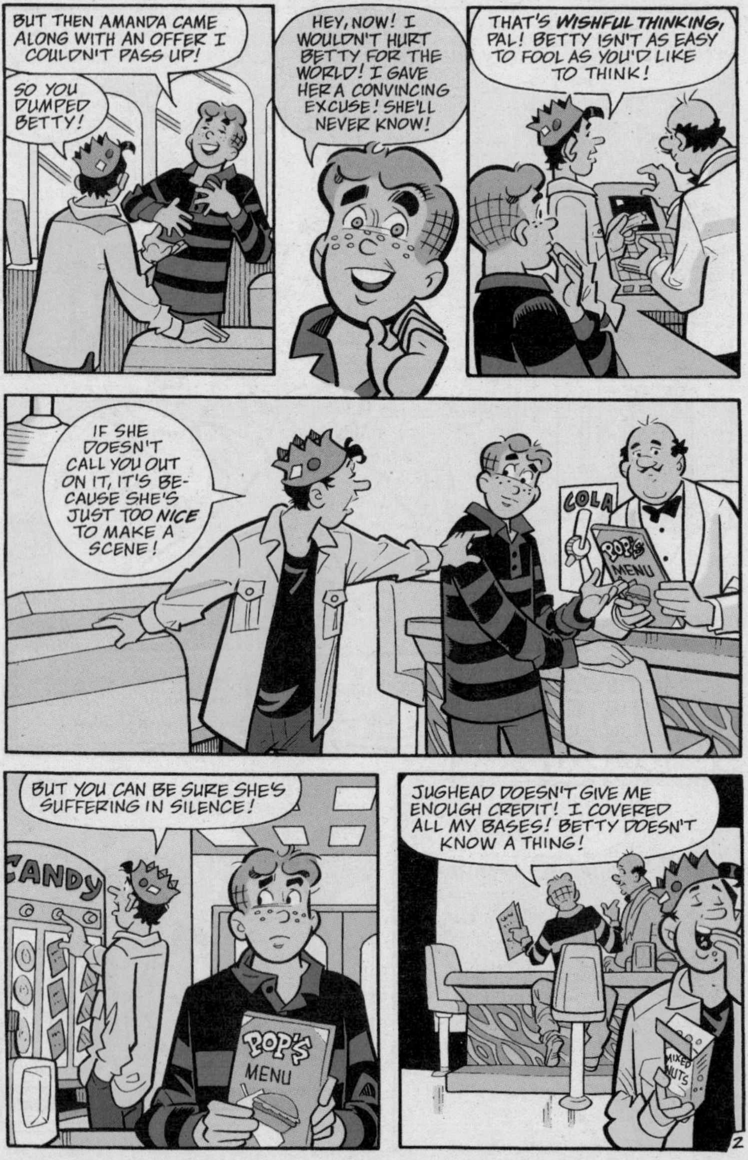

BUT THEN AMANDA CAME ALONG WITH AN OFFER I COULDN'T PASS UP!
SO YOU DUMPED BETTY!
HEY, NOW! I WOULDN'T HURT BETTY FOR THE WORLD! I GAVE HER A CONVINCING EXCUSE! SHE'LL NEVER KNOW!
THAT'S WISHFUL THINKING, PAL! BETTY ISN'T AS EASY TO FOOL AS YOU'D LIKE TO THINK!
IF SHE DOESN'T CALL YOU OUT ON IT, IT'S BE-CAUSE SHE'S JUST TOO NICE TO MAKE A SCENE!
COLA
POP'S MENU
BUT YOU CAN BE SURE SHE'S SUFFERING IN SILENCE!
CANDY
POP'S MENU
JUGHEAD DOESN'T GIVE ME ENOUGH CREDIT! I COVERED ALL MY BASES! BETTY DOESN'T KNOW A THING!
MIXED NUTS

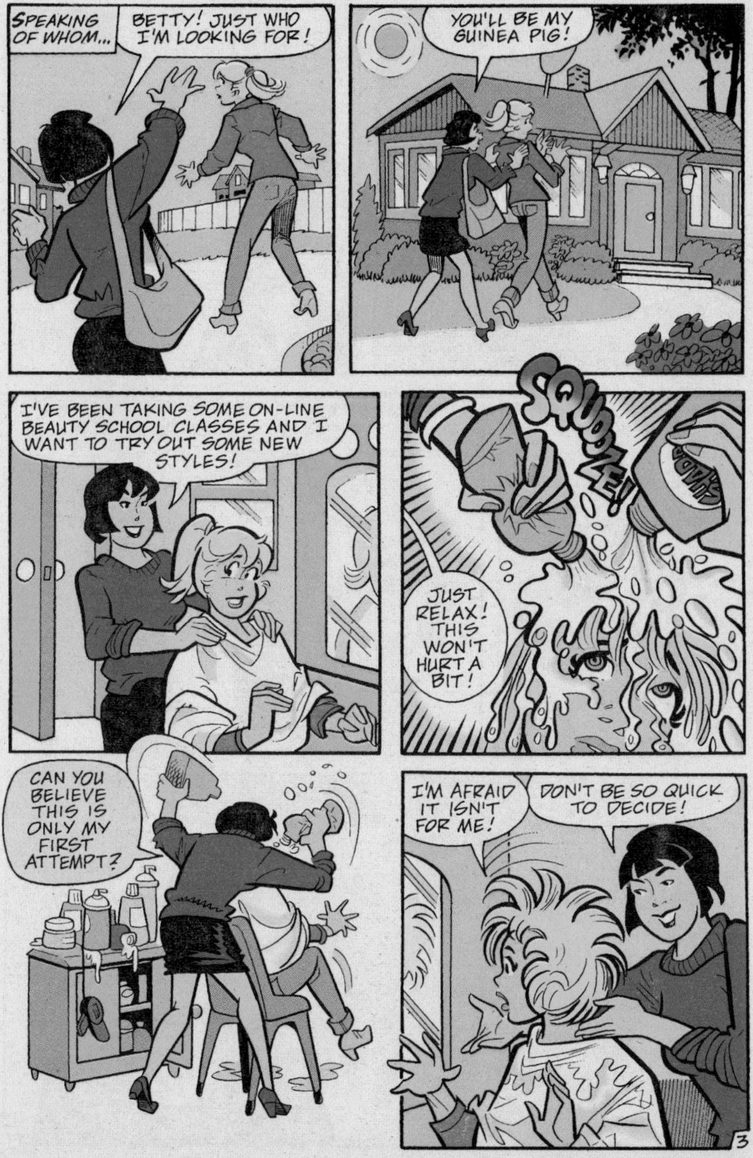
SPEAKING OF WHOM...
BETTY! JUST WHO I'M LOOKING FOR!
YOU'LL BE MY GUINEA PIG!
I'VE BEEN TAKING SOME ON-LINE BEAUTY SCHOOL CLASSES AND I WANT TO TRY OUT SOME NEW STYLES!
SQUOOZE!
JUST RELAX! THIS WON'T HURT A BIT!
CAN YOU BELIEVE THIS IS ONLY MY FIRST ATTEMPT?
I'M AFRAID IT ISN'T FOR ME!
DON'T BE SO QUICK TO DECIDE!

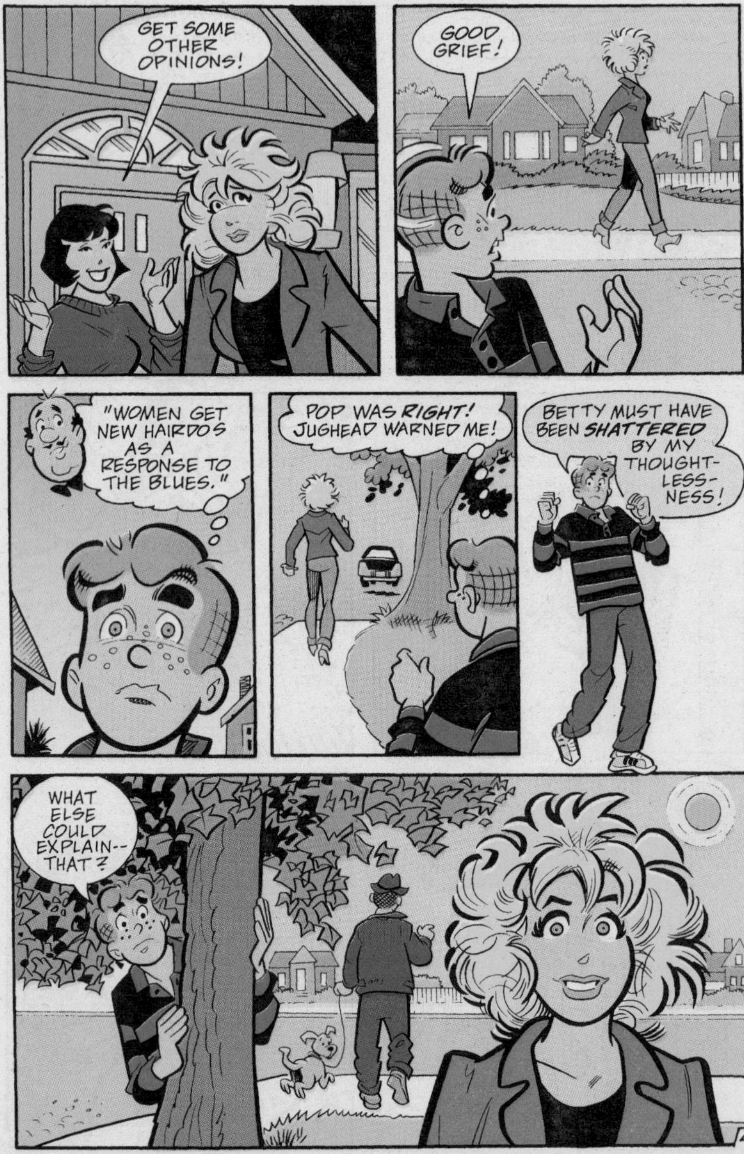
GET SOME OTHER OPINIONS!
GOOD GRIEF!
"WOMEN GET NEW HAIRDOS AS A RESPONSE TO THE BLUES."
POP WAS RIGHT! JUGHEAD WARNED ME!
BETTY MUST HAVE BEEN SHATTERED BY MY THOUGHT-LESS-NESS!
WHAT ELSE COULD EXPLAIN-- THAT?

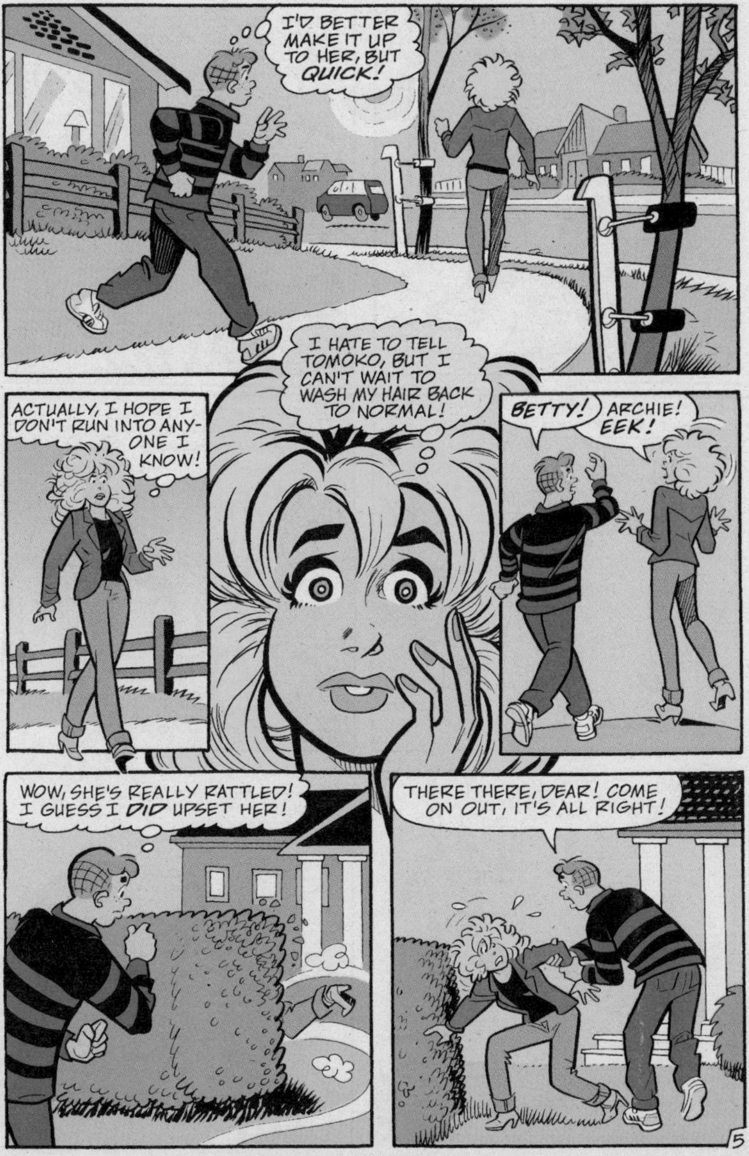
I'D BETTER MAKE IT UP TO HER, BUT QUICK!
I HATE TO TELL TOMOKO, BUT I CAN'T WAIT TO WASH MY HAIR BACK TO NORMAL!
ACTUALLY, I HOPE I DON'T RUN INTO ANYONE I KNOW!
BETTY!
ARCHIE! EEK!
WOW, SHE'S REALLY RATTLED! I GUESS I DID UPSET HER!
THERE THERE, DEAR! COME ON OUT, IT'S ALL RIGHT!

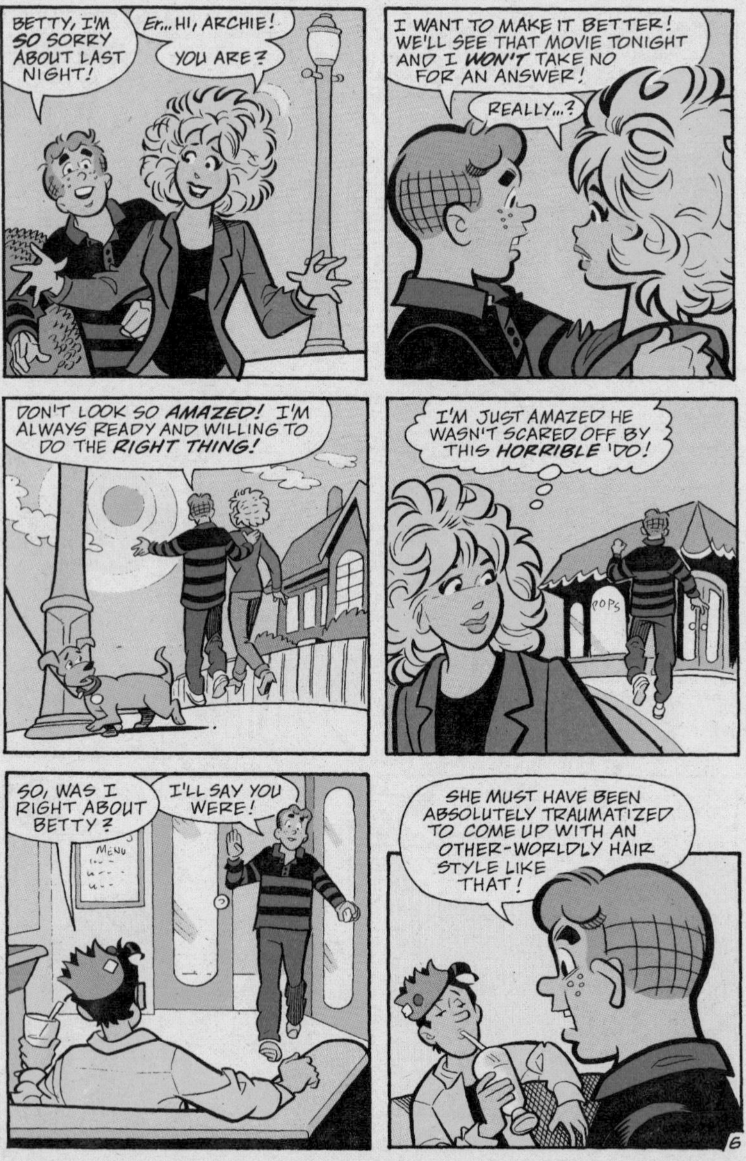
BETTY, I'M SO SORRY ABOUT LAST NIGHT!
Er... HI, ARCHIE!
YOU ARE?
I WANT TO MAKE IT BETTER! WE'LL SEE THAT MOVIE TONIGHT AND I WON'T TAKE NO FOR AN ANSWER!
REALLY...?
DON'T LOOK SO AMAZED! I'M ALWAYS READY AND WILLING TO DO THE RIGHT THING!
I'M JUST AMAZED HE WASN'T SCARED OFF BY THIS HORRIBLE 'DO!
POPS
SO, WAS I RIGHT ABOUT BETTY?
I'LL SAY YOU WERE!
MENU
SHE MUST HAVE BEEN ABSOLUTELY TRAUMATIZED TO COME UP WITH AN OTHER-WORLDLY HAIR STYLE LIKE THAT!

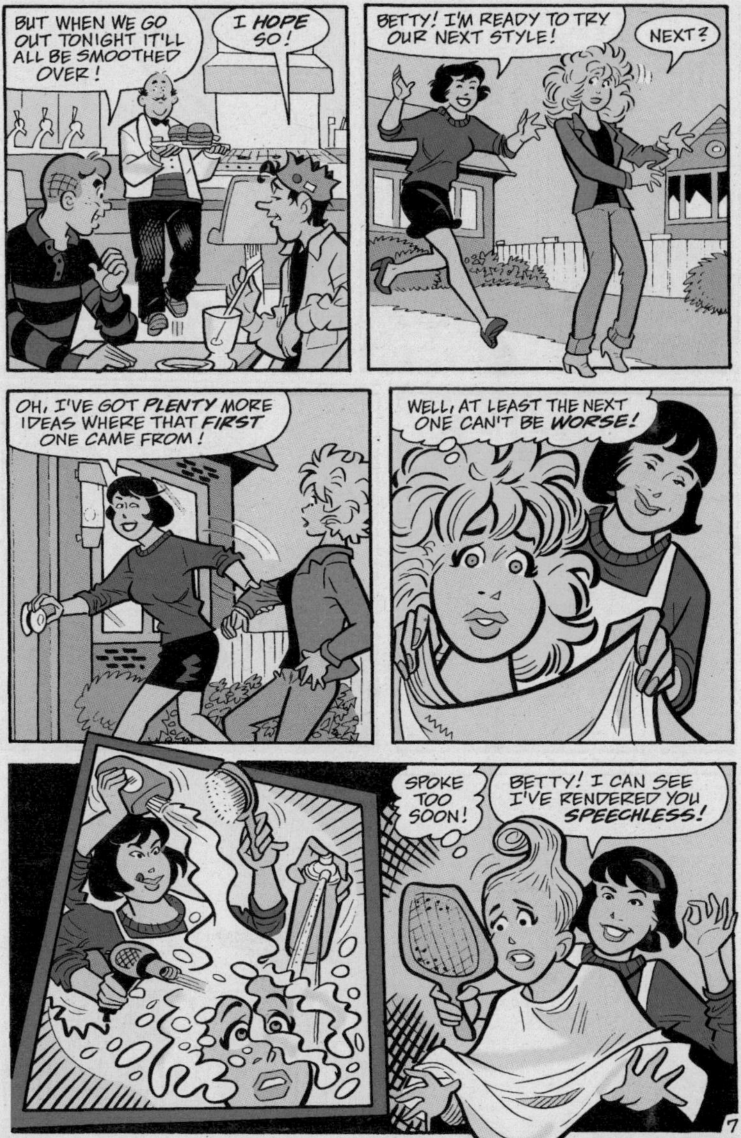

BUT WHEN WE GO OUT TONIGHT IT'LL ALL BE SMOOTHED OVER!
I HOPE SO!
BETTY! I'M READY TO TRY OUR NEXT STYLE!
NEXT?
OH, I'VE GOT PLENTY MORE IDEAS WHERE THAT FIRST ONE CAME FROM!
WELL, AT LEAST THE NEXT ONE CAN'T BE WORSE!
SPOKE TOO SOON!
BETTY! I CAN SEE I'VE RENDERED YOU SPEECHLESS!

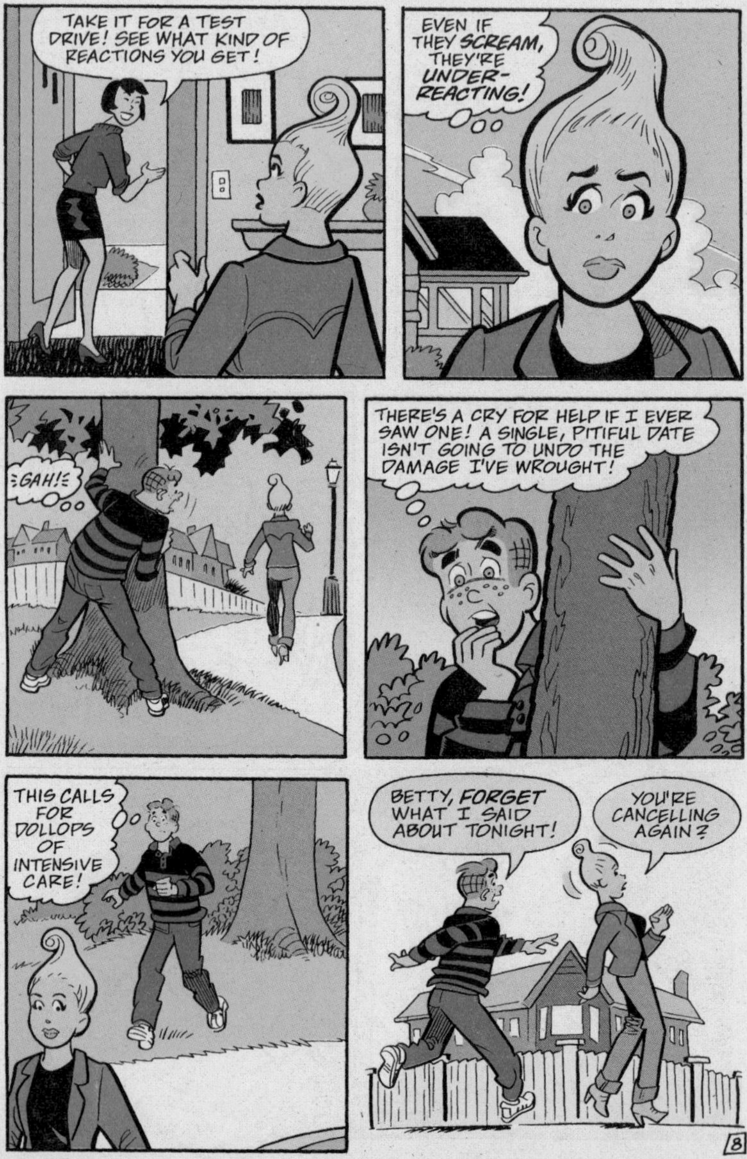
TAKE IT FOR A TEST DRIVE! SEE WHAT KIND OF REACTIONS YOU GET!
EVEN IF THEY SCREAM, THEY'RE UNDER-REACTING!
GAH!
THERE'S A CRY FOR HELP IF I EVER SAW ONE! A SINGLE, PITIFUL DATE ISN'T GOING TO UNDO THE DAMAGE I'VE WROUGHT!
THIS CALLS FOR DOLLOPS OF INTENSIVE CARE!
BETTY, FORGET WHAT I SAID ABOUT TONIGHT!
YOU'RE CANCELLING AGAIN?
8

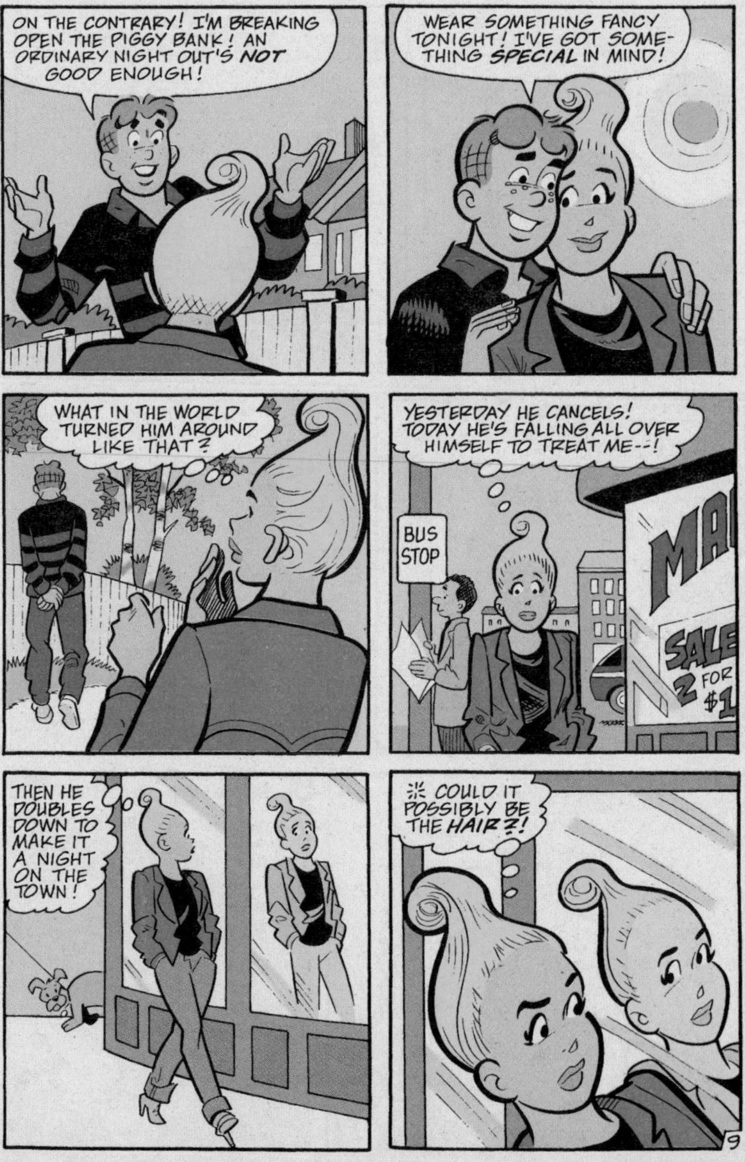
ON THE CONTRARY! I'M BREAKING OPEN THE PIGGY BANK! AN ORDINARY NIGHT OUT'S NOT GOOD ENOUGH!
WEAR SOMETHING FANCY TONIGHT! I'VE GOT SOMETHING SPECIAL IN MIND!
WHAT IN THE WORLD TURNED HIM AROUND LIKE THAT?
YESTERDAY HE CANCELS! TODAY HE'S FALLING ALL OVER HIMSELF TO TREAT ME--!
BUS STOP
SALE
2 FOR
THEN HE DOUBLES DOWN TO MAKE IT A NIGHT ON THE TOWN!
COULD IT POSSIBLY BE THE HAIR?!

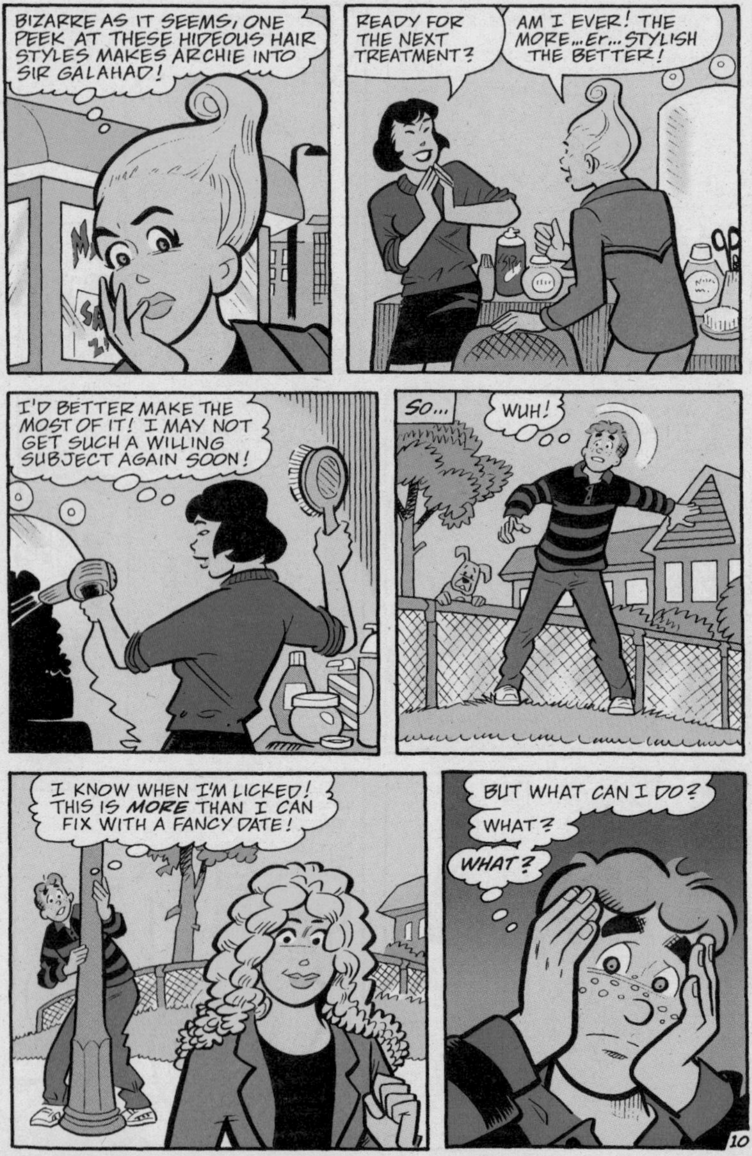

BIZARRE AS IT SEEMS, ONE PEEK AT THESE HIDEOUS HAIR STYLES MAKES ARCHIE INTO SIR GALAHAD!
READY FOR THE NEXT TREATMENT?
AM I EVER! THE MORE...Er...STYLISH THE BETTER!
I'D BETTER MAKE THE MOST OF IT! I MAY NOT GET SUCH A WILLING SUBJECT AGAIN SOON!
SO...
WUH!
I KNOW WHEN I'M LICKED! THIS IS MORE THAN I CAN FIX WITH A FANCY DATE!
BUT WHAT CAN I DO?
WHAT?
WHAT?

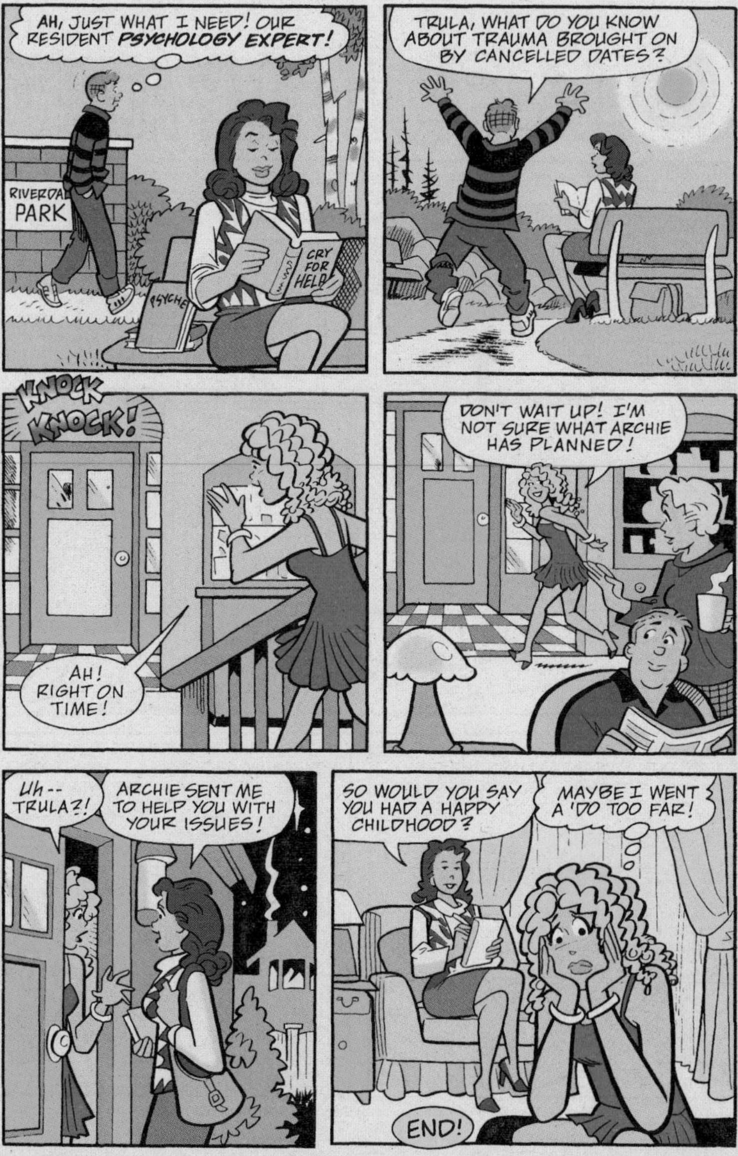
AH, JUST WHAT I NEED! OUR RESIDENT PSYCHOLOGY EXPERT!
RIVERDA
PARK
PSYCHE
CRY FOR HELP
TRULA, WHAT DO YOU KNOW ABOUT TRAUMA BROUGHT ON BY CANCELLED DATES?
KNOCK KNOCK!
AH! RIGHT ON TIME!
DON'T WAIT UP! I'M NOT SURE WHAT ARCHIE HAS PLANNED!
UH-- TRULA?!
ARCHIE SENT ME TO HELP YOU WITH YOUR ISSUES!
SO WOULD YOU SAY YOU HAD A HAPPY CHILDHOOD?
MAYBE I WENT A 'DO TOO FAR!
END!

Archie in "QUIT BELLY-ACHING"

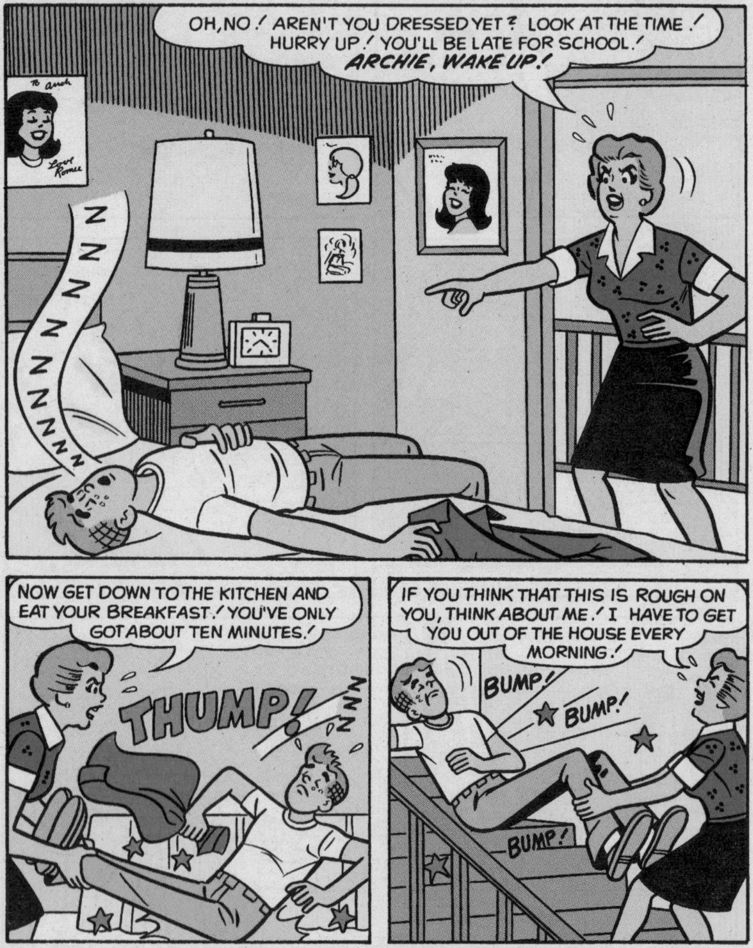

OH, NO! AREN'T YOU DRESSED YET? LOOK AT THE TIME! HURRY UP! YOU'LL BE LATE FOR SCHOOL! ARCHIE, WAKE UP!
NOW GET DOWN TO THE KITCHEN AND EAT YOUR BREAKFAST! YOU'VE ONLY GOT ABOUT TEN MINUTES!
THUMP!
IF YOU THINK THAT THIS IS ROUGH ON YOU, THINK ABOUT ME! I HAVE TO GET YOU OUT OF THE HOUSE EVERY MORNING!
BUMP!
BUMP!
BUMP!

Script & Pencils: Dick Malmgren / Inks: Rudy Lapick / Letters: Bill Yoshida

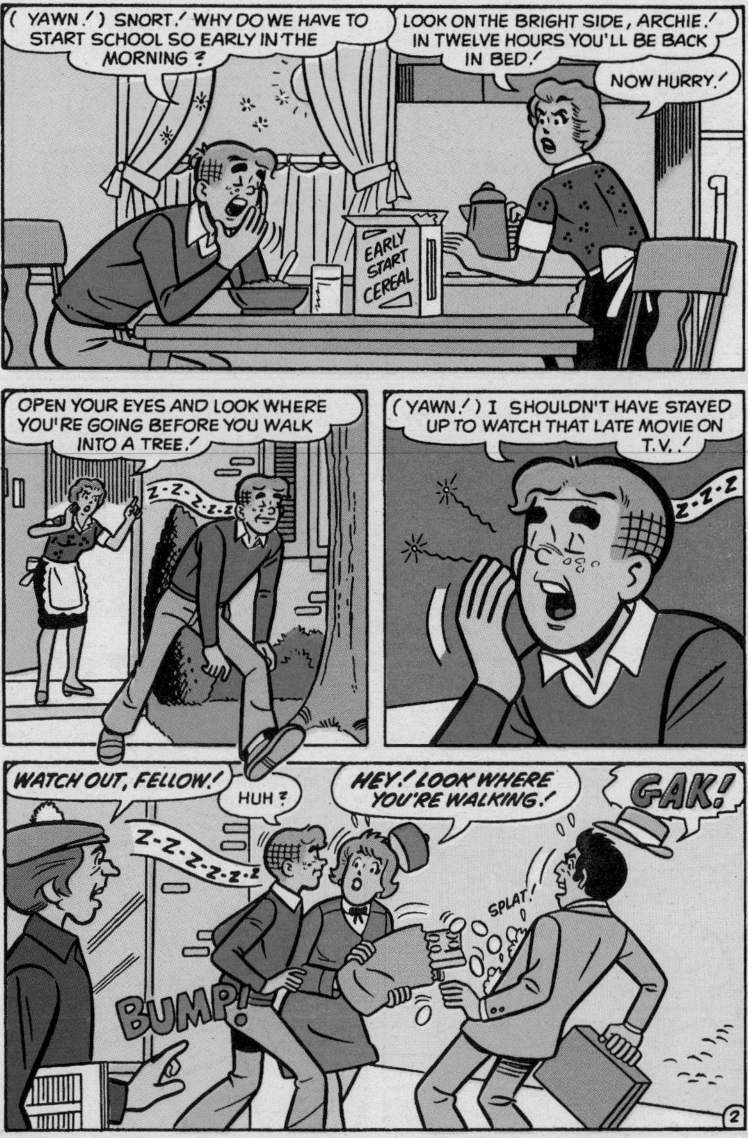

(YAWN.!) SNORT.! WHY DO WE HAVE TO START SCHOOL SO EARLY IN THE MORNING ?
LOOK ON THE BRIGHT SIDE, ARCHIE.! IN TWELVE HOURS YOU'LL BE BACK IN BED.!
NOW HURRY.!
EARLY START CEREAL
OPEN YOUR EYES AND LOOK WHERE YOU'RE GOING BEFORE YOU WALK INTO A TREE.!
Z-Z-Z-Z-Z
(YAWN.!) I SHOULDN'T HAVE STAYED UP TO WATCH THAT LATE MOVIE ON T.V. .!
Z-Z-Z
WATCH OUT, FELLOW.!
HUH ?
HEY.! LOOK WHERE YOU'RE WALKING.!
GAK!
Z-Z-Z-Z-Z-Z
SPLAT!
BUMP!
2

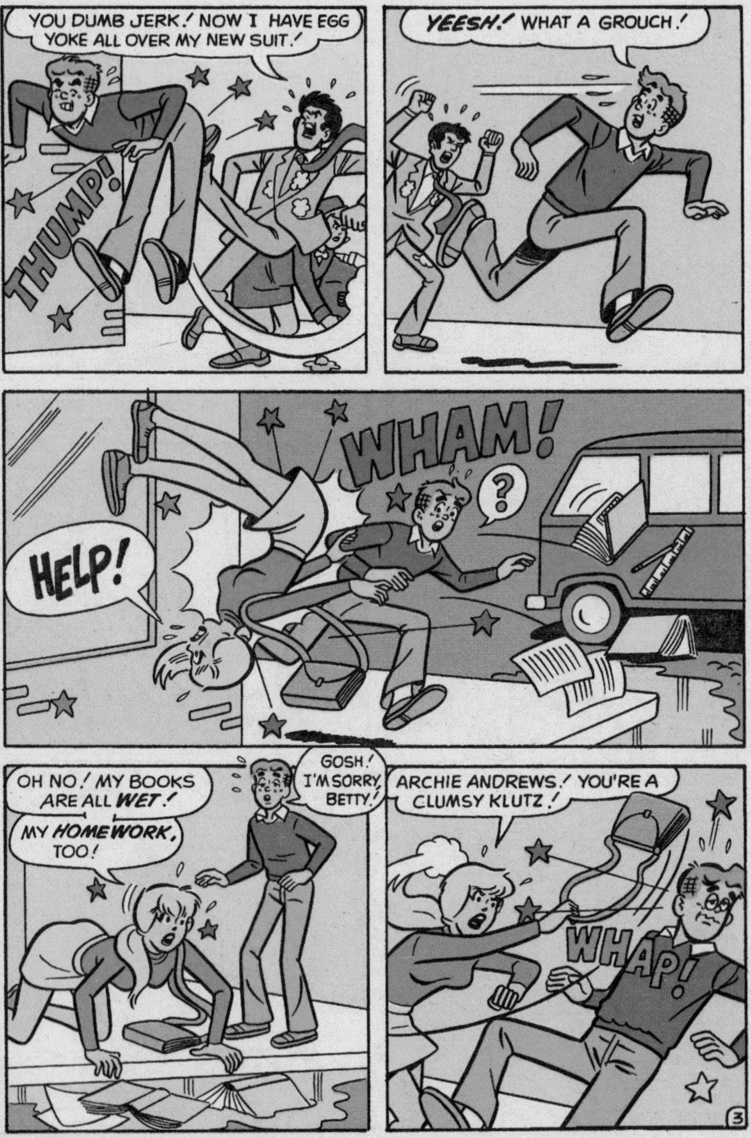
YOU DUMB JERK! NOW I HAVE EGG YOKE ALL OVER MY NEW SUIT!
THUMP!
YEESH! WHAT A GROUCH!
WHAM!
?
HELP!
OH NO! MY BOOKS ARE ALL WET!
MY HOMEWORK, TOO!
GOSH! I'M SORRY, BETTY!
ARCHIE ANDREWS! YOU'RE A CLUMSY KLUTZ!
WHAP!
3

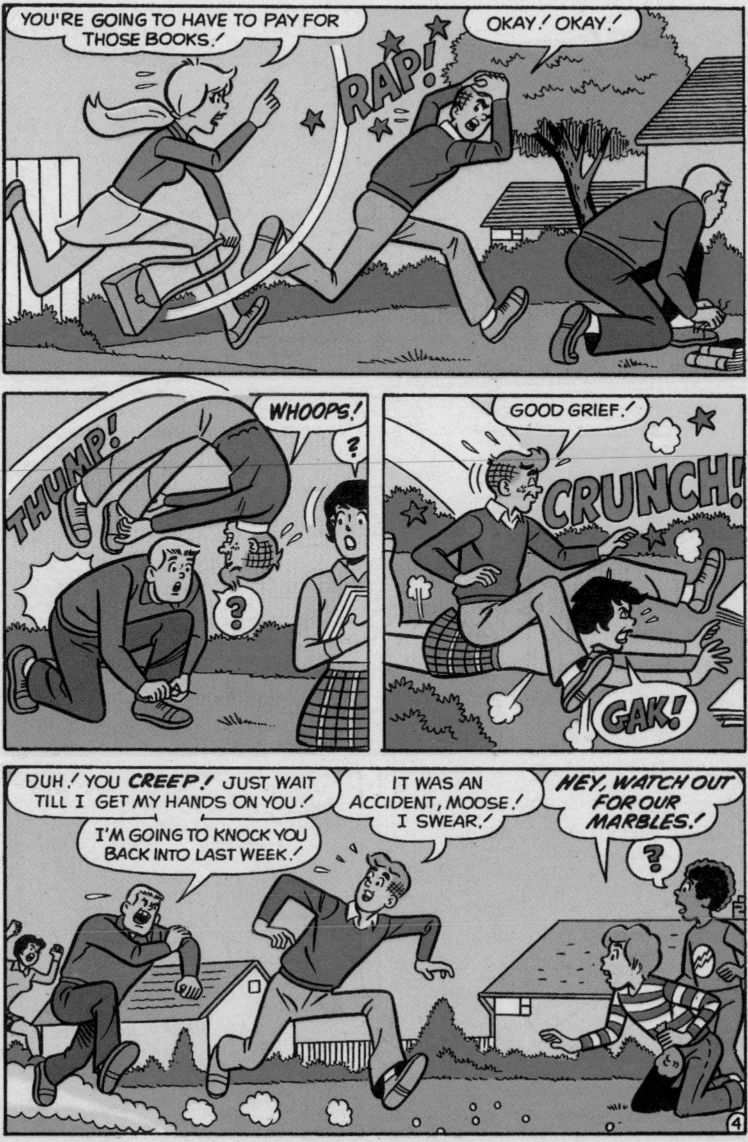
YOU'RE GOING TO HAVE TO PAY FOR THOSE BOOKS!
RAP!
OKAY! OKAY!
THUMP!
WHOOPS!
?
?
GOOD GRIEF!
CRUNCH!
GAK!
DUH! YOU CREEP! JUST WAIT TILL I GET MY HANDS ON YOU!
I'M GOING TO KNOCK YOU BACK INTO LAST WEEK!
IT WAS AN ACCIDENT, MOOSE! I SWEAR!
HEY, WATCH OUT FOR OUR MARBLES!
?
4

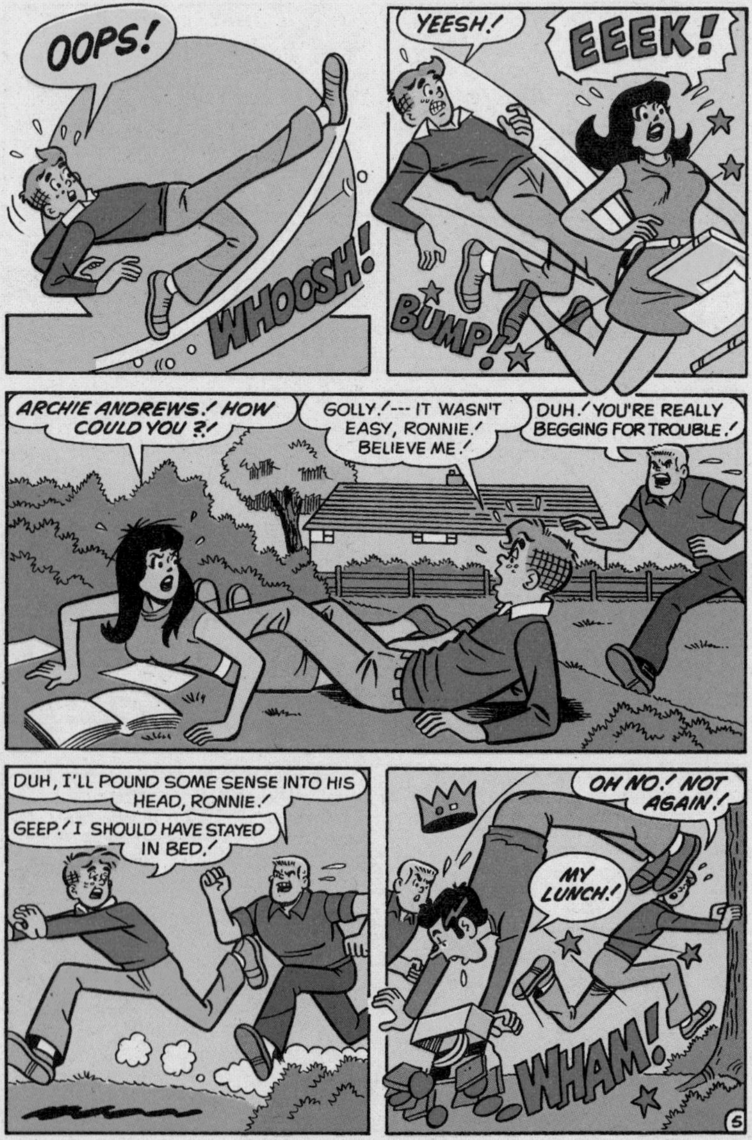
OOPS!
WHOOSH!
YEESH!
EEEK!
BUMP!
ARCHIE ANDREWS! HOW COULD YOU ?!
GOLLY!--- IT WASN'T EASY, RONNIE! BELIEVE ME!
DUH! YOU'RE REALLY BEGGING FOR TROUBLE!
DUH, I'LL POUND SOME SENSE INTO HIS HEAD, RONNIE!
GEEP! I SHOULD HAVE STAYED IN BED!
OH NO! NOT AGAIN!
MY LUNCH!
WHAM!
5

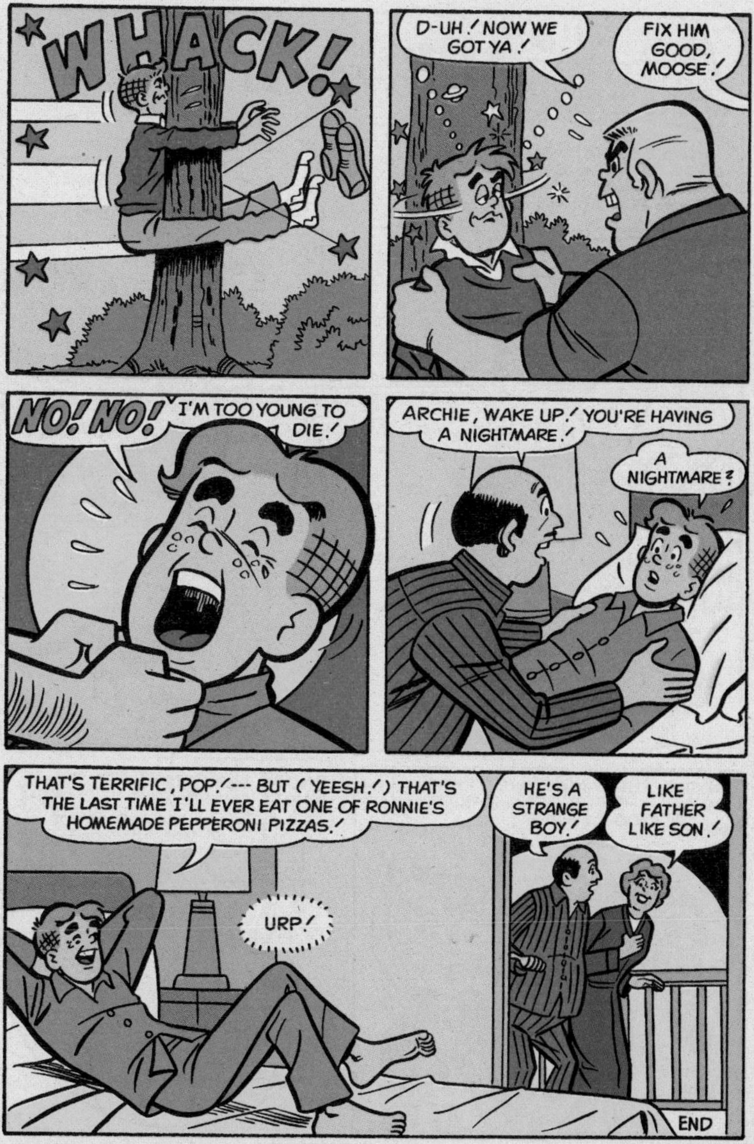
WHACK!
D-UH! NOW WE GOT YA!
FIX HIM GOOD, MOOSE!
NO! NO! I'M TOO YOUNG TO DIE!
ARCHIE, WAKE UP! YOU'RE HAVING A NIGHTMARE!
A NIGHTMARE?
THAT'S TERRIFIC, POP! --- BUT (YEESH!) THAT'S THE LAST TIME I'LL EVER EAT ONE OF RONNIE'S HOMEMADE PEPPERONI PIZZAS!
URP!
HE'S A STRANGE BOY!
LIKE FATHER LIKE SON!
END

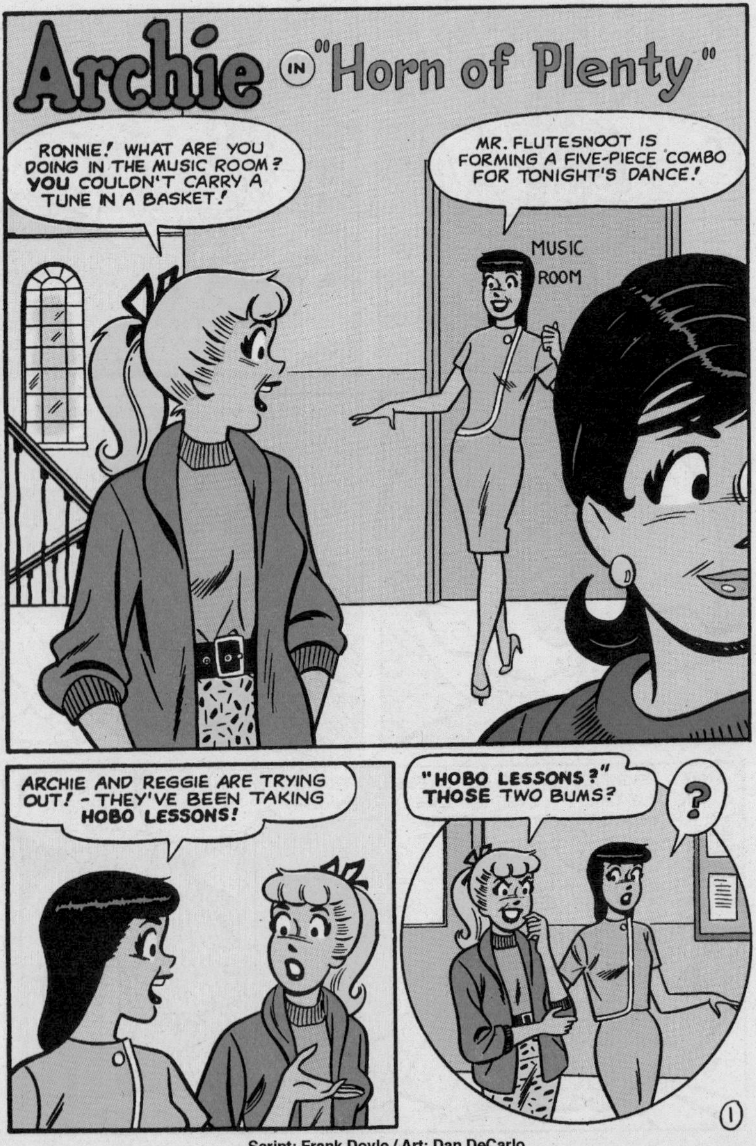
Archie IN "Horn of Plenty"
RONNIE! WHAT ARE YOU DOING IN THE MUSIC ROOM? YOU COULDN'T CARRY A TUNE IN A BASKET!
MR. FLUTESNOOT IS FORMING A FIVE-PIECE COMBO FOR TONIGHT'S DANCE!
MUSIC ROOM
ARCHIE AND REGGIE ARE TRYING OUT! - THEY'VE BEEN TAKING HOBO LESSONS!
"HOBO LESSONS?" THOSE TWO BUMS?
?
1

Script: Frank Doyle / Art: Dan DeCarlo

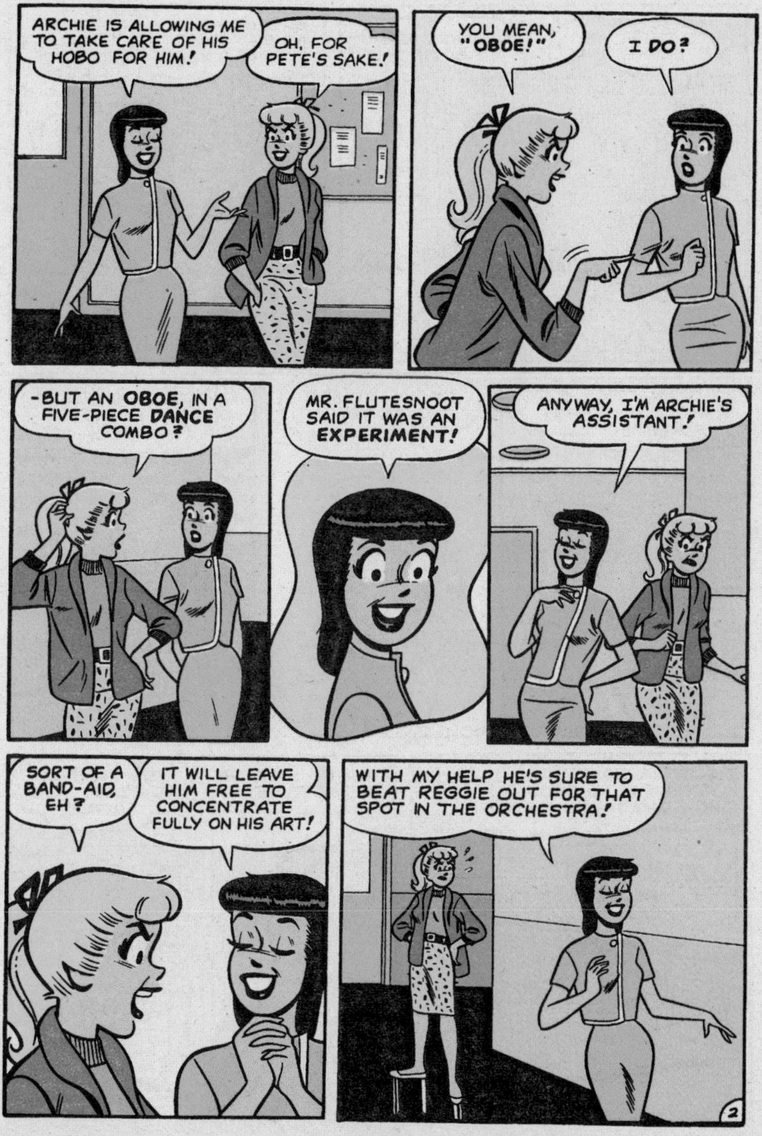
ARCHIE IS ALLOWING ME TO TAKE CARE OF HIS HOBO FOR HIM!
OH, FOR PETE'S SAKE!
YOU MEAN, "OBOE!"
I DO?
-BUT AN OBOE, IN A FIVE-PIECE DANCE COMBO?
MR. FLUTESNOOT SAID IT WAS AN EXPERIMENT!
ANYWAY, I'M ARCHIE'S ASSISTANT!
SORT OF A BAND-AID, EH?
IT WILL LEAVE HIM FREE TO CONCENTRATE FULLY ON HIS ART!
WITH MY HELP HE'S SURE TO BEAT REGGIE OUT FOR THAT SPOT IN THE ORCHESTRA!
2

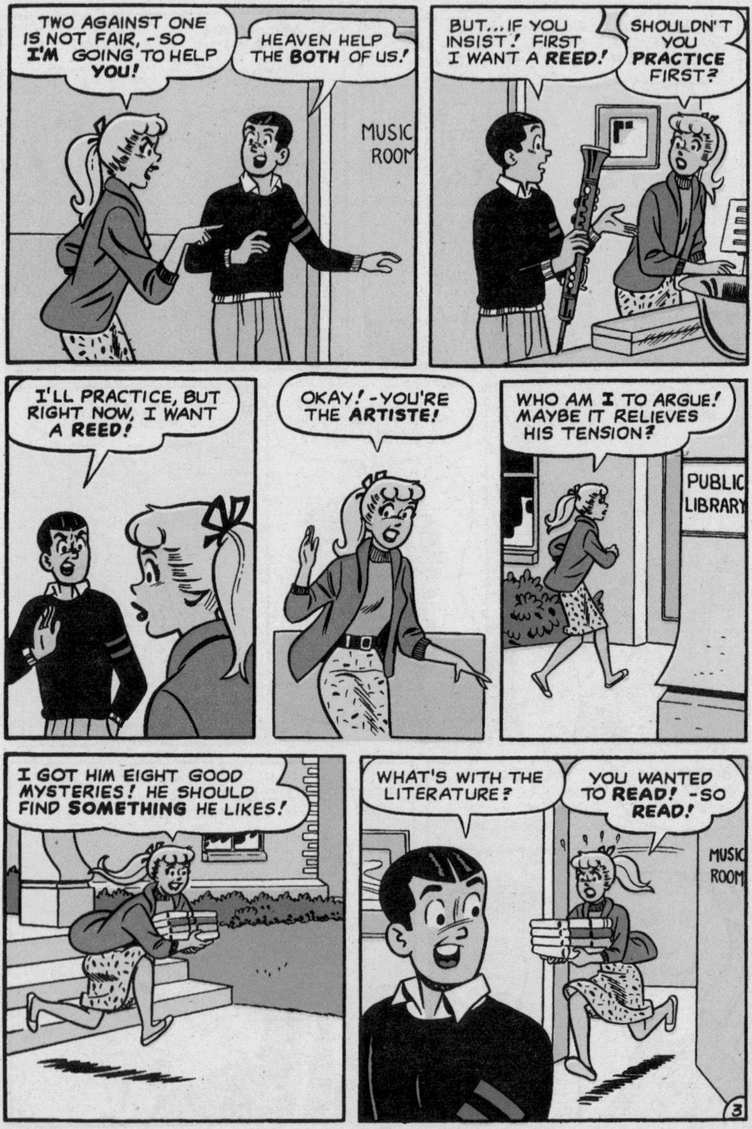

TWO AGAINST ONE IS NOT FAIR, - SO I'M GOING TO HELP YOU!
HEAVEN HELP THE BOTH OF US!
MUSIC ROOM
BUT... IF YOU INSIST! FIRST I WANT A REED!
SHOULDN'T YOU PRACTICE FIRST?
I'LL PRACTICE, BUT RIGHT NOW, I WANT A REED!
OKAY! - YOU'RE THE ARTISTE!
WHO AM I TO ARGUE! MAYBE IT RELIEVES HIS TENSION?
PUBLIC LIBRARY
I GOT HIM EIGHT GOOD MYSTERIES! HE SHOULD FIND SOMETHING HE LIKES!
WHAT'S WITH THE LITERATURE?
YOU WANTED TO READ! - SO READ!
MUSIC ROOM
3

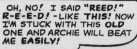

OH, NO! I SAID "REED!" R-E-E-D! -LIKE THIS! NOW I'M STUCK WITH THIS OLD ONE AND ARCHIE WILL BEAT ME EASILY!

WHAT A BRAIN! THE ONLY ONE WHO KNOWS LESS ABOUT MUSIC THAN YOU, IS RONNIE!

SHE IS QUITE A MUSICAL MORON!

HEY! MAYBE WE CAN USE THAT FACT!

HUH?

QUICK! TAKE ALL THESE INSTRUMENTS APART!

W-WHAT ARE YOU DOING?

YOK, YOK! W-WE LEAVE THIS PLUMBER'S NIGHT-MARE BESIDE ARCHIE'S OBOE CASE!

Y-YOU MEAN...

-OF COURSE! RONNIE DOESN'T KNOW AN OBOE FROM A ZULU ZITHER!

4

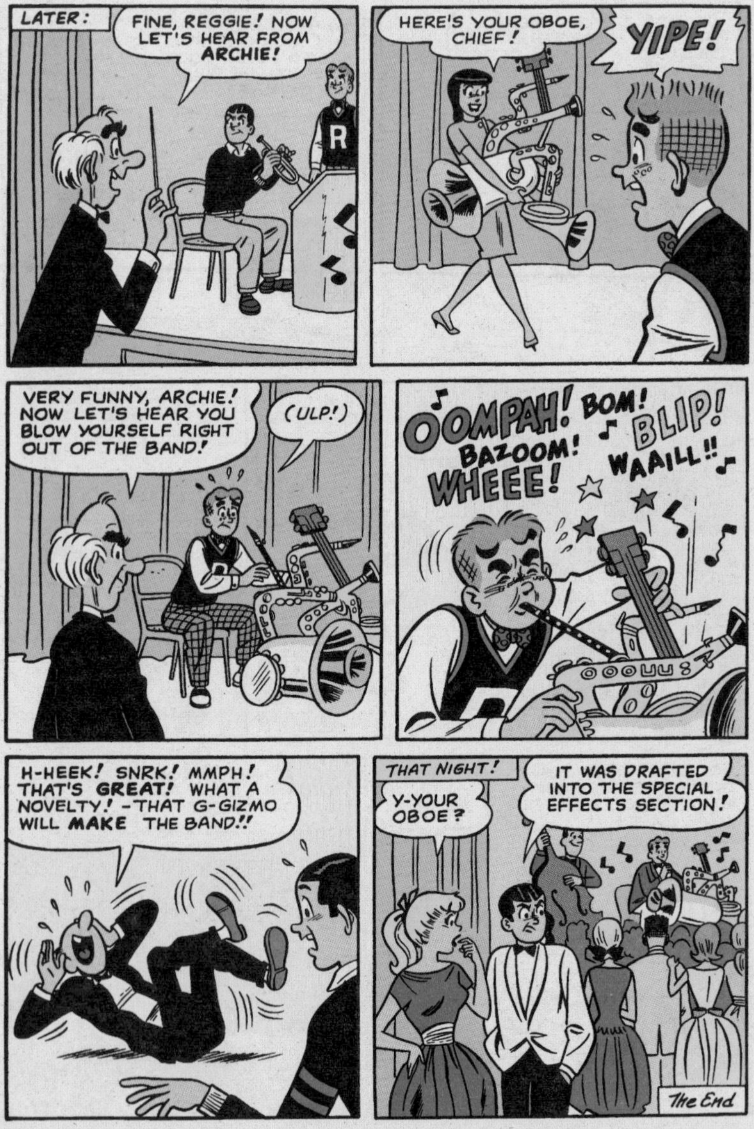
LATER:
FINE, REGGIE! NOW LET'S HEAR FROM ARCHIE!
HERE'S YOUR OBOE, CHIEF!
YIPE!
VERY FUNNY, ARCHIE! NOW LET'S HEAR YOU BLOW YOURSELF RIGHT OUT OF THE BAND!
(ULP!)
OOMPAH! BOM! BLIP! BAZOOM! WHEEE! WAAILL!!
H-HEEK! SNRK! MMPH! THAT'S GREAT! WHAT A NOVELTY! -THAT G-GIZMO WILL MAKE THE BAND!!
THAT NIGHT!
Y-YOUR OBOE?
IT WAS DRAFTED INTO THE SPECIAL EFFECTS SECTION!
The End

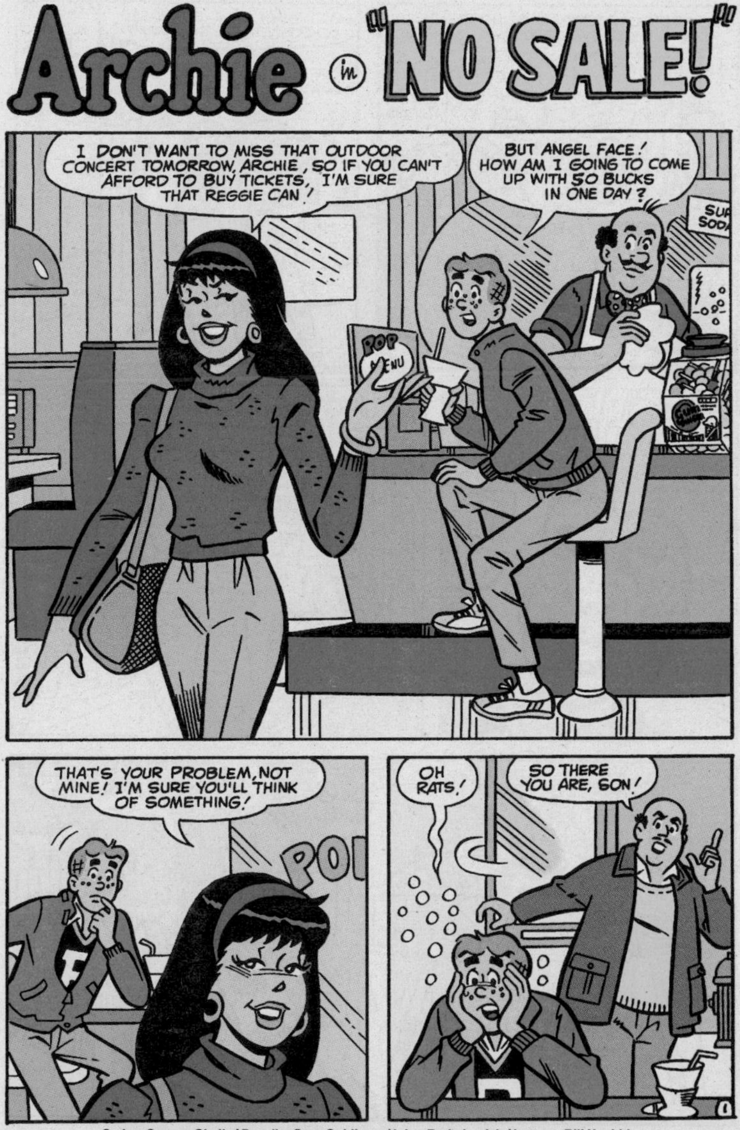
Archie in "NO SALE!"
I DON'T WANT TO MISS THAT OUTDOOR CONCERT TOMORROW, ARCHIE, SO IF YOU CAN'T AFFORD TO BUY TICKETS, I'M SURE THAT REGGIE CAN!
BUT ANGEL FACE! HOW AM I GOING TO COME UP WITH 50 BUCKS IN ONE DAY?
POP MENU
THAT'S YOUR PROBLEM, NOT MINE! I'M SURE YOU'LL THINK OF SOMETHING!
OH RATS!
SO THERE YOU ARE, SON!

Script: George Gladir / Pencils: Stan Goldberg / Inks: Rudy Lapick / Letters: Bill Yoshida

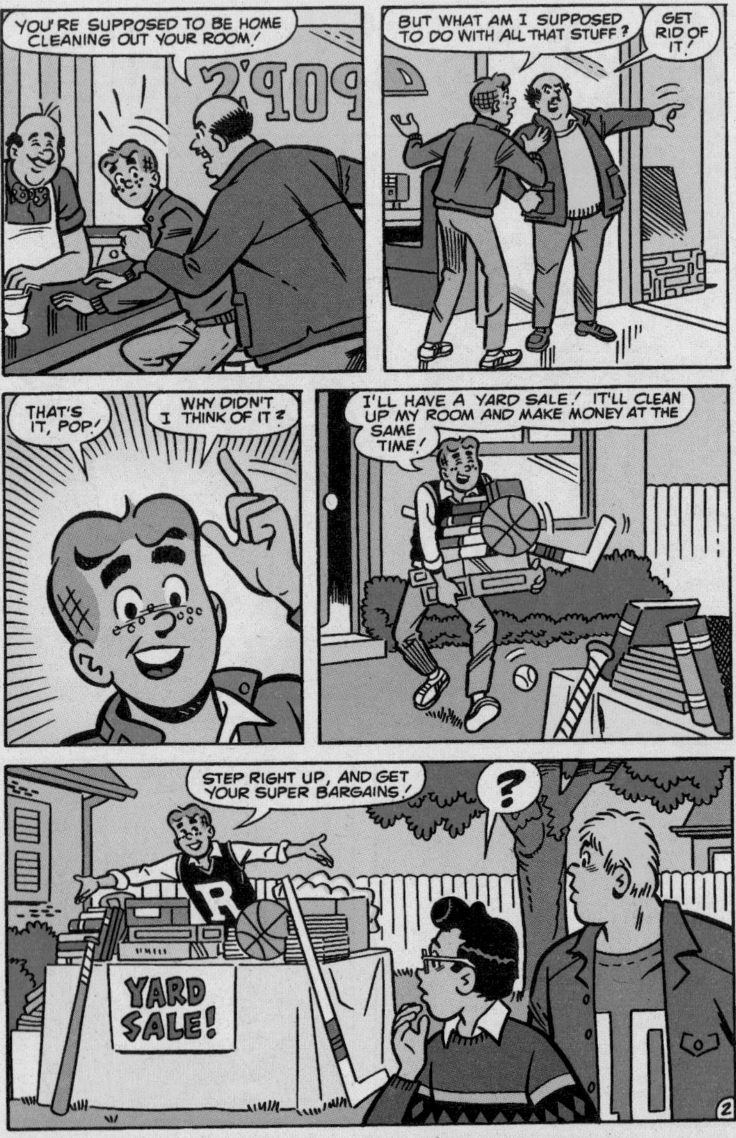
YOU'RE SUPPOSED TO BE HOME CLEANING OUT YOUR ROOM!
POP'S
BUT WHAT AM I SUPPOSED TO DO WITH ALL THAT STUFF?
GET RID OF IT!
THAT'S IT, POP!
WHY DIDN'T I THINK OF IT?
I'LL HAVE A YARD SALE! IT'LL CLEAN UP MY ROOM AND MAKE MONEY AT THE SAME TIME!
STEP RIGHT UP, AND GET YOUR SUPER BARGAINS!
?
R
YARD SALE!
2

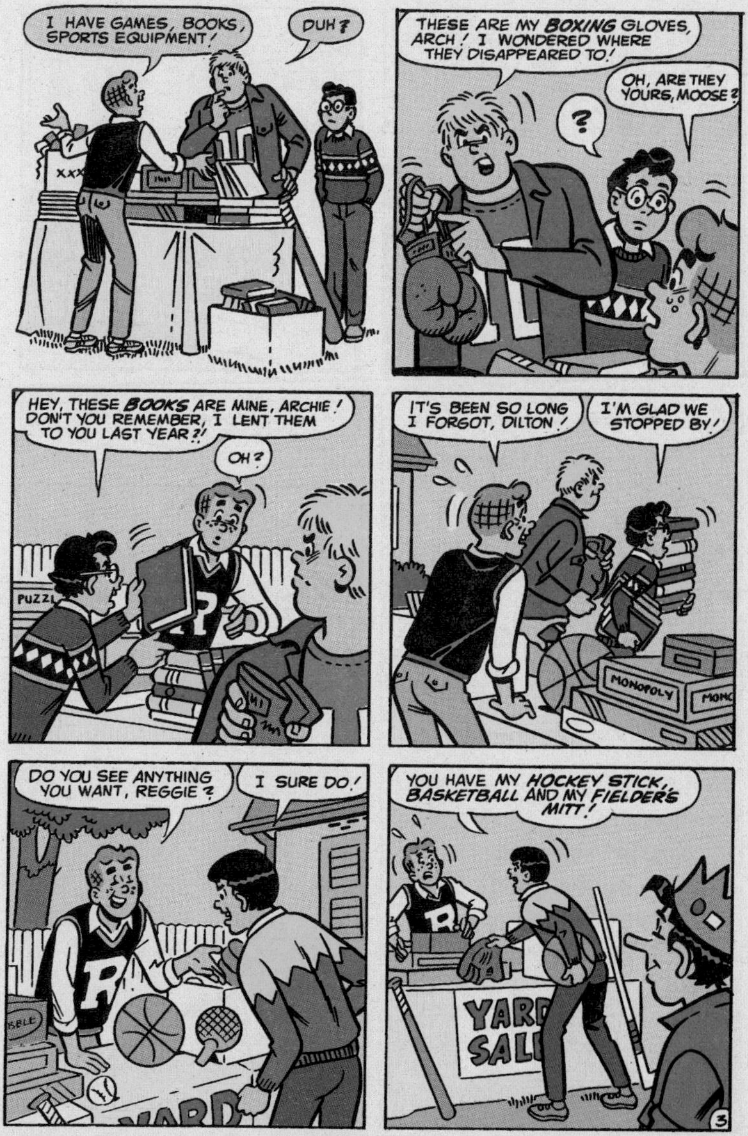
I HAVE GAMES, BOOKS, SPORTS EQUIPMENT!
DUH?
XXX
THESE ARE MY BOXING GLOVES, ARCH! I WONDERED WHERE THEY DISAPPEARED TO!
?
OH, ARE THEY YOURS, MOOSE?
HEY, THESE BOOKS ARE MINE, ARCHIE! DON'T YOU REMEMBER, I LENT THEM TO YOU LAST YEAR?!
OH?
PUZZL
IT'S BEEN SO LONG I FORGOT, DILTON!
I'M GLAD WE STOPPED BY!
MONOPOLY
MONO
DO YOU SEE ANYTHING YOU WANT, REGGIE?
I SURE DO!
YOU HAVE MY HOCKEY STICK, BASKETBALL AND MY FIELDER'S MITT!
YARD SAL
3

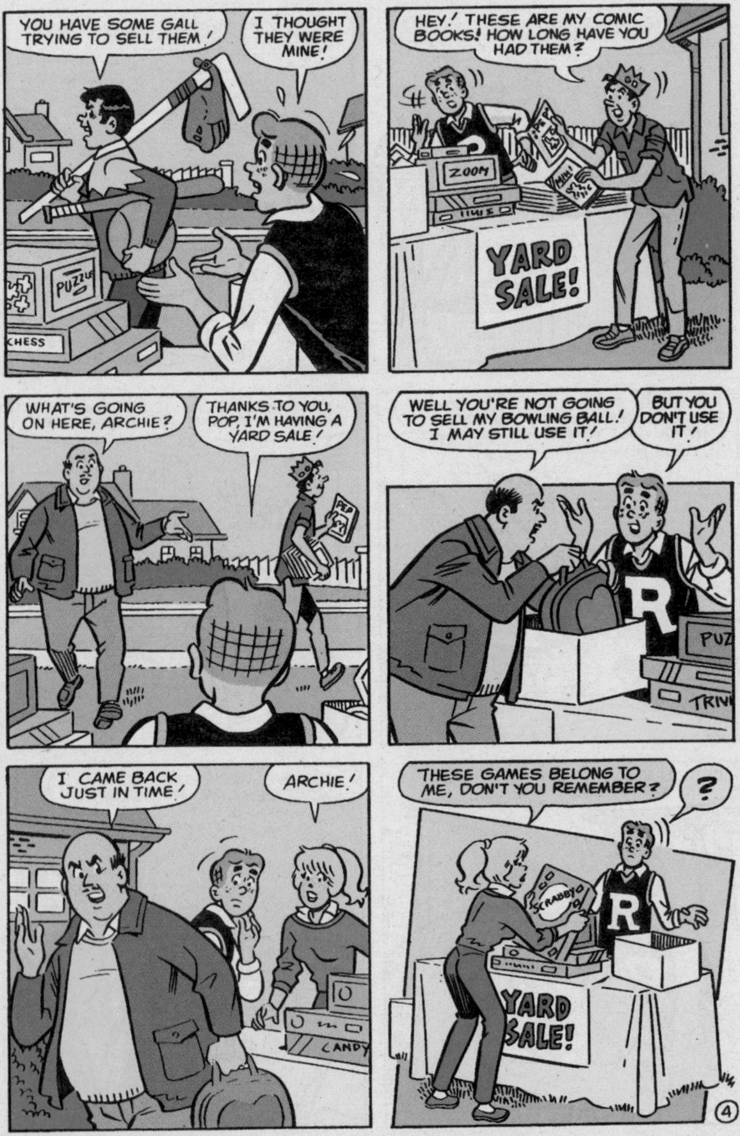

YOU HAVE SOME GALL TRYING TO SELL THEM!
I THOUGHT THEY WERE MINE!
PUZZLE
CHESS
HEY! THESE ARE MY COMIC BOOKS! HOW LONG HAVE YOU HAD THEM?
ZOOM
YARD SALE!
WHAT'S GOING ON HERE, ARCHIE?
THANKS TO YOU, POP, I'M HAVING A YARD SALE!
PEP
WELL YOU'RE NOT GOING TO SELL MY BOWLING BALL! I MAY STILL USE IT!
BUT YOU DON'T USE IT!
R
PUZ
TRIV
I CAME BACK JUST IN TIME!
ARCHIE!
CANDY
THESE GAMES BELONG TO ME, DON'T YOU REMEMBER?
?
SCRABBY
R
YARD SALE!
4

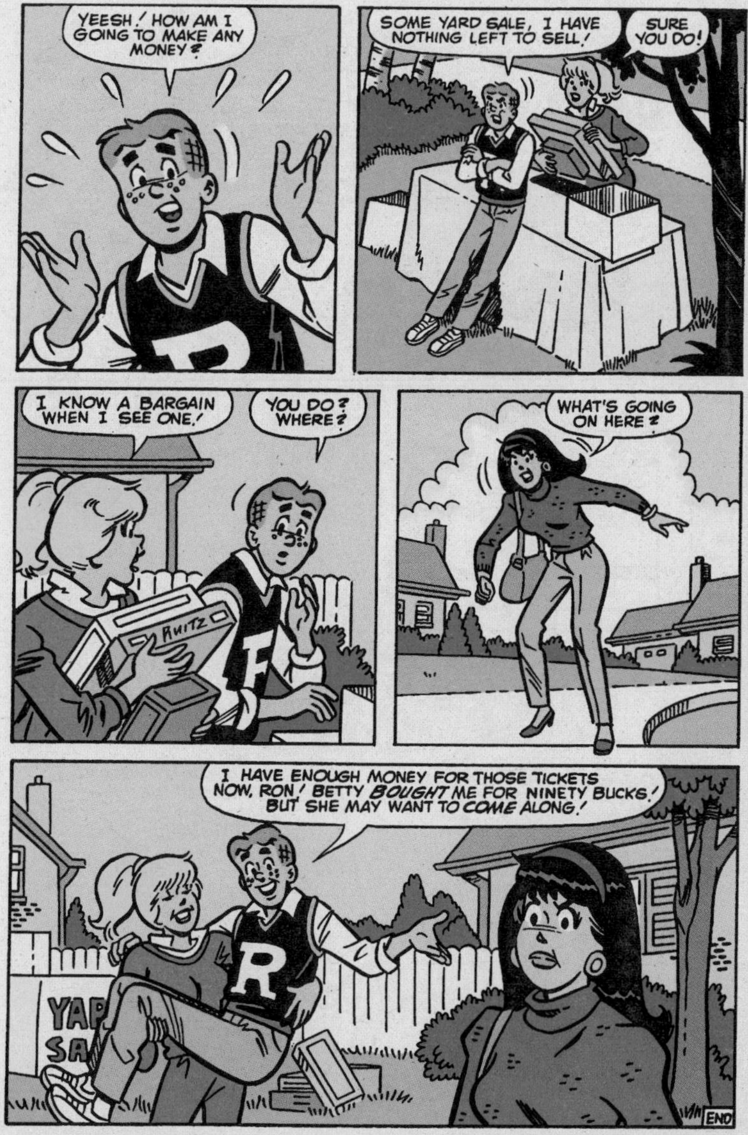
YEESH! HOW AM I GOING TO MAKE ANY MONEY?
SOME YARD SALE, I HAVE NOTHING LEFT TO SELL!
SURE YOU DO!
I KNOW A BARGAIN WHEN I SEE ONE!
YOU DO? WHERE?
RUITZ
WHAT'S GOING ON HERE?
I HAVE ENOUGH MONEY FOR THOSE TICKETS NOW, RON! BETTY *BOUGHT* ME FOR NINETY BUCKS! BUT SHE MAY WANT TO *COME* ALONG!
YA
SA
END

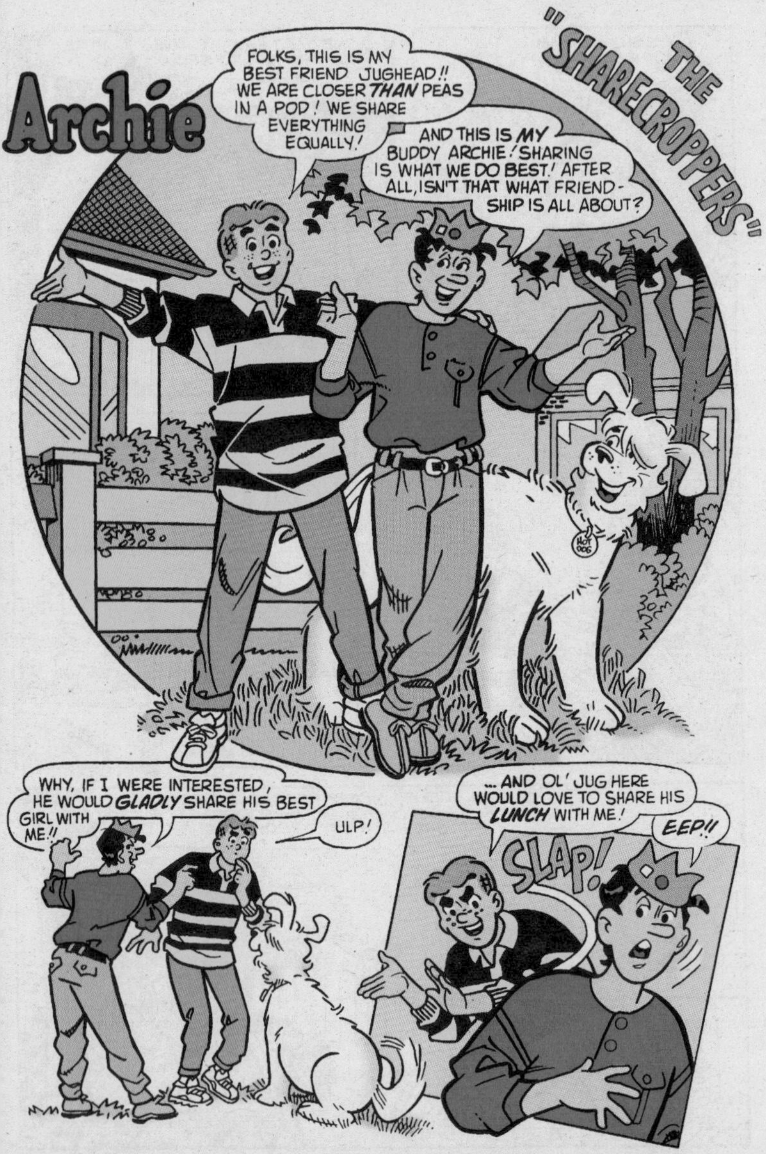
Archie
"THE SHARECROPPERS"
FOLKS, THIS IS MY BEST FRIEND JUGHEAD!! WE ARE CLOSER THAN PEAS IN A POD! WE SHARE EVERYTHING EQUALLY!
AND THIS IS MY BUDDY ARCHIE! SHARING IS WHAT WE DO BEST! AFTER ALL, ISN'T THAT WHAT FRIEND-SHIP IS ALL ABOUT?
HOT DOG
WHY, IF I WERE INTERESTED, HE WOULD GLADLY SHARE HIS BEST GIRL WITH ME!!
ULP!
... AND OL' JUG HERE WOULD LOVE TO SHARE HIS LUNCH WITH ME!
EEP!!
SLAP!

Script: Frank Doyle / Pencils: Stan Goldberg / Inks: Henry Scarpelli / Letters: Bill Yoshida

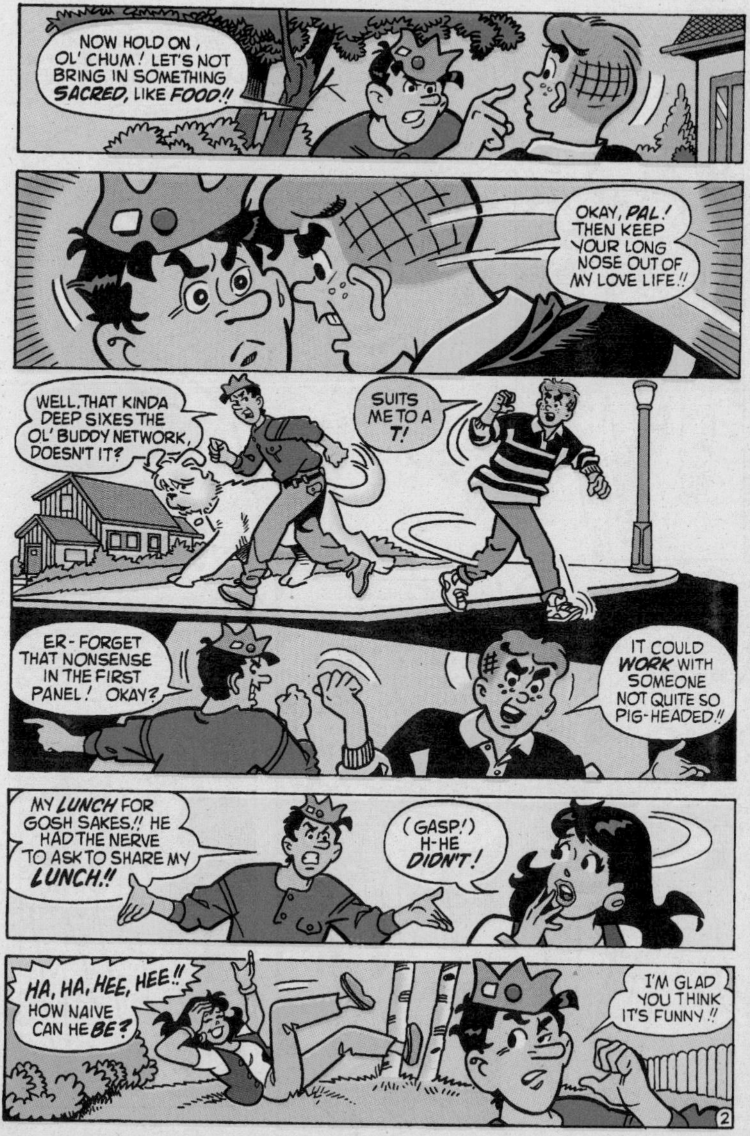
NOW HOLD ON, OL' CHUM! LET'S NOT BRING IN SOMETHING SACRED, LIKE FOOD!!
OKAY, PAL! THEN KEEP YOUR LONG NOSE OUT OF MY LOVE LIFE!!
WELL, THAT KINDA DEEP SIXES THE OL' BUDDY NETWORK, DOESN'T IT?
SUITS ME TO A T!
ER-FORGET THAT NONSENSE IN THE FIRST PANEL! OKAY?
IT COULD WORK WITH SOMEONE NOT QUITE SO PIG-HEADED!!
MY LUNCH FOR GOSH SAKES!! HE HAD THE NERVE TO ASK TO SHARE MY LUNCH!!
(GASP!) H-HE DIDN'T!
HA, HA, HEE, HEE!! HOW NAIVE CAN HE BE?
I'M GLAD YOU THINK IT'S FUNNY!!
2

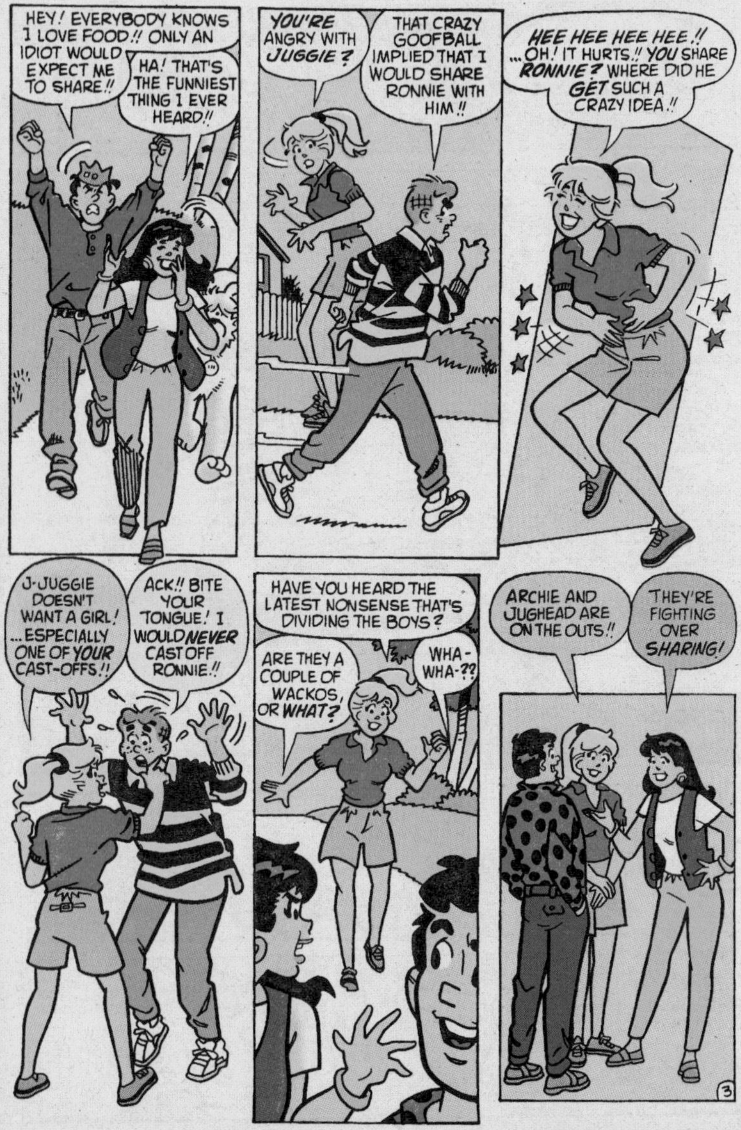

HEY! EVERYBODY KNOWS I LOVE FOOD!! ONLY AN IDIOT WOULD EXPECT ME TO SHARE!!
HA! THAT'S THE FUNNIEST THING I EVER HEARD!!
YOU'RE ANGRY WITH JUGGIE?
THAT CRAZY GOOFBALL IMPLIED THAT I WOULD SHARE RONNIE WITH HIM!!
HEE HEE HEE HEE!! ...OH! IT HURTS!! YOU SHARE RONNIE? WHERE DID HE GET SUCH A CRAZY IDEA!!
J-JUGGIE DOESN'T WANT A GIRL! ...ESPECIALLY ONE OF YOUR CAST-OFFS!!
ACK!! BITE YOUR TONGUE! I WOULD NEVER CAST OFF RONNIE!!
HAVE YOU HEARD THE LATEST NONSENSE THAT'S DIVIDING THE BOYS?
ARE THEY A COUPLE OF WACKOS, OR WHAT?
WHA-WHA-??
ARCHIE AND JUGHEAD ARE ON THE OUTS!!
THEY'RE FIGHTING OVER SHARING!

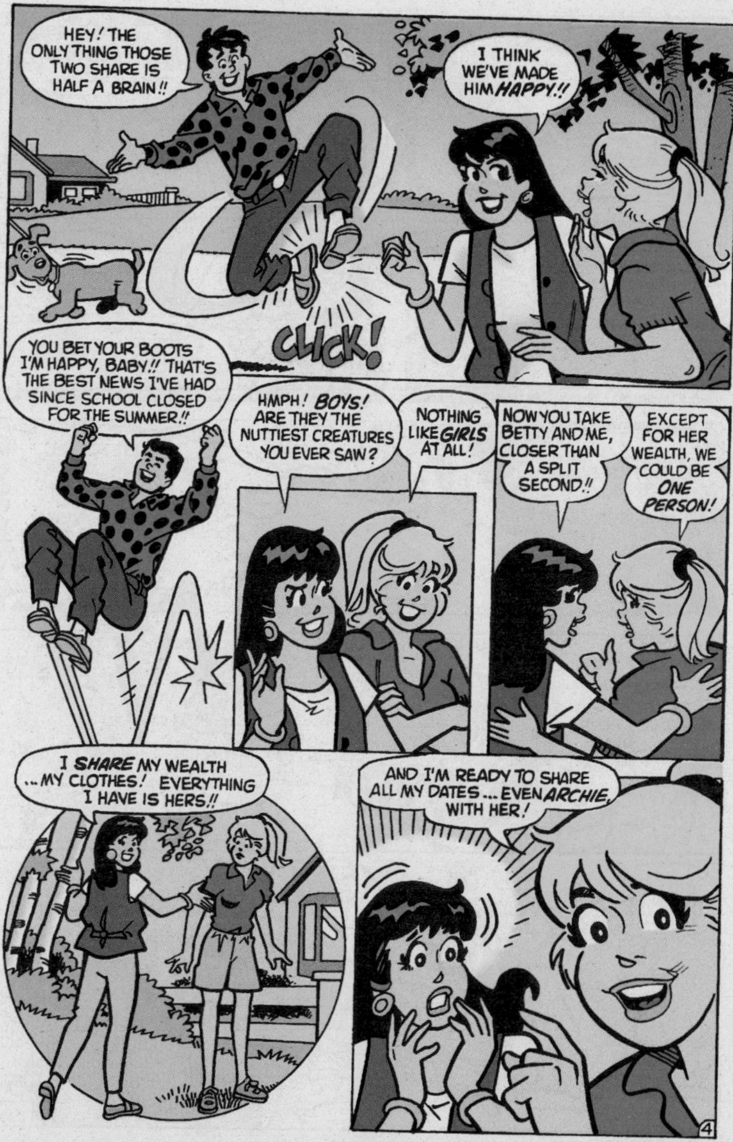
HEY! THE ONLY THING THOSE TWO SHARE IS HALF A BRAIN!!
I THINK WE'VE MADE HIM HAPPY!!
CLICK!
YOU BET YOUR BOOTS I'M HAPPY, BABY!! THAT'S THE BEST NEWS I'VE HAD SINCE SCHOOL CLOSED FOR THE SUMMER!!
HMPH! BOYS! ARE THEY THE NUTTIEST CREATURES YOU EVER SAW?
NOTHING LIKE GIRLS AT ALL!
NOW YOU TAKE BETTY AND ME, CLOSER THAN A SPLIT SECOND!!
EXCEPT FOR HER WEALTH, WE COULD BE ONE PERSON!
I SHARE MY WEALTH ... MY CLOTHES! EVERYTHING I HAVE IS HERS!!
AND I'M READY TO SHARE ALL MY DATES ... EVEN ARCHIE, WITH HER!
4

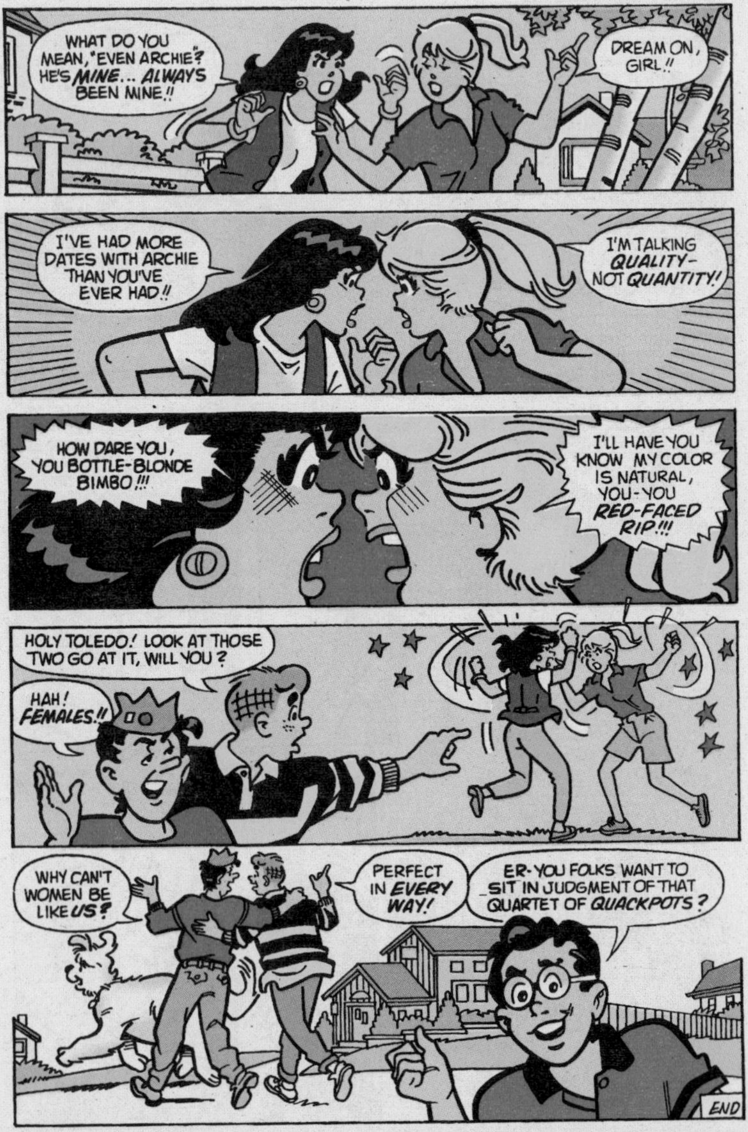
WHAT DO YOU MEAN, "EVEN ARCHIE"? HE'S MINE... ALWAYS BEEN MINE!!
DREAM ON, GIRL!!
I'VE HAD MORE DATES WITH ARCHIE THAN YOU'VE EVER HAD!!
I'M TALKING QUALITY- NOT QUANTITY!
HOW DARE YOU, YOU BOTTLE-BLONDE BIMBO!!!
I'LL HAVE YOU KNOW MY COLOR IS NATURAL, YOU-YOU RED-FACED RIP!!!
HOLY TOLEDO! LOOK AT THOSE TWO GO AT IT, WILL YOU?
HAH! FEMALES!!
WHY CAN'T WOMEN BE LIKE US?
PERFECT IN EVERY WAY!
ER-YOU FOLKS WANT TO SIT IN JUDGMENT OF THAT QUARTET OF QUACKPOTS?
END

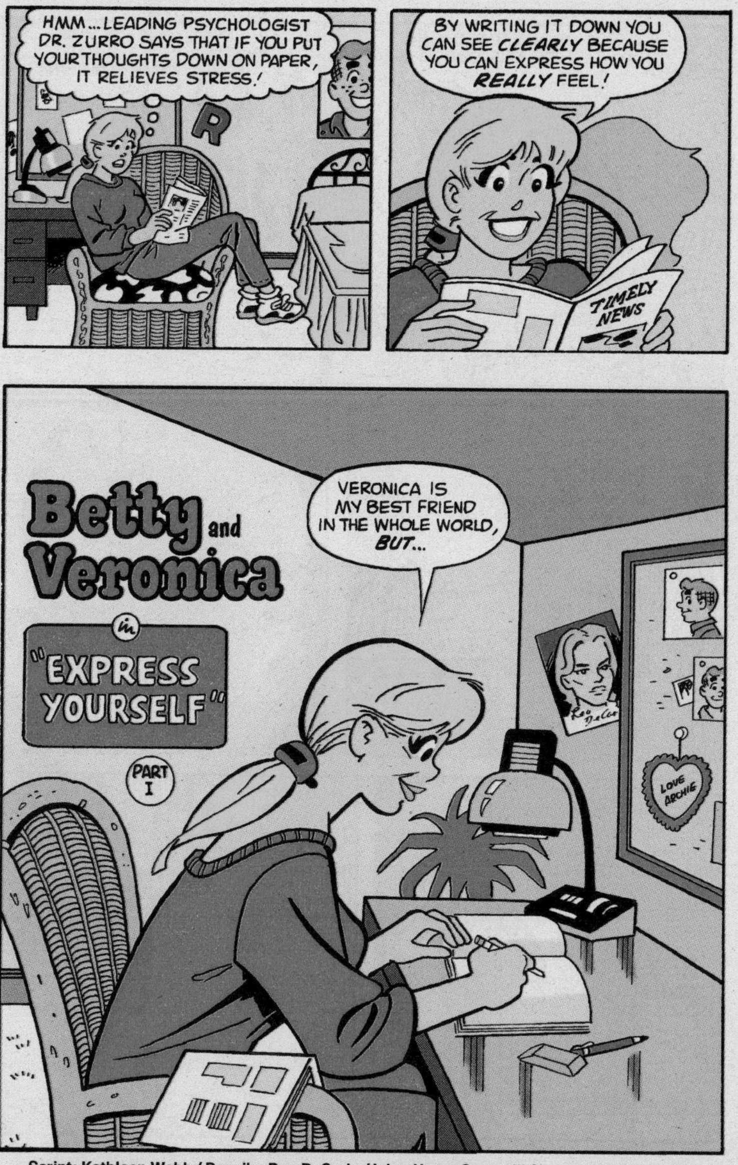
HMM... LEADING PSYCHOLOGIST DR. ZURRO SAYS THAT IF YOU PUT YOUR THOUGHTS DOWN ON PAPER, IT RELIEVES STRESS!
BY WRITING IT DOWN YOU CAN SEE CLEARLY BECAUSE YOU CAN EXPRESS HOW YOU REALLY FEEL!
TIMELY NEWS
Betty and Veronica
in
"EXPRESS YOURSELF"
PART I
VERONICA IS MY BEST FRIEND IN THE WHOLE WORLD, BUT...
LOVE ARCHIE

Script: Kathleen Webb / Pencils: Dan DeCarlo / Inks: Henry Scarpelli / Letters: Bill Yoshida

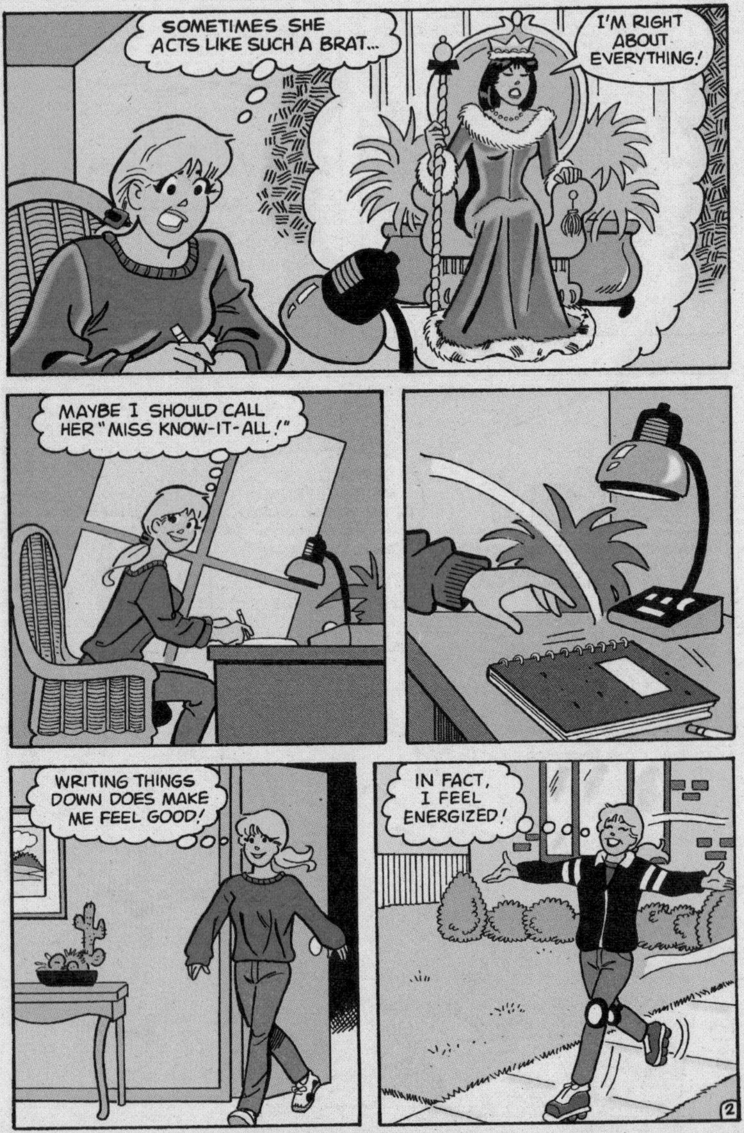
SOMETIMES SHE ACTS LIKE SUCH A BRAT...
I'M RIGHT ABOUT EVERYTHING!
MAYBE I SHOULD CALL HER "MISS KNOW-IT-ALL!"
WRITING THINGS DOWN DOES MAKE ME FEEL GOOD!
IN FACT, I FEEL ENERGIZED!
2

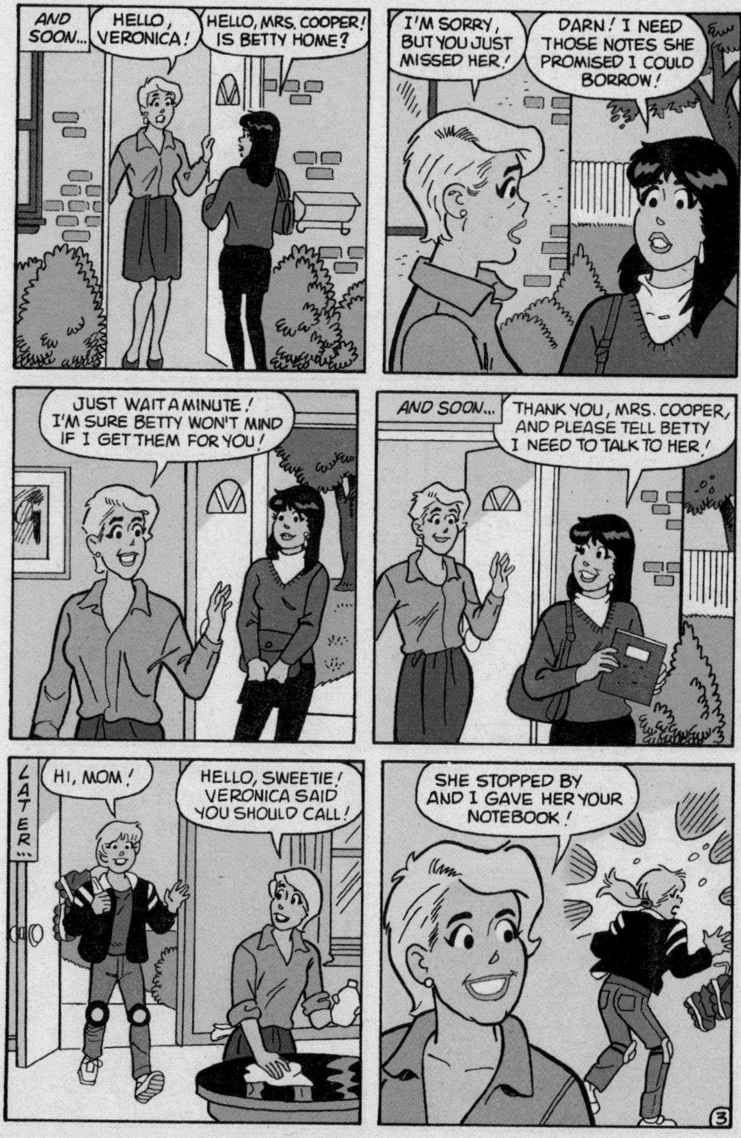
AND SOON...
HELLO, VERONICA!
HELLO, MRS. COOPER! IS BETTY HOME?
I'M SORRY, BUT YOU JUST MISSED HER!
DARN! I NEED THOSE NOTES SHE PROMISED I COULD BORROW!
JUST WAIT A MINUTE! I'M SURE BETTY WON'T MIND IF I GET THEM FOR YOU!
AND SOON...
THANK YOU, MRS. COOPER, AND PLEASE TELL BETTY I NEED TO TALK TO HER!
LATER...
HI, MOM!
HELLO, SWEETIE! VERONICA SAID YOU SHOULD CALL!
SHE STOPPED BY AND I GAVE HER YOUR NOTEBOOK!
3

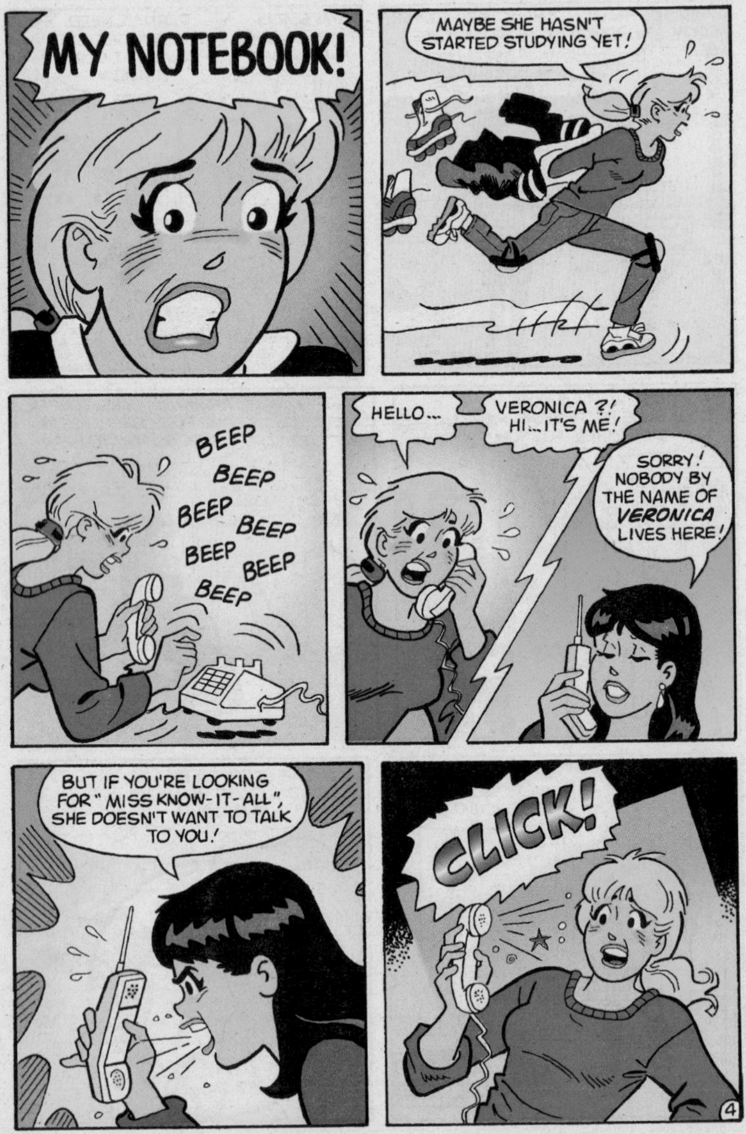
MY NOTEBOOK!
MAYBE SHE HASN'T STARTED STUDYING YET!
BEEP
BEEP
BEEP
BEEP
BEEP
BEEP
BEEP
HELLO...
VERONICA ?! HI... IT'S ME!
SORRY! NOBODY BY THE NAME OF VERONICA LIVES HERE!
BUT IF YOU'RE LOOKING FOR "MISS KNOW-IT-ALL", SHE DOESN'T WANT TO TALK TO YOU!
CLICK!
4

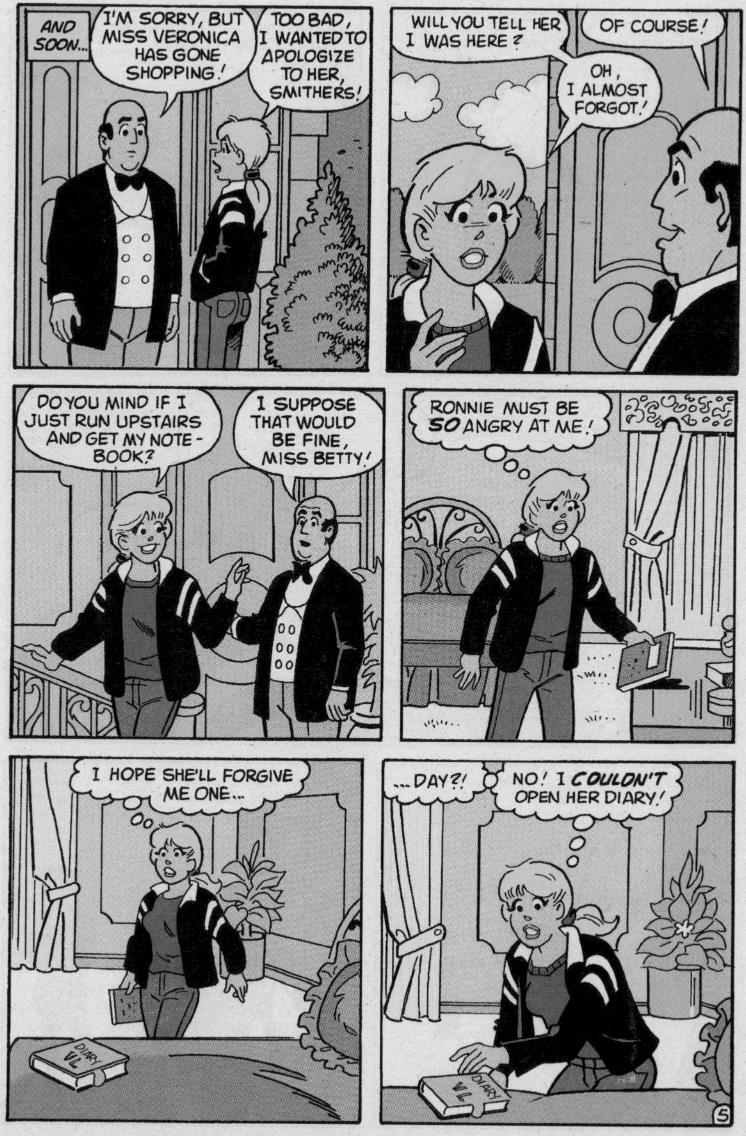
AND SOON...
I'M SORRY, BUT MISS VERONICA HAS GONE SHOPPING!
TOO BAD, I WANTED TO APOLOGIZE TO HER, SMITHERS!
WILL YOU TELL HER I WAS HERE?
OF COURSE!
OH, I ALMOST FORGOT!
DO YOU MIND IF I JUST RUN UPSTAIRS AND GET MY NOTE-BOOK?
I SUPPOSE THAT WOULD BE FINE, MISS BETTY!
RONNIE MUST BE SO ANGRY AT ME!
I HOPE SHE'LL FORGIVE ME ONE...
DIARY
VL
...DAY?!
NO! I COULDN'T OPEN HER DIARY!
DIARY
VL
5

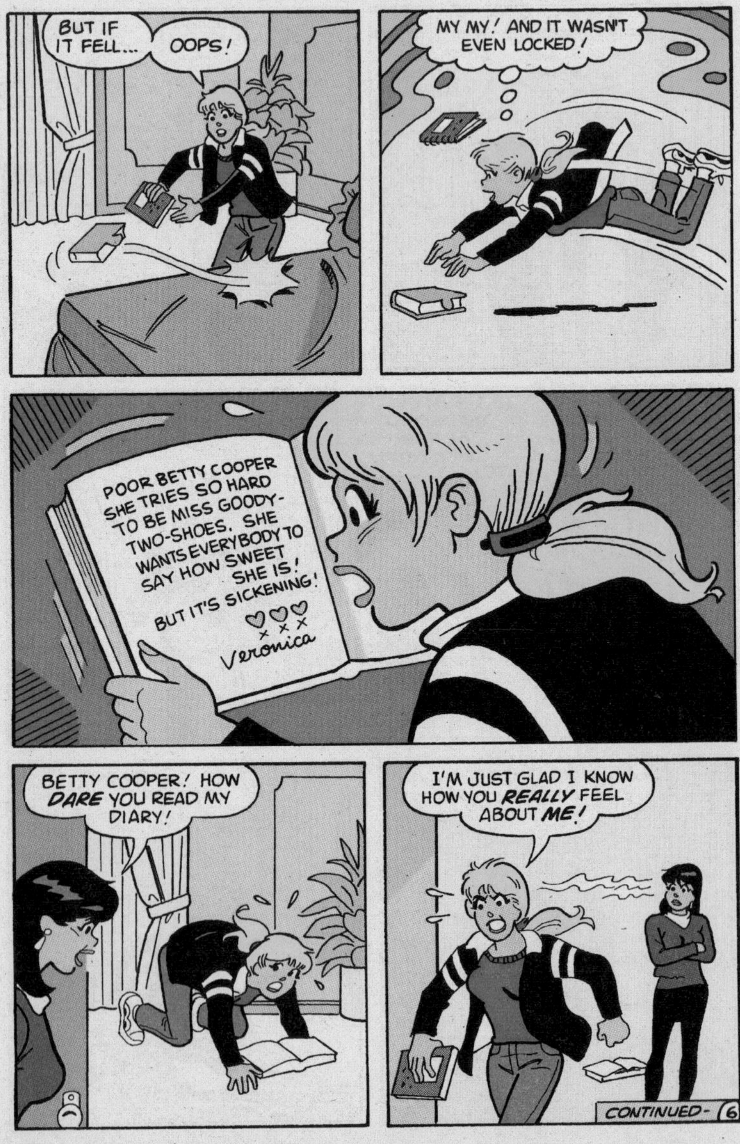
BUT IF IT FELL...
OOPS!
MY MY! AND IT WASN'T EVEN LOCKED!
POOR BETTY COOPER SHE TRIES SO HARD TO BE MISS GOODY-TWO-SHOES. SHE WANTS EVERYBODY TO SAY HOW SWEET SHE IS! BUT IT'S SICKENING!
Veronica
BETTY COOPER! HOW DARE YOU READ MY DIARY!
I'M JUST GLAD I KNOW HOW YOU REALLY FEEL ABOUT ME!
CONTINUED-
6

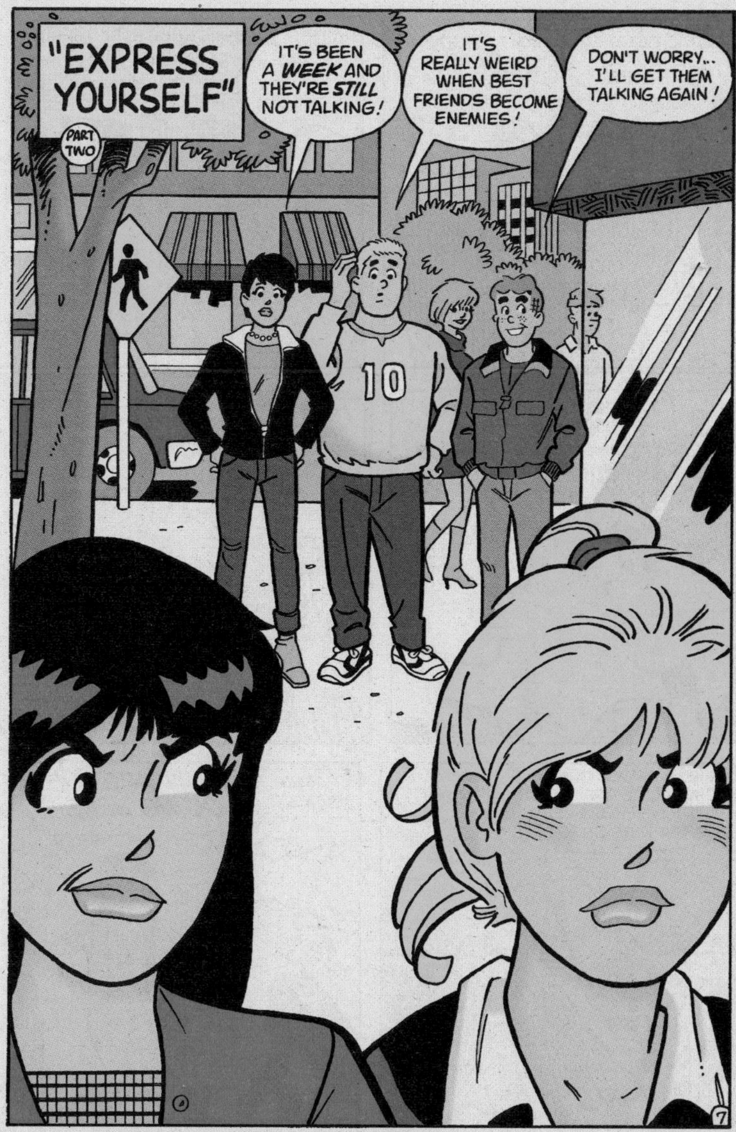
"EXPRESS YOURSELF"
PART TWO
IT'S BEEN A WEEK AND THEY'RE STILL NOT TALKING!
IT'S REALLY WEIRD WHEN BEST FRIENDS BECOME ENEMIES!
DON'T WORRY... I'LL GET THEM TALKING AGAIN!
10
7

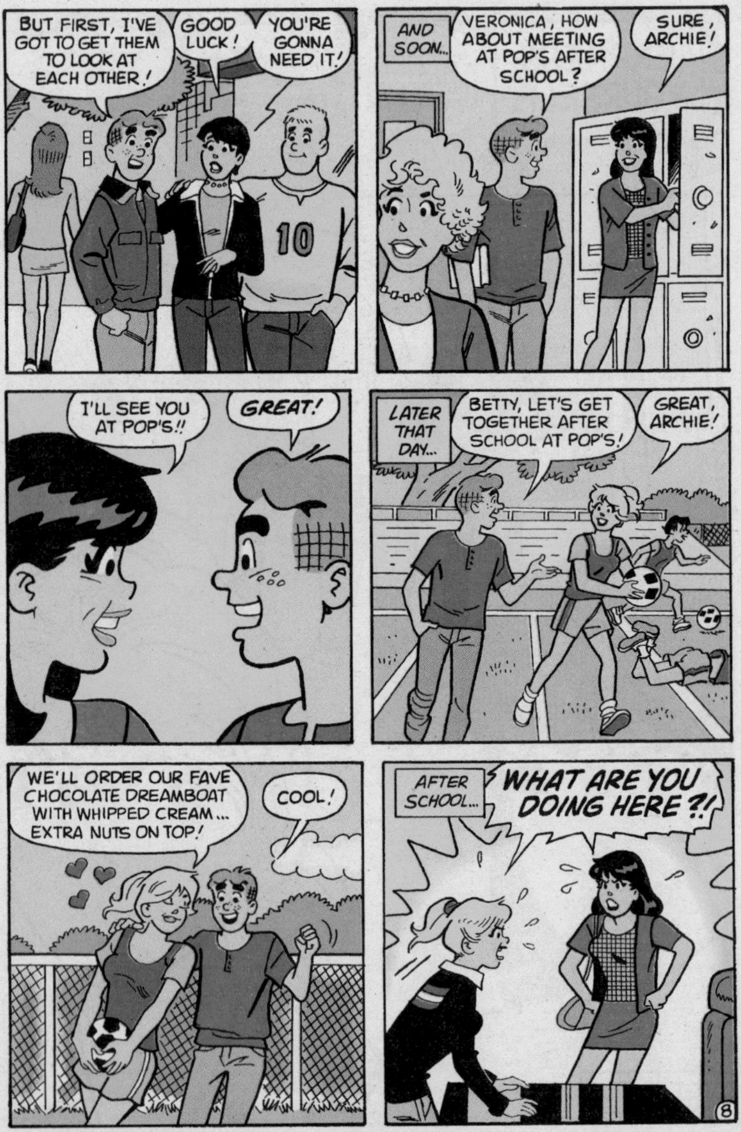

BUT FIRST, I'VE GOT TO GET THEM TO LOOK AT EACH OTHER!
GOOD LUCK!
YOU'RE GONNA NEED IT!
10
AND SOON...
VERONICA, HOW ABOUT MEETING AT POP'S AFTER SCHOOL?
SURE, ARCHIE!
I'LL SEE YOU AT POP'S!!
GREAT!
LATER THAT DAY...
BETTY, LET'S GET TOGETHER AFTER SCHOOL AT POP'S!
GREAT, ARCHIE!
WE'LL ORDER OUR FAVE CHOCOLATE DREAMBOAT WITH WHIPPED CREAM... EXTRA NUTS ON TOP!
COOL!
AFTER SCHOOL...
WHAT ARE YOU DOING HERE?!
8

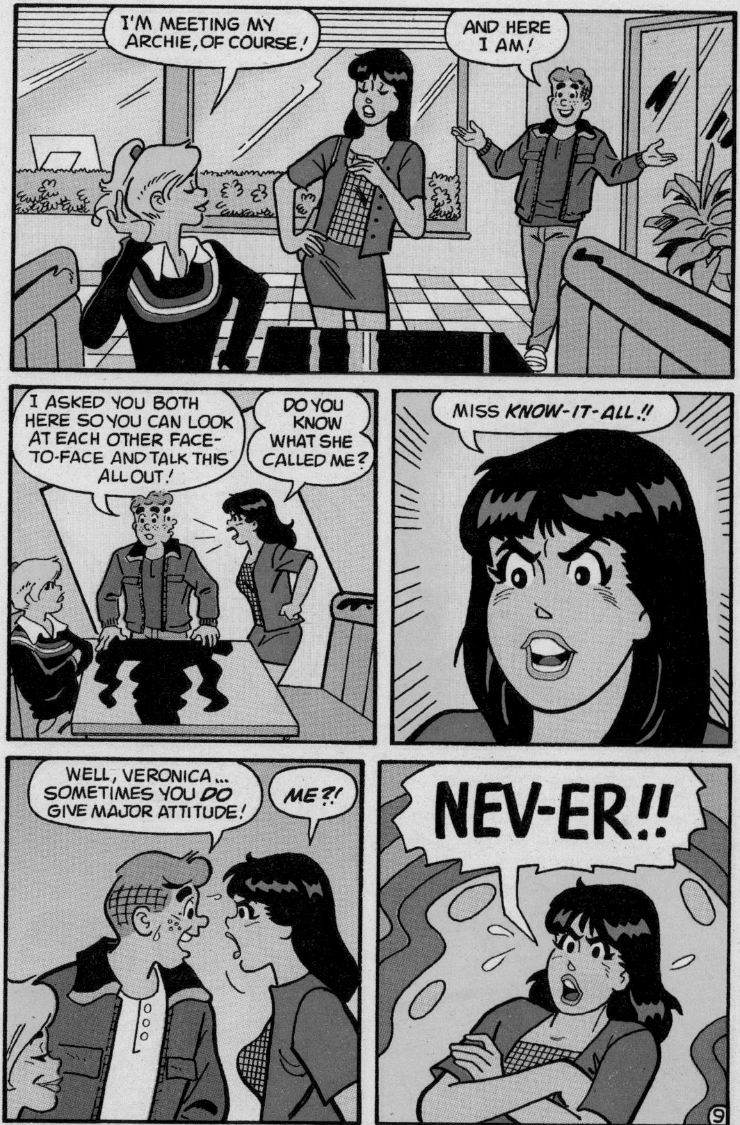
I'M MEETING MY ARCHIE, OF COURSE!
AND HERE I AM!
I ASKED YOU BOTH HERE SO YOU CAN LOOK AT EACH OTHER FACE-TO-FACE AND TALK THIS ALL OUT!
DO YOU KNOW WHAT SHE CALLED ME?
MISS *KNOW-IT-ALL*!!
WELL, VERONICA... SOMETIMES YOU *DO* GIVE MAJOR ATTITUDE!
ME?!
NEV-ER!!

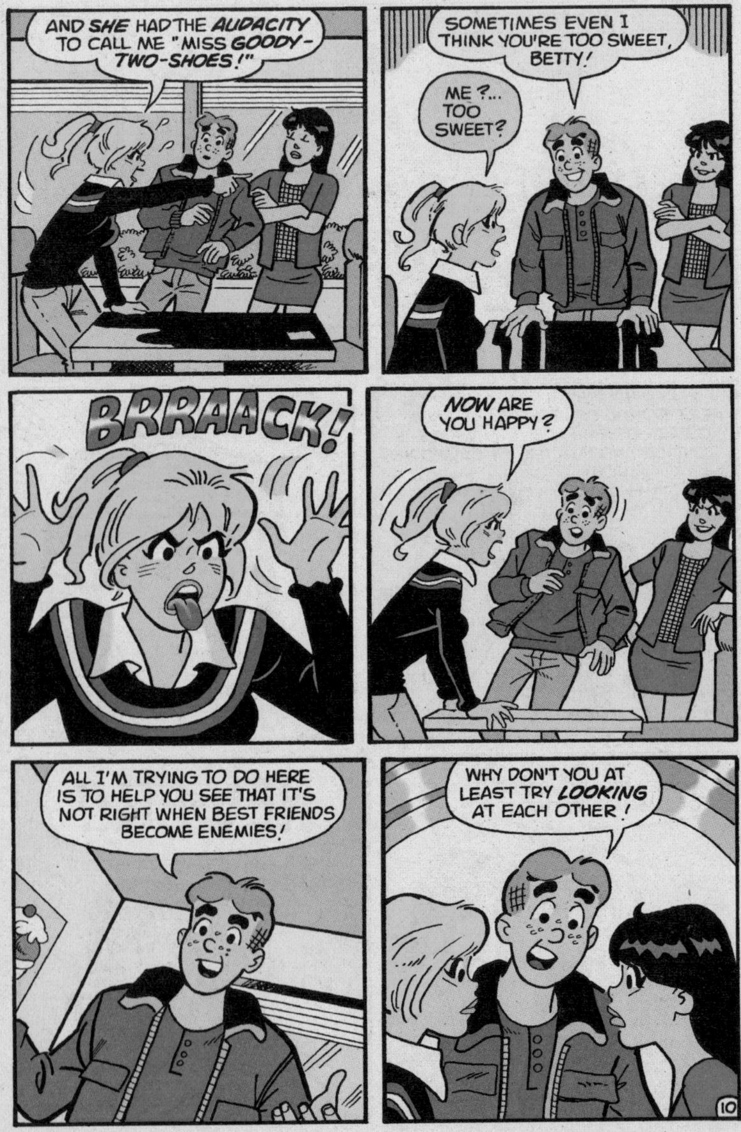
AND SHE HAD THE AUDACITY TO CALL ME "MISS GOODY-TWO-SHOES!"
SOMETIMES EVEN I THINK YOU'RE TOO SWEET, BETTY!
ME ?... TOO SWEET?
BRRAACK!
NOW ARE YOU HAPPY?
ALL I'M TRYING TO DO HERE IS TO HELP YOU SEE THAT IT'S NOT RIGHT WHEN BEST FRIENDS BECOME ENEMIES!
WHY DON'T YOU AT LEAST TRY LOOKING AT EACH OTHER!
10

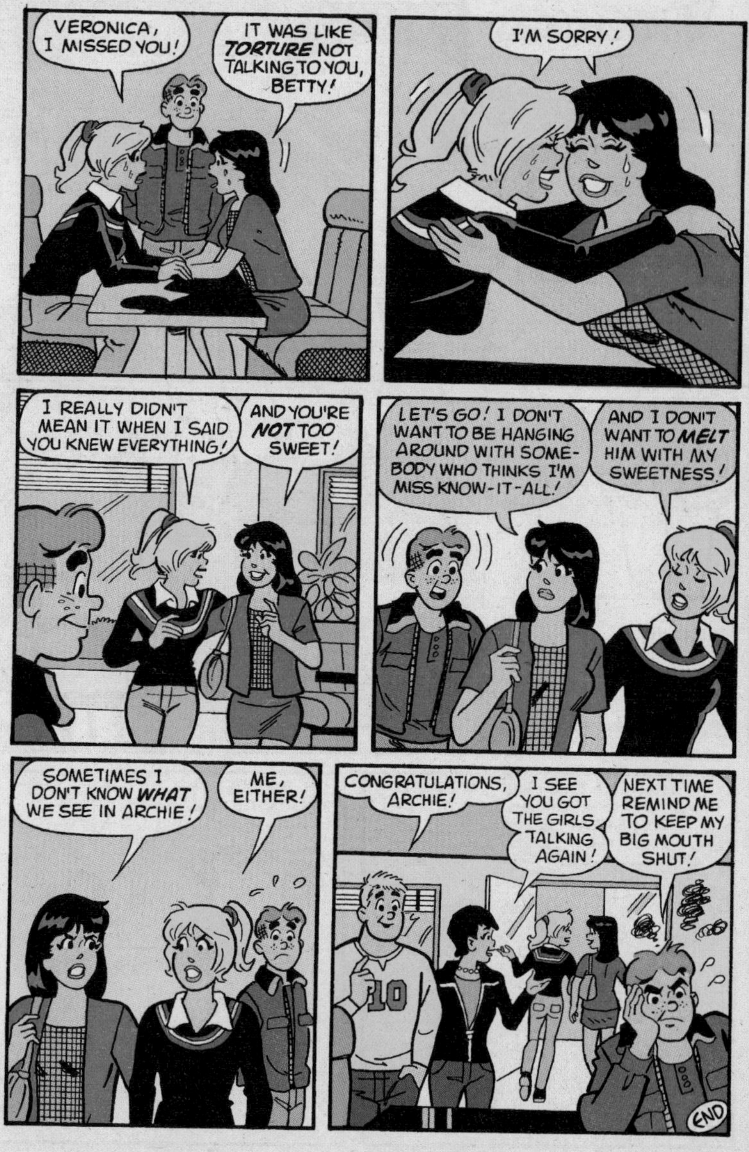
VERONICA, I MISSED YOU!
IT WAS LIKE TORTURE NOT TALKING TO YOU, BETTY!
I'M SORRY!
I REALLY DIDN'T MEAN IT WHEN I SAID YOU KNEW EVERYTHING!
AND YOU'RE NOT TOO SWEET!
LET'S GO! I DON'T WANT TO BE HANGING AROUND WITH SOMEBODY WHO THINKS I'M MISS KNOW-IT-ALL!
AND I DON'T WANT TO MELT HIM WITH MY SWEETNESS!
SOMETIMES I DON'T KNOW WHAT WE SEE IN ARCHIE!
ME, EITHER!
CONGRATULATIONS, ARCHIE!
I SEE YOU GOT THE GIRLS TALKING AGAIN!
NEXT TIME REMIND ME TO KEEP MY BIG MOUTH SHUT!
END

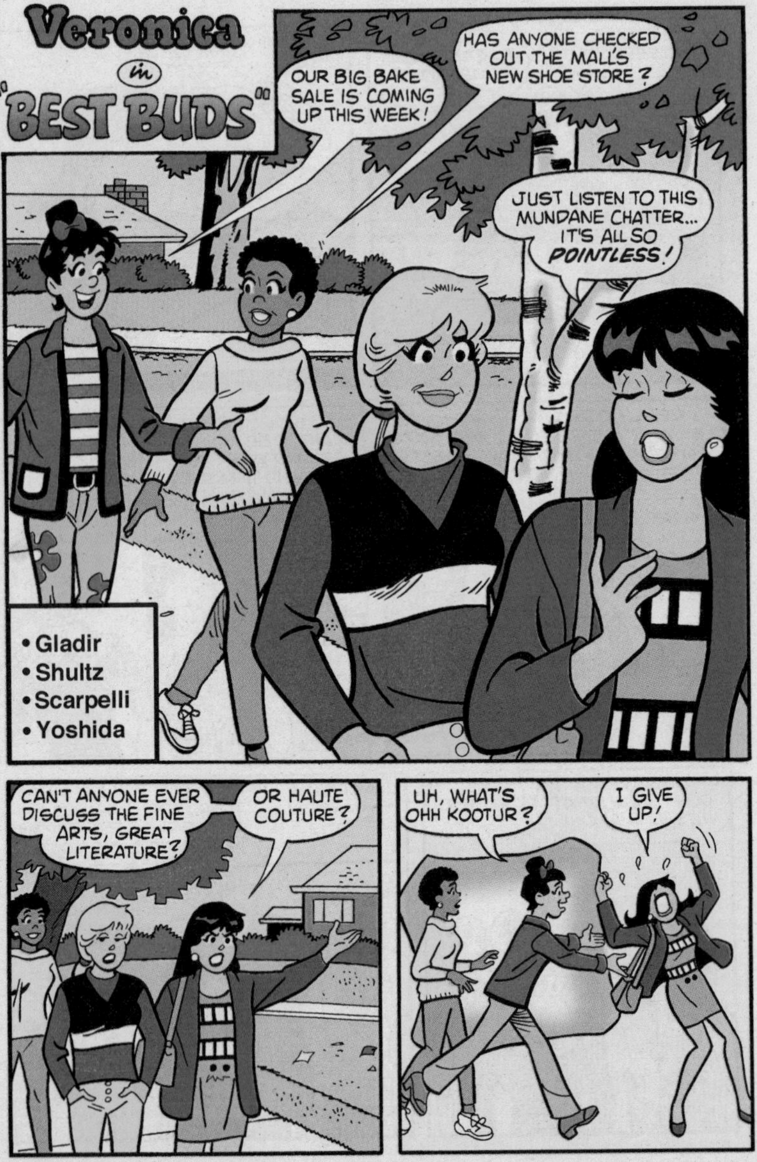
Veronica
in
"BEST BUDS"
OUR BIG BAKE SALE IS COMING UP THIS WEEK!
HAS ANYONE CHECKED OUT THE MALL'S NEW SHOE STORE?
JUST LISTEN TO THIS MUNDANE CHATTER... IT'S ALL SO POINTLESS!
• Gladir
• Shultz
• Scarpelli
• Yoshida
CAN'T ANYONE EVER DISCUSS THE FINE ARTS, GREAT LITERATURE?
OR HAUTE COUTURE?
UH, WHAT'S OHH KOOTUR?
I GIVE UP!

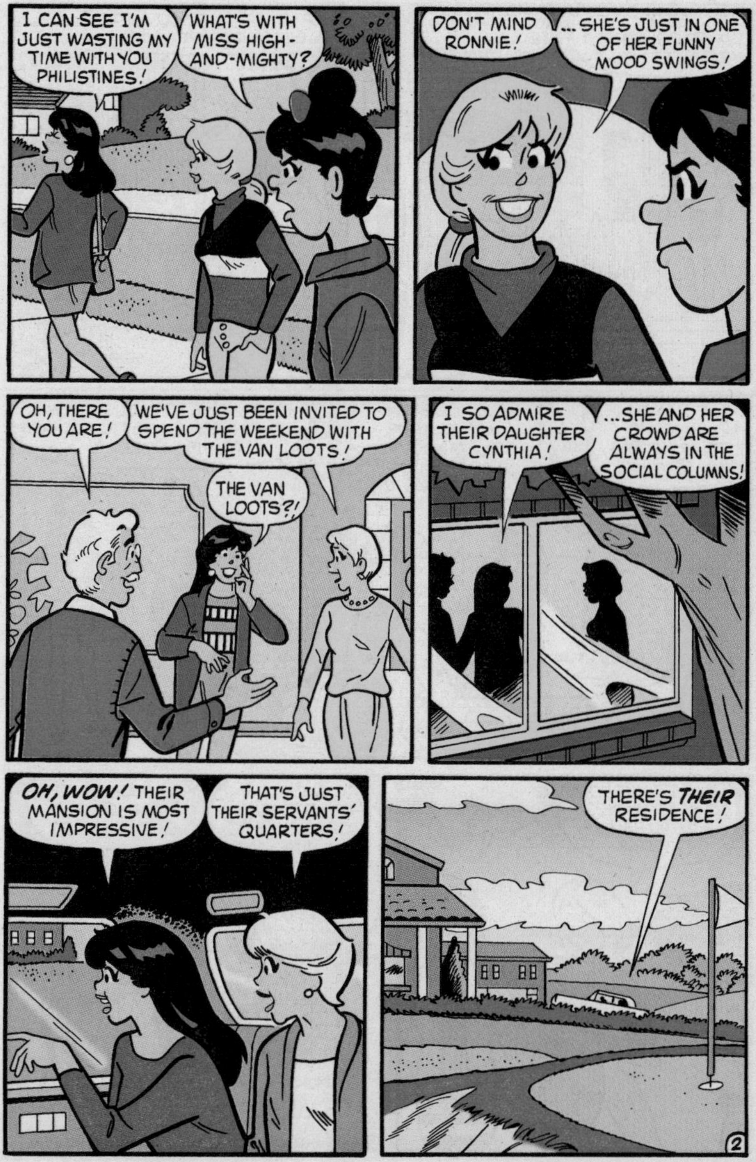
I CAN SEE I'M JUST WASTING MY TIME WITH YOU PHILISTINES!
WHAT'S WITH MISS HIGH-AND-MIGHTY?
DON'T MIND RONNIE!
...SHE'S JUST IN ONE OF HER FUNNY MOOD SWINGS!
OH, THERE YOU ARE!
WE'VE JUST BEEN INVITED TO SPEND THE WEEKEND WITH THE VAN LOOTS!
THE VAN LOOTS?!
I SO ADMIRE THEIR DAUGHTER CYNTHIA!
...SHE AND HER CROWD ARE ALWAYS IN THE SOCIAL COLUMNS!
OH, WOW! THEIR MANSION IS MOST IMPRESSIVE!
THAT'S JUST THEIR SERVANTS' QUARTERS!
THERE'S THEIR RESIDENCE!
2

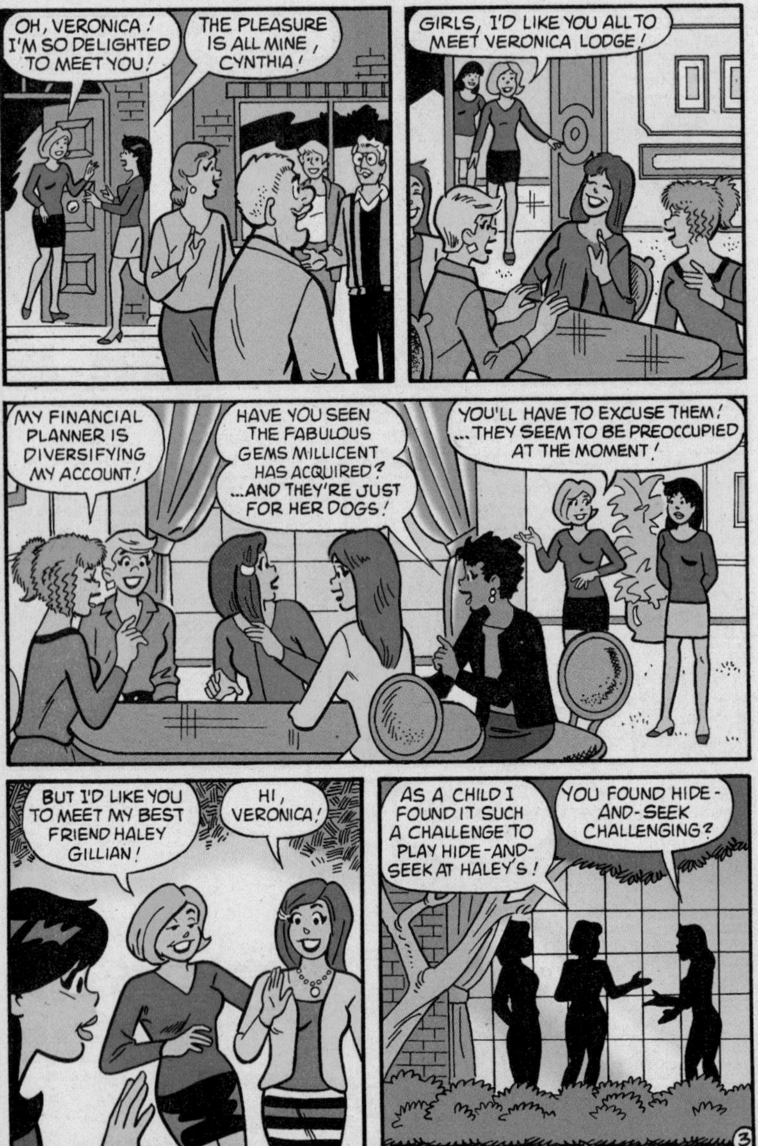
OH, VERONICA! I'M SO DELIGHTED TO MEET YOU!
THE PLEASURE IS ALL MINE, CYNTHIA!
GIRLS, I'D LIKE YOU ALL TO MEET VERONICA LODGE!
MY FINANCIAL PLANNER IS DIVERSIFYING MY ACCOUNT!
HAVE YOU SEEN THE FABULOUS GEMS MILLICENT HAS ACQUIRED? ...AND THEY'RE JUST FOR HER DOGS!
YOU'LL HAVE TO EXCUSE THEM! ...THEY SEEM TO BE PREOCCUPIED AT THE MOMENT!
BUT I'D LIKE YOU TO MEET MY BEST FRIEND HALEY GILLIAN!
HI, VERONICA!
AS A CHILD I FOUND IT SUCH A CHALLENGE TO PLAY HIDE-AND-SEEK AT HALEY'S!
YOU FOUND HIDE-AND-SEEK CHALLENGING?
3

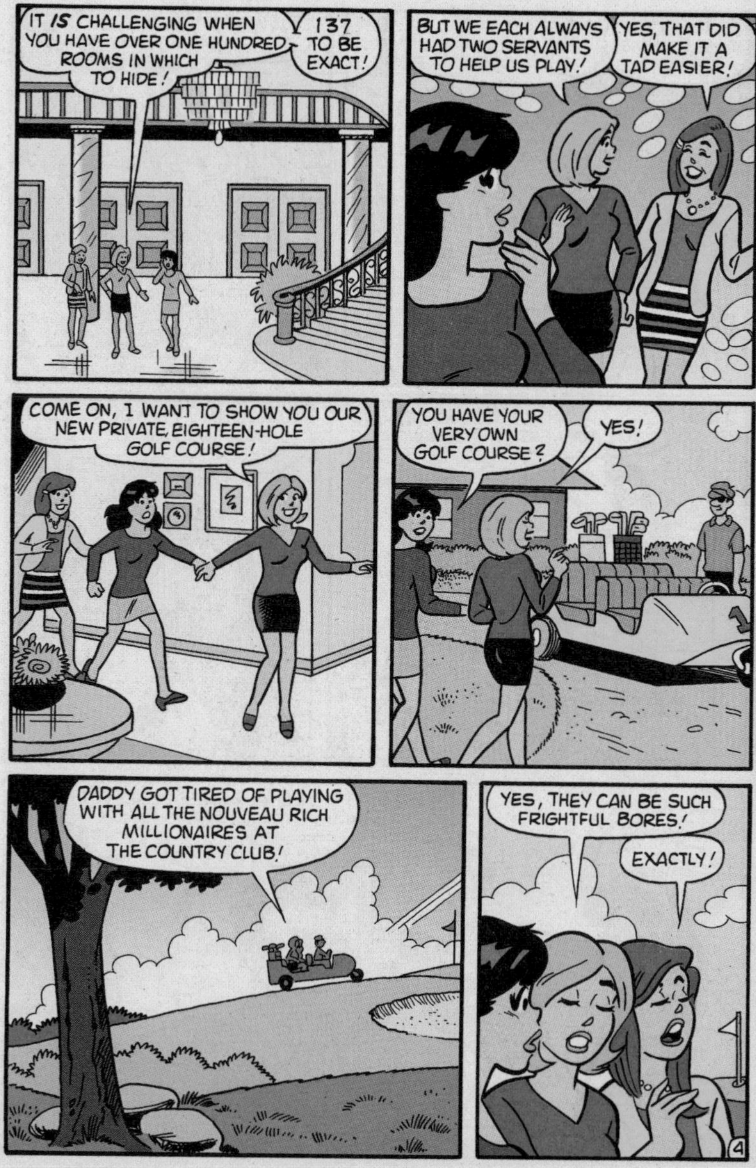
IT IS CHALLENGING WHEN YOU HAVE OVER ONE HUNDRED ROOMS IN WHICH TO HIDE!
137 TO BE EXACT!
BUT WE EACH ALWAYS HAD TWO SERVANTS TO HELP US PLAY!
YES, THAT DID MAKE IT A TAD EASIER!
COME ON, I WANT TO SHOW YOU OUR NEW PRIVATE, EIGHTEEN-HOLE GOLF COURSE!
YOU HAVE YOUR VERY OWN GOLF COURSE?
YES!
DADDY GOT TIRED OF PLAYING WITH ALL THE NOUVEAU RICH MILLIONAIRES AT THE COUNTRY CLUB!
YES, THEY CAN BE SUCH FRIGHTFUL BORES!
EXACTLY!
4

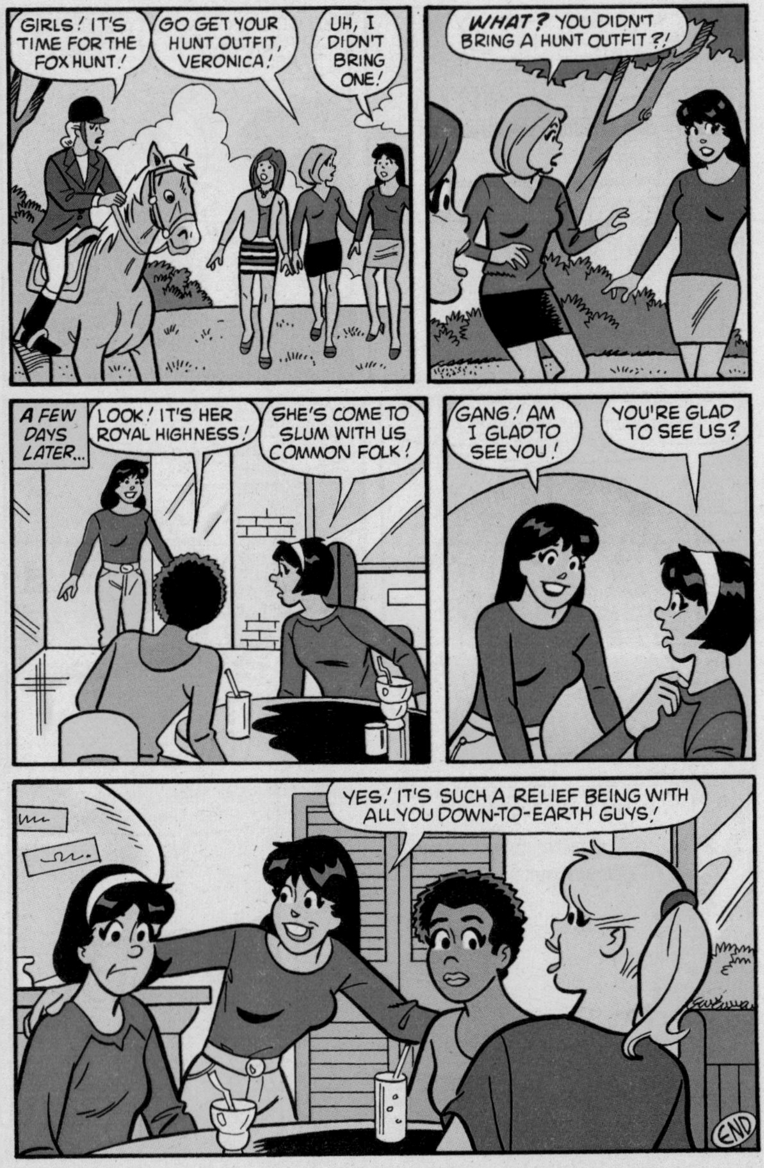
GIRLS! IT'S TIME FOR THE FOX HUNT!
GO GET YOUR HUNT OUTFIT, VERONICA!
UH, I DIDN'T BRING ONE!
WHAT? YOU DIDN'T BRING A HUNT OUTFIT?!
A FEW DAYS LATER...
LOOK! IT'S HER ROYAL HIGHNESS!
SHE'S COME TO SLUM WITH US COMMON FOLK!
GANG! AM I GLAD TO SEE YOU!
YOU'RE GLAD TO SEE US?
YES! IT'S SUCH A RELIEF BEING WITH ALL YOU DOWN-TO-EARTH GUYS!
END

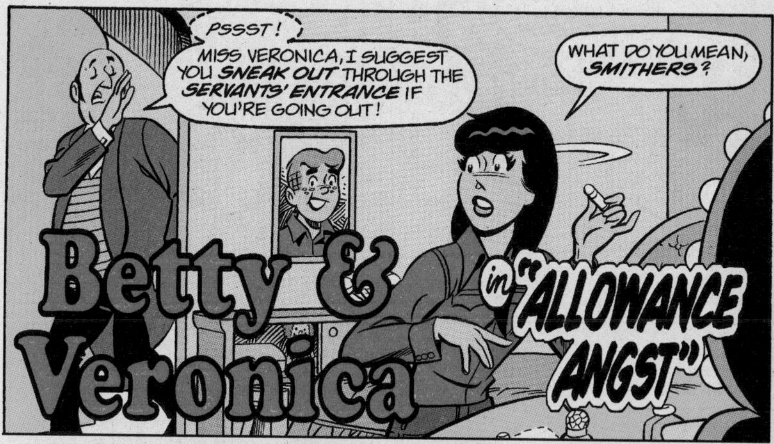
PSSST!
MISS VERONICA, I SUGGEST YOU SNEAK OUT THROUGH THE SERVANTS' ENTRANCE IF YOU'RE GOING OUT!
WHAT DO YOU MEAN, SMITHERS?
Betty & Veronica
in "ALLOWANCE ANGST"

SCRIPT: BILL GOLLIHER PENCILS: BOB BOLLING INKS: AL MILGROM
COLORS: BARRY GROSSMAN LETTERS: VICKIE WILLIAMS

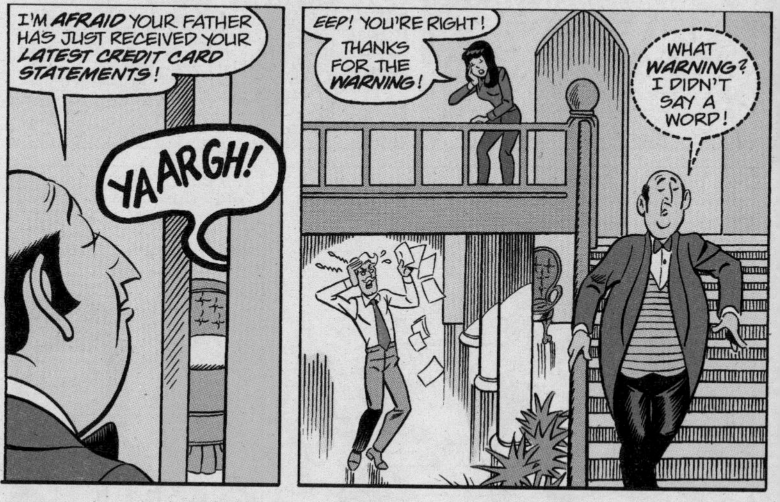
I'M AFRAID YOUR FATHER HAS JUST RECEIVED YOUR LATEST CREDIT CARD STATEMENTS!
YAARGH!
EEP! YOU'RE RIGHT!
THANKS FOR THE WARNING!
WHAT WARNING? I DIDN'T SAY A WORD!

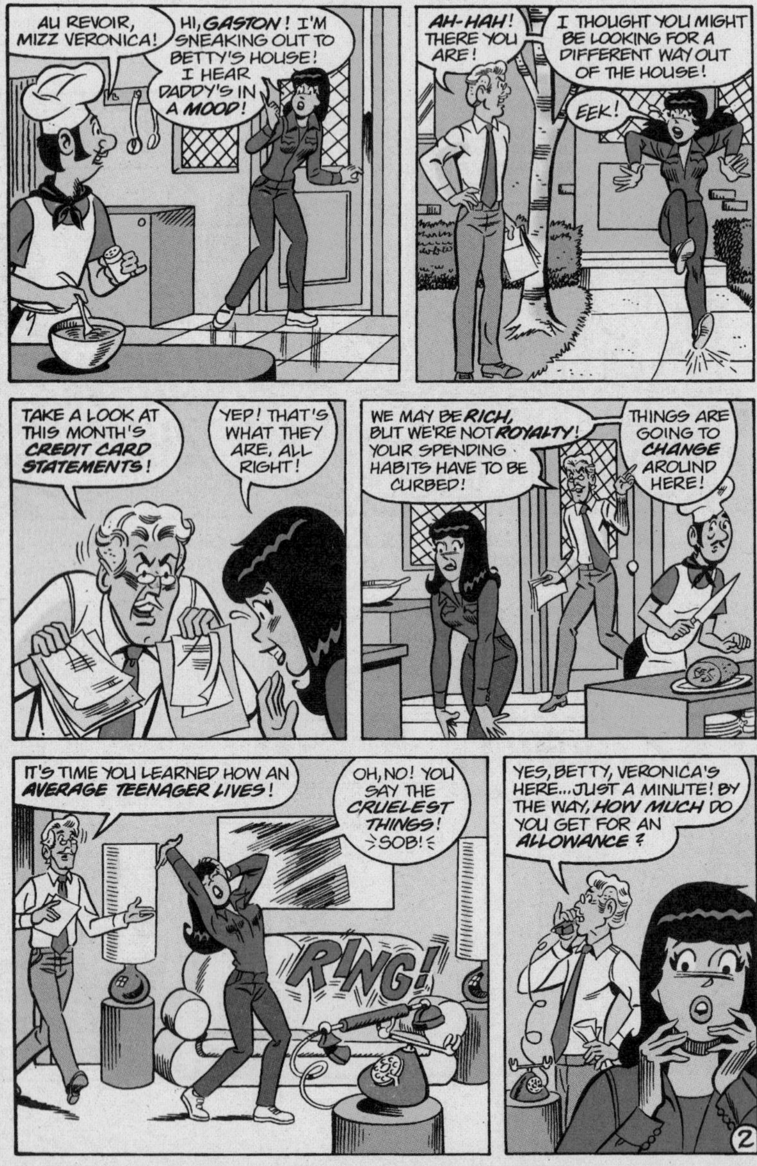

AU REVOIR, MIZZ VERONICA!
HI, GASTON! I'M SNEAKING OUT TO BETTY'S HOUSE! I HEAR DADDY'S IN A MOOD!
AH-HAH! THERE YOU ARE!
I THOUGHT YOU MIGHT BE LOOKING FOR A DIFFERENT WAY OUT OF THE HOUSE!
EEK!
TAKE A LOOK AT THIS MONTH'S CREDIT CARD STATEMENTS!
YEP! THAT'S WHAT THEY ARE, ALL RIGHT!
WE MAY BE RICH, BUT WE'RE NOT ROYALTY! YOUR SPENDING HABITS HAVE TO BE CURBED!
THINGS ARE GOING TO CHANGE AROUND HERE!
IT'S TIME YOU LEARNED HOW AN AVERAGE TEENAGER LIVES!
OH, NO! YOU SAY THE CRUELEST THINGS! SOB!
RING!
YES, BETTY, VERONICA'S HERE...JUST A MINUTE! BY THE WAY, HOW MUCH DO YOU GET FOR AN ALLOWANCE?
2

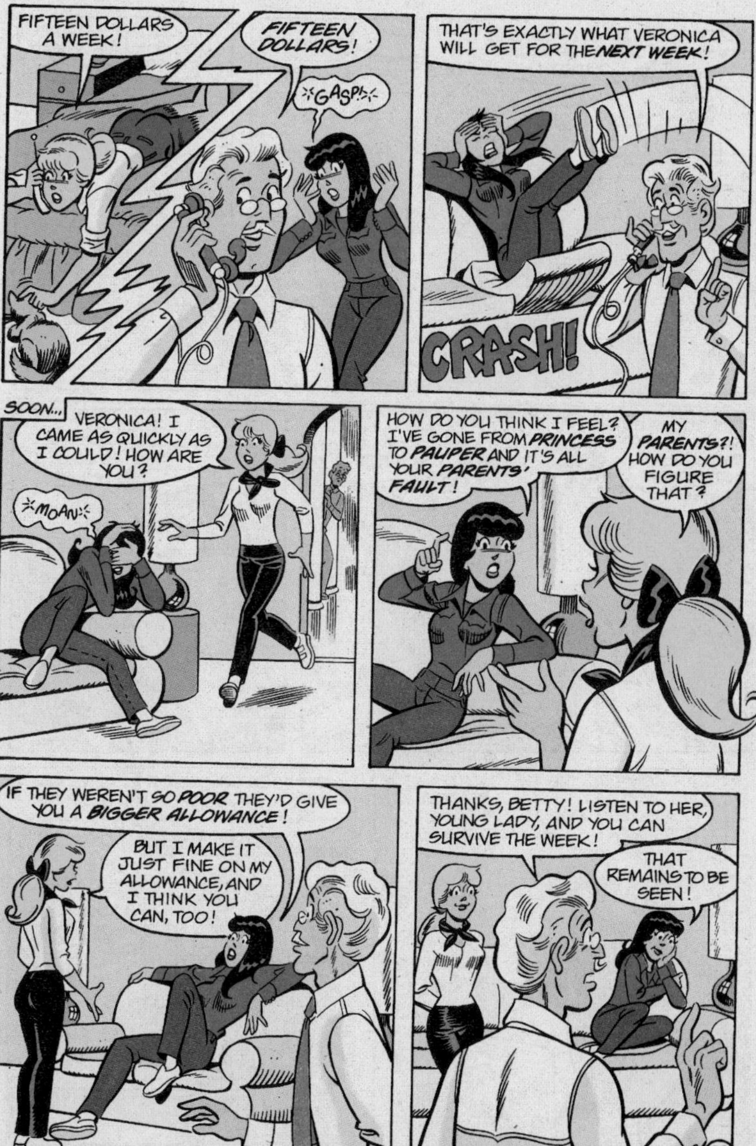
FIFTEEN DOLLARS A WEEK!
FIFTEEN DOLLARS!
GASP!
THAT'S EXACTLY WHAT VERONICA WILL GET FOR THE NEXT WEEK!
CRASH!
SOON...
VERONICA! I CAME AS QUICKLY AS I COULD! HOW ARE YOU?
MOAN
HOW DO YOU THINK I FEEL? I'VE GONE FROM PRINCESS TO PAUPER AND IT'S ALL YOUR PARENTS' FAULT!
MY PARENTS?! HOW DO YOU FIGURE THAT?
IF THEY WEREN'T SO POOR THEY'D GIVE YOU A BIGGER ALLOWANCE!
BUT I MAKE IT JUST FINE ON MY ALLOWANCE, AND I THINK YOU CAN, TOO!
THANKS, BETTY! LISTEN TO HER, YOUNG LADY, AND YOU CAN SURVIVE THE WEEK!
THAT REMAINS TO BE SEEN!
3

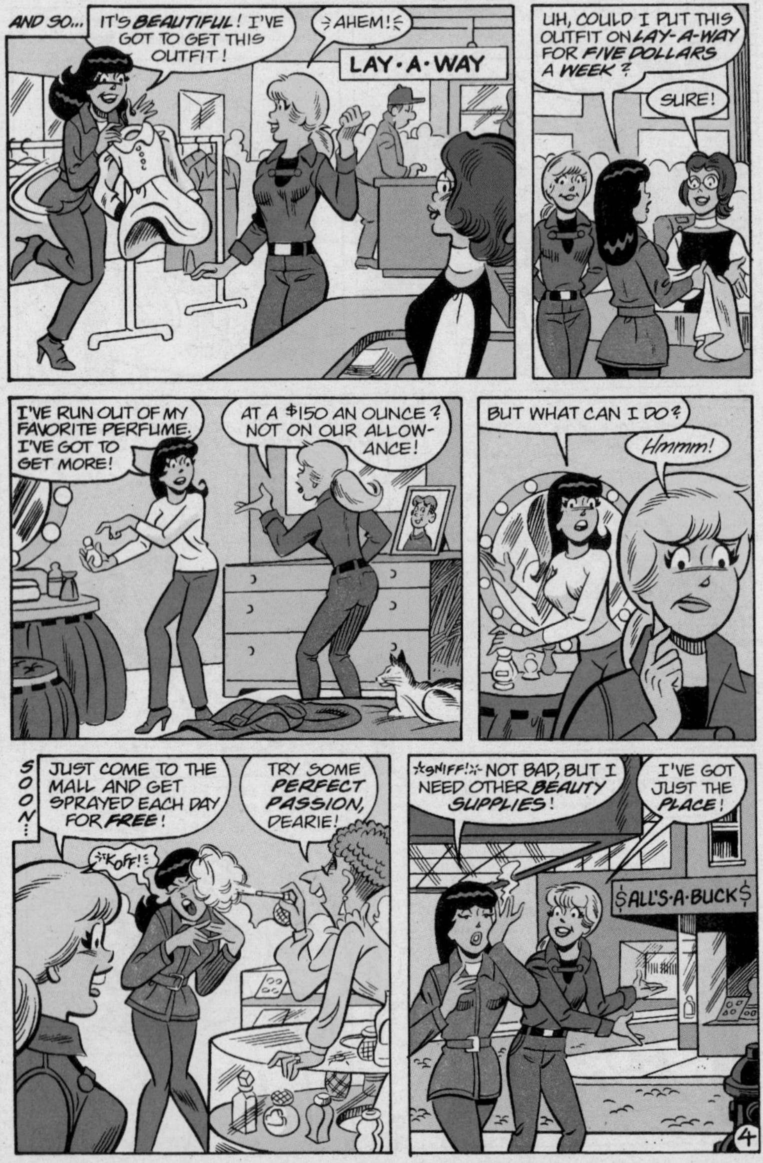
AND SO...
IT'S BEAUTIFUL! I'VE GOT TO GET THIS OUTFIT!
AHEM!
LAY·A·WAY
UH, COULD I PUT THIS OUTFIT ON LAY-A-WAY FOR FIVE DOLLARS A WEEK?
SURE!
I'VE RUN OUT OF MY FAVORITE PERFUME. I'VE GOT TO GET MORE!
AT A $150 AN OUNCE? NOT ON OUR ALLOW-ANCE!
BUT WHAT CAN I DO?
Hmmm!
SOON...
JUST COME TO THE MALL AND GET SPRAYED EACH DAY FOR FREE!
TRY SOME PERFECT PASSION, DEARIE!
KOFF!
SNIFF! NOT BAD, BUT I NEED OTHER BEAUTY SUPPLIES!
I'VE GOT JUST THE PLACE!
$ALL'S·A·BUCK$
4

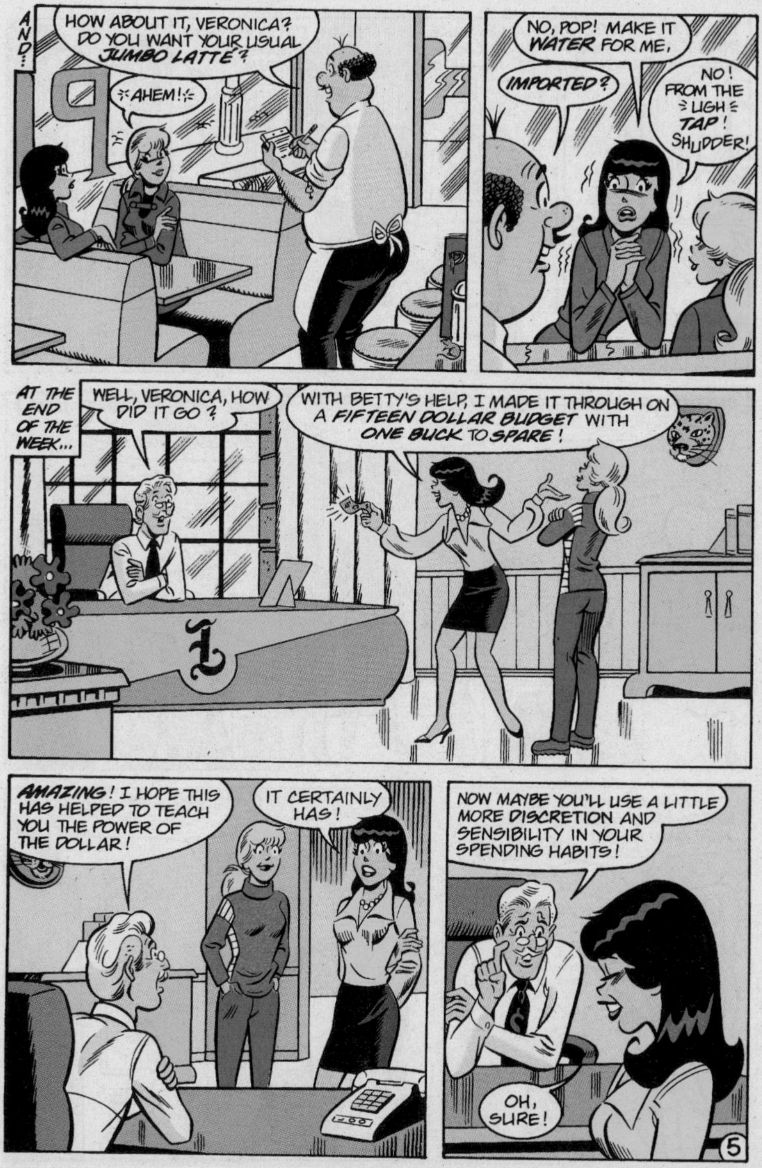
AND...
HOW ABOUT IT, VERONICA? DO YOU WANT YOUR USUAL JUMBO LATTE?
AHEM!
NO, POP! MAKE IT WATER FOR ME.
IMPORTED?
NO! FROM THE UGH TAP! SHUDDER!
AT THE END OF THE WEEK...
WELL, VERONICA, HOW DID IT GO?
WITH BETTY'S HELP, I MADE IT THROUGH ON A FIFTEEN DOLLAR BUDGET WITH ONE BUCK TO SPARE!
AMAZING! I HOPE THIS HAS HELPED TO TEACH YOU THE POWER OF THE DOLLAR!
IT CERTAINLY HAS!
NOW MAYBE YOU'LL USE A LITTLE MORE DISCRETION AND SENSIBILITY IN YOUR SPENDING HABITS!
OH, SURE!
5

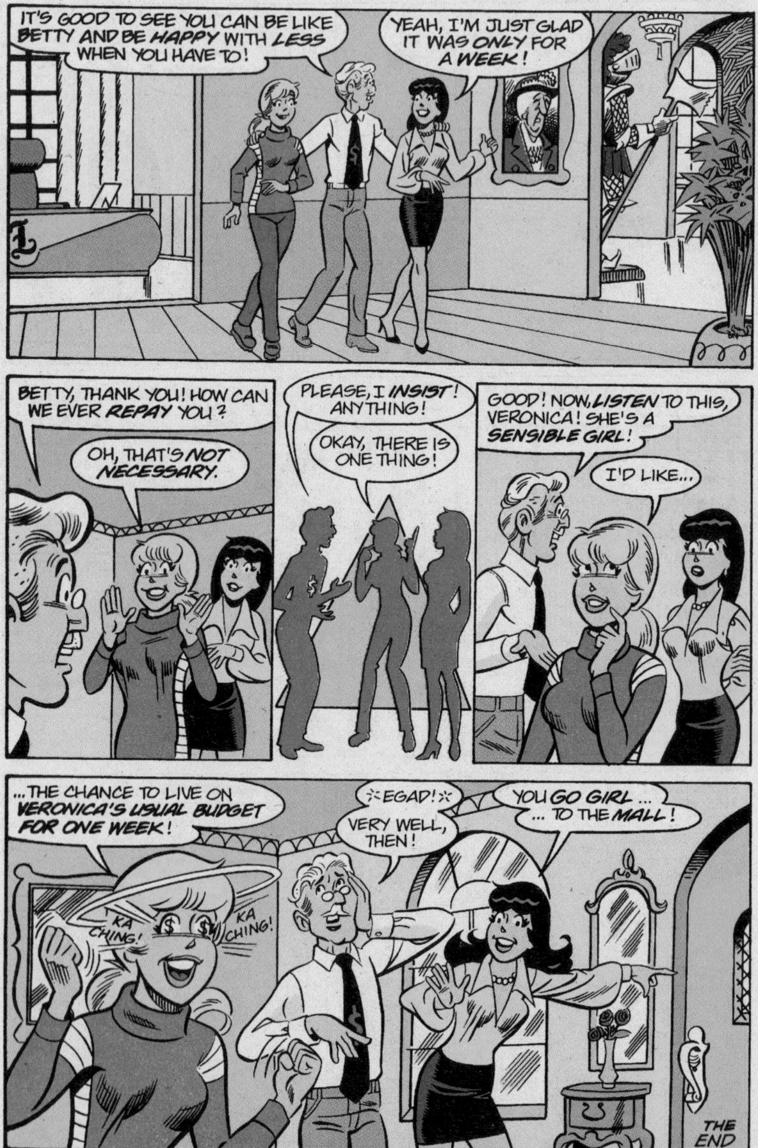
IT'S GOOD TO SEE YOU CAN BE LIKE BETTY AND BE *HAPPY* WITH *LESS* WHEN YOU HAVE TO!
YEAH, I'M JUST GLAD IT WAS *ONLY* FOR A *WEEK*!
BETTY, THANK YOU! HOW CAN WE EVER *REPAY* YOU?
OH, THAT'S *NOT NECESSARY*.
PLEASE, I *INSIST*! ANYTHING!
OKAY, THERE IS ONE THING!
GOOD! NOW, *LISTEN* TO THIS, VERONICA! SHE'S A *SENSIBLE GIRL*!
I'D LIKE...
...THE CHANCE TO LIVE ON *VERONICA'S USUAL BUDGET FOR ONE WEEK*!
KA CHING!
KA CHING!
EGAD!
VERY WELL, THEN!
YOU *GO GIRL* ...
... TO THE *MALL*!
THE END

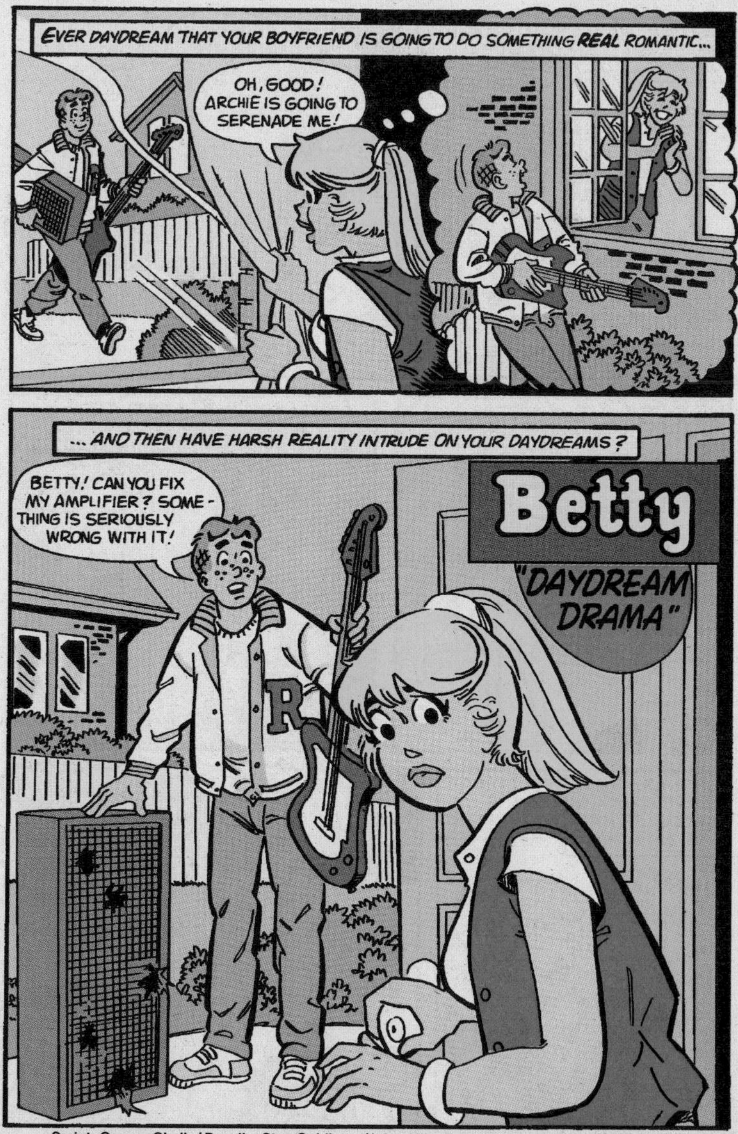
EVER DAYDREAM THAT YOUR BOYFRIEND IS GOING TO DO SOMETHING REAL ROMANTIC...
OH, GOOD! ARCHIE IS GOING TO SERENADE ME!
... AND THEN HAVE HARSH REALITY INTRUDE ON YOUR DAYDREAMS?
BETTY! CAN YOU FIX MY AMPLIFIER? SOME-THING IS SERIOUSLY WRONG WITH IT!
Betty
"DAYDREAM DRAMA"

Script: George Gladir / Pencils: Stan Goldberg / Inks: Mike Esposito / Letters: Bill Yoshida

AND THEN THERE WAS THE TIME... SINCE YOUR BIRTHDAY IS COMING UP I DROPPED ARCHIE A HINT...YOU ARE VERY FOND OF *GOLD*!

HAPPY BIRTHDAY! ♪

14K

DING-DONG!

THAT MUST BE ARCHIE NOW!

HAPPY BIRTHDAY, BETTY! I HEAR YOU'RE INTO GOLD!

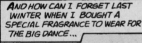

AND HOW CAN I FORGET LAST WINTER WHEN I BOUGHT A SPECIAL FRAGRANCE TO WEAR FOR THE BIG DANCE...

SPRITZ! SPRITZ!

BETTY! YOUR SCENT... IT'S DRIVING ME *WILD*!

DANCE

2

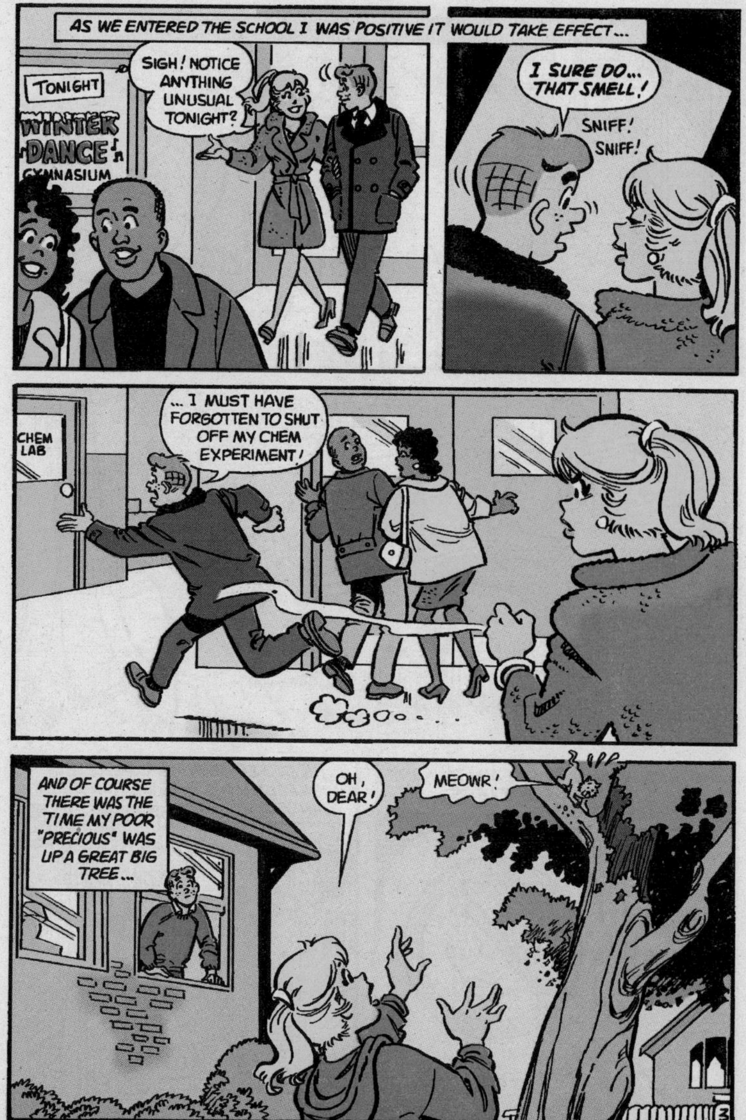
AS WE ENTERED THE SCHOOL I WAS POSITIVE IT WOULD TAKE EFFECT...
TONIGHT
WINTER DANCE
GYMNASIUM
SIGH! NOTICE ANYTHING UNUSUAL TONIGHT?
I SURE DO... THAT SMELL!
SNIFF!
SNIFF!
CHEM LAB
... I MUST HAVE FORGOTTEN TO SHUT OFF MY CHEM EXPERIMENT!
AND OF COURSE THERE WAS THE TIME MY POOR "PRECIOUS" WAS UP A GREAT BIG TREE...
OH, DEAR!
MEOWR!
3

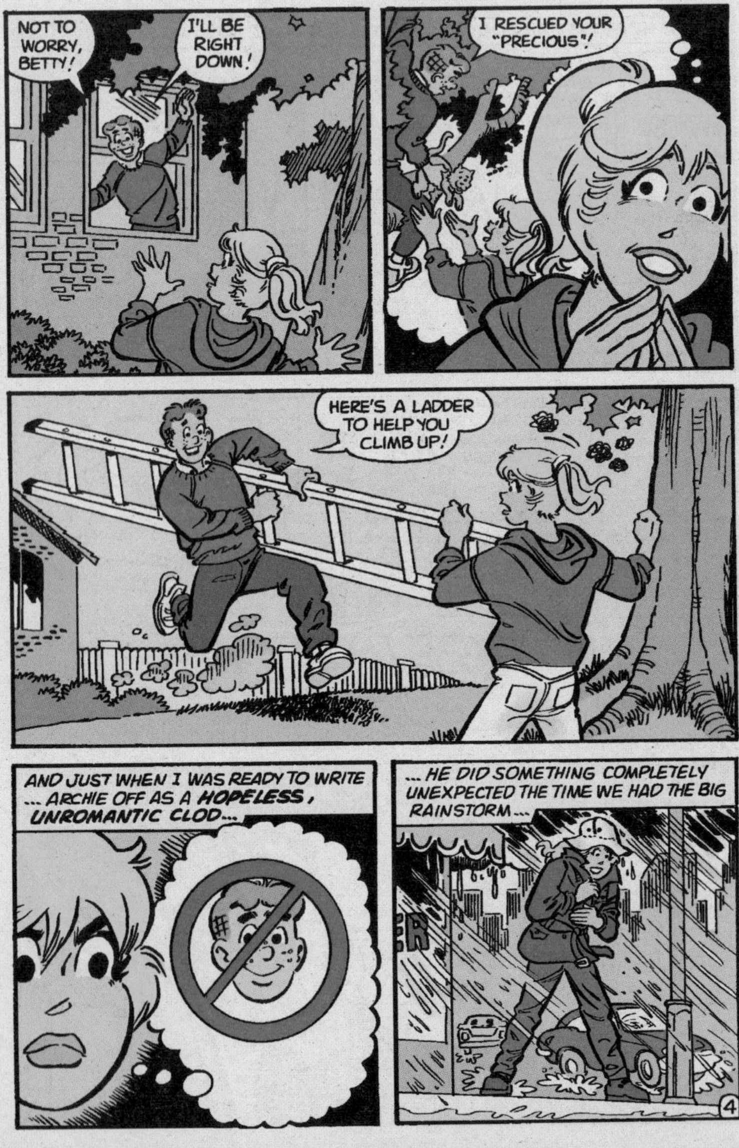
NOT TO WORRY, BETTY!
I'LL BE RIGHT DOWN!
I RESCUED YOUR "PRECIOUS"!
HERE'S A LADDER TO HELP YOU CLIMB UP!
AND JUST WHEN I WAS READY TO WRITE ... ARCHIE OFF AS A HOPELESS, UNROMANTIC CLOD...
... HE DID SOMETHING COMPLETELY UNEXPECTED THE TIME WE HAD THE BIG RAINSTORM...
4

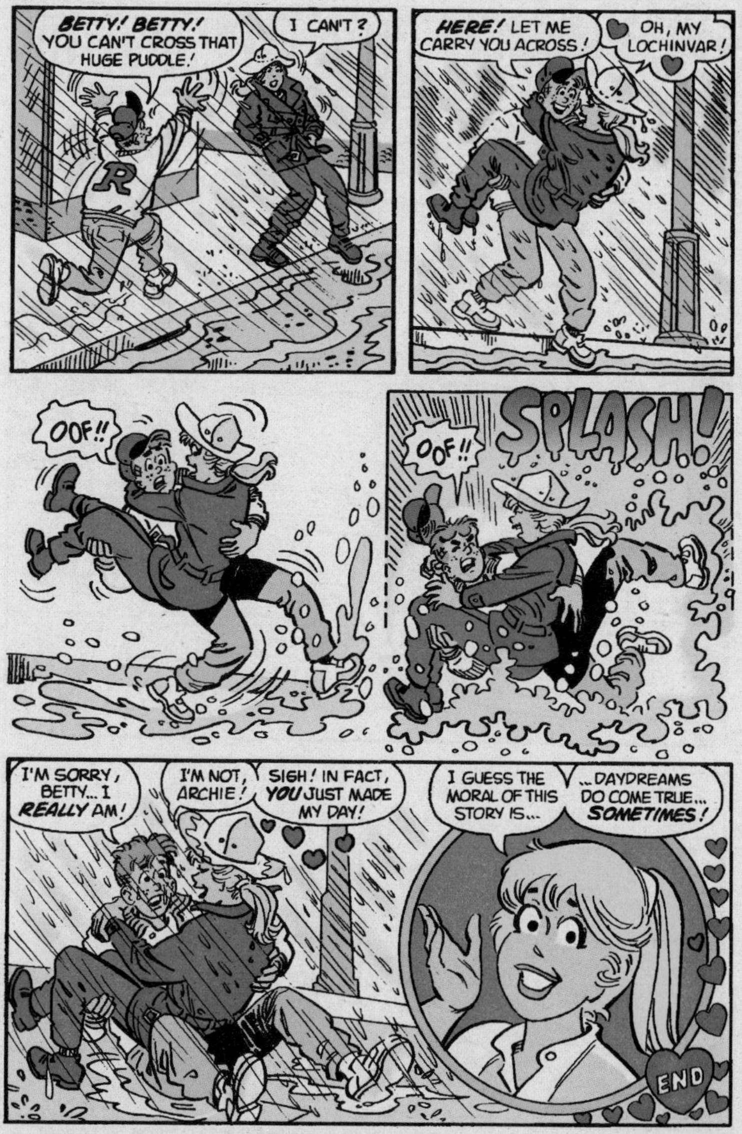
BETTY! BETTY! YOU CAN'T CROSS THAT HUGE PUDDLE!
I CAN'T?
HERE! LET ME CARRY YOU ACROSS!
OH, MY LOCHINVAR!
OOF!!
SPLASH!
OOF!!
I'M SORRY, BETTY... I REALLY AM!
I'M NOT, ARCHIE!
SIGH! IN FACT, YOU JUST MADE MY DAY!
I GUESS THE MORAL OF THIS STORY IS...
...DAYDREAMS DO COME TRUE... SOMETIMES!
END

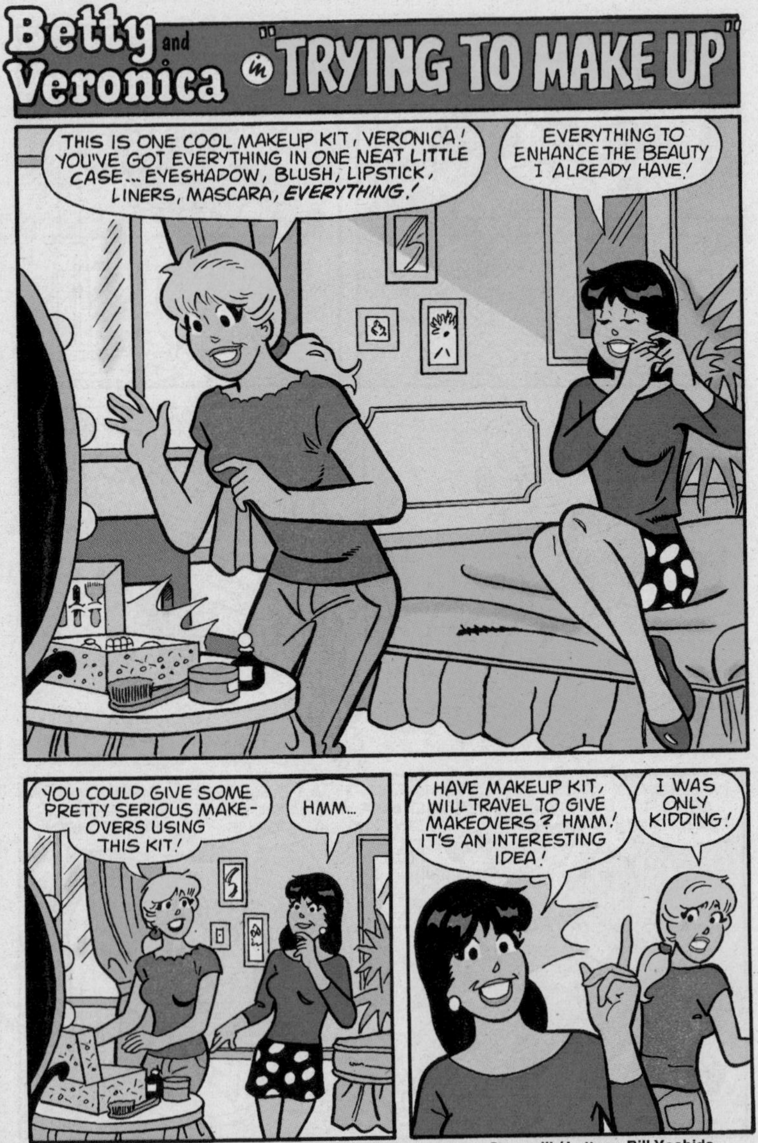
Betty and Veronica in "TRYING TO MAKE UP"
THIS IS ONE COOL MAKEUP KIT, VERONICA! YOU'VE GOT EVERYTHING IN ONE NEAT LITTLE CASE... EYESHADOW, BLUSH, LIPSTICK, LINERS, MASCARA, EVERYTHING!
EVERYTHING TO ENHANCE THE BEAUTY I ALREADY HAVE!
YOU COULD GIVE SOME PRETTY SERIOUS MAKE-OVERS USING THIS KIT!
HMM...
HAVE MAKEUP KIT, WILL TRAVEL TO GIVE MAKEOVERS? HMM! IT'S AN INTERESTING IDEA!
I WAS ONLY KIDDING!

Script: Kathleen Webb / Pencils: Jeff Shultz / Inks: Henry Scarpelli / Letters: Bill Yoshida

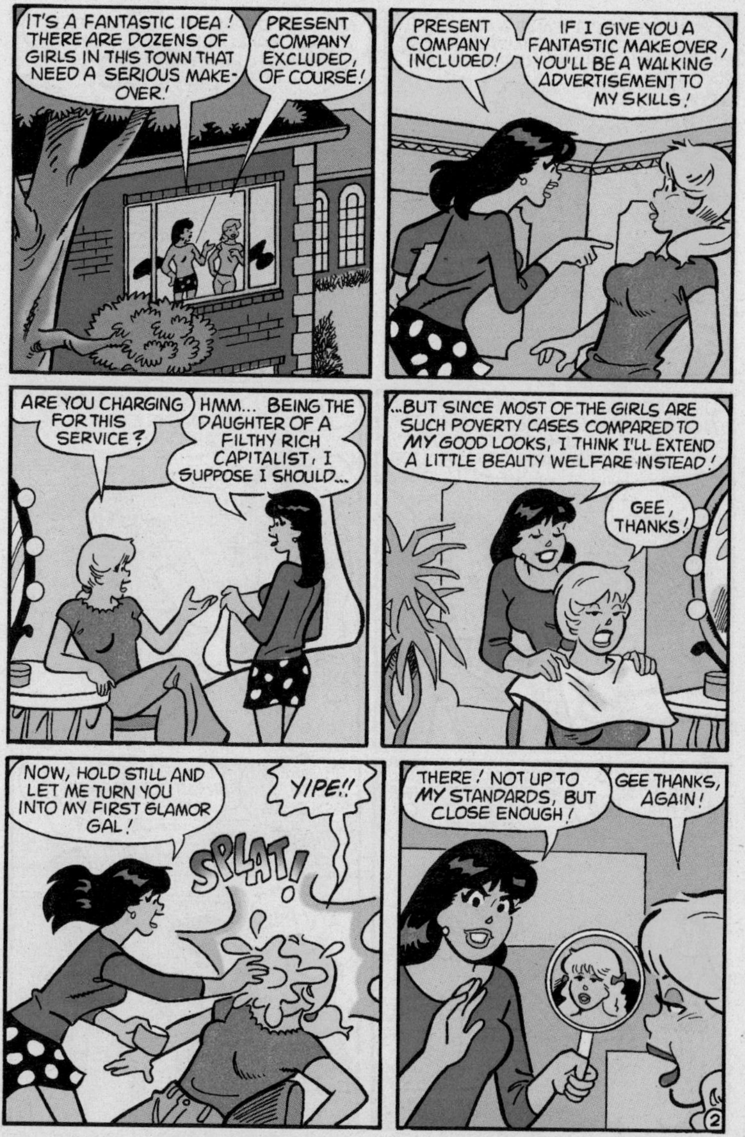

IT'S A FANTASTIC IDEA! THERE ARE DOZENS OF GIRLS IN THIS TOWN THAT NEED A SERIOUS MAKE-OVER!
PRESENT COMPANY EXCLUDED, OF COURSE!
PRESENT COMPANY INCLUDED!
IF I GIVE YOU A FANTASTIC MAKEOVER, YOU'LL BE A WALKING ADVERTISEMENT TO MY SKILLS!
ARE YOU CHARGING FOR THIS SERVICE?
HMM... BEING THE DAUGHTER OF A FILTHY RICH CAPITALIST, I SUPPOSE I SHOULD...
...BUT SINCE MOST OF THE GIRLS ARE SUCH POVERTY CASES COMPARED TO MY GOOD LOOKS, I THINK I'LL EXTEND A LITTLE BEAUTY WELFARE INSTEAD!
GEE, THANKS!
NOW, HOLD STILL AND LET ME TURN YOU INTO MY FIRST GLAMOR GAL!
YIPE!!
SPLAT!
THERE! NOT UP TO MY STANDARDS, BUT CLOSE ENOUGH!
GEE THANKS, AGAIN!
2

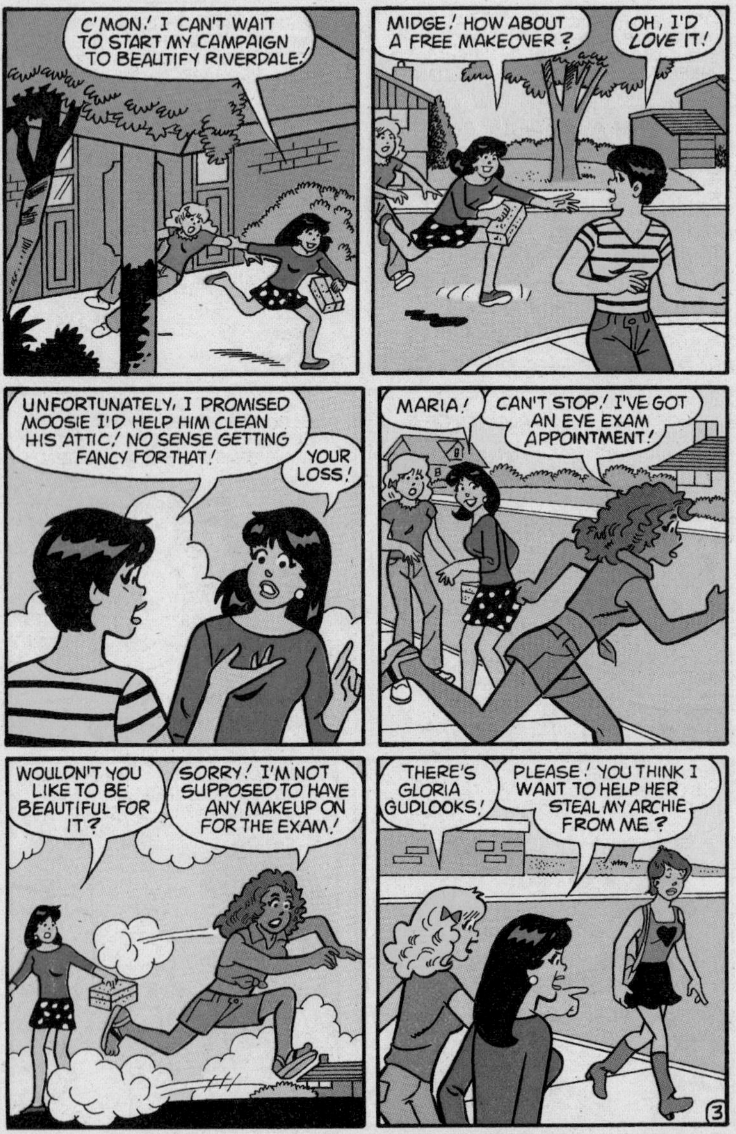
C'MON! I CAN'T WAIT TO START MY CAMPAIGN TO BEAUTIFY RIVERDALE!
MIDGE! HOW ABOUT A FREE MAKEOVER?
OH, I'D LOVE IT!
UNFORTUNATELY, I PROMISED MOOSIE I'D HELP HIM CLEAN HIS ATTIC! NO SENSE GETTING FANCY FOR THAT!
YOUR LOSS!
MARIA!
CAN'T STOP! I'VE GOT AN EYE EXAM APPOINTMENT!
WOULDN'T YOU LIKE TO BE BEAUTIFUL FOR IT?
SORRY! I'M NOT SUPPOSED TO HAVE ANY MAKEUP ON FOR THE EXAM!
THERE'S GLORIA GUDLOOKS!
PLEASE! YOU THINK I WANT TO HELP HER STEAL MY ARCHIE FROM ME?
3

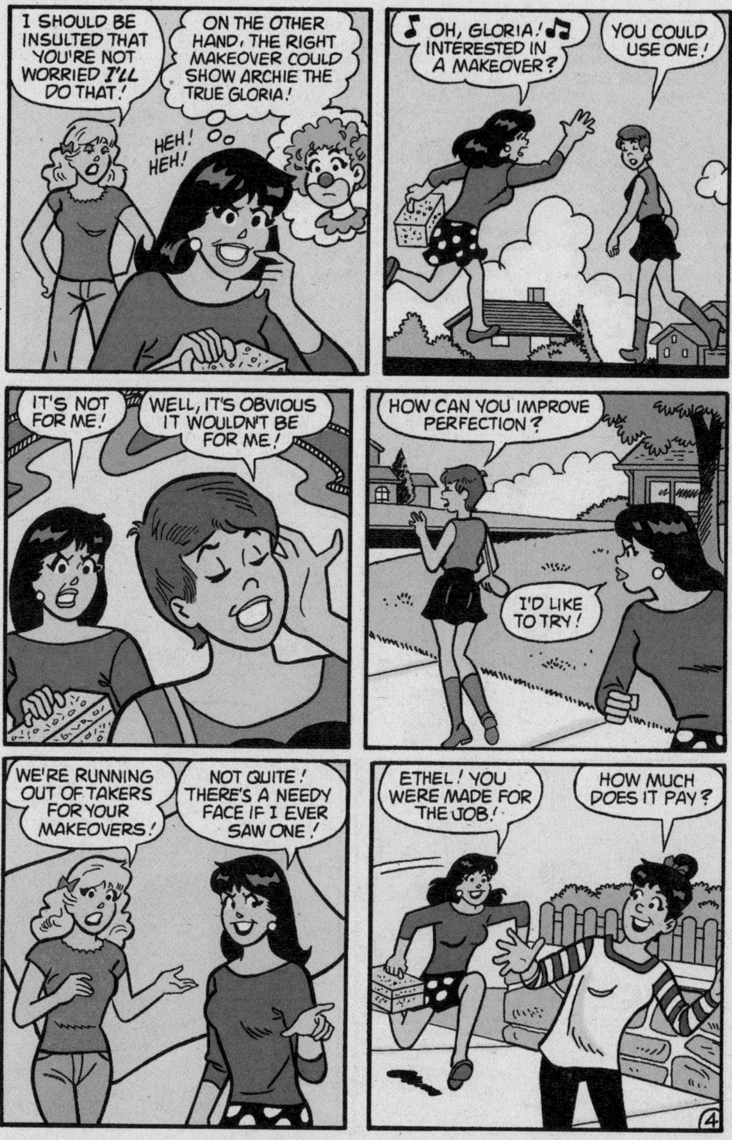
I SHOULD BE INSULTED THAT YOU'RE NOT WORRIED I'LL DO THAT!
ON THE OTHER HAND, THE RIGHT MAKEOVER COULD SHOW ARCHIE THE TRUE GLORIA!
HEH! HEH!
OH, GLORIA! INTERESTED IN A MAKEOVER?
YOU COULD USE ONE!
IT'S NOT FOR ME!
WELL, IT'S OBVIOUS IT WOULDN'T BE FOR ME!
HOW CAN YOU IMPROVE PERFECTION?
I'D LIKE TO TRY!
WE'RE RUNNING OUT OF TAKERS FOR YOUR MAKEOVERS!
NOT QUITE! THERE'S A NEEDY FACE IF I EVER SAW ONE!
ETHEL! YOU WERE MADE FOR THE JOB!
HOW MUCH DOES IT PAY?
4

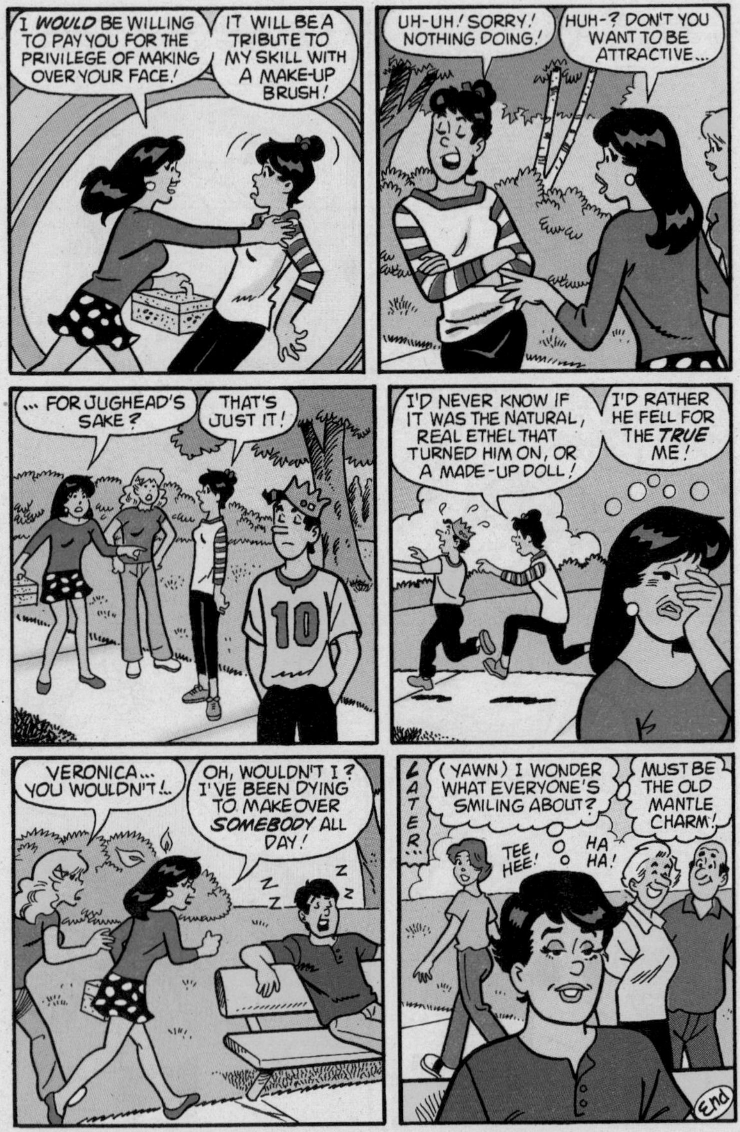
I *WOULD* BE WILLING TO PAY YOU FOR THE PRIVILEGE OF MAKING OVER YOUR FACE!
IT WILL BE A TRIBUTE TO MY SKILL WITH A MAKE-UP BRUSH!
UH-UH! SORRY! NOTHING DOING!
HUH-? DON'T YOU WANT TO BE ATTRACTIVE...
... FOR JUGHEAD'S SAKE?
THAT'S JUST IT!
10
I'D NEVER KNOW IF IT WAS THE NATURAL, REAL ETHEL THAT TURNED HIM ON, OR A MADE-UP DOLL!
I'D RATHER HE FELL FOR THE *TRUE* ME!
VERONICA... YOU WOULDN'T!..
OH, WOULDN'T I? I'VE BEEN DYING TO MAKE OVER *SOMEBODY* ALL DAY!
Z Z Z Z
LATER...
(YAWN) I WONDER WHAT EVERYONE'S SMILING ABOUT?
MUST BE THE OLD MANTLE CHARM!
TEE HEE!
HA HA!
End

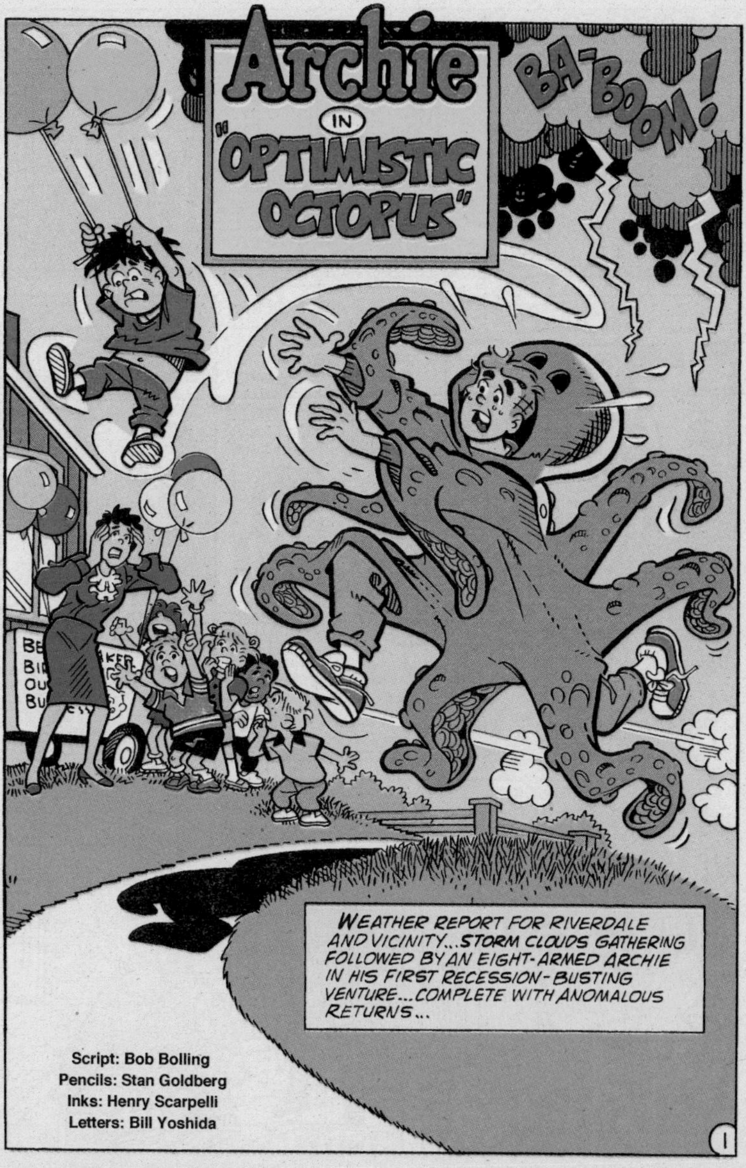
Archie
IN
"OPTIMISTIC OCTOPUS"
BA-BOOM!
WEATHER REPORT FOR RIVERDALE AND VICINITY...STORM CLOUDS GATHERING FOLLOWED BY AN EIGHT-ARMED ARCHIE IN HIS FIRST RECESSION-BUSTING VENTURE...COMPLETE WITH ANOMALOUS RETURNS...
Script: Bob Bolling
Pencils: Stan Goldberg
Inks: Henry Scarpelli
Letters: Bill Yoshida
1

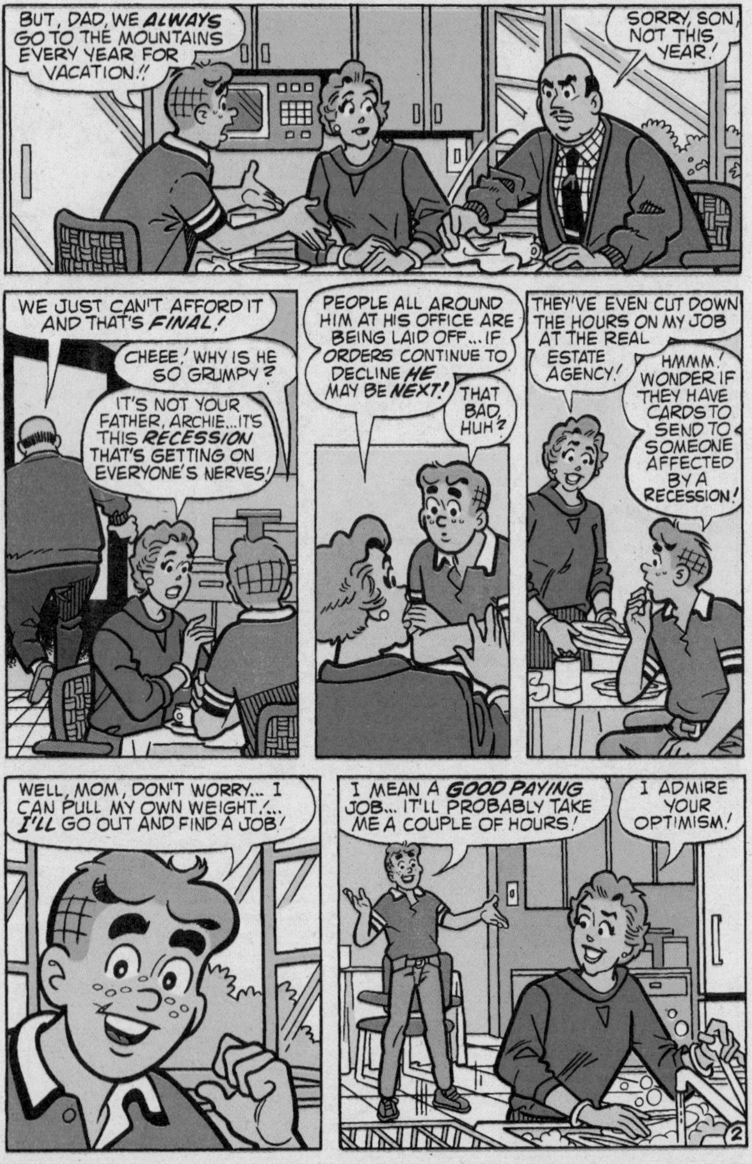
BUT, DAD, WE ALWAYS GO TO THE MOUNTAINS EVERY YEAR FOR VACATION!!
SORRY, SON, NOT THIS YEAR!
WE JUST CAN'T AFFORD IT AND THAT'S FINAL!
CHEEE! WHY IS HE SO GRUMPY?
IT'S NOT YOUR FATHER, ARCHIE...IT'S THIS RECESSION THAT'S GETTING ON EVERYONE'S NERVES!
PEOPLE ALL AROUND HIM AT HIS OFFICE ARE BEING LAID OFF... IF ORDERS CONTINUE TO DECLINE HE MAY BE NEXT!
THAT BAD, HUH?
THEY'VE EVEN CUT DOWN THE HOURS ON MY JOB AT THE REAL ESTATE AGENCY!
HMMM! WONDER IF THEY HAVE CARDS TO SEND TO SOMEONE AFFECTED BY A RECESSION!
WELL, MOM, DON'T WORRY... I CAN PULL MY OWN WEIGHT!... I'LL GO OUT AND FIND A JOB!
I MEAN A GOOD PAYING JOB... IT'LL PROBABLY TAKE ME A COUPLE OF HOURS!
I ADMIRE YOUR OPTIMISM!
2

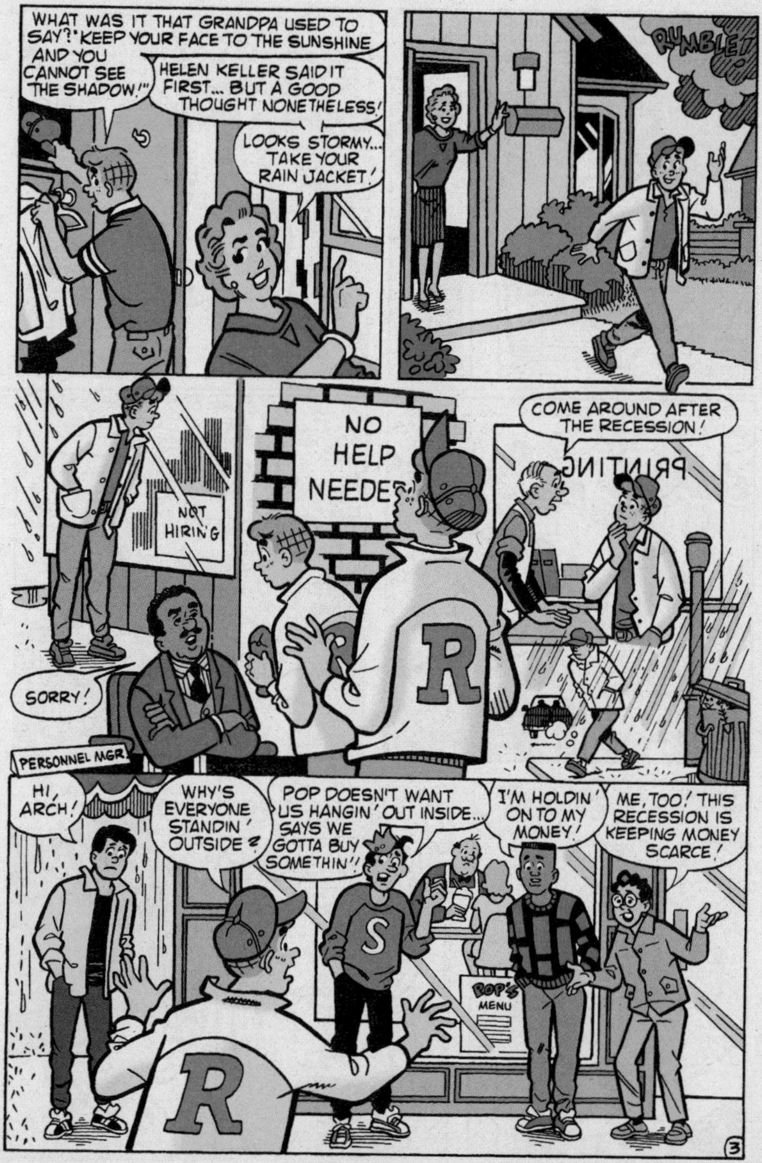

WHAT WAS IT THAT GRANDPA USED TO SAY? "KEEP YOUR FACE TO THE SUNSHINE AND YOU CANNOT SEE THE SHADOW!"
HELEN KELLER SAID IT FIRST... BUT A GOOD THOUGHT NONETHELESS!
LOOKS STORMY... TAKE YOUR RAIN JACKET!
RUMBLE!
NOT HIRING
NO HELP NEEDED
SORRY!
PERSONNEL MGR.
COME AROUND AFTER THE RECESSION!
PRINTING
HI, ARCH!
WHY'S EVERYONE STANDIN' OUTSIDE?
POP DOESN'T WANT US HANGIN' OUT INSIDE... SAYS WE GOTTA BUY SOMETHIN'!
I'M HOLDIN' ON TO MY MONEY!
ME, TOO! THIS RECESSION IS KEEPING MONEY SCARCE!
POP'S MENU

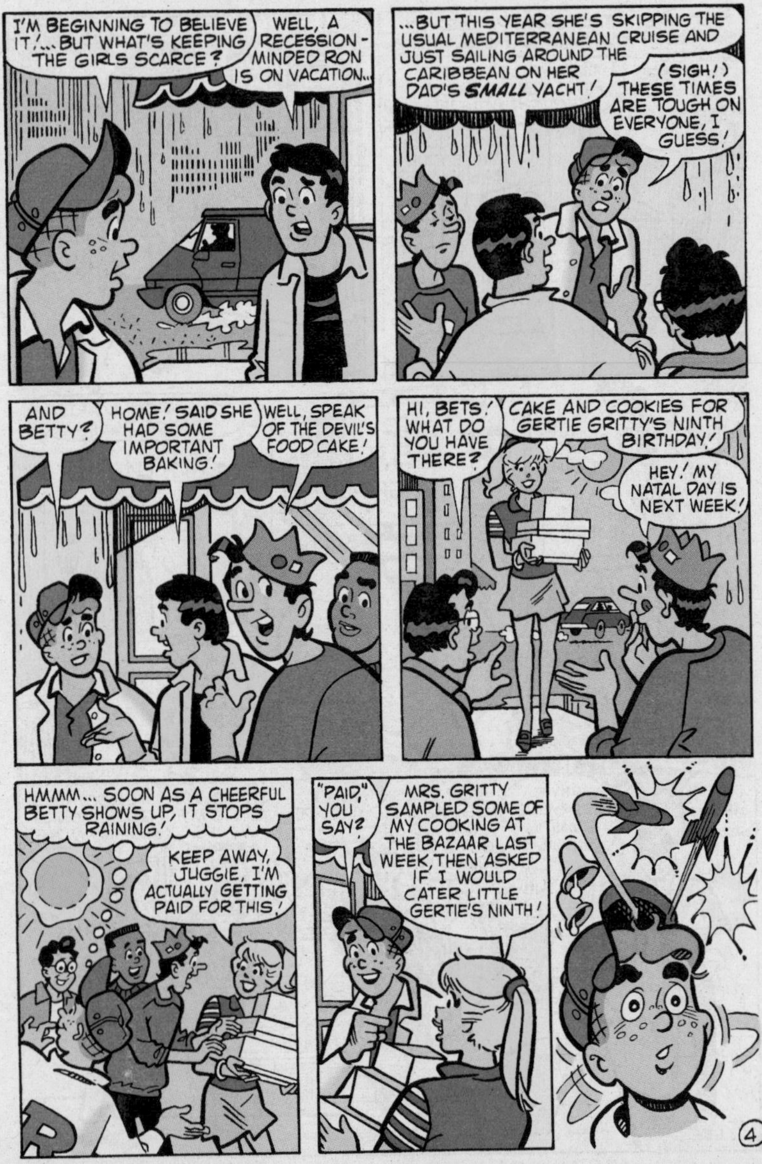
I'M BEGINNING TO BELIEVE IT!... BUT WHAT'S KEEPING THE GIRLS SCARCE?
WELL, A RECESSION-MINDED RON IS ON VACATION...
...BUT THIS YEAR SHE'S SKIPPING THE USUAL MEDITERRANEAN CRUISE AND JUST SAILING AROUND THE CARIBBEAN ON HER DAD'S SMALL YACHT!
(SIGH!) THESE TIMES ARE TOUGH ON EVERYONE, I GUESS!
AND BETTY?
HOME! SAID SHE HAD SOME IMPORTANT BAKING!
WELL, SPEAK OF THE DEVIL'S FOOD CAKE!
HI, BETS! WHAT DO YOU HAVE THERE?
CAKE AND COOKIES FOR GERTIE GRITTY'S NINTH BIRTHDAY!
HEY! MY NATAL DAY IS NEXT WEEK!
HMMM... SOON AS A CHEERFUL BETTY SHOWS UP, IT STOPS RAINING!
KEEP AWAY, JUGGIE, I'M ACTUALLY GETTING PAID FOR THIS!
"PAID," YOU SAY?
MRS. GRITTY SAMPLED SOME OF MY COOKING AT THE BAZAAR LAST WEEK, THEN ASKED IF I WOULD CATER LITTLE GERTIE'S NINTH!
4

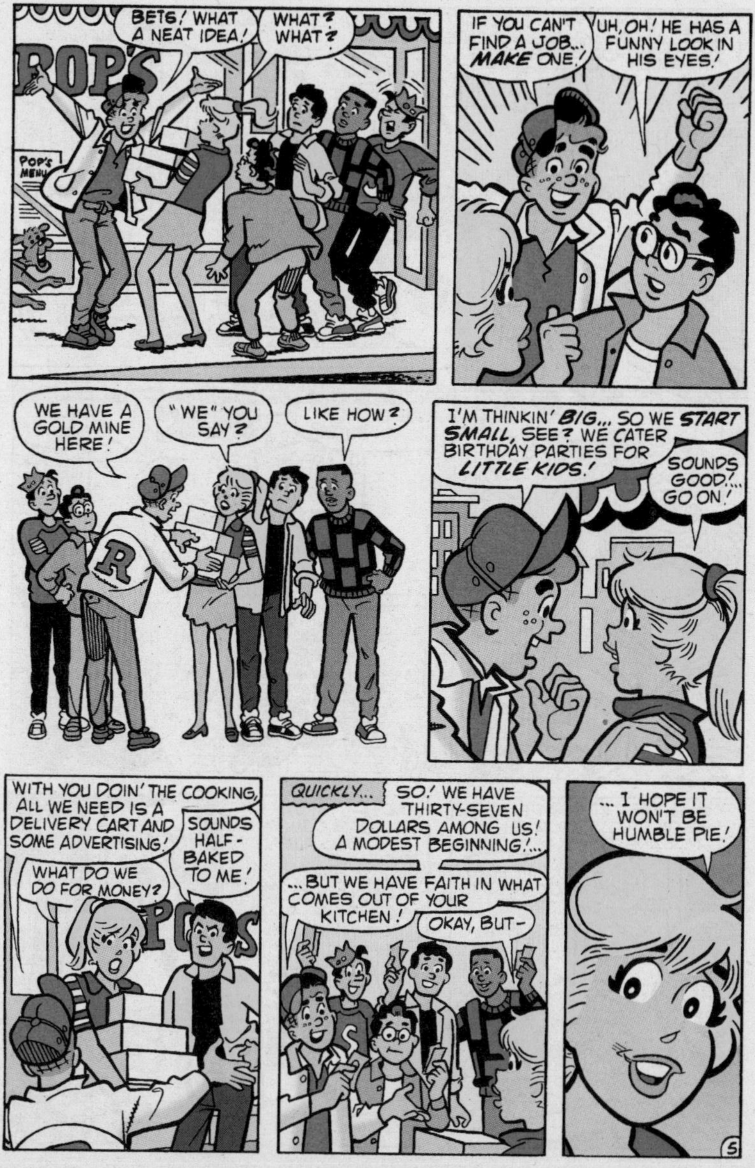
BETS! WHAT A NEAT IDEA!
WHAT? WHAT?
POP'S
POP'S MENU
IF YOU CAN'T FIND A JOB... MAKE ONE!
UH, OH! HE HAS A FUNNY LOOK IN HIS EYES!
WE HAVE A GOLD MINE HERE!
"WE" YOU SAY?
LIKE HOW?
I'M THINKIN' BIG... SO WE START SMALL, SEE? WE CATER BIRTHDAY PARTIES FOR LITTLE KIDS!
SOUNDS GOOD!... GO ON!
WITH YOU DOIN' THE COOKING, ALL WE NEED IS A DELIVERY CART AND SOME ADVERTISING!
SOUNDS HALF-BAKED TO ME!
WHAT DO WE DO FOR MONEY?
QUICKLY...
SO! WE HAVE THIRTY-SEVEN DOLLARS AMONG US! A MODEST BEGINNING!...
...BUT WE HAVE FAITH IN WHAT COMES OUT OF YOUR KITCHEN!
OKAY, BUT-
... I HOPE IT WON'T BE HUMBLE PIE!
5

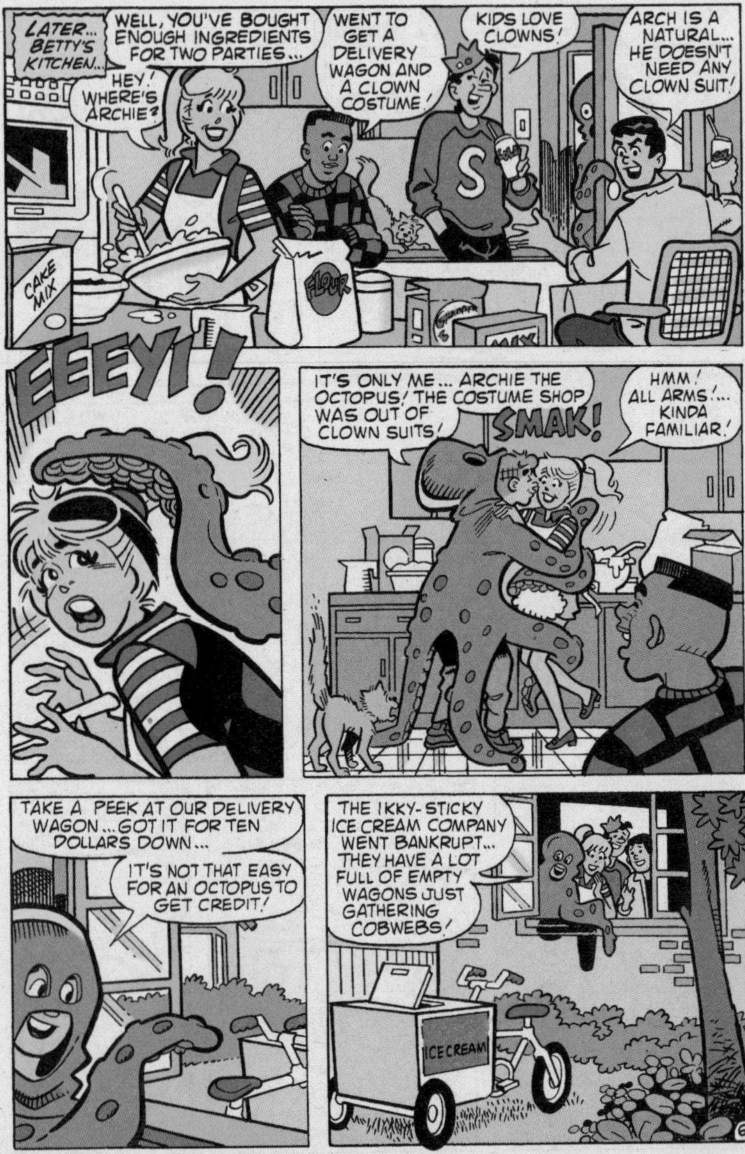
LATER... BETTY'S KITCHEN...
WELL, YOU'VE BOUGHT ENOUGH INGREDIENTS FOR TWO PARTIES...
HEY! WHERE'S ARCHIE?
WENT TO GET A DELIVERY WAGON AND A CLOWN COSTUME!
KIDS LOVE CLOWNS!
ARCH IS A NATURAL... HE DOESN'T NEED ANY CLOWN SUIT!
CAKE MIX
FLOUR
MIX
EEEYI!!
IT'S ONLY ME... ARCHIE THE OCTOPUS! THE COSTUME SHOP WAS OUT OF CLOWN SUITS!
SMAK!
HMM! ALL ARMS!... KINDA FAMILIAR!
TAKE A PEEK AT OUR DELIVERY WAGON... GOT IT FOR TEN DOLLARS DOWN...
IT'S NOT THAT EASY FOR AN OCTOPUS TO GET CREDIT!
THE IKKY-STICKY ICE CREAM COMPANY WENT BANKRUPT... THEY HAVE A LOT FULL OF EMPTY WAGONS JUST GATHERING COBWEBS!
ICE CREAM
6

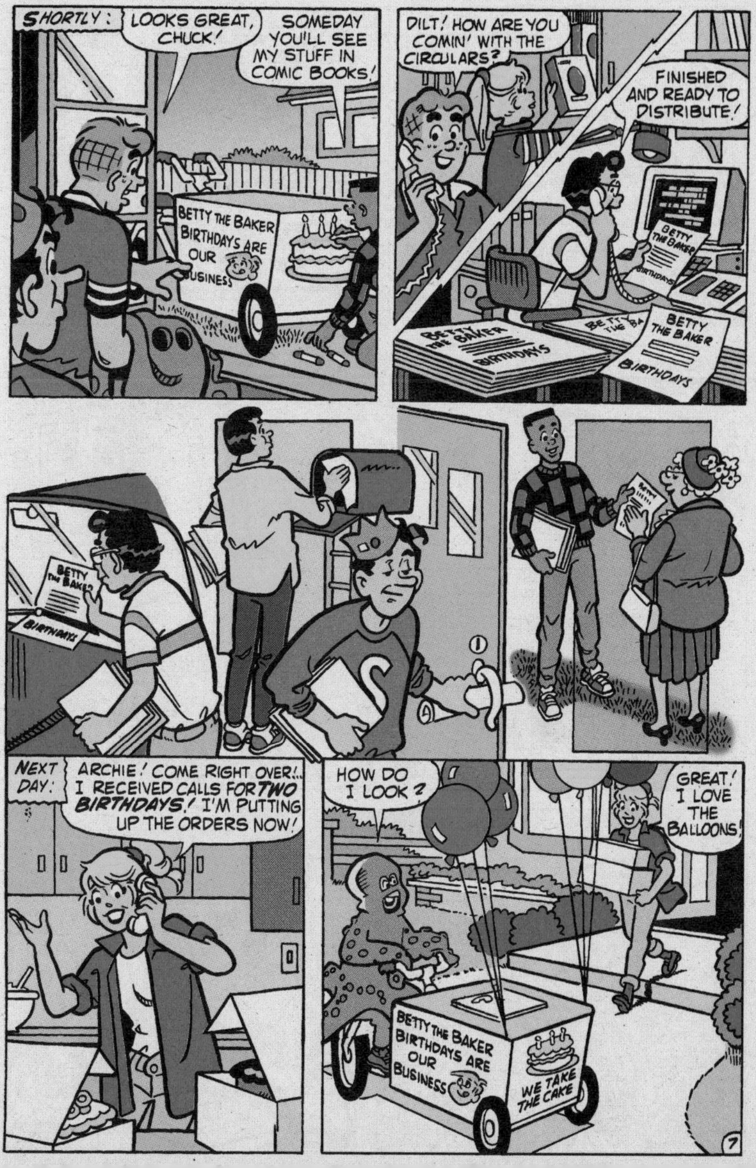
SHORTLY:
LOOKS GREAT, CHUCK!
SOMEDAY YOU'LL SEE MY STUFF IN COMIC BOOKS!
BETTY THE BAKER BIRTHDAYS ARE OUR BUSINESS
DILT! HOW ARE YOU COMIN' WITH THE CIRCULARS?
FINISHED AND READY TO DISTRIBUTE!
BETTY THE BAKER BIRTHDAYS
BETTY THE BAKER BIRTHDAYS
BETTY THE BAKER BIRTHDAYS
NEXT DAY:
ARCHIE! COME RIGHT OVER!... I RECEIVED CALLS FOR TWO BIRTHDAYS! I'M PUTTING UP THE ORDERS NOW!
HOW DO I LOOK?
GREAT! I LOVE THE BALLOONS!
BETTY THE BAKER BIRTHDAYS ARE OUR BUSINESS
WE TAKE THE CAKE
7

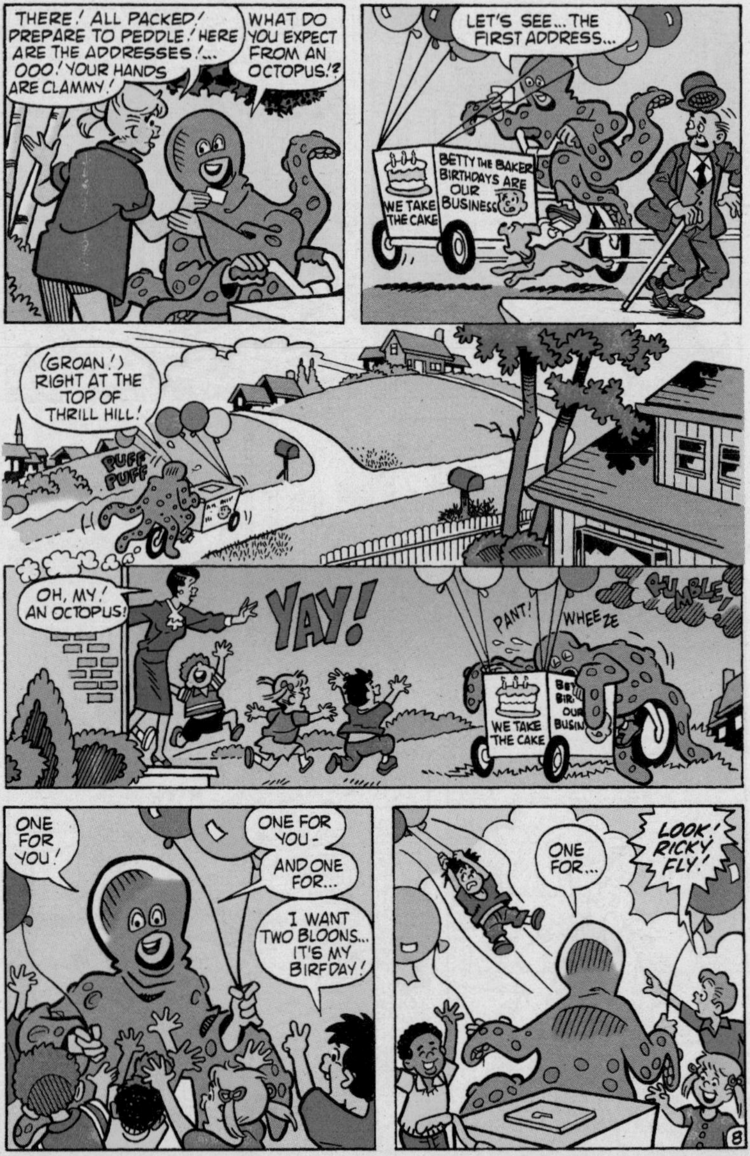

THERE! ALL PACKED! PREPARE TO PEDDLE! HERE ARE THE ADDRESSES!... OOO! YOUR HANDS ARE CLAMMY!
WHAT DO YOU EXPECT FROM AN OCTOPUS!?
LET'S SEE... THE FIRST ADDRESS...
BETTY THE BAKER BIRTHDAYS ARE OUR BUSINESS
WE TAKE THE CAKE
(GROAN!) RIGHT AT THE TOP OF THRILL HILL!
PUFF PUFF
OH, MY! AN OCTOPUS!
YAY!
PANT!
WHEEZE
RUMBLE!
WE TAKE THE CAKE
ONE FOR YOU!
ONE FOR YOU -
AND ONE FOR...
I WANT TWO BLOONS... IT'S MY BIRFDAY!
ONE FOR...
LOOK! RICKY FLY!
8

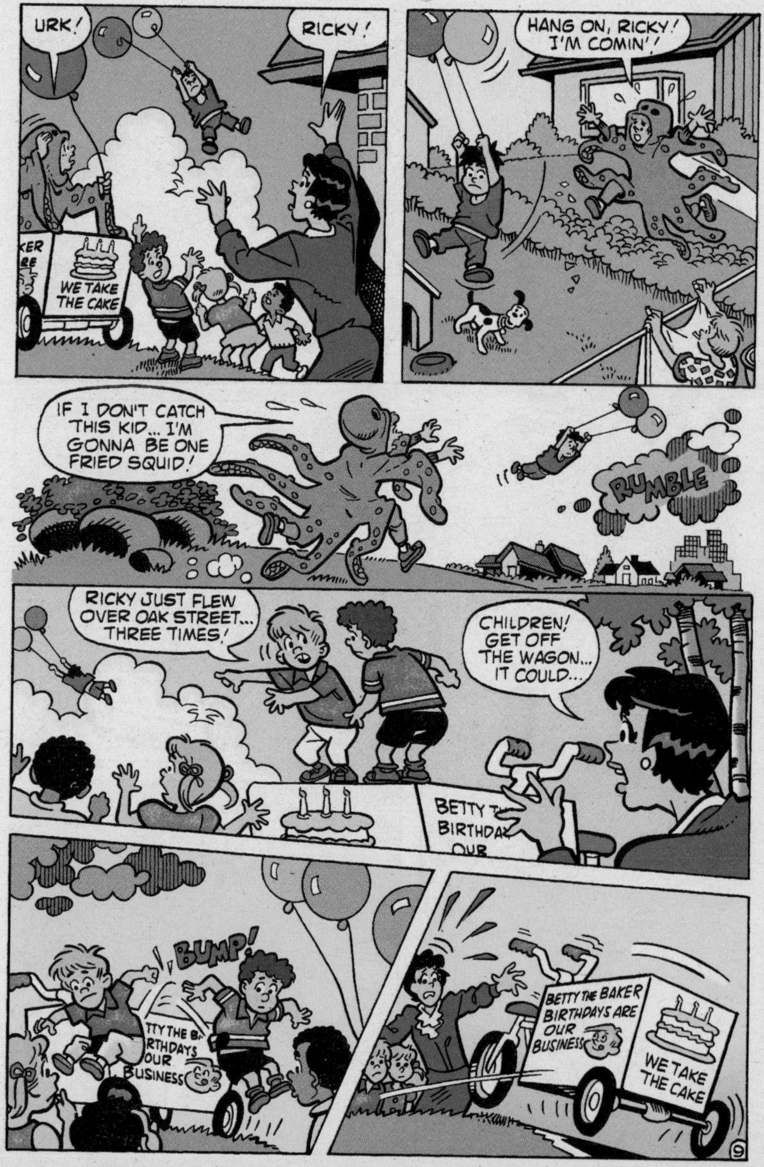
URK!
RICKY!
KER
RE
WE TAKE THE CAKE
HANG ON, RICKY! I'M COMIN'!
IF I DON'T CATCH THIS KID... I'M GONNA BE ONE FRIED SQUID!
RUMBLE
RICKY JUST FLEW OVER OAK STREET... THREE TIMES!
CHILDREN! GET OFF THE WAGON... IT COULD...
BETTY T
BIRTHDA
OUR
BUMP!
TTY THE B
RTHDAYS
OUR
BUSINESS
BETTY THE BAKER
BIRTHDAYS ARE
OUR
BUSINESS
WE TAKE THE CAKE

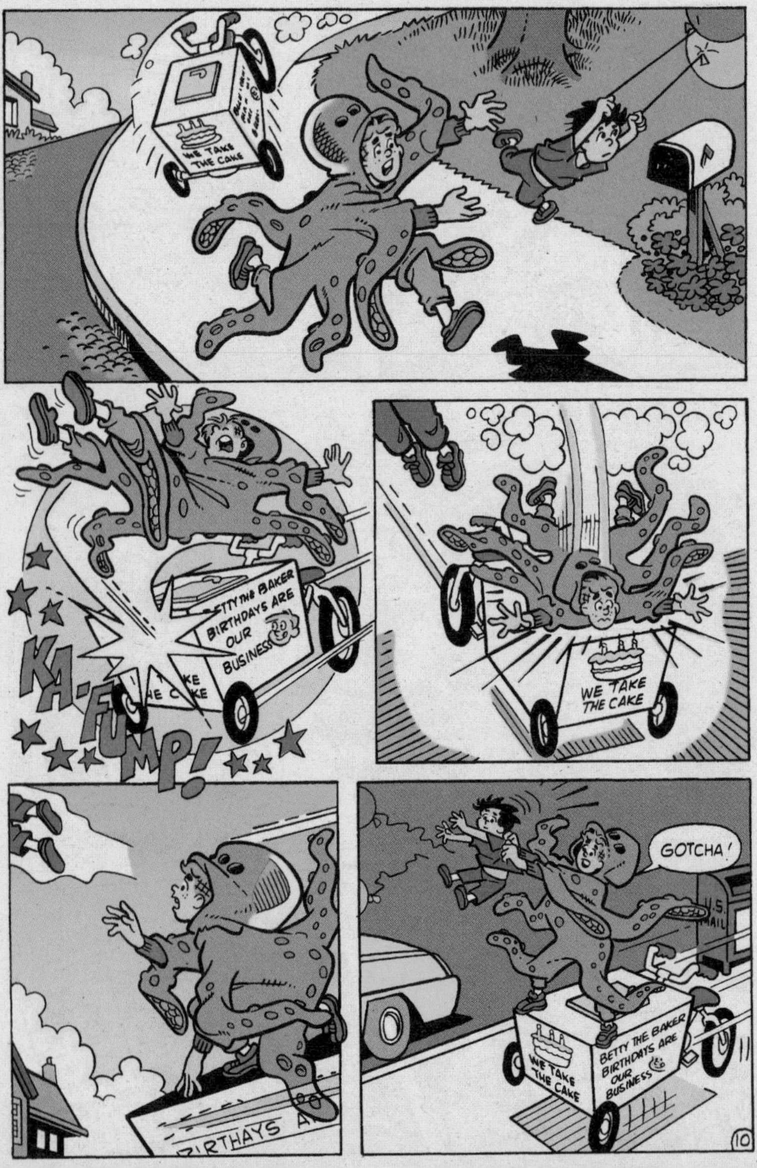
WE TAKE THE CAKE
BETTY THE BAKER BIRTHDAYS ARE OUR BUSINESS
KA-FUMP!
WE TAKE THE CAKE
GOTCHA!
U.S. MAIL
BETTY THE BAKER BIRTHDAYS ARE OUR BUSINESS
WE TAKE THE CAKE

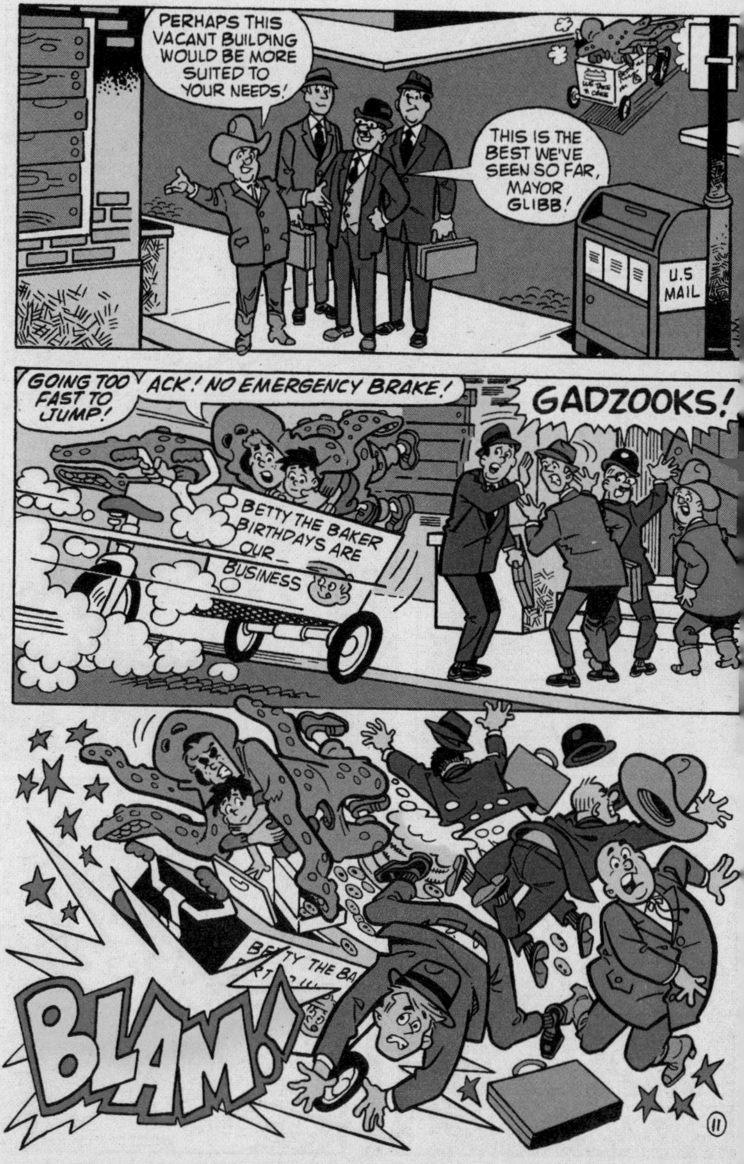

PERHAPS THIS VACANT BUILDING WOULD BE MORE SUITED TO YOUR NEEDS!
THIS IS THE BEST WE'VE SEEN SO FAR, MAYOR GLIBB!
U.S MAIL
GOING TOO FAST TO JUMP!
ACK! NO EMERGENCY BRAKE!
GADZOOKS!
BETTY THE BAKER BIRTHDAYS ARE OUR BUSINESS
BLAM!

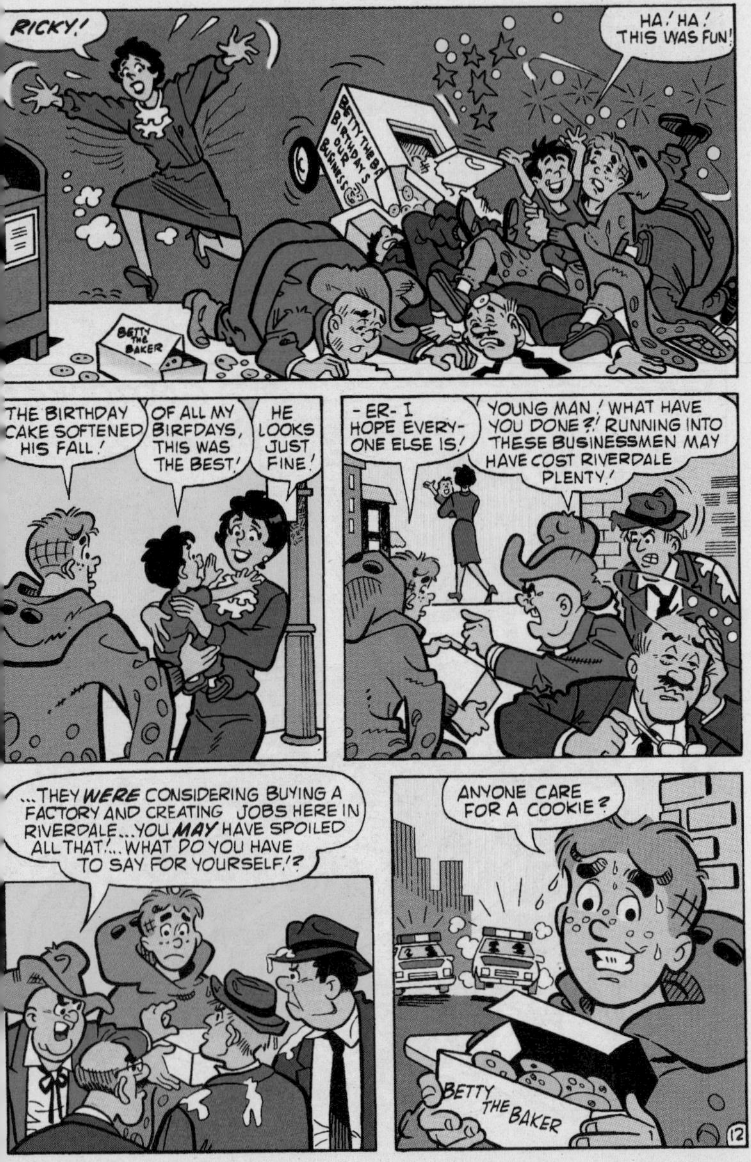
RICKY!
HA! HA! THIS WAS FUN!
BETTY THE BA... BIRTHDAYS OUR BUSINESS
BETTY THE BAKER
THE BIRTHDAY CAKE SOFTENED HIS FALL!
OF ALL MY BIRFDAYS, THIS WAS THE BEST!
HE LOOKS JUST FINE!
-ER- I HOPE EVERY-ONE ELSE IS!
YOUNG MAN! WHAT HAVE YOU DONE?! RUNNING INTO THESE BUSINESSMEN MAY HAVE COST RIVERDALE PLENTY!
...THEY WERE CONSIDERING BUYING A FACTORY AND CREATING JOBS HERE IN RIVERDALE...YOU MAY HAVE SPOILED ALL THAT!...WHAT DO YOU HAVE TO SAY FOR YOURSELF!?
ANYONE CARE FOR A COOKIE?
BETTY THE BAKER
12

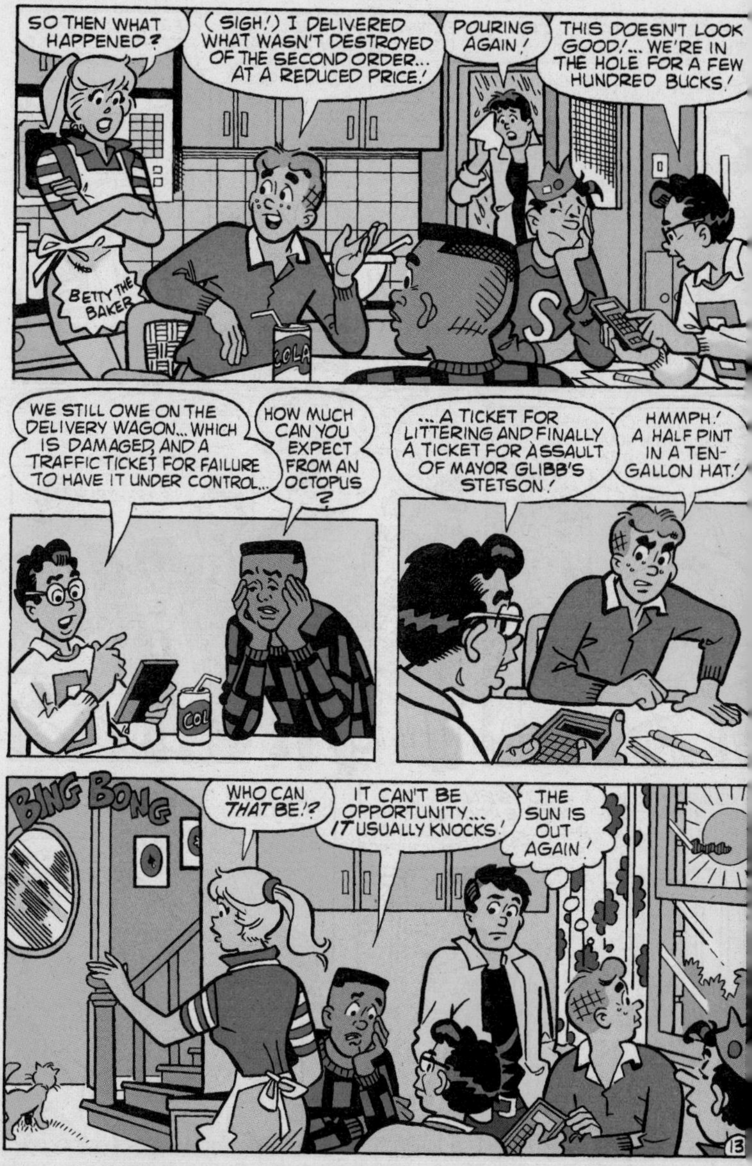
SO THEN WHAT HAPPENED?
(SIGH!) I DELIVERED WHAT WASN'T DESTROYED OF THE SECOND ORDER... AT A REDUCED PRICE!
POURING AGAIN!
THIS DOESN'T LOOK GOOD!... WE'RE IN THE HOLE FOR A FEW HUNDRED BUCKS!
BETTY THE BAKER
COLA
WE STILL OWE ON THE DELIVERY WAGON... WHICH IS DAMAGED, AND A TRAFFIC TICKET FOR FAILURE TO HAVE IT UNDER CONTROL...
HOW MUCH CAN YOU EXPECT FROM AN OCTOPUS?
... A TICKET FOR LITTERING AND FINALLY A TICKET FOR ASSAULT OF MAYOR GLIBB'S STETSON!
HMMPH! A HALF PINT IN A TEN-GALLON HAT!
BING BONG
WHO CAN THAT BE!?
IT CAN'T BE OPPORTUNITY... IT USUALLY KNOCKS!
THE SUN IS OUT AGAIN!

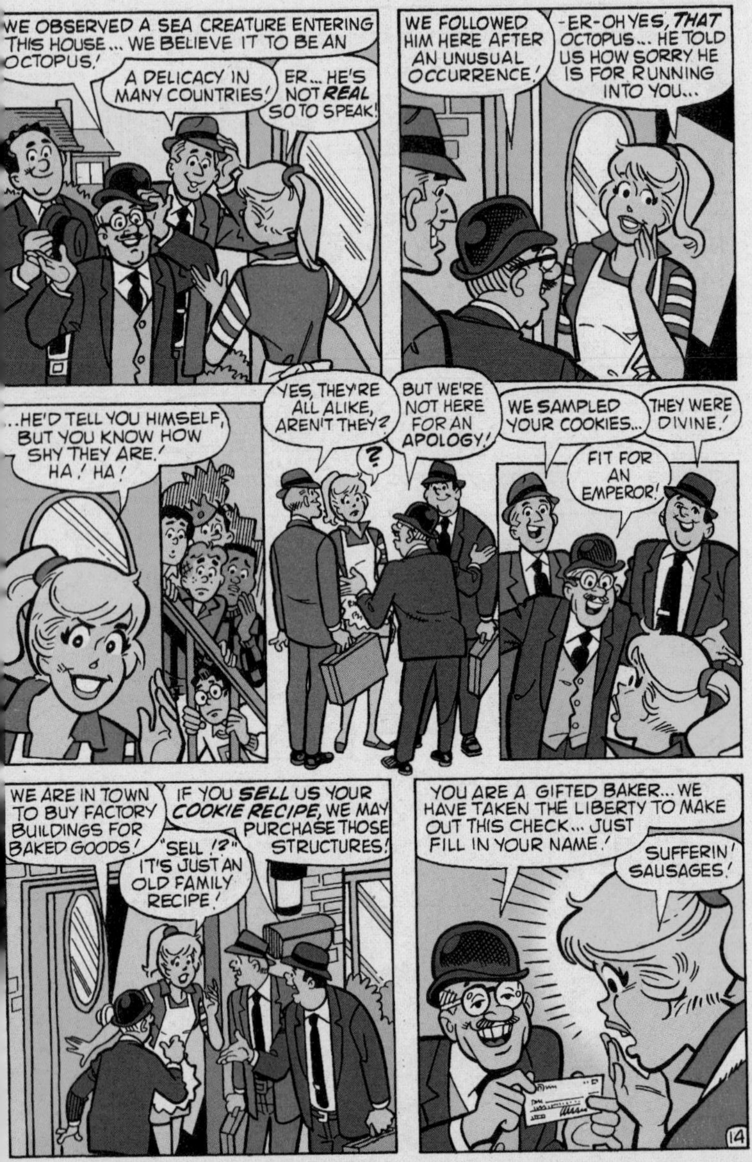
WE OBSERVED A SEA CREATURE ENTERING THIS HOUSE... WE BELIEVE IT TO BE AN OCTOPUS!
A DELICACY IN MANY COUNTRIES!
ER... HE'S NOT REAL SO TO SPEAK!
WE FOLLOWED HIM HERE AFTER AN UNUSUAL OCCURRENCE!
-ER-OH YES, THAT OCTOPUS... HE TOLD US HOW SORRY HE IS FOR RUNNING INTO YOU...
...HE'D TELL YOU HIMSELF, BUT YOU KNOW HOW SHY THEY ARE! HA! HA!
YES, THEY'RE ALL ALIKE, AREN'T THEY?
?
BUT WE'RE NOT HERE FOR AN APOLOGY!
WE SAMPLED YOUR COOKIES...
THEY WERE DIVINE!
FIT FOR AN EMPEROR!
WE ARE IN TOWN TO BUY FACTORY BUILDINGS FOR BAKED GOODS!
IF YOU SELL US YOUR COOKIE RECIPE, WE MAY PURCHASE THOSE STRUCTURES!
"SELL!?" IT'S JUST AN OLD FAMILY RECIPE!
YOU ARE A GIFTED BAKER... WE HAVE TAKEN THE LIBERTY TO MAKE OUT THIS CHECK... JUST FILL IN YOUR NAME!
SUFFERIN' SAUSAGES!
14

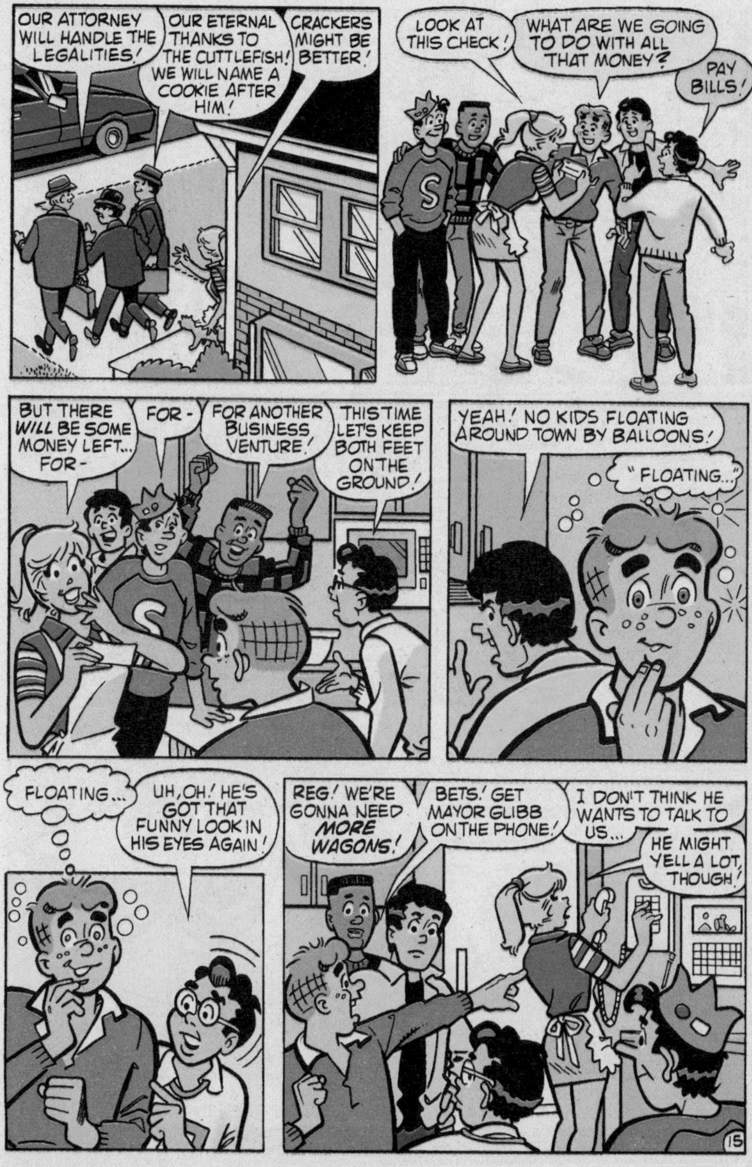
OUR ATTORNEY WILL HANDLE THE LEGALITIES!
OUR ETERNAL THANKS TO THE CUTTLEFISH! WE WILL NAME A COOKIE AFTER HIM!
CRACKERS MIGHT BE BETTER!
LOOK AT THIS CHECK!
WHAT ARE WE GOING TO DO WITH ALL THAT MONEY?
PAY BILLS!
BUT THERE WILL BE SOME MONEY LEFT... FOR-
FOR-
FOR ANOTHER BUSINESS VENTURE!
THIS TIME LET'S KEEP BOTH FEET ON THE GROUND!
YEAH! NO KIDS FLOATING AROUND TOWN BY BALLOONS!
"FLOATING..."
FLOATING...
UH, OH! HE'S GOT THAT FUNNY LOOK IN HIS EYES AGAIN!
REG! WE'RE GONNA NEED MORE WAGONS!
BETS! GET MAYOR GLIBB ON THE PHONE!
I DON'T THINK HE WANTS TO TALK TO US...
HE MIGHT YELL A LOT, THOUGH!
15

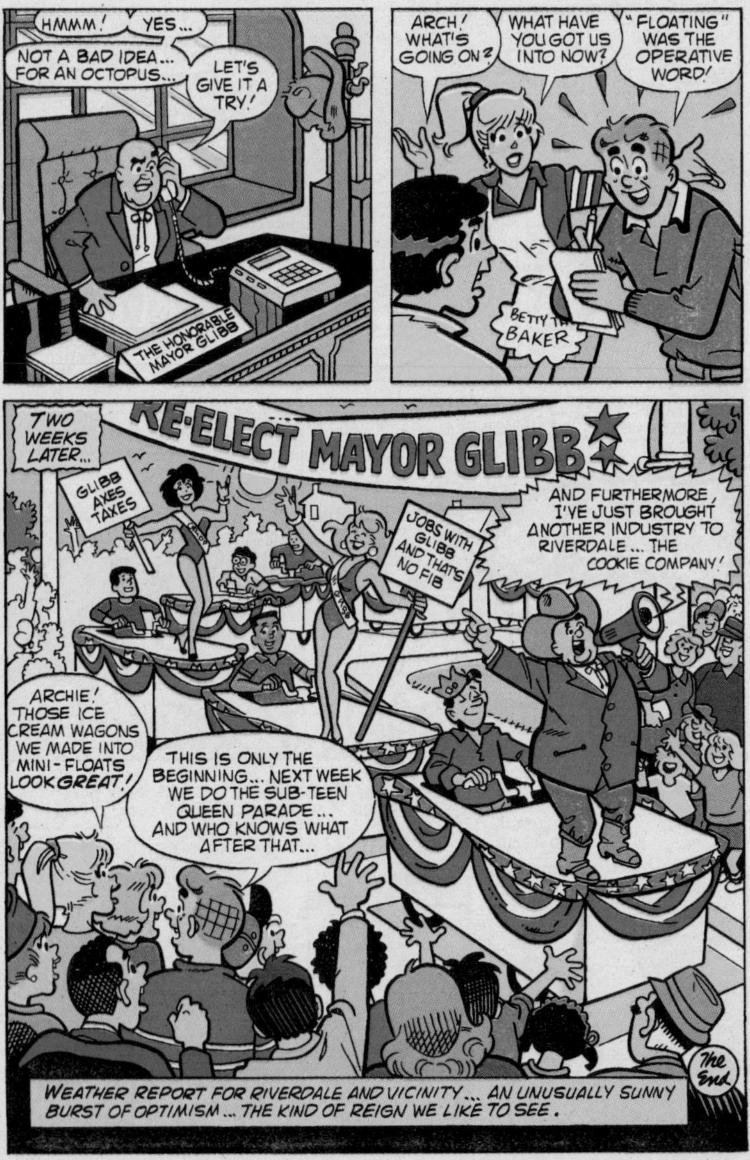
HMMM!
YES...
NOT A BAD IDEA... FOR AN OCTOPUS...
LET'S GIVE IT A TRY!
THE HONORABLE MAYOR GLIBB
ARCH! WHAT'S GOING ON?
WHAT HAVE YOU GOT US INTO NOW?
"FLOATING" WAS THE OPERATIVE WORD!
BAKER
TWO WEEKS LATER...
RE-ELECT MAYOR GLIBB
GLIBB AXES TAXES
JOBS WITH GLIBB AND THAT'S NO FIB
AND FURTHERMORE, I'VE JUST BROUGHT ANOTHER INDUSTRY TO RIVERDALE ... THE COOKIE COMPANY!
ARCHIE! THOSE ICE CREAM WAGONS WE MADE INTO MINI-FLOATS LOOK GREAT!
THIS IS ONLY THE BEGINNING... NEXT WEEK WE DO THE SUB-TEEN QUEEN PARADE... AND WHO KNOWS WHAT AFTER THAT...
The End
WEATHER REPORT FOR RIVERDALE AND VICINITY... AN UNUSUALLY SUNNY BURST OF OPTIMISM... THE KIND OF REIGN WE LIKE TO SEE.

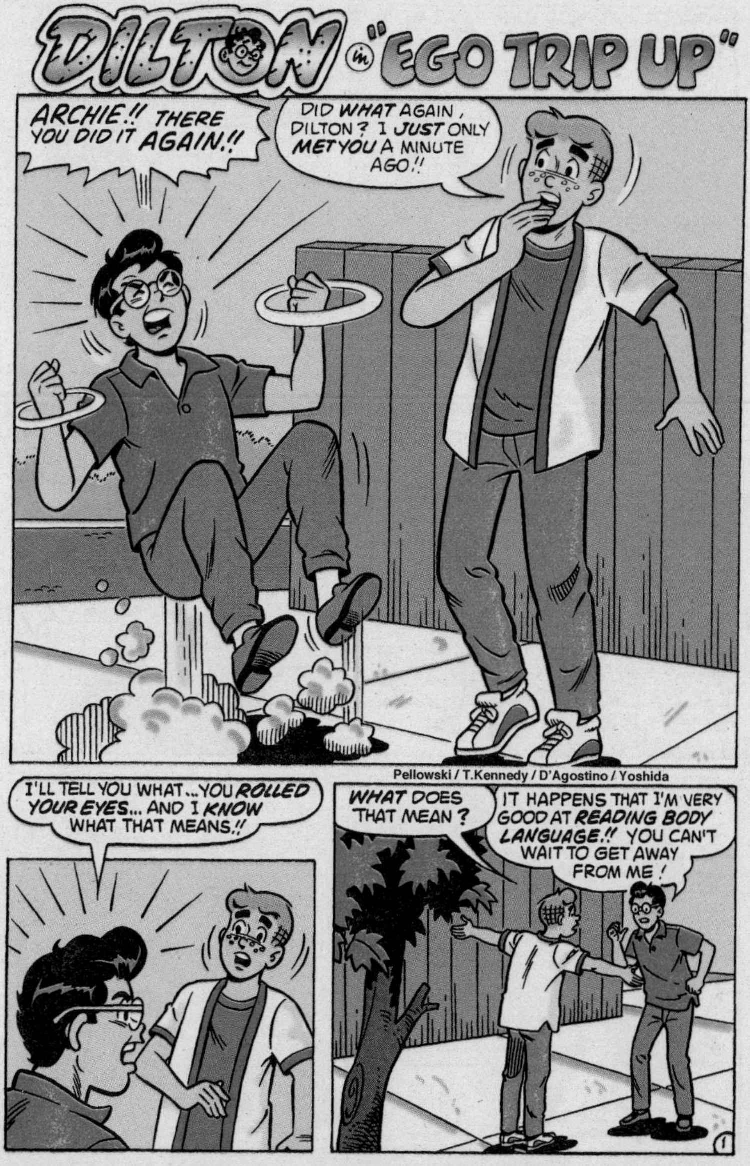
DILTON in "EGO TRIP UP"
ARCHIE!! THERE YOU DID IT AGAIN!!
DID WHAT AGAIN, DILTON? I JUST ONLY MET YOU A MINUTE AGO!!
Pellowski / T.Kennedy / D'Agostino / Yoshida
I'LL TELL YOU WHAT...YOU ROLLED YOUR EYES... AND I KNOW WHAT THAT MEANS!!
WHAT DOES THAT MEAN?
IT HAPPENS THAT I'M VERY GOOD AT READING BODY LANGUAGE!! YOU CAN'T WAIT TO GET AWAY FROM ME!
1

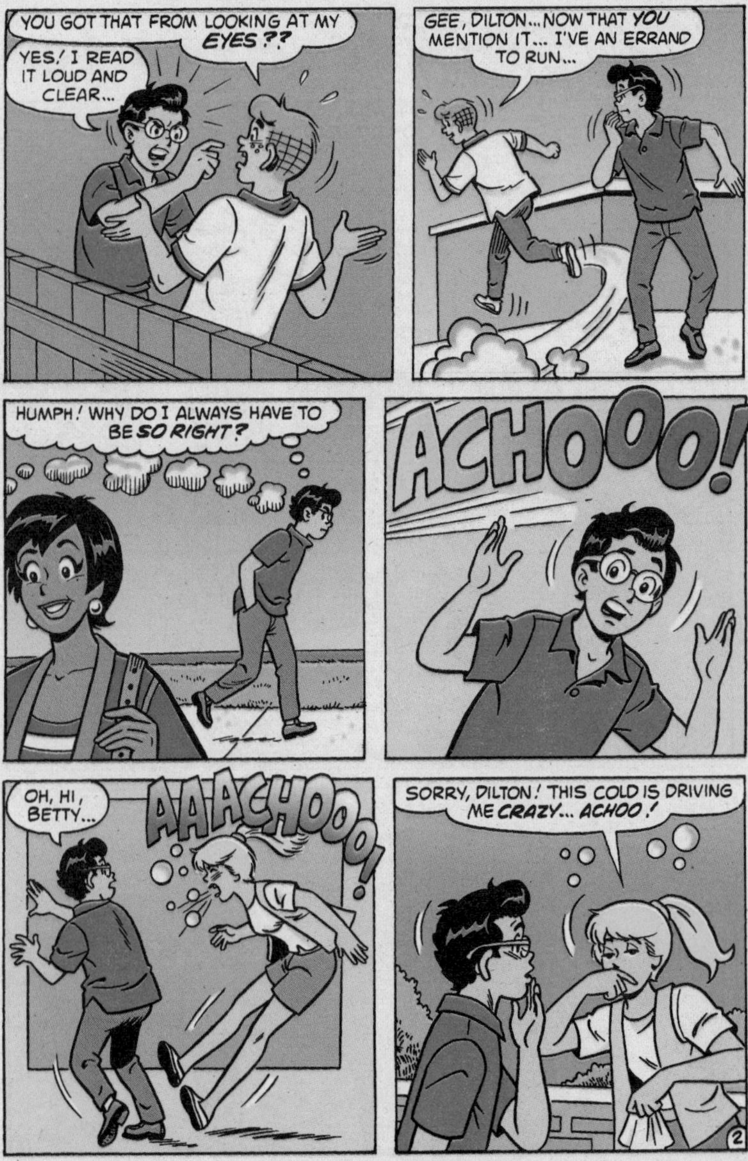
YOU GOT THAT FROM LOOKING AT MY EYES??
YES! I READ IT LOUD AND CLEAR...
GEE, DILTON...NOW THAT YOU MENTION IT... I'VE AN ERRAND TO RUN...
HUMPH! WHY DO I ALWAYS HAVE TO BE SO RIGHT?
ACHOOO!
OH, HI, BETTY...
AAACHOOOO!
SORRY, DILTON! THIS COLD IS DRIVING ME CRAZY... ACHOO!
2

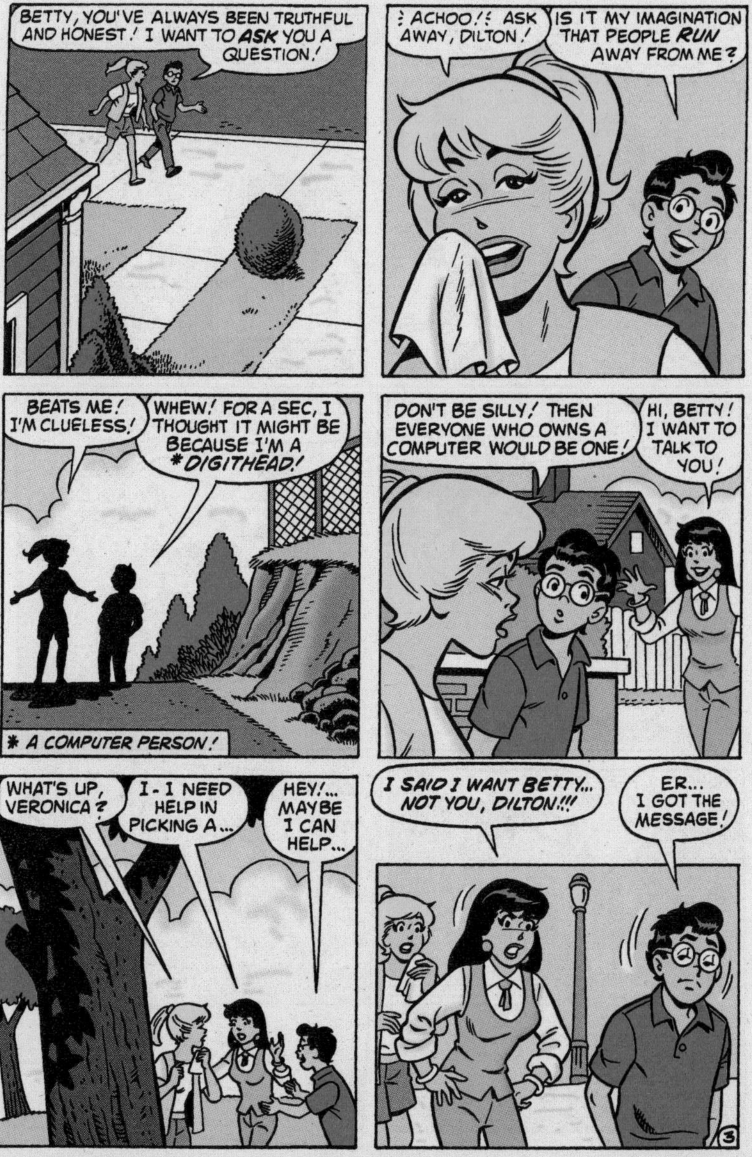
BETTY, YOU'VE ALWAYS BEEN TRUTHFUL AND HONEST! I WANT TO ASK YOU A QUESTION!
ACHOO!! ASK AWAY, DILTON!
IS IT MY IMAGINATION THAT PEOPLE RUN AWAY FROM ME?
BEATS ME! I'M CLUELESS!
WHEW! FOR A SEC, I THOUGHT IT MIGHT BE BECAUSE I'M A *DIGITHEAD!
* A COMPUTER PERSON!
DON'T BE SILLY! THEN EVERYONE WHO OWNS A COMPUTER WOULD BE ONE!
HI, BETTY! I WANT TO TALK TO YOU!
WHAT'S UP, VERONICA?
I - I NEED HELP IN PICKING A...
HEY!... MAYBE I CAN HELP...
I SAID I WANT BETTY... NOT YOU, DILTON!!!
ER... I GOT THE MESSAGE!
3

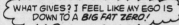

WHAT GIVES? I FEEL LIKE MY EGO IS DOWN TO A *BIG FAT ZERO!*

HUMPH! IF MY EGO ISN'T SHATTERED ENOUGH... HERE COMES REGGIE... THE BIG DEFLATER!

HI, DILTON! HOW IS *MR. KNOW-IT-ALL* TODAY?

WELL, NOW THAT YOU MENTION IT...

ER... NEVER MIND!

I JUST REMEMBERED, I HAVE TO BE SOME PLACE ...*ANY* PLACE BUT HERE!

HUMPH! I FEEL MY *EGO* IS *NOW* *BELOW* ZERO!

HEAD'S UP, DILTON!

WOMP!

④

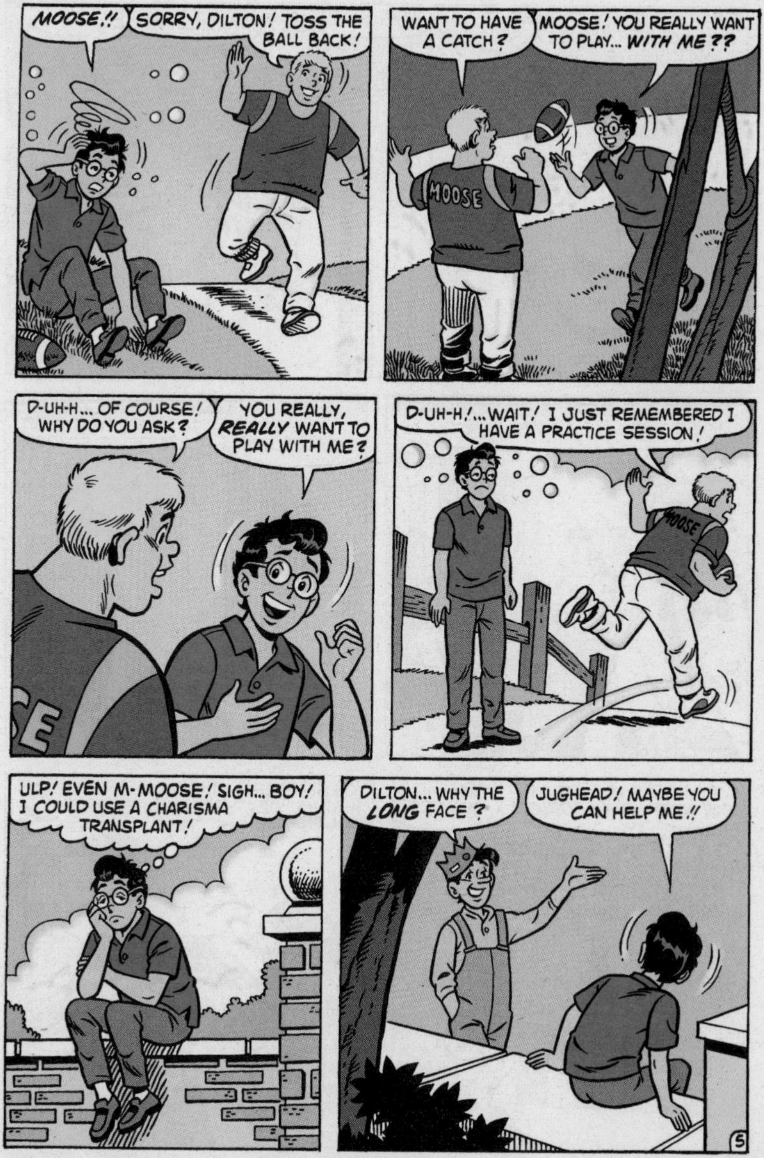
MOOSE!!
SORRY, DILTON! TOSS THE BALL BACK!
WANT TO HAVE A CATCH?
MOOSE! YOU REALLY WANT TO PLAY... WITH ME??
MOOSE
D-UH-H... OF COURSE! WHY DO YOU ASK?
YOU REALLY, REALLY WANT TO PLAY WITH ME?
D-UH-H!... WAIT! I JUST REMEMBERED I HAVE A PRACTICE SESSION!
MOOSE
ULP! EVEN M-MOOSE! SIGH... BOY! I COULD USE A CHARISMA TRANSPLANT!
DILTON... WHY THE LONG FACE?
JUGHEAD! MAYBE YOU CAN HELP ME!!
5

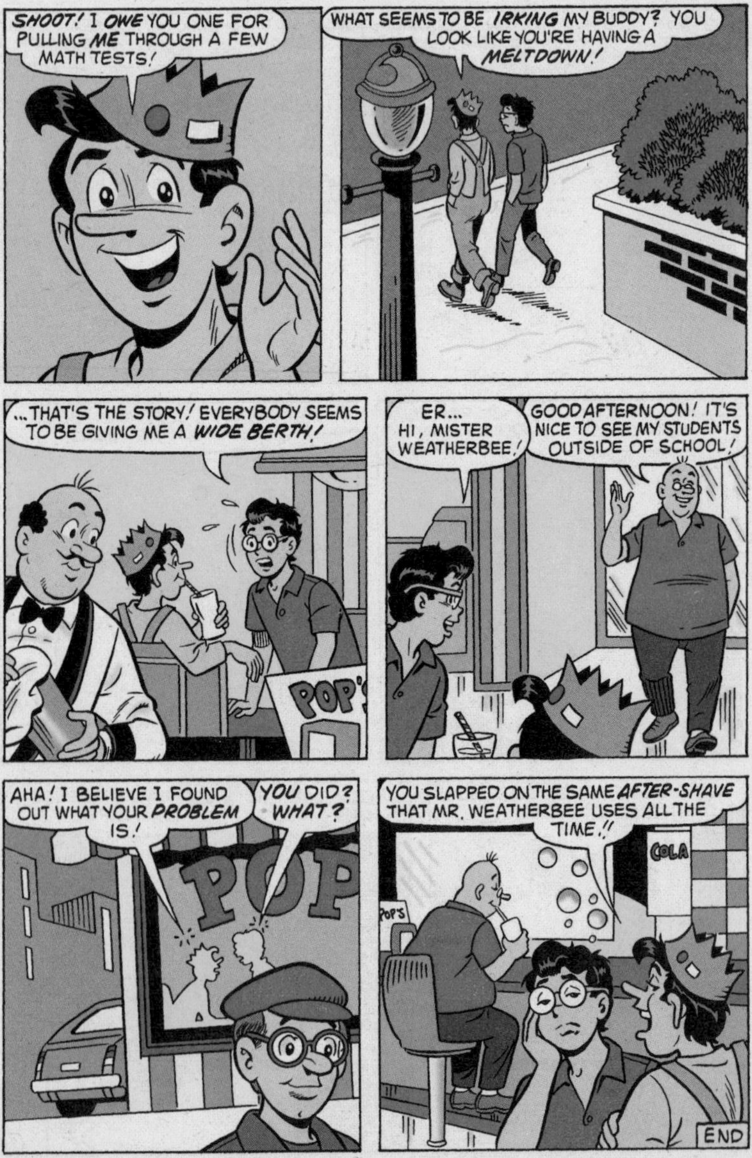
SHOOT! I OWE YOU ONE FOR PULLING ME THROUGH A FEW MATH TESTS!
WHAT SEEMS TO BE IRKING MY BUDDY? YOU LOOK LIKE YOU'RE HAVING A MELTDOWN!
...THAT'S THE STORY! EVERYBODY SEEMS TO BE GIVING ME A WIDE BERTH!
POP'S
ER... HI, MISTER WEATHERBEE!
GOOD AFTERNOON! IT'S NICE TO SEE MY STUDENTS OUTSIDE OF SCHOOL!
AHA! I BELIEVE I FOUND OUT WHAT YOUR PROBLEM IS!
YOU DID? WHAT?
POP
YOU SLAPPED ON THE SAME AFTER-SHAVE THAT MR. WEATHERBEE USES ALL THE TIME!!
COLA
POP'S
END

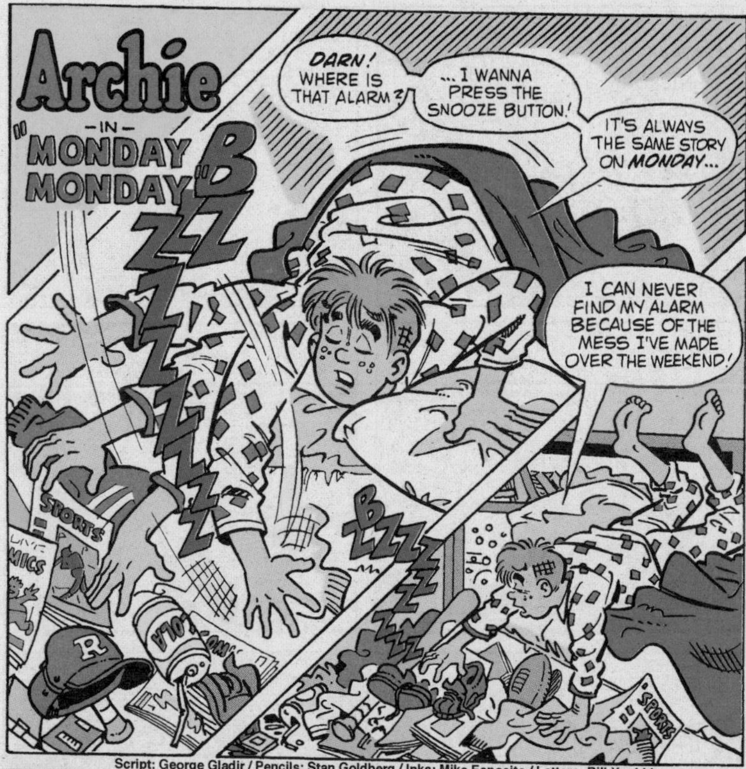
Archie
-IN-
"MONDAY MONDAY"
DARN! WHERE IS THAT ALARM?
...I WANNA PRESS THE SNOOZE BUTTON!
IT'S ALWAYS THE SAME STORY ON MONDAY...
BZZZZZZZZ
I CAN NEVER FIND MY ALARM BECAUSE OF THE MESS I'VE MADE OVER THE WEEKEND!
BZZZZZZZ
SPORTS

Script: George Gladir / Pencils: Stan Goldberg / Inks: Mike Esposito / Letters: Bill Yoshida

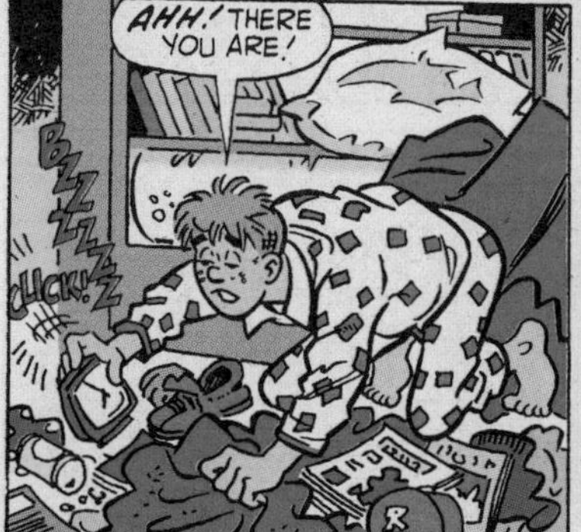
AHH! THERE YOU ARE!
BZZZZZ
CLICK!

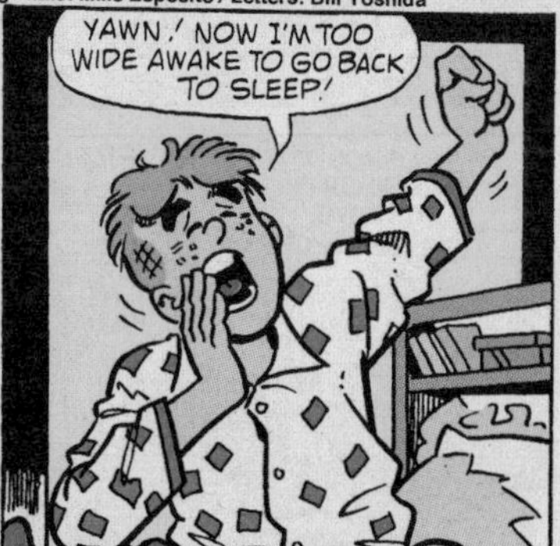
YAWN! NOW I'M TOO WIDE AWAKE TO GO BACK TO SLEEP!

Mom: ARCHIE, COME AND EAT YOUR BREAKFAST!

Archie: I STILL HAVE TO FINISH MY HOMEWORK!

Mr. Andrews: WHY DO YOU PUT IT OFF UNTIL THE LAST MINUTE? YOU HAD ALL WEEKEND TO DO YOUR HOMEWORK!

Archie: THAT'S WHY I KEPT PUTTING IT OFF! I FIGURED I HAD ALL WEEKEND TO DO IT!

Archie: DON'T WORRY, MA! IT'S ONLY ON MONDAYS THAT I HAVE THIS PROBLEM!

Archie: I SEE YOU HAVE MONDAY BLUES, TOO!

Jughead: IN SPADES!

SCHOOL BUS

Archie: THEY SHOULD ABOLISH MONDAYS!

RIVERDALE HIGH SCHOOL

Jughead: YAWN! THE WEEK SHOULD BEGIN WITH A TUESDAY!

MOOS

2

GLORIOUS MONDAY! IT'S *THE DAY* I LOOK FORWARD TO!

... AFTER A BORING WEEKEND I CAN HIT THE BLACKBOARD AGAIN!

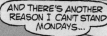

AND THERE'S ANOTHER REASON I CAN'T STAND MONDAYS...

OVER THE WEEKEND I ALWAYS SEEM TO FORGET MY LOCKER COMBINATION!

IS IT 36-18-5 OR 56-5-18?

I'LL TELL YOU SOMETHING ELSE THAT YOU FORGOT OVER THE WEEKEND, ARCHIE!

WHAT?

THAT YOUR LOCKER IS OVER HERE!

3

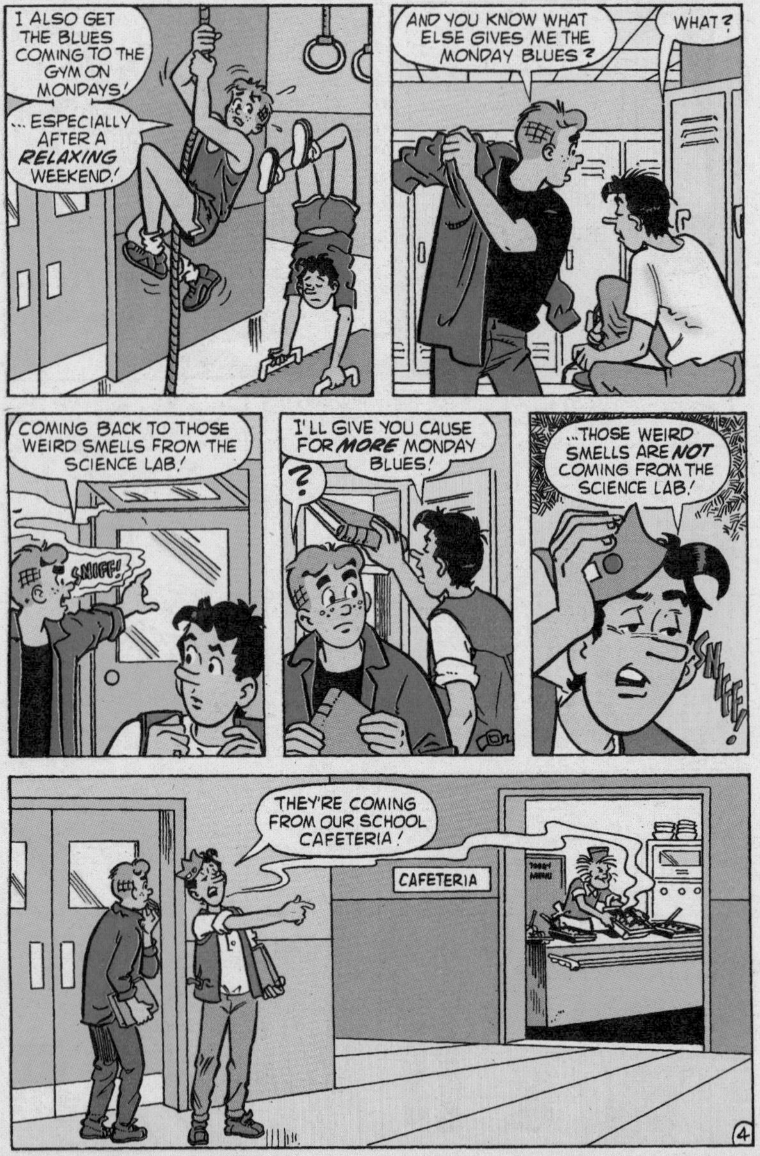

I ALSO GET THE BLUES COMING TO THE GYM ON MONDAYS!
... ESPECIALLY AFTER A *RELAXING* WEEKEND!
AND YOU KNOW WHAT ELSE GIVES ME THE MONDAY BLUES?
WHAT?
COMING BACK TO THOSE WEIRD SMELLS FROM THE SCIENCE LAB!
SNIFF!
I'LL GIVE YOU CAUSE FOR *MORE* MONDAY BLUES!
?
...THOSE WEIRD SMELLS ARE *NOT* COMING FROM THE SCIENCE LAB!
SNIFF!
THEY'RE COMING FROM OUR SCHOOL CAFETERIA!
CAFETERIA
4

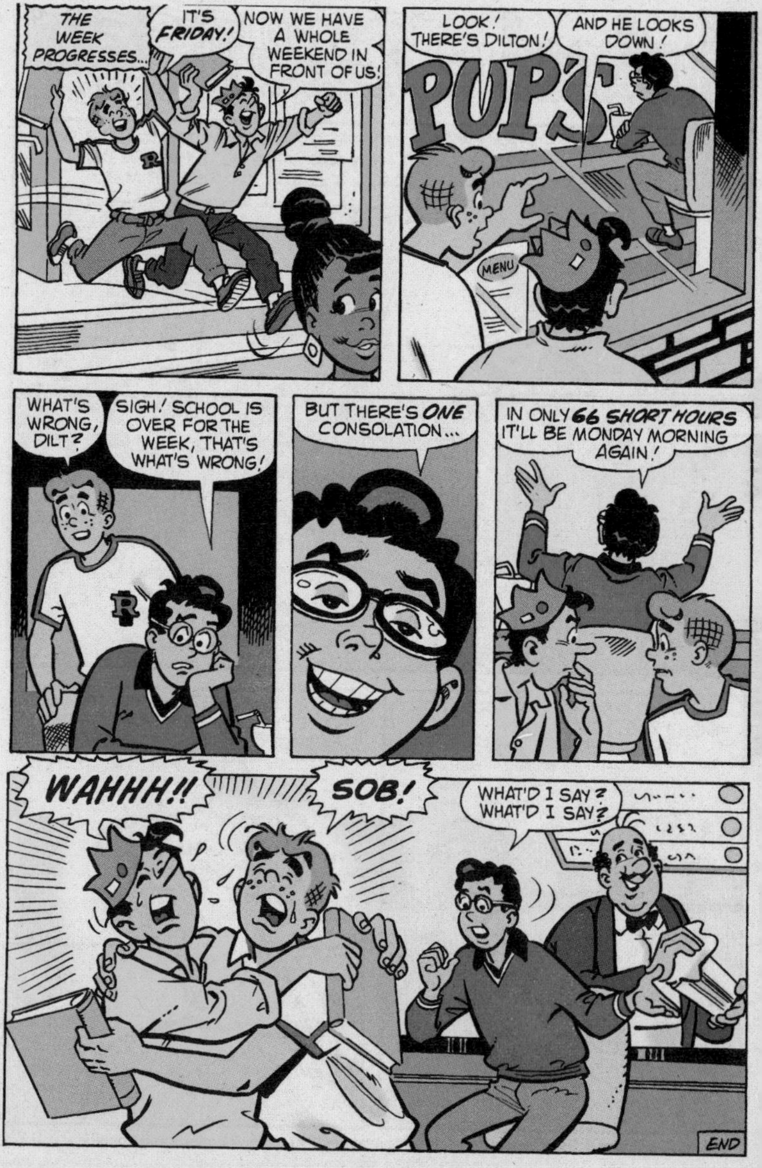
THE WEEK PROGRESSES...
IT'S FRIDAY!
NOW WE HAVE A WHOLE WEEKEND IN FRONT OF US!
LOOK! THERE'S DILTON!
AND HE LOOKS DOWN!
POP'S
MENU
WHAT'S WRONG, DILT?
SIGH! SCHOOL IS OVER FOR THE WEEK, THAT'S WHAT'S WRONG!
BUT THERE'S ONE CONSOLATION...
IN ONLY 66 SHORT HOURS IT'LL BE MONDAY MORNING AGAIN!
WAHHH!!
SOB!
WHAT'D I SAY? WHAT'D I SAY?
END

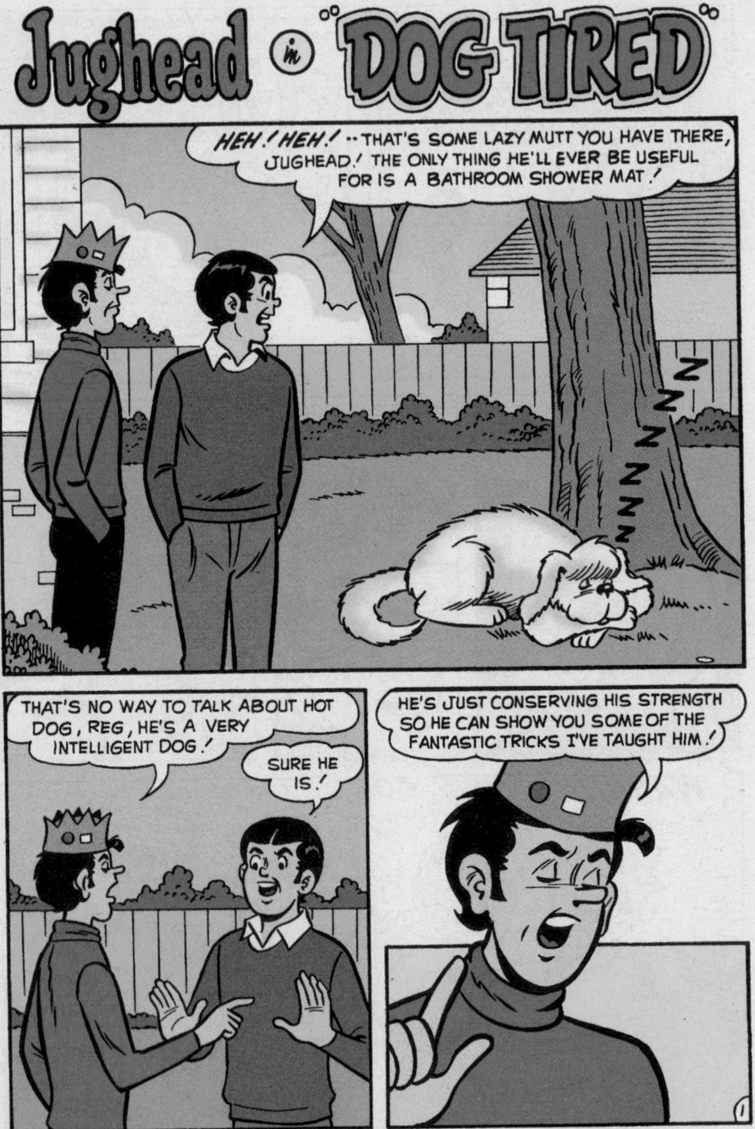
Jughead in "DOG TIRED"
HEH! HEH! --THAT'S SOME LAZY MUTT YOU HAVE THERE, JUGHEAD! THE ONLY THING HE'LL EVER BE USEFUL FOR IS A BATHROOM SHOWER MAT!
Z Z Z Z Z Z
THAT'S NO WAY TO TALK ABOUT HOT DOG, REG, HE'S A VERY INTELLIGENT DOG!
SURE HE IS!
HE'S JUST CONSERVING HIS STRENGTH SO HE CAN SHOW YOU SOME OF THE FANTASTIC TRICKS I'VE TAUGHT HIM!
1

Script & Pencils: Dick Malmgren / Inks: Jon D'Agostino / Letters: Bill Yoshida

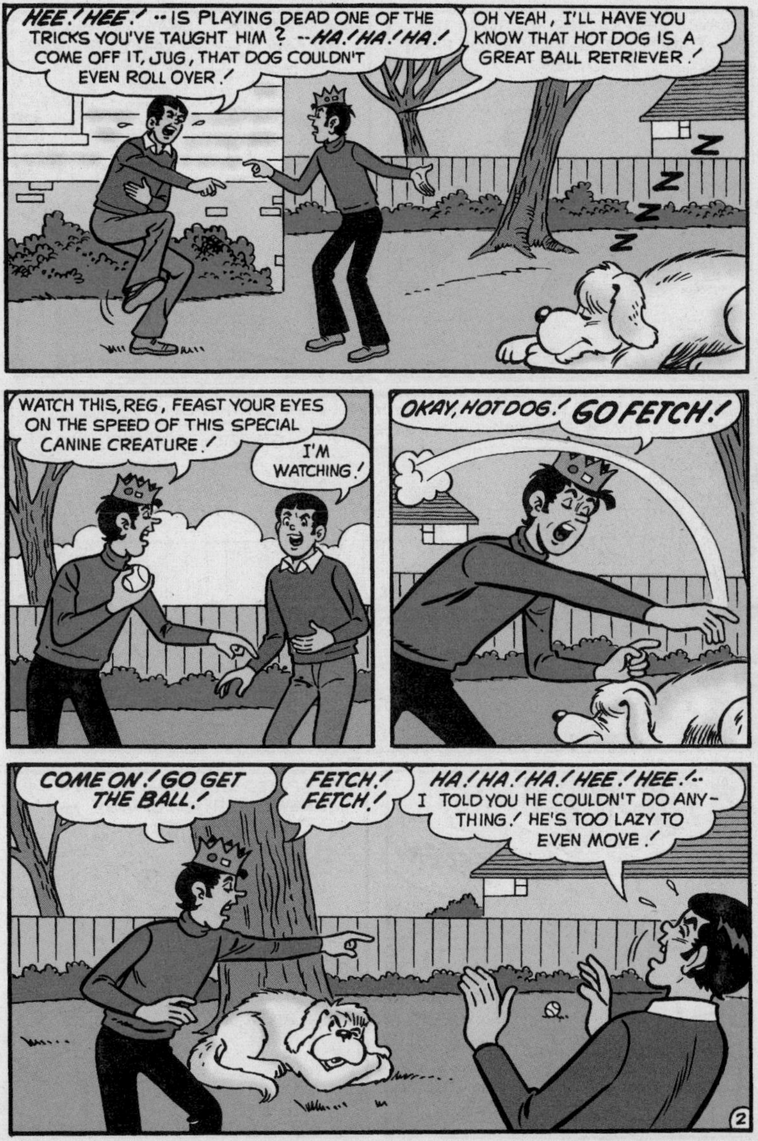
HEE! HEE! --IS PLAYING DEAD ONE OF THE TRICKS YOU'VE TAUGHT HIM? --HA! HA! HA! COME OFF IT, JUG, THAT DOG COULDN'T EVEN ROLL OVER!
OH YEAH, I'LL HAVE YOU KNOW THAT HOT DOG IS A GREAT BALL RETRIEVER!
Z
Z
Z
Z
WATCH THIS, REG, FEAST YOUR EYES ON THE SPEED OF THIS SPECIAL CANINE CREATURE!
I'M WATCHING!
OKAY, HOT DOG! GO FETCH!
COME ON! GO GET THE BALL!
FETCH! FETCH!
HA! HA! HA! HEE! HEE!.. I TOLD YOU HE COULDN'T DO ANY-THING! HE'S TOO LAZY TO EVEN MOVE!
2

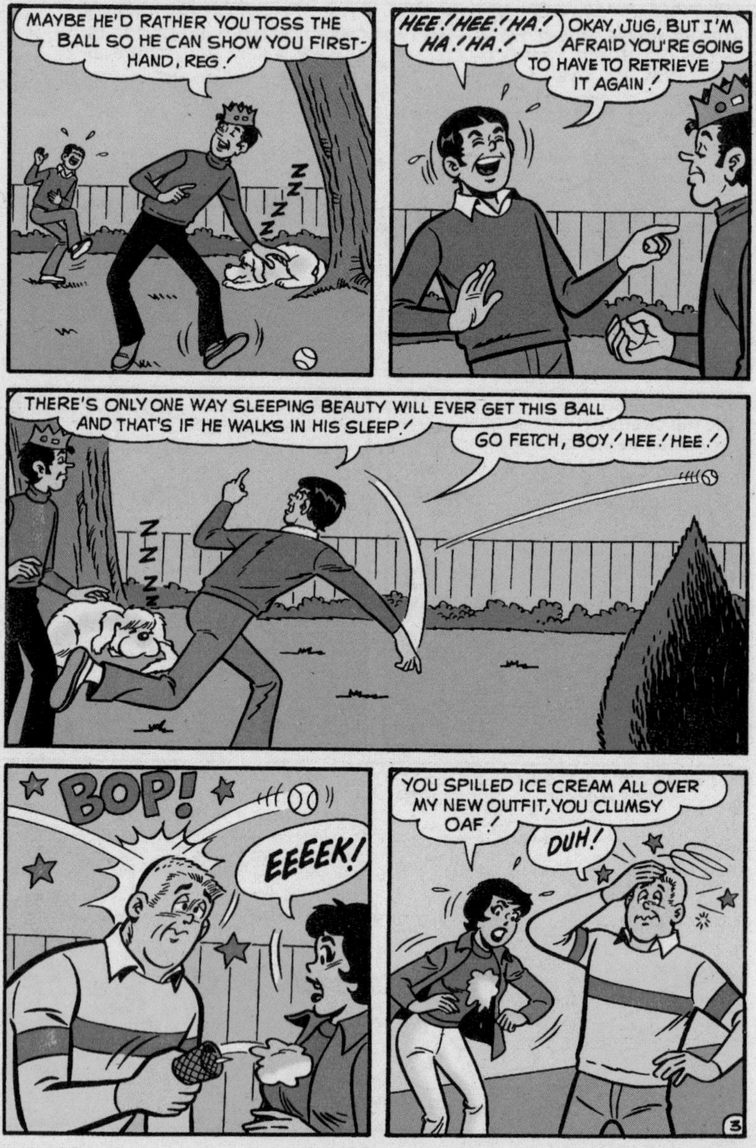
MAYBE HE'D RATHER YOU TOSS THE BALL SO HE CAN SHOW YOU FIRST-HAND, REG!
HEE! HEE! HA! HA! HA!
OKAY, JUG, BUT I'M AFRAID YOU'RE GOING TO HAVE TO RETRIEVE IT AGAIN!
THERE'S ONLY ONE WAY SLEEPING BEAUTY WILL EVER GET THIS BALL AND THAT'S IF HE WALKS IN HIS SLEEP!
GO FETCH, BOY! HEE! HEE!
BOP!
EEEEK!
YOU SPILLED ICE CREAM ALL OVER MY NEW OUTFIT, YOU CLUMSY OAF!
DUH!
3

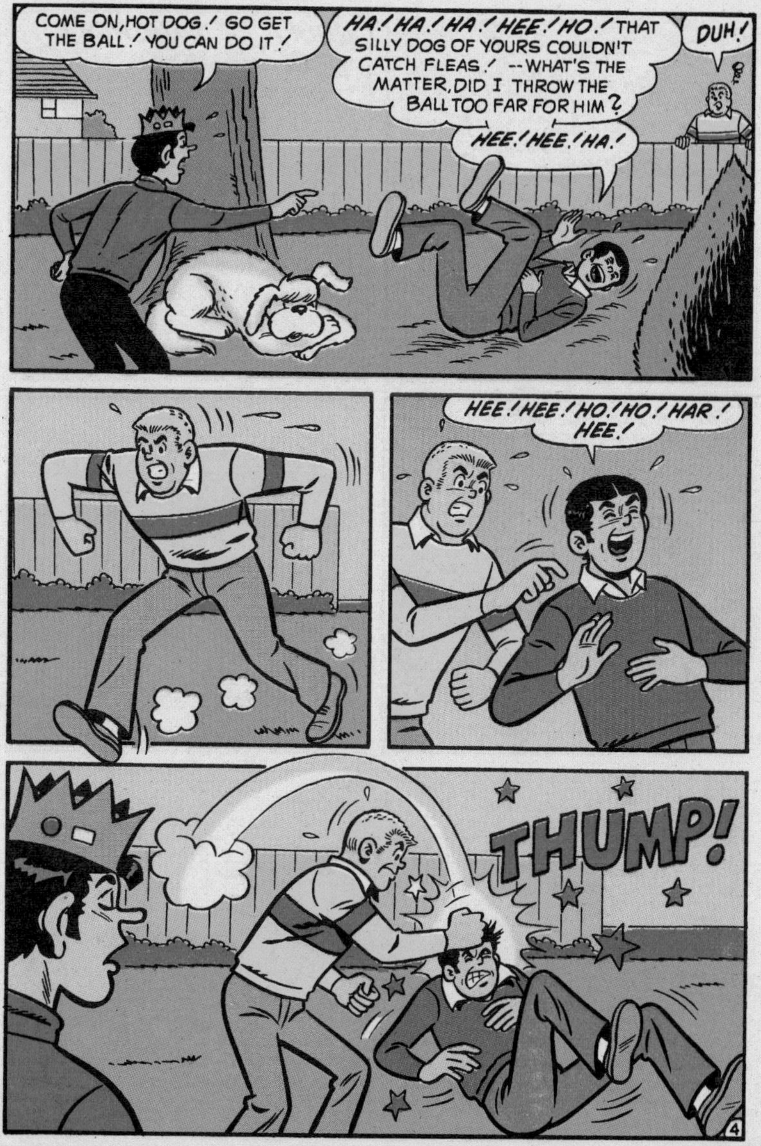
COME ON, HOT DOG! GO GET THE BALL! YOU CAN DO IT!
HA! HA! HA! HEE! HO! THAT SILLY DOG OF YOURS COULDN'T CATCH FLEAS! --WHAT'S THE MATTER, DID I THROW THE BALL TOO FAR FOR HIM?
HEE! HEE! HA!
DUH!
HEE! HEE! HO! HO! HAR! HEE!
THUMP!
4

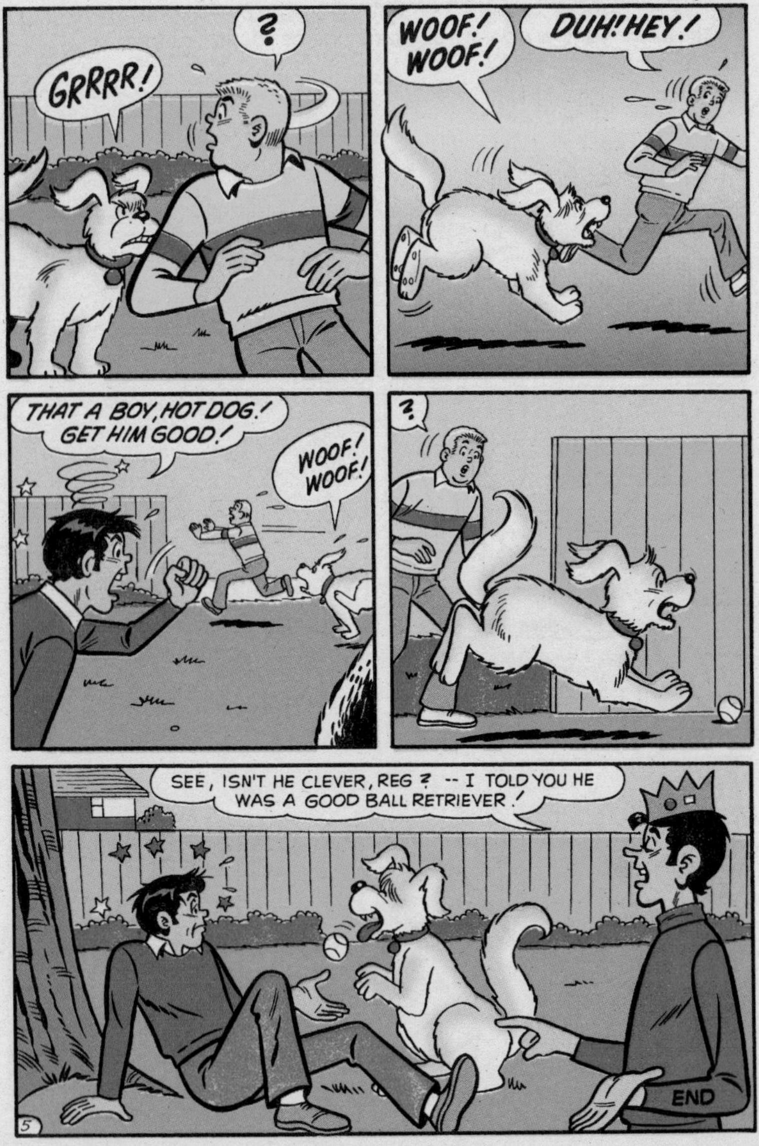
GRRRR!
?
WOOF! WOOF!
DUH! HEY!
THAT A BOY, HOT DOG! GET HIM GOOD!
WOOF! WOOF!
?
SEE, ISN'T HE CLEVER, REG ? -- I TOLD YOU HE WAS A GOOD BALL RETRIEVER!
END
5

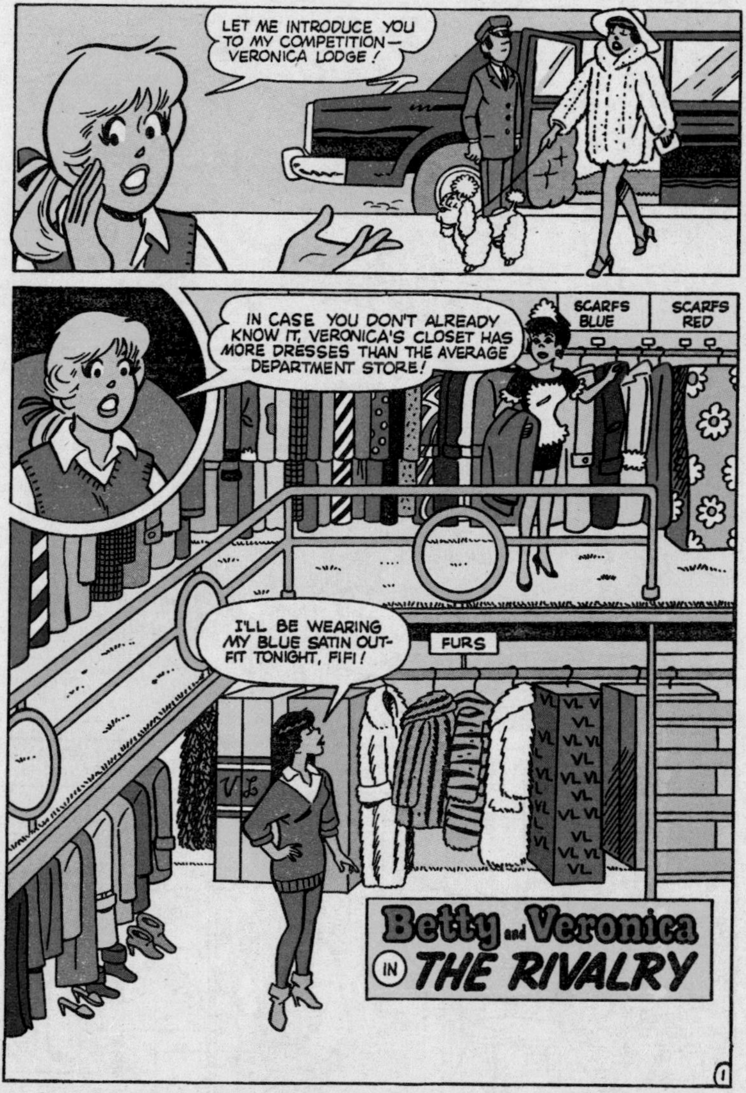
LET ME INTRODUCE YOU TO MY COMPETITION— VERONICA LODGE!
IN CASE YOU DON'T ALREADY KNOW IT, VERONICA'S CLOSET HAS MORE DRESSES THAN THE AVERAGE DEPARTMENT STORE!
SCARFS BLUE
SCARFS RED
I'LL BE WEARING MY BLUE SATIN OUT-FIT TONIGHT, FIFI!
FURS
Betty and Veronica
IN THE RIVALRY
1

Script: George Gladir / Pencils: Dan DeCarlo Jr. / Inks: Jim DeCarlo / Letters: Bill Yoshida

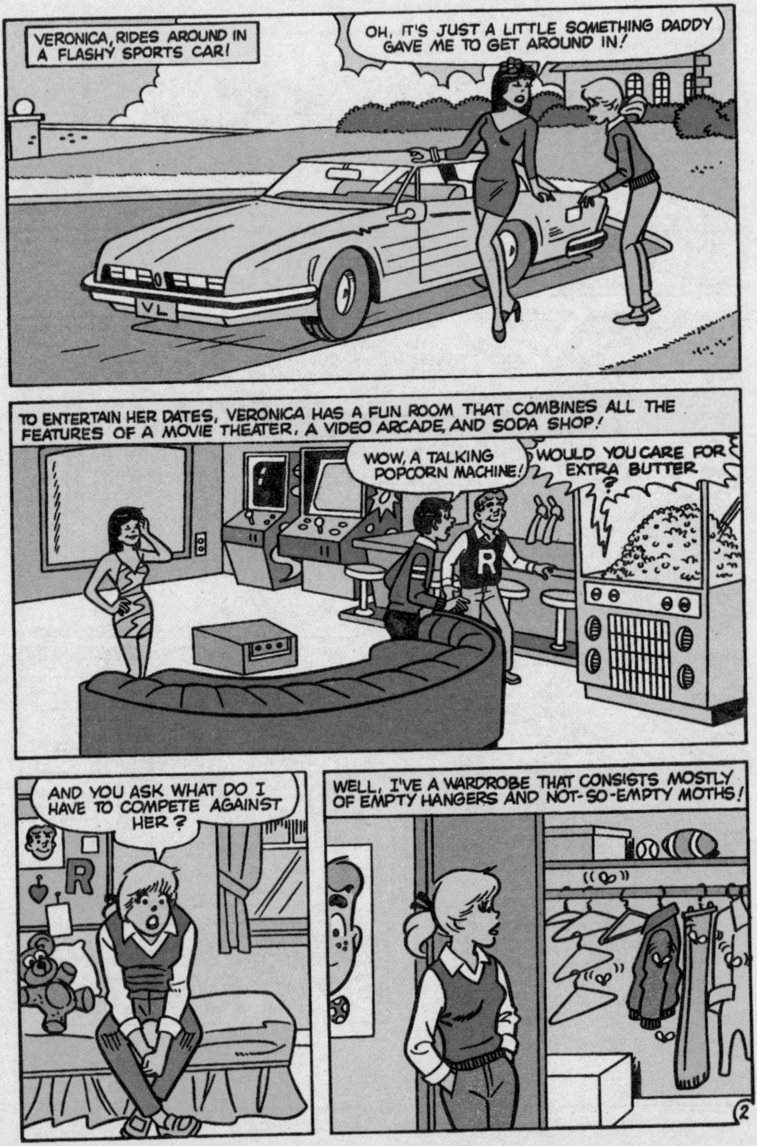
VERONICA, RIDES AROUND IN A FLASHY SPORTS CAR!
OH, IT'S JUST A LITTLE SOMETHING DADDY GAVE ME TO GET AROUND IN!
VL
TO ENTERTAIN HER DATES, VERONICA HAS A FUN ROOM THAT COMBINES ALL THE FEATURES OF A MOVIE THEATER, A VIDEO ARCADE, AND SODA SHOP!
WOW, A TALKING POPCORN MACHINE!
WOULD YOU CARE FOR EXTRA BUTTER ?
R
AND YOU ASK WHAT DO I HAVE TO COMPETE AGAINST HER ?
R
WELL, I'VE A WARDROBE THAT CONSISTS MOSTLY OF EMPTY HANGERS AND NOT-SO-EMPTY MOTHS!

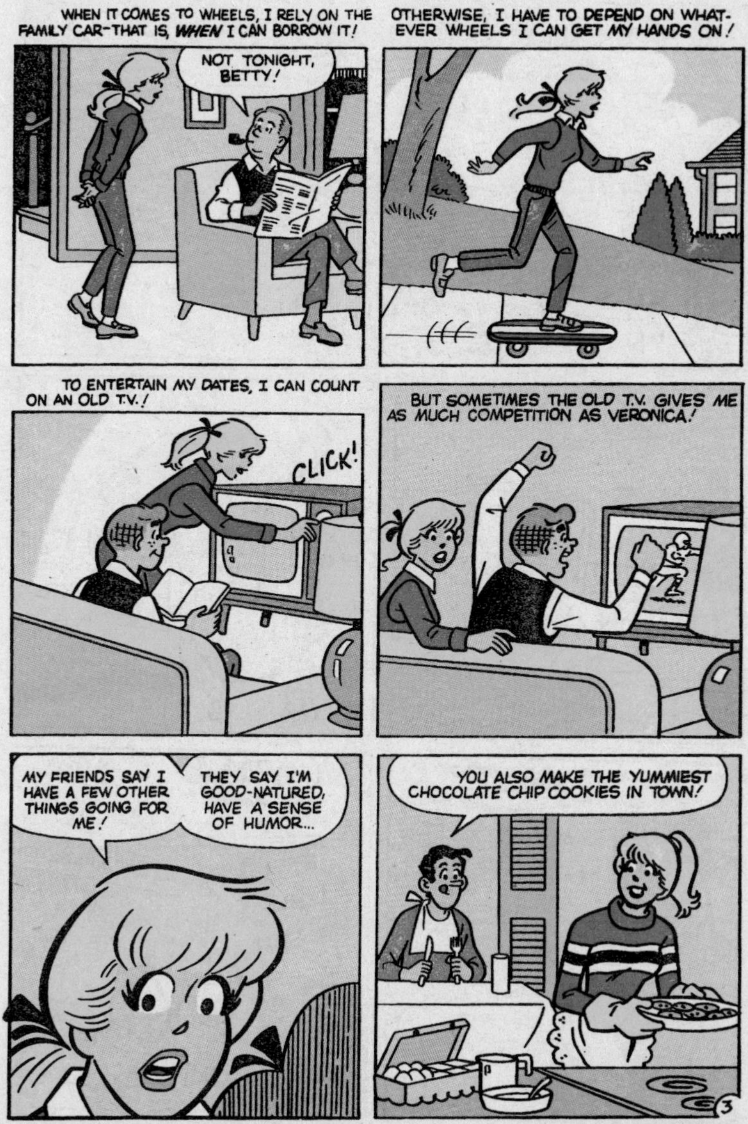

WHEN IT COMES TO WHEELS, I RELY ON THE FAMILY CAR—THAT IS, WHEN I CAN BORROW IT!
NOT TONIGHT, BETTY!
OTHERWISE, I HAVE TO DEPEND ON WHATEVER WHEELS I CAN GET MY HANDS ON!
TO ENTERTAIN MY DATES, I CAN COUNT ON AN OLD T.V.!
CLICK!
BUT SOMETIMES THE OLD T.V. GIVES ME AS MUCH COMPETITION AS VERONICA!
MY FRIENDS SAY I HAVE A FEW OTHER THINGS GOING FOR ME!
THEY SAY I'M GOOD-NATURED, HAVE A SENSE OF HUMOR...
YOU ALSO MAKE THE YUMMIEST CHOCOLATE CHIP COOKIES IN TOWN!
3

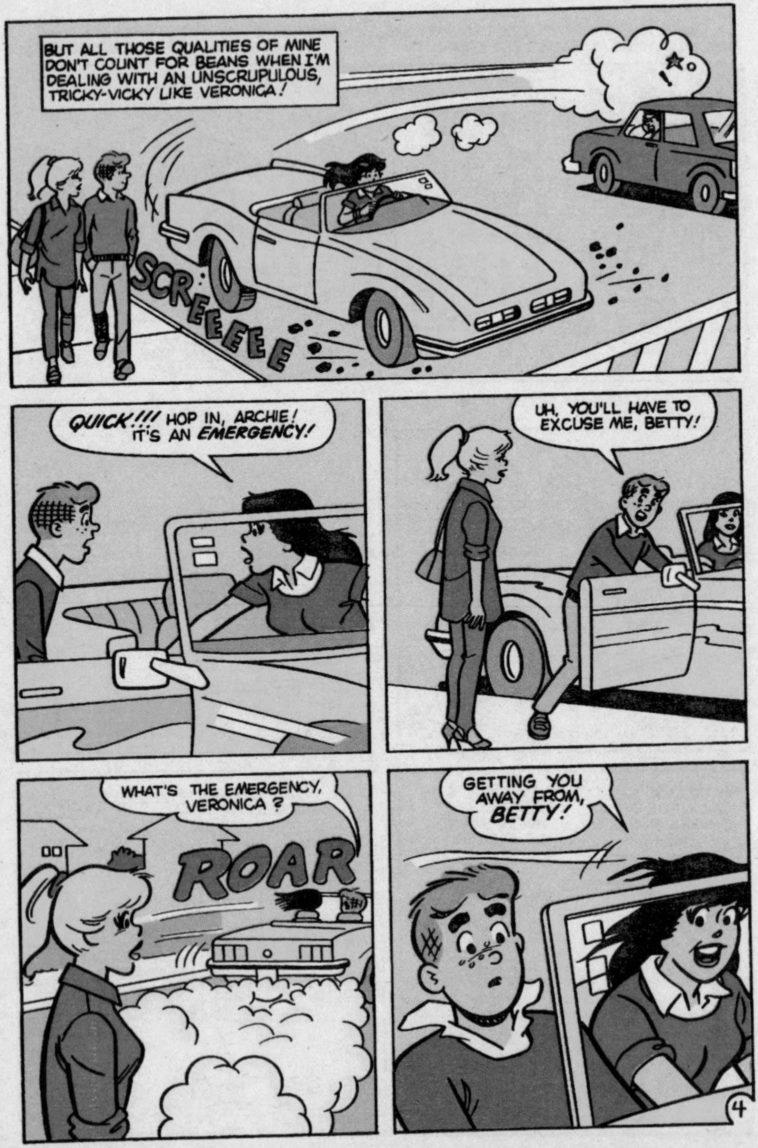

BUT ALL THOSE QUALITIES OF MINE DON'T COUNT FOR BEANS WHEN I'M DEALING WITH AN UNSCRUPULOUS, TRICKY-VICKY LIKE VERONICA!
SCREEEEEE
QUICK!!!! HOP IN, ARCHIE! IT'S AN EMERGENCY!
UH, YOU'LL HAVE TO EXCUSE ME, BETTY!
WHAT'S THE EMERGENCY, VERONICA?
ROAR
GETTING YOU AWAY FROM, BETTY!
4

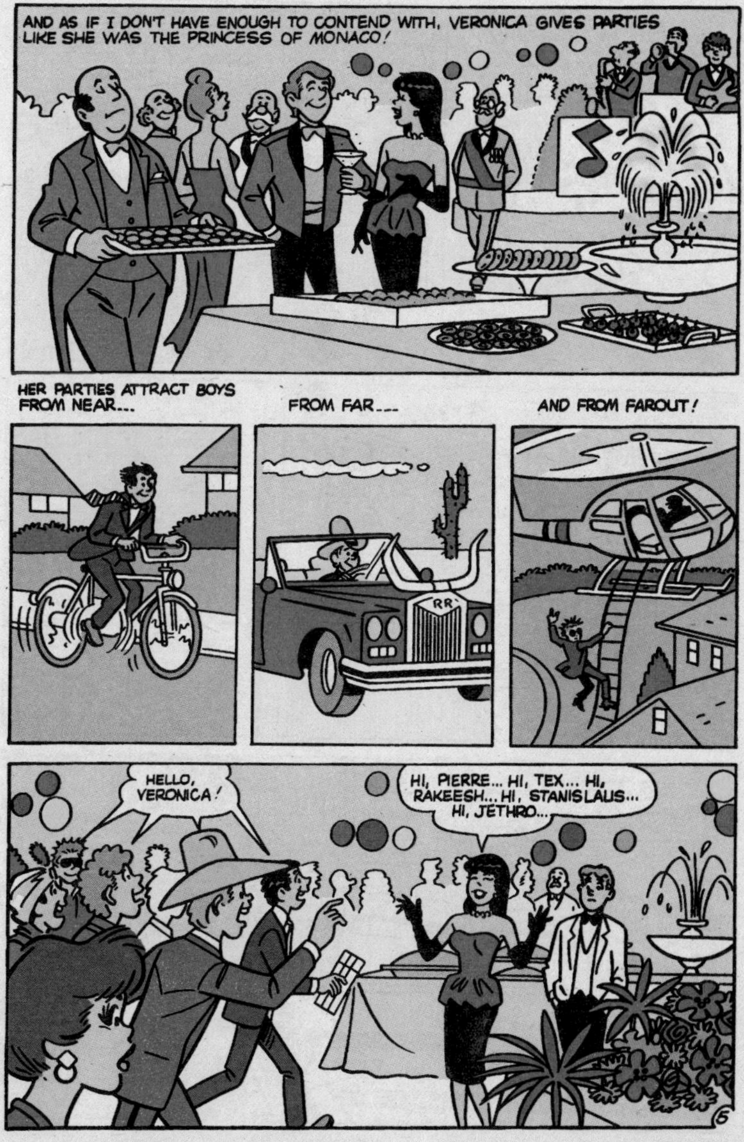
AND AS IF I DON'T HAVE ENOUGH TO CONTEND WITH, VERONICA GIVES PARTIES LIKE SHE WAS THE PRINCESS OF MONACO!
HER PARTIES ATTRACT BOYS FROM NEAR...
FROM FAR...
AND FROM FAROUT!
RR
HELLO, VERONICA!
HI, PIERRE... HI, TEX... HI, RAKEESH... HI, STANISLAUS... HI, JETHRO...
5

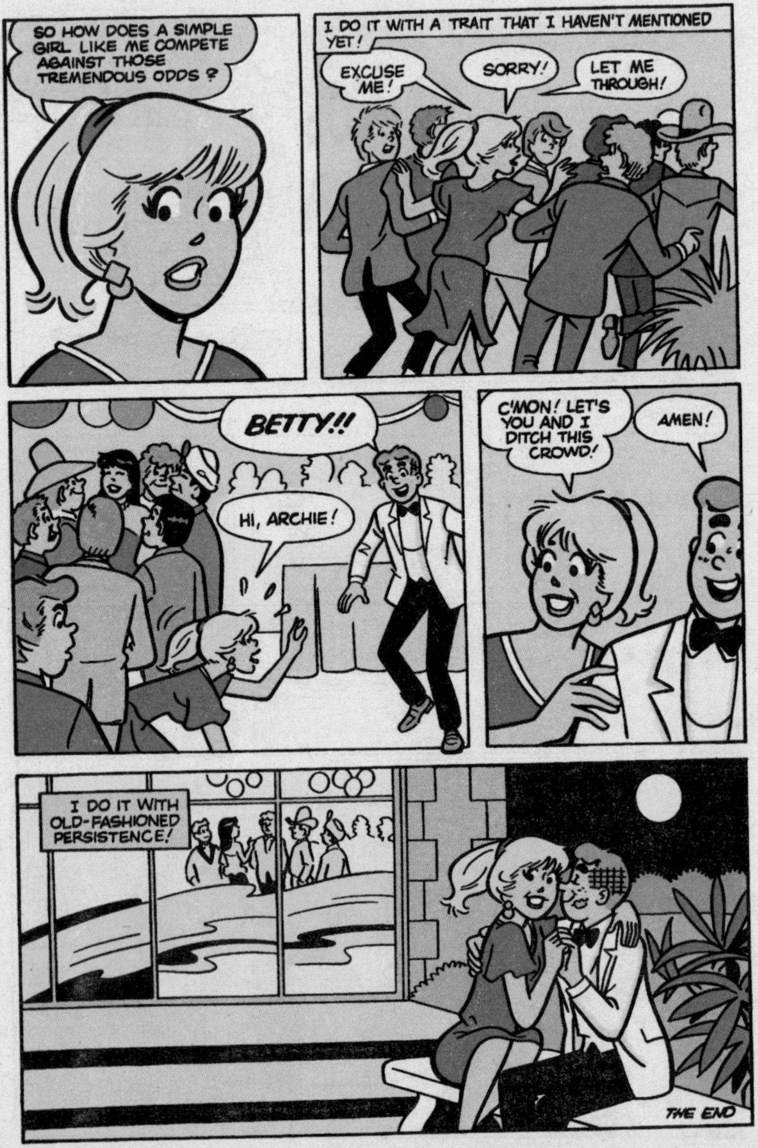
SO HOW DOES A SIMPLE GIRL LIKE ME COMPETE AGAINST THOSE TREMENDOUS ODDS ?
I DO IT WITH A TRAIT THAT I HAVEN'T MENTIONED YET!
EXCUSE ME!
SORRY!
LET ME THROUGH!
BETTY!!
HI, ARCHIE!
C'MON! LET'S YOU AND I DITCH THIS CROWD!
AMEN!
I DO IT WITH OLD-FASHIONED PERSISTENCE!
THE END

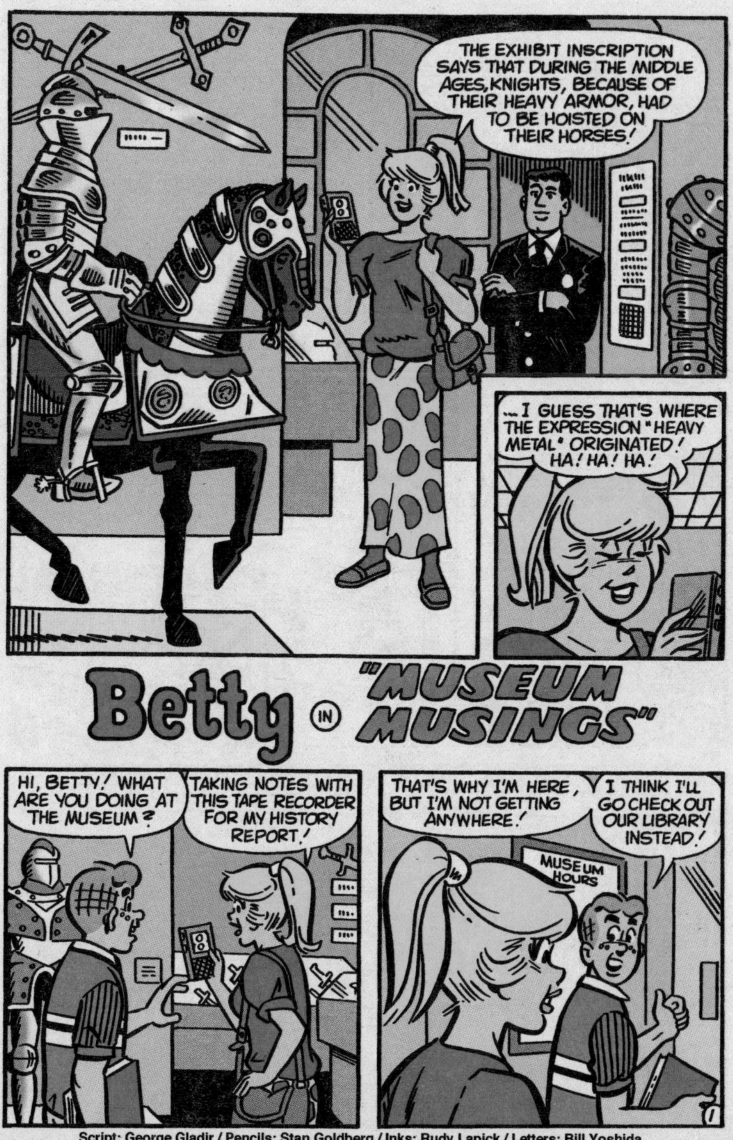
THE EXHIBIT INSCRIPTION SAYS THAT DURING THE MIDDLE AGES, KNIGHTS, BECAUSE OF THEIR HEAVY ARMOR, HAD TO BE HOISTED ON THEIR HORSES!
...I GUESS THAT'S WHERE THE EXPRESSION "HEAVY METAL" ORIGINATED! HA! HA! HA!
Betty IN "MUSEUM MUSINGS"
HI, BETTY! WHAT ARE YOU DOING AT THE MUSEUM?
TAKING NOTES WITH THIS TAPE RECORDER FOR MY HISTORY REPORT!
THAT'S WHY I'M HERE, BUT I'M NOT GETTING ANYWHERE!
I THINK I'LL GO CHECK OUT OUR LIBRARY INSTEAD!
MUSEUM HOURS
1

Script: George Gladir / Pencils: Stan Goldberg / Inks: Rudy Lapick / Letters: Bill Yoshida

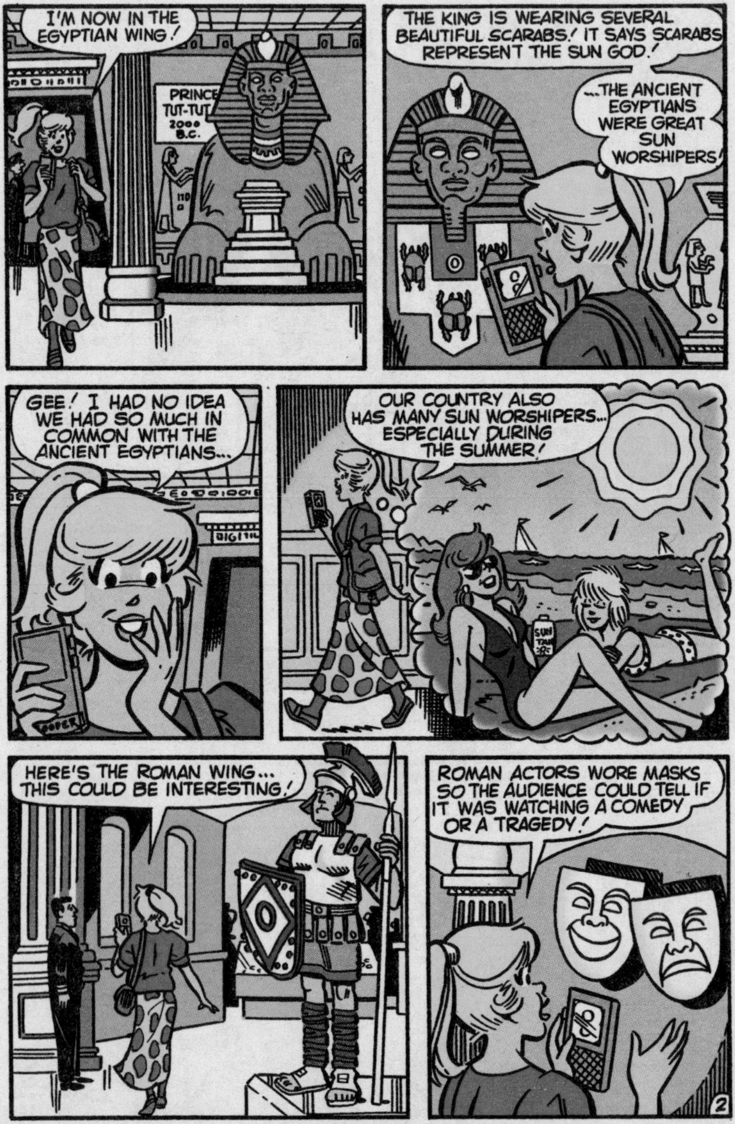
I'M NOW IN THE EGYPTIAN WING!
PRINCE TUT-TUT 2000 B.C.
THE KING IS WEARING SEVERAL BEAUTIFUL SCARABS! IT SAYS SCARABS REPRESENT THE SUN GOD!
...THE ANCIENT EGYPTIANS WERE GREAT SUN WORSHIPERS!
GEE! I HAD NO IDEA WE HAD SO MUCH IN COMMON WITH THE ANCIENT EGYPTIANS...
OUR COUNTRY ALSO HAS MANY SUN WORSHIPERS... ESPECIALLY DURING THE SUMMER!
SUN TAN
HERE'S THE ROMAN WING... THIS COULD BE INTERESTING!
ROMAN ACTORS WORE MASKS SO THE AUDIENCE COULD TELL IF IT WAS WATCHING A COMEDY OR A TRAGEDY!
2

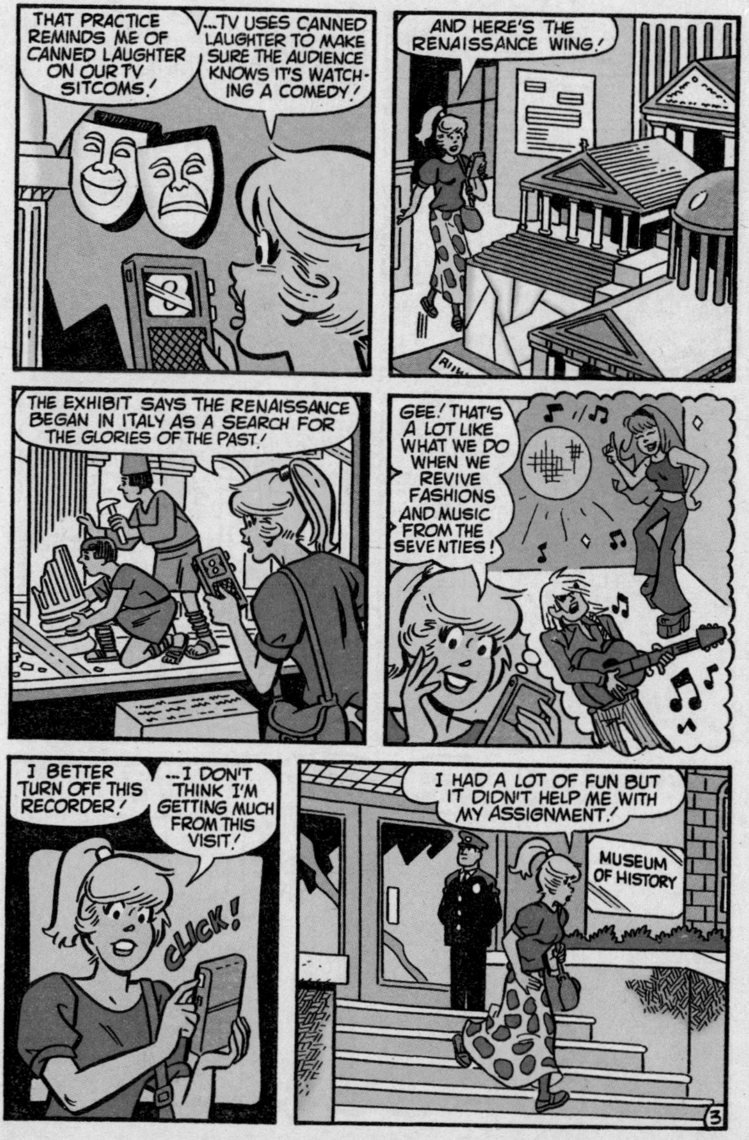
THAT PRACTICE REMINDS ME OF CANNED LAUGHTER ON OUR TV SITCOMS!
...TV USES CANNED LAUGHTER TO MAKE SURE THE AUDIENCE KNOWS IT'S WATCHING A COMEDY!
AND HERE'S THE RENAISSANCE WING!
THE EXHIBIT SAYS THE RENAISSANCE BEGAN IN ITALY AS A SEARCH FOR THE GLORIES OF THE PAST!
GEE! THAT'S A LOT LIKE WHAT WE DO WHEN WE REVIVE FASHIONS AND MUSIC FROM THE SEVENTIES!
I BETTER TURN OFF THIS RECORDER!
...I DON'T THINK I'M GETTING MUCH FROM THIS VISIT!
CLICK!
I HAD A LOT OF FUN BUT IT DIDN'T HELP ME WITH MY ASSIGNMENT!
MUSEUM OF HISTORY
3

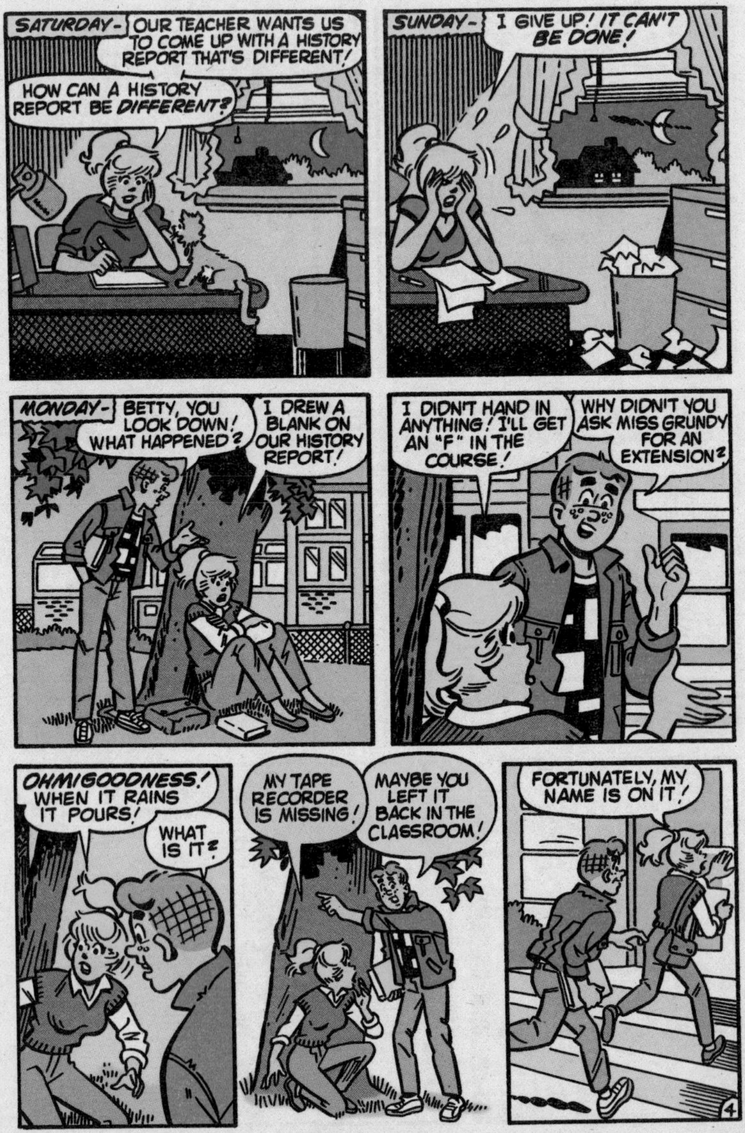

SATURDAY-
OUR TEACHER WANTS US TO COME UP WITH A HISTORY REPORT THAT'S DIFFERENT!
HOW CAN A HISTORY REPORT BE DIFFERENT?
SUNDAY-
I GIVE UP! IT CAN'T BE DONE!
MONDAY-
BETTY, YOU LOOK DOWN! WHAT HAPPENED?
I DREW A BLANK ON OUR HISTORY REPORT!
I DIDN'T HAND IN ANYTHING! I'LL GET AN "F" IN THE COURSE!
WHY DIDN'T YOU ASK MISS GRUNDY FOR AN EXTENSION?
OHMIGOODNESS! WHEN IT RAINS IT POURS!
WHAT IS IT?
MY TAPE RECORDER IS MISSING!
MAYBE YOU LEFT IT BACK IN THE CLASSROOM!
FORTUNATELY, MY NAME IS ON IT!

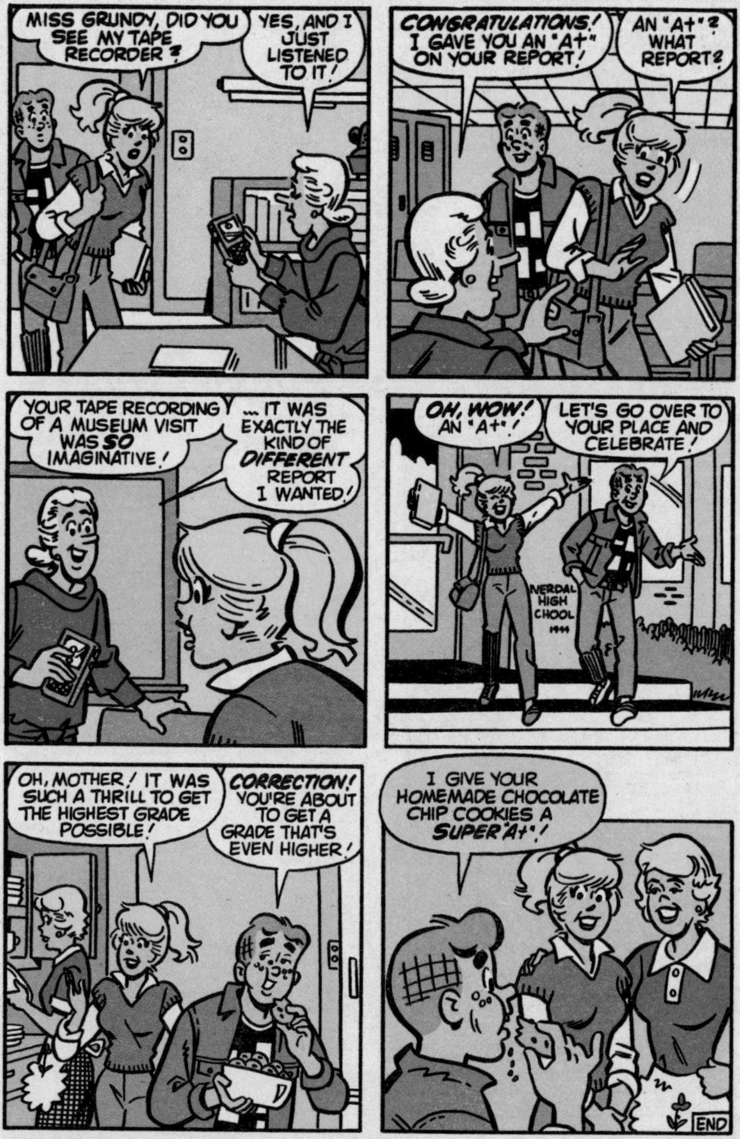
MISS GRUNDY, DID YOU SEE MY TAPE RECORDER ?
YES, AND I JUST LISTENED TO IT!
CONGRATULATIONS! I GAVE YOU AN "A+" ON YOUR REPORT!
AN "A+" ? WHAT REPORT?
YOUR TAPE RECORDING OF A MUSEUM VISIT WAS SO IMAGINATIVE!
... IT WAS EXACTLY THE KIND OF DIFFERENT REPORT I WANTED!
OH, WOW! AN "A+"!
LET'S GO OVER TO YOUR PLACE AND CELEBRATE!
NERDAL HIGH CHOOL 1944
OH, MOTHER! IT WAS SUCH A THRILL TO GET THE HIGHEST GRADE POSSIBLE!
CORRECTION! YOU'RE ABOUT TO GET A GRADE THAT'S EVEN HIGHER!
I GIVE YOUR HOMEMADE CHOCOLATE CHIP COOKIES A SUPER "A+"!
END

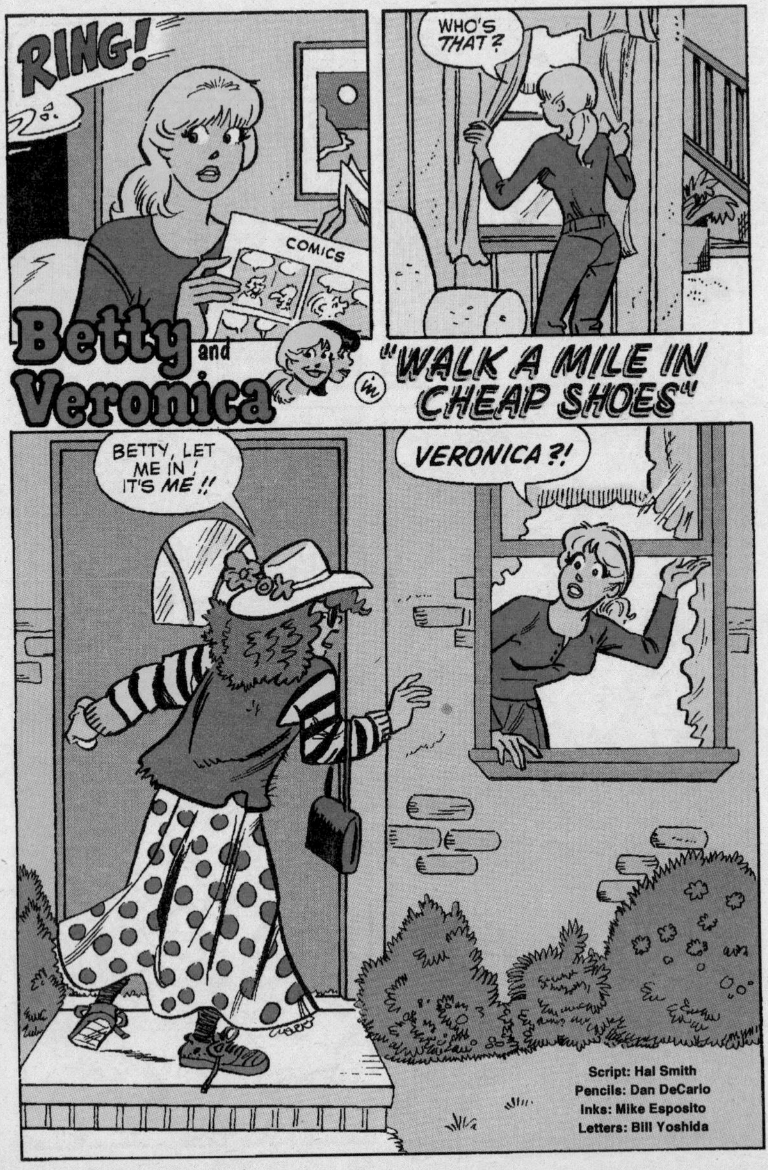
RING!
COMICS
WHO'S THAT?
Betty and Veronica
in
"WALK A MILE IN CHEAP SHOES"
BETTY, LET ME IN! IT'S ME!!
VERONICA?!
Script: Hal Smith
Pencils: Dan DeCarlo
Inks: Mike Esposito
Letters: Bill Yoshida

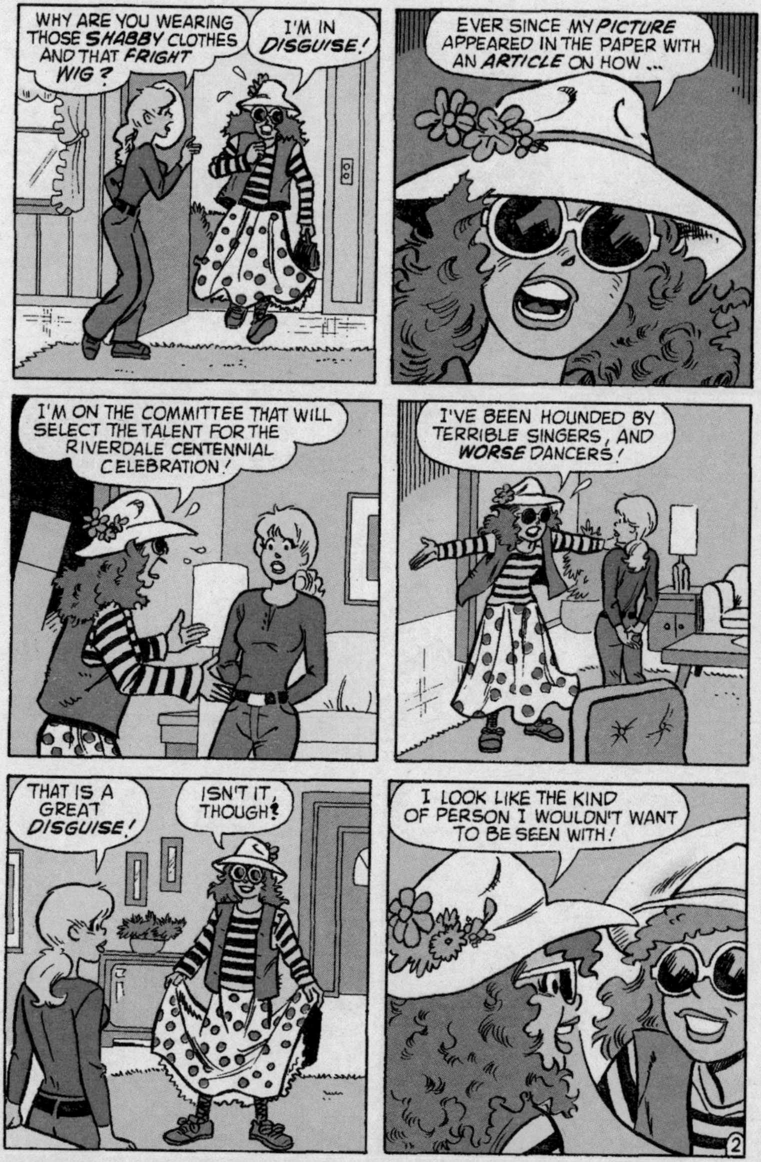
WHY ARE YOU WEARING THOSE SHABBY CLOTHES AND THAT FRIGHT WIG?
I'M IN DISGUISE!
EVER SINCE MY PICTURE APPEARED IN THE PAPER WITH AN ARTICLE ON HOW ...
I'M ON THE COMMITTEE THAT WILL SELECT THE TALENT FOR THE RIVERDALE CENTENNIAL CELEBRATION!
I'VE BEEN HOUNDED BY TERRIBLE SINGERS, AND WORSE DANCERS!
THAT IS A GREAT DISGUISE!
ISN'T IT, THOUGH?
I LOOK LIKE THE KIND OF PERSON I WOULDN'T WANT TO BE SEEN WITH!
2

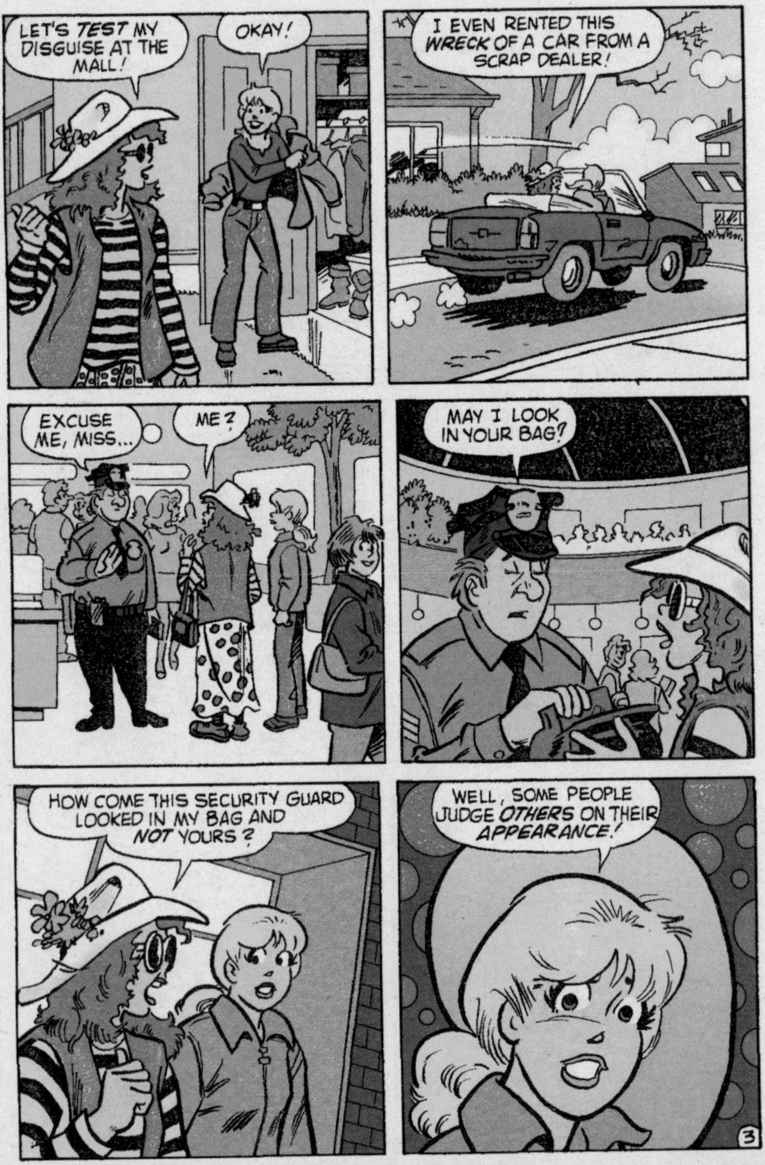
LET'S TEST MY DISGUISE AT THE MALL!
OKAY!
I EVEN RENTED THIS WRECK OF A CAR FROM A SCRAP DEALER!
EXCUSE ME, MISS...
ME?
MAY I LOOK IN YOUR BAG?
HOW COME THIS SECURITY GUARD LOOKED IN MY BAG AND NOT YOURS?
WELL, SOME PEOPLE JUDGE OTHERS ON THEIR APPEARANCE!
3

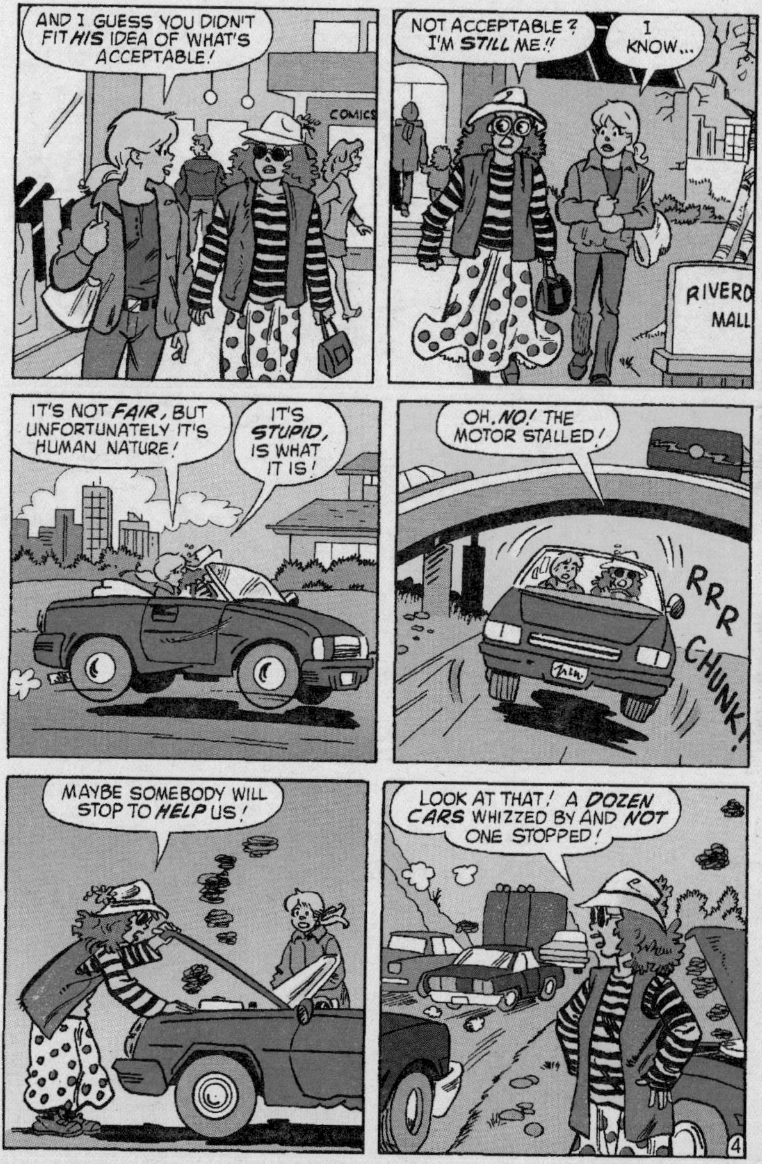
AND I GUESS YOU DIDN'T FIT HIS IDEA OF WHAT'S ACCEPTABLE!
COMICS
NOT ACCEPTABLE? I'M STILL ME!!
I KNOW...
RIVERD
MALL
IT'S NOT FAIR, BUT UNFORTUNATELY IT'S HUMAN NATURE!
IT'S STUPID, IS WHAT IT IS!
OH, NO! THE MOTOR STALLED!
RRR
CHUNK!
MAYBE SOMEBODY WILL STOP TO HELP US!
LOOK AT THAT! A DOZEN CARS WHIZZED BY AND NOT ONE STOPPED!
4

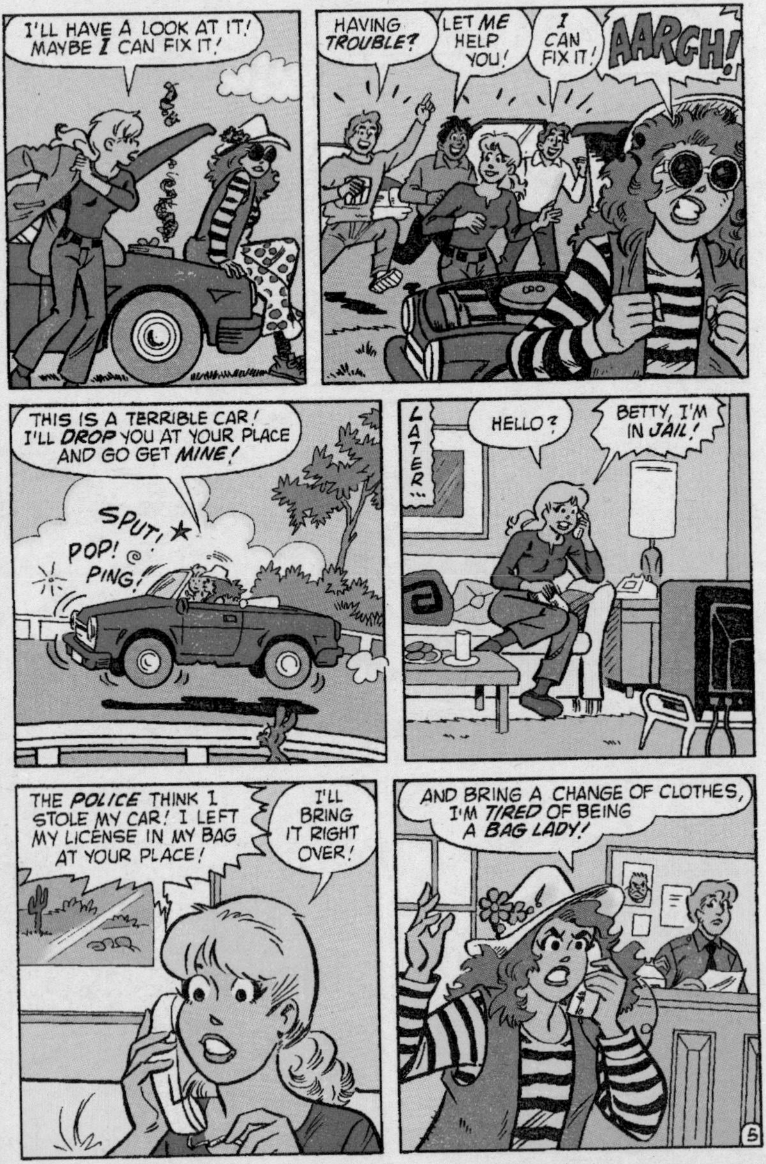
I'LL HAVE A LOOK AT IT! MAYBE I CAN FIX IT!
HAVING TROUBLE?
LET ME HELP YOU!
I CAN FIX IT!
AARGH!
THIS IS A TERRIBLE CAR! I'LL DROP YOU AT YOUR PLACE AND GO GET MINE!
SPUT!
POP!
PING!
LATER...
HELLO?
BETTY, I'M IN JAIL!
THE POLICE THINK I STOLE MY CAR! I LEFT MY LICENSE IN MY BAG AT YOUR PLACE!
I'LL BRING IT RIGHT OVER!
AND BRING A CHANGE OF CLOTHES, I'M TIRED OF BEING A BAG LADY!
5

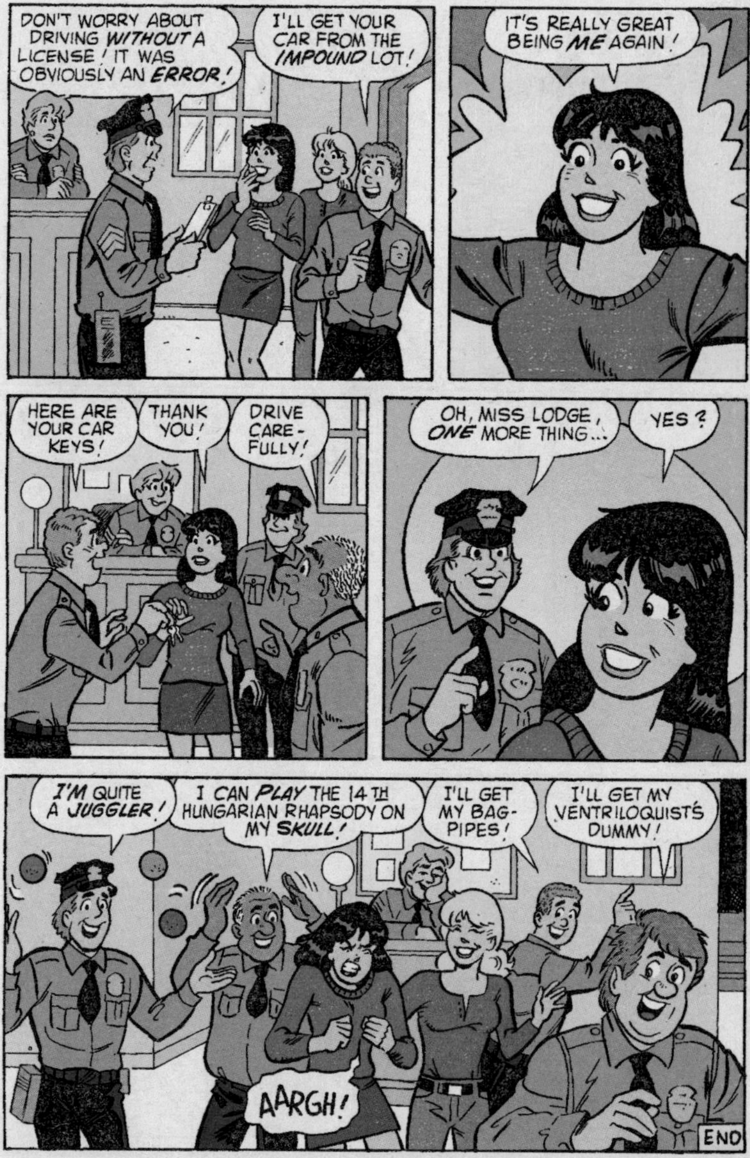
DON'T WORRY ABOUT DRIVING WITHOUT A LICENSE! IT WAS OBVIOUSLY AN ERROR!
I'LL GET YOUR CAR FROM THE IMPOUND LOT!
IT'S REALLY GREAT BEING ME AGAIN!
HERE ARE YOUR CAR KEYS!
THANK YOU!
DRIVE CARE-FULLY!
OH, MISS LODGE, ONE MORE THING...
YES?
I'M QUITE A JUGGLER!
I CAN PLAY THE 14TH HUNGARIAN RHAPSODY ON MY SKULL!
I'LL GET MY BAG-PIPES!
I'LL GET MY VENTRILOQUIST'S DUMMY!
AARGH!
END

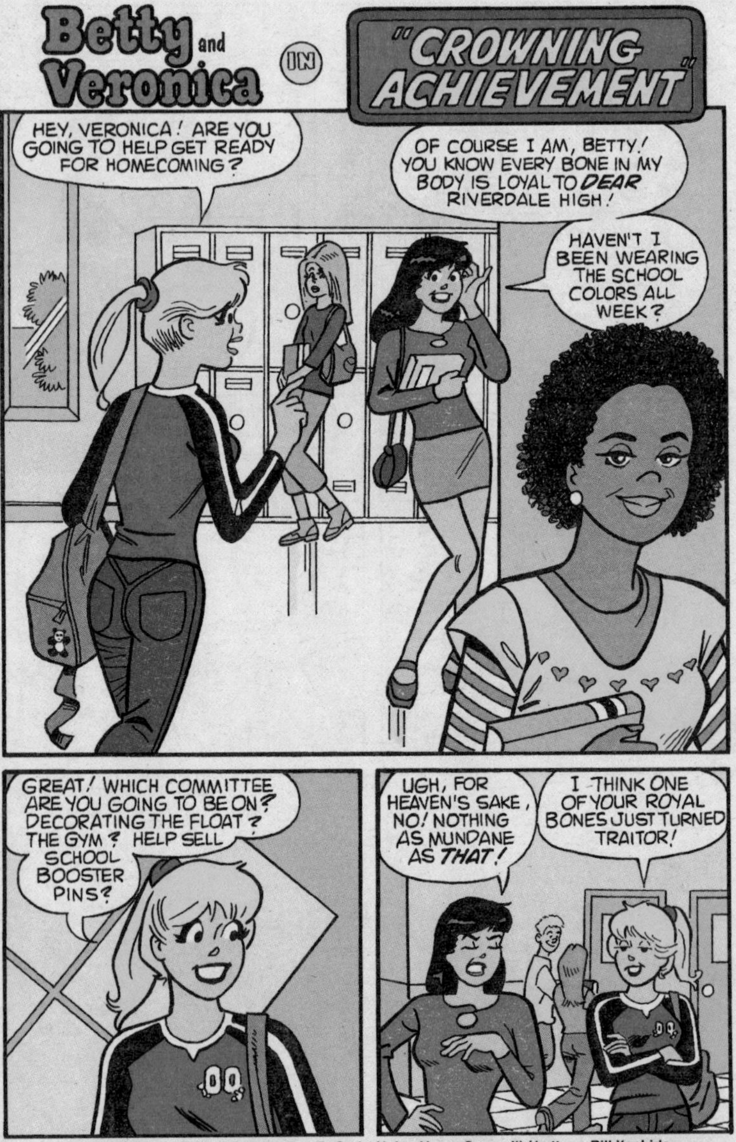

Betty and Veronica
IN
"CROWNING ACHIEVEMENT"
HEY, VERONICA! ARE YOU GOING TO HELP GET READY FOR HOMECOMING?
OF COURSE I AM, BETTY! YOU KNOW EVERY BONE IN MY BODY IS LOYAL TO DEAR RIVERDALE HIGH!
HAVEN'T I BEEN WEARING THE SCHOOL COLORS ALL WEEK?
GREAT! WHICH COMMITTEE ARE YOU GOING TO BE ON? DECORATING THE FLOAT? THE GYM? HELP SELL SCHOOL BOOSTER PINS?
UGH, FOR HEAVEN'S SAKE, NO! NOTHING AS MUNDANE AS THAT!
I THINK ONE OF YOUR ROYAL BONES JUST TURNED TRAITOR!

Script: Kathleen Webb / Pencils: Dan DeCarlo / Inks: Henry Scarpelli / Letters: Bill Yoshida

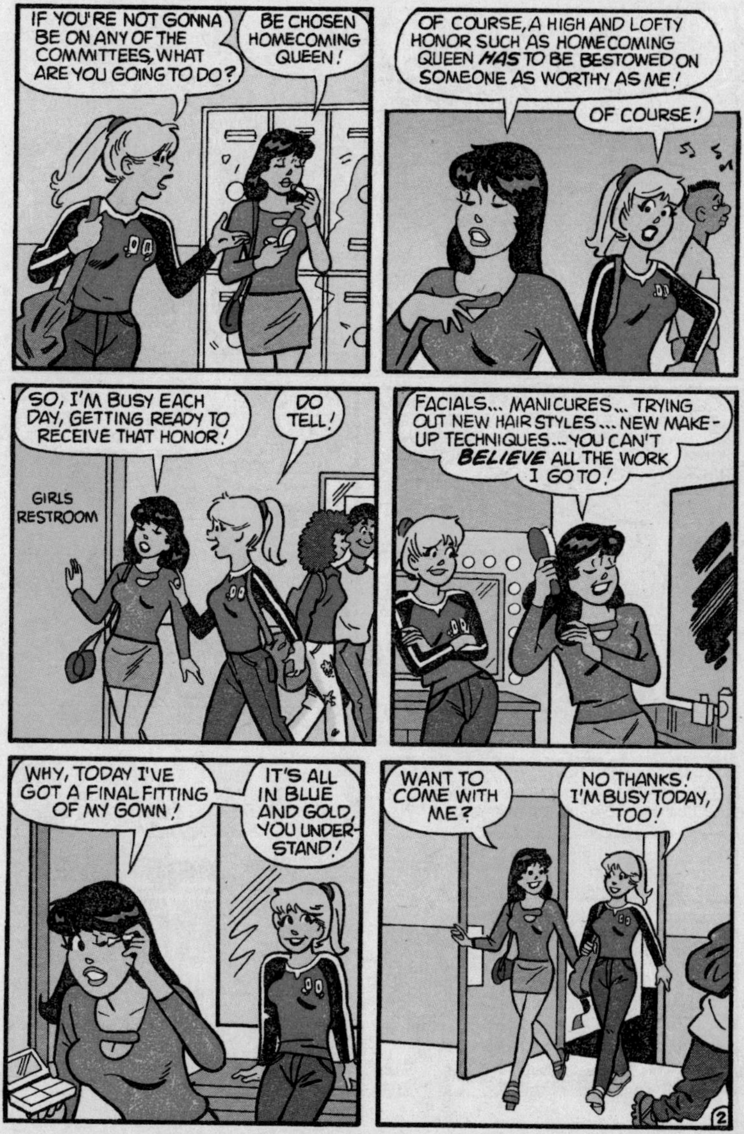

IF YOU'RE NOT GONNA BE ON ANY OF THE COMMITTEES, WHAT ARE YOU GOING TO DO?
BE CHOSEN HOMECOMING QUEEN!
OF COURSE, A HIGH AND LOFTY HONOR SUCH AS HOMECOMING QUEEN *HAS* TO BE BESTOWED ON SOMEONE AS WORTHY AS ME!
OF COURSE!
SO, I'M BUSY EACH DAY, GETTING READY TO RECEIVE THAT HONOR!
DO TELL!
GIRLS RESTROOM
FACIALS... MANICURES... TRYING OUT NEW HAIR STYLES... NEW MAKE-UP TECHNIQUES... YOU CAN'T *BELIEVE* ALL THE WORK I GO TO!
WHY, TODAY I'VE GOT A FINAL FITTING OF MY GOWN!
IT'S ALL IN BLUE AND GOLD, YOU UNDERSTAND!
WANT TO COME WITH ME?
NO THANKS! I'M BUSY TODAY, TOO!
2

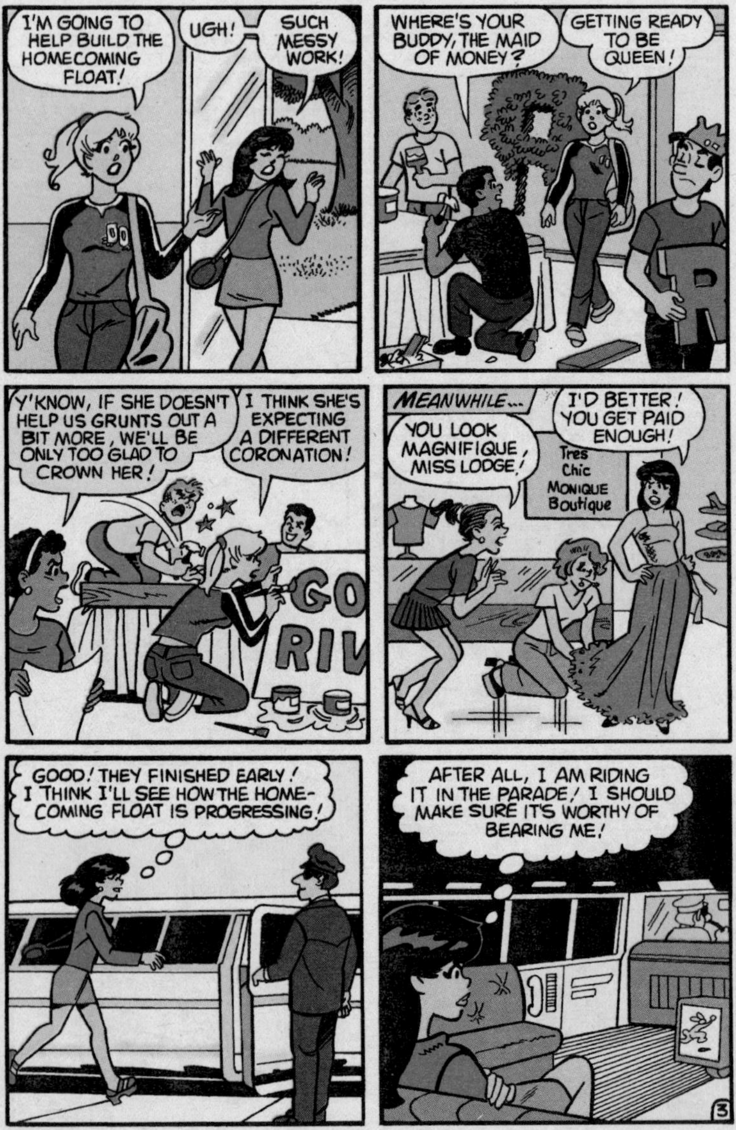
I'M GOING TO HELP BUILD THE HOMECOMING FLOAT!
UGH!
SUCH MESSY WORK!
WHERE'S YOUR BUDDY, THE MAID OF MONEY?
GETTING READY TO BE QUEEN!
Y'KNOW, IF SHE DOESN'T HELP US GRUNTS OUT A BIT MORE, WE'LL BE ONLY TOO GLAD TO CROWN HER!
I THINK SHE'S EXPECTING A DIFFERENT CORONATION!
GO
RIV
MEANWHILE...
YOU LOOK MAGNIFIQUE, MISS LODGE!
I'D BETTER! YOU GET PAID ENOUGH!
Tres Chic
MONIQUE Boutique
GOOD! THEY FINISHED EARLY! I THINK I'LL SEE HOW THE HOME-COMING FLOAT IS PROGRESSING!
AFTER ALL, I AM RIDING IT IN THE PARADE! I SHOULD MAKE SURE IT'S WORTHY OF BEARING ME!
3

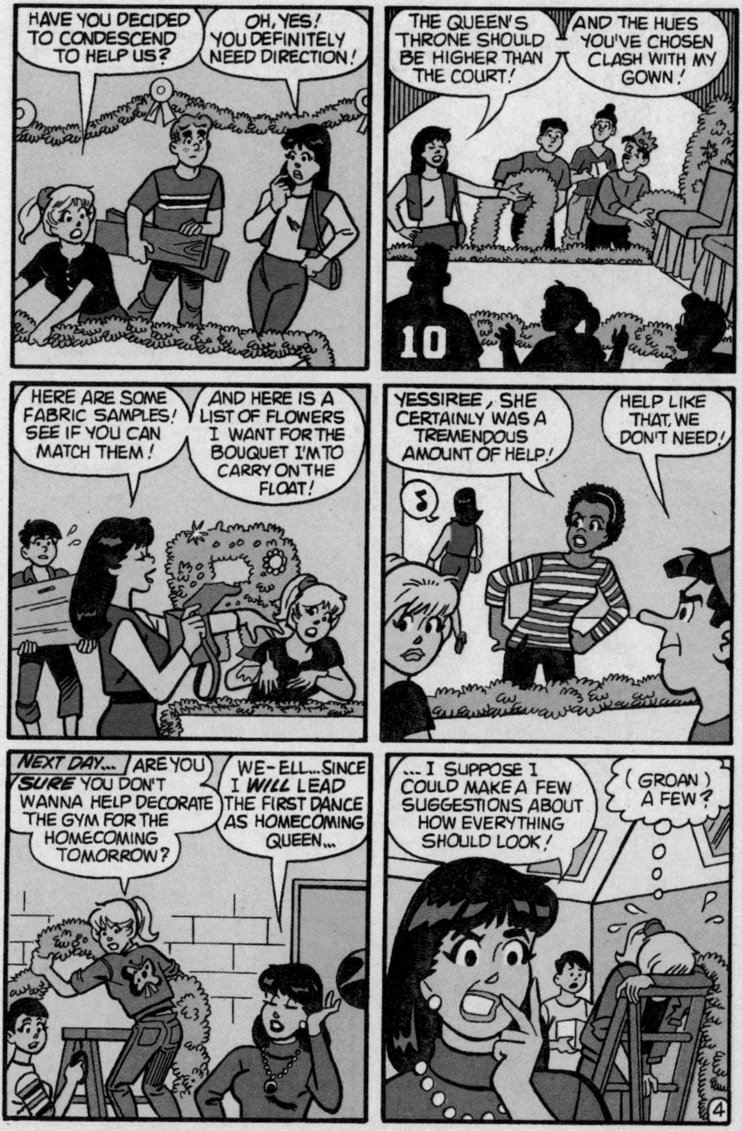
HAVE YOU DECIDED TO CONDESCEND TO HELP US?
OH, YES! YOU DEFINITELY NEED DIRECTION!
THE QUEEN'S THRONE SHOULD BE HIGHER THAN THE COURT!
AND THE HUES YOU'VE CHOSEN CLASH WITH MY GOWN!
10
HERE ARE SOME FABRIC SAMPLES! SEE IF YOU CAN MATCH THEM!
AND HERE IS A LIST OF FLOWERS I WANT FOR THE BOUQUET I'M TO CARRY ON THE FLOAT!
YESSIREE, SHE CERTAINLY WAS A TREMENDOUS AMOUNT OF HELP!
HELP LIKE THAT, WE DON'T NEED!
NEXT DAY...
ARE YOU SURE YOU DON'T WANNA HELP DECORATE THE GYM FOR THE HOMECOMING TOMORROW?
WE-ELL... SINCE I WILL LEAD THE FIRST DANCE AS HOMECOMING QUEEN...
... I SUPPOSE I COULD MAKE A FEW SUGGESTIONS ABOUT HOW EVERYTHING SHOULD LOOK!
(GROAN) A FEW?

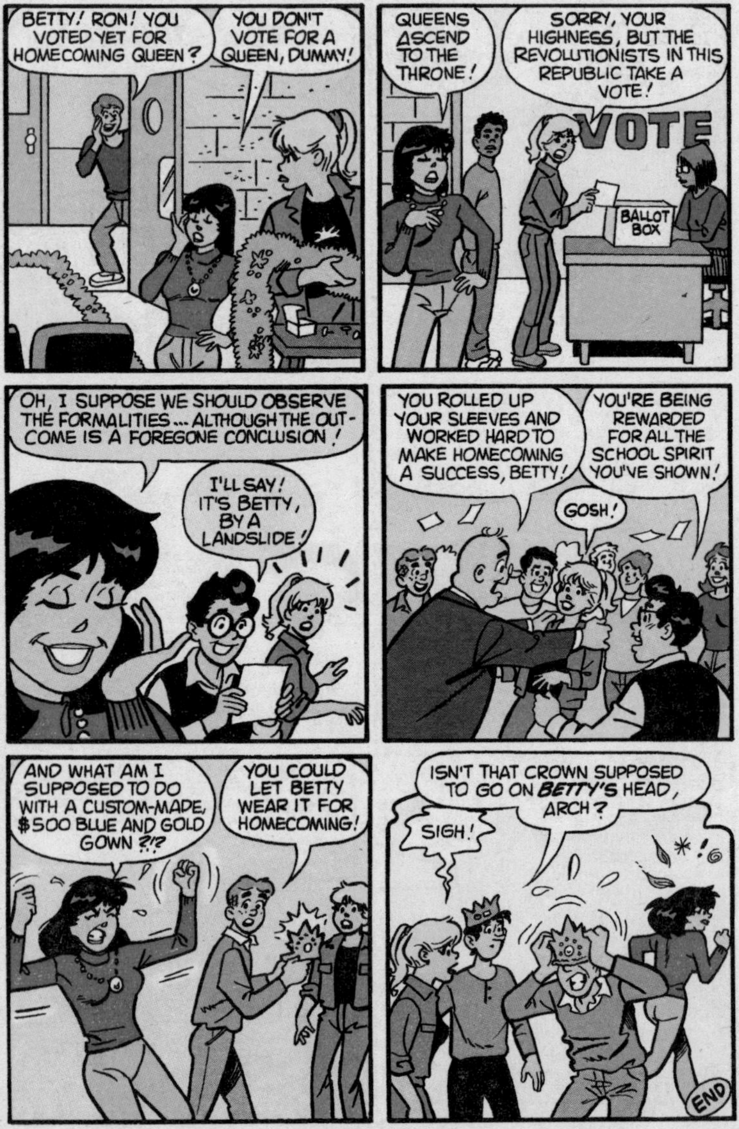
BETTY! RON! YOU VOTED YET FOR HOMECOMING QUEEN?
YOU DON'T VOTE FOR A QUEEN, DUMMY!
QUEENS ASCEND TO THE THRONE!
SORRY, YOUR HIGHNESS, BUT THE REVOLUTIONISTS IN THIS REPUBLIC TAKE A VOTE!
VOTE
BALLOT BOX
OH, I SUPPOSE WE SHOULD OBSERVE THE FORMALITIES... ALTHOUGH THE OUT-COME IS A FOREGONE CONCLUSION!
I'LL SAY! IT'S BETTY, BY A LANDSLIDE!
YOU ROLLED UP YOUR SLEEVES AND WORKED HARD TO MAKE HOMECOMING A SUCCESS, BETTY!
YOU'RE BEING REWARDED FOR ALL THE SCHOOL SPIRIT YOU'VE SHOWN!
GOSH!
AND WHAT AM I SUPPOSED TO DO WITH A CUSTOM-MADE, $500 BLUE AND GOLD GOWN?!?
YOU COULD LET BETTY WEAR IT FOR HOMECOMING!
ISN'T THAT CROWN SUPPOSED TO GO ON BETTY'S HEAD, ARCH?
SIGH!
END

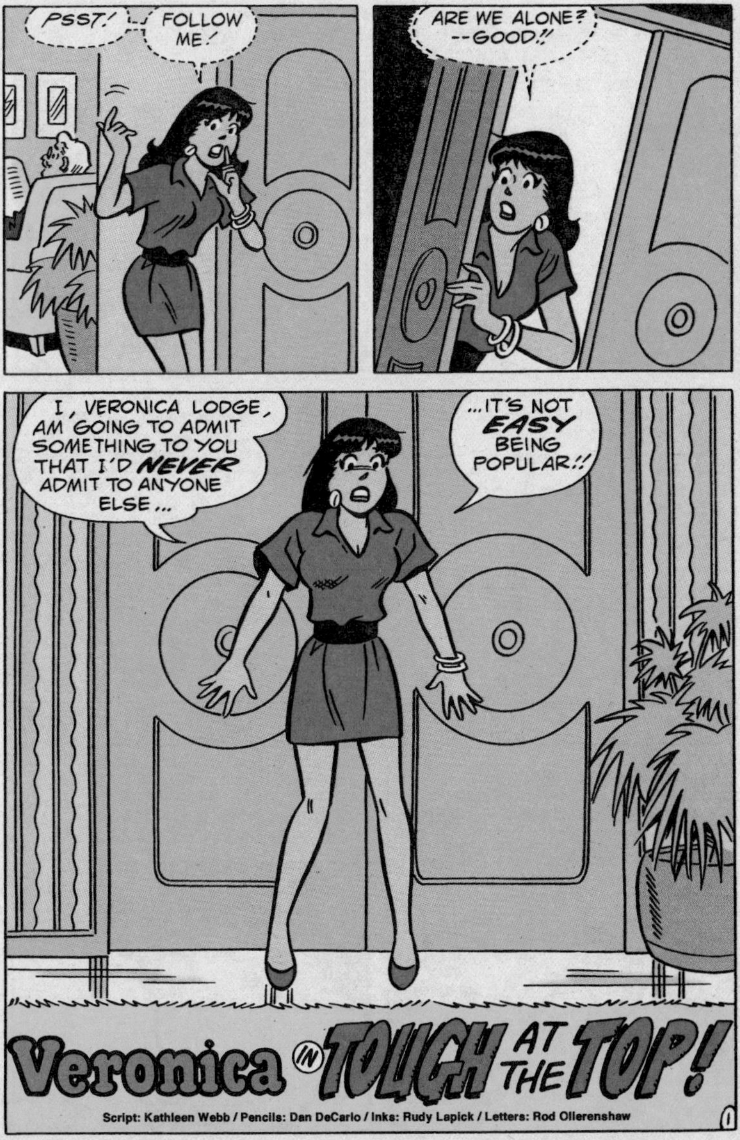
PSST!
FOLLOW ME!
ARE WE ALONE? --GOOD!!
I, VERONICA LODGE, AM GOING TO ADMIT SOMETHING TO YOU THAT I'D NEVER ADMIT TO ANYONE ELSE...
...IT'S NOT EASY BEING POPULAR!!
Veronica IN TOUGH AT THE TOP!
Script: Kathleen Webb / Pencils: Dan DeCarlo / Inks: Rudy Lapick / Letters: Rod Ollerenshaw
1

OH, SURE, I ADORE BEING LOOKED UPON AS A FASHION TRENDSETTER... WHO WOULDN'T?

EVERYTHING I WEAR, NO MATTER *HOW* OUTLANDISH, IS COPIED BY MY ADORING PUBLIC!

AND IT'S MARVELOUS TO HAVE PEOPLE SEEK MY VALUED OPINION ON THINGS!

RON, I NEED YOUR HELP WITH A FASHION DECISION!

VERONICA, WHAT'S YOUR OPINION ON THE COMING TRENDS?

RON! HELP ME WITH A ROMANCE QUESTION!

FANTASTIC, BEING ASSURED AN INVITATION TO PARTIES, DANCES, AND OTHER SOCIAL EVENTS!

SATURDAY NIGHT? LET ME CHECK WITH MY SOCIAL SECRETARY FIRST!

CALENDAR AT A GLANCE

	THUR	FRI	SAT
EO	DAN	STAN	BILL
VIC	MAR	SAM	AL
WE	DEX	BAM	TED
FRO	JIM	GEO	LOU
NE			

--NOT TO MENTION BEING GUARANTEED AN APPOINTMENT ON EVERY IMPORTANT SCHOOL COMMITTEE!

RON! YOU'RE ON THE DECORATING COMMITTEE!

YOU'VE BEEN ELECTED FRENCH CLUB PRESIDENT!

¿YAWN? SO WHAT *ELSE* IS NEW?

I'M ACCEPTED, ADMIRED, HAVE A TIGHT CIRCLE OF FRIENDS, PLUS THE POWER TO START NEW TRENDS AND STYLES, *BUT...*

2

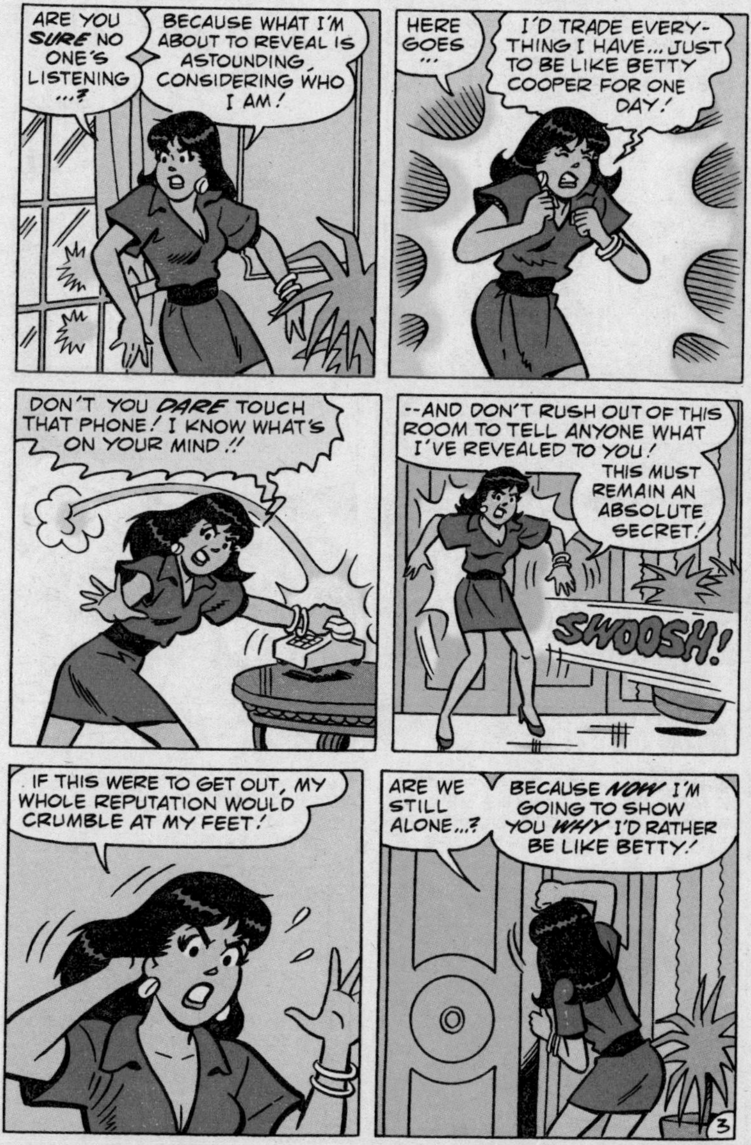

ARE YOU SURE NO ONE'S LISTENING ...?
BECAUSE WHAT I'M ABOUT TO REVEAL IS ASTOUNDING, CONSIDERING WHO I AM!
HERE GOES ...
I'D TRADE EVERY-THING I HAVE... JUST TO BE LIKE BETTY COOPER FOR ONE DAY!
DON'T YOU DARE TOUCH THAT PHONE! I KNOW WHAT'S ON YOUR MIND!!
--AND DON'T RUSH OUT OF THIS ROOM TO TELL ANYONE WHAT I'VE REVEALED TO YOU!
THIS MUST REMAIN AN ABSOLUTE SECRET!
SWOOSH!
IF THIS WERE TO GET OUT, MY WHOLE REPUTATION WOULD CRUMBLE AT MY FEET!
ARE WE STILL ALONE...?
BECAUSE NOW I'M GOING TO SHOW YOU WHY I'D RATHER BE LIKE BETTY!
3

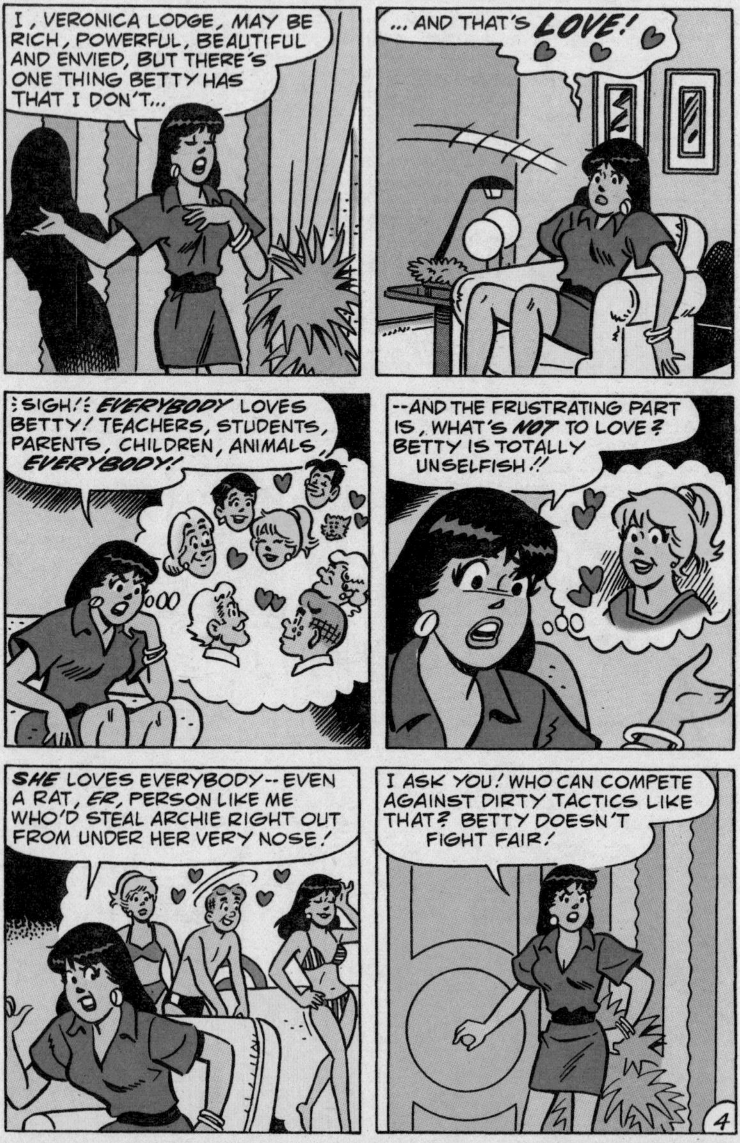
I, VERONICA LODGE, MAY BE RICH, POWERFUL, BEAUTIFUL AND ENVIED, BUT THERE'S ONE THING BETTY HAS THAT I DON'T...
... AND THAT'S LOVE!
SIGH! EVERYBODY LOVES BETTY! TEACHERS, STUDENTS, PARENTS, CHILDREN, ANIMALS, EVERYBODY!
--AND THE FRUSTRATING PART IS, WHAT'S NOT TO LOVE? BETTY IS TOTALLY UNSELFISH!!
SHE LOVES EVERYBODY-- EVEN A RAT, ER, PERSON LIKE ME WHO'D STEAL ARCHIE RIGHT OUT FROM UNDER HER VERY NOSE!
I ASK YOU! WHO CAN COMPETE AGAINST DIRTY TACTICS LIKE THAT? BETTY DOESN'T FIGHT FAIR!
4

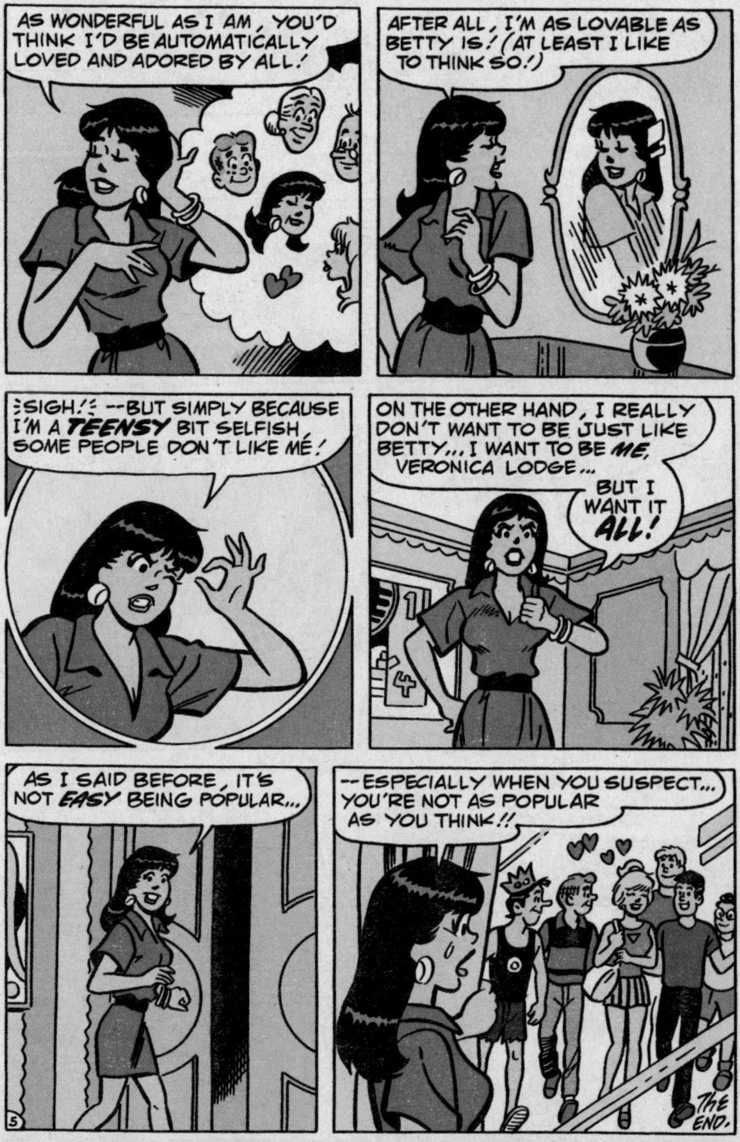
AS WONDERFUL AS I AM, YOU'D THINK I'D BE AUTOMATICALLY LOVED AND ADORED BY ALL!
AFTER ALL, I'M AS LOVABLE AS BETTY IS! (AT LEAST I LIKE TO THINK SO!)
SIGH! --BUT SIMPLY BECAUSE I'M A TEENSY BIT SELFISH, SOME PEOPLE DON'T LIKE ME!
ON THE OTHER HAND, I REALLY DON'T WANT TO BE JUST LIKE BETTY... I WANT TO BE ME, VERONICA LODGE...
BUT I WANT IT ALL!
AS I SAID BEFORE, IT'S NOT EASY BEING POPULAR...
--ESPECIALLY WHEN YOU SUSPECT... YOU'RE NOT AS POPULAR AS YOU THINK!!
5
THE END.

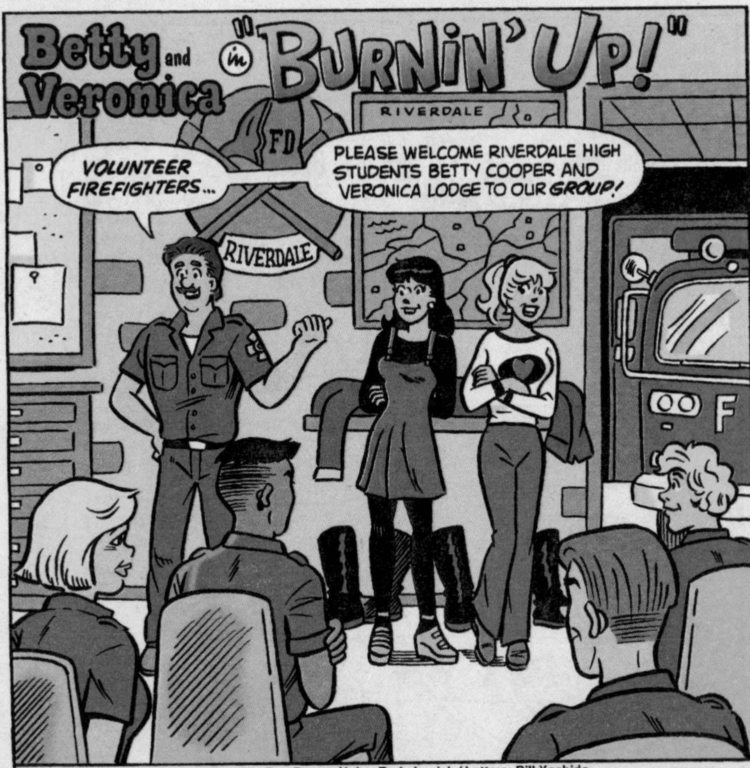
Betty and Veronica
in "BURNIN' UP!"
RIVERDALE
FD
VOLUNTEER FIREFIGHTERS...
PLEASE WELCOME RIVERDALE HIGH STUDENTS BETTY COOPER AND VERONICA LODGE TO OUR GROUP!
RIVERDALE
F

Script & Pencils: Dan Parent / Inks: Rudy Lapick / Letters: Bill Yoshida

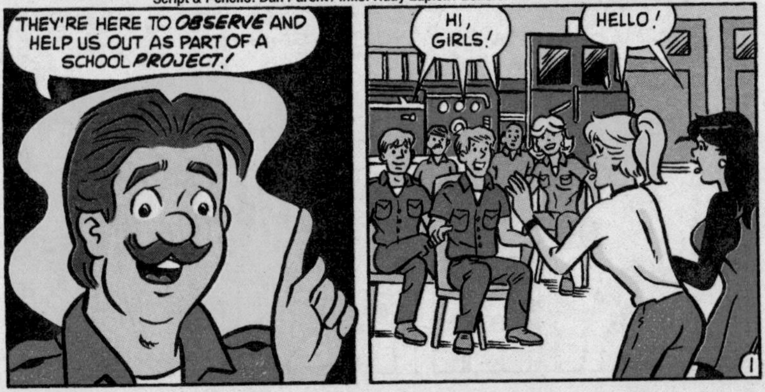
THEY'RE HERE TO OBSERVE AND HELP US OUT AS PART OF A SCHOOL PROJECT!
HI, GIRLS!
HELLO!

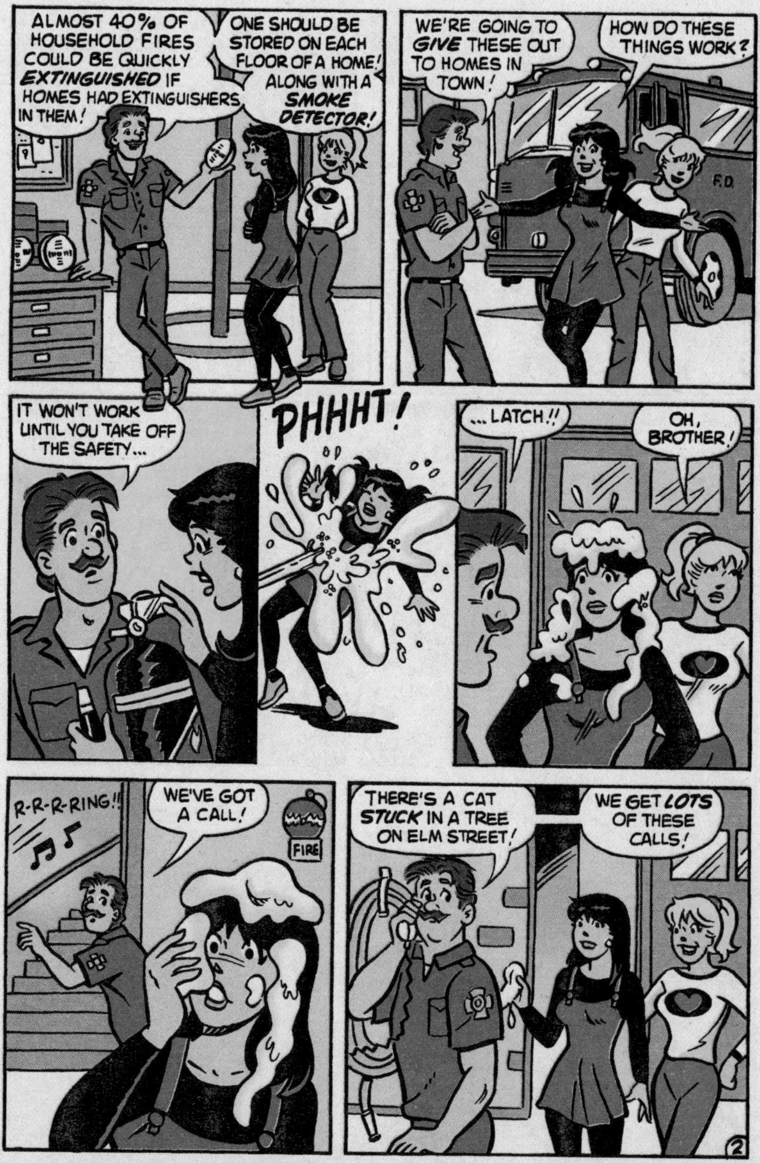
ALMOST 40% OF HOUSEHOLD FIRES COULD BE QUICKLY EXTINGUISHED IF HOMES HAD EXTINGUISHERS IN THEM!
ONE SHOULD BE STORED ON EACH FLOOR OF A HOME! ALONG WITH A SMOKE DETECTOR!
WE'RE GOING TO GIVE THESE OUT TO HOMES IN TOWN!
HOW DO THESE THINGS WORK?
F.D.
IT WON'T WORK UNTIL YOU TAKE OFF THE SAFETY...
PHHHT!
...LATCH!!
OH, BROTHER!
R-R-R-RING!!
WE'VE GOT A CALL!
FIRE
THERE'S A CAT STUCK IN A TREE ON ELM STREET!
WE GET LOTS OF THESE CALLS!
2

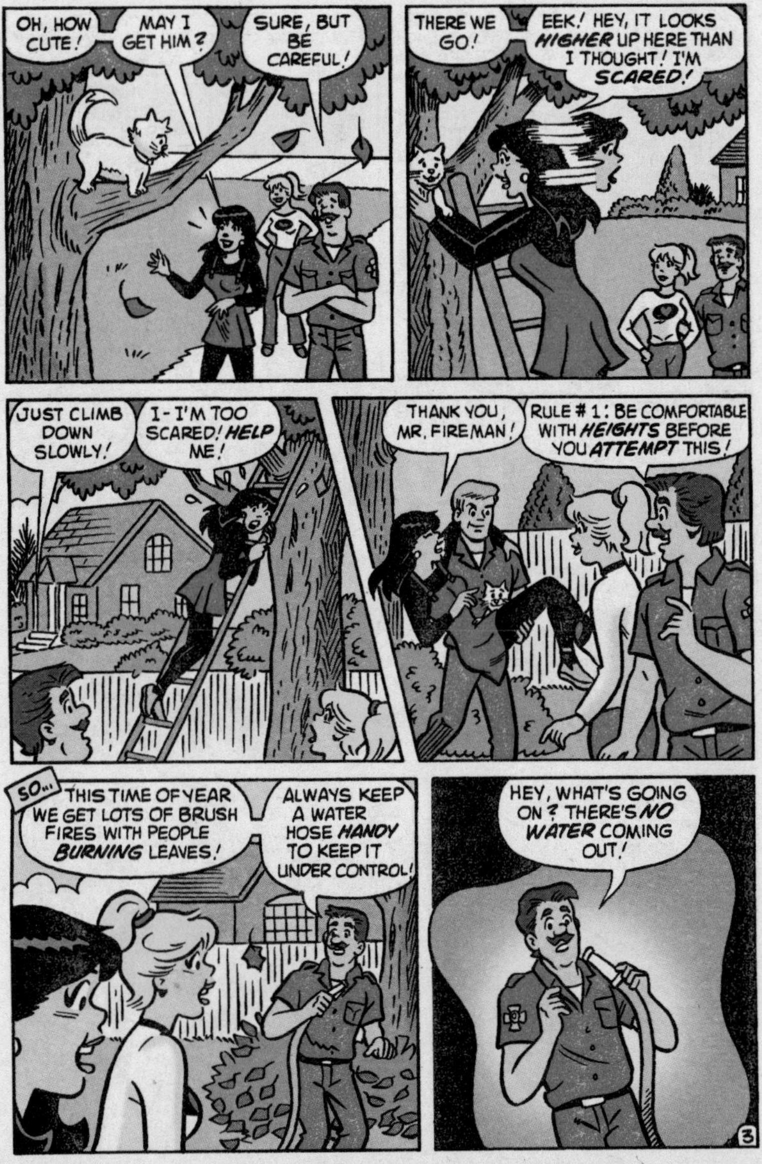

OH, HOW CUTE!
MAY I GET HIM?
SURE, BUT BE CAREFUL!
THERE WE GO!
EEK! HEY, IT LOOKS HIGHER UP HERE THAN I THOUGHT! I'M SCARED!
JUST CLIMB DOWN SLOWLY!
I-I'M TOO SCARED! HELP ME!
THANK YOU, MR. FIREMAN!
RULE # 1: BE COMFORTABLE WITH HEIGHTS BEFORE YOU ATTEMPT THIS!
SO...
THIS TIME OF YEAR WE GET LOTS OF BRUSH FIRES WITH PEOPLE BURNING LEAVES!
ALWAYS KEEP A WATER HOSE HANDY TO KEEP IT UNDER CONTROL!
HEY, WHAT'S GOING ON? THERE'S NO WATER COMING OUT!
3

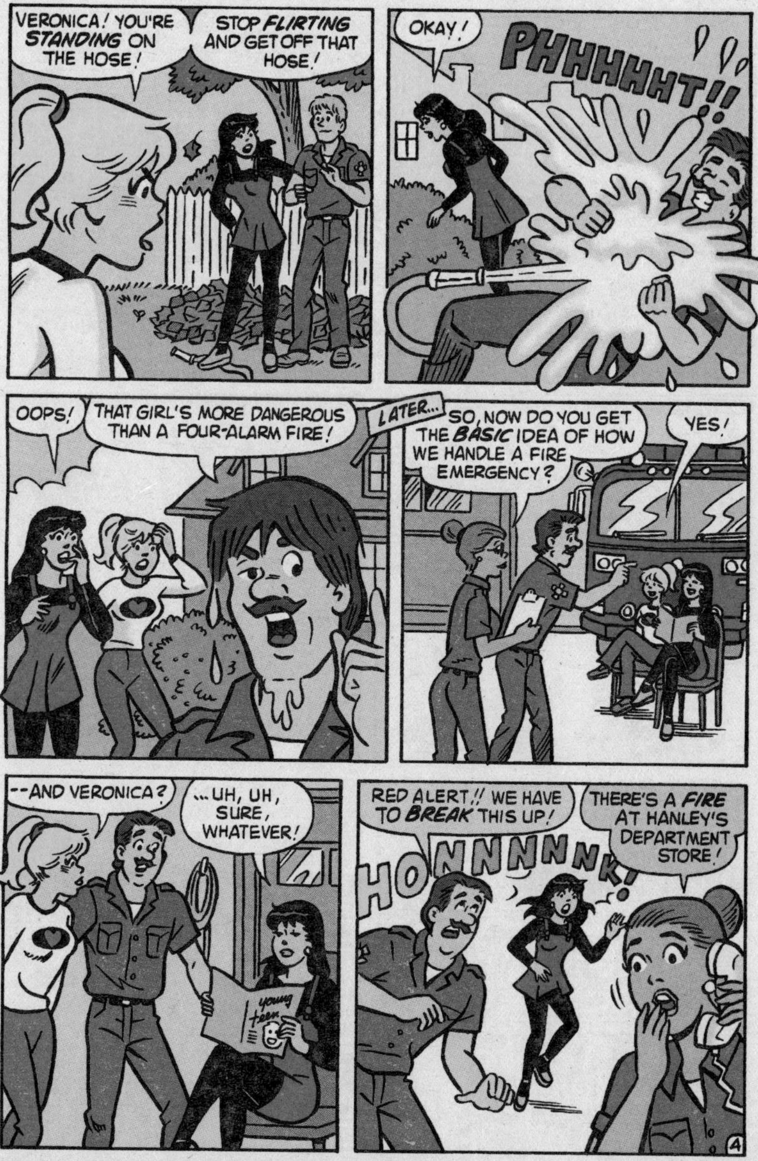
VERONICA! YOU'RE STANDING ON THE HOSE!
STOP FLIRTING AND GET OFF THAT HOSE!
OKAY!
PHHHHHT!!
OOPS!
THAT GIRL'S MORE DANGEROUS THAN A FOUR-ALARM FIRE!
LATER...
SO, NOW DO YOU GET THE BASIC IDEA OF HOW WE HANDLE A FIRE EMERGENCY?
YES!
--AND VERONICA?
...UH, UH, SURE, WHATEVER!
young teen
RED ALERT!! WE HAVE TO BREAK THIS UP!
HONNNNNK!
THERE'S A FIRE AT HANLEY'S DEPARTMENT STORE!
4

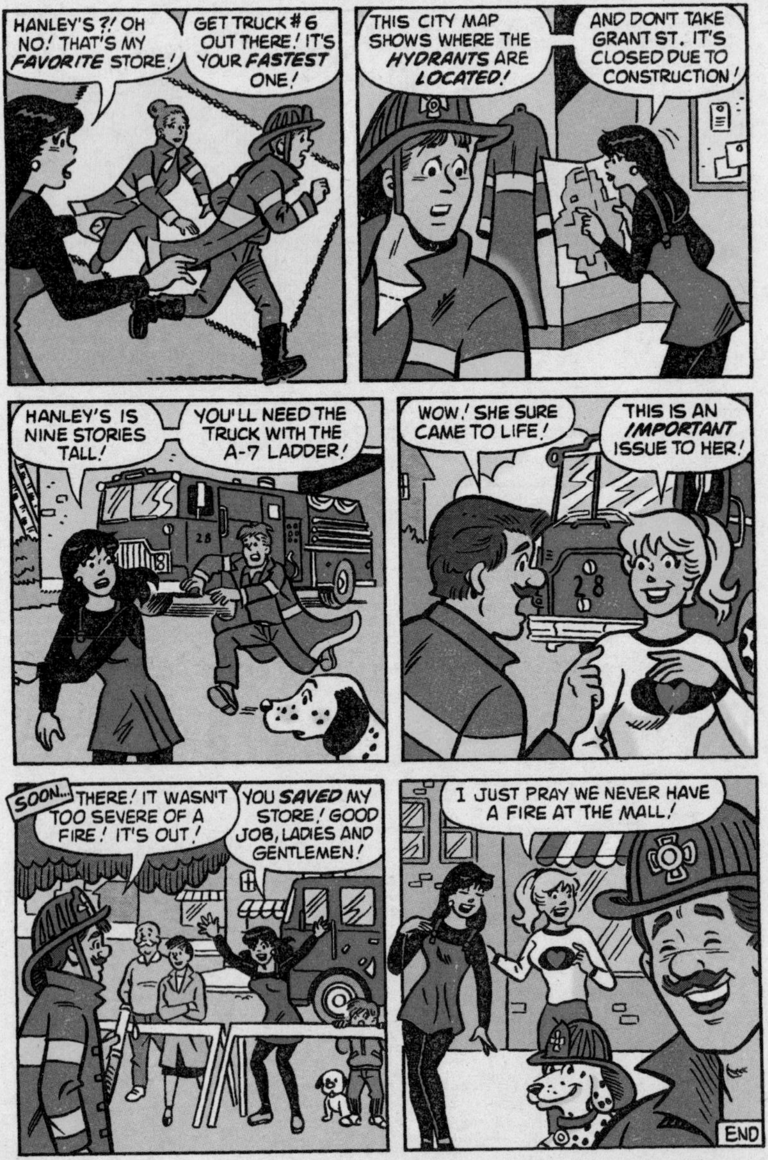
HANLEY'S ?! OH NO! THAT'S MY FAVORITE STORE!
GET TRUCK # 6 OUT THERE! IT'S YOUR FASTEST ONE!
THIS CITY MAP SHOWS WHERE THE HYDRANTS ARE LOCATED!
AND DON'T TAKE GRANT ST. IT'S CLOSED DUE TO CONSTRUCTION!
HANLEY'S IS NINE STORIES TALL!
YOU'LL NEED THE TRUCK WITH THE A-7 LADDER!
WOW! SHE SURE CAME TO LIFE!
THIS IS AN IMPORTANT ISSUE TO HER!
SOON...
THERE! IT WASN'T TOO SEVERE OF A FIRE! IT'S OUT!
YOU SAVED MY STORE! GOOD JOB, LADIES AND GENTLEMEN!
I JUST PRAY WE NEVER HAVE A FIRE AT THE MALL!
END

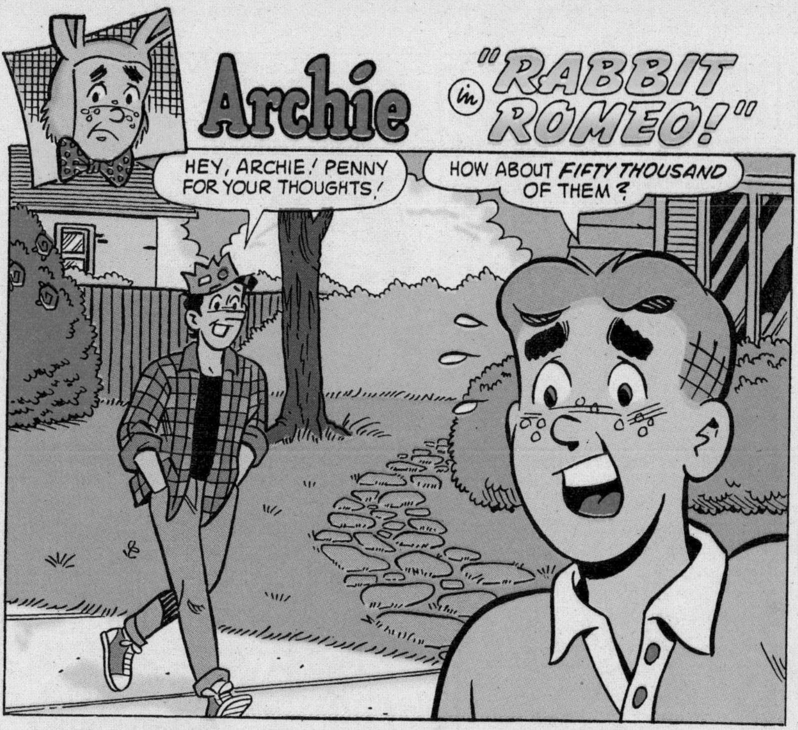
Archie
in "RABBIT ROMEO!"
HEY, ARCHIE! PENNY FOR YOUR THOUGHTS!
HOW ABOUT FIFTY THOUSAND OF THEM?

Script & Pencils: Fernando Ruiz / Inks: Jim Amash / Letters: Bill Yoshida

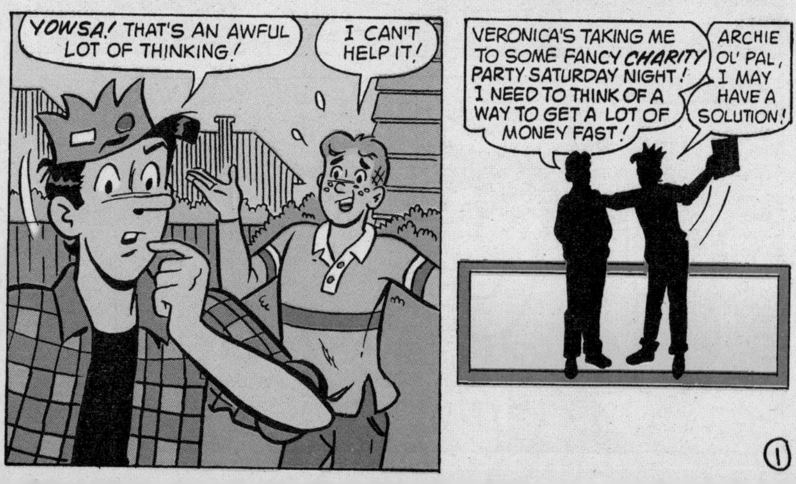
YOWSA! THAT'S AN AWFUL LOT OF THINKING!
I CAN'T HELP IT!
VERONICA'S TAKING ME TO SOME FANCY CHARITY PARTY SATURDAY NIGHT! I NEED TO THINK OF A WAY TO GET A LOT OF MONEY FAST!
ARCHIE OL' PAL, I MAY HAVE A SOLUTION!

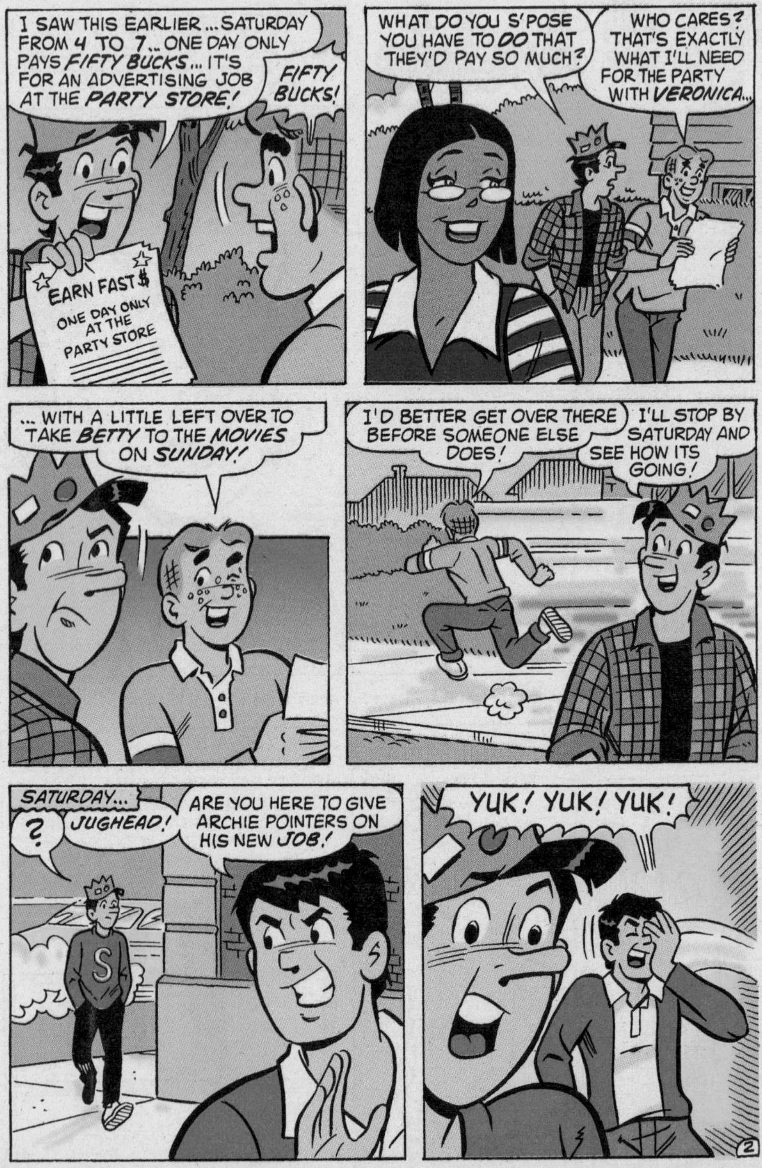
I SAW THIS EARLIER ... SATURDAY FROM 4 TO 7... ONE DAY ONLY PAYS FIFTY BUCKS... IT'S FOR AN ADVERTISING JOB AT THE PARTY STORE!
FIFTY BUCKS!
EARN FAST $
ONE DAY ONLY AT THE PARTY STORE
WHAT DO YOU S'POSE YOU HAVE TO DO THAT THEY'D PAY SO MUCH?
WHO CARES? THAT'S EXACTLY WHAT I'LL NEED FOR THE PARTY WITH VERONICA...
... WITH A LITTLE LEFT OVER TO TAKE BETTY TO THE MOVIES ON SUNDAY!
I'D BETTER GET OVER THERE BEFORE SOMEONE ELSE DOES!
I'LL STOP BY SATURDAY AND SEE HOW ITS GOING!
SATURDAY...
?
JUGHEAD!
ARE YOU HERE TO GIVE ARCHIE POINTERS ON HIS NEW JOB!
YUK! YUK! YUK!
2

GOSH!

ER... HI, FELLAS!

YOU FINALLY FOUND A PERFECT CAREER, ANDREWS! BEING A *DUMB BUNNY!*

ALL YOUR P NEEDS
DONS · FAVOR
COSTUMES

HAVE A BALL at the PARTY STORE

THIS IS A *GREAT* JOB! I BRING JOY TO CHILDREN, HAPPINESS TO OLD PEOPLE AND *ALL* THE GIRLS *NOTICE* ME!

WELL THEN, WE WON'T KEEP YOU! *HOP TO IT!*

LATER...

POP

HAVE A BALL at the PARTY STORE

HAVE A BALL at the PARTY

GRRR!

HAVE A BALL at the PARTY

③

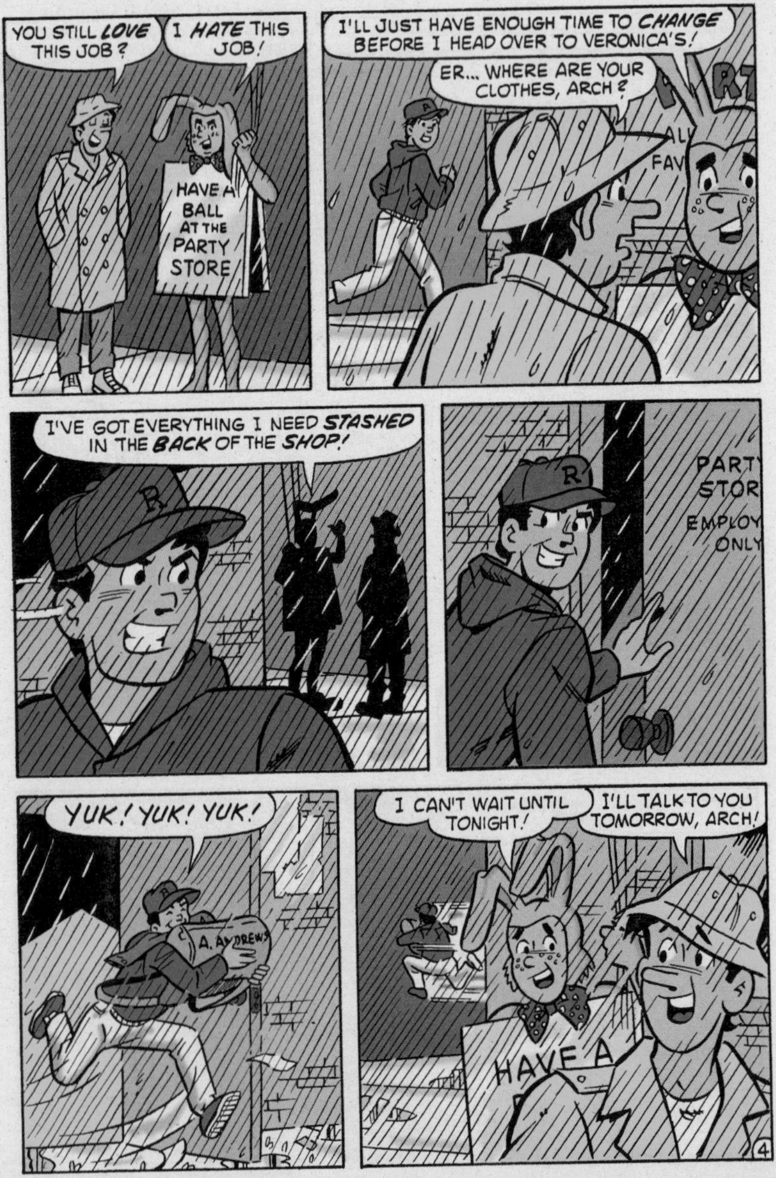

YOU STILL LOVE THIS JOB?
I HATE THIS JOB!
HAVE A BALL AT THE PARTY STORE
I'LL JUST HAVE ENOUGH TIME TO CHANGE BEFORE I HEAD OVER TO VERONICA'S!
ER... WHERE ARE YOUR CLOTHES, ARCH?
I'VE GOT EVERYTHING I NEED STASHED IN THE BACK OF THE SHOP!
YUK! YUK! YUK!
A. ANDREWS
I CAN'T WAIT UNTIL TONIGHT!
I'LL TALK TO YOU TOMORROW, ARCH!
HAVE A
4

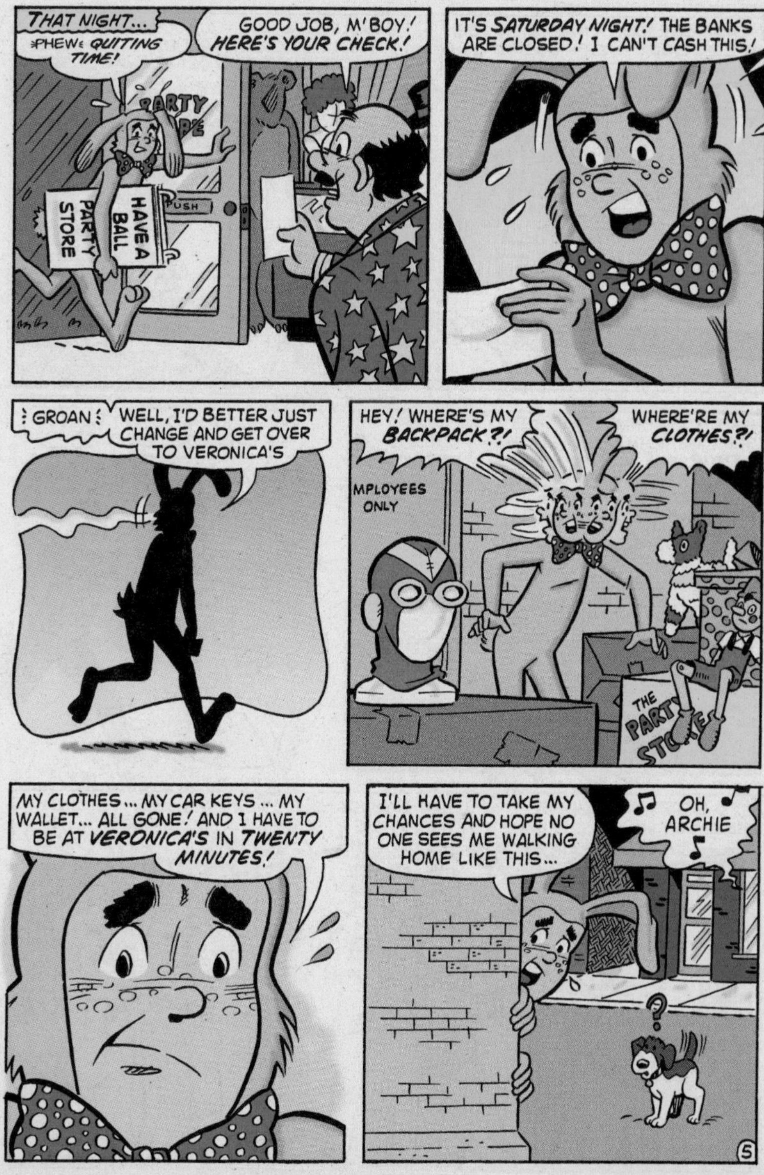
THAT NIGHT...
PHEW! QUITING TIME!
GOOD JOB, M'BOY! HERE'S YOUR CHECK!
PARTY
PUSH
HAVE A BALL PARTY STORE
IT'S SATURDAY NIGHT! THE BANKS ARE CLOSED! I CAN'T CASH THIS!
GROAN
WELL, I'D BETTER JUST CHANGE AND GET OVER TO VERONICA'S
HEY! WHERE'S MY BACKPACK?!
WHERE'RE MY CLOTHES?!
MPLOYEES ONLY
THE PARTY STORE
MY CLOTHES... MY CAR KEYS ... MY WALLET... ALL GONE! AND I HAVE TO BE AT VERONICA'S IN TWENTY MINUTES!
I'LL HAVE TO TAKE MY CHANCES AND HOPE NO ONE SEES ME WALKING HOME LIKE THIS...
OH, ARCHIE
5

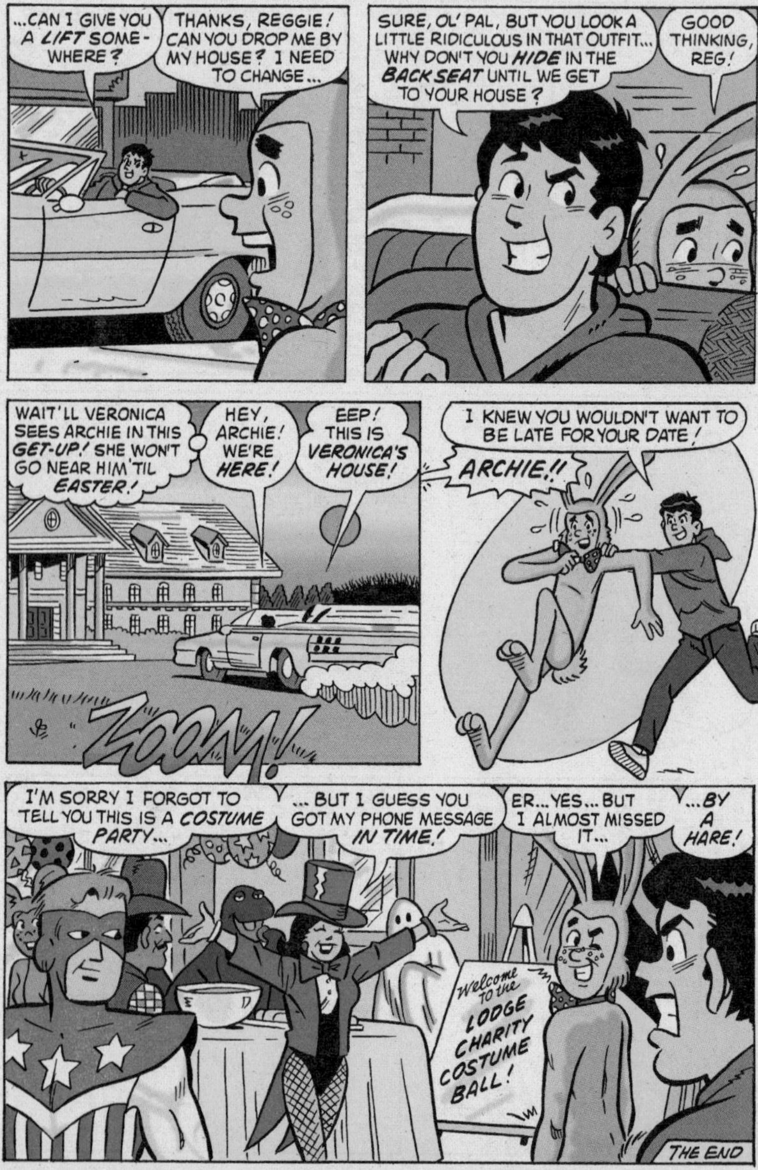
...CAN I GIVE YOU A LIFT SOME-WHERE?
THANKS, REGGIE! CAN YOU DROP ME BY MY HOUSE? I NEED TO CHANGE...
SURE, OL' PAL, BUT YOU LOOK A LITTLE RIDICULOUS IN THAT OUTFIT... WHY DON'T YOU HIDE IN THE BACK SEAT UNTIL WE GET TO YOUR HOUSE?
GOOD THINKING, REG!
WAIT'LL VERONICA SEES ARCHIE IN THIS GET-UP! SHE WON'T GO NEAR HIM 'TIL EASTER!
HEY, ARCHIE! WE'RE HERE!
EEP! THIS IS VERONICA'S HOUSE!
ZOOM!
I KNEW YOU WOULDN'T WANT TO BE LATE FOR YOUR DATE!
ARCHIE!!
I'M SORRY I FORGOT TO TELL YOU THIS IS A COSTUME PARTY...
... BUT I GUESS YOU GOT MY PHONE MESSAGE IN TIME!
ER...YES... BUT I ALMOST MISSED IT...
...BY A HARE!
Welcome to the LODGE CHARITY COSTUME BALL!
THE END

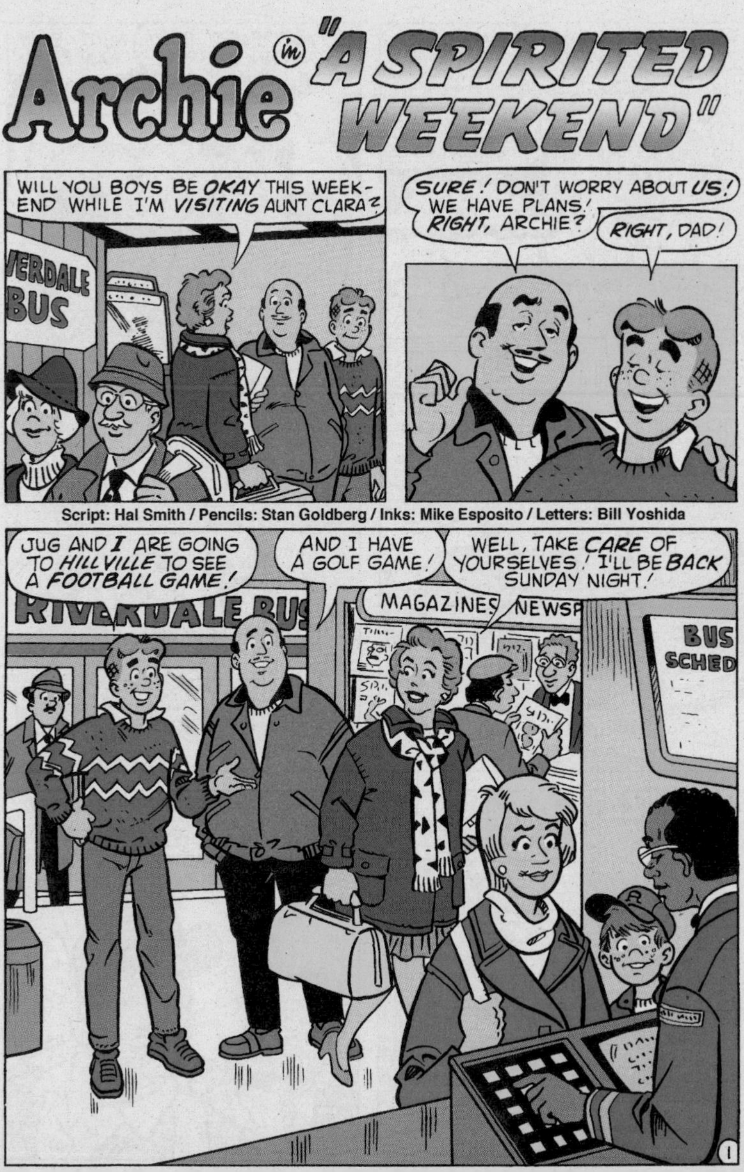

Archie in "A SPIRITED WEEKEND"
WILL YOU BOYS BE OKAY THIS WEEK-END WHILE I'M VISITING AUNT CLARA?
ERDALE BUS
SURE! DON'T WORRY ABOUT US! WE HAVE PLANS! RIGHT, ARCHIE?
RIGHT, DAD!
Script: Hal Smith / Pencils: Stan Goldberg / Inks: Mike Esposito / Letters: Bill Yoshida
JUG AND I ARE GOING TO HILLVILLE TO SEE A FOOTBALL GAME!
AND I HAVE A GOLF GAME!
WELL, TAKE CARE OF YOURSELVES! I'LL BE BACK SUNDAY NIGHT!
RIVERDALE BUS
MAGAZINES NEWSP
BUS SCHED
1

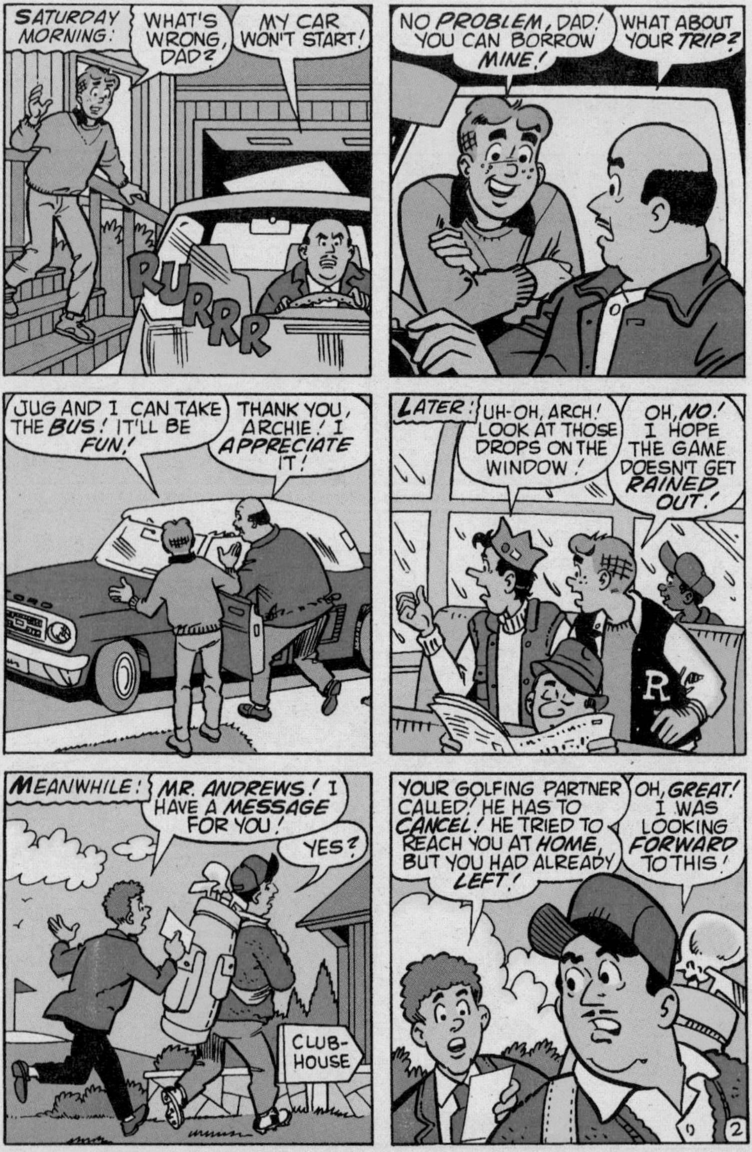
SATURDAY MORNING:
WHAT'S WRONG, DAD?
MY CAR WON'T START!
RURRR
NO PROBLEM, DAD! YOU CAN BORROW MINE!
WHAT ABOUT YOUR TRIP?
JUG AND I CAN TAKE THE BUS! IT'LL BE FUN!
THANK YOU, ARCHIE! I APPRECIATE IT!
LATER:
UH-OH, ARCH! LOOK AT THOSE DROPS ON THE WINDOW!
OH, NO! I HOPE THE GAME DOESN'T GET RAINED OUT!
MEANWHILE:
MR. ANDREWS! I HAVE A MESSAGE FOR YOU!
YES?
CLUB-HOUSE
YOUR GOLFING PARTNER CALLED! HE HAS TO CANCEL! HE TRIED TO REACH YOU AT HOME, BUT YOU HAD ALREADY LEFT!
OH, GREAT! I WAS LOOKING FORWARD TO THIS!
2

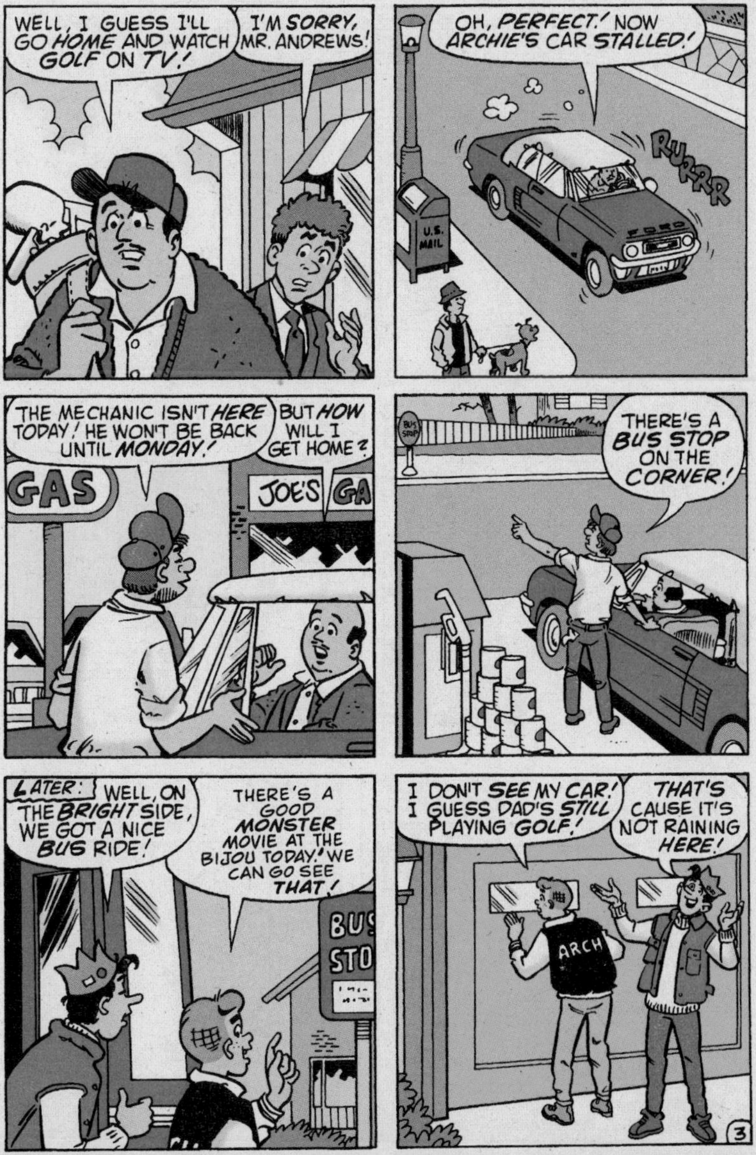
WELL, I GUESS I'LL GO HOME AND WATCH GOLF ON TV!
I'M SORRY, MR. ANDREWS!
OH, PERFECT! NOW ARCHIE'S CAR STALLED!
RURRR
U.S. MAIL
FORD
THE MECHANIC ISN'T HERE TODAY! HE WON'T BE BACK UNTIL MONDAY!
BUT HOW WILL I GET HOME?
GAS
JOE'S GA
THERE'S A BUS STOP ON THE CORNER!
LATER:
WELL, ON THE BRIGHT SIDE, WE GOT A NICE BUS RIDE!
THERE'S A GOOD MONSTER MOVIE AT THE BIJOU TODAY! WE CAN GO SEE THAT!
BUS STO
I DON'T SEE MY CAR! I GUESS DAD'S STILL PLAYING GOLF!
THAT'S CAUSE IT'S NOT RAINING HERE!
ARCH

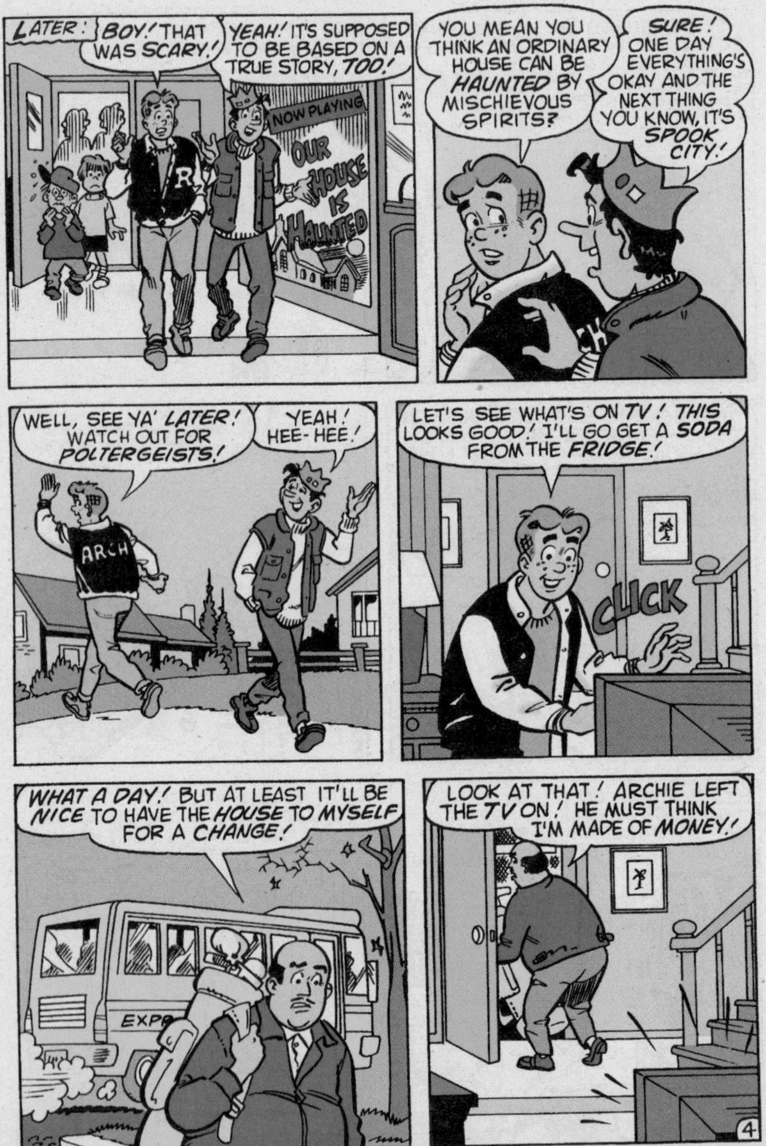
LATER:
BOY! THAT WAS SCARY!
YEAH! IT'S SUPPOSED TO BE BASED ON A TRUE STORY, TOO!
NOW PLAYING
OUR HOUSE IS HAUNTED
YOU MEAN YOU THINK AN ORDINARY HOUSE CAN BE HAUNTED BY MISCHIEVOUS SPIRITS?
SURE! ONE DAY EVERYTHING'S OKAY AND THE NEXT THING YOU KNOW, IT'S SPOOK CITY!
WELL, SEE YA' LATER! WATCH OUT FOR POLTERGEISTS!
YEAH! HEE-HEE!
ARCH
LET'S SEE WHAT'S ON TV! THIS LOOKS GOOD! I'LL GO GET A SODA FROM THE FRIDGE!
CLICK
WHAT A DAY! BUT AT LEAST IT'LL BE NICE TO HAVE THE HOUSE TO MYSELF FOR A CHANGE!
EXP
LOOK AT THAT! ARCHIE LEFT THE TV ON! HE MUST THINK I'M MADE OF MONEY!
4

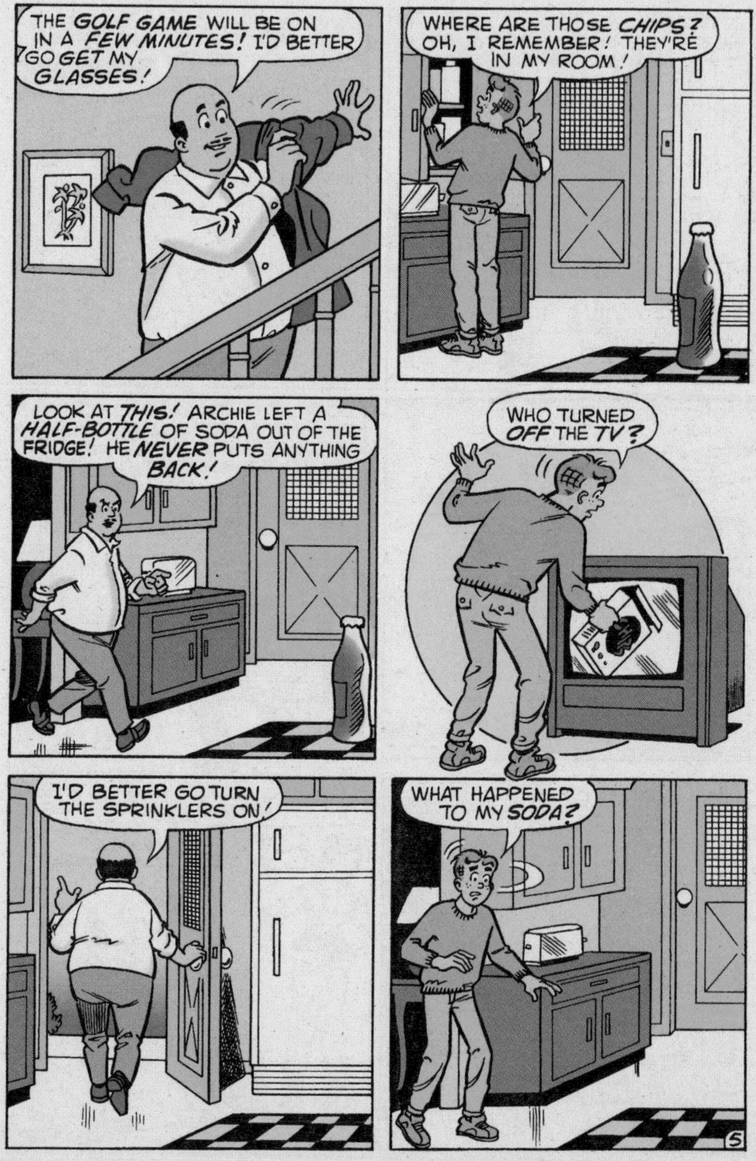
THE GOLF GAME WILL BE ON IN A FEW MINUTES! I'D BETTER GO GET MY GLASSES!
WHERE ARE THOSE CHIPS? OH, I REMEMBER! THEY'RE IN MY ROOM!
LOOK AT THIS! ARCHIE LEFT A HALF-BOTTLE OF SODA OUT OF THE FRIDGE! HE NEVER PUTS ANYTHING BACK!
WHO TURNED OFF THE TV?
I'D BETTER GO TURN THE SPRINKLERS ON!
WHAT HAPPENED TO MY SODA?

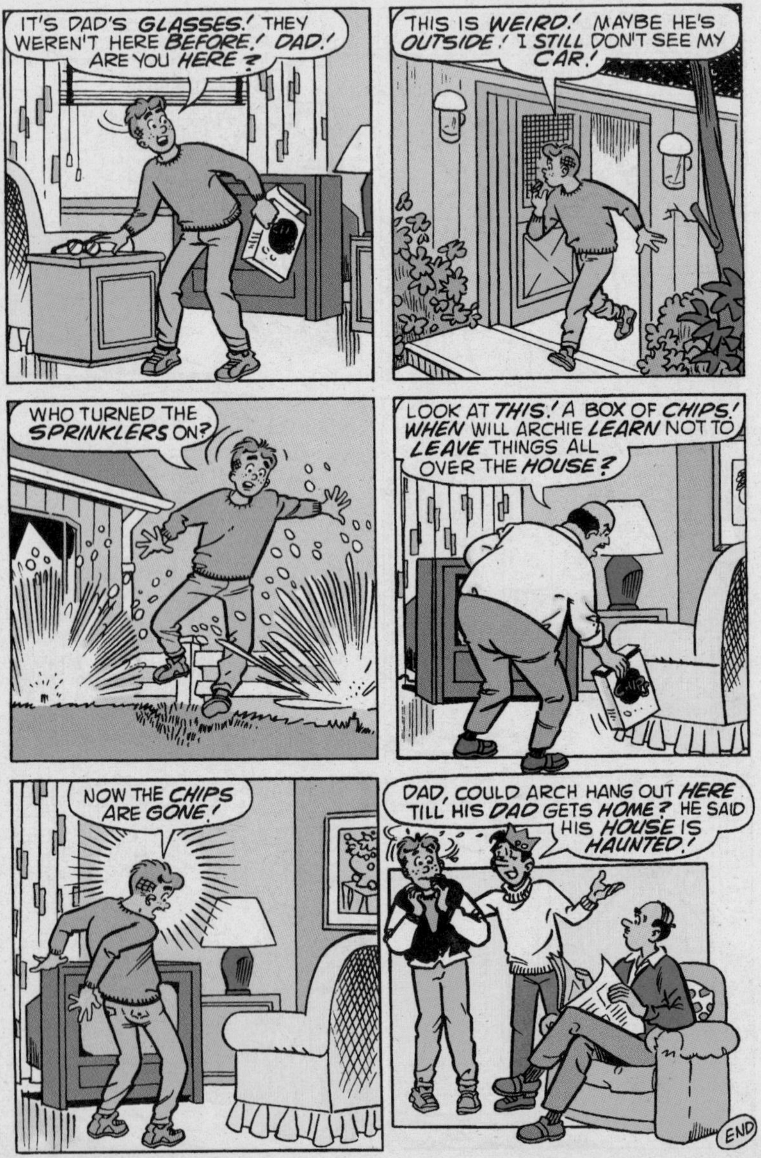
IT'S DAD'S GLASSES! THEY WEREN'T HERE BEFORE! DAD! ARE YOU HERE?
THIS IS WEIRD! MAYBE HE'S OUTSIDE! I STILL DON'T SEE MY CAR!
WHO TURNED THE SPRINKLERS ON?
LOOK AT THIS! A BOX OF CHIPS! WHEN WILL ARCHIE LEARN NOT TO LEAVE THINGS ALL OVER THE HOUSE?
NOW THE CHIPS ARE GONE!
DAD, COULD ARCH HANG OUT HERE TILL HIS DAD GETS HOME? HE SAID HIS HOUSE IS HAUNTED!
END

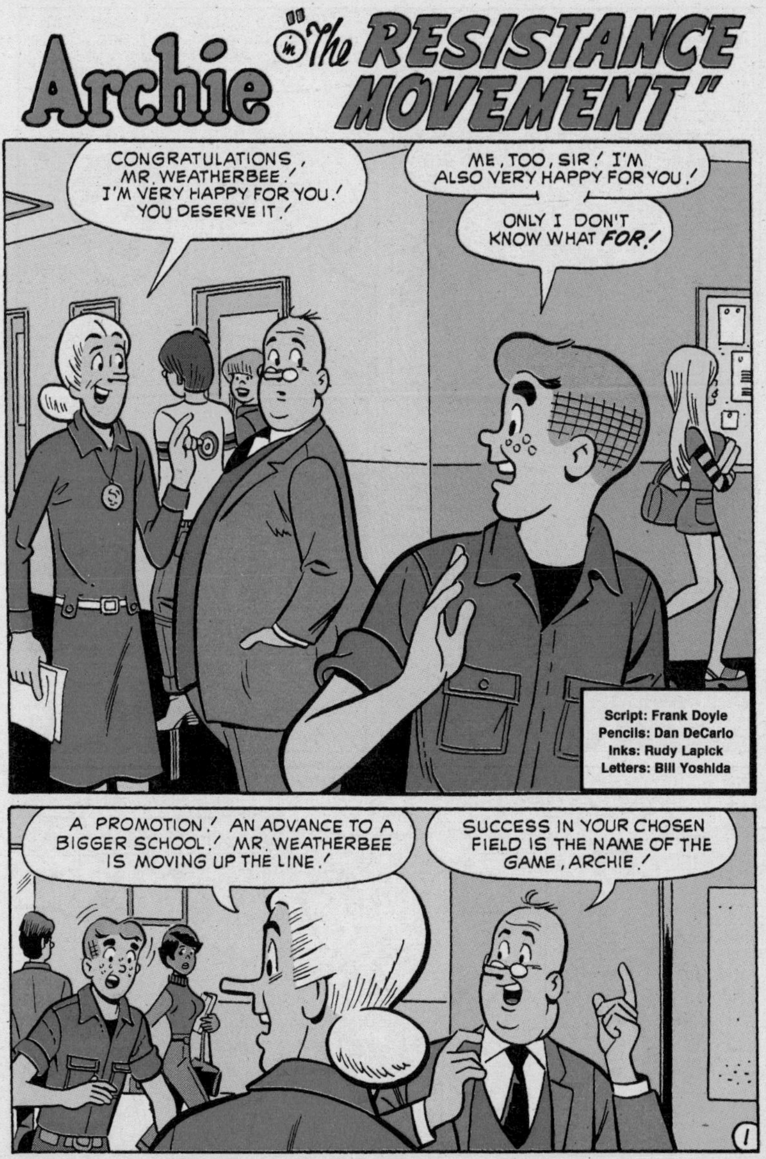
Archie in "The RESISTANCE MOVEMENT"
CONGRATULATIONS, MR. WEATHERBEE! I'M VERY HAPPY FOR YOU! YOU DESERVE IT!
ME, TOO, SIR! I'M ALSO VERY HAPPY FOR YOU!
ONLY I DON'T KNOW WHAT FOR!
Script: Frank Doyle
Pencils: Dan DeCarlo
Inks: Rudy Lapick
Letters: Bill Yoshida
A PROMOTION! AN ADVANCE TO A BIGGER SCHOOL! MR. WEATHERBEE IS MOVING UP THE LINE!
SUCCESS IN YOUR CHOSEN FIELD IS THE NAME OF THE GAME, ARCHIE!
1

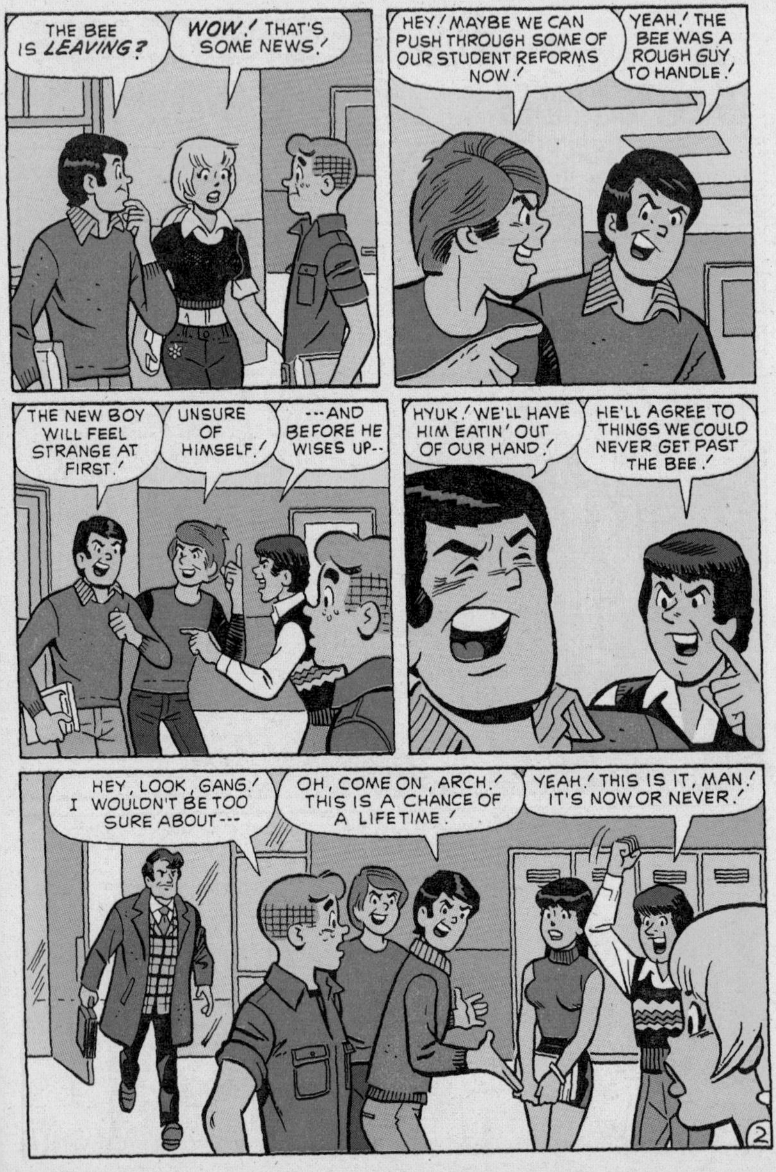
THE BEE IS LEAVING?
WOW! THAT'S SOME NEWS!
HEY! MAYBE WE CAN PUSH THROUGH SOME OF OUR STUDENT REFORMS NOW!
YEAH! THE BEE WAS A ROUGH GUY TO HANDLE!
THE NEW BOY WILL FEEL STRANGE AT FIRST!
UNSURE OF HIMSELF!
---AND BEFORE HE WISES UP--
HYUK! WE'LL HAVE HIM EATIN' OUT OF OUR HAND!
HE'LL AGREE TO THINGS WE COULD NEVER GET PAST THE BEE!
HEY, LOOK, GANG! I WOULDN'T BE TOO SURE ABOUT---
OH, COME ON, ARCH! THIS IS A CHANCE OF A LIFETIME!
YEAH! THIS IS IT, MAN! IT'S NOW OR NEVER!
2

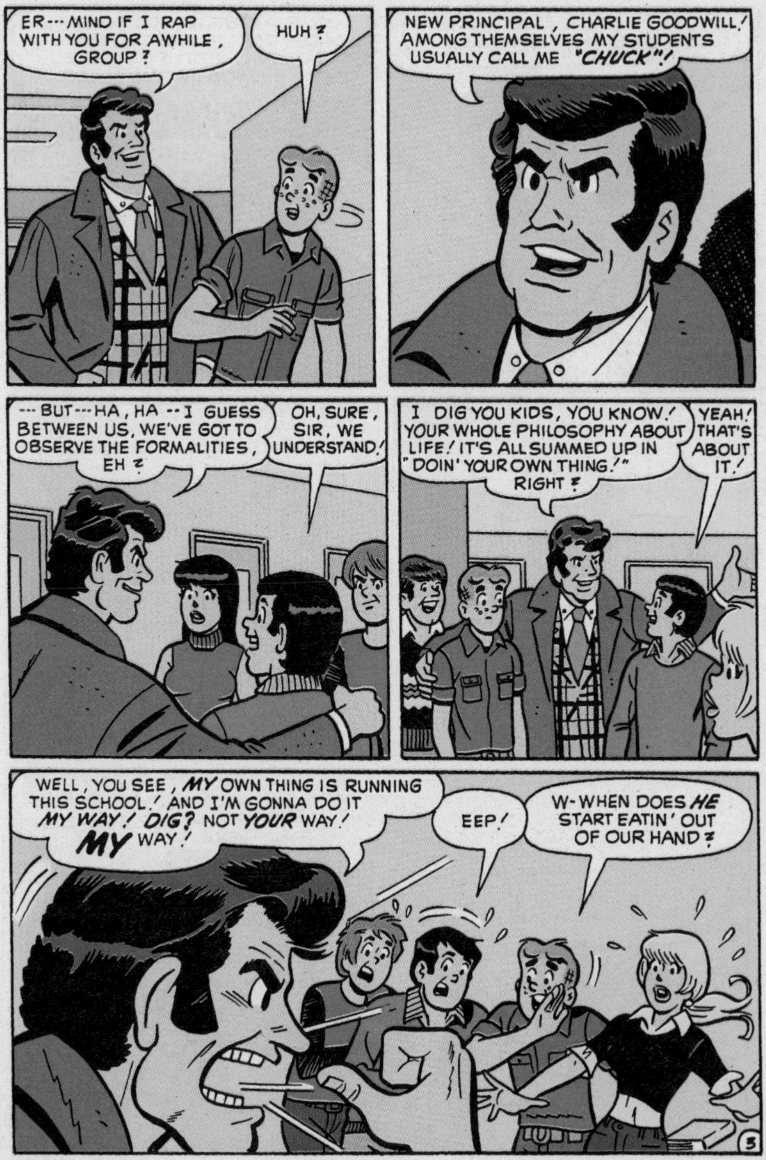

ER--- MIND IF I RAP WITH YOU FOR AWHILE, GROUP?
HUH?
NEW PRINCIPAL, CHARLIE GOODWILL! AMONG THEMSELVES MY STUDENTS USUALLY CALL ME "CHUCK"!
--- BUT--- HA, HA -- I GUESS BETWEEN US, WE'VE GOT TO OBSERVE THE FORMALITIES, EH?
OH, SURE, SIR, WE UNDERSTAND!
I DIG YOU KIDS, YOU KNOW! YOUR WHOLE PHILOSOPHY ABOUT LIFE! IT'S ALL SUMMED UP IN "DOIN' YOUR OWN THING!" RIGHT?
YEAH! THAT'S ABOUT IT!
WELL, YOU SEE, MY OWN THING IS RUNNING THIS SCHOOL! AND I'M GONNA DO IT MY WAY! DIG? NOT YOUR WAY! MY WAY!
EEP!
W-WHEN DOES HE START EATIN' OUT OF OUR HAND?
3

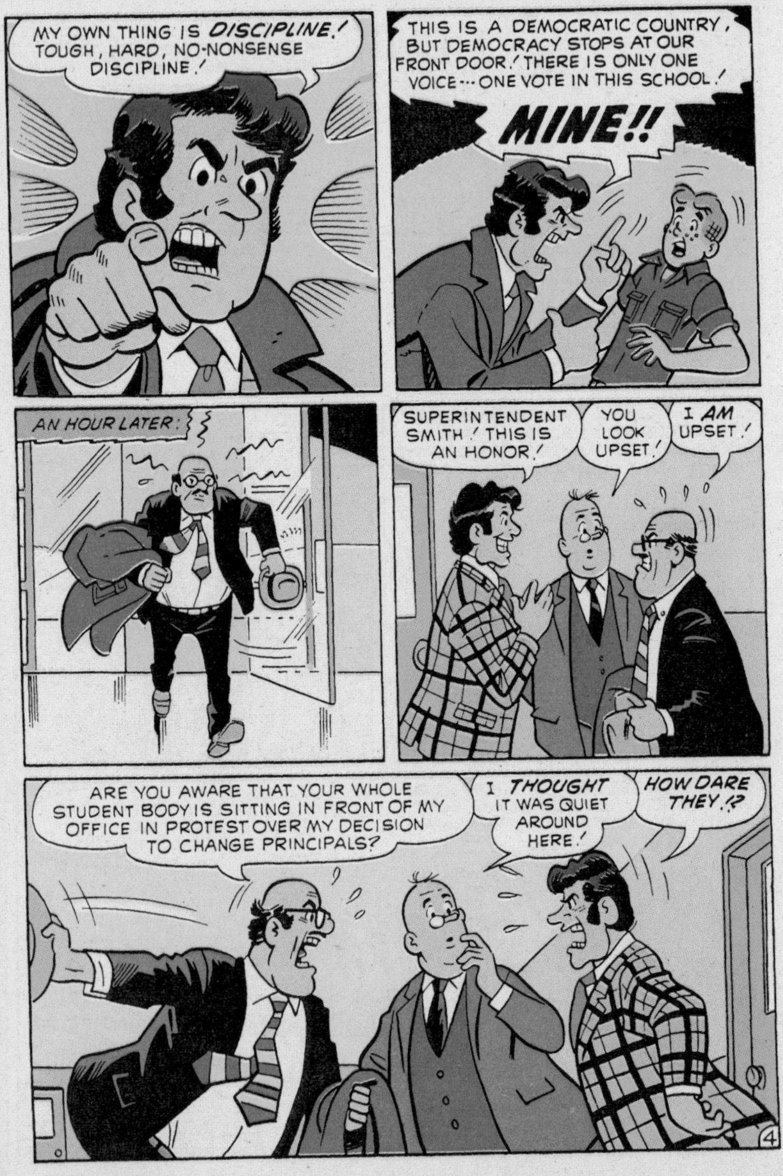

MY OWN THING IS DISCIPLINE! TOUGH, HARD, NO-NONSENSE DISCIPLINE!
THIS IS A DEMOCRATIC COUNTRY, BUT DEMOCRACY STOPS AT OUR FRONT DOOR! THERE IS ONLY ONE VOICE--- ONE VOTE IN THIS SCHOOL!
MINE!!
AN HOUR LATER:
SUPERINTENDENT SMITH! THIS IS AN HONOR!
YOU LOOK UPSET!
I AM UPSET!
ARE YOU AWARE THAT YOUR WHOLE STUDENT BODY IS SITTING IN FRONT OF MY OFFICE IN PROTEST OVER MY DECISION TO CHANGE PRINCIPALS?
I THOUGHT IT WAS QUIET AROUND HERE!
HOW DARE THEY!?
4

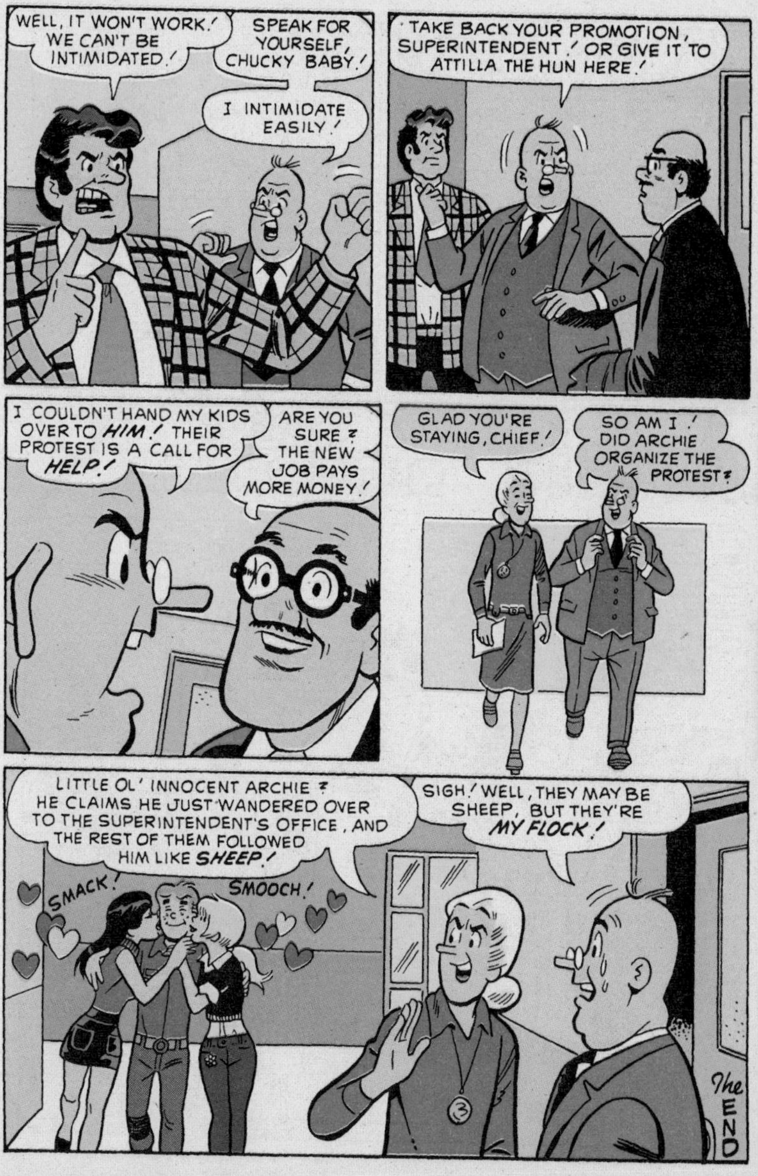

WELL, IT WON'T WORK! WE CAN'T BE INTIMIDATED!
SPEAK FOR YOURSELF, CHUCKY BABY!
I INTIMIDATE EASILY!
TAKE BACK YOUR PROMOTION, SUPERINTENDENT! OR GIVE IT TO ATTILLA THE HUN HERE!
I COULDN'T HAND MY KIDS OVER TO HIM! THEIR PROTEST IS A CALL FOR HELP!
ARE YOU SURE? THE NEW JOB PAYS MORE MONEY!
GLAD YOU'RE STAYING, CHIEF!
SO AM I! DID ARCHIE ORGANIZE THE PROTEST?
LITTLE OL' INNOCENT ARCHIE? HE CLAIMS HE JUST WANDERED OVER TO THE SUPERINTENDENT'S OFFICE, AND THE REST OF THEM FOLLOWED HIM LIKE SHEEP!
SMACK!
SMOOCH!
SIGH! WELL, THEY MAY BE SHEEP, BUT THEY'RE MY FLOCK!
The END

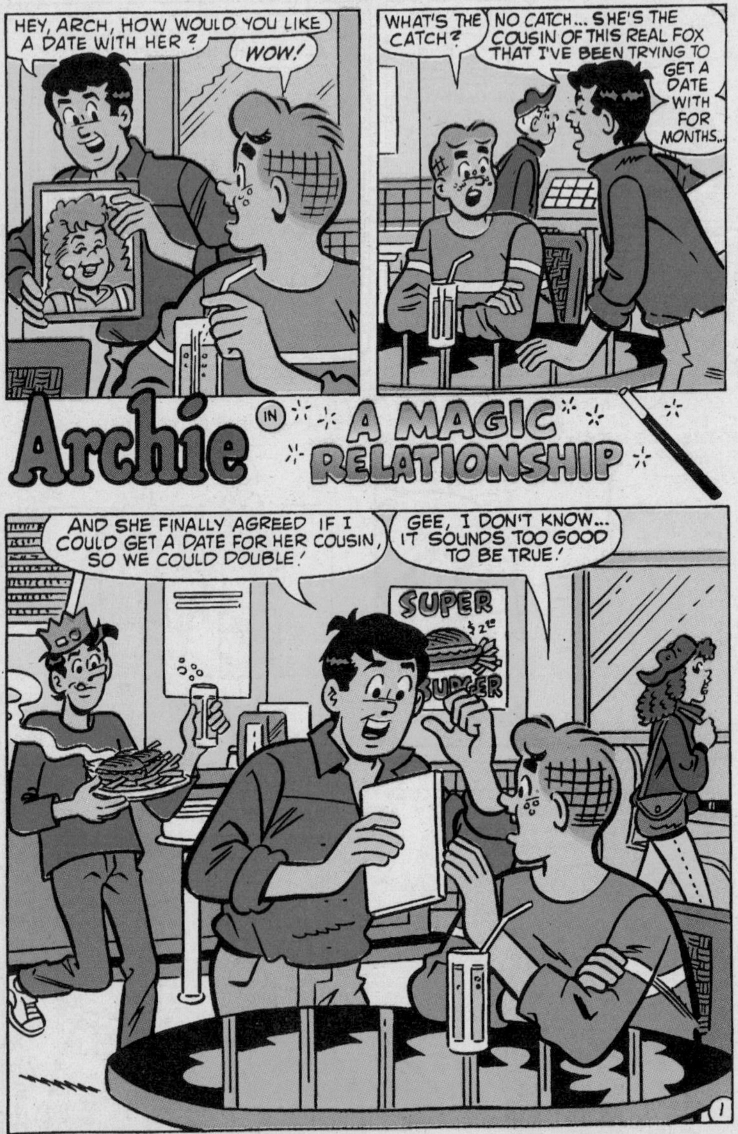
HEY, ARCH, HOW WOULD YOU LIKE A DATE WITH HER?
WOW!
WHAT'S THE CATCH?
NO CATCH... SHE'S THE COUSIN OF THIS REAL FOX THAT I'VE BEEN TRYING TO GET A DATE WITH FOR MONTHS...
Archie
IN
A MAGIC RELATIONSHIP
AND SHE FINALLY AGREED IF I COULD GET A DATE FOR HER COUSIN, SO WE COULD DOUBLE!
GEE, I DON'T KNOW... IT SOUNDS TOO GOOD TO BE TRUE!
SUPER
$2.00
BURGER
1

Script: Hal Smith / Pencils: Tim Kennedy / Inks: Rudy Lapick / Letters: Bill Yoshida

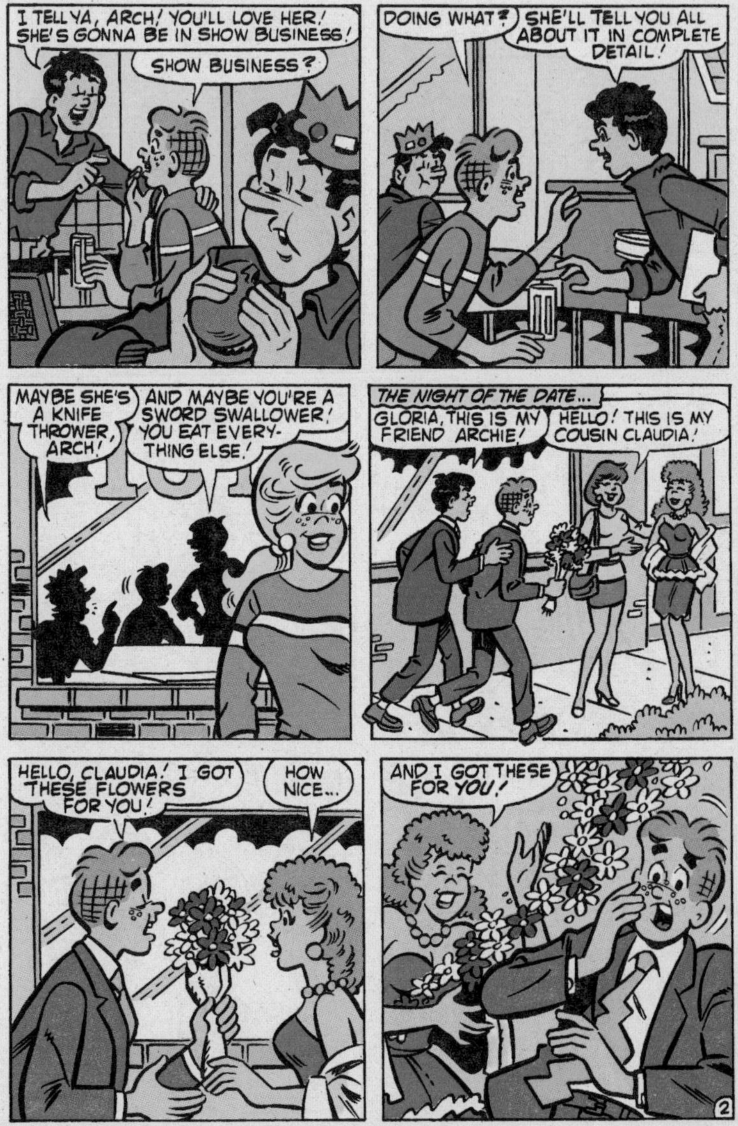
I TELL YA, ARCH! YOU'LL LOVE HER! SHE'S GONNA BE IN SHOW BUSINESS!
SHOW BUSINESS?
DOING WHAT?
SHE'LL TELL YOU ALL ABOUT IT IN COMPLETE DETAIL!
MAYBE SHE'S A KNIFE THROWER, ARCH!
AND MAYBE YOU'RE A SWORD SWALLOWER! YOU EAT EVERYTHING ELSE!
THE NIGHT OF THE DATE...
GLORIA, THIS IS MY FRIEND ARCHIE!
HELLO! THIS IS MY COUSIN CLAUDIA!
HELLO, CLAUDIA! I GOT THESE FLOWERS FOR YOU!
HOW NICE...
AND I GOT THESE FOR YOU!
2

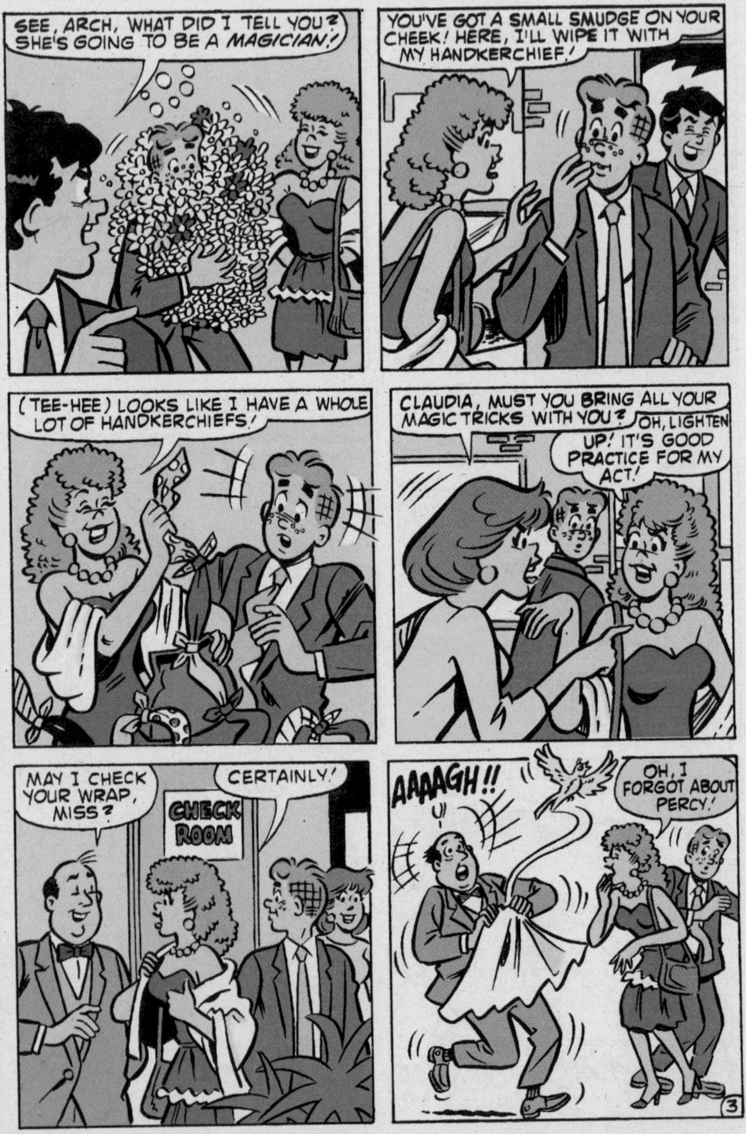
SEE, ARCH, WHAT DID I TELL YOU? SHE'S GOING TO BE A *MAGICIAN*!
YOU'VE GOT A SMALL SMUDGE ON YOUR CHEEK! HERE, I'LL WIPE IT WITH MY HANDKERCHIEF!
(TEE-HEE) LOOKS LIKE I HAVE A WHOLE LOT OF HANDKERCHIEFS!
CLAUDIA, MUST YOU BRING ALL YOUR MAGIC TRICKS WITH YOU?
OH, LIGHTEN UP! IT'S GOOD PRACTICE FOR MY ACT!
MAY I CHECK YOUR WRAP, MISS?
CHECK ROOM
CERTAINLY!
AAAAGH!!
U!
OH, I FORGOT ABOUT PERCY!
3

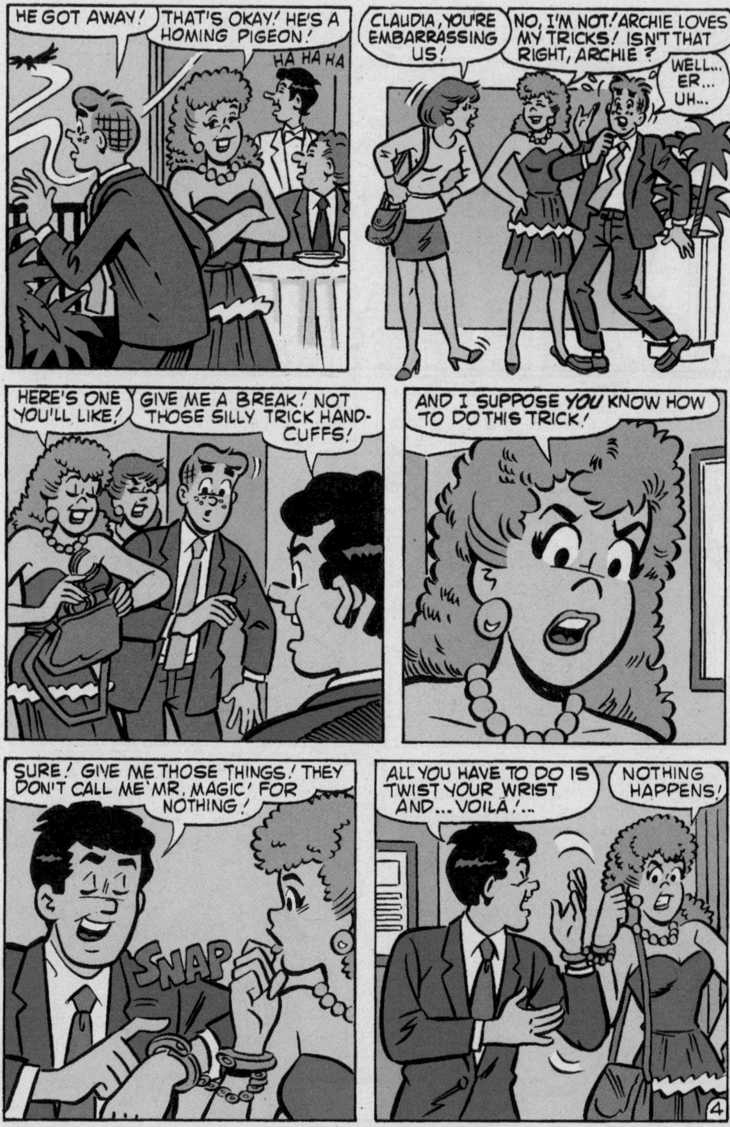

HE GOT AWAY!
THAT'S OKAY! HE'S A HOMING PIGEON!
HA HA HA
CLAUDIA, YOU'RE EMBARRASSING US!
NO, I'M NOT! ARCHIE LOVES MY TRICKS! ISN'T THAT RIGHT, ARCHIE?
WELL... ER... UH...
HERE'S ONE YOU'LL LIKE!
GIVE ME A BREAK! NOT THOSE SILLY TRICK HAND-CUFFS!
AND I SUPPOSE YOU KNOW HOW TO DO THIS TRICK!
SURE! GIVE ME THOSE THINGS! THEY DON'T CALL ME 'MR. MAGIC' FOR NOTHING!
SNAP
ALL YOU HAVE TO DO IS TWIST YOUR WRIST AND... VOILÀ!...
NOTHING HAPPENS!
4

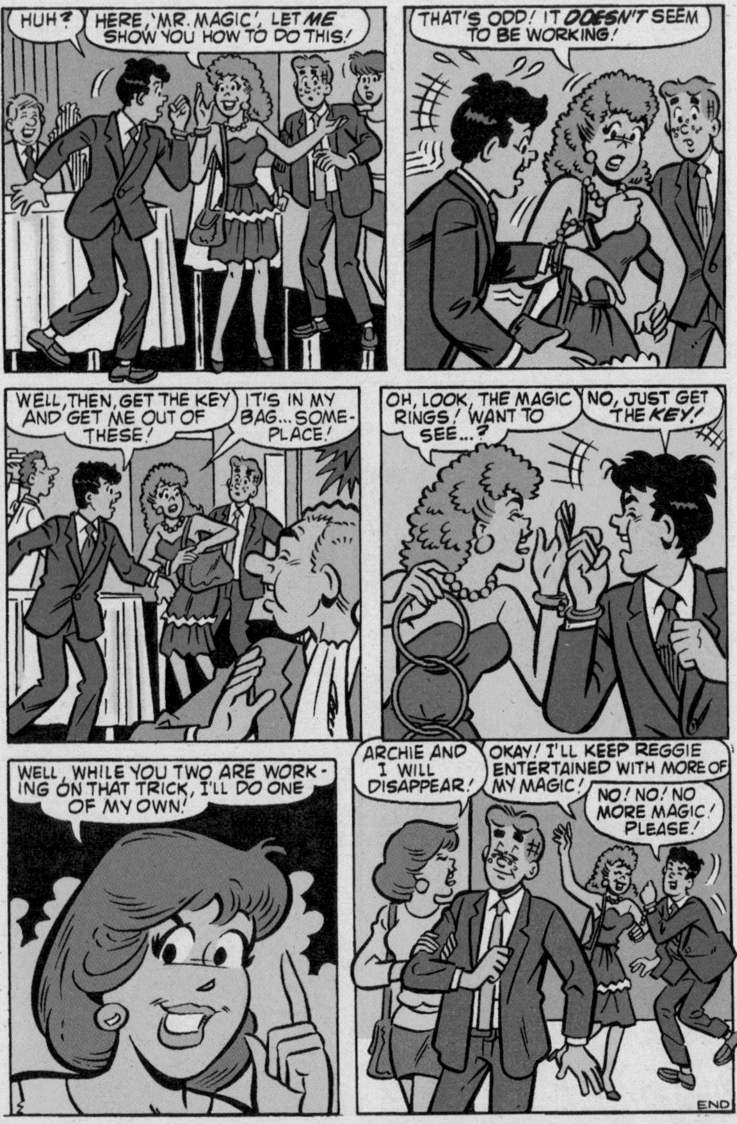
HUH?
HERE, 'MR. MAGIC', LET ME SHOW YOU HOW TO DO THIS!
THAT'S ODD! IT DOESN'T SEEM TO BE WORKING!
WELL, THEN, GET THE KEY AND GET ME OUT OF THESE!
IT'S IN MY BAG... SOME-PLACE!
OH, LOOK, THE MAGIC RINGS! WANT TO SEE...?
NO, JUST GET THE KEY!
WELL, WHILE YOU TWO ARE WORK-ING ON THAT TRICK, I'LL DO ONE OF MY OWN!
ARCHIE AND I WILL DISAPPEAR!
OKAY! I'LL KEEP REGGIE ENTERTAINED WITH MORE OF MY MAGIC!
NO! NO! NO MORE MAGIC! PLEASE!
END

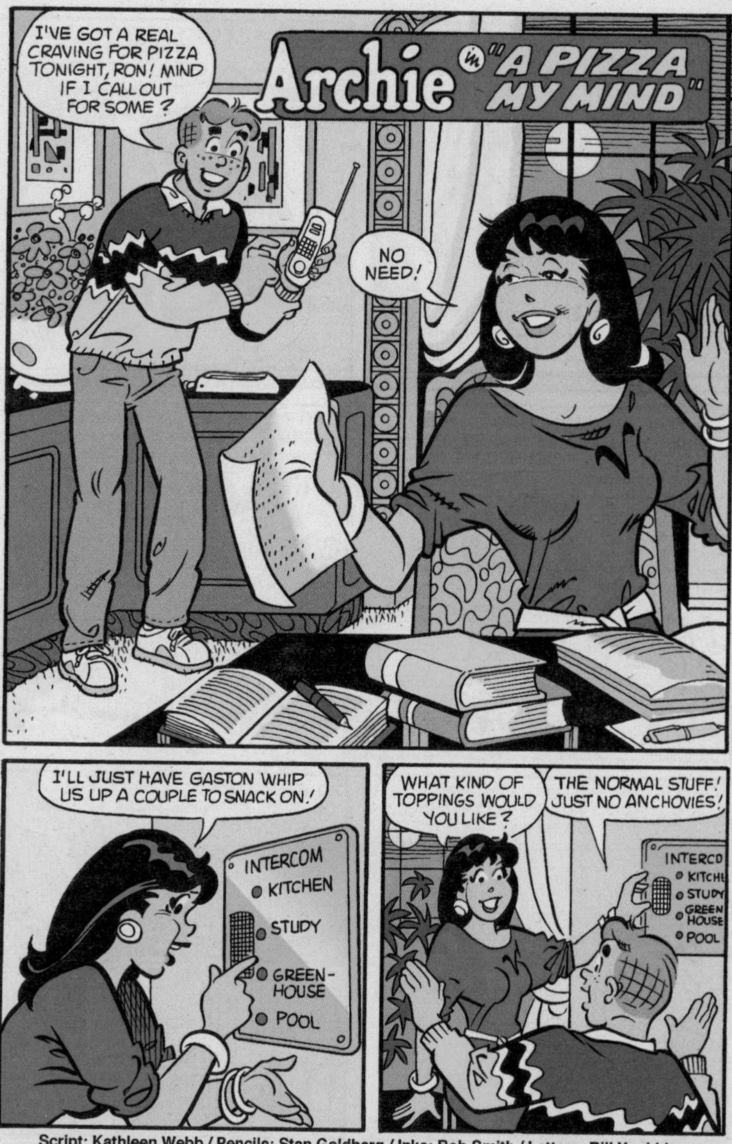
I'VE GOT A REAL CRAVING FOR PIZZA TONIGHT, RON! MIND IF I CALL OUT FOR SOME?
Archie in "A PIZZA MY MIND"
NO NEED!
I'LL JUST HAVE GASTON WHIP US UP A COUPLE TO SNACK ON!
INTERCOM
KITCHEN
STUDY
GREEN-HOUSE
POOL
WHAT KIND OF TOPPINGS WOULD YOU LIKE?
THE NORMAL STUFF! JUST NO ANCHOVIES!

Script: Kathleen Webb / Pencils: Stan Goldberg / Inks: Bob Smith / Letters: Bill Yoshida

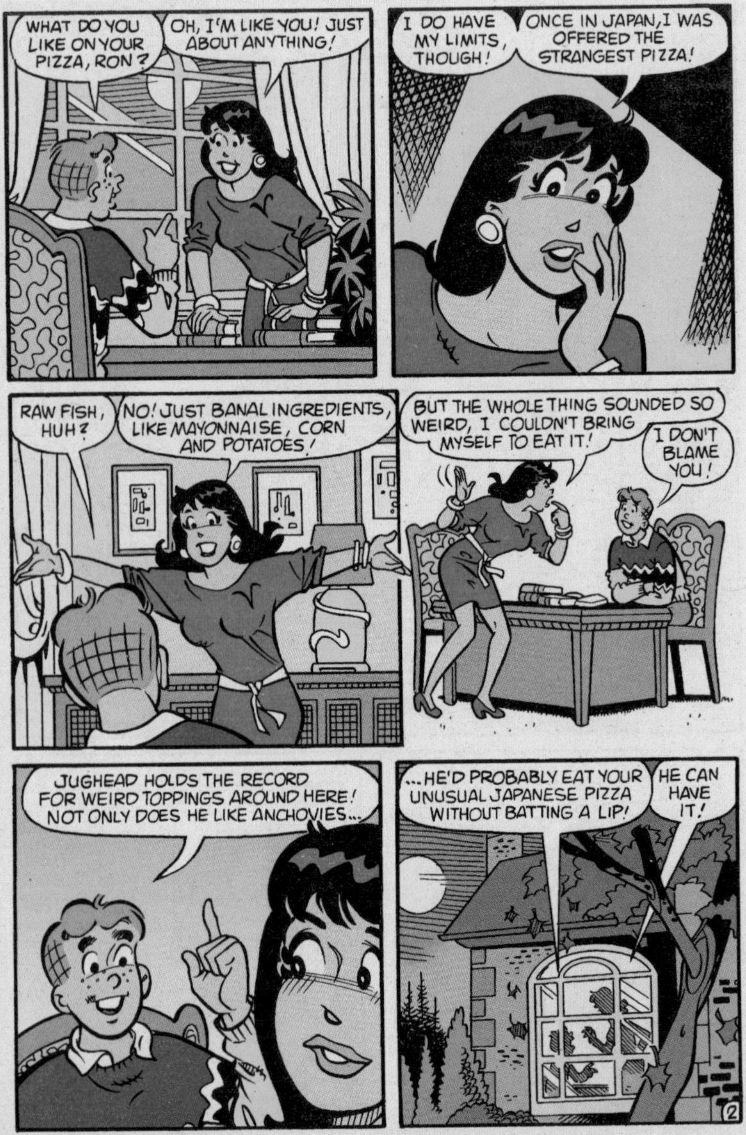
WHAT DO YOU LIKE ON YOUR PIZZA, RON?
OH, I'M LIKE YOU! JUST ABOUT ANYTHING!
I DO HAVE MY LIMITS, THOUGH!
ONCE IN JAPAN, I WAS OFFERED THE STRANGEST PIZZA!
RAW FISH, HUH?
NO! JUST BANAL INGREDIENTS, LIKE MAYONNAISE, CORN AND POTATOES!
BUT THE WHOLE THING SOUNDED SO WEIRD, I COULDN'T BRING MYSELF TO EAT IT!
I DON'T BLAME YOU!
JUGHEAD HOLDS THE RECORD FOR WEIRD TOPPINGS AROUND HERE! NOT ONLY DOES HE LIKE ANCHOVIES...
...HE'D PROBABLY EAT YOUR UNUSUAL JAPANESE PIZZA WITHOUT BATTING A LIP!
HE CAN HAVE IT!
2

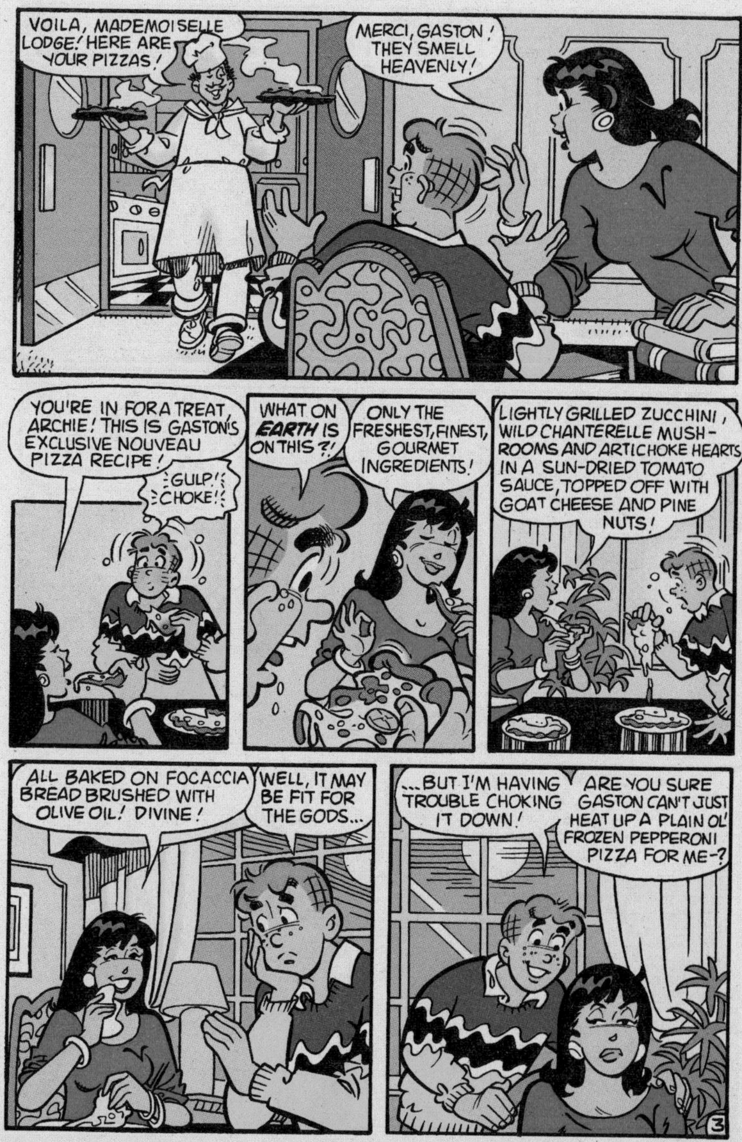

VOILA, MADEMOISELLE LODGE! HERE ARE YOUR PIZZAS!
MERCI, GASTON! THEY SMELL HEAVENLY!
YOU'RE IN FOR A TREAT, ARCHIE! THIS IS GASTON'S EXCLUSIVE NOUVEAU PIZZA RECIPE!
GULP! CHOKE!
WHAT ON EARTH IS ON THIS?!
ONLY THE FRESHEST, FINEST, GOURMET INGREDIENTS!
LIGHTLY GRILLED ZUCCHINI, WILD CHANTERELLE MUSH-ROOMS AND ARTICHOKE HEARTS IN A SUN-DRIED TOMATO SAUCE, TOPPED OFF WITH GOAT CHEESE AND PINE NUTS!
ALL BAKED ON FOCACCIA BREAD BRUSHED WITH OLIVE OIL! DIVINE!
WELL, IT MAY BE FIT FOR THE GODS...
...BUT I'M HAVING TROUBLE CHOKING IT DOWN!
ARE YOU SURE GASTON CAN'T JUST HEAT UP A PLAIN OL' FROZEN PEPPERONI PIZZA FOR ME-?
3

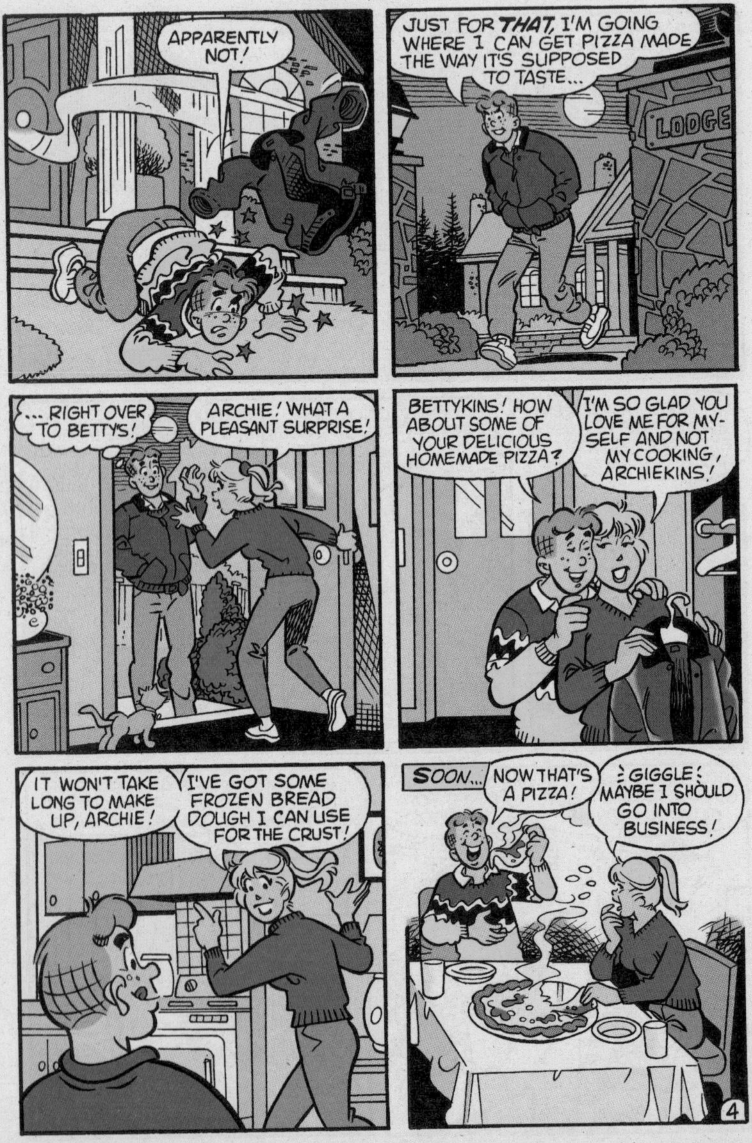

APPARENTLY NOT!
JUST FOR ***THAT,*** I'M GOING WHERE I CAN GET PIZZA MADE THE WAY IT'S SUPPOSED TO TASTE...
LODGE
... RIGHT OVER TO BETTY'S!
ARCHIE! WHAT A PLEASANT SURPRISE!
BETTYKINS! HOW ABOUT SOME OF YOUR DELICIOUS HOMEMADE PIZZA?
I'M SO GLAD YOU LOVE ME FOR MY-SELF AND NOT MY COOKING, ARCHIEKINS!
IT WON'T TAKE LONG TO MAKE UP, ARCHIE!
I'VE GOT SOME FROZEN BREAD DOUGH I CAN USE FOR THE CRUST!
SOON...
NOW THAT'S A PIZZA!
⁝GIGGLE⁝ MAYBE I SHOULD GO INTO BUSINESS!
4

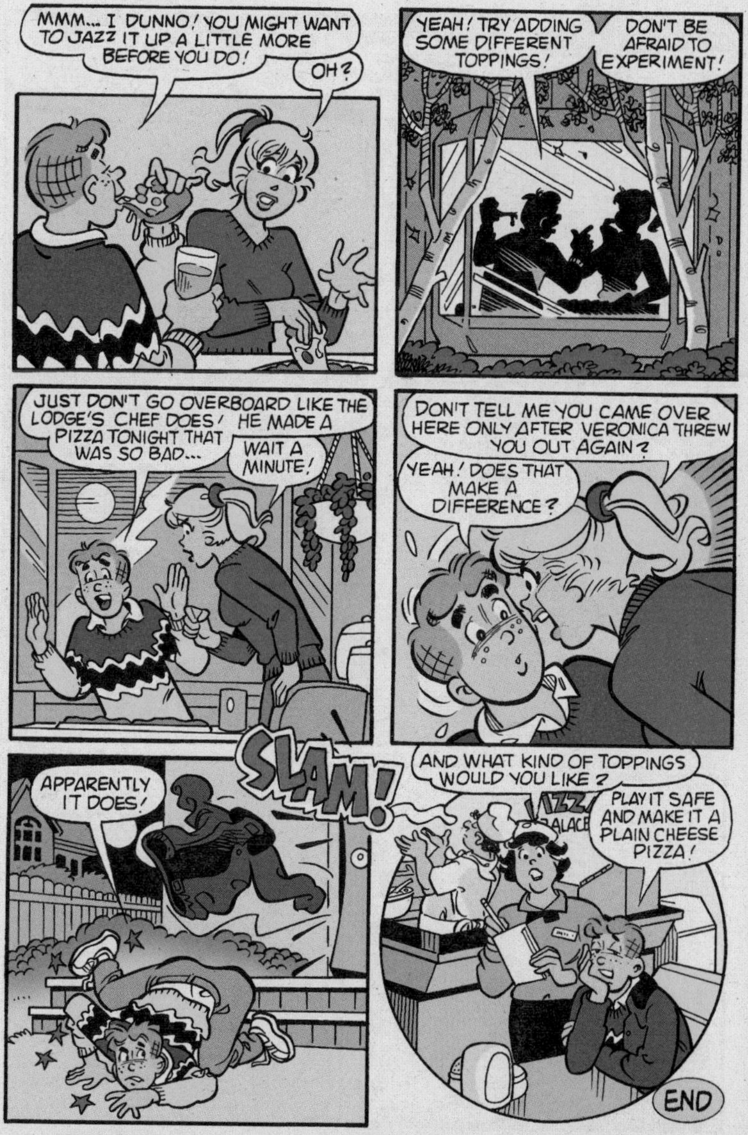
MMM... I DUNNO! YOU MIGHT WANT TO JAZZ IT UP A LITTLE MORE BEFORE YOU DO!
OH?
YEAH! TRY ADDING SOME DIFFERENT TOPPINGS!
DON'T BE AFRAID TO EXPERIMENT!
JUST DON'T GO OVERBOARD LIKE THE LODGE'S CHEF DOES! HE MADE A PIZZA TONIGHT THAT WAS SO BAD...
WAIT A MINUTE!
DON'T TELL ME YOU CAME OVER HERE ONLY AFTER VERONICA THREW YOU OUT AGAIN?
YEAH! DOES THAT MAKE A DIFFERENCE?
SLAM!
APPARENTLY IT DOES!
AND WHAT KIND OF TOPPINGS WOULD YOU LIKE?
PLAY IT SAFE AND MAKE IT A PLAIN CHEESE PIZZA!
END

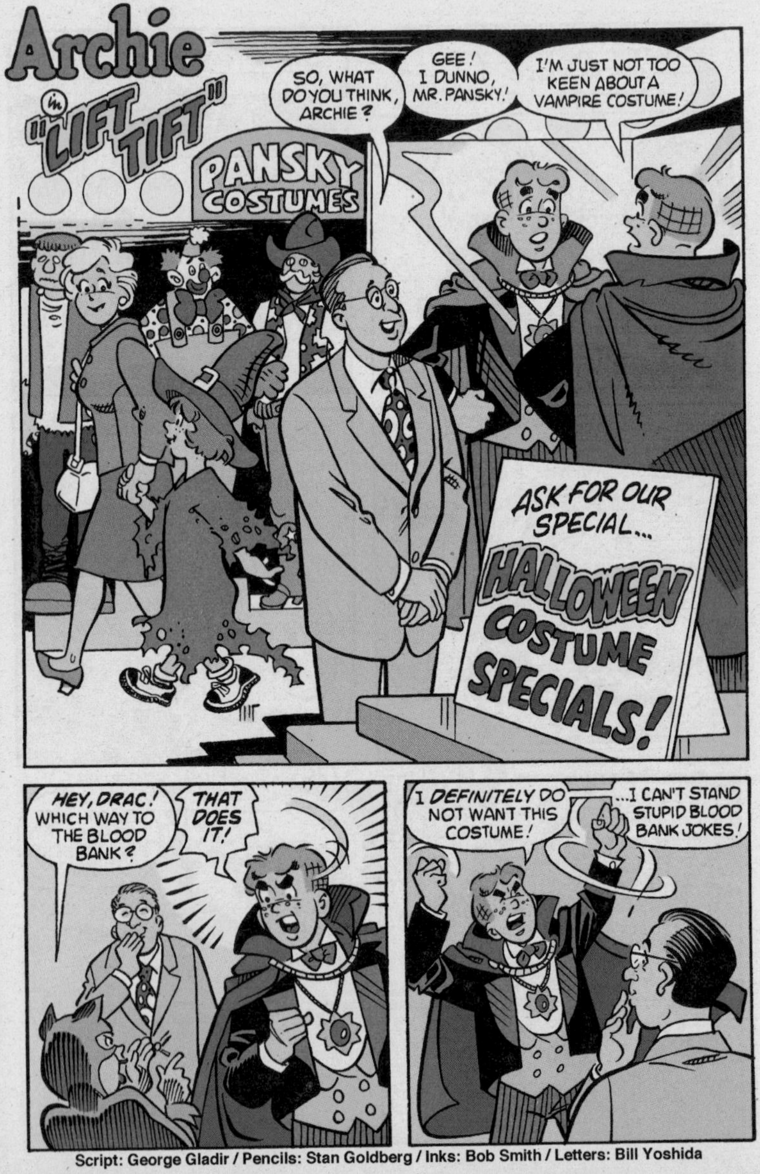
Archie
in "LIFT TIFT"
PANSKY COSTUMES
SO, WHAT DO YOU THINK, ARCHIE?
GEE! I DUNNO, MR. PANSKY!
I'M JUST NOT TOO KEEN ABOUT A VAMPIRE COSTUME!
ASK FOR OUR SPECIAL... HALLOWEEN COSTUME SPECIALS!
HEY, DRAC! WHICH WAY TO THE BLOOD BANK?
THAT DOES IT!
I DEFINITELY DO NOT WANT THIS COSTUME!
...I CAN'T STAND STUPID BLOOD BANK JOKES!

Script: George Gladir / Pencils: Stan Goldberg / Inks: Bob Smith / Letters: Bill Yoshida

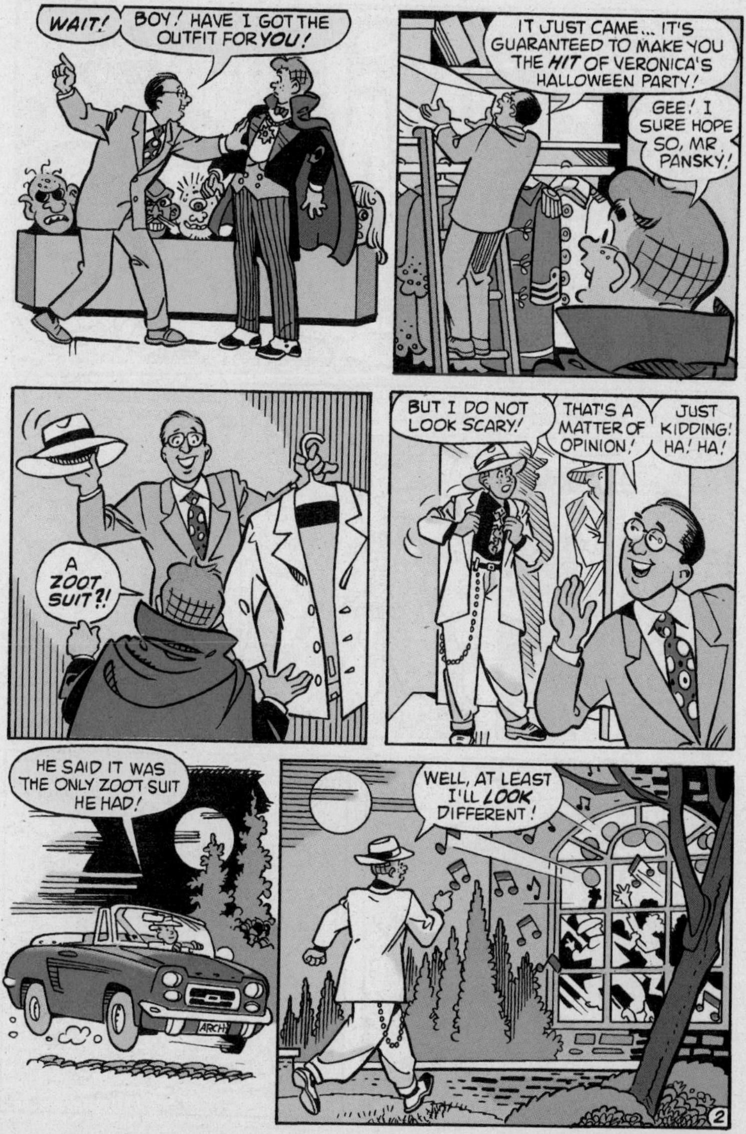

WAIT!
BOY! HAVE I GOT THE OUTFIT FOR YOU!
IT JUST CAME... IT'S GUARANTEED TO MAKE YOU THE HIT OF VERONICA'S HALLOWEEN PARTY!
GEE! I SURE HOPE SO, MR. PANSKY!
A ZOOT SUIT?!
BUT I DO NOT LOOK SCARY!
THAT'S A MATTER OF OPINION!
JUST KIDDING! HA! HA!
HE SAID IT WAS THE ONLY ZOOT SUIT HE HAD!
ARCH
WELL, AT LEAST I'LL LOOK DIFFERENT!
2

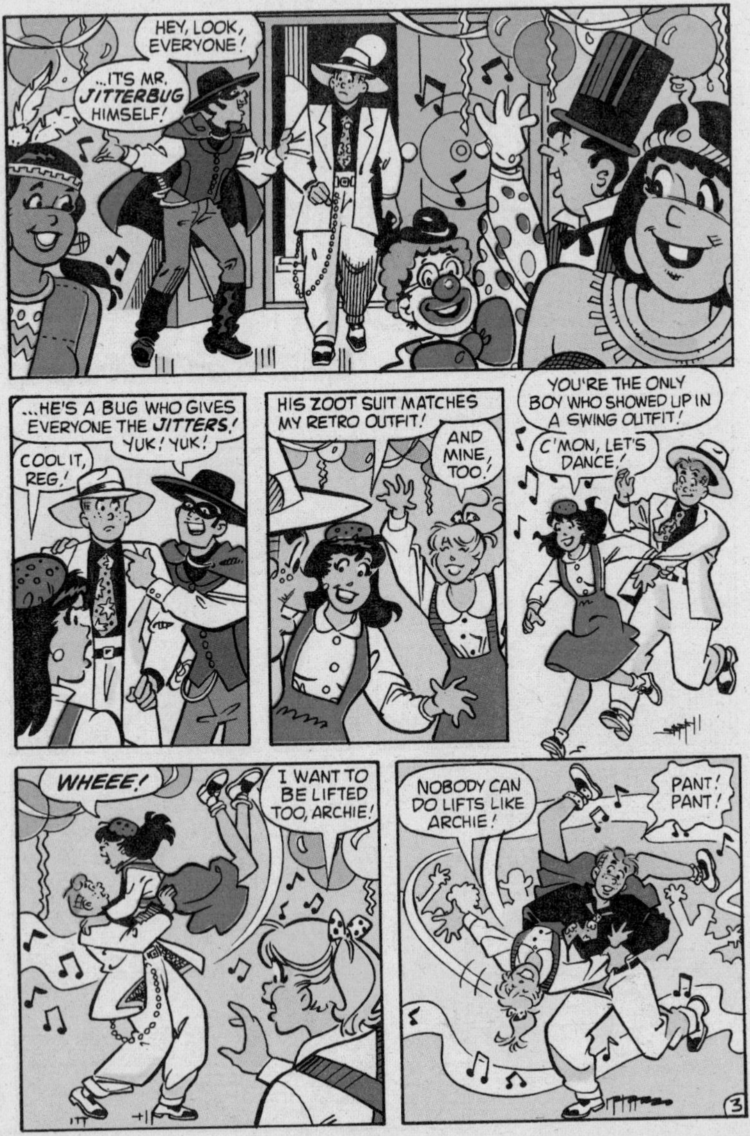
HEY, LOOK, EVERYONE!
...IT'S MR. JITTERBUG HIMSELF!
...HE'S A BUG WHO GIVES EVERYONE THE JITTERS! YUK! YUK!
COOL IT, REG!
HIS ZOOT SUIT MATCHES MY RETRO OUTFIT!
AND MINE, TOO!
YOU'RE THE ONLY BOY WHO SHOWED UP IN A SWING OUTFIT!
C'MON, LET'S DANCE!
WHEEE!
I WANT TO BE LIFTED TOO, ARCHIE!
NOBODY CAN DO LIFTS LIKE ARCHIE!
PANT! PANT!
3

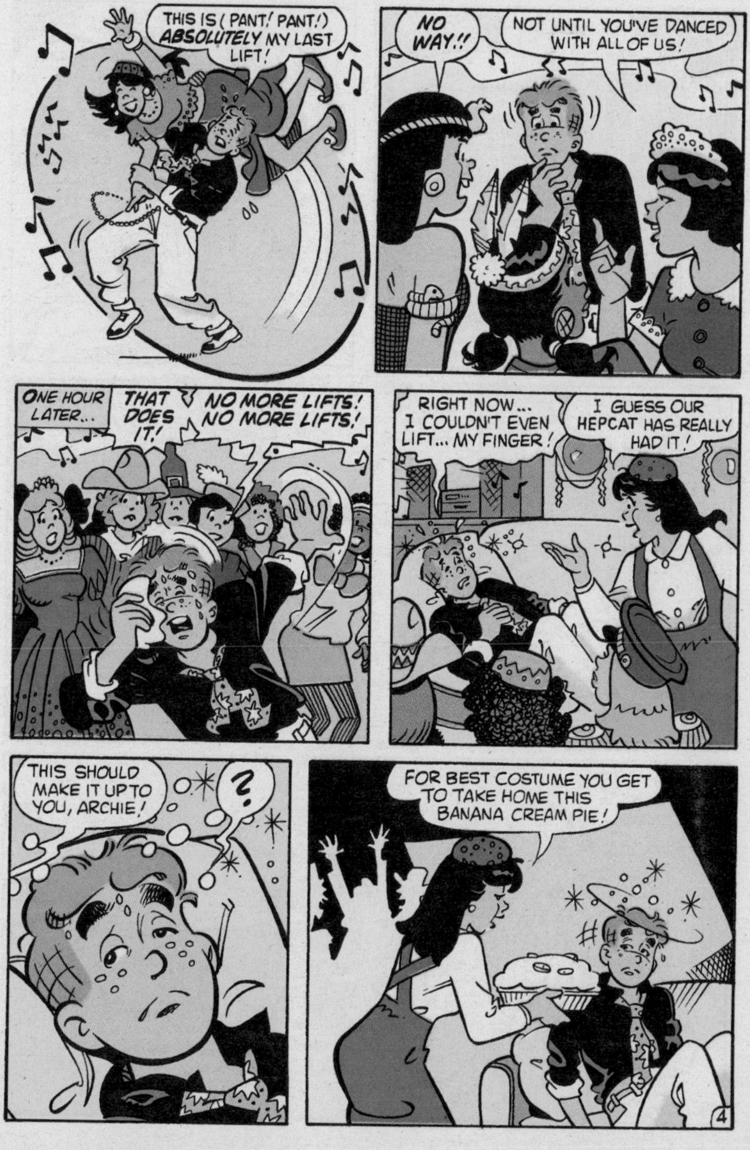

THIS IS (PANT! PANT!) ABSOLUTELY MY LAST LIFT!
NO WAY!!
NOT UNTIL YOU'VE DANCED WITH ALL OF US!
ONE HOUR LATER...
THAT DOES IT!
NO MORE LIFTS! NO MORE LIFTS!
RIGHT NOW... I COULDN'T EVEN LIFT... MY FINGER!
I GUESS OUR HEPCAT HAS REALLY HAD IT!
THIS SHOULD MAKE IT UP TO YOU, ARCHIE!
?
FOR BEST COSTUME YOU GET TO TAKE HOME THIS BANANA CREAM PIE!
4

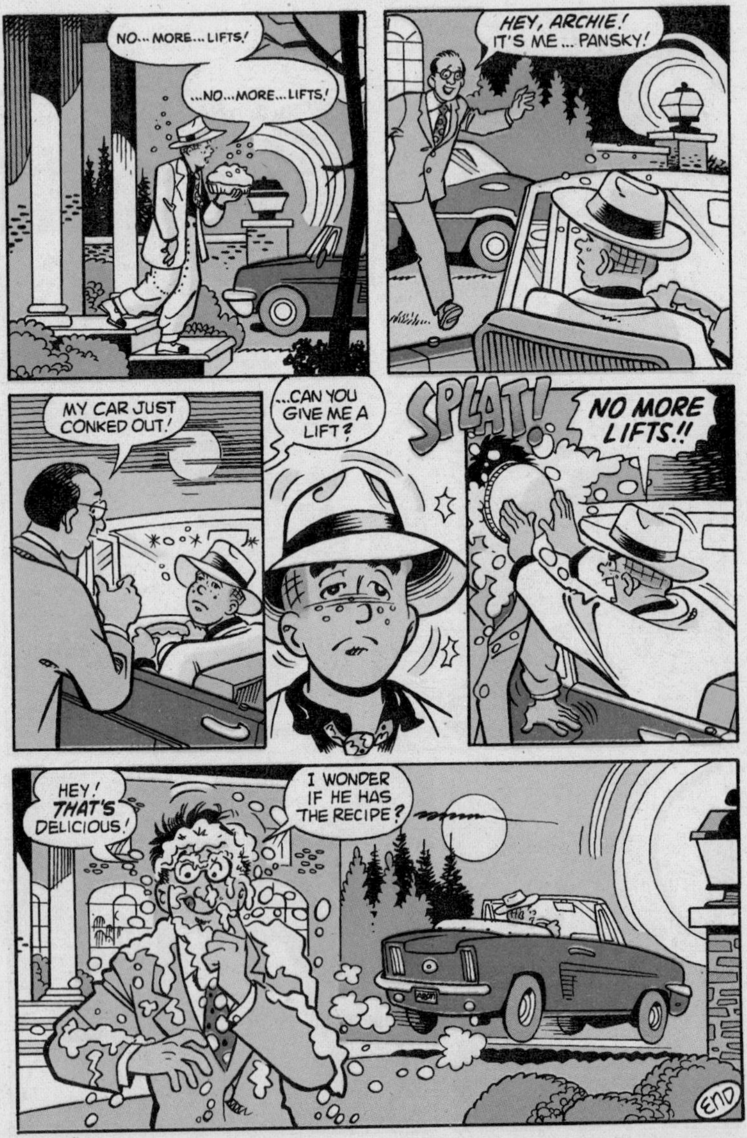

NO... MORE... LIFTS!
...NO... MORE... LIFTS!
HEY, ARCHIE! IT'S ME ... PANSKY!
MY CAR JUST CONKED OUT!
...CAN YOU GIVE ME A LIFT?
SPLAT!
NO MORE LIFTS!!
HEY! THAT'S DELICIOUS!
I WONDER IF HE HAS THE RECIPE?
END

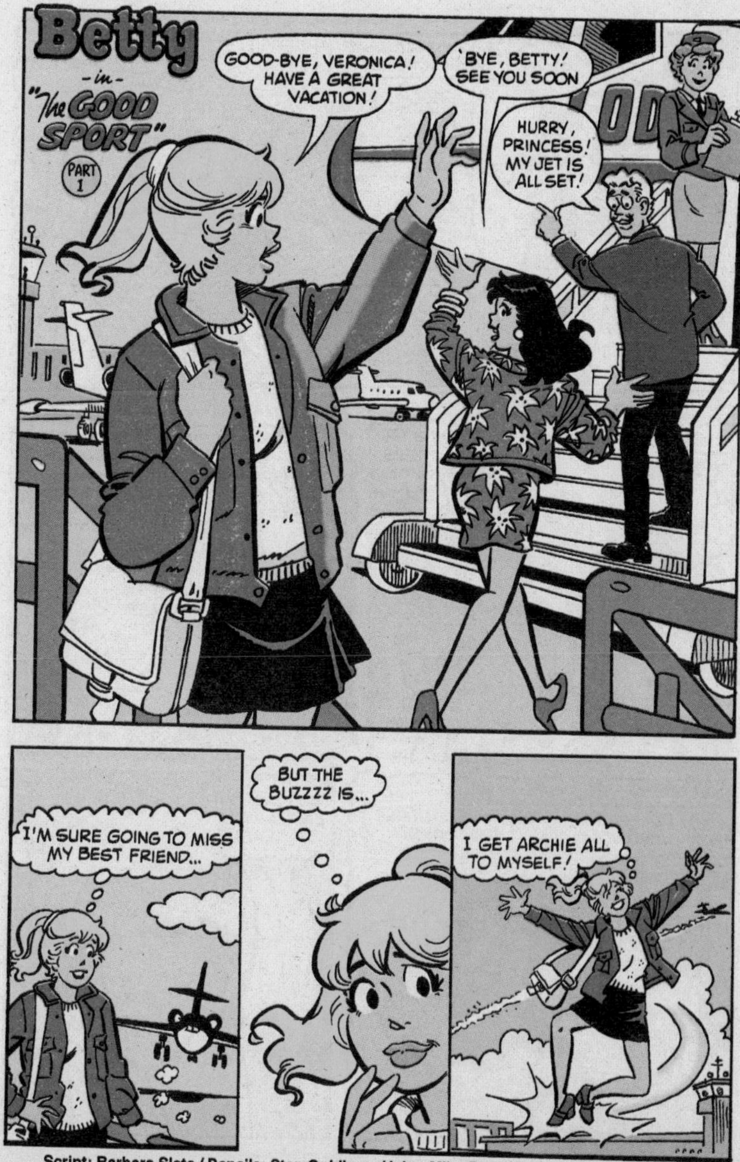
Betty
-in-
"The GOOD SPORT"
PART 1
GOOD-BYE, VERONICA! HAVE A GREAT VACATION!
'BYE, BETTY! SEE YOU SOON
HURRY, PRINCESS! MY JET IS ALL SET!
I'M SURE GOING TO MISS MY BEST FRIEND...
BUT THE BUZZZZ IS...
I GET ARCHIE ALL TO MYSELF!

Script: Barbara Slate / Pencils: Stan Goldberg / Inks: Mike Esposito / Letters: Bill Yoshida

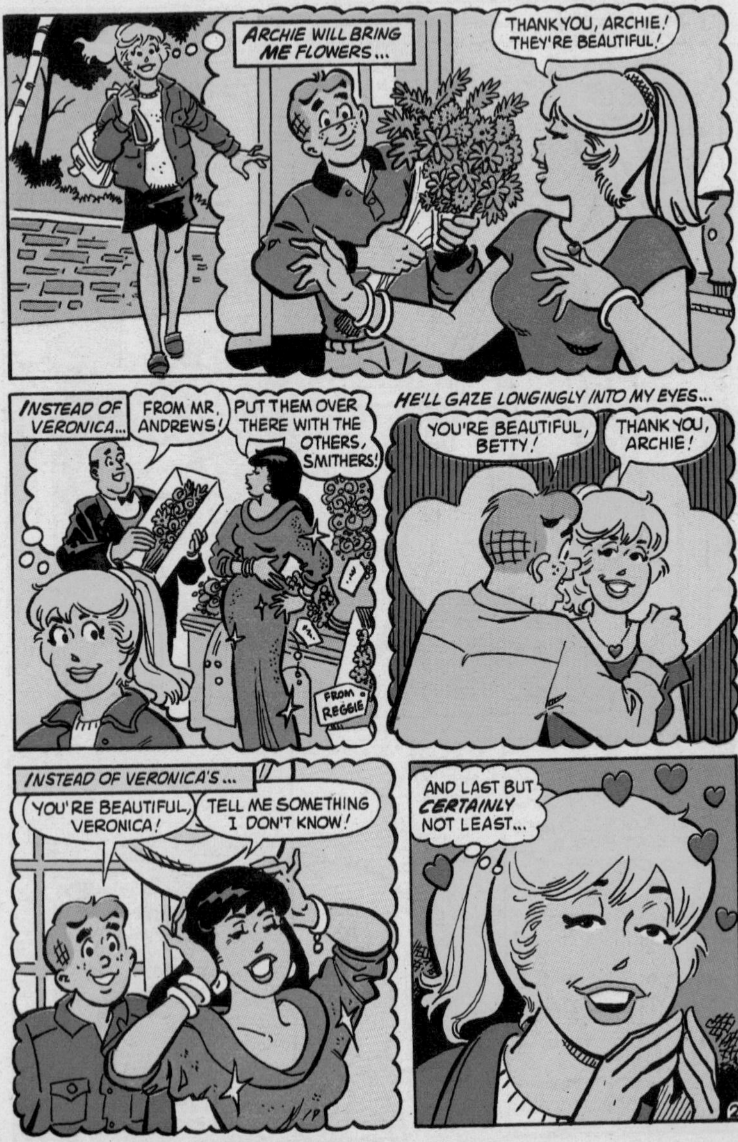
ARCHIE WILL BRING ME FLOWERS...
THANK YOU, ARCHIE! THEY'RE BEAUTIFUL!
INSTEAD OF VERONICA...
FROM MR. ANDREWS!
PUT THEM OVER THERE WITH THE OTHERS, SMITHERS!
FROM REGGIE
HE'LL GAZE LONGINGLY INTO MY EYES...
YOU'RE BEAUTIFUL, BETTY!
THANK YOU, ARCHIE!
INSTEAD OF VERONICA'S...
YOU'RE BEAUTIFUL, VERONICA!
TELL ME SOMETHING I DON'T KNOW!
AND LAST BUT CERTAINLY NOT LEAST...
2

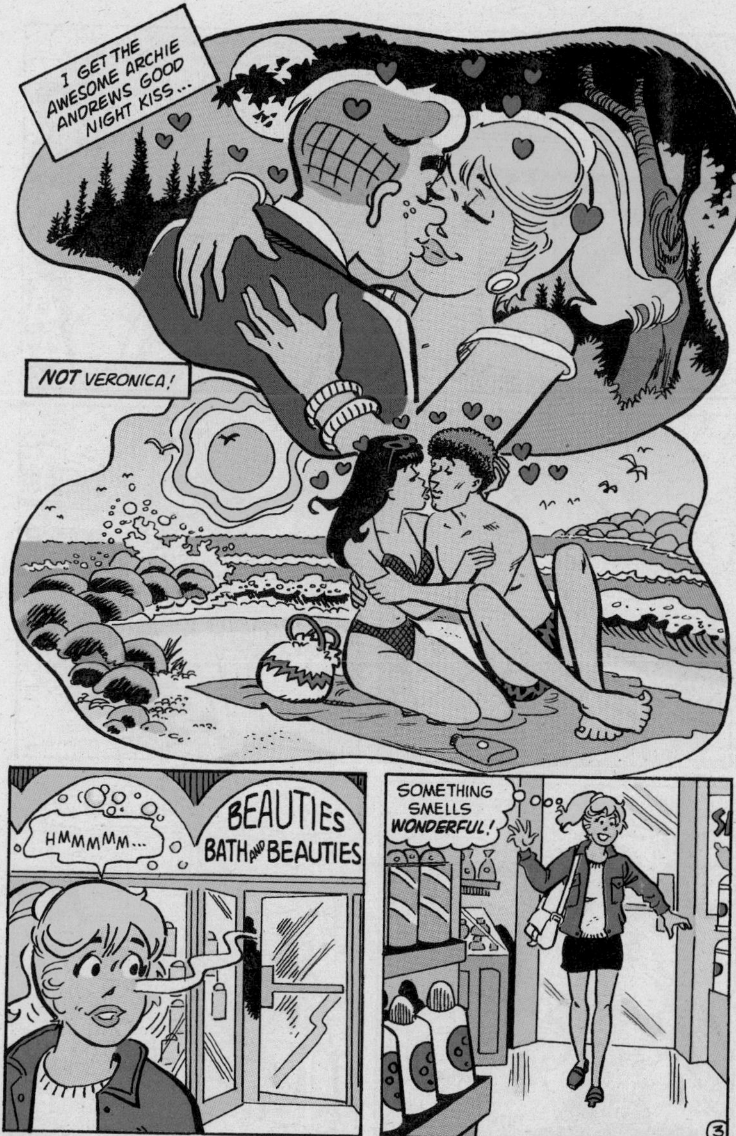
I GET THE AWESOME ARCHIE ANDREWS GOOD NIGHT KISS...
NOT VERONICA!
HMMMMM...
BEAUTIES
BATH AND BEAUTIES
SOMETHING SMELLS WONDERFUL!
3

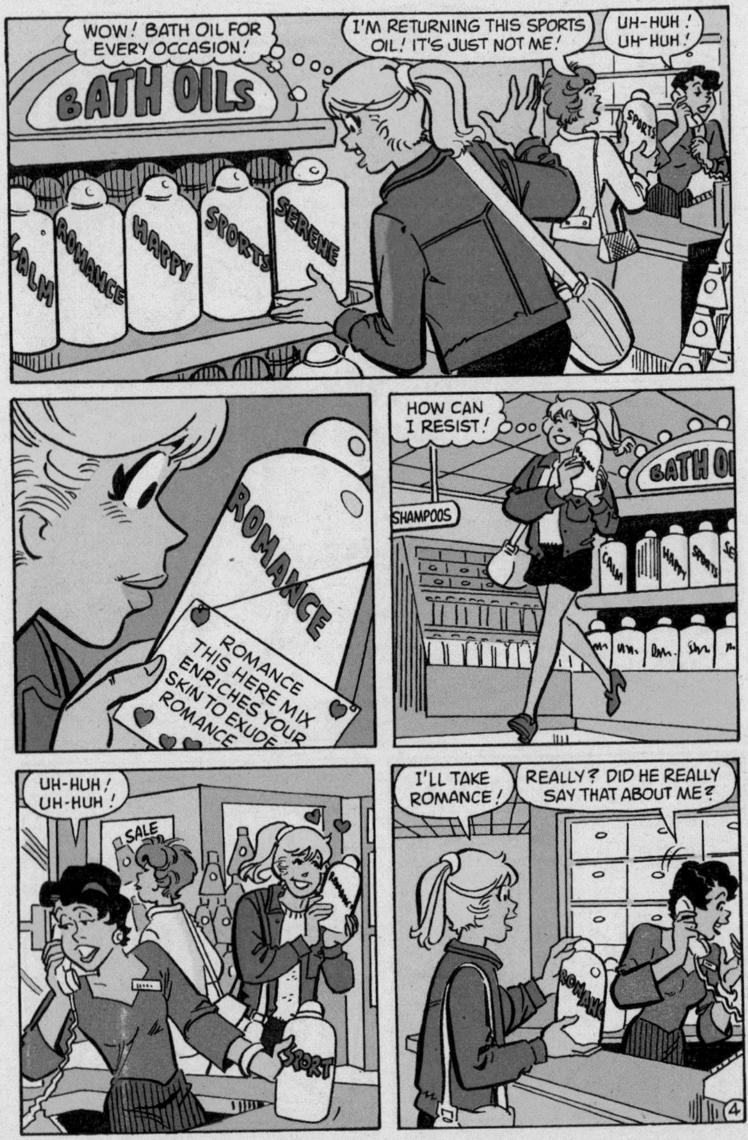
WOW! BATH OIL FOR EVERY OCCASION!
BATH OILS
CALM
ROMANCE
HAPPY
SPORTS
SERENE
I'M RETURNING THIS SPORTS OIL! IT'S JUST NOT ME!
SPORTS
UH-HUH! UH-HUH!
ROMANCE
ROMANCE THIS HERE MIX ENRICHES YOUR SKIN TO EXUDE ROMANCE
HOW CAN I RESIST!
BATH OI
SHAMPOOS
CALM
HAPPY
SPORTS
UH-HUH! UH-HUH!
SALE
SPORT
I'LL TAKE ROMANCE!
REALLY? DID HE REALLY SAY THAT ABOUT ME?
ROMANC
4

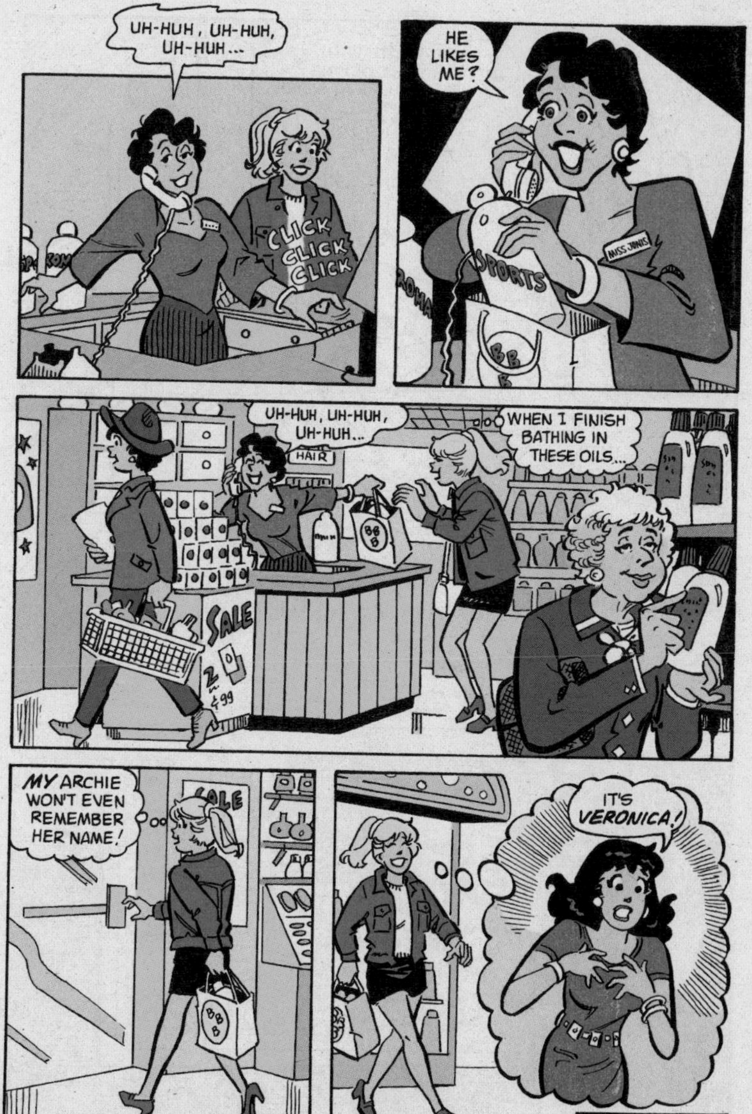

UH-HUH, UH-HUH, UH-HUH...
CLICK CLICK CLICK
HE LIKES ME?
SPORTS
UH-HUH, UH-HUH, UH-HUH...
HAIR
WHEN I FINISH BATHING IN THESE OILS...
SALE
MY ARCHIE WON'T EVEN REMEMBER HER NAME!
IT'S VERONICA!
CONTINUED- 5

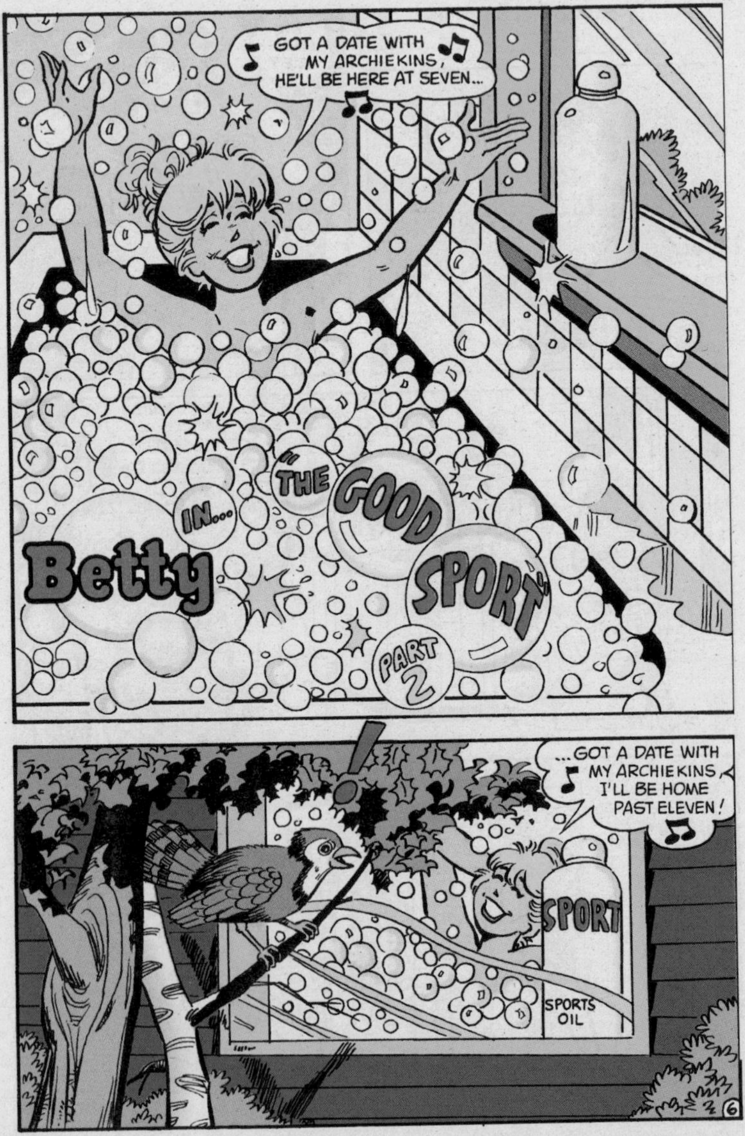

GOT A DATE WITH MY ARCHIEKINS, HE'LL BE HERE AT SEVEN...
Betty
IN...
"THE GOOD SPORT"
PART 2
!
...GOT A DATE WITH MY ARCHIEKINS, I'LL BE HOME PAST ELEVEN!
SPORT
SPORTS OIL
6

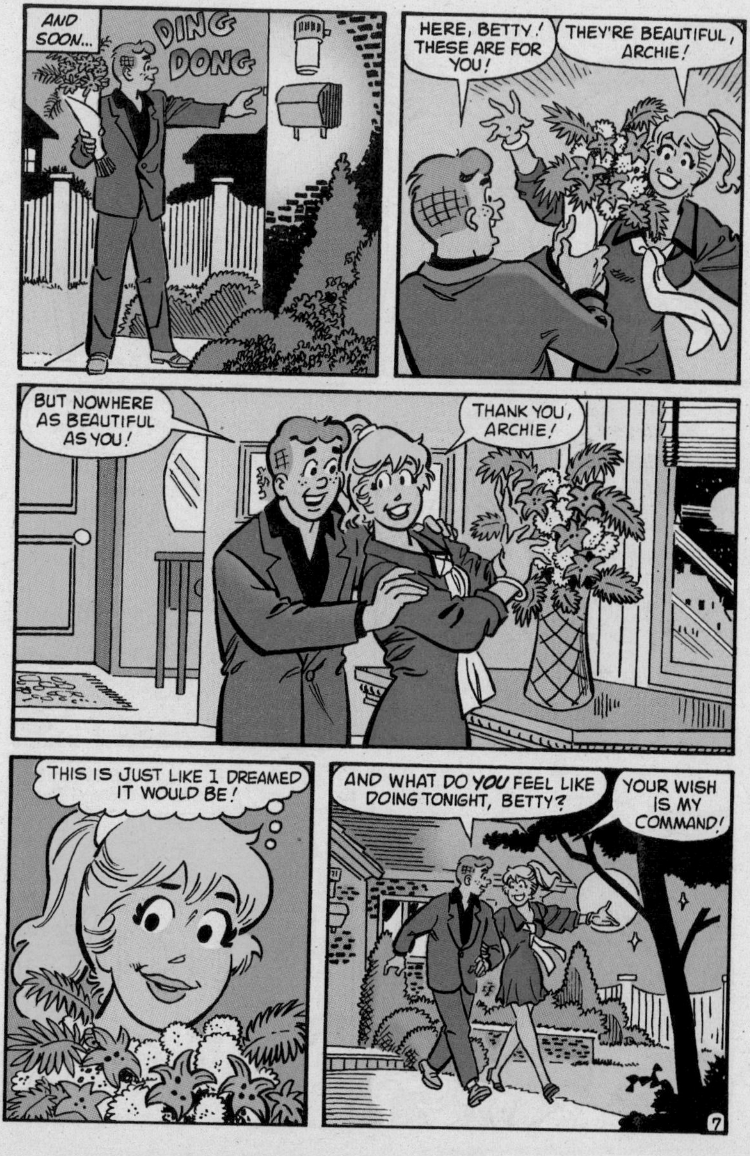
AND SOON...
DING DONG
HERE, BETTY! THESE ARE FOR YOU!
THEY'RE BEAUTIFUL, ARCHIE!
BUT NOWHERE AS BEAUTIFUL AS YOU!
THANK YOU, ARCHIE!
THIS IS JUST LIKE I DREAMED IT WOULD BE!
AND WHAT DO YOU FEEL LIKE DOING TONIGHT, BETTY?
YOUR WISH IS MY COMMAND!
7

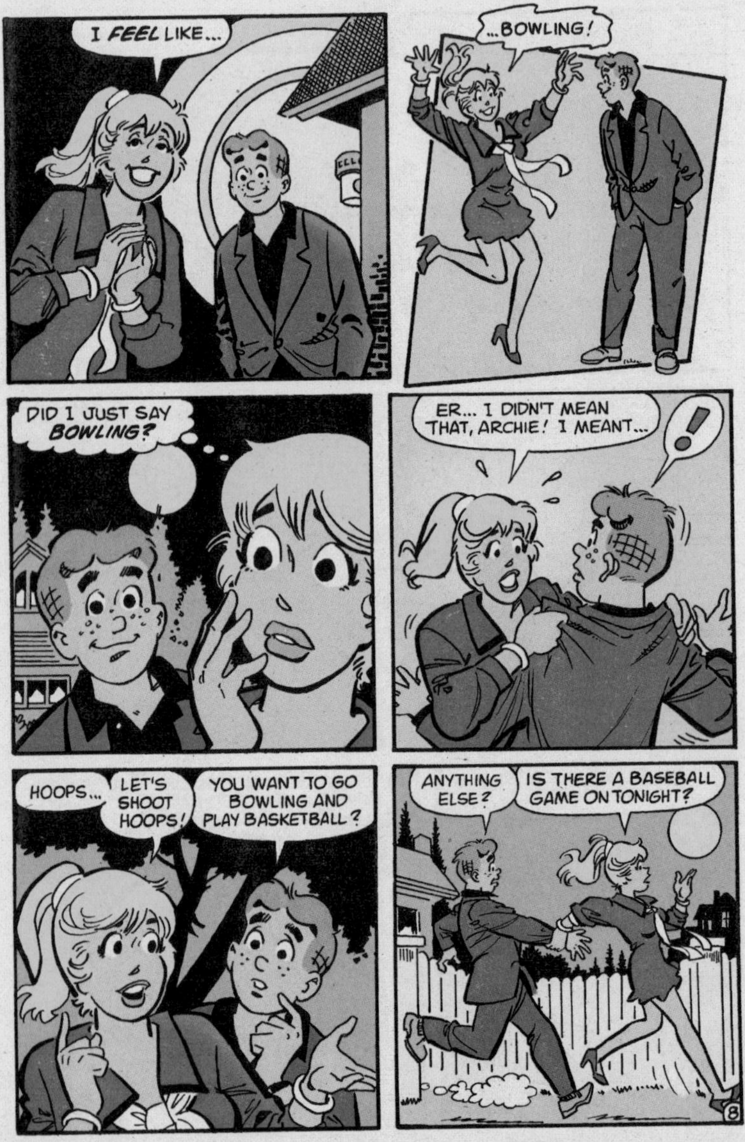
I FEEL LIKE...
...BOWLING!
DID I JUST SAY BOWLING?
ER... I DIDN'T MEAN THAT, ARCHIE! I MEANT...
!
HOOPS...
LET'S SHOOT HOOPS!
YOU WANT TO GO BOWLING AND PLAY BASKETBALL?
ANYTHING ELSE?
IS THERE A BASEBALL GAME ON TONIGHT?
8

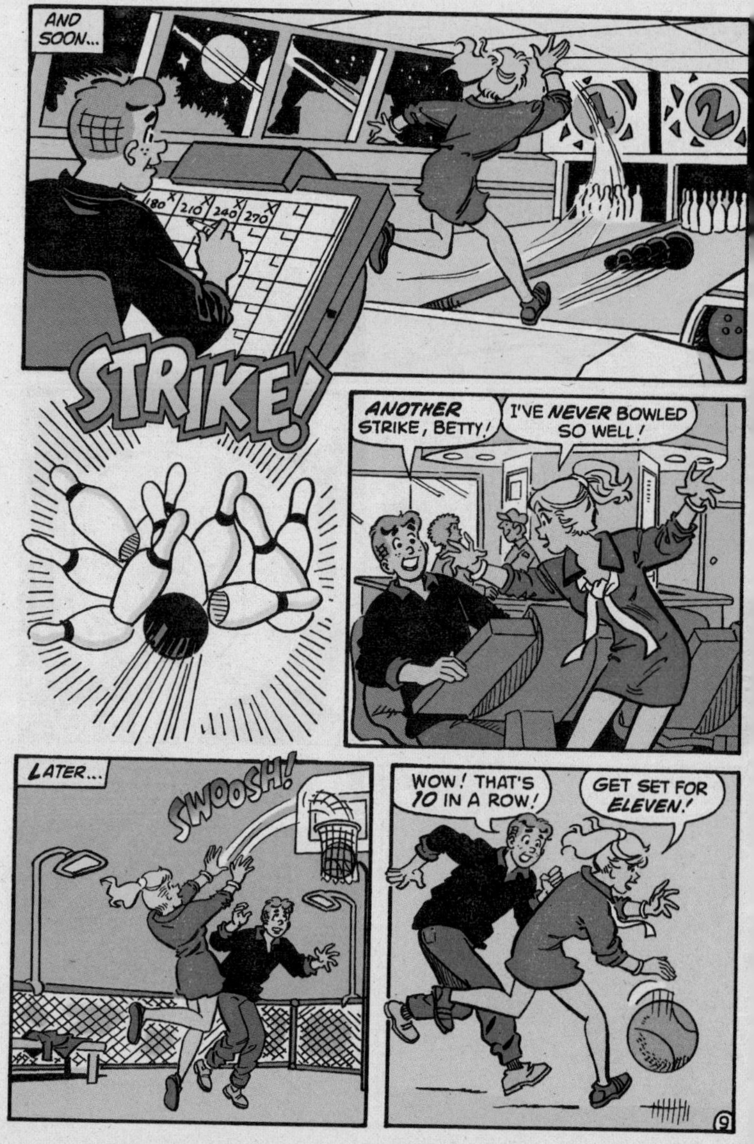

AND SOON...
180
210
240
270
STRIKE!
ANOTHER STRIKE, BETTY!
I'VE NEVER BOWLED SO WELL!
LATER...
SWOOSH!
WOW! THAT'S 10 IN A ROW!
GET SET FOR ELEVEN!

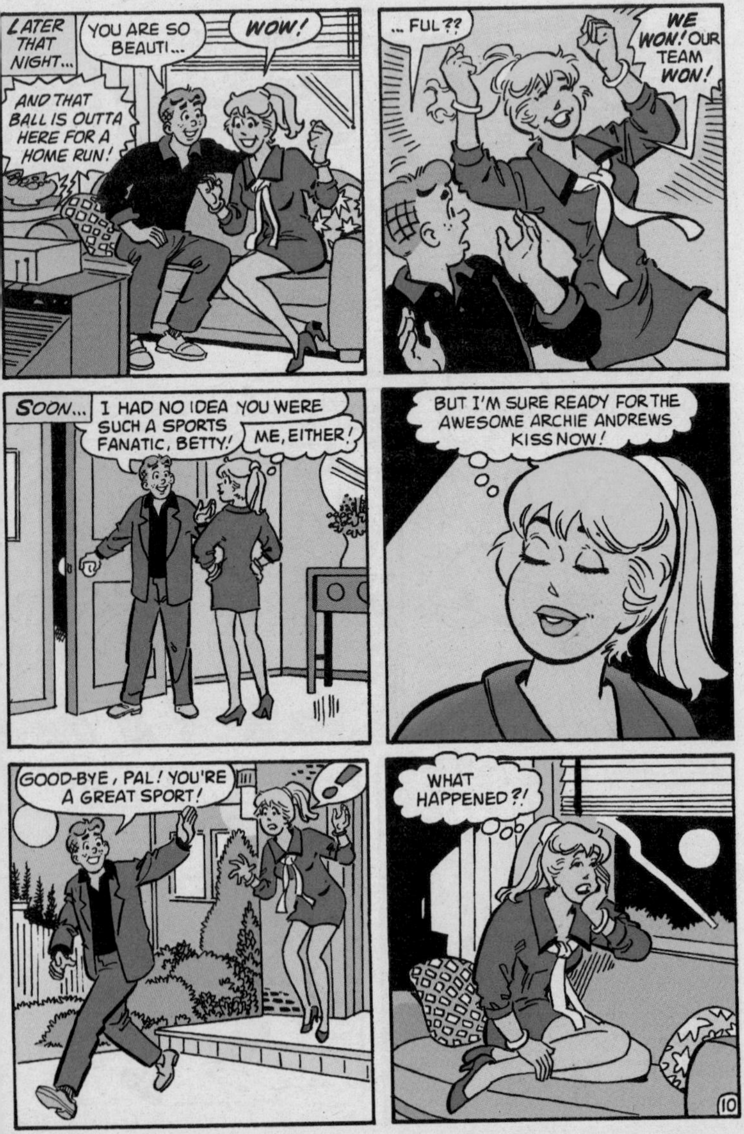
LATER THAT NIGHT...
YOU ARE SO BEAUTI...
WOW!
AND THAT BALL IS OUTTA HERE FOR A HOME RUN!
... FUL??
WE WON! OUR TEAM WON!
SOON...
I HAD NO IDEA YOU WERE SUCH A SPORTS FANATIC, BETTY!
ME, EITHER!
BUT I'M SURE READY FOR THE AWESOME ARCHIE ANDREWS KISS NOW!
GOOD-BYE, PAL! YOU'RE A GREAT SPORT!
!
WHAT HAPPENED?!
10

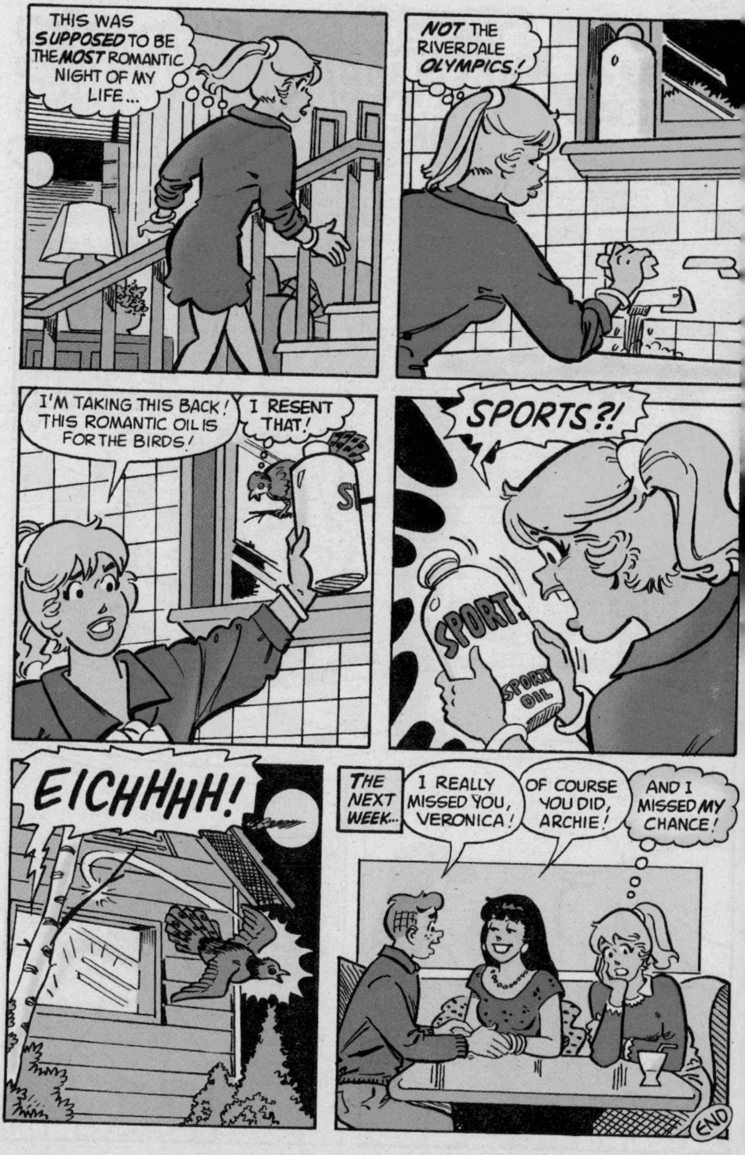

THIS WAS SUPPOSED TO BE THE MOST ROMANTIC NIGHT OF MY LIFE...
NOT THE RIVERDALE OLYMPICS!
I'M TAKING THIS BACK! THIS ROMANTIC OIL IS FOR THE BIRDS!
I RESENT THAT!
SPORTS?!
SPORTS
SPORTS OIL
EICHHHH!
THE NEXT WEEK...
I REALLY MISSED YOU, VERONICA!
OF COURSE YOU DID, ARCHIE!
AND I MISSED MY CHANCE!
END

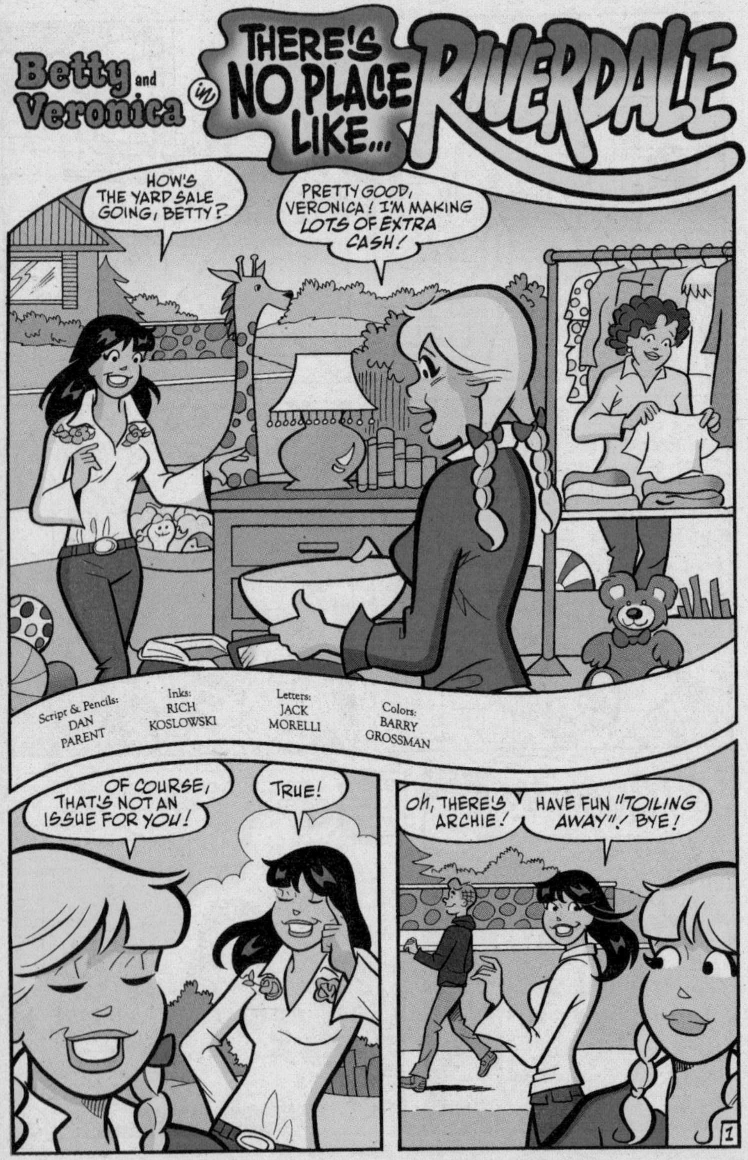

Betty and Veronica in
THERE'S NO PLACE LIKE... RIVERDALE
HOW'S THE YARD SALE GOING, BETTY?
PRETTY GOOD, VERONICA! I'M MAKING LOTS OF EXTRA CASH!
Script & Pencils: DAN PARENT
Inks: RICH KOSLOWSKI
Letters: JACK MORELLI
Colors: BARRY GROSSMAN
OF COURSE, THAT'S NOT AN ISSUE FOR YOU!
TRUE!
OH, THERE'S ARCHIE!
HAVE FUN "TOILING AWAY"! BYE!
1

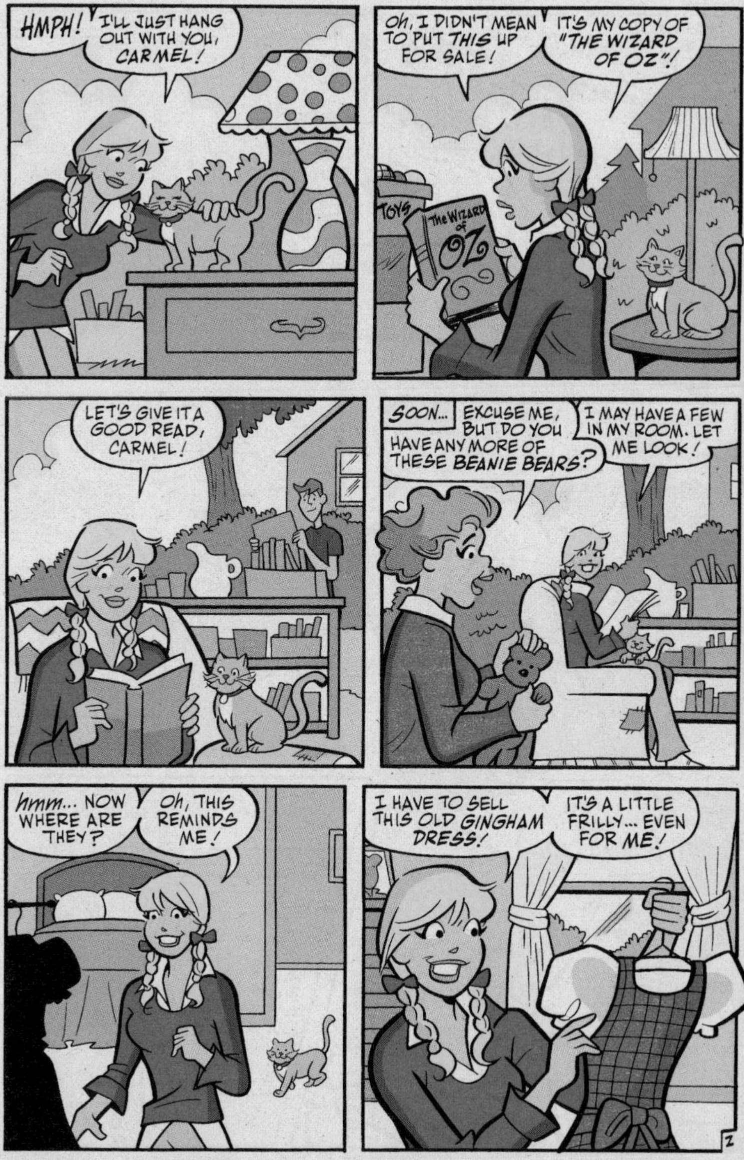
HMPH!
I'LL JUST HANG OUT WITH YOU, CARMEL!
Oh, I DIDN'T MEAN TO PUT THIS UP FOR SALE!
IT'S MY COPY OF "THE WIZARD OF OZ"!
TOYS
The Wizard of OZ
LET'S GIVE IT A GOOD READ, CARMEL!
SOON...
EXCUSE ME, BUT DO YOU HAVE ANY MORE OF THESE BEANIE BEARS?
I MAY HAVE A FEW IN MY ROOM. LET ME LOOK!
hmm... NOW WHERE ARE THEY?
Oh, THIS REMINDS ME!
I HAVE TO SELL THIS OLD GINGHAM DRESS!
IT'S A LITTLE FRILLY... EVEN FOR ME!
2

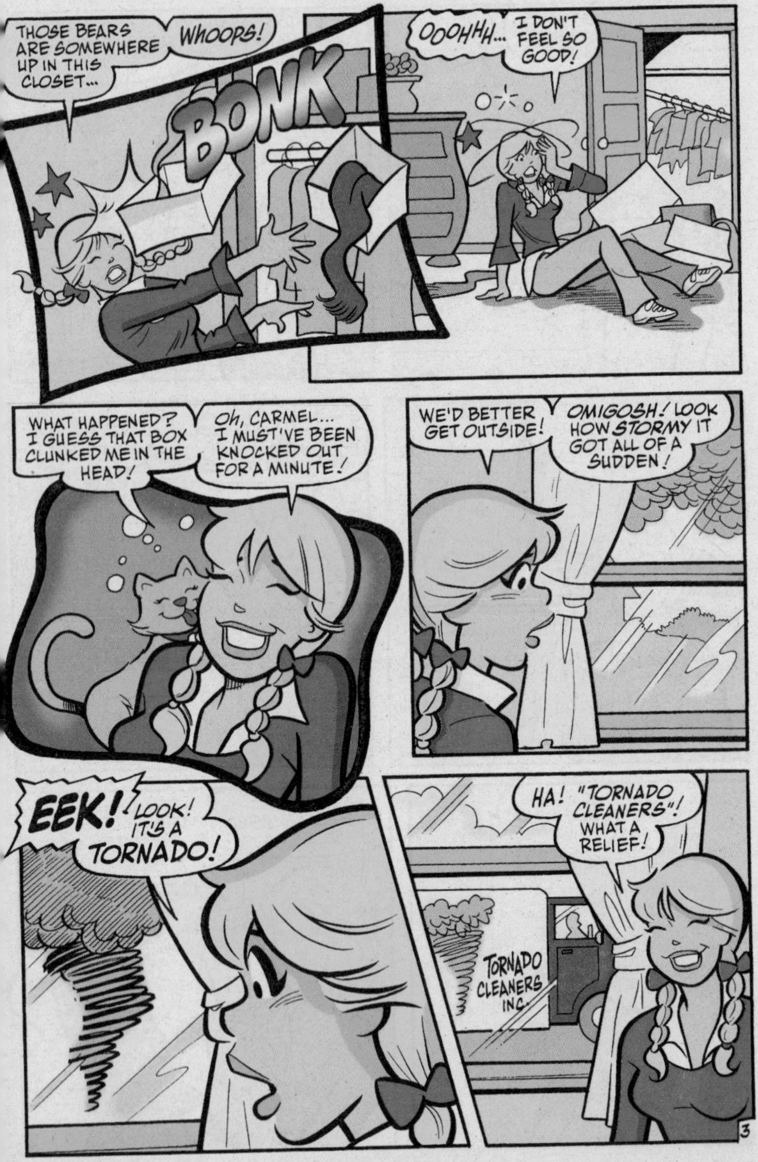
THOSE BEARS ARE SOMEWHERE UP IN THIS CLOSET...
WHOOPS!
BONK
OOOHHH... I DON'T FEEL SO GOOD!
WHAT HAPPENED? I GUESS THAT BOX CLUNKED ME IN THE HEAD!
Oh, CARMEL... I MUST'VE BEEN KNOCKED OUT FOR A MINUTE!
WE'D BETTER GET OUTSIDE!
OMIGOSH! LOOK HOW STORMY IT GOT ALL OF A SUDDEN!
EEK!
LOOK! IT'S A TORNADO!
HA! "TORNADO CLEANERS"! WHAT A RELIEF!
TORNADO CLEANERS INC.
3

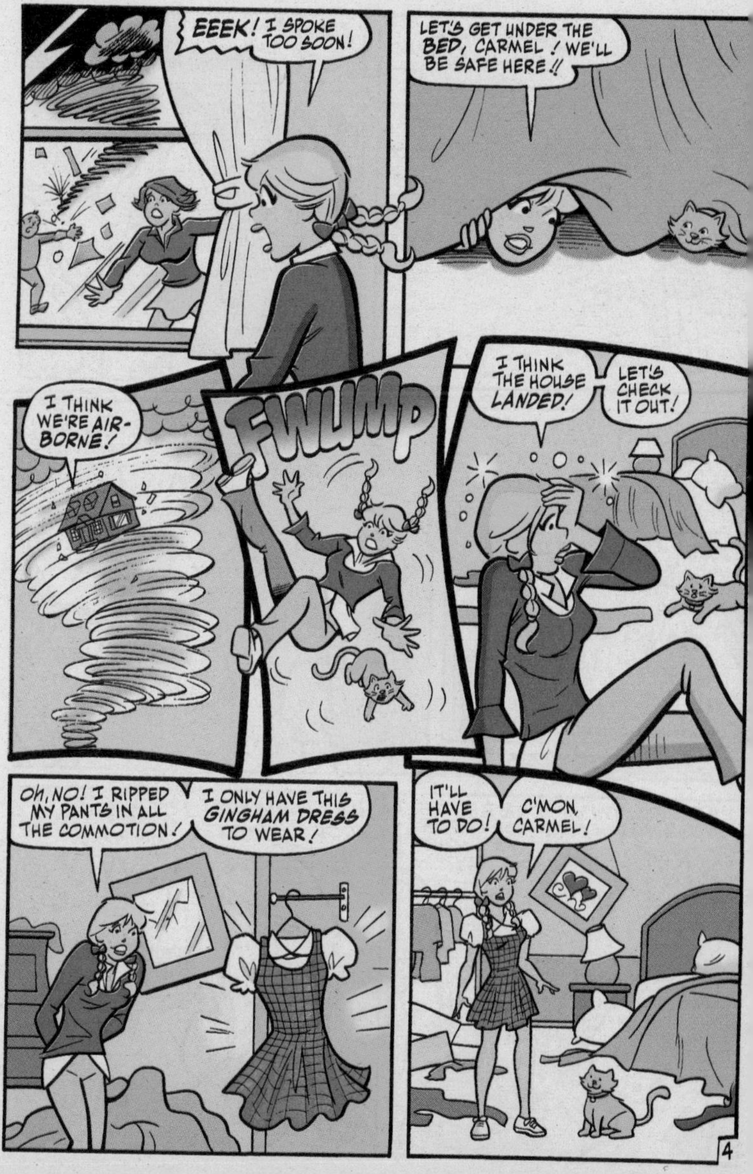
EEEK! I SPOKE TOO SOON!
LET'S GET UNDER THE BED, CARMEL! WE'LL BE SAFE HERE!!
I THINK WE'RE AIR-BORNE!
FWUMP
I THINK THE HOUSE LANDED!
LET'S CHECK IT OUT!
OH, NO! I RIPPED MY PANTS IN ALL THE COMMOTION!
I ONLY HAVE THIS GINGHAM DRESS TO WEAR!
IT'LL HAVE TO DO!
C'MON, CARMEL!

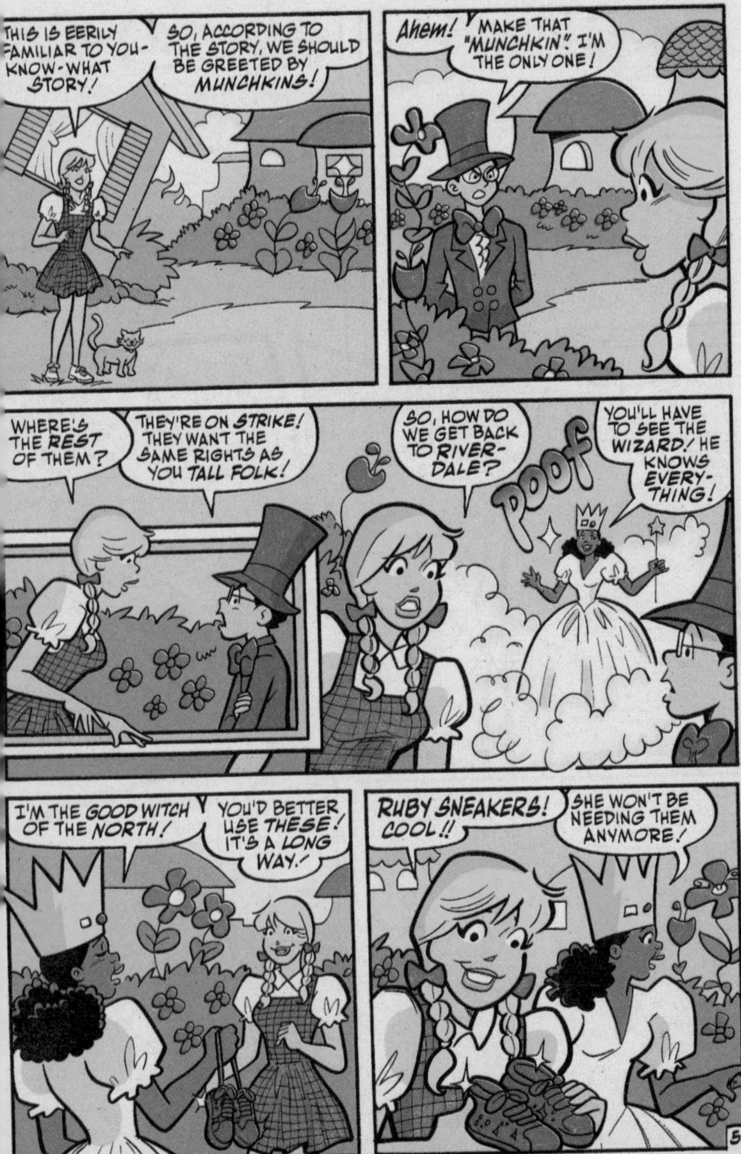
THIS IS EERILY FAMILIAR TO YOU-KNOW-WHAT STORY!
SO, ACCORDING TO THE STORY, WE SHOULD BE GREETED BY MUNCHKINS!
Ahem!
MAKE THAT "MUNCHKIN"! I'M THE ONLY ONE!
WHERE'S THE REST OF THEM?
THEY'RE ON STRIKE! THEY WANT THE SAME RIGHTS AS YOU TALL FOLK!
SO, HOW DO WE GET BACK TO RIVERDALE?
POOF
YOU'LL HAVE TO SEE THE WIZARD! HE KNOWS EVERYTHING!
I'M THE GOOD WITCH OF THE NORTH!
YOU'D BETTER USE THESE! IT'S A LONG WAY!
RUBY SNEAKERS! COOL!!
SHE WON'T BE NEEDING THEM ANYMORE!
5

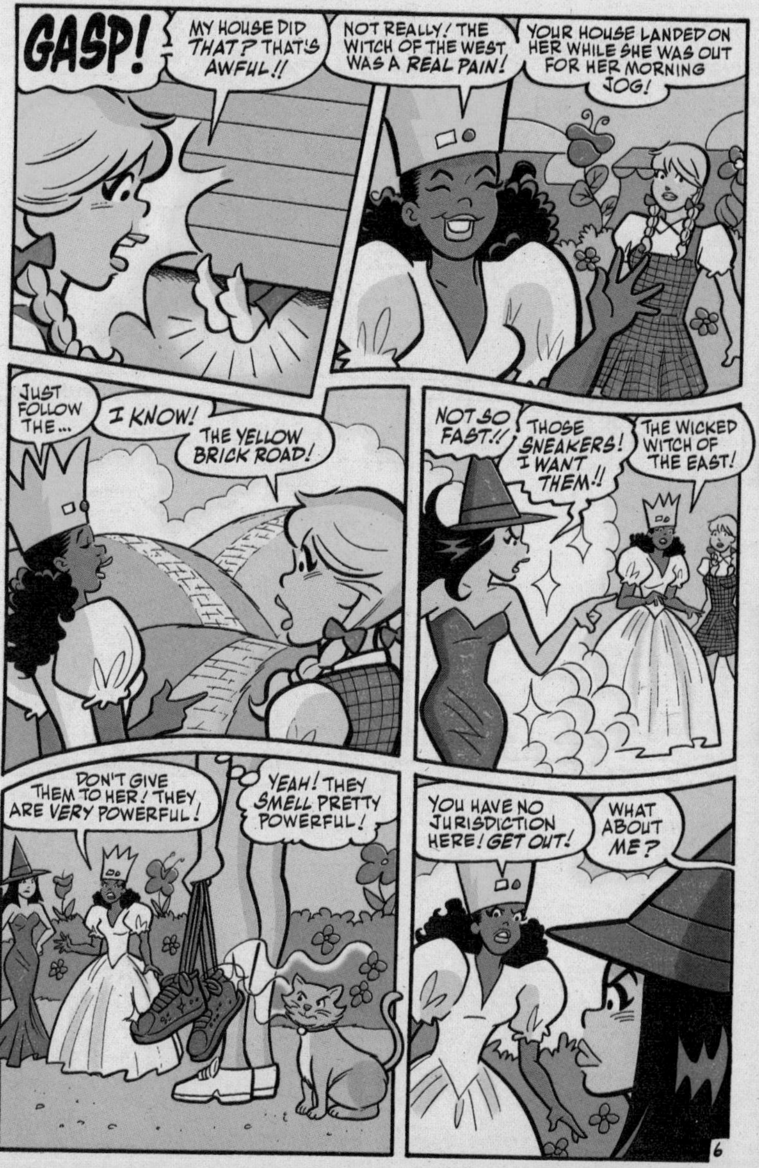
GASP!
MY HOUSE DID THAT? THAT'S AWFUL!!
NOT REALLY! THE WITCH OF THE WEST WAS A REAL PAIN!
YOUR HOUSE LANDED ON HER WHILE SHE WAS OUT FOR HER MORNING JOG!
JUST FOLLOW THE...
I KNOW!
THE YELLOW BRICK ROAD!
NOT SO FAST!!
THOSE SNEAKERS! I WANT THEM!!
THE WICKED WITCH OF THE EAST!
DON'T GIVE THEM TO HER! THEY ARE VERY POWERFUL!
YEAH! THEY SMELL PRETTY POWERFUL!
YOU HAVE NO JURISDICTION HERE! GET OUT!
WHAT ABOUT ME?

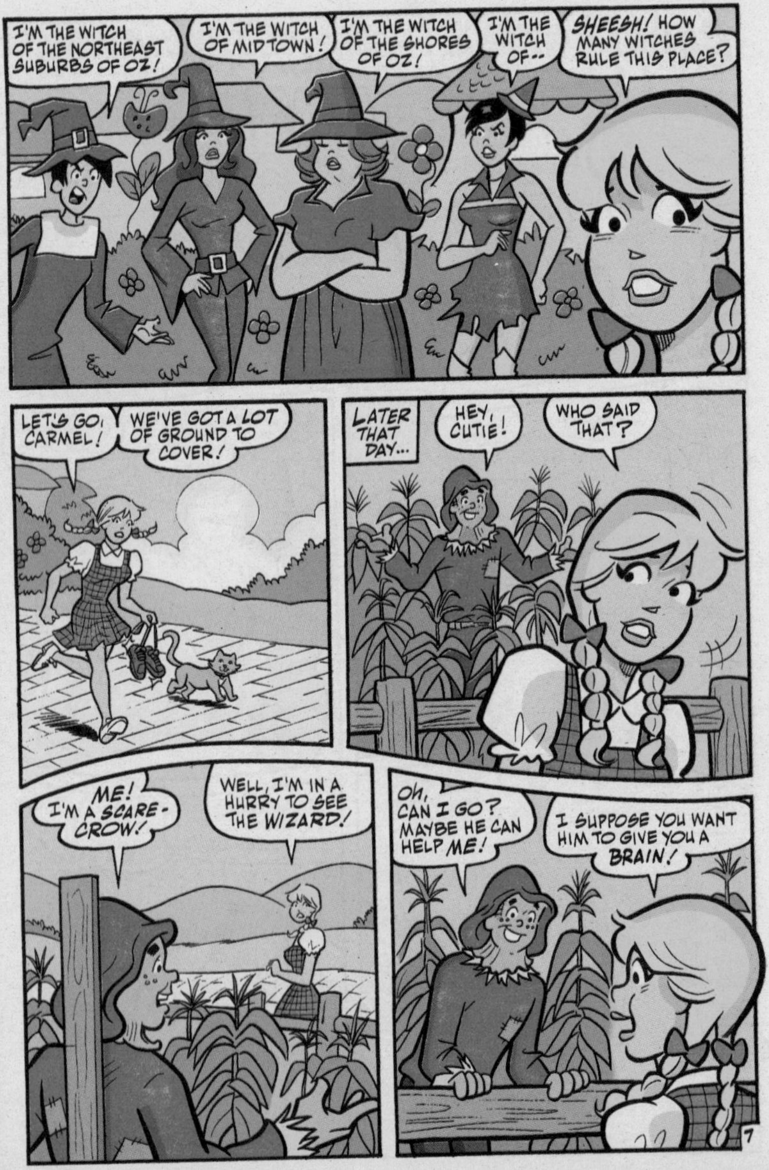
I'M THE WITCH OF THE NORTHEAST SUBURBS OF OZ!
I'M THE WITCH OF MIDTOWN!
I'M THE WITCH OF THE SHORES OF OZ!
I'M THE WITCH OF--
SHEESH! HOW MANY WITCHES RULE THIS PLACE?
LET'S GO, CARMEL!
WE'VE GOT A LOT OF GROUND TO COVER!
LATER THAT DAY...
HEY, CUTIE!
WHO SAID THAT?
ME! I'M A SCARE-CROW!
WELL, I'M IN A HURRY TO SEE THE WIZARD!
OH, CAN I GO? MAYBE HE CAN HELP ME!
I SUPPOSE YOU WANT HIM TO GIVE YOU A BRAIN!
7

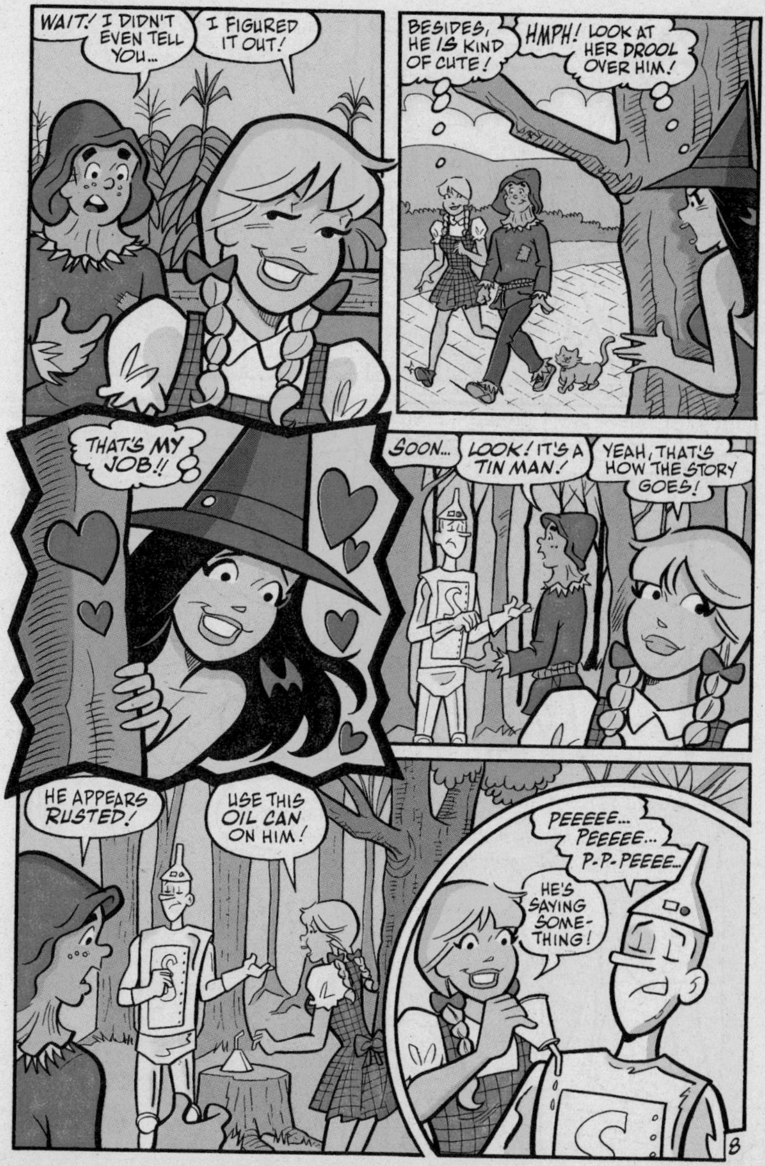
WAIT! I DIDN'T EVEN TELL YOU...
I FIGURED IT OUT!
BESIDES, HE IS KIND OF CUTE!
HMPH! LOOK AT HER DROOL OVER HIM!
THAT'S MY JOB!!
SOON...
LOOK! IT'S A TIN MAN!
YEAH, THAT'S HOW THE STORY GOES!
HE APPEARS RUSTED!
USE THIS OIL CAN ON HIM!
PEEEEE... PEEEEE... P-P-PEEEE...
HE'S SAYING SOME-THING!
8

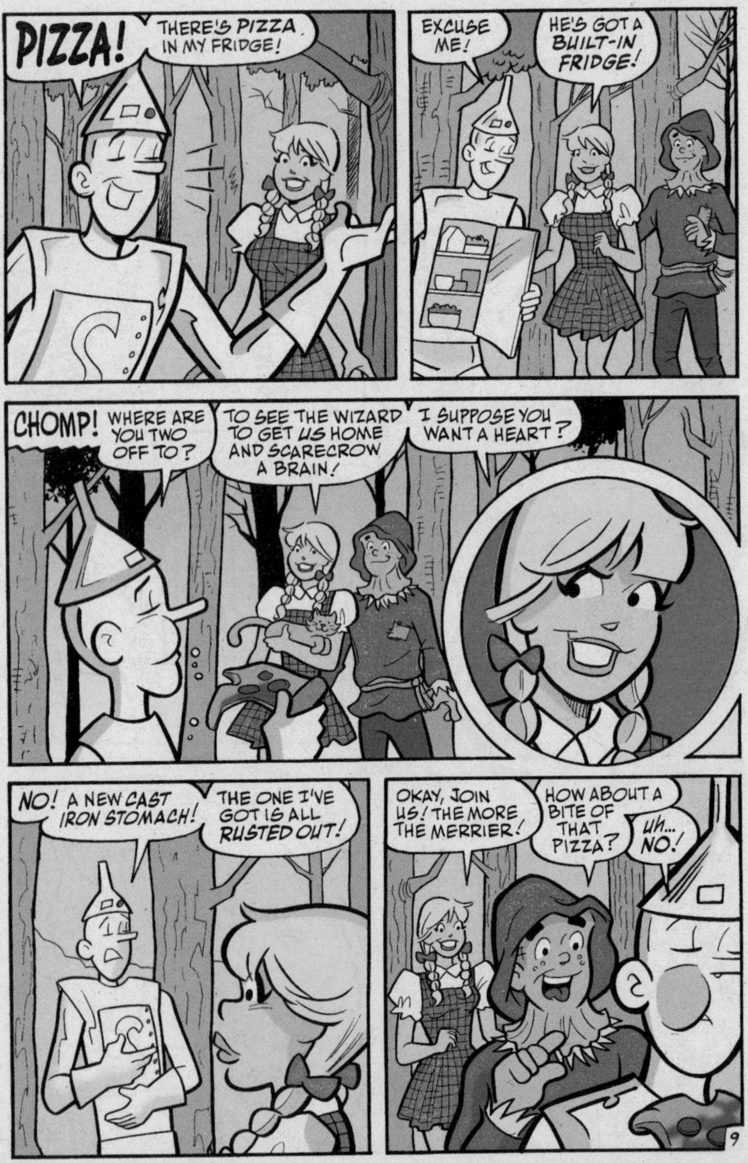
PIZZA!
THERE'S PIZZA IN MY FRIDGE!
EXCUSE ME!
HE'S GOT A BUILT-IN FRIDGE!
CHOMP!
WHERE ARE YOU TWO OFF TO?
TO SEE THE WIZARD TO GET US HOME AND SCARECROW A BRAIN!
I SUPPOSE YOU WANT A HEART?
NO! A NEW CAST IRON STOMACH!
THE ONE I'VE GOT IS ALL RUSTED OUT!
OKAY, JOIN US! THE MORE THE MERRIER!
HOW ABOUT A BITE OF THAT PIZZA?
UH... NO!

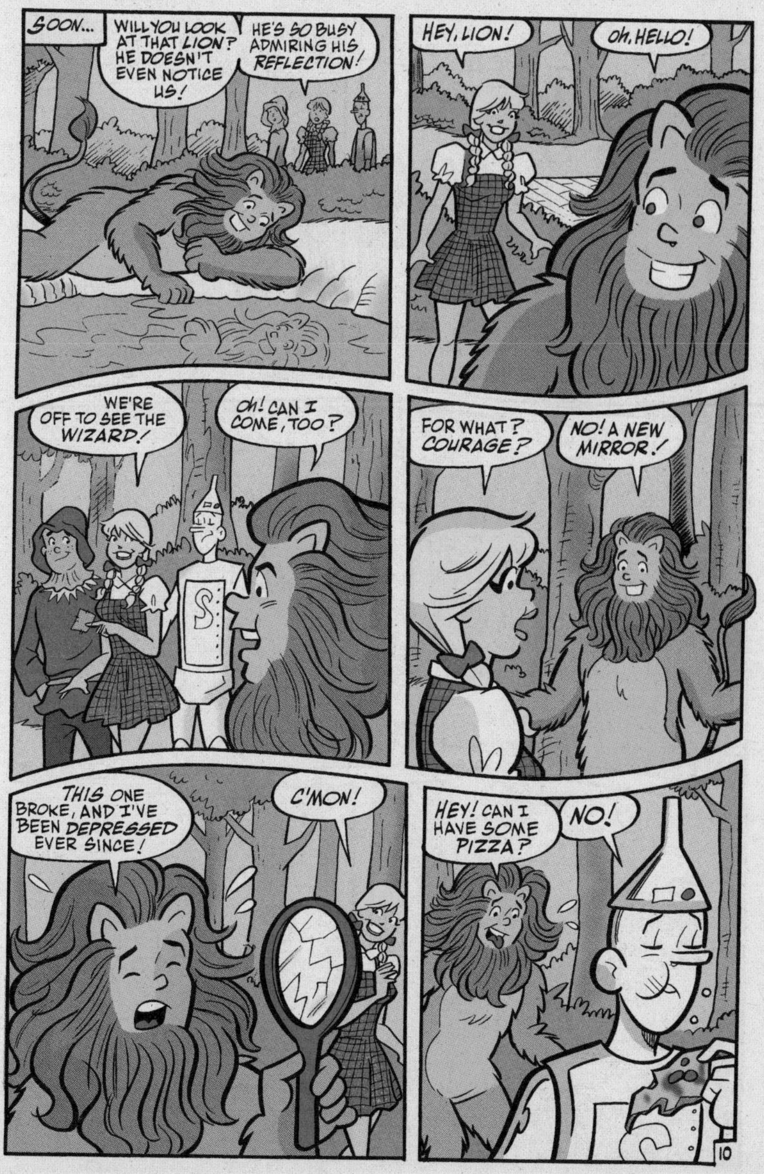
SOON...
WILL YOU LOOK AT THAT LION? HE DOESN'T EVEN NOTICE US!
HE'S SO BUSY ADMIRING HIS REFLECTION!
HEY, LION!
OH, HELLO!
WE'RE OFF TO SEE THE WIZARD!
OH! CAN I COME, TOO?
FOR WHAT? COURAGE?
NO! A NEW MIRROR!
THIS ONE BROKE, AND I'VE BEEN DEPRESSED EVER SINCE!
C'MON!
HEY! CAN I HAVE SOME PIZZA?
NO!

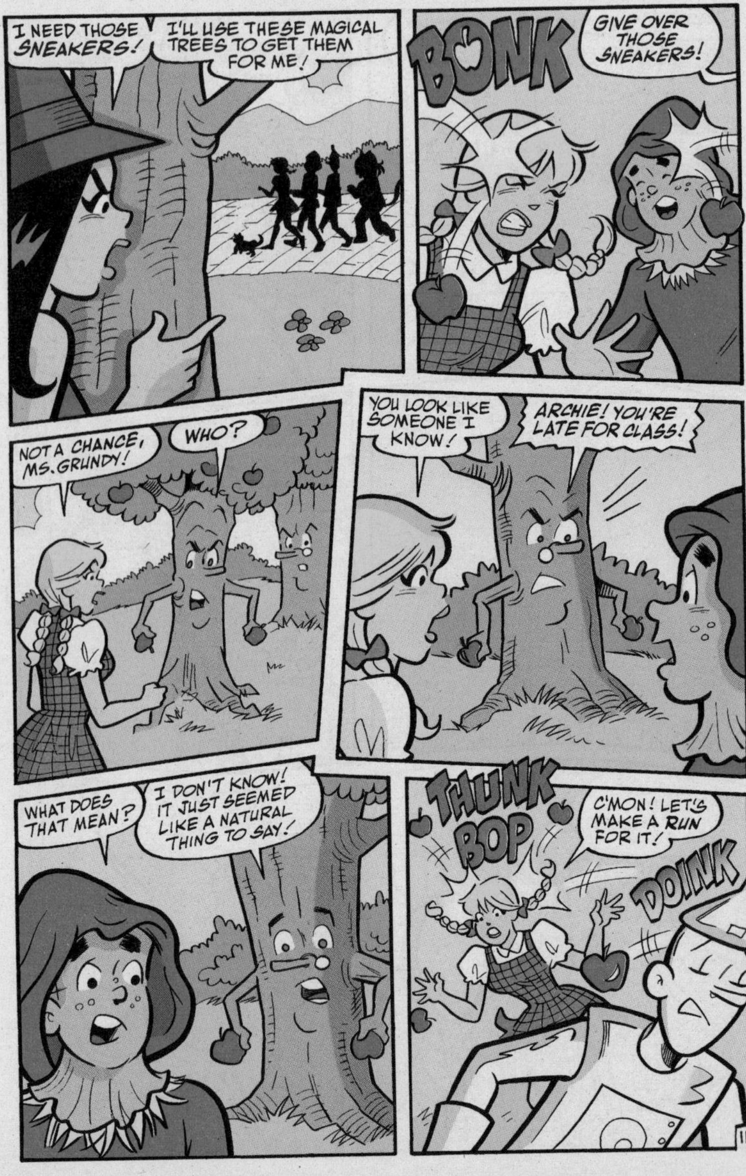
I NEED THOSE SNEAKERS!
I'LL USE THESE MAGICAL TREES TO GET THEM FOR ME!
BONK
GIVE OVER THOSE SNEAKERS!
NOT A CHANCE, MS. GRUNDY!
WHO?
YOU LOOK LIKE SOMEONE I KNOW!
ARCHIE! YOU'RE LATE FOR CLASS!
WHAT DOES THAT MEAN?
I DON'T KNOW! IT JUST SEEMED LIKE A NATURAL THING TO SAY!
THUNK
BOP
C'MON! LET'S MAKE A RUN FOR IT!
DOINK

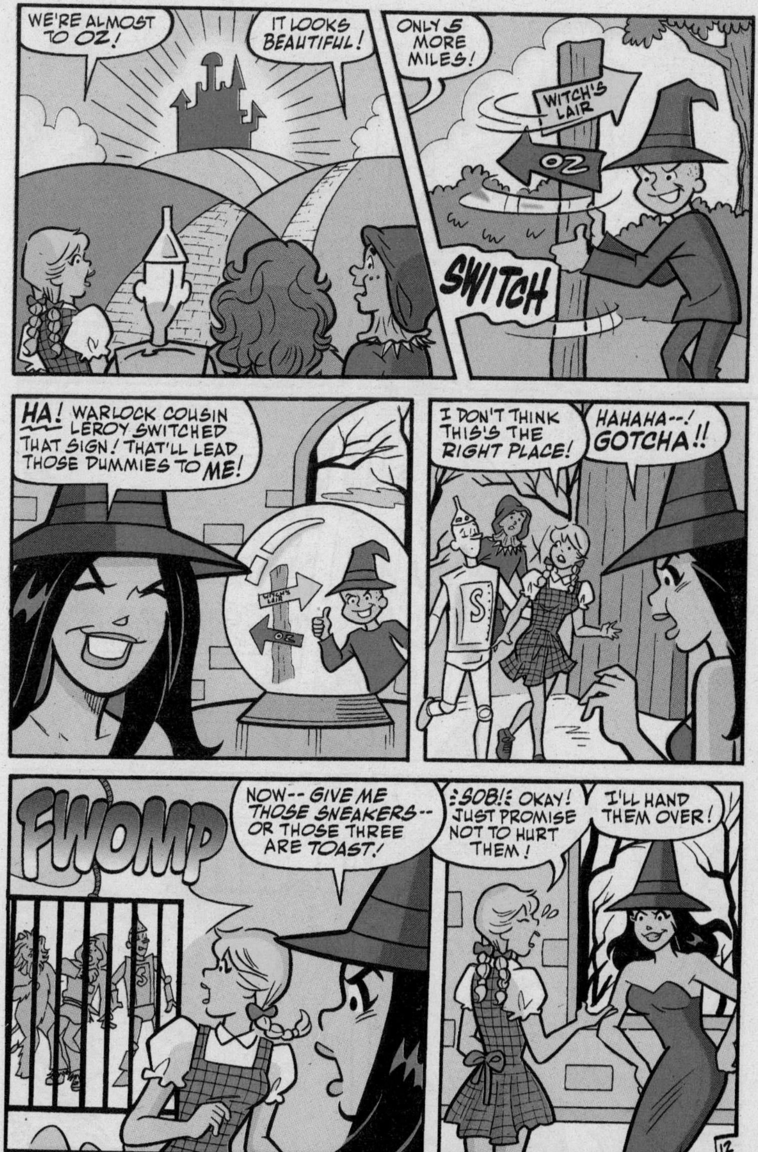

WE'RE ALMOST TO OZ!
IT LOOKS BEAUTIFUL!
ONLY 5 MORE MILES!
WITCH'S LAIR
OZ
SWITCH
HA! WARLOCK COUSIN LEROY SWITCHED THAT SIGN! THAT'LL LEAD THOSE DUMMIES TO ME!
I DON'T THINK THIS'S THE RIGHT PLACE!
HAHAHA--! GOTCHA!!
FWOMP
NOW-- GIVE ME THOSE SNEAKERS-- OR THOSE THREE ARE TOAST!
SOB! OKAY! JUST PROMISE NOT TO HURT THEM!
I'LL HAND THEM OVER!
12

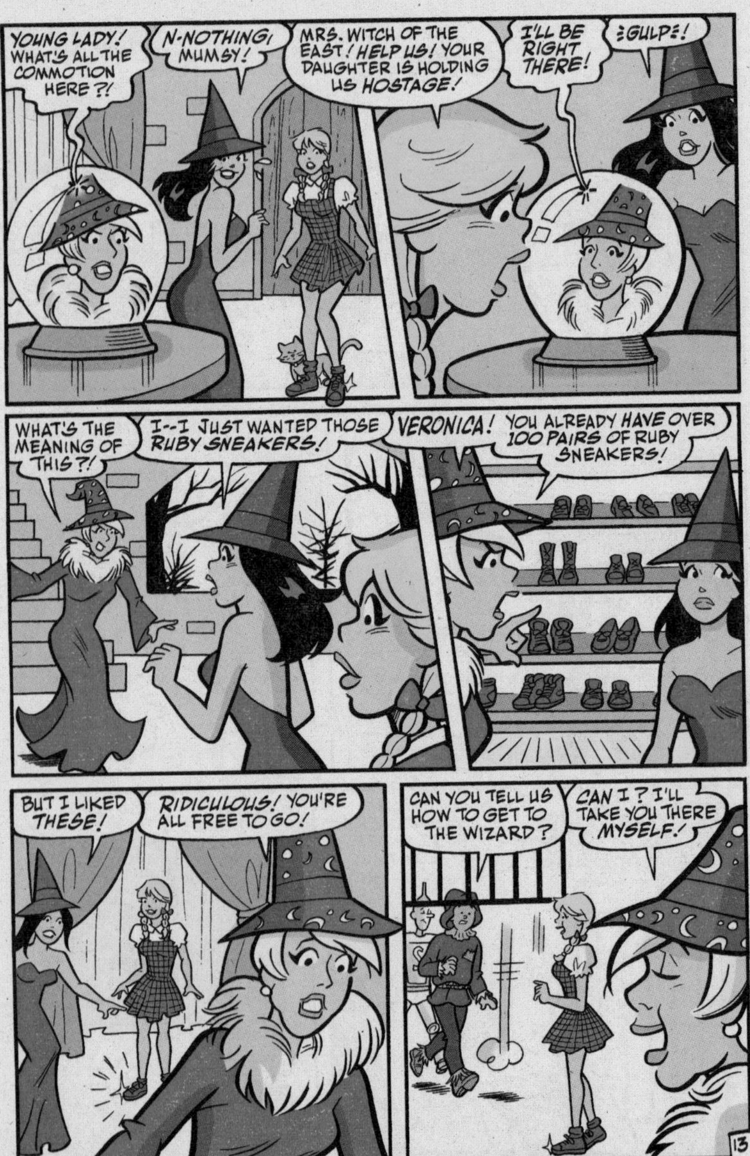
YOUNG LADY! WHAT'S ALL THE COMMOTION HERE?!
N-NOTHING, MUMSY!
MRS. WITCH OF THE EAST! HELP US! YOUR DAUGHTER IS HOLDING US HOSTAGE!
I'LL BE RIGHT THERE!
GULP!
WHAT'S THE MEANING OF THIS?!
I--I JUST WANTED THOSE RUBY SNEAKERS!
VERONICA!
YOU ALREADY HAVE OVER 100 PAIRS OF RUBY SNEAKERS!
BUT I LIKED THESE!
RIDICULOUS! YOU'RE ALL FREE TO GO!
CAN YOU TELL US HOW TO GET TO THE WIZARD?
CAN I? I'LL TAKE YOU THERE MYSELF!

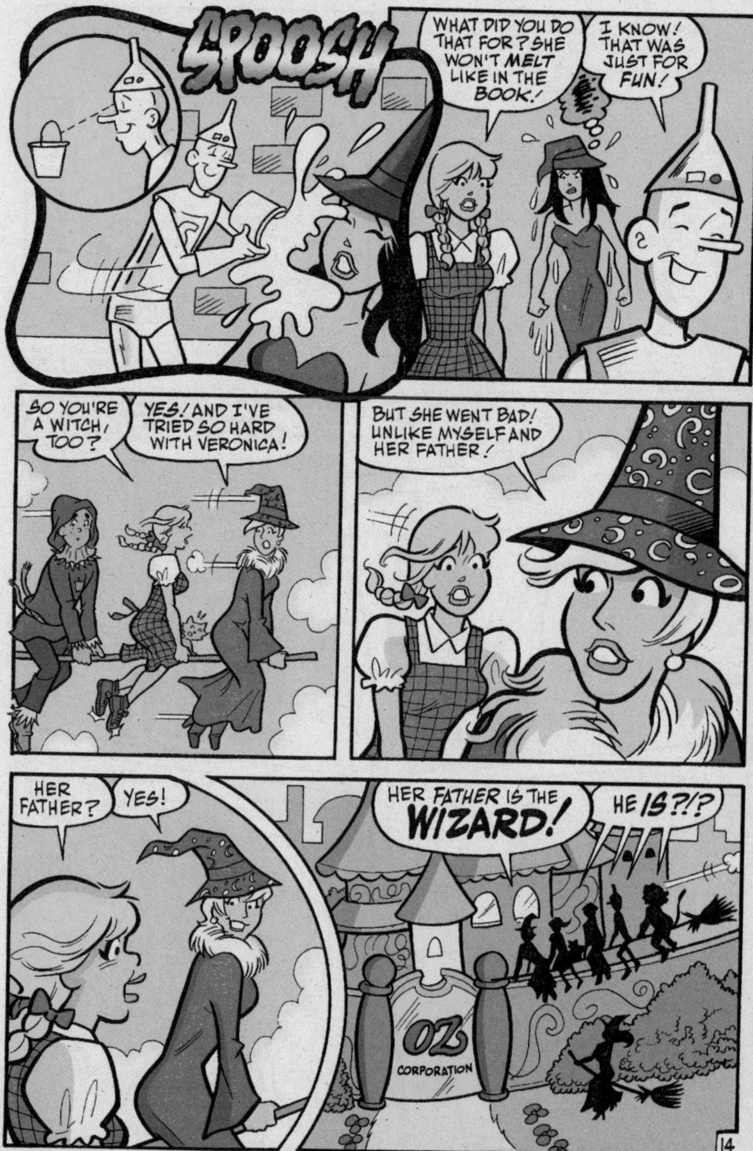
SPOOSH
WHAT DID YOU DO THAT FOR? SHE WON'T MELT LIKE IN THE BOOK!
I KNOW! THAT WAS JUST FOR FUN!
SO YOU'RE A WITCH, TOO?
YES! AND I'VE TRIED SO HARD WITH VERONICA!
BUT SHE WENT BAD! UNLIKE MYSELF AND HER FATHER!
HER FATHER?
YES!
HER FATHER IS THE WIZARD!
HE IS?!?
OZ
CORPORATION

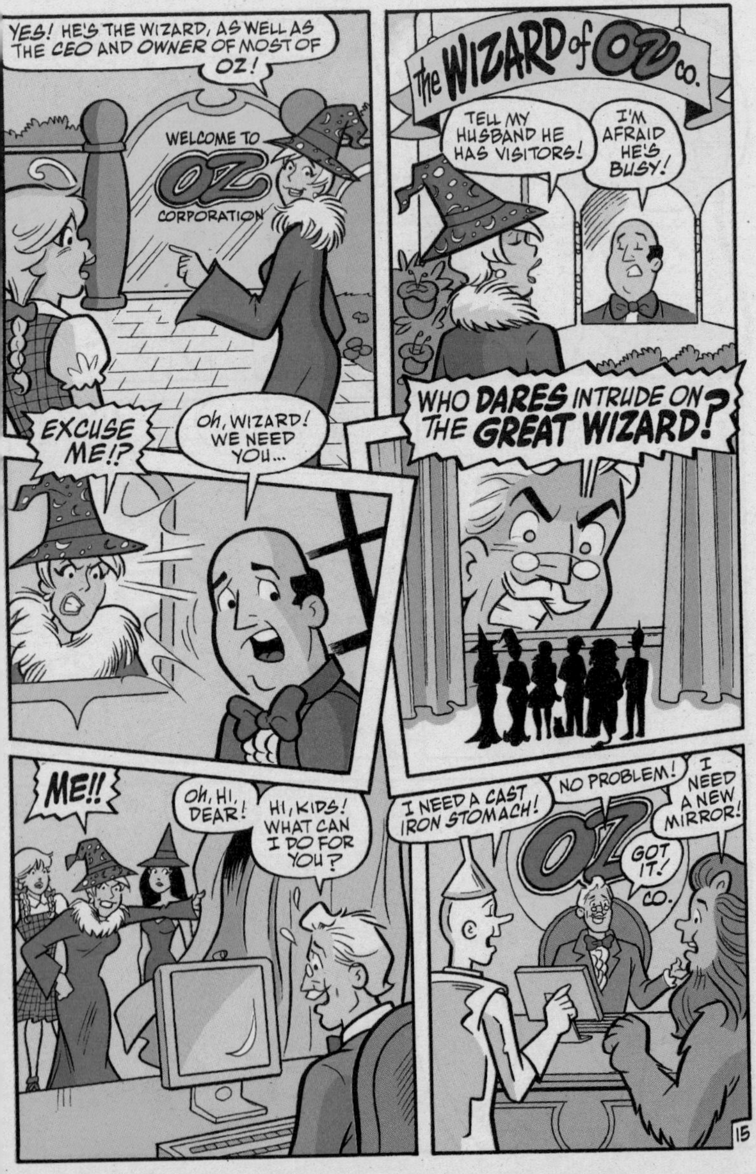
YES! HE'S THE WIZARD, AS WELL AS THE CEO AND OWNER OF MOST OF OZ!
WELCOME TO OZ CORPORATION
the WIZARD of OZ co.
TELL MY HUSBAND HE HAS VISITORS!
I'M AFRAID HE'S BUSY!
EXCUSE ME!?
Oh, WIZARD! WE NEED YOU...
WHO DARES INTRUDE ON THE GREAT WIZARD?
ME!!
Oh, HI, DEAR!
HI, KIDS! WHAT CAN I DO FOR YOU?
I NEED A CAST IRON STOMACH!
NO PROBLEM!
I NEED A NEW MIRROR!
GOT IT!
OZ CO.

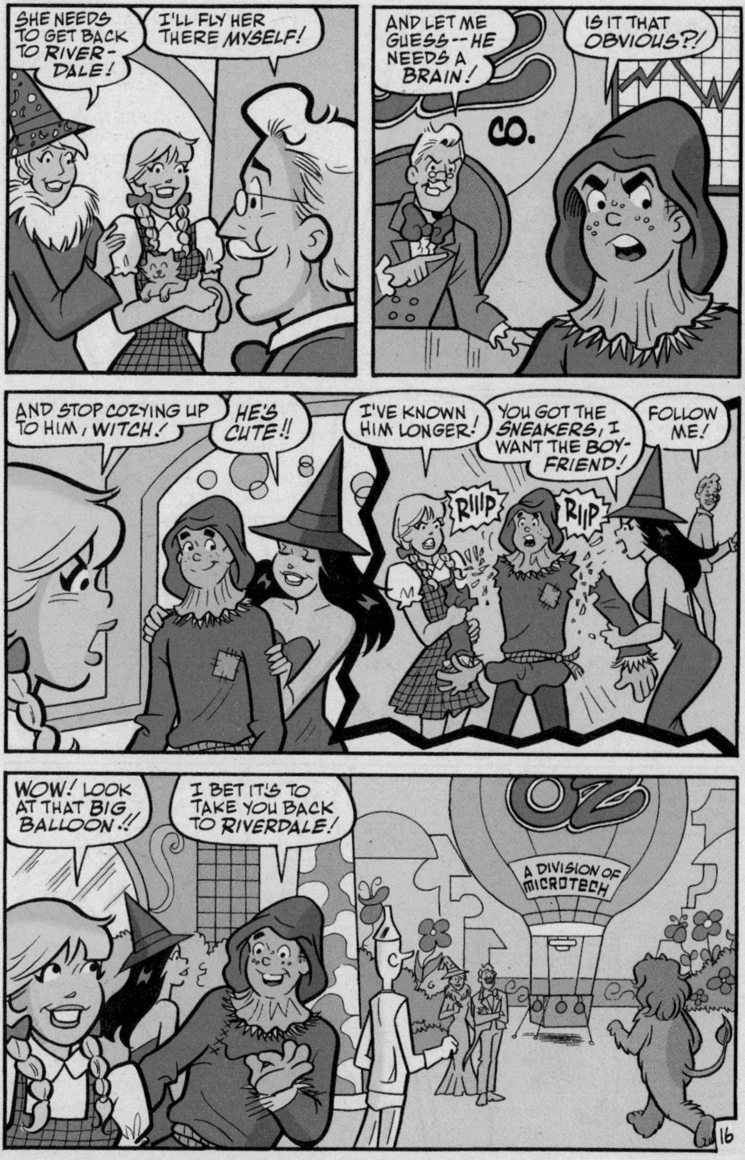
SHE NEEDS TO GET BACK TO RIVER-DALE!
I'LL FLY HER THERE MYSELF!
AND LET ME GUESS-- HE NEEDS A BRAIN!
IS IT THAT OBVIOUS?!
CO.
AND STOP COZYING UP TO HIM, WITCH!
HE'S CUTE!!
I'VE KNOWN HIM LONGER!
YOU GOT THE SNEAKERS, I WANT THE BOY-FRIEND!
FOLLOW ME!
RIIIP
RIIP
WOW! LOOK AT THAT BIG BALLOON!!
I BET IT'S TO TAKE YOU BACK TO RIVERDALE!
OZ
A DIVISION OF MICROTECH

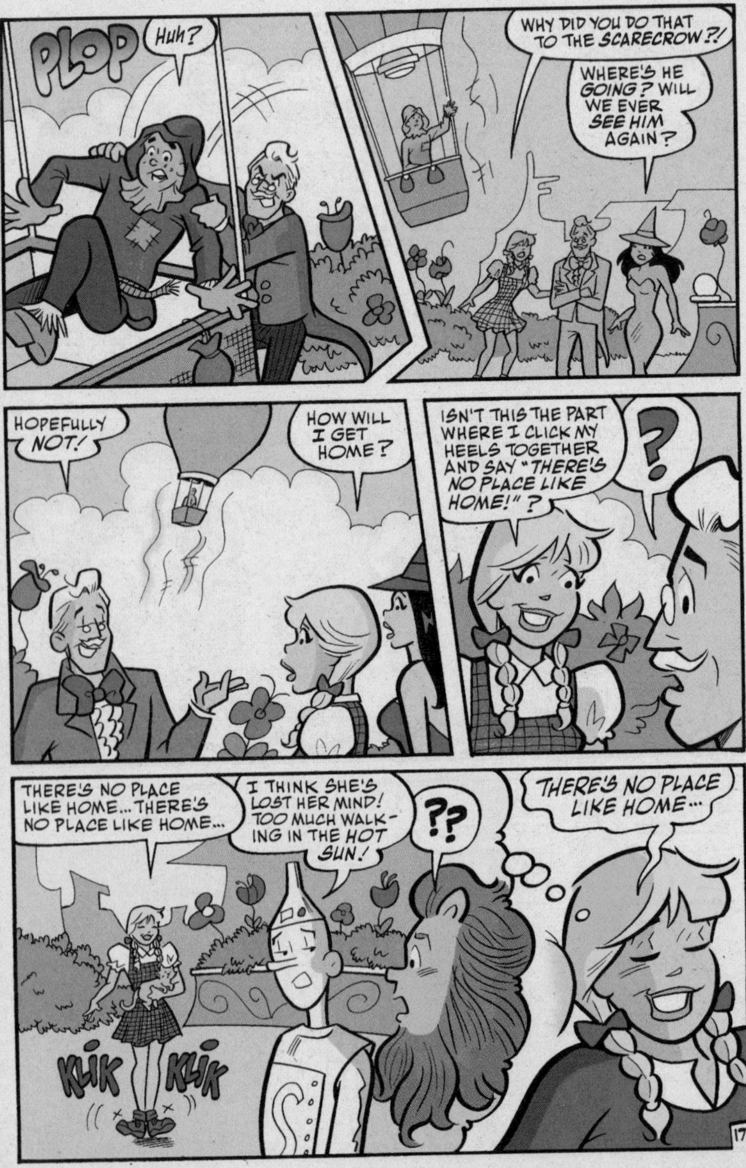
PLOP
Huh?
WHY DID YOU DO THAT TO THE SCARECROW?!
WHERE'S HE GOING? WILL WE EVER SEE HIM AGAIN?
HOPEFULLY NOT!
HOW WILL I GET HOME?
ISN'T THIS THE PART WHERE I CLICK MY HEELS TOGETHER AND SAY "THERE'S NO PLACE LIKE HOME!"?
?
THERE'S NO PLACE LIKE HOME... THERE'S NO PLACE LIKE HOME...
I THINK SHE'S LOST HER MIND! TOO MUCH WALKING IN THE HOT SUN!
??
THERE'S NO PLACE LIKE HOME...
KLIK KLIK
17

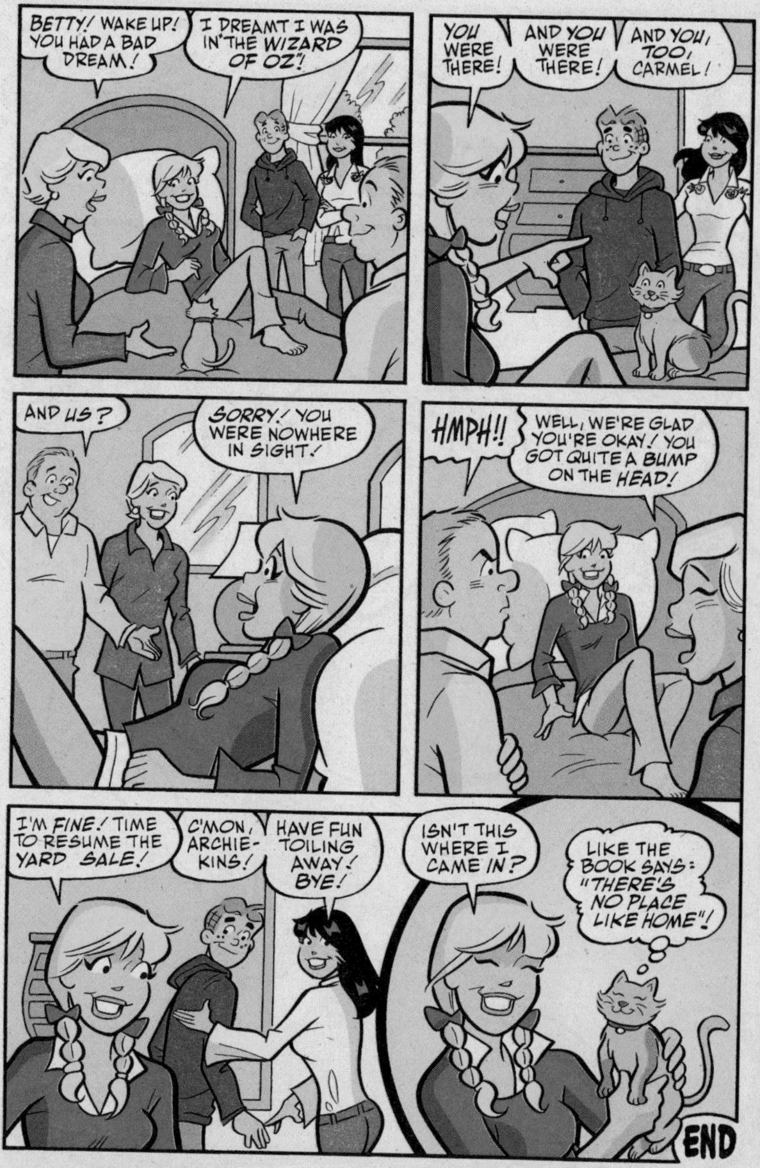
BETTY! WAKE UP! YOU HAD A BAD DREAM!
I DREAMT I WAS IN "THE WIZARD OF OZ"!
YOU WERE THERE!
AND YOU WERE THERE!
AND YOU, TOO, CARMEL!
AND US?
SORRY! YOU WERE NOWHERE IN SIGHT!
HMPH!!
WELL, WE'RE GLAD YOU'RE OKAY! YOU GOT QUITE A BUMP ON THE HEAD!
I'M FINE! TIME TO RESUME THE YARD SALE!
C'MON, ARCHIE-KINS!
HAVE FUN TOILING AWAY! BYE!
ISN'T THIS WHERE I CAME IN?
LIKE THE BOOK SAYS: "THERE'S NO PLACE LIKE HOME"!
END

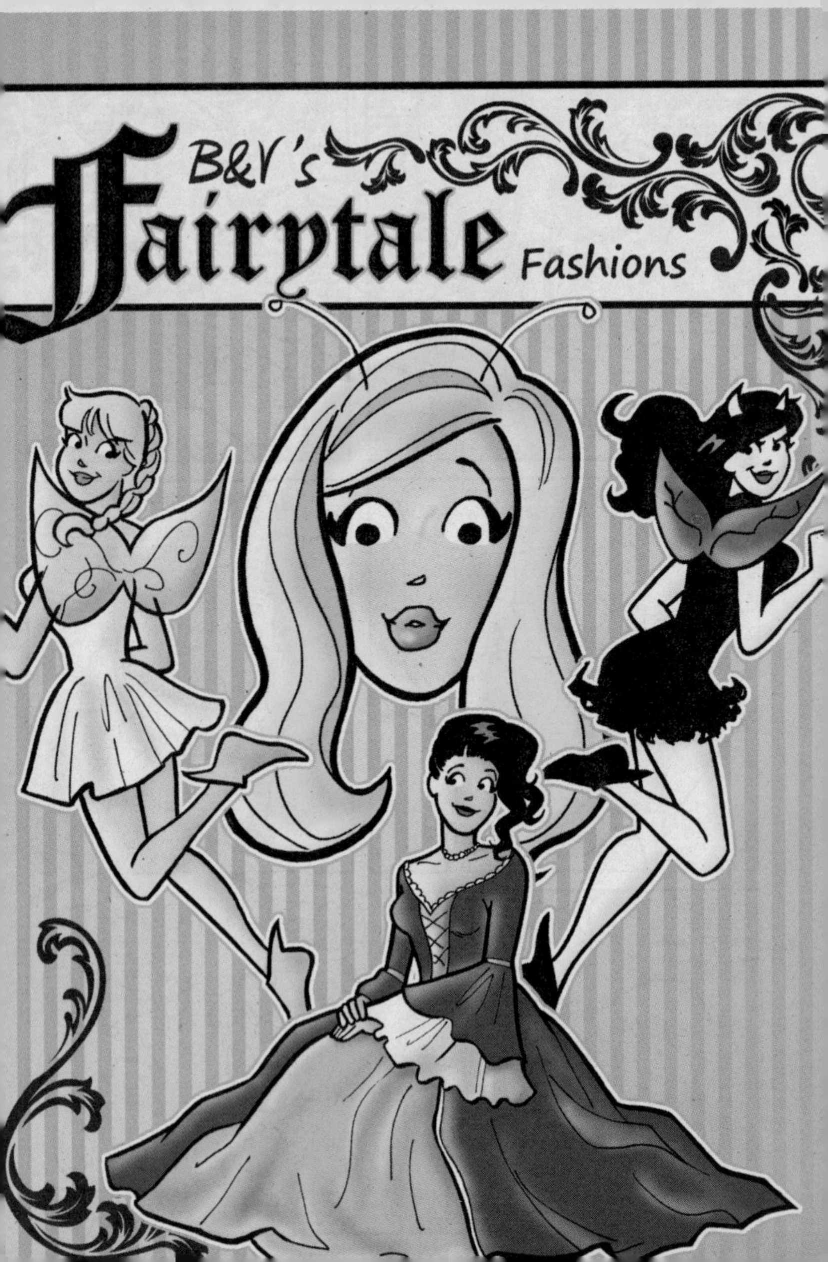
B&V's
Fairytale
Fashions

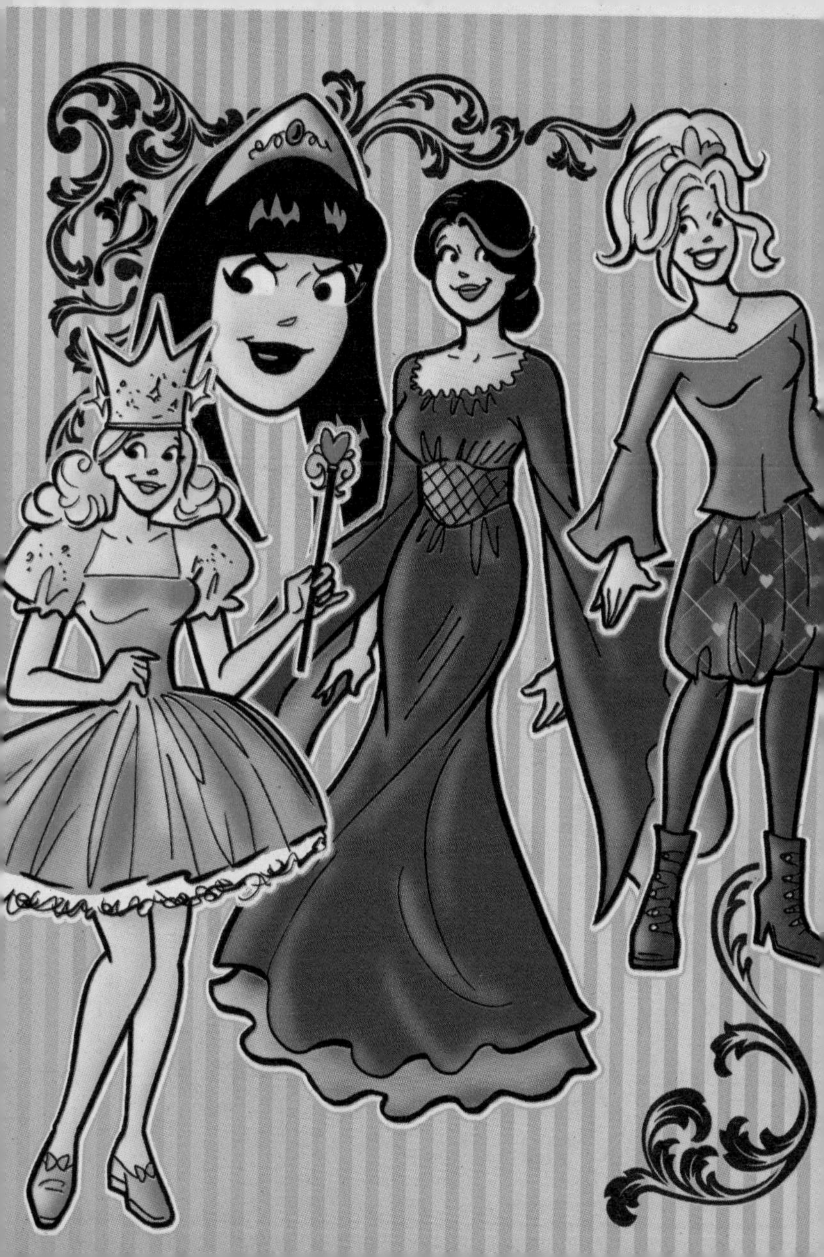

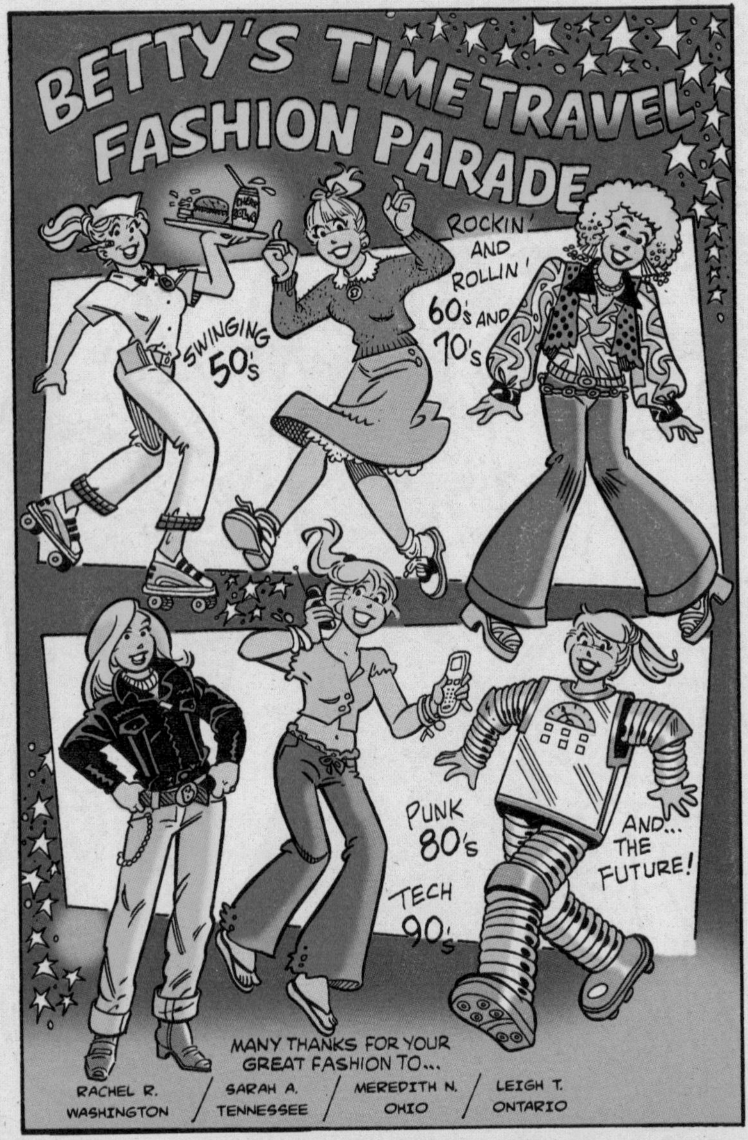
BETTY'S TIME TRAVEL FASHION PARADE
CHERRY COLA
SWINGING 50's
ROCKIN' AND ROLLIN' 60's AND 70's
PUNK 80's
TECH 90's
AND... THE FUTURE!
MANY THANKS FOR YOUR GREAT FASHION TO...
RACHEL R. WASHINGTON
SARAH A. TENNESSEE
MEREDITH N. OHIO
LEIGH T. ONTARIO

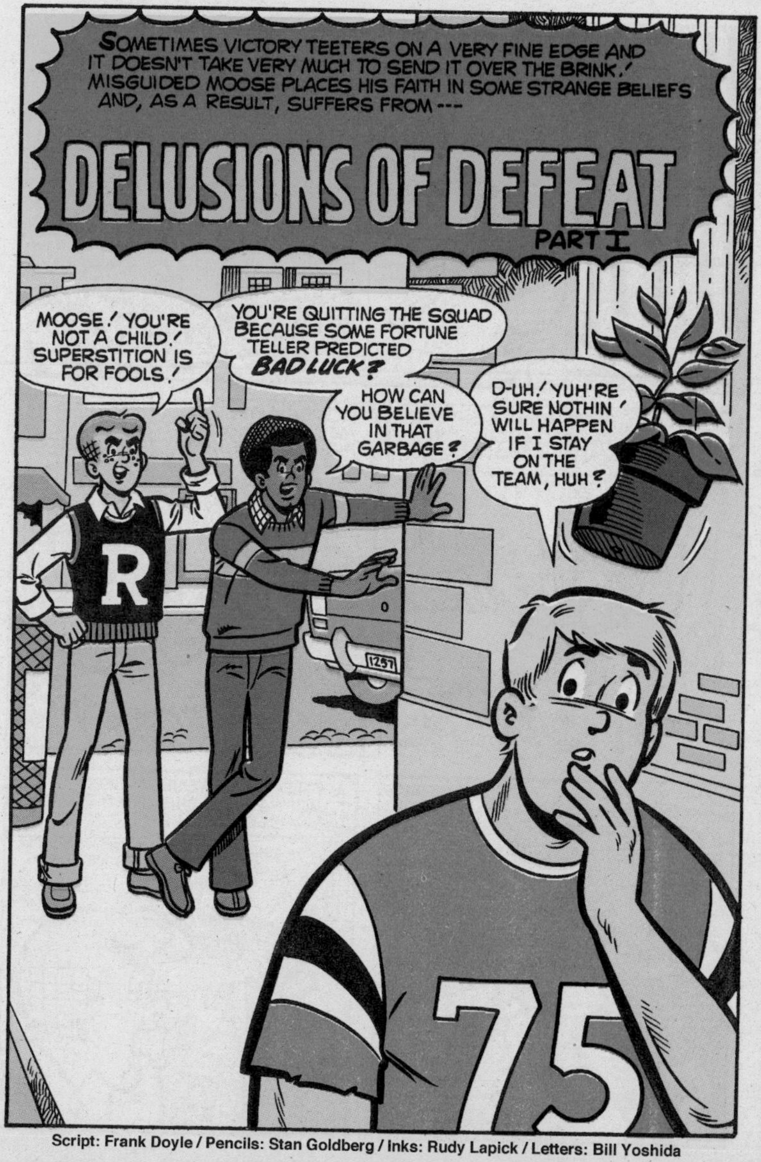
SOMETIMES VICTORY TEETERS ON A VERY FINE EDGE AND IT DOESN'T TAKE VERY MUCH TO SEND IT OVER THE BRINK! MISGUIDED MOOSE PLACES HIS FAITH IN SOME STRANGE BELIEFS AND, AS A RESULT, SUFFERS FROM ---
DELUSIONS OF DEFEAT
PART I
MOOSE! YOU'RE NOT A CHILD! SUPERSTITION IS FOR FOOLS!
YOU'RE QUITTING THE SQUAD BECAUSE SOME FORTUNE TELLER PREDICTED BAD LUCK?
HOW CAN YOU BELIEVE IN THAT GARBAGE?
D-UH! YUH'RE SURE NOTHIN' WILL HAPPEN IF I STAY ON THE TEAM, HUH?
R
75

Script: Frank Doyle / Pencils: Stan Goldberg / Inks: Rudy Lapick / Letters: Bill Yoshida

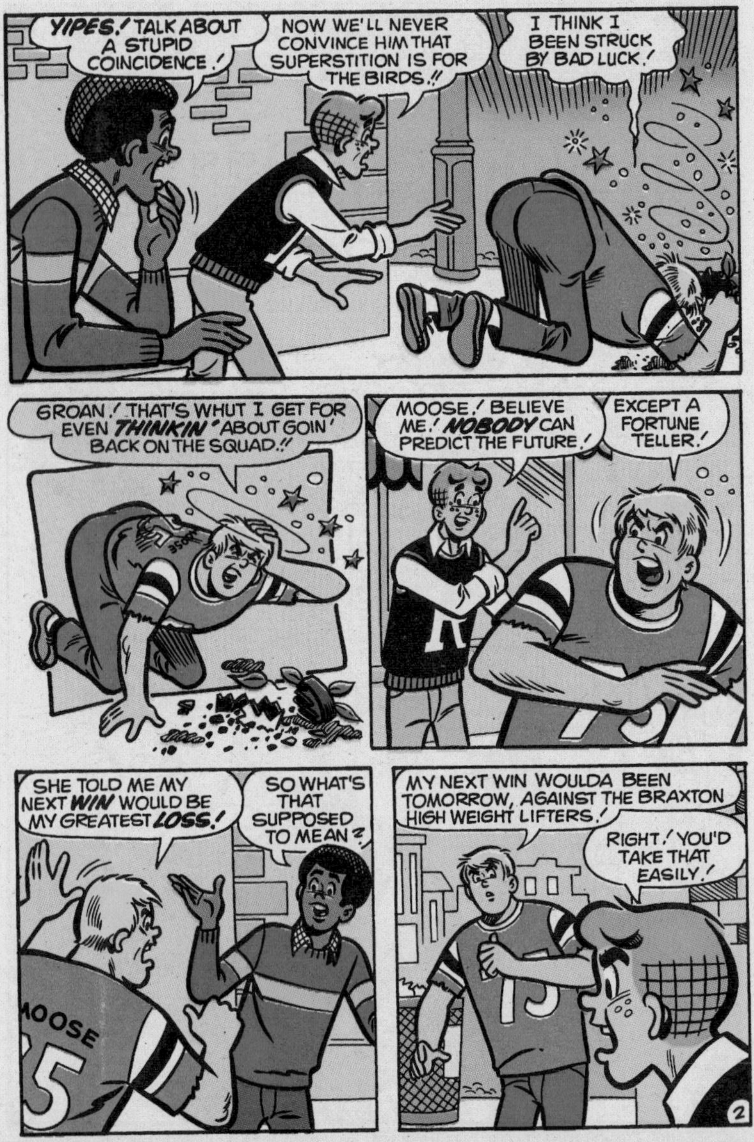
YIPES! TALK ABOUT A STUPID COINCIDENCE!
NOW WE'LL NEVER CONVINCE HIM THAT SUPERSTITION IS FOR THE BIRDS!!
I THINK I BEEN STRUCK BY BAD LUCK!
GROAN! THAT'S WHUT I GET FOR EVEN THINKIN' ABOUT GOIN' BACK ON THE SQUAD!!
MOOSE! BELIEVE ME! NOBODY CAN PREDICT THE FUTURE!
EXCEPT A FORTUNE TELLER!
SHE TOLD ME MY NEXT WIN WOULD BE MY GREATEST LOSS!
SO WHAT'S THAT SUPPOSED TO MEAN?
MY NEXT WIN WOULDA BEEN TOMORROW, AGAINST THE BRAXTON HIGH WEIGHT LIFTERS!
RIGHT! YOU'D TAKE THAT EASILY!
2

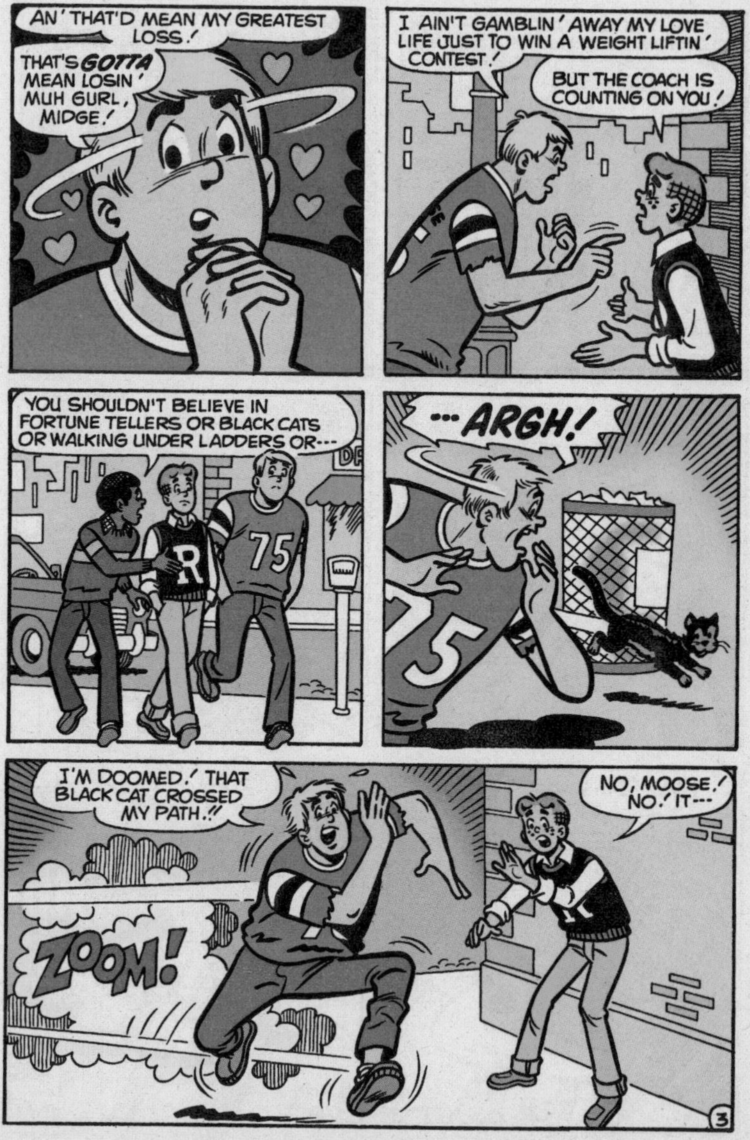

AN' THAT'D MEAN MY GREATEST LOSS.!
THAT'S GOTTA MEAN LOSIN' MUH GURL, MIDGE.!
I AIN'T GAMBLIN' AWAY MY LOVE LIFE JUST TO WIN A WEIGHT LIFTIN' CONTEST.!
BUT THE COACH IS COUNTING ON YOU!
YOU SHOULDN'T BELIEVE IN FORTUNE TELLERS OR BLACK CATS OR WALKING UNDER LADDERS OR---
---ARGH!
I'M DOOMED.! THAT BLACK CAT CROSSED MY PATH.!!
NO, MOOSE.! NO.! IT---
ZOOM!

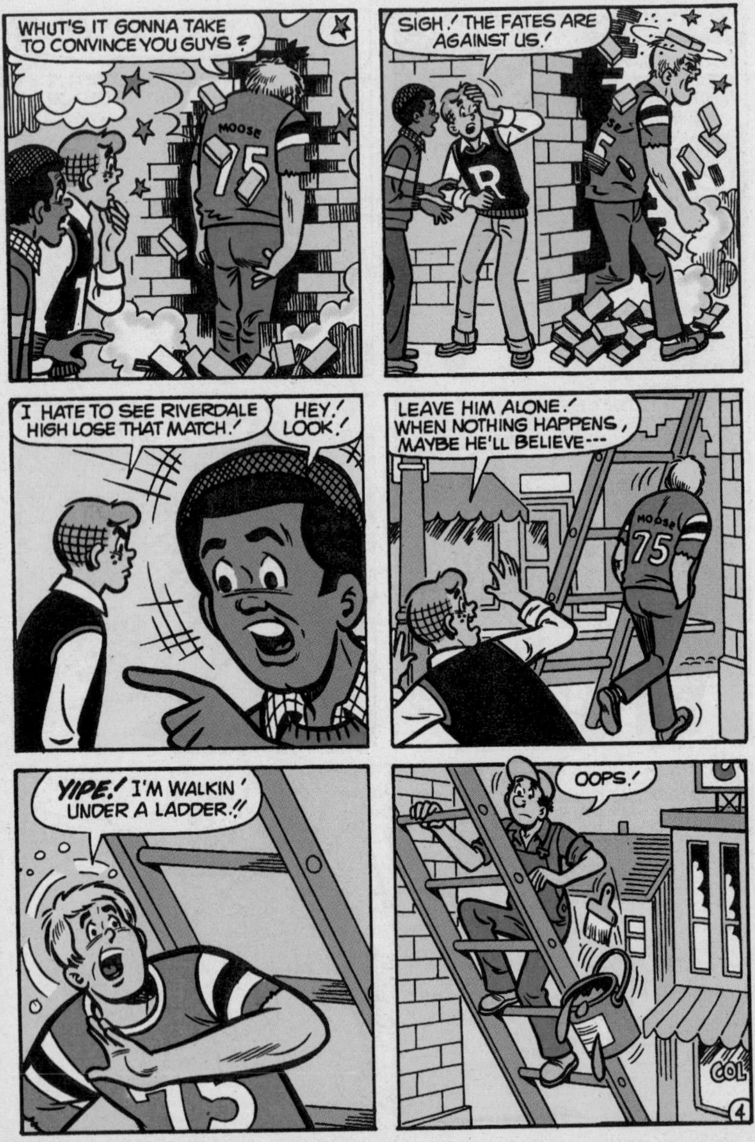
WHUT'S IT GONNA TAKE TO CONVINCE YOU GUYS ?
MOOSE
75
SIGH! THE FATES ARE AGAINST US!
R
I HATE TO SEE RIVERDALE HIGH LOSE THAT MATCH!
HEY! LOOK!
LEAVE HIM ALONE! WHEN NOTHING HAPPENS, MAYBE HE'LL BELIEVE---
MOOSE
75
YIPE! I'M WALKIN' UNDER A LADDER!!
OOPS!
COL
4

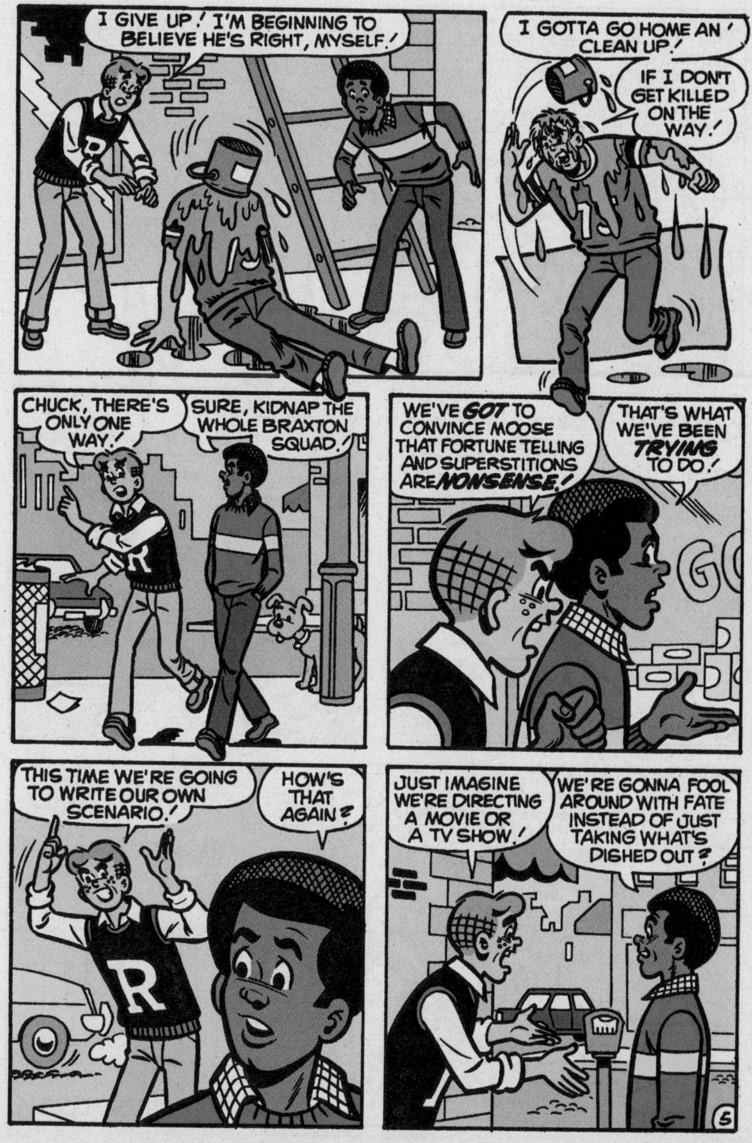
I GIVE UP! I'M BEGINNING TO BELIEVE HE'S RIGHT, MYSELF!
I GOTTA GO HOME AN' CLEAN UP!
IF I DON'T GET KILLED ON THE WAY!
CHUCK, THERE'S ONLY ONE WAY!
SURE, KIDNAP THE WHOLE BRAXTON SQUAD!
WE'VE GOT TO CONVINCE MOOSE THAT FORTUNE TELLING AND SUPERSTITIONS ARE NONSENSE!
THAT'S WHAT WE'VE BEEN TRYING TO DO!
THIS TIME WE'RE GOING TO WRITE OUR OWN SCENARIO!
HOW'S THAT AGAIN?
JUST IMAGINE WE'RE DIRECTING A MOVIE OR A TV SHOW!
WE'RE GONNA FOOL AROUND WITH FATE INSTEAD OF JUST TAKING WHAT'S DISHED OUT?
5

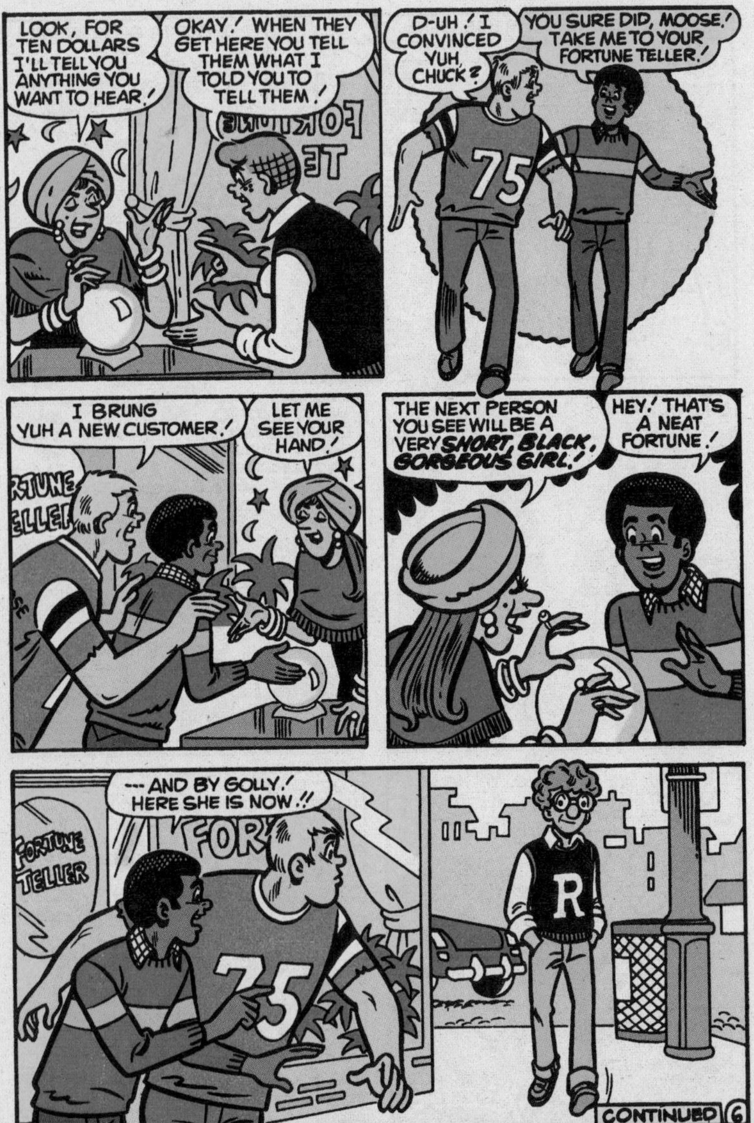
LOOK, FOR TEN DOLLARS I'LL TELL YOU ANYTHING YOU WANT TO HEAR!
OKAY! WHEN THEY GET HERE YOU TELL THEM WHAT I TOLD YOU TO TELL THEM!
D-UH! I CONVINCED YUH, CHUCK?
YOU SURE DID, MOOSE! TAKE ME TO YOUR FORTUNE TELLER!
I BRUNG YUH A NEW CUSTOMER!
LET ME SEE YOUR HAND!
FORTUNE TELLER
THE NEXT PERSON YOU SEE WILL BE A VERY SHORT, BLACK, GORGEOUS GIRL!
HEY! THAT'S A NEAT FORTUNE!
--- AND BY GOLLY! HERE SHE IS NOW!!
FORTUNE TELLER
CONTINUED
6

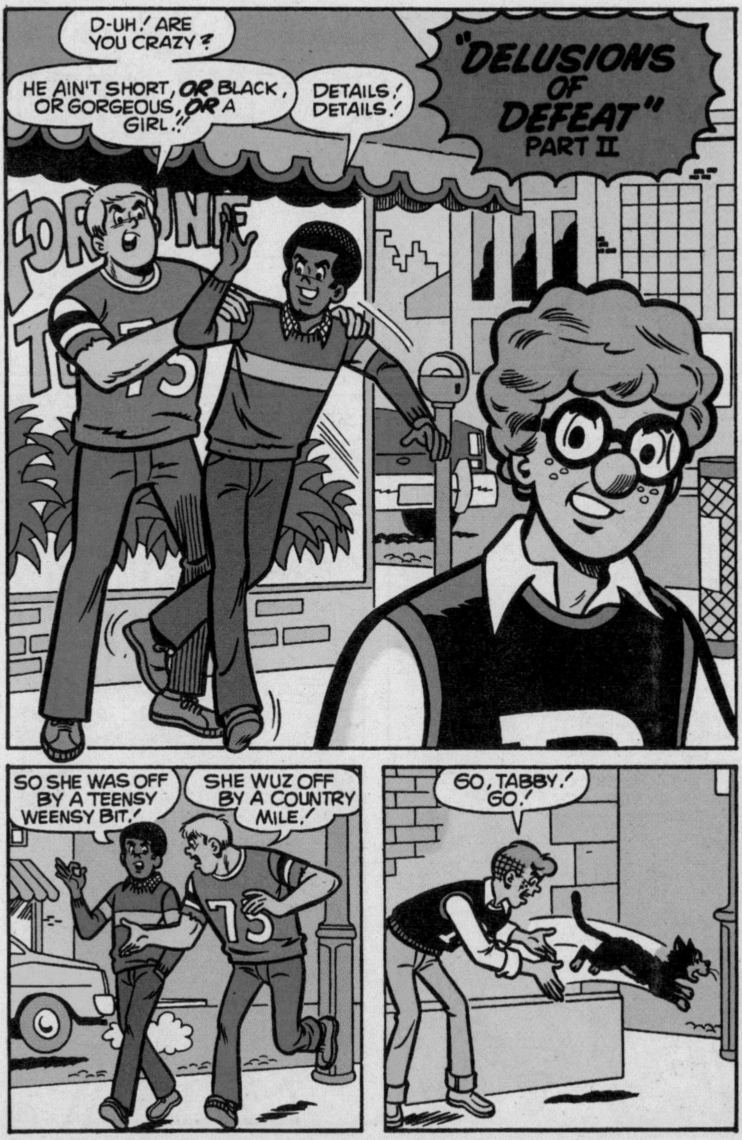
D-UH! ARE YOU CRAZY?
HE AIN'T SHORT, OR BLACK, OR GORGEOUS, OR A GIRL!!
DETAILS! DETAILS!
"DELUSIONS OF DEFEAT" PART II
SO SHE WAS OFF BY A TEENSY WEENSY BIT!
SHE WUZ OFF BY A COUNTRY MILE!
GO, TABBY! GO!

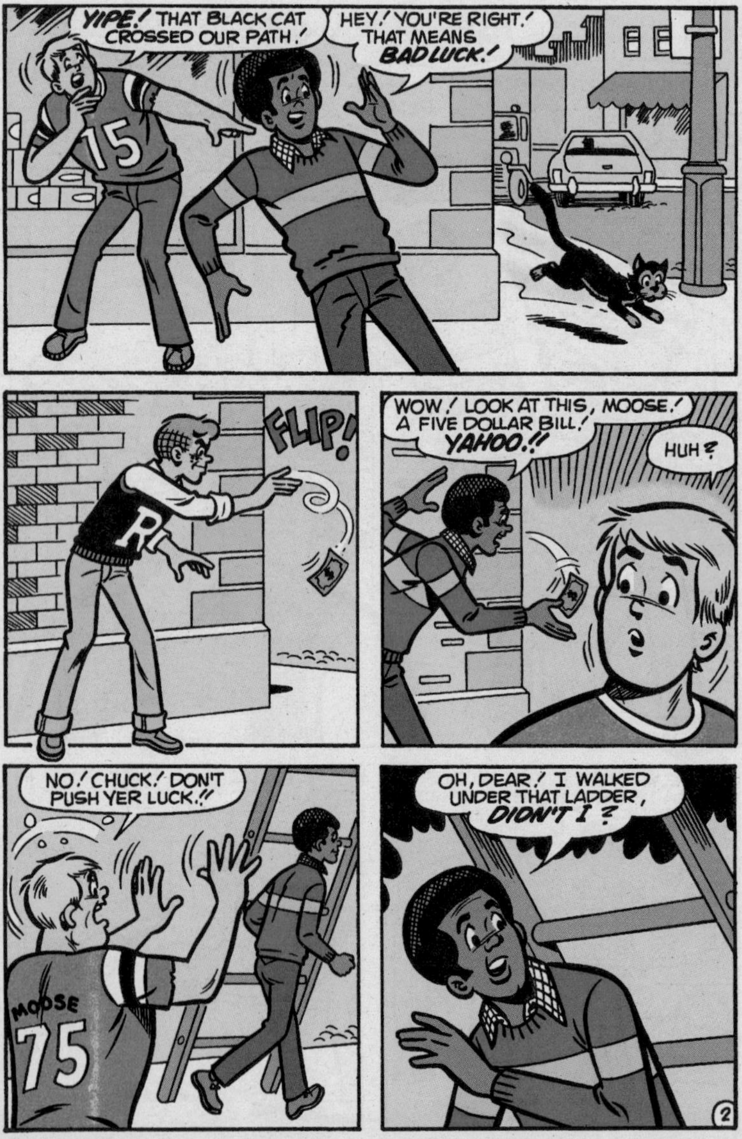

YIPE! THAT BLACK CAT CROSSED OUR PATH!
HEY! YOU'RE RIGHT! THAT MEANS BAD LUCK!
FLIP!
WOW! LOOK AT THIS, MOOSE! A FIVE DOLLAR BILL! YAHOO!!
HUH?
NO! CHUCK! DON'T PUSH YER LUCK!!
MOOSE
75
OH, DEAR! I WALKED UNDER THAT LADDER, DIDN'T I?

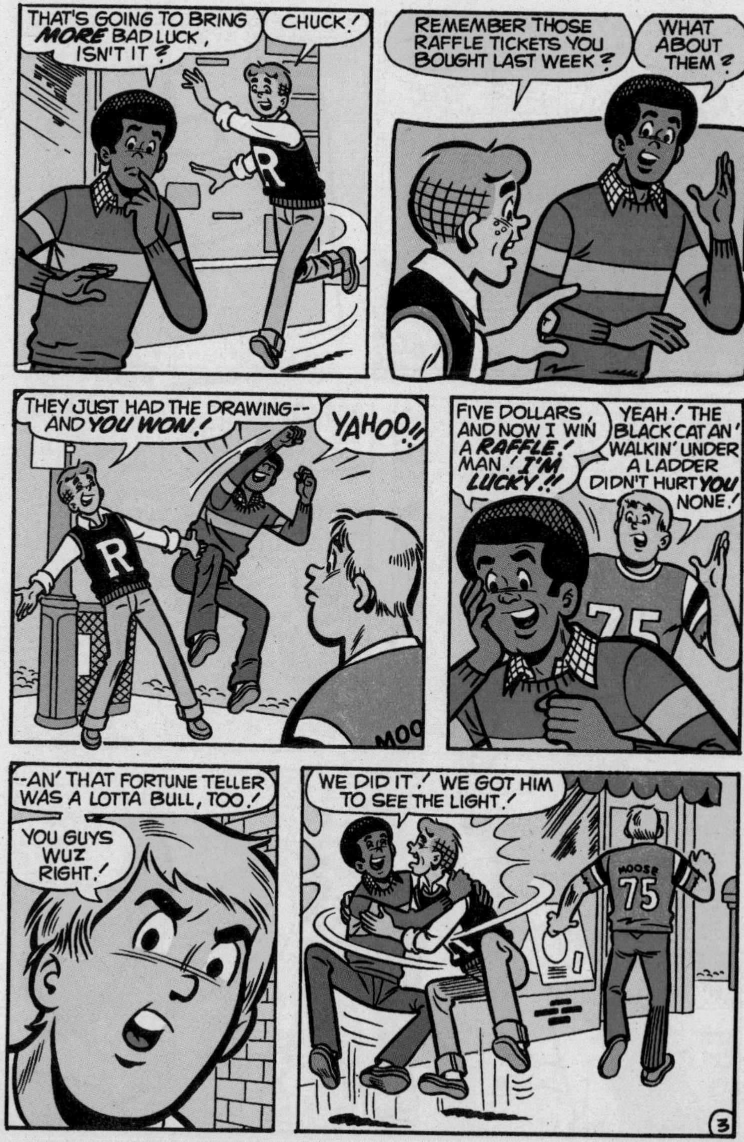

THAT'S GOING TO BRING MORE BAD LUCK, ISN'T IT ?
CHUCK !
REMEMBER THOSE RAFFLE TICKETS YOU BOUGHT LAST WEEK ?
WHAT ABOUT THEM ?
THEY JUST HAD THE DRAWING-- AND YOU WON !
YAHOO!!
MOO
FIVE DOLLARS, AND NOW I WIN A RAFFLE ! MAN ! I'M LUCKY !!
YEAH ! THE BLACK CAT AN' WALKIN' UNDER A LADDER DIDN'T HURT YOU NONE !
75
--AN' THAT FORTUNE TELLER WAS A LOTTA BULL, TOO !
YOU GUYS WUZ RIGHT !
WE DID IT ! WE GOT HIM TO SEE THE LIGHT !
MOOSE
75

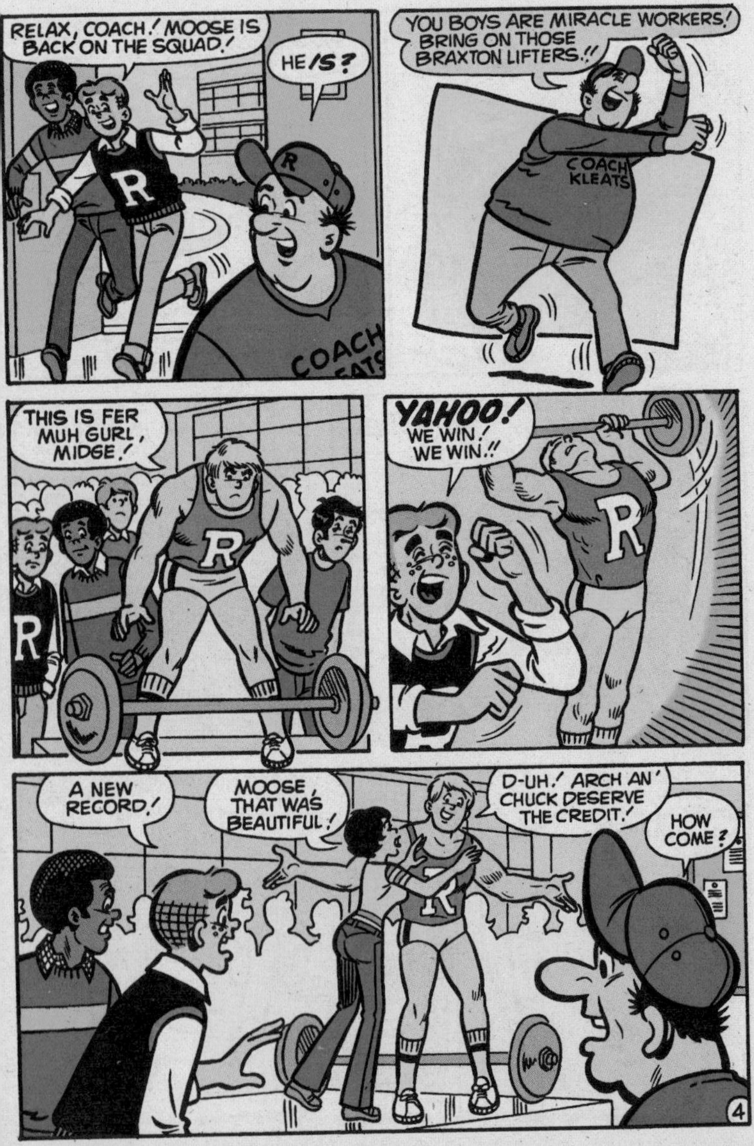
RELAX, COACH! MOOSE IS BACK ON THE SQUAD!
HE IS?
COACH
YOU BOYS ARE MIRACLE WORKERS! BRING ON THOSE BRAXTON LIFTERS!!
COACH KLEATS
THIS IS FER MUH GURL, MIDGE!
YAHOO! WE WIN! WE WIN!!
A NEW RECORD!
MOOSE, THAT WAS BEAUTIFUL!
D-UH! ARCH AN' CHUCK DESERVE THE CREDIT!
HOW COME?
4

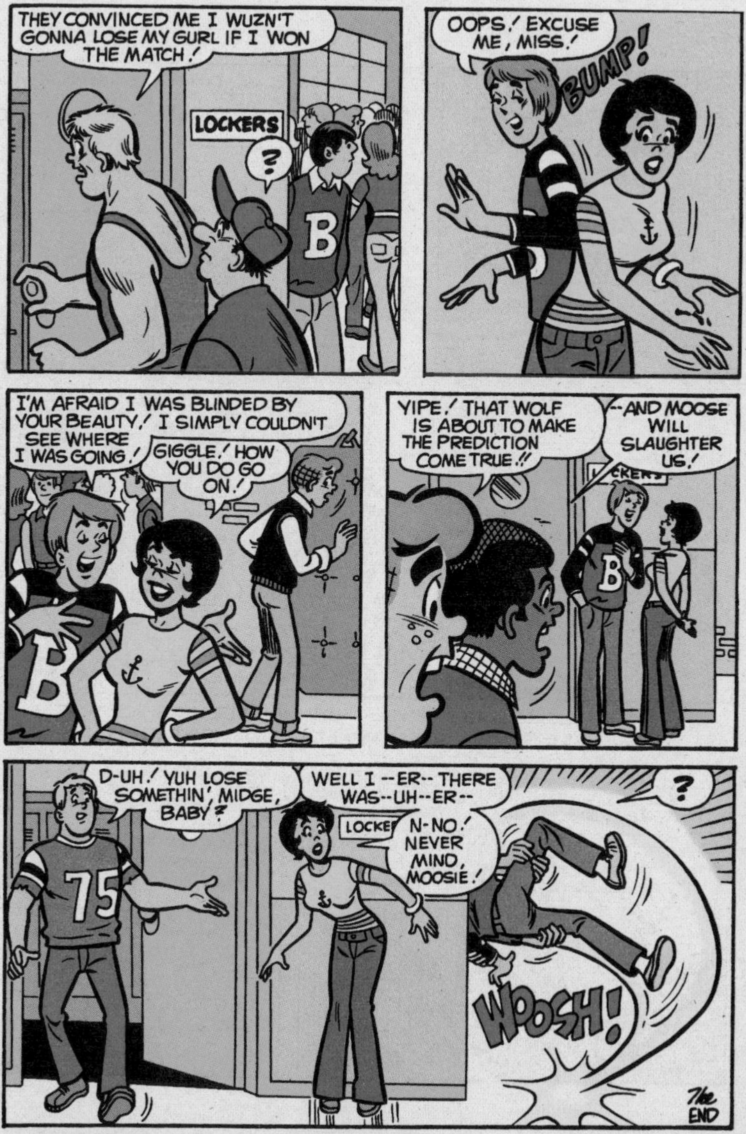
THEY CONVINCED ME I WUZN'T GONNA LOSE MY GURL IF I WON THE MATCH!
LOCKERS
?
OOPS! EXCUSE ME, MISS!
BUMP!
I'M AFRAID I WAS BLINDED BY YOUR BEAUTY! I SIMPLY COULDN'T SEE WHERE I WAS GOING!
GIGGLE! HOW YOU DO GO ON!
YIPE! THAT WOLF IS ABOUT TO MAKE THE PREDICTION COME TRUE!!
--AND MOOSE WILL SLAUGHTER US!
D-UH! YUH LOSE SOMETHIN', MIDGE, BABY?
WELL I --ER-- THERE WAS--UH--ER--
N-NO! NEVER MIND, MOOSIE!
?
WOOSH!
The END

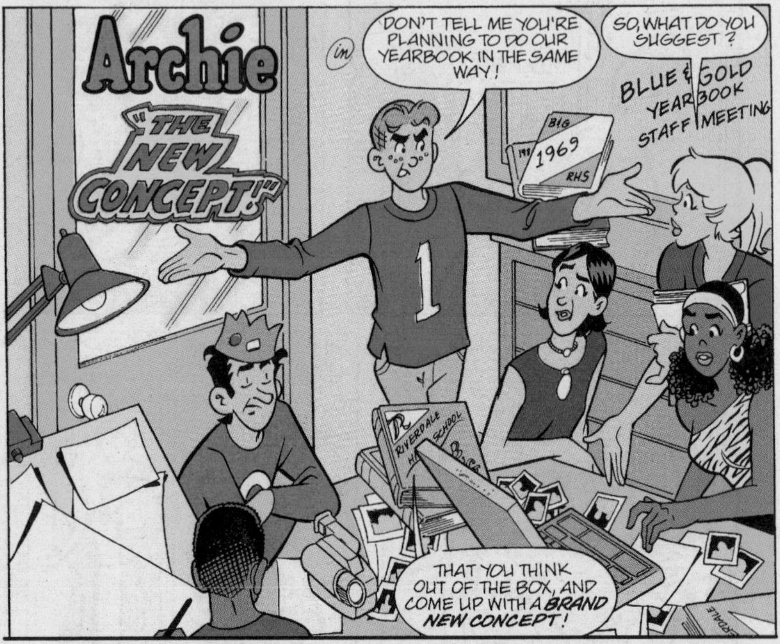
Archie
in
"THE NEW CONCEPT!"
DON'T TELL ME YOU'RE PLANNING TO DO OUR YEARBOOK IN THE SAME WAY!
SO, WHAT DO YOU SUGGEST?
BLUE & GOLD YEARBOOK STAFF MEETING
BIG 1969 RHS
THAT YOU THINK OUT OF THE BOX, AND COME UP WITH A ***BRAND NEW CONCEPT***!

SCRIPT: GEORGE GLADIR PENCILS: FERNANDO RUIZ INKS: BOB SMITH
COLORS: BARRY GROSSMAN LETTERS: VICKIE WILLIAMS

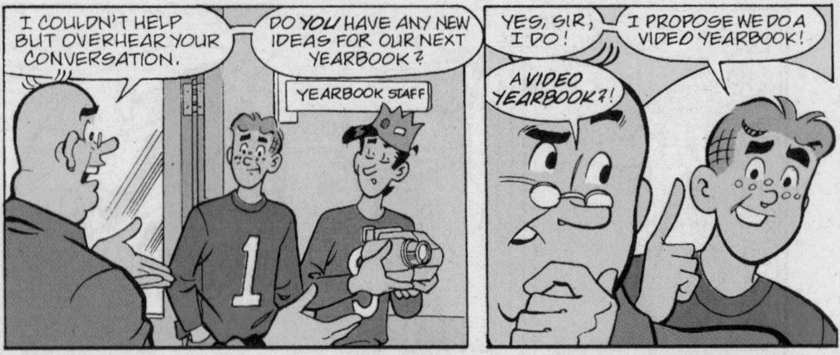
I COULDN'T HELP BUT OVERHEAR YOUR CONVERSATION.
DO ***YOU*** HAVE ANY NEW IDEAS FOR OUR NEXT YEARBOOK?
YEARBOOK STAFF
YES, SIR, I DO!
I PROPOSE WE DO A VIDEO YEARBOOK!
A ***VIDEO YEARBOOK***?!

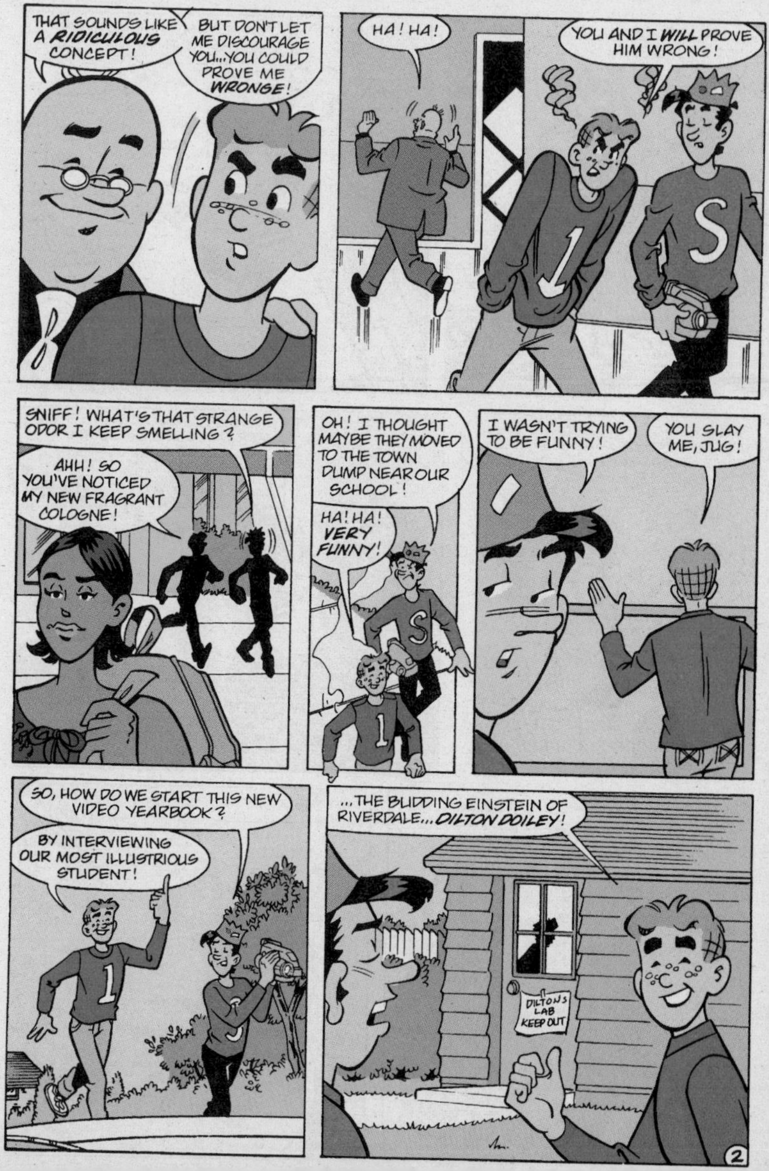

THAT SOUNDS LIKE A RIDICULOUS CONCEPT!
BUT DON'T LET ME DISCOURAGE YOU...YOU COULD PROVE ME WRONGE!
HA! HA!
YOU AND I WILL PROVE HIM WRONG!
SNIFF! WHAT'S THAT STRANGE ODOR I KEEP SMELLING?
AHH! SO YOU'VE NOTICED MY NEW FRAGRANT COLOGNE!
OH! I THOUGHT MAYBE THEY MOVED TO THE TOWN DUMP NEAR OUR SCHOOL!
HA! HA! VERY FUNNY!
I WASN'T TRYING TO BE FUNNY!
YOU SLAY ME, JUG!
SO, HOW DO WE START THIS NEW VIDEO YEARBOOK?
BY INTERVIEWING OUR MOST ILLUSTRIOUS STUDENT!
...THE BUDDING EINSTEIN OF RIVERDALE... DILTON DOILEY!
DILTONS LAB KEEP OUT

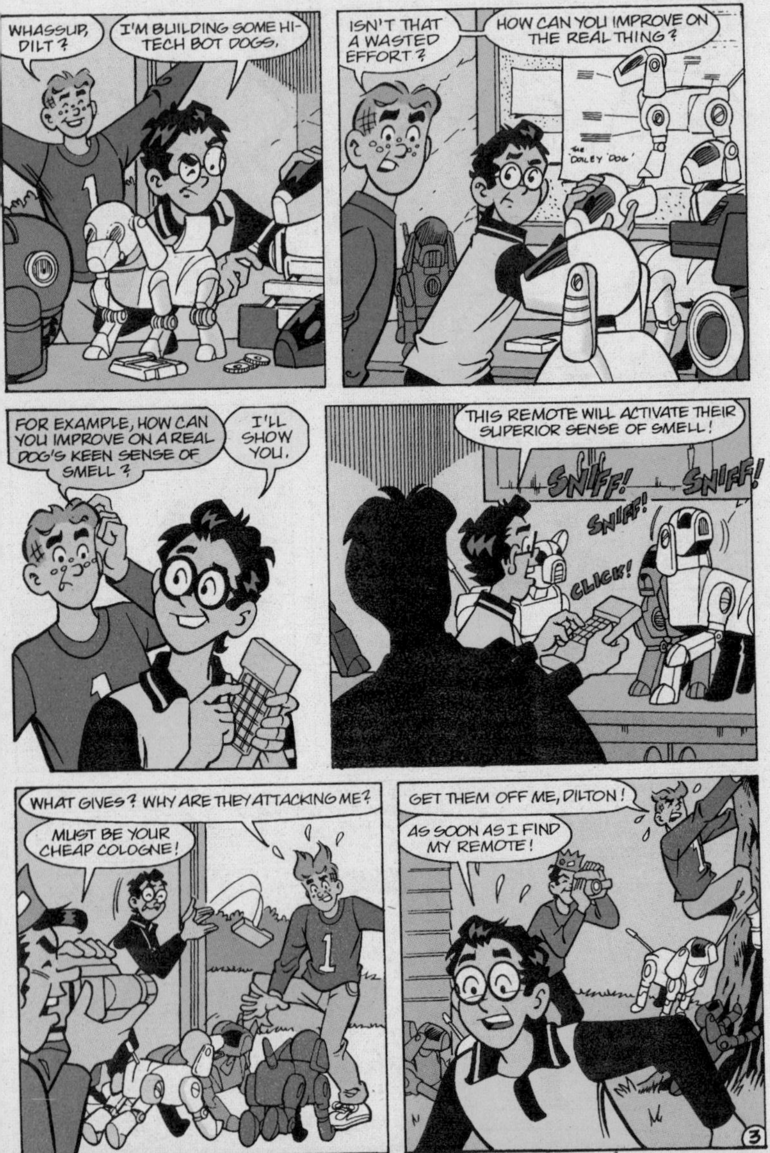
WHASSUP, DILT?
I'M BUILDING SOME HI-TECH BOT DOGS.
ISN'T THAT A WASTED EFFORT?
HOW CAN YOU IMPROVE ON THE REAL THING?
THE 'DOILEY DOG'
FOR EXAMPLE, HOW CAN YOU IMPROVE ON A REAL DOG'S KEEN SENSE OF SMELL?
I'LL SHOW YOU.
THIS REMOTE WILL ACTIVATE THEIR SUPERIOR SENSE OF SMELL!
SNIFF!
SNIFF!
SNIFF!
CLICK!
WHAT GIVES? WHY ARE THEY ATTACKING ME?
MUST BE YOUR CHEAP COLOGNE!
GET THEM OFF ME, DILTON!
AS SOON AS I FIND MY REMOTE!
3

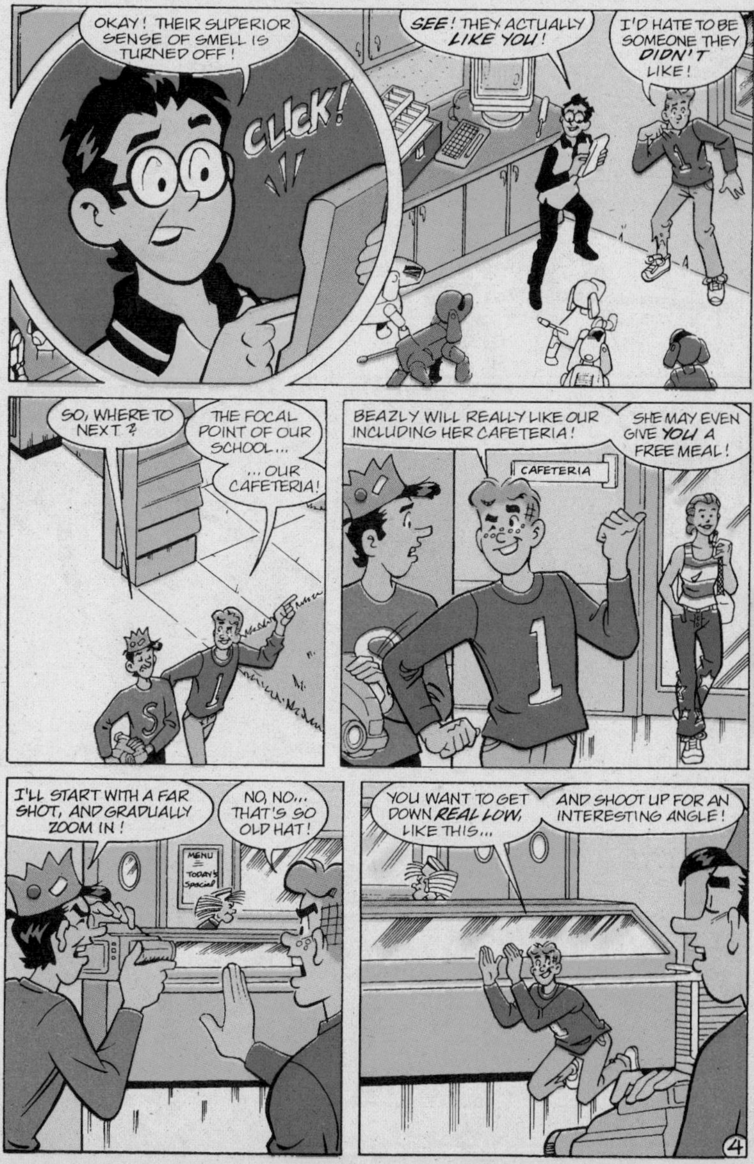
OKAY! THEIR SUPERIOR SENSE OF SMELL IS TURNED OFF!
CLICK!
SEE! THEY ACTUALLY LIKE YOU!
I'D HATE TO BE SOMEONE THEY DIDN'T LIKE!
SO, WHERE TO NEXT?
THE FOCAL POINT OF OUR SCHOOL...
...OUR CAFETERIA!
BEAZLY WILL REALLY LIKE OUR INCLUDING HER CAFETERIA!
CAFETERIA
SHE MAY EVEN GIVE YOU A FREE MEAL!
I'LL START WITH A FAR SHOT, AND GRADUALLY ZOOM IN!
NO, NO... THAT'S SO OLD HAT!
MENU
TODAY'S Special
YOU WANT TO GET DOWN REAL LOW, LIKE THIS...
AND SHOOT UP FOR AN INTERESTING ANGLE!

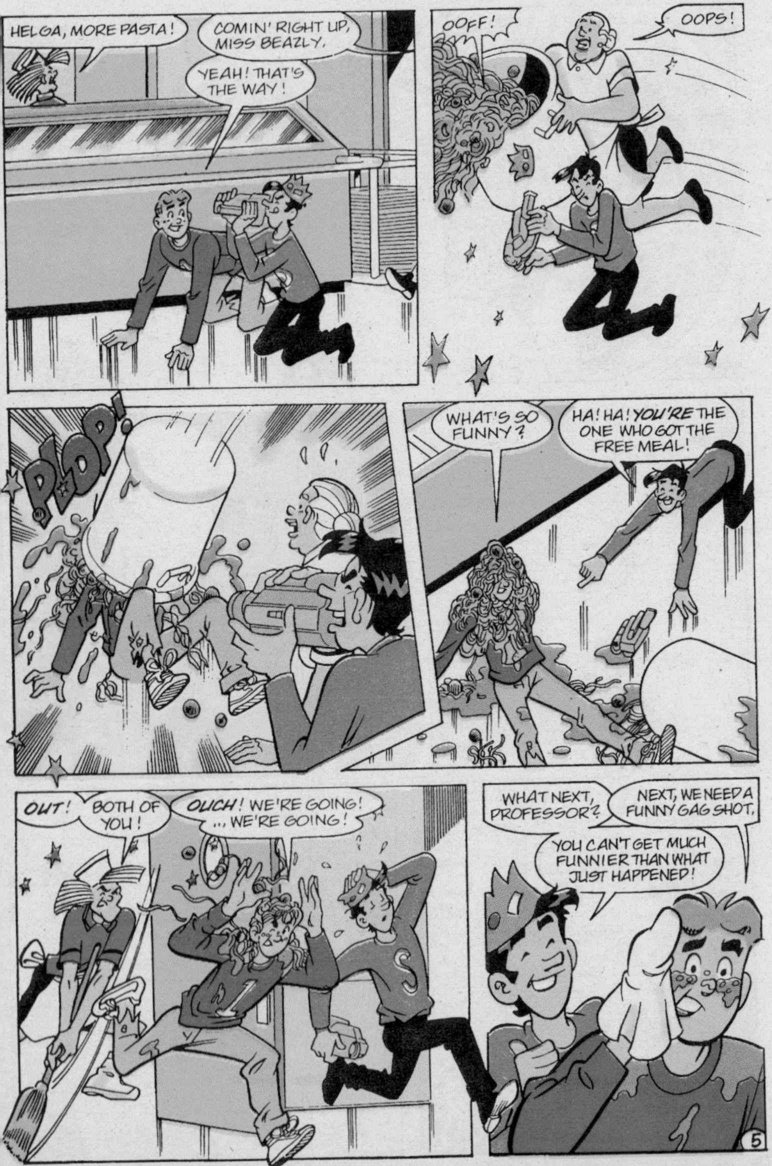
HELGA, MORE PASTA!
COMIN' RIGHT UP, MISS BEAZLY.
YEAH! THAT'S THE WAY!
OOFF!
OOPS!
PLOP!
WHAT'S SO FUNNY?
HA! HA! YOU'RE THE ONE WHO GOT THE FREE MEAL!
OUT! BOTH OF YOU!
OUCH! WE'RE GOING! ... WE'RE GOING!
WHAT NEXT, PROFESSOR?
NEXT, WE NEED A FUNNY GAG SHOT.
YOU CAN'T GET MUCH FUNNIER THAN WHAT JUST HAPPENED!
5

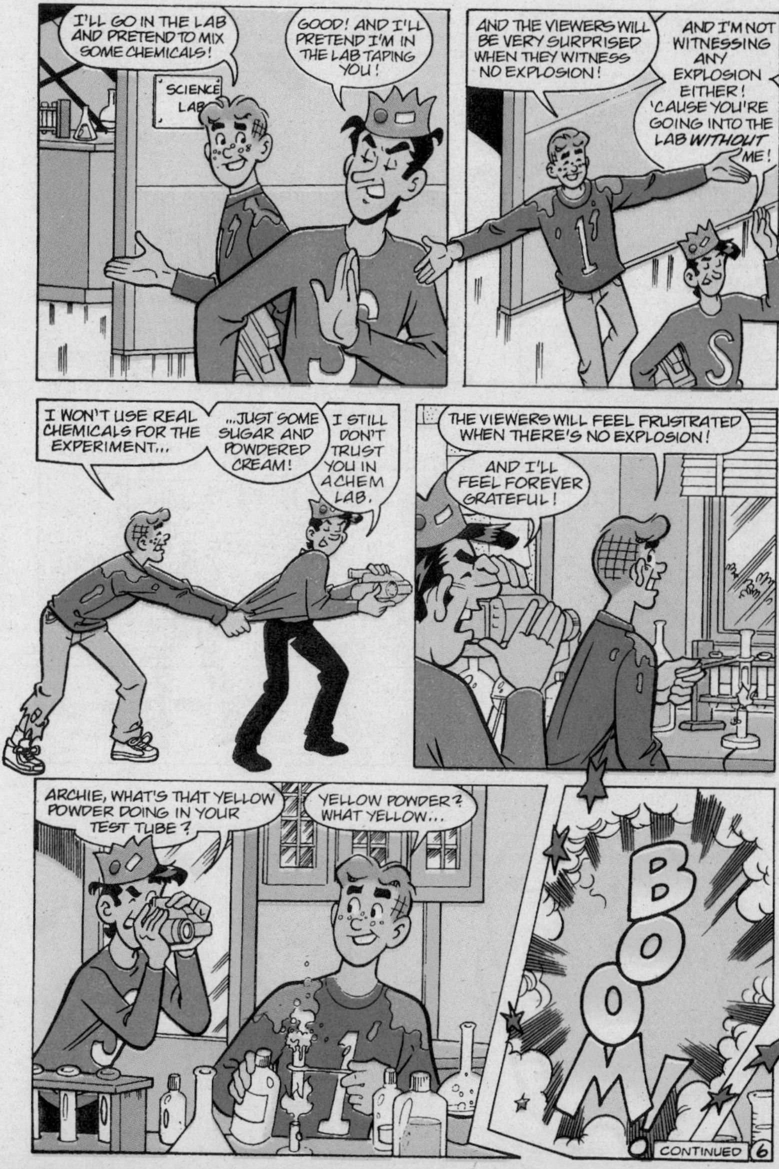
I'LL GO IN THE LAB AND PRETEND TO MIX SOME CHEMICALS!
GOOD! AND I'LL PRETEND I'M IN THE LAB TAPING YOU!
SCIENCE LAB
AND THE VIEWERS WILL BE VERY SURPRISED WHEN THEY WITNESS NO EXPLOSION!
AND I'M NOT WITNESSING ANY EXPLOSION EITHER! 'CAUSE YOU'RE GOING INTO THE LAB WITHOUT ME!
I WON'T USE REAL CHEMICALS FOR THE EXPERIMENT...
...JUST SOME SUGAR AND POWDERED CREAM!
I STILL DON'T TRUST YOU IN A CHEM LAB.
THE VIEWERS WILL FEEL FRUSTRATED WHEN THERE'S NO EXPLOSION!
AND I'LL FEEL FOREVER GRATEFUL!
ARCHIE, WHAT'S THAT YELLOW POWDER DOING IN YOUR TEST TUBE?
YELLOW POWDER? WHAT YELLOW...
BOOM!
CONTINUED

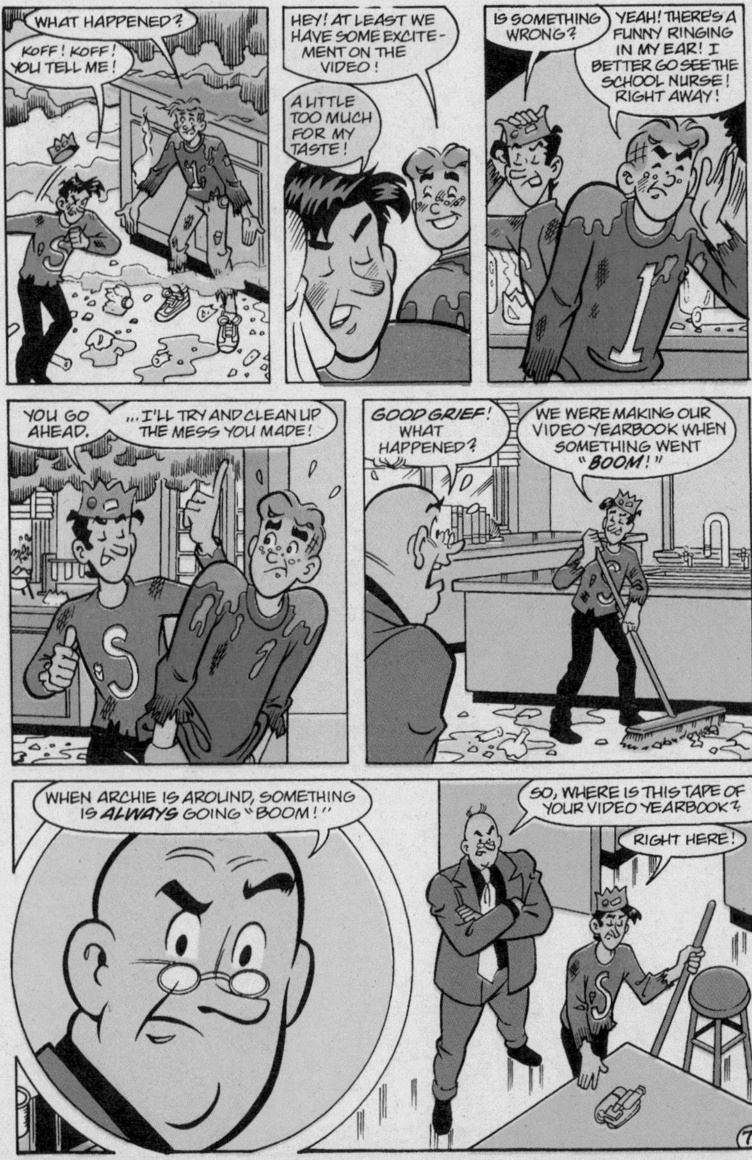
WHAT HAPPENED?
KOFF! KOFF! YOU TELL ME!
HEY! AT LEAST WE HAVE SOME EXCITE-MENT ON THE VIDEO!
A LITTLE TOO MUCH FOR MY TASTE!
IS SOMETHING WRONG?
YEAH! THERE'S A FUNNY RINGING IN MY EAR! I BETTER GO SEE THE SCHOOL NURSE! RIGHT AWAY!
YOU GO AHEAD.
...I'LL TRY AND CLEAN UP THE MESS YOU MADE!
GOOD GRIEF! WHAT HAPPENED?
WE WERE MAKING OUR VIDEO YEARBOOK WHEN SOMETHING WENT "BOOM!"
WHEN ARCHIE IS AROUND, SOMETHING IS ALWAYS GOING "BOOM!"
SO, WHERE IS THIS TAPE OF YOUR VIDEO YEARBOOK?
RIGHT HERE!

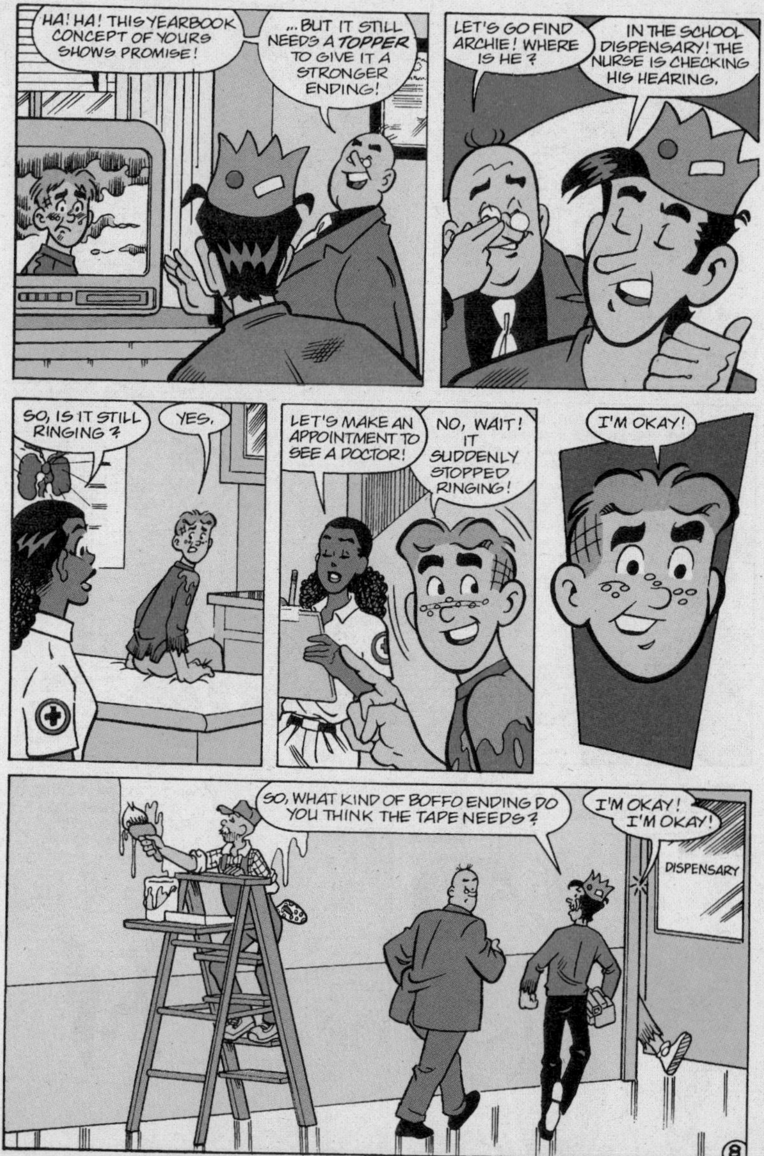
HA! HA! THIS YEARBOOK CONCEPT OF YOURS SHOWS PROMISE!
...BUT IT STILL NEEDS A *TOPPER* TO GIVE IT A STRONGER ENDING!
LET'S GO FIND ARCHIE! WHERE IS HE?
IN THE SCHOOL DISPENSARY! THE NURSE IS CHECKING HIS HEARING.
SO, IS IT STILL RINGING?
YES.
LET'S MAKE AN APPOINTMENT TO SEE A DOCTOR!
NO, WAIT! IT SUDDENLY STOPPED RINGING!
I'M OKAY!
SO, WHAT KIND OF BOFFO ENDING DO YOU THINK THE TAPE NEEDS?
I'M OKAY! I'M OKAY!
DISPENSARY

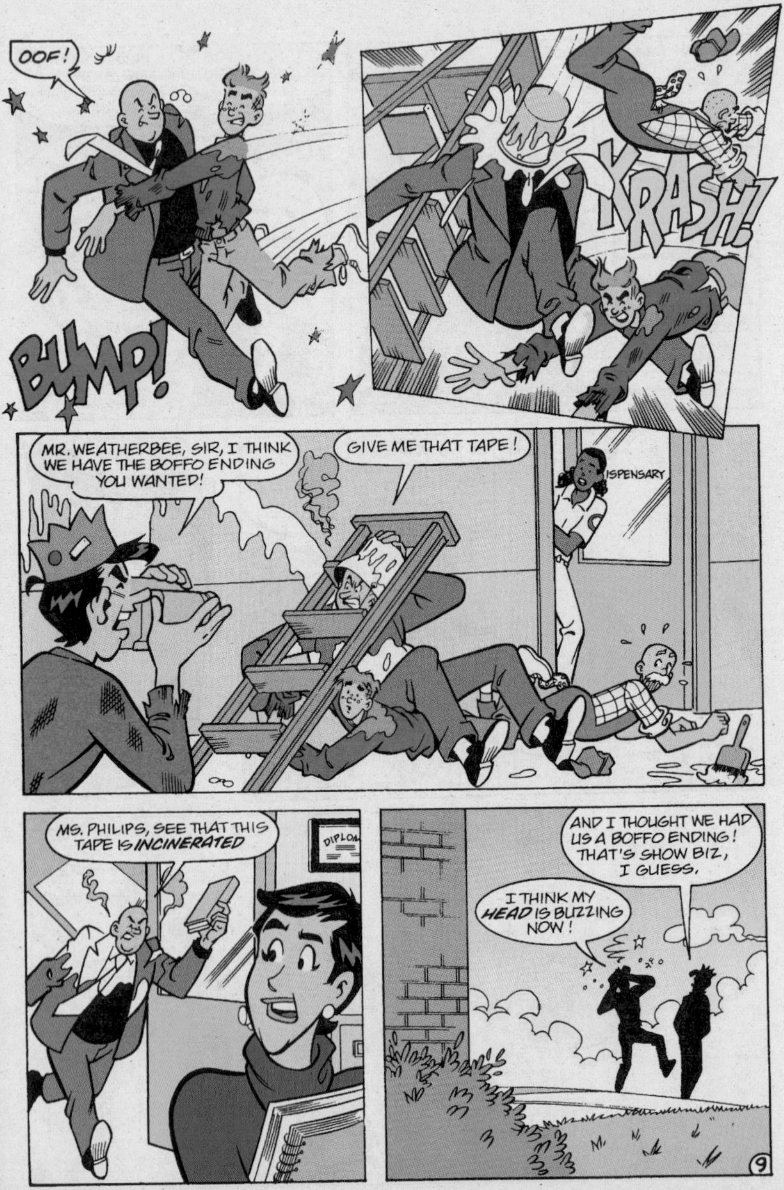
OOF!
BUMP!
KRASH!
MR. WEATHERBEE, SIR, I THINK WE HAVE THE BOFFO ENDING YOU WANTED!
GIVE ME THAT TAPE!
ISPENSARY
MS. PHILIPS, SEE THAT THIS TAPE IS INCINERATED
DIPLOM
AND I THOUGHT WE HAD US A BOFFO ENDING! THAT'S SHOW BIZ, I GUESS.
I THINK MY HEAD IS BUZZING NOW!
9

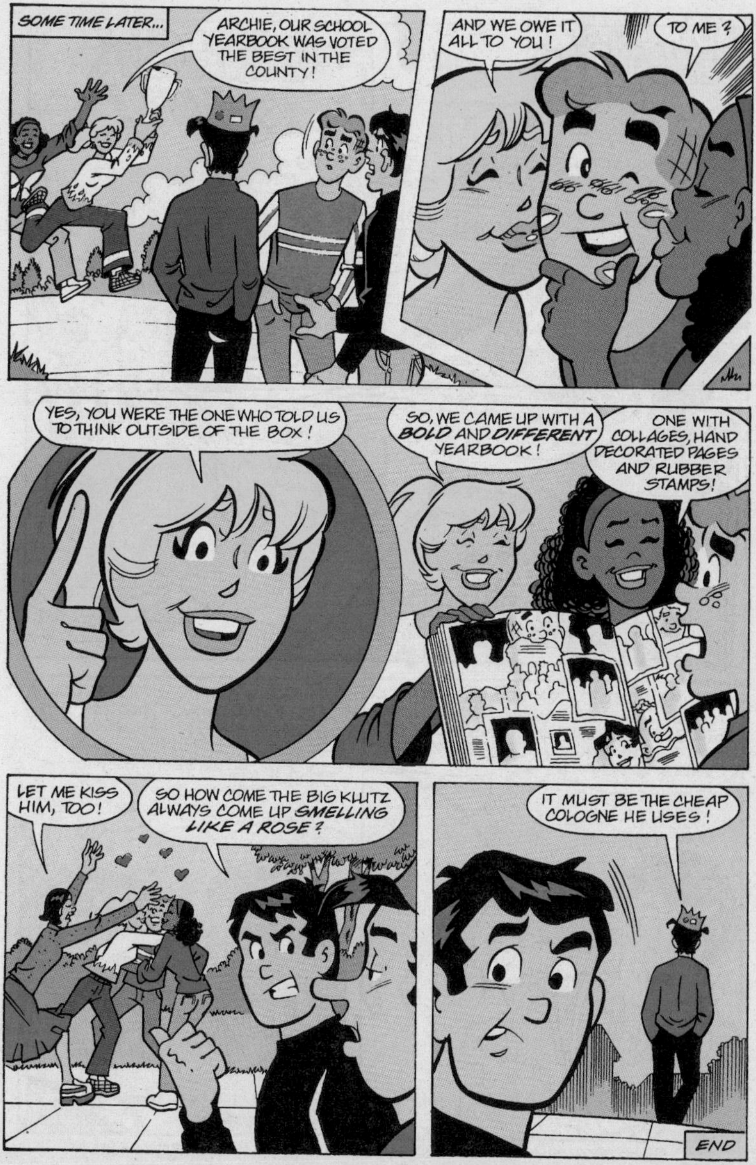

SOME TIME LATER...
ARCHIE, OUR SCHOOL YEARBOOK WAS VOTED THE BEST IN THE COUNTY!
AND WE OWE IT ALL TO YOU!
TO ME?
YES, YOU WERE THE ONE WHO TOLD US TO THINK OUTSIDE OF THE BOX!
SO, WE CAME UP WITH A BOLD AND DIFFERENT YEARBOOK!
ONE WITH COLLAGES, HAND DECORATED PAGES AND RUBBER STAMPS!
LET ME KISS HIM, TOO!
SO HOW COME THE BIG KLUTZ ALWAYS COME UP SMELLING LIKE A ROSE?
IT MUST BE THE CHEAP COLOGNE HE USES!
END

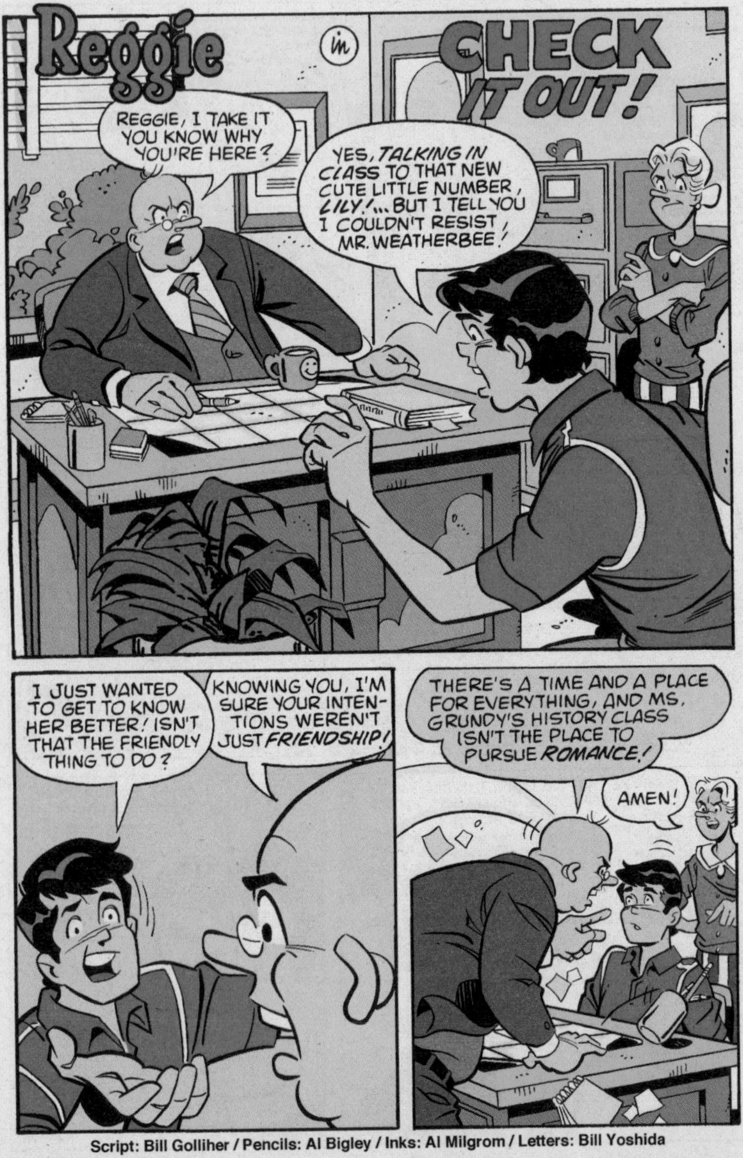
Reggie in
CHECK IT OUT!
REGGIE, I TAKE IT YOU KNOW WHY YOU'RE HERE?
YES, TALKING IN CLASS TO THAT NEW CUTE LITTLE NUMBER, LILY!... BUT I TELL YOU I COULDN'T RESIST, MR. WEATHERBEE!
I JUST WANTED TO GET TO KNOW HER BETTER! ISN'T THAT THE FRIENDLY THING TO DO?
KNOWING YOU, I'M SURE YOUR INTENTIONS WEREN'T JUST FRIENDSHIP!
THERE'S A TIME AND A PLACE FOR EVERYTHING, AND MS. GRUNDY'S HISTORY CLASS ISN'T THE PLACE TO PURSUE ROMANCE!
AMEN!

Script: Bill Golliher / Pencils: Al Bigley / Inks: Al Milgrom / Letters: Bill Yoshida

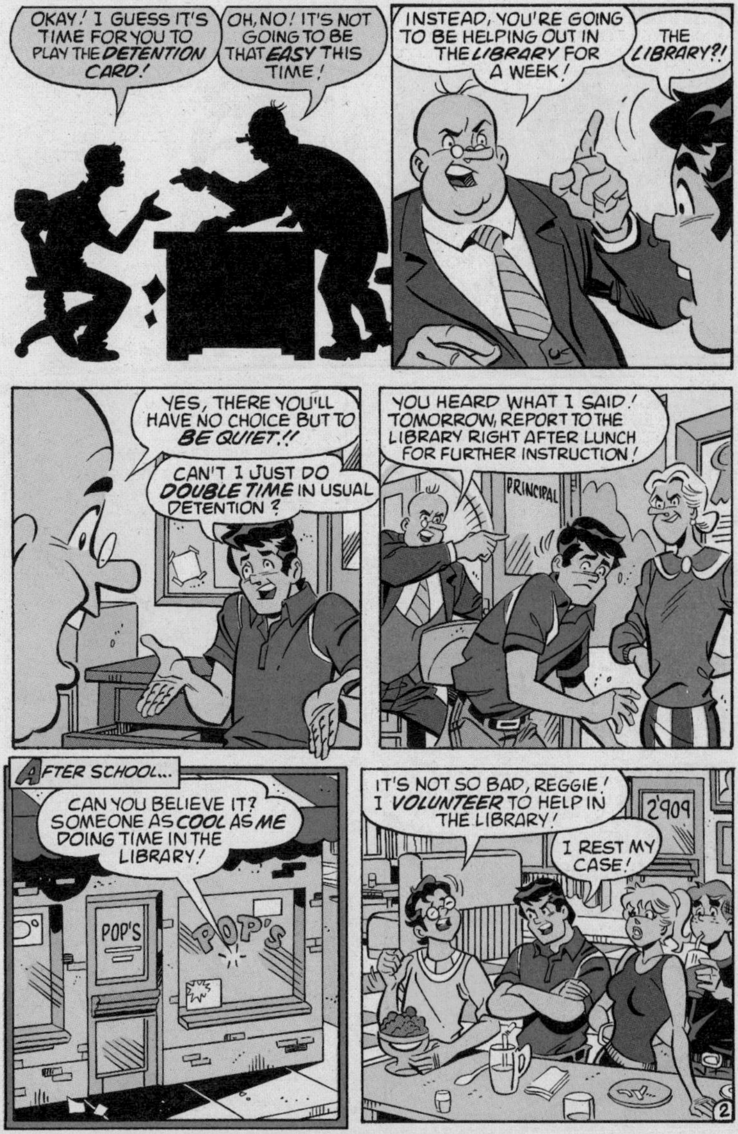
OKAY! I GUESS IT'S TIME FOR YOU TO PLAY THE DETENTION CARD!
OH, NO! IT'S NOT GOING TO BE THAT EASY THIS TIME!
INSTEAD, YOU'RE GOING TO BE HELPING OUT IN THE LIBRARY FOR A WEEK!
THE LIBRARY?!
YES, THERE YOU'LL HAVE NO CHOICE BUT TO BE QUIET!!
CAN'T I JUST DO DOUBLE TIME IN USUAL DETENTION?
YOU HEARD WHAT I SAID! TOMORROW, REPORT TO THE LIBRARY RIGHT AFTER LUNCH FOR FURTHER INSTRUCTION!
PRINCIPAL
AFTER SCHOOL...
CAN YOU BELIEVE IT? SOMEONE AS COOL AS ME DOING TIME IN THE LIBRARY!
POP'S
POP'S
IT'S NOT SO BAD, REGGIE! I VOLUNTEER TO HELP IN THE LIBRARY!
I REST MY CASE!
POP'S
2

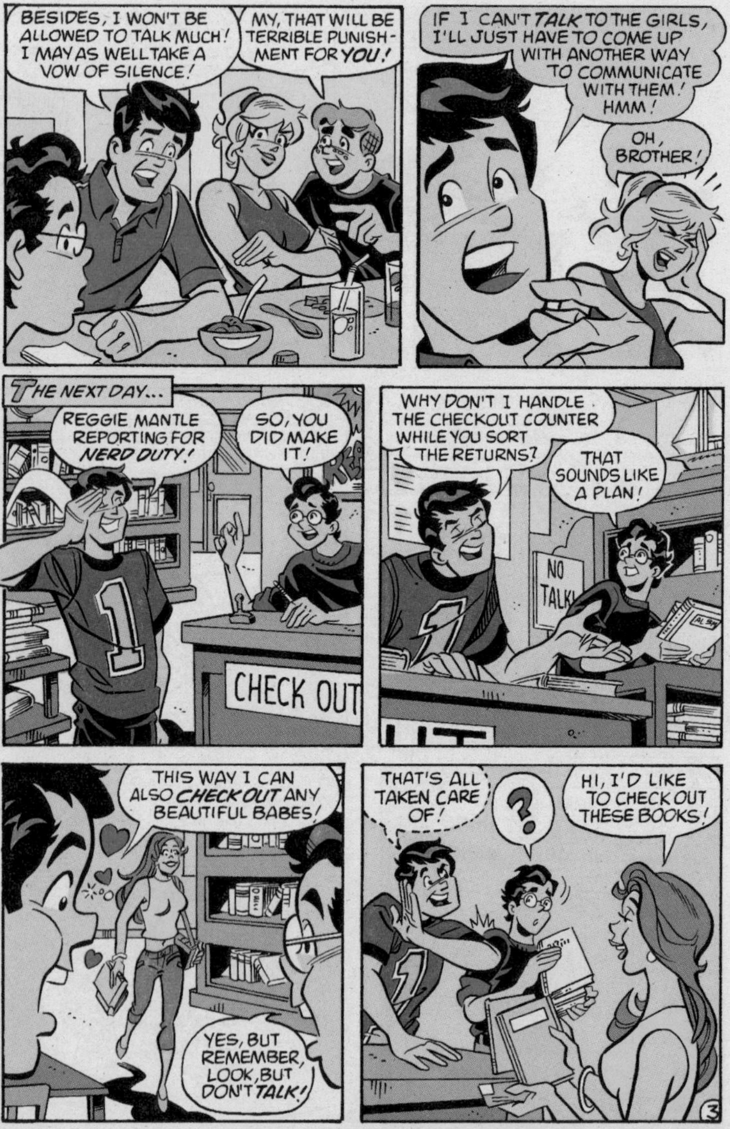
BESIDES, I WON'T BE ALLOWED TO TALK MUCH! I MAY AS WELL TAKE A VOW OF SILENCE!
MY, THAT WILL BE TERRIBLE PUNISH-MENT FOR YOU!
IF I CAN'T TALK TO THE GIRLS, I'LL JUST HAVE TO COME UP WITH ANOTHER WAY TO COMMUNICATE WITH THEM! HMM!
OH, BROTHER!
THE NEXT DAY...
REGGIE MANTLE REPORTING FOR NERD DUTY!
SO, YOU DID MAKE IT!
CHECK OUT
WHY DON'T I HANDLE THE CHECKOUT COUNTER WHILE YOU SORT THE RETURNS?
THAT SOUNDS LIKE A PLAN!
NO TALK
THIS WAY I CAN ALSO CHECK OUT ANY BEAUTIFUL BABES!
YES, BUT REMEMBER, LOOK, BUT DON'T TALK!
THAT'S ALL TAKEN CARE OF!
?
HI, I'D LIKE TO CHECK OUT THESE BOOKS!
3

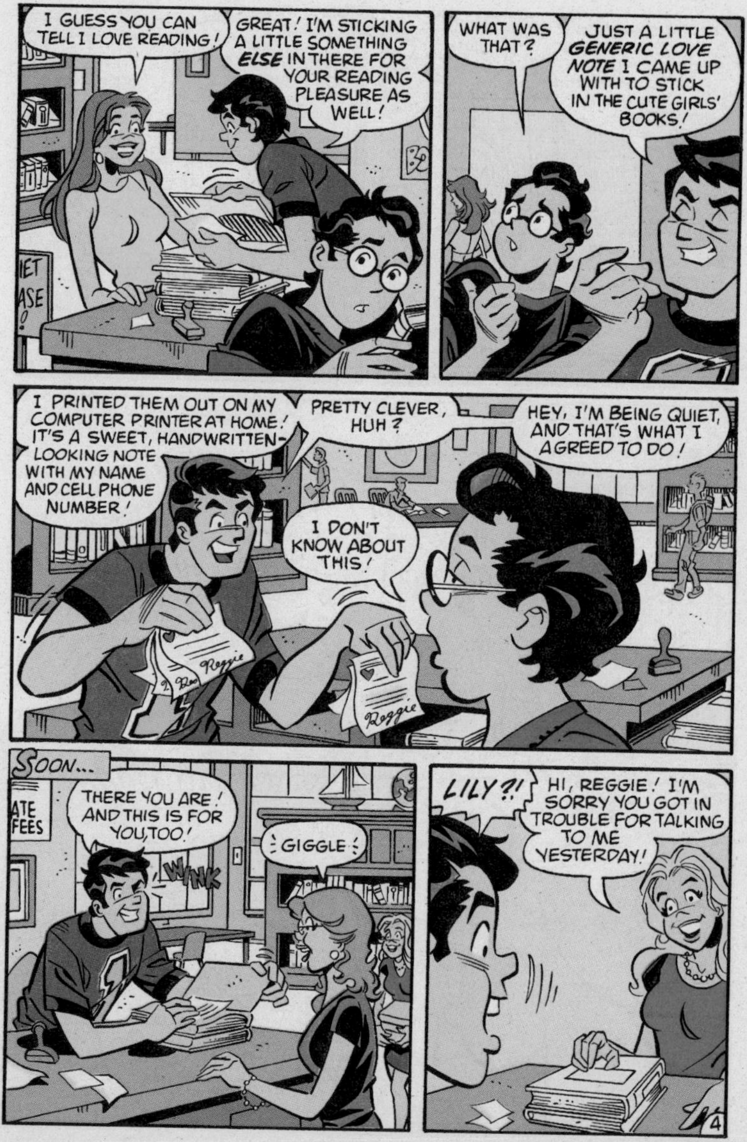
I GUESS YOU CAN TELL I LOVE READING!
GREAT! I'M STICKING A LITTLE SOMETHING *ELSE* IN THERE FOR YOUR READING PLEASURE AS WELL!
WHAT WAS THAT?
JUST A LITTLE *GENERIC LOVE NOTE* I CAME UP WITH TO STICK IN THE CUTE GIRLS' BOOKS!
I PRINTED THEM OUT ON MY COMPUTER PRINTER AT HOME! IT'S A SWEET, HANDWRITTEN-LOOKING NOTE WITH MY NAME AND CELL PHONE NUMBER!
PRETTY CLEVER, HUH?
HEY, I'M BEING QUIET, AND THAT'S WHAT I AGREED TO DO!
I DON'T KNOW ABOUT THIS!
Reggie
Reggie
SOON...
ATE FEES
THERE YOU ARE! AND THIS IS FOR YOU, TOO!
WINK
GIGGLE
LILY?!
HI, REGGIE! I'M SORRY YOU GOT IN TROUBLE FOR TALKING TO ME YESTERDAY!
4

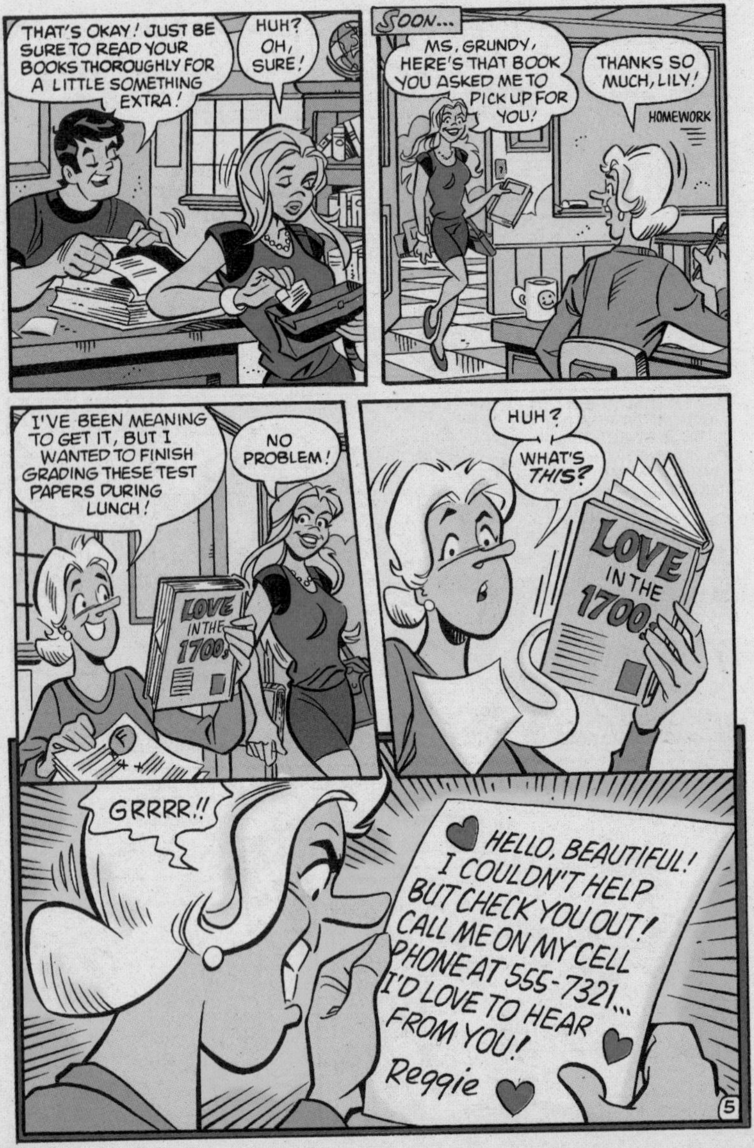
THAT'S OKAY! JUST BE SURE TO READ YOUR BOOKS THOROUGHLY FOR A LITTLE SOMETHING EXTRA!
HUH? OH, SURE!
SOON...
MS. GRUNDY, HERE'S THAT BOOK YOU ASKED ME TO PICK UP FOR YOU!
THANKS SO MUCH, LILY!
HOMEWORK
I'VE BEEN MEANING TO GET IT, BUT I WANTED TO FINISH GRADING THESE TEST PAPERS DURING LUNCH!
NO PROBLEM!
LOVE IN THE 1700s
F
HUH?
WHAT'S THIS?
LOVE IN THE 1700s
GRRRR!!
HELLO, BEAUTIFUL! I COULDN'T HELP BUT CHECK YOU OUT! CALL ME ON MY CELL PHONE AT 555-7321... I'D LOVE TO HEAR FROM YOU!
Reggie
5

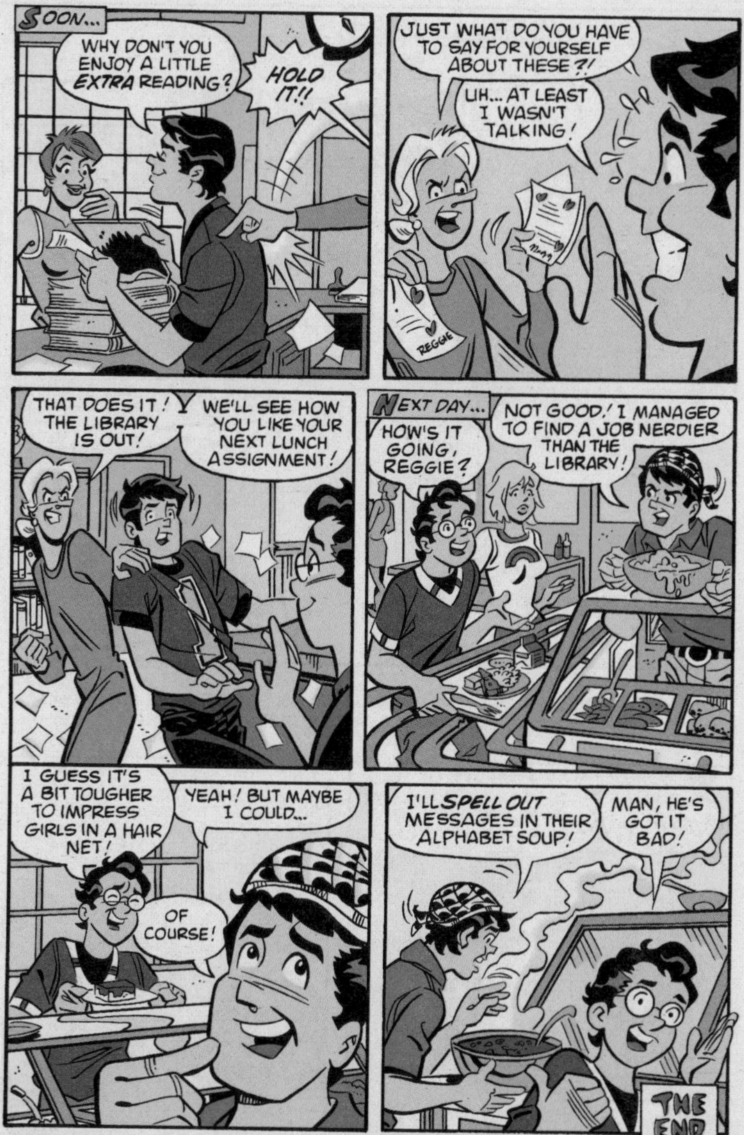
SOON...
WHY DON'T YOU ENJOY A LITTLE EXTRA READING?
HOLD IT!!
JUST WHAT DO YOU HAVE TO SAY FOR YOURSELF ABOUT THESE?!
UH... AT LEAST I WASN'T TALKING!
REGGIE
THAT DOES IT! THE LIBRARY IS OUT!
WE'LL SEE HOW YOU LIKE YOUR NEXT LUNCH ASSIGNMENT!
NEXT DAY...
HOW'S IT GOING, REGGIE?
NOT GOOD! I MANAGED TO FIND A JOB NERDIER THAN THE LIBRARY!
I GUESS IT'S A BIT TOUGHER TO IMPRESS GIRLS IN A HAIR NET!
YEAH! BUT MAYBE I COULD...
OF COURSE!
I'LL SPELL OUT MESSAGES IN THEIR ALPHABET SOUP!
MAN, HE'S GOT IT BAD!
THE END

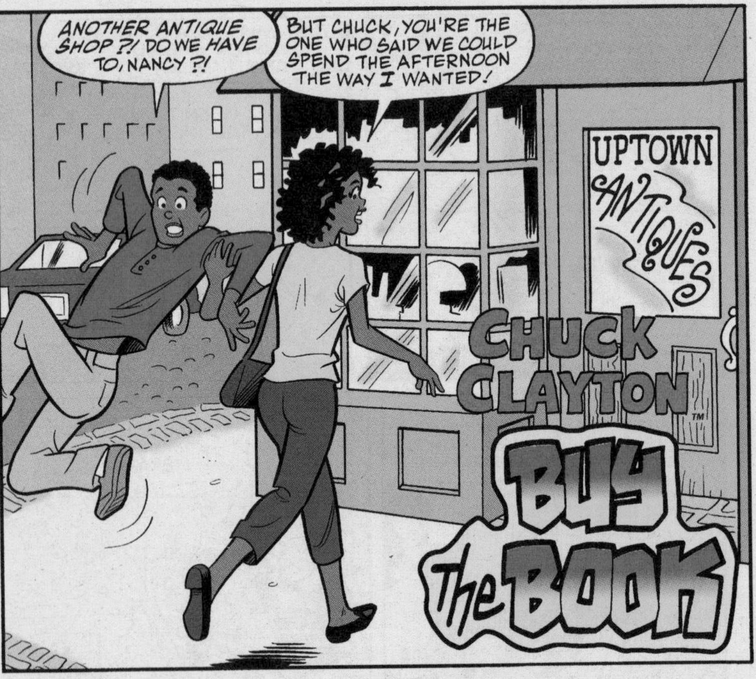
ANOTHER ANTIQUE SHOP ?! DO WE HAVE TO, NANCY ?!
BUT CHUCK, YOU'RE THE ONE WHO SAID WE COULD SPEND THE AFTERNOON THE WAY I WANTED!
UPTOWN ANTIQUES
CHUCK CLAYTON™
BUY THE BOOK

SCRIPT: BILL GOLLIHER PENCILS: JEFF SHULTZ INKS: RICH KOSLOWSKI
COLORS: BARRY GROSSMAN LETTERS: JACK MORELLI

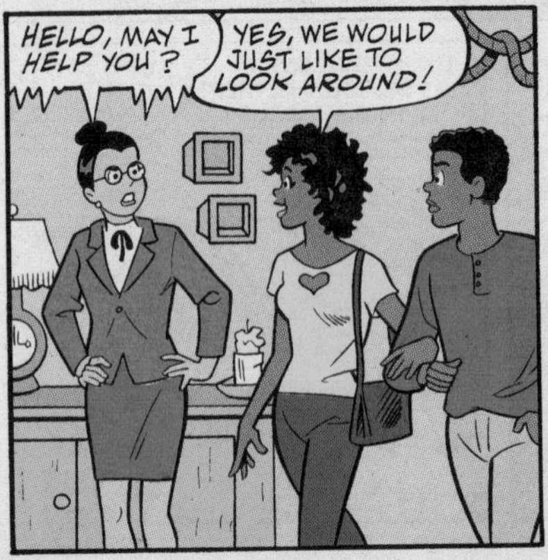
HELLO, MAY I HELP YOU ?
YES, WE WOULD JUST LIKE TO LOOK AROUND!

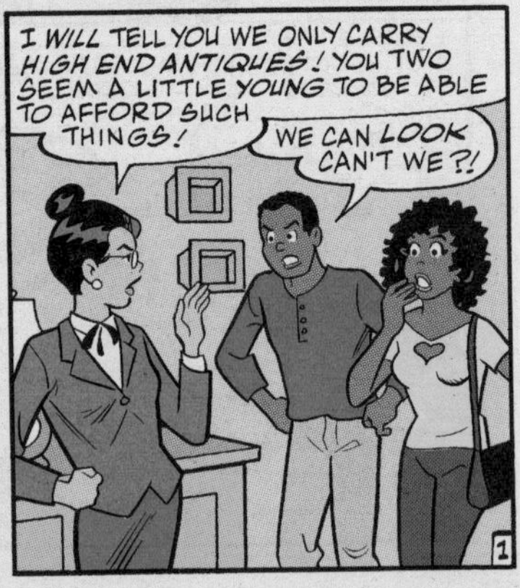
I WILL TELL YOU WE ONLY CARRY HIGH END ANTIQUES! YOU TWO SEEM A LITTLE YOUNG TO BE ABLE TO AFFORD SUCH THINGS!
WE CAN LOOK CAN'T WE ?!

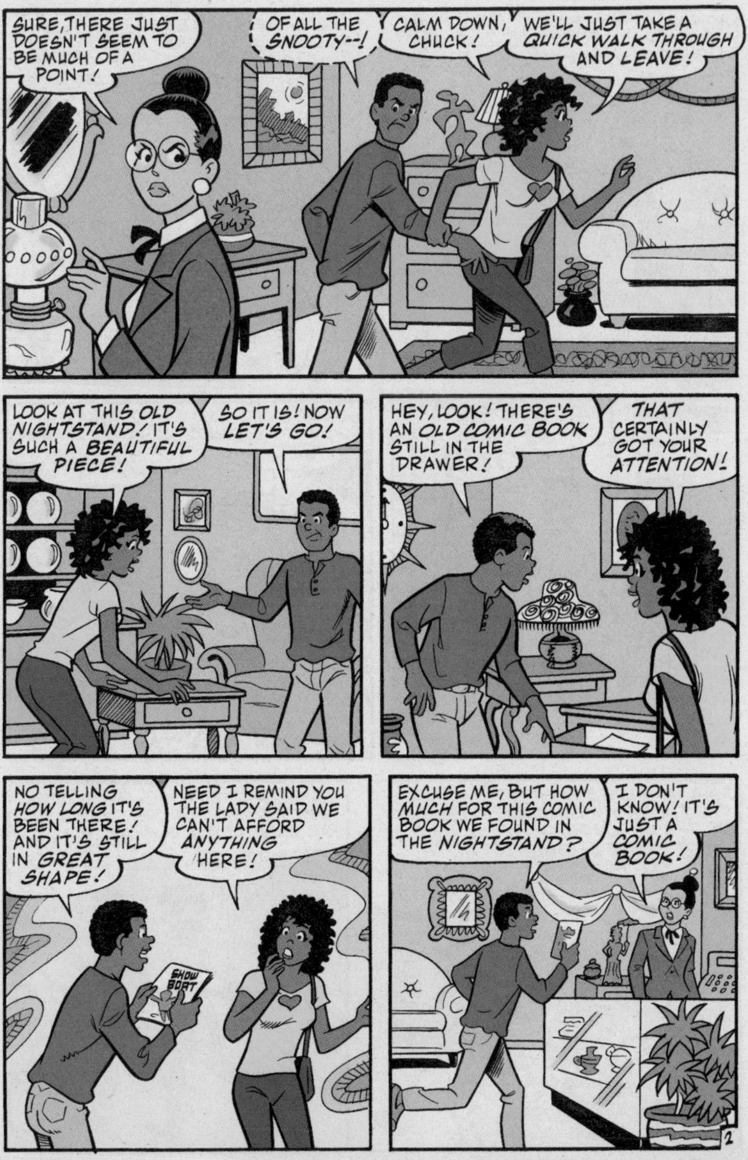

SURE, THERE JUST DOESN'T SEEM TO BE MUCH OF A POINT!
OF ALL THE SNOOTY--!
CALM DOWN, CHUCK!
WE'LL JUST TAKE A QUICK WALK THROUGH AND LEAVE!
LOOK AT THIS OLD NIGHTSTAND! IT'S SUCH A BEAUTIFUL PIECE!
SO IT IS! NOW LET'S GO!
HEY, LOOK! THERE'S AN OLD COMIC BOOK STILL IN THE DRAWER!
THAT CERTAINLY GOT YOUR ATTENTION!
NO TELLING HOW LONG IT'S BEEN THERE! AND IT'S STILL IN GREAT SHAPE!
NEED I REMIND YOU THE LADY SAID WE CAN'T AFFORD ANYTHING HERE!
SHOW BOAT
EXCUSE ME, BUT HOW MUCH FOR THIS COMIC BOOK WE FOUND IN THE NIGHTSTAND?
I DON'T KNOW! IT'S JUST A COMIC BOOK!

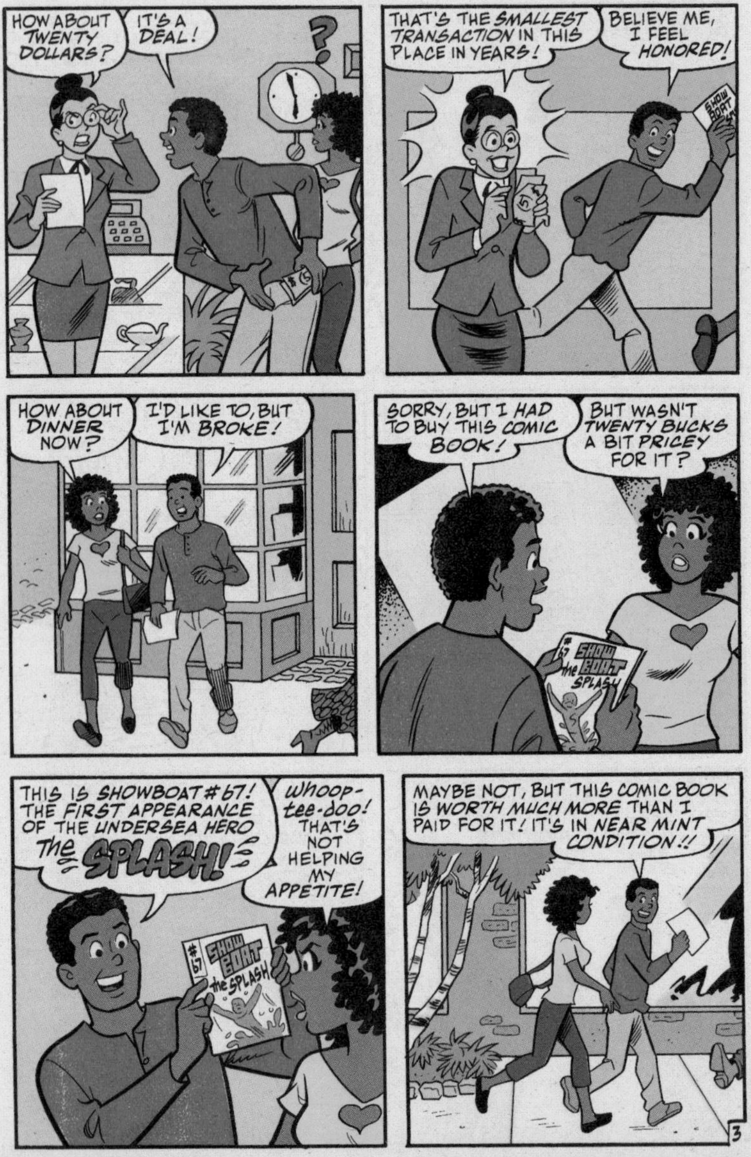

HOW ABOUT TWENTY DOLLARS?
IT'S A DEAL!
?
THAT'S THE SMALLEST TRANSACTION IN THIS PLACE IN YEARS!
BELIEVE ME, I FEEL HONORED!
HOW ABOUT DINNER NOW?
I'D LIKE TO, BUT I'M BROKE!
SORRY, BUT I HAD TO BUY THIS COMIC BOOK!
BUT WASN'T TWENTY BUCKS A BIT PRICEY FOR IT?
THIS IS SHOWBOAT #67! THE FIRST APPEARANCE OF THE UNDERSEA HERO The SPLASH!
Whoop-tee-doo! THAT'S NOT HELPING MY APPETITE!
#67 SHOW BOAT the SPLASH
MAYBE NOT, BUT THIS COMIC BOOK IS WORTH MUCH MORE THAN I PAID FOR IT! IT'S IN NEAR MINT CONDITION!!
3

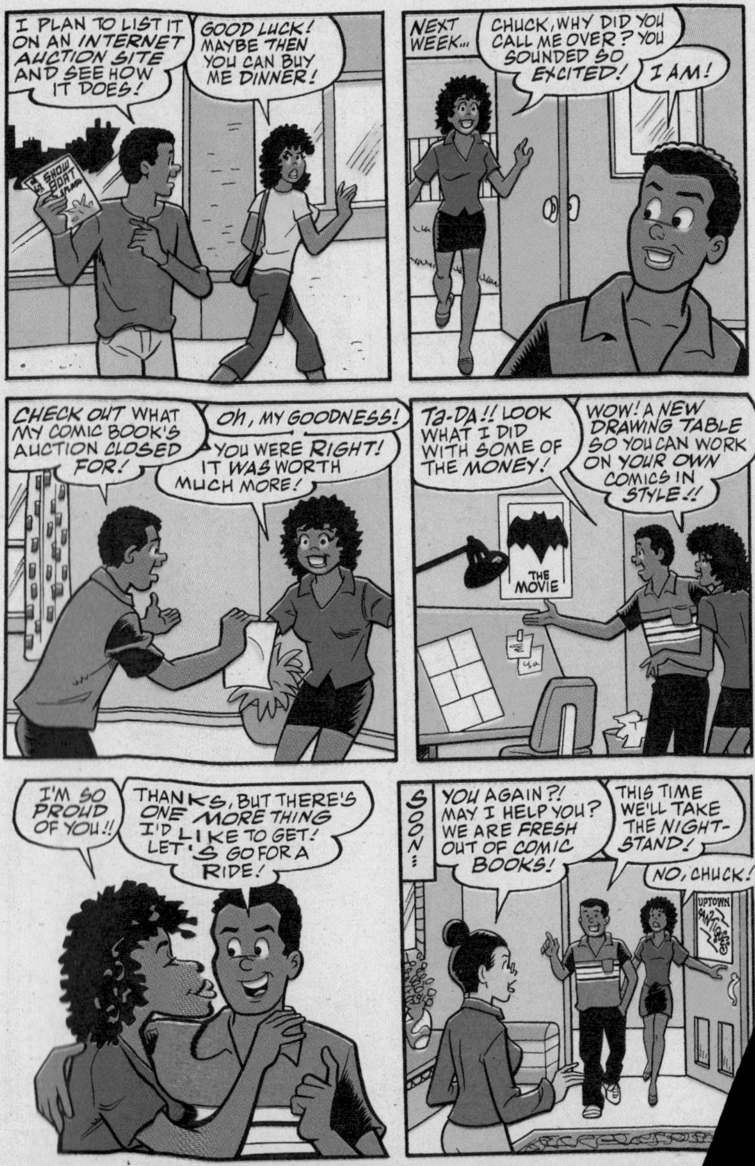
I PLAN TO LIST IT ON AN INTERNET AUCTION SITE AND SEE HOW IT DOES!
GOOD LUCK! MAYBE THEN YOU CAN BUY ME DINNER!
SHOW BOAT
NEXT WEEK...
CHUCK, WHY DID YOU CALL ME OVER? YOU SOUNDED SO EXCITED!
I AM!
CHECK OUT WHAT MY COMIC BOOK'S AUCTION CLOSED FOR!
Oh, MY GOODNESS!
YOU WERE RIGHT! IT WAS WORTH MUCH MORE!
Ta-DA!! LOOK WHAT I DID WITH SOME OF THE MONEY!
WOW! A NEW DRAWING TABLE SO YOU CAN WORK ON YOUR OWN COMICS IN STYLE!!
THE MOVIE
I'M SO PROUD OF YOU!!
THANKS, BUT THERE'S ONE MORE THING I'D LIKE TO GET! LET'S GO FOR A RIDE!
SOON...
YOU AGAIN?! MAY I HELP YOU? WE ARE FRESH OUT OF COMIC BOOKS!
THIS TIME WE'LL TAKE THE NIGHT-STAND!
NO, CHUCK!
UPTOWN

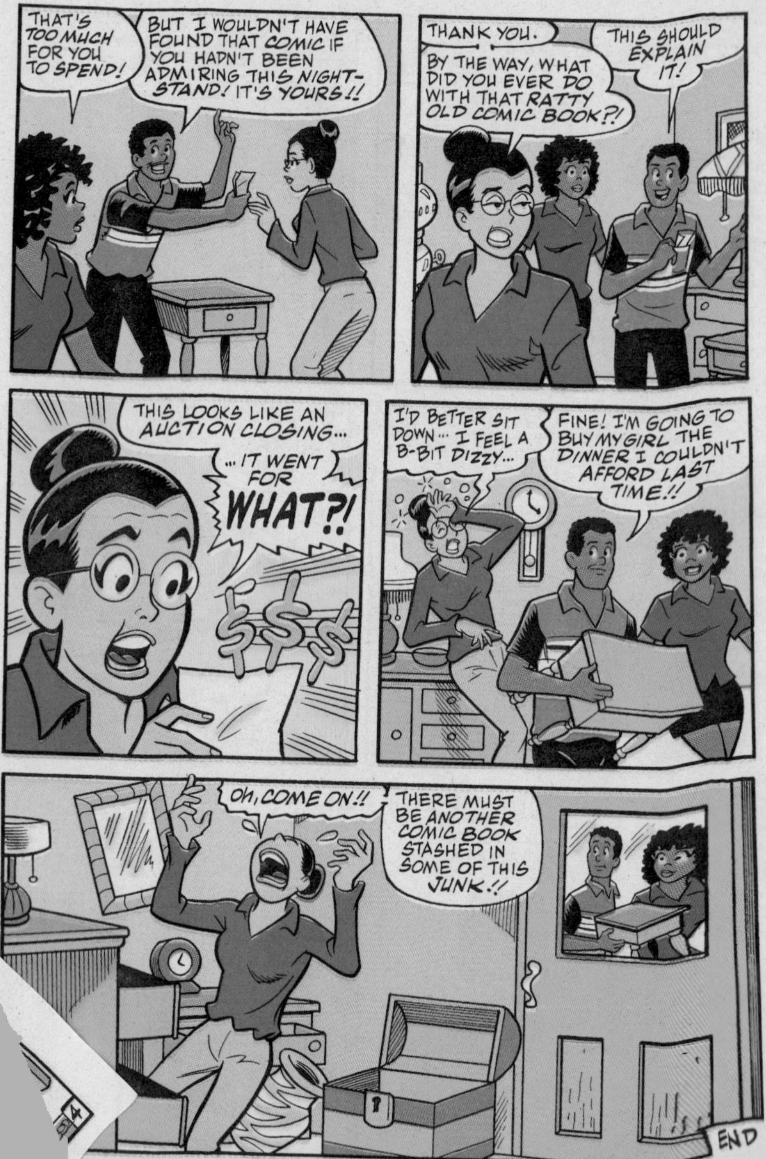
THAT'S TOO MUCH FOR YOU TO SPEND!
BUT I WOULDN'T HAVE FOUND THAT COMIC IF YOU HADN'T BEEN ADMIRING THIS NIGHT-STAND! IT'S YOURS!!
THANK YOU.
BY THE WAY, WHAT DID YOU EVER DO WITH THAT RATTY OLD COMIC BOOK?!
THIS SHOULD EXPLAIN IT!
THIS LOOKS LIKE AN AUCTION CLOSING...
...IT WENT FOR WHAT?!
I'D BETTER SIT DOWN... I FEEL A B-BIT DIZZY...
FINE! I'M GOING TO BUY MY GIRL THE DINNER I COULDN'T AFFORD LAST TIME!!
Oh, COME ON!!
THERE MUST BE ANOTHER COMIC BOOK STASHED IN SOME OF THIS JUNK!!
4
END